A Book
of Bones

Also by John Connolly

The Charlie Parker Stories
Every Dead Thing
Dark Hollow
The Killing Kind
The White Road
The Reflecting Eye (novella in the *Nocturnes* collection)
The Black Angel
The Unquiet
The Reapers
The Lovers
The Whisperers
The Burning Soul
The Wrath of Angels
The Wolf in Winter
A Song of Shadows
A Time of Torment
A Game of Ghosts
The Woman in the Woods

Other Works
Bad Men
The Book of Lost Things
he: A Novel

Short Stories
Nocturnes
Night Music: Nocturnes Volume II

The Samuel Johnson Stories (for Young Adults)
The Gates
Hell's Bells
The Creeps

The Chronicles of the Invaders (with Jennifer Ridyard)
Conquest
Empire
Dominion

Non-Fiction
Books to Die For: The World's Greatest Mystery Writers on the
World's Greatest Mystery Novels (as editor, with Declan Burke)
Parker: A Miscellany
Midnight Movie Monographs: Horror Express

John
Connolly

A Book
of Bones

HODDER &
STOUGHTON

First published in Great Britain in 2019 by Hodder & Stoughton
An Hachette UK company

1

Copyright © Bad Dog Books Limited 2019

The right of John Connolly to be identified as the
Author of the Work has been asserted by him in accordance
with the Copyright, Designs and Patents Act 1988.

A CIP catalogue record for this title is available from the British Library

Hardback ISBN 978 1 473 64201 0
Trade Paperback ISBN 978 1 473 64202 7
eBook ISBN 978 1 473 64200 3

Typeset in Sabon LT Std by
Palimpsest Book Production Ltd, Falkirk, Stirlingshire

Printed and bound in Great Britain by Clays Ltd, Elcograf S.p.A.

Hodder & Stoughton policy is to use papers that are natural, renewable
and recyclable products and made from wood grown in sustainable forests.
The logging and manufacturing processes are expected to conform
to the environmental regulations of the country of origin.

Hodder & Stoughton Ltd
Carmelite House
50 Victoria Embankment
London EC4Y 0DZ

www.hodder.co.uk

To Paul Johnston, for beating the odds.

ACKNOWLEDGEMENTS

Grateful acknowledgement is made for permission to reprint from the following copyrighted works:

'Casualty' was taken from: *New Selected Poems, 1966-1987* by Seamus Heaney. Copyright © Seamus Heaney. Published by Faber & Faber.

'German Requiem' was taken from: *Selected Poems* by James Fenton. Copyright © James Fenton. Published by Penguin. Used by permission of United Agents.

'Lady Lazarus' was taken from: *Collected Poems* by Sylvia Plath. Copyright © Sylvia Plath. Published by Faber & Faber. Used by permission.

'Hawk Roosting' was taken from: *Collected Animal Poems Vol 1–4* by Ted Hughes. Copyright © Ted Hughes. Published by Faber & Faber. Used by permission.

'Little Gidding' was taken from: *Four Quartets* by T.S. Eliot. Copyright © T. S. Eliot. Published by Faber & Faber. Used by permission.

'Decorating and Insurance Factors' by Bill Griffiths, first published in *Jacket* magazine (1999), and later in *Durham & Other Sequences* (West House Books, 2002).

I

Waneth the watch, but the world holdeth.

Anonymous, 'The Seafarer'

I

Desert, scrub, and a city in the sunlight: Phoenix, Arizona.
'Business?' asked the woman sitting next to Parker, as the plane made its final approach. They hadn't spoken since the flight left Texas, but Parker had registered her curiosity. He'd passed her as he was being escorted to the gate, bypassing security entirely, a federal agent to either side of him, their weapons visible. He was surprised it had taken her so long to strike up a conversation. Her self-discipline was admirable.

'I'm sorry?' he said.

She was in her early forties, he estimated, and recently divorced. The pale circle around her ring finger was visible against her southwestern coloration. Her hair was dark, and her eyes were kind, if wary. The separation had probably been painful.

'I was wondering if you're here on business.'

'Yes.'

Parker returned his gaze to the window, but she was persistent.

'Do you mind if I ask what it is you do?'

The correct reply should have been 'yes' for a second time, but he didn't want to appear rude. It would make her feel bad, and he wouldn't feel much better.

'I hunt,' said Parker. He was surprised to hear the words emerge, as though spoken by another in his stead.

'Oh.' Her disapproval was obvious.

'But not animals,' he added, as the voice decided to make the situation yet more complicated.

'Oh,' she said again.

He could almost hear the cogs turning.

'So, you hunt . . . people?'

'Sometimes.'

3

The wheels came down, and the plane hit the ground with a jolt that caused someone at the back to yelp in the manner of a wounded dog.

'Like a bounty hunter?' asked the woman.

'Like a bounty hunter.'

'So that's what you are?'

'No.'

'Oh,' she said, for the third time. 'I guess I shouldn't have asked, but I saw the people with you at the airport, and . . .'

She trailed off. She was holding a magazine in her hands, which she now opened and pretended to read as they taxied to the terminal. Parker had set aside his own book, a copy of Montaigne's *Essays* gifted to him by Louis. It was the first time Louis had ever passed on a book to him. Lately, Louis had become quite the bibliophile. They both had, because in recent months they'd been learning a lot about old volumes.

Parker wasn't entirely clear why the *Essays* should have particularly engaged Louis, although he had to concede that Montaigne wasn't short of opinions on just about every subject under the sun, from thumbs to cannibals. Initially Parker had persisted with the book because of its giver, but now Montaigne was getting under his skin. Montaigne knew a lot, yet his essays weren't about displaying what he knew so much as working toward some understanding of all he didn't know, which made him an unusual individual by any reckoning. Since the flight had been delayed by almost an hour, he'd had plenty of time to spend in Montaigne's company.

The plane came to a halt, but Parker didn't rush to get up. He was seated in the second row, was traveling only with cabin bags, and knew that more federal agents would be waiting for him at the gate. He would be in a car and on his way from the airport before most of his fellow travelers had even claimed their baggage.

The door opened, and the first passengers began to disembark. The woman who had been sitting beside him was now wrestling an overfilled case from the compartment. He helped her to free it, and she thanked him.

'I'm sorry for prying,' she said.

'It's okay.'

He followed her from the plane, and she fell into step beside him.

'Look,' she said, 'if you're in town for a few days, maybe you might like to meet for a drink. I'll buy, as an apology, and I promise I won't ask any more questions about what you do for a living. At least, I'll try not to.'

'That's very generous of you,' said Parker, 'but I won't be staying long.'

They reached the gate. As predicted, two more federal agents were hovering by the desk. Parker saw them react as he appeared, and the woman picked up on it.

'I guess it didn't hurt to ask,' she said.

'No.'

She handed him a business card. Her name was Tonya Nichols, and she was the vice-president of a bank in Tempe.

'In case your schedule changes,' she said. 'Good luck with your hunting.'

Parker had never come to terms with Arizona. He did not have the desert gene, and Phoenix Sky Harbor was one of his least favorite airports, even by the low standards of Brutalist architecture. Back in the late 1990s, the then-mayor of Phoenix, Skip Rimsza, had proposed renaming the entire airport after Barry Goldwater. The proposal didn't have enough support to go through, but Terminal 4, at which Parker had arrived, was still named in honor of the former Republican senator and UFO nut who'd had his ass handed to him by Lyndon Johnson in the 1964 presidential election. But Parker's grandfather, a staunch northeastern Democrat, had always retained a degree of affection for Goldwater, mostly because the latter had once advised all good Christians to line up and kick the televangelist Jerry Falwell in the seat of his pants.

The two agents marching alongside Parker didn't look old enough to remember Goldwater's funeral, which had only taken place in 1998, and were probably still being carded in bars. Parker wondered if the FBI was now recruiting straight out of high school. The agents, who introduced themselves as Skal and Crist, were very polite, and one of them insisted on carrying Parker's case, leaving him to manage only his leather messenger bag unaided. Their solicitude made Parker feel old, and their height caused him to resemble an adopted mascot. Skal was north of six feet tall, and built entirely from blocks. Crist made him appear dainty by comparison.

'Where does the name Skal come from?' Parker asked.

'Denmark, sir.'

'Isn't it some kind of toast?'

'Yes, sir. I believe the derivation is from a cup or bowl.'

Parker wasn't used to being addressed so politely by federal agents. It made him nervous.

'Do you mind not calling me "sir"?' he asked.

Skal looked at Crist, who shrugged helplessly, as though to suggest that the ways of men remained mysterious to him, but he'd back his colleague to the hilt if the decision to drop the 'sir' came back to bite him somewhere down the line.

'I'll try not to,' said Skal.

By now they were at the terminal door. A heavy-duty Chevy Suburban was parked in the area reserved for law enforcement personnel, a Phoenix PD cruiser idling nearby just in case anyone became alarmed.

'I take it Ross is already here.'

'*SAC* Ross is at the scene,' Crist corrected. His voice might have come from the bowels of the earth, so deep was the rumble.

'Did he say anything before he sent you to pick me up?'

It was Skal who answered the question.

'Sir' – and the word held an additional unspoken apology for its return – 'he told us not to let you shoot anyone.'

'He was pretty clear on that,' Crist added.

Neither of the agents offered even the hint of a smile. If anything, they bore the slightly fretful demeanor of two straight-A students who had somehow fallen in with a bad element, and were certain it was going to impact on their report cards come the end of semester.

'Well, I wouldn't want to get you into any trouble,' said Parker.

'Thank you,' said Skal.

'Yes,' said Crist, 'thank you very much. We wouldn't want you to get us into any trouble either.'

The three men stood awkwardly by the Suburban for a moment.

'If you're waiting for a hug . . .' said Parker.

Skal bounded to open the rear door of the Suburban as quickly as he could.

Clearly, thought Parker, he wasn't the hugging kind.

II

The call had come through that morning, while Parker was taking a break from listening to an attorney attempt to convince a federal judge in Houston, Texas, of the inadmissibility of evidence Parker was scheduled to give. The case in question concerned a pair of counselors accused of sexually assaulting a series of vulnerable teenagers in at least three states over a period of ten years, sometimes after incapacitating them with narcotics, whether ingested either willingly or unknowingly. The men, Bruer and Seben, had most recently operated as licensed 'conversion therapists' in Maine, their clients referred to them by parents or guardians who viewed the children's sexual orientation as a perversion or aberration, and sought to have it dealt with coercively. Bruer and Seben's state-acquired shingle had effectively permitted them to abuse children under its aegis, and earn good money along the way.

But one of the Maine victims, a girl named Lacey Smith from Old Orchard Beach, had committed suicide in the aftermath of her 'treatment', and Moxie Castin, Parker's lawyer, occasional employer, and possibly even friend, had been engaged by her family to obtain proof that could be used to force a prosecution by the state. By then the counselors had already left Maine to seek fresh prey elsewhere, but Parker tracked them to Texas, where he spent a week monitoring them with the aid of a pair of local PIs. Eventually the counselors made an error, which was why Parker was now sitting in a Texan courtroom, waiting to add his testimony to the weight of evidence mounting against the abusers.

Their defense attorneys had already tried unsuccessfully to have Parker's testimony shot down on the grounds that their clients had a reasonable expectation of privacy when they were recorded at a bar in Baytown comparing notes on the oral rape of a sixteen-year-old boy. Parker had used an acoustic vector sensor to listen to, and record, the conversation, which had subsequently required only a minimal digital wash to be made entirely comprehensible. It had barely been worth the prosecution's time to point out that the two men could have no expectation of privacy under such circumstances, as the booth of a bar could not be construed as a private place, and the evidence had not been gathered in a way that broke any law.

Now the defense was altering its plan of attack, focusing instead on Parker's character, and calling into question his credibility by documenting a pattern of illegality during previous investigations, along with what the attorney described as 'a propensity for violent acts up to, and including, homicide'. Parker didn't particularly relish having his character traduced in court, but couldn't disagree with some of what was being said, not that anyone was asking his opinion of himself. The judge announced a brief adjournment to consider the arguments, and Parker went to get coffee and some air, which was when his cell phone rang. He recognized the number, and paused for a moment before answering. From bitter experience, he knew that little good could come of what would follow.

'Agent Ross,' said Parker. 'What a pleasure.'

SAC Edgar Ross of the Federal Bureau of Investigation was based at Federal Plaza in New York, and had coordinated the FBI's internal inquiry into its handling of the hunt for the Traveling Man, the killer who had taken the lives of Parker's wife and first child, and whom Parker had killed in turn. Since then, the paths taken by Parker and Ross had grown increasingly intertwined. As a consequence, Parker now banked a monthly retainer from the FBI as a consultant, and had been more than useful to Ross on occasion, if sometimes only on grounds of plausible deniability. Meanwhile, Ross offered Parker a degree of protection, in addition to improving his financial situation considerably. Parker didn't entirely trust Ross, and Ross didn't entirely trust Parker, but they were allies, of a kind.

'Where are you?' said Ross.

'Houston, Texas. I'm waiting to see if a federal judge thinks I can be trusted to give evidence against a pair of sexual predators. It seems to be a question of my character.'

'That's unfortunate for you. Maybe you should try bribery.'

'Wouldn't that just confirm the truth of the allegation?'

'Only if the bribe is refused.'

'I think I'll let justice run its course. Is this a social call?'

'You'll have to wait a while longer for that particular first. We have a body. It may be that of Mors.'

A month earlier, a woman who went by the name of Pallida Mors had cut a bloody swathe from Indiana to Maine, killing men, women, and one unborn child in an effort to secure older vellum pages bound into an edition of *Grimm's Fairy Tales* dating from the early part of the previous century, and illustrated by Arthur Rackham. Mors was working for an Englishman named Quayle, who may or may not have been a lawyer. Both had subsequently escaped from Maine with the pages, although not before Louis injured Mors in a gunfight, and was wounded in turn. No trace of Quayle and Mors had been found since then, and there was no record of them having left the country.

'Where?' Parker asked.

'Near Gila Bend, Arizona.' He heard Ross speak to someone else on the other end of the line. 'We've booked you on an American Airlines flight departing at two-forty.'

'In the movies you send private jets.'

'Movies tend to leave out the boring parts about budgets and congressional oversight.'

'It's already after one-thirty.'

'Then you'd better hurry.'

'What about the court case?'

'I'll take care of it. Who knows, I may even manage to present your character in a favorable light. We'll have agents waiting for you at George Bush. They'll get you to the gate on time. Expect a call from one of them in about twenty minutes.'

Ross hung up just as a federal prosecutor named Tracey Ermenthal emerged from the courthouse.

10

'Problem?' she asked.

'I have to go to Arizona.'

'Wait, we need you here. We didn't fly you from Maine for dinner and a show.'

Parker told her about his conversation with Ross, and gave her the first of two cell phone numbers he possessed for the agent. The second was changed regularly, and rarely used. It was strictly for off-the-books business.

'Fucking feds,' said Ermenthal, as she dialed the number.

'Wait a minute,' said Parker. 'Aren't you—?'

'Don't even think of finishing that question,' said Ermenthal, and then she was shouting at Ross, and Parker could hear Ross shouting back in turn.

He left them to it, and caught a cab to the airport.

III

Parker and the two agents put Phoenix behind them, heading west to I-85, which they followed south toward Gila Bend. After about an hour's drive, conducted mostly in silence, the Chevy took a left turn down a road pitted and rutted by the passage of trucks. By now it was almost six and, in anticipation of night, the route was already illuminated by lights strung from a series of posts set at irregular intervals, their bulbs occasionally dimming to the barest flicker as the Chevy passed before returning to semi-brightness once it was gone, as though the lighting itself were complicit in some greater scheme to dissuade the strangers from approaching their destination.

Eventually they came to it: a junkyard set in a desert hollow, fenced in to discourage thieves. Parker could discern the remains of refrigerators and stoves, computers and microwaves, the husks of old vehicles, and what might have been the carcass of a light aircraft. The yard was lit in a similar fashion to the road, down to the guttering of the bulbs. Here, though, further illumination was provided by the headlights of two more Chevys, along with the full array of a pair of cruisers from the Maricopa County Sheriff's Office, and an additional set of high-intensity lamps. All the beams were directed toward one spot, where a chest freezer stood at one remove from a small mountain of white goods.

They pulled up at the gate of the junkyard, in a spot beside a vehicle from the Maricopa County Office of the State Medical Examiner. Parker got out just in time to prevent Crist from opening the door for him. Next thing, the agent would have been offering to lift him down.

Parker wondered how long all these people had been here. He

counted at least thirty individuals, including deputies, federal agents, and the ME's staff, and that didn't include a handful of Latino workers who sat or stood at one remove, sheltered by a makeshift lean-to as they watched in silence all that was unfolding. A couple of the Latinos looked more miserable than the rest, and Parker guessed they might be illegals cursing their bad luck to have become caught up in some gringo business that would ultimately bring them to the attention of *la migra*. Behind them, a deputy slouched against the hood of a cruiser, his arms folded, making sure everyone stayed where they were for now. A plastic picnic table inside the gates was littered with the remains of meals from McDonald's, probably bought in Gila Bend for those on the scene. At least they'd fed the workers, too: Parker could see bags folded neatly beside the Latinos, and a couple were still sipping sodas.

Parker sniffed the air. It smelled of chemicals, and tasted metallic. There was a feeling of inertia about the scene, a sense of those involved being trapped in limbo, like diners anticipating the arrival of a final guest before the meal can proceed. From the looks he was receiving, Parker thought he might well be that visitant.

Skal and Crist led him through the gates, past a prefabricated hut where a hairless man, his skin tempered to terracotta by the sun, sat in a plastic chair, smoking a cheroot while a pair of mongrel dogs dozed at his feet. In the doorway of the hut lounged a Latino woman who looked too young to be in the company of such a person, unless she was his daughter. The manner of her dress, which barely concealed her breasts, and the way she was using the toes of her right foot to stroke the inside of his left thigh, her ankle nudging his groin, suggested otherwise.

The man removed the cheroot from his mouth as Parker walked by.

'Are you the one they've been waiting for?' he called out.

'Maybe.'

'About fucking time.'

Parker felt Skal bristle beside him.

'Deviant,' Skal muttered, as they moved on. 'Earlier, he closed

13

his office door and had sex with that girl while some of us were drinking iced teas.'

'At least he did close the door,' said Parker.

'We told him he could go home,' said Crist, 'but he insisted on staying. Said he wanted to be sure we didn't steal anything.'

'Well, you can't be too careful,' said Parker.

'We're federal agents.'

'Like I said, you can't be too careful.'

They advanced deeper into the yard, and Parker saw Ross. The SAC was speaking with a trio of agents in windbreakers who stood in the shadow of a small tower of oil drums. Further back, the bodies of innumerable cars lay discarded like great skulls, and Parker picked out a second road winding through the premises from a distant gate to the west. The yard was much larger than it had first appeared, descending in a series of declivities to a massive pit at its heart, where Parker glimpsed a fire burning. Previously hidden from view, but visible as he advanced, were more huts, each devoted to a particular item, or a selection of related salvaged goods: engines and exhausts; wheels and tires; glass panes of every conceivable shape and size; piles of wiring and connectors – whatever one might require, it was not inconceivable that it might be found somewhere in here, as long as one was familiar with the order of the place. Yet every scavenged part bore a patina of sand and dust, and seen up close the rubber on the tires had hardened and degraded to such an extent as to render them useless. No car appeared to be of more recent vintage than the end of the last century, and it would have been no surprise had the television screens bloomed into life to reveal only ancient and unloved shows transmitting in black and white.

Parker turned his attention back to the chest freezer, but did not approach it. Instead he waited for Ross to conclude his conversation, and thought about finding a room for the night. He didn't want to stay in Arizona longer than necessary. He had obligations back in Portland, not to mention the case left hanging in Houston. He'd called Ermenthal on the way from Sky Harbor, to be informed that the court hadn't taken kindly to one of the witnesses in the case vanishing into the blue while the judge was contemplating said witness's character over coffee and a cinnamon roll. Still, it appeared that Ross had managed to give a better account of Parker than the defense, and his testimony would be heard, but the clock was ticking.

Ross's voice pulled Parker from his thoughts.

'Good flight?'

'A woman on the plane tried to pick me up.'

'She has my sympathies.'

Even though it had only been a couple of weeks since he and Ross last spoke face-to-face, Parker thought the FBI man had aged disproportionately during that time. New lines showed at the corners of his eyes, and his skin was mottled: illness perhaps, or more likely stress. It was the face of a man who wasn't sleeping enough, and when he did, dreamed unpleasant dreams.

'You look like you need a vacation,' said Parker.

'That's why I came down here. I thought a little sunshine might help, and I figured it couldn't hurt you either.'

'I don't like the sun. I'm a winter person. You know, you could have just told me everything I needed to know over the phone, and saved me a trip.'

'I don't trust technology,' said Ross. 'I've always preferred the personal touch.'

Parker waited. Ross was hardly known for his warmth.

'And?'

'I think you were meant to see this. When you're done, we'll talk. The federal government may even spring for dinner and a drink, along with a bed for the night.'

'I don't eat at McDonald's, and I'm not sharing a room.'

'We'll do better than fast food, if you still have an appetite, and I'll see what we can do about upgrading you to the presidential suite.'

Ross began walking toward the chest freezer. Parker noticed that all activity around the junkyard had ceased. The attention of agents, deputies, medical staff, workers, and the hairless man and his concubine, was now focused on him. Even the dogs roused themselves from their slumber and turned circles as they barked, until their master aimed a booted foot first at one, then the other, but failed to connect with either. Behind him, the young woman reached for his groin with her left hand and kneaded what she found there, her eyes distant and desolate.

'I hate Arizona,' said Parker softly, before following Ross to the body.

IV

F ar to the northeast, over land and ocean, in another country – and, perhaps, another time – a woman knelt on cold ground beneath a waning moon. Her hands were bound behind her back, and her mouth was sealed by layers of tape. She had spent the last hours breathing only through her nose, inhaling and exhaling in the shadow of suffocation. She had given up trying to make herself comprehensible through the gag. He understood what she was trying to say, and it had done her no good.

She did not know this place. She would never know this place.

She thought of her mother and father, of her sister, of men who had whispered her name in the dark. She saw other lives, a delicate tracery of paths not taken, of alternative existences rejected, the pattern of them like the veins beneath her skin or the buried roots of a tree. She held infants that had never been born, walked fields with sons that had no name, and consoled daughters without histories. She became unmoored from this spot, from the final moments of her life, floating backward to unmake decisions: turning right instead of left, going up instead of down, saying yes instead of no, no instead of yes, so that this other self, the one about to die, might yet be designated the phantom, an ephemeral product of errors not made but merely considered and rejected.

I would have had children, she thought. *I always wanted them. They would have had children of their own, and their babies would have made babies, but now none of this will come to pass, and how much smaller this universe will be without them.*

His footsteps moved behind her. She could hear the sound of his breathing, and smell his aftershave: masculine, and probably expensive, but not overpowering. She had liked that about him.

He had seemed so clean. Perhaps he was a little uncouth in his speech, a fraction rough in his bearing, but she had been with men who boasted an education at the finest schools, men with old names and old money, while under their silk suits and their veneer of fine manners they were no better than rapists.

I should have stayed with Simon. He was decent and honest, but I thought I wanted something more. I mistook gentleness for dullness, and kindness for weakness. I realize my error now. Late, too late.

A hand in her hair. A knee against her back.

Mum, I am sorry for all those times I hurt you. I am sorry for not being a better daughter. I would have tried harder, had I lived. Dad, I—

The world changed around her. Where formerly there had been only bare ground and distant trees she saw the stones of an old church, its walls rising to encompass her, and the earth turned to flagstones against her bare legs. The chapel was a small, primitive construct, but she felt no sense of the Divine there, as though God had turned His back on it, or it had never been raised in His name to begin with, for she could see no crosses, no Christian carvings. There were faces on the walls, but they were leering, hostile presences, born of wood and branch, tree and leaf. If they demanded worship, they offered no love in return, only the deferral of some inevitable retribution.

And yet even they feared something more terrible than themselves.

'You see it?' he asked. 'You do, don't you?'

She could not help but nod.

Yes, I see it.

Yes, I see them.

Daddy, oh Daddy.

As the blade commenced its explorations, and the agony began to unfold.

18

V

It was not the first body Parker had viewed, and certainly not in such a state of disfigurement, but he was more familiar with remains yielded by northern ground, not the fruits of this arid place. Still, he knew a little about such matters, enough to feel troubled from the moment he bore witness.

The rate of decomposition of a corpse is affected by a number of factors, but all are linked to the environment in which the remains are situated, and the way in which they were deposited. Is there water or oxygen in the vicinity? What is the temperature? Is the ground acidic? Has the body been exposed to insects, animals, or the actions of men? These are the most basic questions that must be asked when investigating the natural ruination of a deceased human being. Of these factors, the most important are temperature, insects, and depth of burial, and of these, in turn, burial may be the principal. A body interred in shallow ground will decay in a manner different from one exposed to the elements. Similarly, a deep burial will result in a singular pattern of decomposition.

The portable lights surrounding the freezer offered Parker a clear view of the remains, but he still accepted Ross's offer of a flashlight, and a smear of Olbas oil for his upper lip to offer some protection from odors. The woman lay on her side at the base of the freezer, her legs drawn up against her chest, her mouth open. Parker could see no signs of clothing. As he leaned in, he discerned the recession of the lips and gums, the marbling of the skin, the bloating around the abdomen, and – even through the oil – the smell of her. Her teeth had been removed, probably with a hammer or other tool; jagged and broken edges were embedded in the jaws. Both hands were gone, the severance marks rough at the wrists, as though it might have taken a number of blows to complete the work. Parker didn't have to ask if the teeth or hands had been found with the body. As soon as he saw the empty mouth, he knew they had been disposed of elsewhere. There would be no hope of identification using dental records or fingerprints, and DNA testing would only help if samples were available for comparison. He detected signs of insect activity – flies mostly, probably first generation. There was a crack in the floor of the freezer, large enough to admit bugs. There should have been more of them, though.

Parker shifted position, and saw what might have been entry and exit wounds to the left of the abdomen and the upper left thigh respectively. Louis believed that he had hit Mors when he fired at her. If these were her remains, he was right.

He switched his attention to the woman's hair. It was silver-gray, like that of an older person, but Parker estimated that Mors was probably in her thirties, and the absence of pigmentation to her skin might have been caused by some disease of the thyroid or pituitary. The hair of the woman in the freezer was artificially colored, darkening significantly at the roots.

Finally, he shone the light on what lay against her breast, clasped in her crossed arms. Whoever was responsible for putting her in the chest had taken the time to wrap wire around the limbs, holding the book in place. It consisted of loose pages – and the cover – of an early twentieth-century hardback copy of *Grimm's Fairy Tales*, illustrated by Arthur Rackham. Quayle's little joke: he had come to Maine seeking this very book, one into which had been sewn the older vellum pages he desired. Now he had left his discards.

Parker stepped back.

'I take it you haven't examined the book yet?' he said.

'Haven't touched it,' said Ross. 'I thought we'd wait until we got her inside. Thoughts?'

'Isn't that why you have a medical examiner?' Parker looked past Ross to where two of the ME's team were waiting by their vehicle. He understood now why they had brought their largest truck: the freezer would be coming with the body. They wouldn't risk removing her from it out here.

'The ME's been and gone, so I know what she thinks, for now. I'd like to hear what *you* think.'

Parker killed the flashlight. A discovery of this kind would usually have fallen under the remit of the Homicide Unit of the Maricopa County Sheriff's Office, but they were unlikely to object if the FBI was willing to take a potential homicide off their hands.

'She wasn't put in the chest immediately after she died,' said Parker. 'I know enough about the actions of moisture and humidity to make that assertion. The body was exposed to the elements, maybe for a couple of weeks, before being placed inside. There are signs of disturbance, although I can't say for sure if they occurred when the freezer was dumped here, or before. I'll be curious to read the entomology report, because I'd have expected more insect activity. It's odd – off, somehow.'

'Do you think this is Mors?'

'The gunshot wounds and the presence of the book might suggest it. Even allowing for anomalies, the body looks to be in about the right state of decay.'

'But?'

Parker hit the flashlight again, and shone it on the woman's head. In the aftermath of the killings in Indiana and Maine, descriptions of Mors and Quayle had been red-flagged to every law enforcement office in the country. Mors's hair was certainly her most identifiable feature.

'I don't believe Mors dyed her hair.'

'Evidence?'

'None, or not much beyond seeing her up close, and then only for a short time. The night was dark, and she had just kicked me in the balls, so I admit I was distracted, but her eyebrows were a similar color to her hair, and she had very fine down on her upper lip and her cheeks, as though someone had sprinkled silver filings over her skin. This woman's face looks smooth.'

'Not definitive.'

'No,' Parker admitted, 'not at all. How was the body discovered?'

'Last night, a male caller contacted the owner of the yard –

that's Mr Lagnier, the fornicator, who you probably met as you entered. The caller said he'd noticed a chest freezer when he was searching for stove parts a few days back, and thought it might have an element worth scavenging. He asked Lagnier to set it aside so he could take a closer look.'

The light was fading rapidly, and the temperature was falling: not so much as yet to be uncomfortable, but enough to be noticeable. The sky was cloudless, and already stars were visible. A slight breeze had arisen, blowing the smell of smoke in Parker's direction. It would cling to his clothes, he thought, but not like the burning of wood. These fumes were unclean.

'What are the chances Lagnier killed her?' said Parker, if only for the sake of asking.

'Pretty low, unless he's either massively dumb or incredibly clever. My sense is he's smart, but not that smart.'

Parker took in the junkyard again.

'It doesn't look as though business is booming.'

'I doubt he has an oligarch's tastes, but the Maricopa County sheriff believes Lagnier may be supplementing his income by unlawful means.'

This close to the border, it had to be at least one of three commodities: drugs, guns, or people.

'Not worth the bust?' said Parker.

'As I said already, Lagnier's smart.'

'But also, like you said, not that smart.'

Ross put on his best poker face.

'He has a rabbi?' said Parker.

'Maybe.'

'One of yours?'

'No.'

So Lagnier was being protected by another agency. Down here, that meant the Drug Enforcement Administration, the Bureau of Alcohol, Tobacco, Fire Arms and Explosives, or maybe even Immigration and Customs Enforcement, although informants like Lagnier weren't really ICE's style. Under the deal, Lagnier probably kept a listening ear for large-scale movements of contraband, and in return was allowed some leeway in his own affairs. Not guns – that would be too risky for all involved – which left only people and low-level narcotics.

'Did Lagnier call the police when he found the body?'

'Eventually, but I can't say for sure how much time went between the discovery of it and his coming forward. We got a heads up to say we'd be hearing from him about ten minutes before he called.'

Ross softly whistled a couple of bars of the *Batman* theme, confirming the source of Lagnier's protection. He was under the wing of the ATF: the Batmen, the damned rev'nooers. Lagnier would first have contacted his rabbi after finding the body.

'Do you mind if I talk to him?' said Parker.

'No,' said Ross. 'But I wouldn't go making a habit of it – not that you're likely to. I think you'll find one conversation with Mr Lagnier is more than sufficient for a lifetime.'

Lagnier had made a concession to the departure of the day's warmth by donning a filthy white cardigan. He had also lit himself a fresh cheroot, which he smoked as he leaned against the door-frame of his office, watching Parker and Ross approach. His dogs had resumed their station at his feet, joined by the woman, who had recommenced her rhythmic squeezing of his groin, or perhaps had never stopped.

Seen up close, Lagnier presented an even more unprepossessing figure than when viewed at a distance, and Parker hadn't thought much of him then. The bulb above the door revealed a skin covered in tiny lumps, like the carcass of a plucked chicken, and his eyes were a faded brown, as though exposure to the desert sun were progressively draining them of color. His bare pate was without blemish or indentation, resembling a skull stripped of flesh prior to being painted. The teeth that gripped the cheroot were too white and even to be natural. His limbs were emaciated, and his waist small. His clothing hung from his frame as of one being eaten away by illness, but who refuses to concede that death may take him before he can grow back into them again. Parker estimated that he was in his fifties, but it was hard to be certain, so strange was his aspect. Meanwhile, the woman sitting beside him was even younger than she had first appeared. She could have been out of her teens, but not by much, and Parker and Ross might as well not have been present for all the attention she gave them.

Squeeze, relax.

Squeeze, relax.

The interior of the hut was furnished with a desk, a lamp, a chair upholstered in imitation leather, which was leaking stuffing, and a worn gray couch with a pillow at one end. The wall behind the desk was adorned with pornographic images of women, many of them represented only by their most intimate body parts. The collage reached to the ceiling, and for all Parker knew might well have extended to cover the entire office.

Squeeze, relax.

Squeeze, relax.

'You think you could ask her to stop doing that?' said Parker.

'What do you suggest she should do instead?' Lagnier asked.

'If I were her, I'd clean my hand. There must be battery acid round here somewhere.'

'You're being impolite.'

'Tell her,' said Parker, 'to stop.'

Lagnier placed his hand over the girl's, and gently removed it from his private parts. It dropped heavily into her lap, as though it were not her limb but that of another. She stared at it almost in disbelief, perhaps appalled by the uses to which it had so recently been put.

'You going to introduce yourself,' said Lagnier, 'now that you've insulted my woman and me?'

'My name is Parker.'

'You FBI too?'

'No.'

'Police?'

Parker thought back to the woman on the plane. He hadn't expected to be involved in a similar conversation quite so soon.

'No.'

'So I don't have to speak with you if I don't care to?'

'That's correct.'

'Then I choose not to.'

'That's unfortunate.'

'You say so?'

'I do.'

'And why would that be, allowing as how I'm now extending to you the continued courtesy of discourse?'

'Because the mutilated body of a woman has just been discovered on your property, and we only have your word that you didn't put her there.'

Lagnier rolled the cheroot along his lips. He was smiling.

'I called the police. Why would I do that if I'd killed her?'

'I don't know, but you could spend a long time in a holding cell while investigators tried to come up with an answer to that question.'

'Yet as I recall, you're not a cop, and you're not a fed, so you can go fuck yourself. And I already answered a shitload of questions.'

Parker shrugged, and began to walk away. He was out of practice, and out of sorts. Lagnier might have been an asshole – in fact, there was no doubt about it – but Parker had aggravated him more than he'd intended. The situation could easily be remedied, but it would require Ross's assistance.

'I told you it was a waste of time,' he said to Ross.

'Maybe if you weren't so rude to the man to begin with.'

'I don't need your lessons in etiquette. I did you a favor by coming down here.'

'Jesus, take it easy.'

'This guy isn't my problem. It's like some folks just enjoy giving money to lawyers.'

Ross gave a shrug, and a sigh that went on for so long Parker was afraid the agent might grow lightheaded.

'Mr Lagnier,' said Ross, 'I really don't want to have to take you all the way to Phoenix to answer further questions about matters that could easily be dealt with here, but Mr Parker has been engaged as a consultant by the bureau. He possesses certain talents, and is familiar with aspects of this case.'

Parker kicked up some dirt and watched Lagnier's brain

working. Yes, he had shade from the ATF, but his handler would certainly have advised him to cooperate in every way possible with the investigation into the woman's remains, and that handler wouldn't relish being called on to intervene in the event of any recalcitrance on Lagnier's part. The ATF had already done enough in letting the feds know that they were about to come into contact with a source, although the handler would also have checked that Lagnier wasn't holding any contraband of his own on the premises – or if he was, that he found a way to get rid of it fast.

'Fuck it,' said Lagnier. 'I got nothing to hide. I'll answer his questions, just like I answered yours. I just don't much care for his manner.'

'Not many people do,' said Ross, which Parker felt was rubbing it in some, but he let it go.

'*Dos sillas*,' Lagnier told the woman. She disappeared into the hut, and returned moments later with a pair of lawn chairs, which she unfolded for Parker and Ross.

'You know,' said Lagnier, once they were all settled, 'you two ought to do Shakespeare.'

VI

Ernest Lagnier was fifty-nine years old, and had inherited the junkyard from his father, also Ernest. Lagnier owned a home about a mile east of the yard, but rarely spent more than half his time in it, if that. His office had a bathroom, a TV, and a couch that doubled as a bed, as the investigators had learned to their cost during the earlier coital interlude. A ramshackle structure out back contained a primitive shower, and when Lagnier needed hot water, he filled a tin basin and dropped in a heating element. He had no siblings, and had never married. This scavenger life was all he had ever known.

'It's a big yard,' said Parker.

'Biggest in southern Arizona.'

'You have employees?'

'Over there.' Lagnier used his cheroot to indicate the assembled Latinos. 'Casual labor, mostly.'

'Are they all legal?'

'They said so when I asked them.'

'You didn't check?'

'Let's say the cultural and linguistic barriers have yet to be overcome where some of them are concerned. They earn clean money from dirty work, the kind no white man will do. If we build the Wall, we'll have to start scrubbing our own toilets. They're right with Jesus, which is good enough for me. You "consulting" for Immigration too?'

'Just curious. How familiar are you with the contents of your yard?'

'I walk it every day, even when the sun is splitting the stones. Someone comes in here looking for parts, they don't want to wait around for hours while I go digging without a map. I know where most everything is at – if not exactly, then within a foot or two. Some yards, they got computerized inventory. Me, I got a file cabinet I never use, and this.' He tapped his right temple with the butt of the cheroot.

'What about new junk?'

'See, I know you don't mean to sound ignorant, but you do. For me, this is *not* junk. Junk is the stuff even I can't use. Junk has no purpose. Junk is useless. Everything you see here has worth. It's just waiting to be turned into cash money.

'But in answer to your original question, nothing comes in here that I haven't agreed to take. I decide what's worth accepting, and I determine what to offer for it, but the secret of a place like this is to get as much as you can for nothing at all. I don't produce my wallet to hand over money unless I can be damn sure I'm going to get a good return on my investment. Most of what you see here, nobody else wanted. They were happy for me just to take it away so they didn't have to look at it no more, and they paid me for the privilege. Then I brought it here, figured out what to keep and what to discard, and found a spot for the valuables.'

'When did you acquire the chest freezer?' Parker asked.

'Like I told the police and the federal agents, I didn't.'

'So it was dumped?'

'It wasn't dumped either. Folks around here know that I don't approve of stuff just being thrown on my doorstep, no more than they would on theirs. It happens sometimes, but I don't like it. If the yard is open, and I'm not around, they can leave it with one of the men, long as they pay him, and it goes over there, in that space beside the tires. That's where new material is stored until I decide where it should go.'

'Then how did the freezer get in your yard?'

'I don't know. No civilian is allowed to go further than this office, not without me or someone else from the yard keeping him company. Folks steal, or they go clambering and nosing about where they shouldn't, and get hurt. I have to be careful, or I'll be ass-deep in lawyers.'

'And how come you didn't spot the freezer on one of your rounds?'

'Because it was in the wrong place. It wasn't with the other white goods. It was hidden with the real trash.'

'Real trash?' said Parker.

The freezer looked too big to be hidden comfortably amid garbage, but who knew how much of it was contained in Lagnier's junkyard?

'When I say "trash", I mean the stuff that even I can't sell, or vehicles that have been stripped of all useable parts.'

'Junk.'

'See, you're learning. Yeah, junk. Merrill and Sons, out of Tucson, come up here once a month with a mobile baling press and shredder, and take away the leavings. They got a hammer mill, and sell that shit by the ton.'

'And when did they last make a collection?'

'A week ago, but they couldn't take everything on account of how they'd made two stops before they got to me, and only had room for maybe three-quarters of what was on offer.'

'And the freezer wasn't there when they came?'

'No, it would have stood out.'

So the freezer had been placed in the yard sometime in the last week.

'Could one of your employees have concealed it?'

'You see that man over there, the one with the beard?' Lagnier pointed to an older Latino sitting slightly apart from the rest. 'That's Miguel Ángel. He's been with me for twenty years. If I'm away, he's here, and if he's away, I'm here. I tell you now: Miguel Ángel did not conceal no chest freezer behind busted truck exhausts, and he would permit no one else to do so, either.'

Lagnier leaned forward, now giving his attention only to Ross.

'By the way, you think you're nearly done treating my men like criminals? You've left them sitting in that shelter for a long time.'

'They've been questioned,' said Ross, 'but we have no way of checking the identities of some of them, or even being sure of where they live. And the bureau isn't their problem. It's Border Patrol.'

'What about the rest?' said Lagnier. 'Miguel Ángel, Francisco,

Gerardo, they're all legal. What you're doing to them is wrong. You wouldn't treat them like that if they was white.'

Ross called over one of his agents.

'Go talk to the Border Patrol. Tell them anyone legal can go home.'

The agent looked puzzled.

'You mean back to Mexico?'

'Are you trying to get fired?' Ross asked.

The agent reconsidered the order, and quickly figured out the correct answer.

'No, sir. Sorry.'

'Have them hold the rest for now.'

The agent hurried off, and Lagnier thanked Ross.

'Other than Miguel Ángel, how long have the others been working for you?' Parker asked.

'Francisco and Gerardo have been with me for five years. They're brothers. The rest are temporary, so anything from a few weeks to a couple of months.'

'Do they have access to the yard out of hours?'

'No. Only Miguel Ángel and I have keys. And then there's the dogs.'

Parker took in the two mongrels dozing at Lagnier's feet. One of them opened an eye, as though sensing his regard, before closing it again when Parker did nothing interesting.

'They seem pretty docile.'

'That's because I'm here.'

'And if you weren't?'

'Assuming Miguel Ángel wasn't here either, they'd have torn you up, or you'd have had to shoot them. There are two more just like them over by the far gate. We got them chained up for now, but we'll set them to roaming once you're done.'

'Yet it looks like someone got past them.'

Lagnier looked troubled.

'I don't see no other explanation for it,' he conceded.

'Could they have been drugged?' Ross asked.

'They're trained to take food from no one but me or Miguel Ángel.'

30

'What about the girl?' said Parker, indicating the woman seated by Lagnier's chair. Like the dogs, she now appeared to be asleep.

'What about her?'

'Would the dogs attack her?'

'I don't know. She's never been here without me.'

'What's her name?'

'Leticia.'

Ross interrupted before Parker could continue this line of questioning.

'Leticia doesn't speak,' he said.

'She got her tongue torn out,' said Lagnier.

'Who by?' Parker asked.

Lagnier shrugged. 'Mexicans.'

'What kind of Mexicans?'

Lagnier picked at a scab on his hand. 'The other kind.'

Once again, Parker wished that he were elsewhere, and not in the company of a man who saw only two kinds of Mexicans – two kinds of everyone, probably.

'When?' he said.

'Well, she's been with me for three years, and she was bleeding when I found her, so I'd say about three years back.'

Parker stared at Lagnier without speaking. Seconds passed. Finally, Parker said, 'I have to confess that your thought processes are confusing to me.'

'That's because you're trying to make the world more complicated than it already is,' said Lagnier. 'You ought not to contemplate it so much.'

Parker stood and thanked Lagnier for his time. Three of the Latino workers drifted over: the one called Miguel Ángel, and two younger men who Parker took to be Francisco and Gerardo.

'*Vete a casa*,' Lagnier told them.

Francisco and Gerardo nodded and walked away, but Miguel Ángel remained where he was, his eyes returning to the freezer before shifting away again, but only for a time, as though in some future hell he would forever be forced to look upon the body within.

'It was Miguel Ángel who found her,' Lagnier said. 'He was the one that pulled out the freezer.'

Parker introduced himself, apologized to Miguel Ángel for not having much Spanish, and asked if he spoke English. Parker recognized his own politeness as some attempt to make recompense for the earlier treatment of the workers, but also as penance for his rudeness to Lagnier, and what he had subsequently learned about Leticia. Sometimes, his own rush to judgment was a source of shame to him.

'Yes, I speak English,' said Miguel Ángel.

'Is there anything you can tell us about the discovery of the woman's body, anything that struck you as particularly unusual?'

Miguel Ángel thought.

'The freezer was too light.'

'Even with the body inside?'

'Yes. It should have weighed more.'

'Why didn't it?'

'It had no parts. Just the woman.'

Parker retrieved his flashlight.

'Would you mind coming with me?' he asked Miguel Ángel, who did seem to mind but followed him anyway.

Parker knelt by the vent at the bottom of the freezer and shone the light inside. Miguel Ángel was correct: the appliance had not been fitted with any of its internal workings, not even a condenser. It was essentially a redundant white box, and also relatively new. It had acquired some dents, and a patina of dust, but that was all. He checked the brand name – COOL-A – but didn't recognize it.

'They're made in Juárez for the domestic market,' said Lagnier, who had joined them. 'We don't see too many this side of the border.'

Parker got to his feet.

'She was brought from Mexico,' he said to Ross.

'Which means she didn't die here,' said Ross.

'Because why transport a dead woman to Mexico only to carry her back to the United States again a few weeks later?'

Parker stared down for the final time at the body, as he and Ross spoke the same words simultaneously.

'It's not Mors.'

VII

The Border Patrol wanted to get the suspected illegals over to sector headquarters in Tucson as quickly as possible in order to process them before, in all likelihood, sending them back across the border, assuming they weren't wanted for any crimes in the United States. But Ross didn't particularly care to spend two hours driving to Tucson just to hear what he already knew or suspected: that these men had nothing to do with the body in the freezer.

Nevertheless, it made sense to be certain. After some discussion, it was agreed that questioning should take place at the sheriff's office in Gila Bend, where the first two Mexican workers to be interviewed claimed, through an interpreter, that they indeed knew nothing about the woman's body, and had only crossed the border in the last week. A call to Lagnier confirmed that they had first shown up at his yard about four days earlier, which didn't necessarily mean they were telling the truth, but Lagnier said he'd got 'no bad vibes' from them, and he was a man who knew his vibes.

'He may be right about those two,' said a border patrol agent named Zaleski, once all interested parties – with the obvious exception of the Mexicans themselves – had convened in the main office. She had arrived later than her colleagues, and worked Intelligence for the sector. 'They say they're uncle and nephew, and they're clean: no tattoos. That third one, though – he's a keeper.'

The third man had given his name as José Hernández, which was the equivalent of a Caucasian claiming to be called John Smith. He had not been picked up in the sweep of the yard, but a couple of hours later, supposedly as he waited on a bus to Tucson, although it was more likely he was waiting for a ride back to Mexico, since the next bus for Tucson wasn't scheduled to leave until the following morning. He was smaller and leaner than the others, and had so far done his best not to make eye contact with any of his interrogators. He was also the only one who had been wearing a long-sleeved shirt, fully buttoned, when detained.

'What did Lagnier have to say about him?' Ross asked.

'Beyond the fact that Hernández had been working for him on and off for about five days,' said Zaleski, 'Mr Lagnier had nothing to say about him at all, and that's "nothing" with a heavy emphasis.'

'Meaning?'

'Meaning Lagnier knew better than to ask about José's background. It's probably not the first time Lagnier's done a solid for some friends from across the border: a place for cousins to sleep, a little work to replenish funds before they head further north. But sometimes . . .'

Zaleski let it hang. Parker figured everyone in the room now knew that Lagnier had an arrangement with the ATF, and if they didn't, they had no business being there.

'Sometimes it's a more substantial favor,' finished Newton, one of the Maricopa detectives. 'One he doesn't share with his handler.'

'Not unless Lagnier wants to try holding his silverware without thumbs,' said Zaleski. 'This whole territory belongs to the Sinaloa cartel, and nothing moves in or out without their knowledge. Young José in there has himself a collection of tattoos under that shirt. He didn't much approve of us having a look-see, but he knew better than to kick up a fuss.'

Zaleski took out her phone, and displayed a series of photographs of Hernández's adornments. The man was a walking skin gallery of devils, clowns, and death's-head virgins, but pride of place went to the number '13' on his back.

'He's Mara Salvatrucha Thirteen,' said Zaleski, mostly to Parker. 'You know what that is?'

'Gang member – and not just any gang.'

The mainly El Salvadoran MS-13 had emerged out of Los Angeles in the 1980s, where it initially went head-to-head with its rivals, principally the Mexicans. When the United States began deporting the El Salvadorans, it also effectively exported MS-13 to Central America, facilitating the expansion of its activities – notably human trafficking, especially children and young women destined for the sex trade. The gang's motto was *mata, viola, controla*, or 'kill, rape, control', and it favored knives and machetes over guns for the purposes of maiming and murdering. MS-13 quickly came to a series of mutually beneficial arrangements with the Mexican cartels, and was now firmly embedded within *la Eme*, the Mafia Mexicana. MS-13 members formed the foot soldiers of the Sinaloa cartel.

'You think Hernández put that body in the freezer?' said Ross.

'He might have done,' said Zaleski, 'or helped get it into the yard. Lagnier was kind of vague on when Hernández began working for him, but that may be deliberate forgetfulness on his part, not that I'd blame him. These guys eat people alive, but they like to play with their food first. Even if Hernández wasn't directly responsible for dumping the body, he may have been the lookout. He could have been placed at the yard to make sure the victim wasn't found until the right time.'

'It still doesn't explain how they got the freezer past those dogs,' said Newton.

'I think I can answer that,' said Parker. 'Mors did it.'

'Wait a second,' said Newton. 'We still haven't established for certain that the victim isn't this Mors woman.'

'And we're going to have trouble doing that,' said Parker, 'because we don't have any of Mors's DNA to check against the remains from the freezer. But my guess is she was directly involved in getting that freezer into the yard.'

Mors had been both careful and lucky in her activities. She had probably suffered a facial injury from a key in Cadillac, Indiana, after one of her intended victims successfully fought her off, but the young woman in question hadn't thought to preserve the key with the blood intact. Searches of the other houses occupied by Mors and Quayle had come up with nothing useable, and while the wound, or wounds, inflicted on Mors by Louis had almost certainly resulted in bleeding, rainfall had washed

35

away the blood before an evidence team could even get to the scene.

One of the more curious aspects of the DNA that *had* been recovered – in this case, from a cabin in northwestern Maine temporarily used by Quayle and Mors – was the condition of two hair samples containing the Y chromosome, indicating that they came from a male. The DNA was degraded, like tissue obtained from a dead body. The hair also contained traces of black dye, and while the dye on Quayle's hair had been notice-able to all who encountered him – or the ones that had survived the contact – the lawyer appeared to be a living, breathing specimen. The only logical conclusion to be drawn was that the hairs had not come from Quayle, and the body of an unknown decedent had been present in the cabin at some point. Still, it was peculiar.

'You think she was in the country until recently?' Ross asked Parker.

'Louis thinks he hit Mors with at least one bullet, possibly two, and I wouldn't doubt his word. It would have been hard for her to travel, so she probably found somewhere safe to hole up while she was being treated. Quayle may have remained with her, but it's more likely he left without her, because he'd draw less attention to himself that way. But before he goes, Quayle pays for a favor: the killing of a woman, one roughly similar in age and build to Mors, who can be used to lay a false trail.'

'Even if that's the case,' said Zaleski, 'and you have a whole lot of supposition in there, it still doesn't explain how they got the freezer past Lagnier's dogs.'

'Look, it seems to me that there are two possibilities,' said Parker. 'The first is that Lagnier or his assistant, Miguel Ángel, facilitated the storage of the freezer, but unless you have strong feelings to the contrary, that doesn't seem likely. It's one thing tossing a little work and a few dollars to illegals passing through Gila Bend, and another letting a body decay in a yard. Had they brought the freezer in with Lagnier's knowledge, I believe he'd have taken a look inside as soon as possible, no matter how many warnings he'd been given to mind his own business. Narcotics may end up stored at Lagnier's place on occasion, but I bet they don't stay there for long. A container of any kind left on his premises for more than a day or two would have given Lagnier cause for concern.'

'I'm inclined to agree with Mr Parker,' said Newton. 'I was one of the first on the scene after the body was discovered. Lagnier was shaken, Miguel Ángel too. I don't think they knew about that freezer until a few minutes before Miguel started removing it from under their trash.'

'But Lagnier must have been suspicious when Hernández started hanging around,' said Ross. 'He wasn't there just to earn some cash by sorting junk.'

'Lagnier still wasn't going to raise any objections,' said Zaleski. 'I guarantee that he likes his balls attached to his body.'

'Maybe it wasn't just about Lagnier himself,' said Parker. 'There's also Leticia, that girl he has with him.'

'Story I heard is that she may have been cut by the Jalisco New Generation,' said Zaleski. 'No love lost between them and Sinaloa.'

'Why did they hurt her?' asked Parker.

'Who knows? Just because: because she turned down the wrong guy; because she objected to being raped; because she opened her mouth when she shouldn't have; because someone in her family didn't show enough respect; because she's a woman; or because a narco was bored one afternoon. So: just because.'

'And Lagnier took her in?'

'He found her out in the desert, paid for her medical care,' said Newton. 'I'm not saying that he did it entirely out of the goodness of his heart – Lagnier's no looker, and he'd been hurting for some female company for a long time – but he's not keeping her captive, and she seems to like him, far as anyone can tell. Lagnier's a strange guy. There's a lot of bad to him, but that's not all there is.'

'So Lagnier does what he's told by Sinaloa,' said Parker.

'While trying to stay righteous with the ATF, mostly by feeding them anyone dumb enough to trespass on Sinaloa's territory,' said

Zaleski. 'In return, nobody mentions to the JNG that he's sheltering a girl they mutilated. But I agree that Lagnier's still going to draw the line at bodies stinking up his yard.'

'Which leaves Mors,' said Parker. 'We think she may have killed a woman named Connie White up in Piscataquis County. White had a dog that was all mean, but when we found White's body, the dog was inside with it, alive and well and still all mean. If Mors did murder Connie White, then she may have a way with animals.'

'Enough to charm Lagnier's junkyard curs?' asked Ross.

'It's possible.'

Ross returned his attention to Zaleski.

'What about Hernández? Can you lean on him?'

'We can try,' said Zaleski. 'We'll run his prints and see if they've ended up on the handle of the wrong blade. If we get a match, we can use it to pry him open, but mostly I think we'll be wasting our time. He'll know better than to say anything. Bad enough that we picked him up before he could slip back across the border, and we only did that because one of the sheriff's deputies remembered seeing him around Lagnier's place, so Lagnier couldn't deny all knowledge of him. If Hernández keeps his mouth shut, and hasn't left evidence of his involvement in any crime, then we only have him for alleged gang membership based on the tattoos. We'll check with the Mexicans, and the El Salvadorans and Guatemalans too. Who knows, if he's pissed off any of them, he might prefer to take his chances with us rather than be shipped south. But even if he does talk, all we'll get from him is the name of whoever sent him to Lagnier to start with, and that guy probably just received a phone call telling him the check had cleared.'

'Which is what Quayle wants us to do,' Parker said to Ross. 'He'd like nothing better than to have us chasing dead-end leads in Mexico.'

'You mean have *you* chasing dead-end leads,' said Ross. 'I'm not going down to Mexico. That's why you're on retainer.'

'Thanks,' said Parker. 'I always wondered.'

'That's assuming no one down in cartel land takes offense at your line of questioning, and decides to bring it to an end by cutting off your head,' said Zaleski.

'Yeah, assuming that,' said Parker.

Newton raised a hand.

'I got a question,' he said.

They all looked at him.

'Just who the fuck is Quayle?'

VIII

Pallida Mors stood in the quarters of the lawyer Quayle, the accumulated burden of the past imposing itself upon her as though the gloom of these spaces were less a function of the absence of light than a physical manifestation of darkness itself, a material accumulation of centuries of night. It accentuated her own pallor, so that she perceived herself as a ghost reflected in the glass front of the bookcases behind Quayle's desk.

Not that this place was in need of more ghosts, not by any means.

The room, like the rest of Quayle's living area, was entirely windowless, the only light being bequeathed by a pair of lamps, one on the desk, the other freestanding in a corner; the former illuminated a small circle of embossed leather, and the latter, hampered by a heavy red and cream shade, imbued its territory with a filtered, amniotic phosphorescence. This was the lair of one who hunted, and was now being hunted in turn. It lay in Holborn, close to the heart of London's legal community, which was an organ that beat just the faintest of rhythms – if it truly beat at all, some might have said – and pumped only cold blood. Once, Quayle's chambers had formed part of a little courtyard, the exterior walls wretched in appearance, blackened by the soot and pollution of ages. A narrow passageway from Chancery Lane had permitted access to the core, but it became locked and gated between the First and Second World Wars. Finally, in 1940, a German bomb did what plague and fire had signally failed to do, and laid waste to the courtyard, leaving only one building standing. In time, this was subsumed by newer structures, slowly fading from the city's memory; forgotten by most, perhaps, but not entirely lost. A complicated series of trusts and bequests, a quagmire of deeds and transfers of ownership, meant that this architectural relic, and its fossilized chambers, remained beyond the reach of developers. Eventually, as is often the case, it largely ceased to be noticed at all, which suited its occupant perfectly.

Officially, the last of the Quayle line had been rendered into dust sometime during the 1940s, although no one could say precisely when. Unofficially, he – or some figure resembling him: a distant scion, a bastard son, for the original must surely have long since ceased delighting even the worms – remained above ground, his footsteps occasionally echoing on the cobbles of Lincoln's Inn, his breath pluming in the winter air of the Temple, his solitude now broken only by the visits of a woman with unnaturally white skin and prematurely silver hair who trailed the stink of moral and corporeal corruption.

'So they've found the body,' said Quayle, not turning from the glass. His eyes were cast downward, their gaze fixed not at the books on the shelves but on a single volume occupying its own plinth: the Fractured Atlas, its recovered vellum pages now restored to the whole; the work that would, he believed, bring this world to an end.

And yet still, it was not complete.

'It seemed the right moment had come,' said Mors. 'The Americans were asking questions about passports.'

She was glad to have left the United States behind, glad to be back here where she belonged: in London, by Quayle's side.

'It won't fool them for long,' he said.

'Possibly not,' Mors agreed, 'but it may divert them. Let them travel to Mexico. Let them hunt for leads in the desert. They'll find nothing, and more time will slip away. Time stolen from them is time gifted to you.'

Quayle's right hand reached out and touched the Atlas, gently stroking it as one might a living creature. The pages responded to the contact. He glimpsed within them an image of his own hand, as though mirrored in glass, and beyond them his face, and the lineaments of his rooms. The magic of it never ceased to entrance him.

'He will come, in the end,' said Quayle.

'Parker?'

'Who else? I'm surprised he has not done so already.'

'He won't find you.'

'I wouldn't be too sure of that.'

Quayle closed the Atlas. He was now unrecognizable as the man who had, with the help of Mors, butchered his way across the United States only a month earlier. He had dispensed with dye, so that his hair was almost entirely restored to its natural white, and a rough, silver beard obscured much of his lower face. The prosthetics that had subtly altered the shape of ears and eyes, the colored lenses, all were gone. Even the Botox injections to conceal his wrinkles were wearing off. He now resembled what he was: an old, old man who had lived far, far too long.

'And even if you're right,' he continued, 'I can't remain hidden behind these walls until a way is found to rid ourselves of him. There is work to be done.'

But it was more than that. This was his city, his world. Versions of him breathed in the dust of the Blitz, minute fragments of the living and the dead alike reduced to spores in the sunlight; regarded the maimed returning from the trenches of the Somme; smelled the blood of dead whores in Whitechapel; and watched a king's head fall before the Banqueting House in Whitehall. Quayle understood that no real distinction existed between what is and what once had been. The past was alive in the present, and the seeds of the present were lodged in the past. What was gone before had a habit of manifesting itself over and over again, sometimes without even bothering to find new raiment. And Quayle was the living proof. He was both his own self and all his former selves. Their paths lay parallel to his, and their footsteps echoed in unison.

On the desk before him lay a copy of *The Times*, open to an article detailing the discovery of the body of a young woman named Helen Wylie, who had disappeared from her flat in Ealing one week earlier. Her remains had recently been found in the grounds of the Church of St Martin in Canterbury, Kent, eighty miles from her home. St Martin's was the oldest church in England. It had been in use as a place of worship since the sixth century, although the site dated back to Roman times, and parts of the building were constructed from salvaged Roman brick. Helen Wylie had been killed close to the exterior of the apse, with stabbing as the cause of death, although it would have been more accurate to say that a serrated knife had been used to prize her open from abdomen to chest. One additional detail had not been revealed to the press: the nature of the item recovered from the dead woman's mouth.

But Quayle knew of it, because he had ordered it to be placed there.

Helen Wylie was the first to be revealed.

It had begun.

IX

Zaleski and Newton – with Parker and Ross in attendance, although seated further back from the others – gave eliciting information from Hernández the good old college try, but received only silence for their efforts. Parker did notice Hernández's attention occasionally drifting to him, even when the questions were coming from elsewhere. The rest of the time, the gang member preferred to keep his eyes fixed on the surface of the table to which his cuffs were attached. But he blanked Zaleski entirely, as though, as a woman, she was beneath contempt, so the two interrogators tried a different tack.

'I don't think José likes women much,' said Newton.

'I was wondering about that,' said Zaleski. 'I always feel that men with excessive tattoos are trying to hide something, or make up for some deficiency.'

Hernández seemingly paid them no heed.

'What about it, José?' said Newton. 'Want to tell us why you're working the gang shit so hard?'

'He's no gangster,' said Zaleski. 'He's just small time. You know what?'

'What?'

'I suspect our friend José here is a *huachicolero*.' She looked at Parker. 'Means he steals gasoline. Gets his mouth around a length of pipe and, man, just sucks all that good stuff out.'

'No!' Newton feigned shock, and grinned at Hernández. 'Is that what you are, José? You a gas guzzler? That explains it all.'

But goading Hernández by impugning his sexuality didn't work either, although the dead light in his eyes suggested that some of the barbs had stuck, and if he ever got the chance, he'd make

Zaleski and Newton pay for them. But Zaleski had also picked up on Hernández's interest in Parker.

'Either he finds you attractive,' said Zaleski, 'or he's aware of who you are.'

'How good is his English?' said Parker.

'Better than he's letting us know.'

'You mind if I talk to him?'

'You can try. You want me to translate, just in case?'

'Sure.'

Parker moved his chair closer to the table. Hernández chose to ignore his approach.

'Mr Hernández,' said Parker. He tapped an index finger on the table, and Hernández gave him his attention. 'This is what I think happened. You helped a woman with silver hair dump that body in the junkyard.'

He gave Zaleski time to translate, but saw that Hernández understood what was being said without help. It would make sense for MS-13 to install someone at the yard who could speak both English and Spanish.

'She wanted us to believe she was dead, but you've just confirmed that she was alive and well when last you saw her,' said Parker. 'You shared with us that she walked like she'd been hurt, smelled bad, and kept Lagnier's dogs at bay while the freezer was moved into position.'

Hernández's eyes widened, even before Zaleski began offering the Spanish version.

'You've been really helpful, and we appreciate it,' Parker went on. 'You probably saw those news vans as we were leaving the yard. Well, those reporters are now waiting outside, and we're going to let them film you as you're put in a Border Patrol car bound for Tucson. We'll let them know that, thanks to you, we believe the body in the yard to be a decoy, designed to derail the search for a woman named Pallida Mors, who is wanted for questioning in connection with multiple homicides. We'll tell them what a sport you've been, and how all you ever wanted was to put your gang days behind you and open a little bodega in the United States before the Wall goes up. But times being what they are, and you with your tattoos and your bad rep, we thought it would be best for all concerned if you fulfilled your culinary ambitions closer to home, which is why we'll be shipping you back across the border, no questions asked, as a reward for your assistance. We may even throw in a "Make America Great Again" cap, just so you don't forget us.'

Parker leaned in closer, so he could smell the other man's sweat.

'Now you tell me, Mr Hernández, what do you estimate your life expectancy will be once you're dropped off in Nogales, maybe with a couple of hundred dollars in your pocket so you can celebrate your homecoming with all your buddies?'

Hernández tested his cuffed hands, as though willing the restraints to break so he could go for Parker's throat. He even went so far as to give them a single hard yank. If nothing else, Hernández remained an optimist.

'*Qué quieres?*' he said, once it became clear that no other option was about to present itself.

'What do you want?' Zaleski translated, and nodded her assent for Parker to continue with the questioning.

'First, for you to speak English,' said Parker, 'since you obviously understand it.'

Hernández nodded.

'Where is the woman who hired you, the one with the silver hair?'

'Gone.'

'Where?'

'South.'

'South, where?'

'*No sé.*'

I don't know. Parker understood that much.

'How long ago?'

Hernández shrugged, then raised his right hand, the fingers spread.

'Five days?'

'*Sí, mas o menos.*'

More or less.

'Was she wounded?'

Another nod.

'Where?'

'The side, the leg. *Como la muerta.*'

Like the corpse in the yard.

'But she'd recovered enough to travel?'

Nod.

'Was there an older man with her?'

'*Sí*, but before.'

'How long before?'

'*Dos, tres semanas.*'

Two or three weeks.

'Did he have a name?'

'*No he oído.*'

He didn't hear a name.

'You're sure?'

'Yes. *Nunca lo conocí.*'

I never met him.

'Where had she been while she recovered from her wounds?'

'*No sé.*'

'Where did you meet her?'

'Casa Grande.'

'Where in Casa Grande?'

'*Una parada de descanso.*'

Parker looked to Zaleski for a translation.

'A rest stop,' said Zaleski.

Parker turned back to Hernández.

'When?'

'When we bring to her *la muerta.*'

'What day? Which rest stop?'

'*No recuerdo.*'

'He says he doesn't remember,' said Zaleski.

'You don't remember the day, or the rest stop?'

Hernández was sweating more profusely now. He'd made an error by opening his mouth to begin with, and knew it, even if he'd been given no choice. Now there was no turning back.

'*No sé. Tal vez el lunes.*'

'He thinks that maybe it was a Monday,' said Zaleski.

'And the rest stop?'

'*Tal vez Sacaton.*'

'That's on Interstate Ten,' said Newton. 'There are cameras mounted east- and westbound. We might get something from them.'

'How did you get there?'

'*En una van.*'

A van.

'What van?'

'*Robada.*'

Stolen.

'What type?'

'*No sé.* Buick?'

'Are you asking us or telling us?' said Parker.

'Buick,' said Hernández, with something like conviction.

'What color?'

'Blue.'

'Light or dark?'

'Light.'

'What about the woman? How did she get to the rest stop?'

'She was waiting for us.'

'In a car, a van?'

'Nothing. Just waiting.'

'Alone?'

Hernández shrugged again.

'*Creo que alguien estaba mirando.*'

'He says maybe someone was watching,' Zaleski translated.

'Who?'

'*No sé.*'

'Jesus,' said Newton. 'He doesn't know much, does he? We should just put him on the fucking bus to Nogales right now.'

'*No sé,*' Hernández repeated, with more force.

'What then?' said Parker.

'I think maybe she want to see *el cuerpo.*'

'So you knew there was a body in there when you brought the freezer to her?'

Hernández shook his head.

'*No lo sabía. El otro, el sabe.*'

Parker understood, even if he didn't believe.

'Back to this other man, the one who knew about the body. Tell us about him.'

'*No sé nada de él.*'

I know nothing of him.

'There's a surprise,' said Ross, speaking for the first time.

'Right out of left field,' Newton agreed.

Hernández ignored them. So, for now, did Parker.

'And why do you think she wanted to examine the corpse?'

'To be certain. *El pelo.*'

Hernández gestured at his own head, even though it was entirely shaven. The hair: Mors wanted to be sure that it looked right.

'The body had been prepared in advance of the meeting?'

'*Sí.*'

'How long before?'

Three more fingers, but wavering.

'*Tal vez dos semanas, o un poco mas.*'

Two weeks, maybe, or a little more.

'Who told him to do this?'

'*El jefe.*'

The boss.

'Who is he?'

'*No sé.*'

This was accompanied by a vigorous shake of the head. They certainly weren't going to get that name from Hernández.

'And the woman was pleased with what had been done with the body?'

'*Sí.*'

'And after that?'

'*Fuimos al depósito de chatarra.*'

Zaleski: 'They went to the junkyard.'

'The woman went with you?'

Nod.

'In daylight, or at night?'

'Night.'

'How did you get in?'
'Estaba abierto.'
Zaleski: 'It was unlocked.'
'Who unlocked it?'
'Hice una llava.'
I made a key.
'Did the woman take care of the dogs?'
'Sí.'
'They didn't attack her?'
'No.'
'And after?'
'I stay. She go.'
'South?'
Nod.
Parker sat back.
'Who is the dead woman?'
'No sé, pero . . .'
'What?'
'Una gringa, tal vez.'
A white American, maybe.
'And who killed her?' asked Parker.
Hernández looked Parker in the eye, and let him see the lie.
'No sé.'

The four men convened once more outside the interview room.
'I hate this guy,' said Newton.
'There's not a whole lot about him to like,' Zaleski concurred, before addressing Parker. 'You got more out of him than I expected, but most of it you already knew, or guessed.'

Which was that Mors remained alive, but was probably no longer in the United States, or even in the Americas. If she had recovered enough to assist in the disposal of a body, she had also recovered sufficiently to return whence she came, which was presumably the same place as Quayle: England.

'At least he confirmed it,' said Parker.
'Assuming even half of what he said was true,' said Newton. 'The lying fuck.'

'You really don't like him, do you?'

'Didn't I mention it? Must have slipped my mind.'

'He killed the woman in the freezer,' said Parker.

'Yeah?'

'I saw it in his eyes. He wanted me to.'

'So he knows who she is?' said Ross.

'Maybe,' said Zaleski. 'No guarantee. But a young white American woman would be worth something to these guys. They'd have charged a premium to kill her to order – and more if they had to abduct her first, which seems likely if the victim was required to match a particular body profile.'

'Which means there's probably a missing person report on her somewhere,' said Newton. 'The absence of teeth and hands are a problem. That'll slow things up.'

'She deserves a name,' said Parker. 'And the people who love her should be able to mourn her.'

Zalinksi looked at Ross and Newton.

'It's your call,' she said. 'We can charge him and see what sticks, or . . .'

She let the option hang.

'Hard to prove he knew what was in the freezer before it was dumped,' said Ross. 'Not impossible, but hard.'

'And if you charge him, you may not get anything else out of him,' said Zaleski. 'He won't cut a deal once he's been processed. His life wouldn't be worth a nickel.'

'So?' said Newton.

'He gives us a name,' said Ross, 'and Border Patrol sends him back.'

'No questions asked?'

'No questions asked.'

'I got to tell you,' said Newton, 'that doesn't please me.'

'You have a stake in this,' said Ross. 'If you feel strongly enough about it, give us another option.'

Newton spent a long time staring at his feet. Finally he said, 'Get the name. I'll take an extra Ambien for a couple of nights, until the guilt starts to wear off.'

'Will Hernández go for it?' Parker asked Zaleski.

Zaleski shrugged.

'Let's ask him.'

Hernández took the deal. He didn't alter his story, but only added that he might have heard *el otro* mention a name to the silver-haired woman when they were examining the contents of the freezer – the contents of which he knew nothing about, having been paid only to transport it from Sierra Vista to a junkyard in Gila Bend, a journey of two hundred miles, past any number of equally suitable junkyards, before keeping an eye on it until the time came for the freezer to be discovered.

But never mind.

The name? Barbonne, which was unusual enough to be checked easily. It took Newton only minutes to confirm that a missing person report on an Adrienne Barbonne, 30, had been filed in El Paso just over three weeks earlier. Barbonne was a nurse at the city's University Medical Center. El Paso was a twenty-minute ride across the border from Ciudad Juárez, where COOL-A freezers were assembled

'*Es verdad?*' Hernández asked, once Parker and Zaleski had returned to the interview room.

'Yes,' said Zaleski, 'it's true.'

'*Siento, pero teníamos un trato.*'

'Like hell you're sorry, but we'll keep to the deal. We'll send you back in the morning.'

Hernández jangled his cuffs.

'*¡Ahora!*'

'Nobody wants to take you south now. We just want to go home and get your stink off our clothes and skin. *Mañana*. I hear the food at the Eloy Detention Center has improved a lot. They'll even give you beans for breakfast.'

Hernández swore some, but mostly for the sake of appearances. He'd probably been behind bars enough times in his life for Eloy to hold no terrors. They left him in the interview room, and joined Ross and Newton for the final time.

'Done?' said Newton.

'Done. We'll send him back tomorrow.'

'I'd rather see him gone sooner.'

'Well,' said Zalinksi, 'I'd like that too, but first I want to let all those reporters outside know what a big help he's been in identifying the victim, so they can be sure to get some good shots of Mr Hernández, and spell his name right in the newspapers. Then tomorrow I'm going to dump him on the streets of Nogales with a couple of hundred dollars in his pocket, and let his friends welcome him home. I'll also do my best to find him that baseball cap.'

For the first time since Parker had arrived in Arizona, he saw Newton smile.

'Man,' said Newton, 'I love America.'

X

This is what you must understand: the ground is polluted, befouled. We walk on blighted soil. It holds within it the record of blood spilled, of villages and towns that thrived once but exist no longer, of all who have lived and all who have died in those places.

The earth remembers.

And just as a dormant seed may be revived by rain, so too older presences, lying in troubled rest among the hollows of the honeycomb world, may be woken from their sleep, whether deliberately, by the actions of the malicious; or accidentally, by the explorations of the careless and the curious.

Mostly, all it takes is a little blood.

XI

For so long, Sellars recalled, there had been nothing to this city – well, nothing but pride, pride in the face of poverty and decay. What the Germans started, the natives finished, helped by governments in London that couldn't see further than the Orbital – or if they did, cared little for what was revealed to them there. They wanted the north of England to die because there were no votes for them in its great industrial cities. Best to let a generation or two fade away from neglect before starting again with fresh meat.

Then along came the IRA. Fucking Paddies. As if Manchester didn't have enough of them already without their relatives taking the ferry over to join them for a few days, and plant a bomb or two while they were about it, all because they couldn't keep their troubles to themselves and their little patch of bog land across the Irish Sea. A Saturday morning in 1996: three thousand pounds and more of Semtex mixed with ammonium nitrate, packed into a Ford van parked on Corporation Street. The bastards had tried before, of course: firebombs in the 1970s, and an attack on the Magistrates' Court; another attempt in 1992, targeting people just going about their daily lives, women and kids who'd never done any harm to them, never even wished them any harm. Jesus, some of them were even their own kind, or a mixed-breed version of it, Celtic blood running through their veins from way back, English accents bearing Irish names. Not that the IRA cared. He'd tried to explain that to an American once, some loudmouth in a bar who couldn't have found Ireland on a map if you'd held a gun to his head, talking gibberish about freedom fighters, British oppression, legitimate targets, as though the fucking IRA had gone around tapping pedestrians on their shoulders to ask if they were Catholic or Irish before deciding whether or not to blow them and their children into the next world.

The ignorance of it all.

He'd been close to the Arndale that Saturday morning, he and his mum. They always went into town on Saturdays, and she'd buy him an American comic book at WH Smith's – he loved them – and a bite of lunch later. When he was little, she used to take him to the restaurant in Woolworth's on Piccadilly, but it went up in flames in 1979 because someone threw a cigarette butt into a pile of sofas, and ten people died of cyanide inhalation when the foam filling inside the furniture ignited. The store reopened nine months later, but he and his mum never went back there. Nobody they knew did, and eventually the Woolworth's closed forever, which was for the best. It was a hotel now, and he wondered how many of the guests knew what had happened in 1979. Hardly any of them, he supposed, and that was probably for the best, too.

God, he hadn't thought of Woolworth's in years, yet now he could almost taste the food in his mouth, the juiciness of the sausages and the smell of the frying fat. Strange the tricks memory played.

But the Arndale: even now he could remember the explosion, like a fist from the heavens impacting on the earth. At least the IRA had given a warning, which was something. Previously they hadn't bothered with such niceties. Mind you, for all their bombs they'd still never managed to kill anyone in Manchester; they'd injured a few, which was bad enough, but nobody died. Fleet of foot, your Mancs. Have to be quick to nail one.

He and his mum had been at Marks & Spencer when the announcement came that everyone was to evacuate the area, the police and security guards hustling folk away from the shops, sending them outside the cordon that had been formed about a quarter of a mile from the van.

And then what had the people done?

Well, they'd all stood and watched, which was what you did, he clinging tightly to his mum's right hand, because it wasn't often that you got to see something explode in real life. Except, of course, no one knew just how much explosive was in the van, and even had someone been able to confirm that estimate of three thousand pounds, most people wouldn't have had the slightest notion of what kind of blast this might cause – except maybe the ones who had lived through the Blitz, who could have told you that three thousand pounds of high explosive represented more than twice the destructive power of the largest bomb dropped by the Germans during the war, and that bomb had razed entire streets. In other words, no one had any business being within a quarter of a mile of the van when it went up.

No one.

It was shortly after 11 a.m. when the bomb squad started running from the scene, and 11.17 a.m. when the van exploded. He had never heard a sound like it, not before and not since. It struck his body with physical force, and might even have lifted him off his feet for a moment, because he was only a little lad back then. His ears rang, and his eyes hurt. A great cloud of smoke and debris rose a thousand feet into the air, and –

Of course, what goes up must come down. His mum realized that quicker than most. She was always a smart one, his mum. She lifted him into her arms and began to put as much distance between her and the bomb crater as she could, although it still wasn't enough because glass and wood and brick and dust and bits of plastic began to descend upon them. Suddenly, he and his mum were on the ground, and he was crying because she'd landed on top of him, knocking the wind from his lungs. She rolled off, and he saw that her hair was spangled with crystals of glass, and her coat was covered in dirt, and then blood began to flow down her face from all the little cuts in her scalp, and he cried harder, even as she picked him up again and continued on her way, tottering because she was in shock and didn't know it, not until a woman came out of a drapery shop with a blanket in her arms, which she put over his mum as she guided her gently inside and made her sit down. The woman's name was Daphne, he remembered. She'd made them both a cup of tea, and cleaned the blood from his mum's face. She even managed to get most of the glass out of his mum's scalp, too, using a pair of tweezers and a bottle of TCP antiseptic.

His mum was gone now. She'd died nine years back. Heart attack at 10 a.m. Apparently, most heart attacks occur between nine and eleven in the morning. He hadn't known that until his mum died. She was slap bang in the middle of the scale. Mrs Average. Story of her life: extraordinary only in her ordinariness, extraordinary only because she was his mum.

He wondered what she'd think of him now. She hadn't lived to see him get married, and produce two girls of his own, seven and six, Kelly and Louise, although their mum, Lauren, had chosen the names, not him. He'd get to name the boys, if they ever had any more kids. That was the deal. He wasn't sure they would, though. He and Lauren weren't getting along so well. They bickered, and when they weren't bickering they were giving each other the silent treatment. There were arguments over the kids, her family, and the time he spent on the road. Small things, mostly, but they added up. The marriage was tottering now, like a boxer on his last legs, waiting for the final strike to put him down. Wouldn't take much, just a glancing blow.

Oh, and he'd started killing women: there was that as well. Obviously, Lauren didn't know anything about this – it wasn't the kind of pastime a husband generally discussed with his wife – although she'd probably sensed some change in him, because it was a difficult thing to do, killing a woman, without being altered by it. It had to affect a man somehow. Only made sense. Lauren probably thought he was having an affair, but he wasn't. He'd been unfaithful to her in the past, but that was all behind him now. Anyway, his sex drive had begun to dwindle since the first murder. He'd half-expected it to grow stronger, because he'd read that some killers of women got sexual gratification from their actions, but it wasn't like that for him. He wasn't in it for the kicks. It was more like a job – no, a vocation, and one that he wanted to perform as best he could. He'd always been that way, ever since he was a kid. He liked things to be done right.

He wanted to return to the northeast. He wanted to visit the sleeping god of the Familists. He'd try to find a way to get back there soon. He'd just tell Lauren that a pick-up was going to require an overnight stay, and use the extra time to make a pilgrimage. Yes, that was it. He was a pilgrim, and pilgrims made sacrifices. They offered things up to their gods: their own suffering and, in his case, the sufferings of others.

He wished he'd been able to kill that last one himself, the one in Northumbria, but Mors had convinced him it would be a bad idea, and he always listened to Mors, because not listening to her would also be a bad idea.

A very bad idea.

He shifted Louise on his chest, because one of her elbows was digging into his ribs. She was all sharp edges, that child. Lauren said that giving birth to her had been like forcing out a bag of tools. She didn't sleep well, either – not like Kelly, who had slept through right from the start. No, Louise seemed to exist in a constant state of disturbance. For a while he'd been worried that there might be something wrong with her, but the doctors couldn't find anything amiss. She was probably just one of those kids, they said. She'd settle down in time. He wished she'd hurry up, though. He didn't want to make a habit of sitting up with her in the dead of night, watching fucking cartoons. Not that he could complain on this occasion, because Lauren had done duty on the previous three nights, and by now was so tired that she couldn't have risen from her bed even if she'd wanted to, which she most certainly did not.

Louise grew still at last. Sellars found the remote, muted the television, and lay with his daughter in his arms.

He'd have to kill another woman soon. Time was pressing. Mors had told him so. He didn't mind. He was doing it for a god.

His god.

XII

Skal and Crist were waiting for Parker when he emerged from the sheriff's office. They'd put in a hell of a long day, but neither of them betrayed any signs of tiredness. Even their suits looked fresh. Parker, by contrast, was dead on his feet, and dozed all the way to Phoenix, where a room was waiting for him at the Westin downtown. He would have gone straight to bed, if that had been possible, but Ross had asked to meet later in the bar. According to Crist, Ross was about half an hour behind them, which meant that Parker would have just enough time to shower, and change into a fresh shirt.

'Are Ross and I the only ones staying here?' Parker asked, as Crist held open the door of the Chevy. This time, Parker didn't bother to complain. He was only a breath, and some dignity, away from asking Crist to carry him upstairs and tuck him into bed.

Crist shuffled awkwardly.

'I don't believe the Westin is one of our approved hotels,' he said.

'Then who's covering the tab?'

'SAC Ross said he'd take care of it.'

Parker had heard some of the rumors about Ross: that he was independently wealthy, and wasn't shy about using it to make his life more comfortable. Parker had been careful about delving too deeply into Ross's affairs, since the FBI man had a sixth sense when it came to inquisitiveness on the part of others, but in recent years Parker had learned more about him through careful inquiry. The money came from investment banking, dating back to the growth of the 'Yankee houses' at the end of the nineteenth century, and the dominance of the American oligarchs – J.P. Morgan;

Kuhn, Loeb; Brown Brothers; Kidder, Peabody – in the early decades of the twentieth. Ross's family was no longer involved in finance, mostly because there was no family left to be involved; Ross was the last of the direct line, and could therefore have lived comfortably off the proceeds of various funds without doing anything more arduous with his days than selecting a suitable wine for dinner. Instead, he had carved out his own idiosyncratic enclave in a corner of Federal Plaza, from which he continued to involve himself in Parker's affairs. At least, on this occasion, Parker was benefiting from Ross's attentions in the form of a nice room.

'So where are you guys?' Parker asked.

'The Red Roof Inn, just west of here,' said Crist.

'Red Roof Plus,' Skal reminded him. 'We get a bigger TV.'

Parker thought about tipping them, just to see how they might react, but settled on thanking them for the ride.

'We'll be back to pick you up in the morning,' said Crist. 'You're booked on the 7.15 a.m. American Airlines flight to Houston. We'll swing by around 5.30.'

Then they were gone. Parker checked into the Westin, although he didn't need to hand over a credit card since everything was covered. While he was at the desk, he asked the concierge to have a bottle of good champagne, a six-pack of beer, and a couple of pizzas delivered to Skal and Crist at the Red Roof Plus, and charge it all to the Westin account – oh, and the concierge should add a thirty-dollar tip for himself. Parker would have thrown in some flowers as well, but he didn't think a florist would be open so late. This done, he went to his room and showered, resisting the urge to lie down and take the phone off the hook. The shower made him feel marginally more human, and gave him a burst of energy that he knew wouldn't last longer than an hour.

He thought about Adrienne Barbonne, the dead woman in the freezer. According to Newton, her parents lived in Magdalena, just northwest of San Antonio. Soon, police officers or federal agents would arrive at their home to notify them that a body had been found, and ask for DNA samples in order to assist in identifying the remains. For now, the Barbonnes remained the parents of a missing daughter, still retaining some hope that she might be returned safely to them. In a few hours, they would be mother and father to a dead child, all because their offspring bore a passing resemblance to the wrong woman.

The phone in his room rang. He answered, and heard Ross's voice.

Parker said he'd be right down.

II

Dawn-sniffing revenant,
Plodder through midnight rain,
Question me again.

Seamus Heaney, 'Casualty'

XIII

Quayle took to the streets of London while most of its inhabitants were still in their beds. A heavy rain was falling, sluicing the byways of filth and debris, and keeping downcast the heads of the few people he passed, which suited him greatly. This was his London, just as it had been for centuries, yet he felt less secure here than ever before.

Parker had done this to him. Quayle had underestimated the private investigator, initially dismissing him as merely a jumped-up colonial, another mongrel in a nation replete with them. Even as Quayle had left the United States behind, barely escaping with his life, he persisted in regarding the detective as a temporary inconvenience, one that would not trouble him again. After all, Quayle had returned home with the final pages of the Atlas in his possession, or so he believed. With those pages now restored, the Atlas could finish reordering the world in its image, and Quayle would be given his reward: nothingness, oblivion. He would be permitted to die at last, to sleep without waking.

But the Atlas remained unfinished. Despite all Quayle's research, all his years of hunting, it appeared that more than two leaves had been missing. Could Parker be in possession of the additional contents? It was possible, Quayle felt, but unlikely. All his studies had led him to believe that the copy of *Grimm's Fairy Tales* contained only those two leaves, which he now possessed. The Atlas should already have been a tome entire, but it was not.

If this had not been sufficient to discompose Quayle, there was the matter of Parker himself. At the end of March, a series of clues had appeared in the cryptic crossword of *The Times*, the solutions to which had created a pattern that read CHARLIE

PARKER HUNTING QUAYLE. Placing the clues had been quite an achievement, Quayle thought, even as he resented their impact on one of his greatest pleasures, since he could now no longer enjoy the newspaper's crossword. Thus had Parker given notice of his intention to come after Quayle, but as yet there was no sign of his presence in London. Quayle suspected this to be a deliberate strategy on the part of the investigator: to sound the horn for the hunt but delay the release of the hounds, leaving the silence to whittle away at the quarry's peace of mind, waiting to see how it would respond, and where it would choose to run. But Quayle would not run, not unless given no other option. He had come close to being trapped before, and had survived. He knew how to play this game. Still, it was a disconcerting position in which to be placed after all this time.

And Parker was different. He carried about him a numinous aspect, and a knowledge of liminal spaces. Quayle was not yet ready to accept that Parker might be more than mortal, but he was prepared to concede his singularity.

Mors wanted to kill Parker, but she could not return to the United States to do so. She had always been distinctive in appearance, but had learned from Quayle certain modes of concealment, a practiced unobtrusiveness. But recent events in Indiana and Maine, and the bodies left behind, meant that even the shadows were now inimical to Mors. It had been her decision to use the remains of another woman to throw the police off the scent, but ultimately it would not keep Parker from these shores.

Quayle had tried to explain all this to Mors, because he was beginning to understand the dilemma faced by all those who came into conflict with the investigator. Yes, one could try to kill him, but if one failed, one would face retribution, just like those who had failed in the past; and even if one were somehow to succeed in the endeavor, there were Parker's allies to consider. They might not have been as exceptional as he was, but the more Quayle found out about them, the greater the threat they represented – and those were only the ones Quayle could identify, because Parker had other confederates, protectors in the highest echelons of law enforcement. He would not otherwise have been allowed to operate as a free agent, not with his record of lethality.

'But what,' Mors had suggested, 'if we were to threaten his family?'

She was naked beside him, offering her warmth. He could have entered her if he wished, but it was enough for him to have her skin against his, to draw heat from her. She would not be able to tolerate this intimacy for long, though. Quayle's coldness was the kind that bred pain in the bone, freezing the marrow.

'Do you really think threats would dissuade him? One might as well provoke a wolf and expect it not to bite.'

'We could abduct his daughter.'

'Then what: hold her indefinitely? Return her to him piece by piece, a little for every month he keeps his distance from us?'

Quayle had pulled away from her then, wearied by her foolishness. He noted signs of relief on her part, a wince at the release.

'So we should just wait and see if he comes?'

'He will come,' said Quayle, 'whether we choose to wait or not. But here we have the advantage. He will be on unfamiliar ground, far from home. This is our ground, *my* ground.'

Whatever Parker's strangeness, he could have no real conception of time, or not of the kind possessed by Quayle. Parker had not lived as long, and so could not comprehend how the ruins of a Saxon settlement might provide the foundations for a Roman garrison, that garrison give way to a Norman fortress, the fortress to a medieval town, and the town to a city, the old apparently succumbing to the new, yet always with the persistence of the past. Each cycle left its mark, the ancient lingering in the umbrous folds of the modern, all its pain and fury, its bloodshed and grief, still present at the periphery of consciousness. When he landed at last, Parker would not only be facing Quayle and Mors. He would be pitting himself against the weight of the past, a creature of the New World trespassing carelessly on the Old.

I am not afraid of you.

'What did you say?' asked Mors, and Quayle realized he had whispered the words loudly enough for her to hear.

'I said that it is he who should be afraid,' said Quayle, and

Mors let her doubt go unremarked because Quayle was returning to her side, and when he entered her she thought that he had never felt so cold, but she tolerated it because it was this man's essence, and she loved him in her way, and now he was in her and of her, and she of him, but as he moved deep inside her the pain grew sharper and fiercer, and the chill gripped her innards, spreading from her groin to her belly and into her chest so that it seemed set to still her heart, and she wanted to beg him to stop but all speech was frozen, each syllable a fragment of ice that could not be joined to another, and she cried but her tears turned to crystals in her eyes and on her cheeks, and her very soul was rimy.

And this, she understood, was what it would be like to die.

Now Mors was sleeping while Quayle wandered the city, its modernity imperfectly concealed by the dark, so that it was just possible for him, if he kept to old paths, to walk with his other selves through lost times.

It was probably as well that Mors should remain unconscious for as long as she could, he thought, because she would be in pain when she woke. He had almost killed her earlier. What his own essence, his profound algor could not do, his bare hands might have accomplished. She was more conspicuous than he, and so her existence jeopardized his own, but he would need her in order to deal with Parker. Quayle would miss her once she was gone. She asked so little of him, and gave so much. Sometimes, when he was with her, he forgot the loneliness of the very old.

But then, he had always been of a melancholic disposition.

He passed a pharmacy, with its clean white shelves, its cheap perfumes and generic medicines, and brought to mind the stores that had preceded it, back to the apothecary who had tended to Quayle's afflictions in another century, another version of this city. The apothecary was an old fraud, even by the standards of his profession. For Quayle's melancholy he had recommended swallow water, specially created for him by a woman in Cornwall, or so he claimed: fifty baby swallows sourced from their nests before they could take their first flight, ground to a pulp and combined in a solution of castor and vinegar, with a little sugar added to ease the consumption of the whole, guaranteed to make the heart take wing and ease one's sorrows.

Any doubts Quayle might have entertained about the contents of the bottle were laid to rest when he discovered a fragment of feather in the liquid on his spoon, and even though he had been in the deepest of desponds, still he had cast the swallow water aside as so much humbug, and instead medicated himself with Madeira wine. The apothecary had died some months later, along with his family: a wife and two daughters, killed in their beds. Rumors of rape. All very unpleasant. Despite the apothecary's deficiencies, Quayle had regretted his passing. His commitment to quackery had been almost admirable. Quayle had bribed the constable in order to be permitted to view the bodies before they were removed from the premises, and was struck by the extent of the butchery, particularly the injuries inflicted on the females. They were startling in their savagery.

A century later, a man named Hatton murdered his mistress in a similar manner in the same building, claiming to have been advised do so by the voices in the walls. Then, during World War One, a French merchant and his wife, who had taken rooms on the top floor, were assaulted and killed in the course of what appeared to be a botched robbery, their assailant or assailants never to be identified. Bricks and mortar could be contaminated just as easily as stone and soil – more so, perhaps, because there was form and substance to hold the memories.

All these old places.

All these old acts.

All this old blood.

XIV

The bar of the Westin was quiet when Parker entered. He counted three couples, two single women, and a group of young businessmen drinking bourbon by the window. Ross had taken a corner table, where he could neither be overlooked nor overheard. He had not changed his clothes, and Parker caught traces of sand in his hair and on the shoulders of his jacket, and thought he could still smell the smoke of Lagnier's junkyard about him, although that might have been his own imagination playing on memories of the day. Having resisted the lure of his bed, Parker was feeling hungry. He and Ross both ordered steak sandwiches, and Ross opted for a beer over Parker's red wine.

A sheaf of papers contained in an anonymous manila envelope lay on the table in front of Ross. He left it unopened as he and Parker sat waiting for their food.

'You didn't need me at that junkyard today,' said Parker, 'or at that farce of an interview with Hernández.'

'I told you: I thought you should see the body, and you spotted things we hadn't.'

'You'd have figured them out, sooner or later – probably sooner.'

'That hint of doubt is noted. As for Hernández, by your presence we were able to confirm that he knew who you were. Mors must have warned him about you.'

'Well, thanks for that, because no harm can come from spending time with a member of MS-13, right? They seem like good guys.'

'Mr Hernández won't live long enough to be a problem for you or anyone else,' said Ross. 'He'll be dead by this time tomorrow, either at the hands of his own people or those of the Federales.'

'Is that how justice works now?'

'It is down there, and forgive me if I bristle at being lectured about extrajudicial killings by you.'

Their food arrived, and Ross ordered another beer. Parker had barely sipped his wine.

'Aren't you going to ask me what's in the folder?' said Ross, once he'd made some inroads into his sandwich and fries.

'If it makes you happy. What's in the folder, Agent Ross?'

'Why don't you take a look?'

Parker did, revealing copies of two passport pages, along with blurred photographs of a man making his way through what appeared to be an airport terminal with signs in Spanish and English. The pictures had been pulled from a security camera. Most were poor – the man was careful to keep his head down, and seemed to have an instinct for surveillance – apart from the final one. It had clearly been taken at an immigration desk, with the subject facing the camera. His hair was white, matched by a thin beard, his glasses thick-framed, exaggerating the size of his green eyes, but he was still recognizable as the man who had instigated a campaign of carnage from Indiana to Maine.

'It's Quayle,' said Parker.

'You're sure?'

'Yes. The eye color is different, and the hair and beard, but it's him. Where was this taken?'

'El Salvador International, shortly before the end of March.'

Parker examined the reproductions of the passport pages. *Koninkrijk der Nederlanden*: Kingdom of the Netherlands, issued two years earlier in the name of Axel de Bruijn by the *Burgemeester van Amsterdam.*

'Was he flying to the Netherlands?'

'Paris.'

'Is this the same passport he used to enter the United States?'

'No, there's no immigration record for this Axel de Bruijn. Take a look at the rest of the papers, see what you think.'

Parker dug deeper into the file, and found Customs and Border Protection data on a dozen men and six women. He went through it slowly, and when he was done the information on two men and one woman had been set aside.

'Quayle could be either of these two men: possibly the first, but more likely the second. The woman is definitely Mors.'

The first man, Ernst Bourdon, had arrived in the United States early the previous December on a French passport; the second, Hans Herbert Haffner, had come in on an eight-year-old Dutch passport at about the same time. Both were of similar age and build, but Bourdon looked unwell, and his face was a little thinner than Quayle's. Haffner, by contrast, appeared healthy: his cheeks were fuller, and his eyes brighter. Parker couldn't have said for certain that it was Quayle, not without more than these images to go on, but there was something familiar about Haffner.

The woman, meanwhile, was named Angelika Piek, and her hair was dark brown, with silver visible at the roots. The alterations to her aspect had been less successful than Quayle's, assuming Haffner was indeed Quayle, perhaps because Mors was so much more distinctive in appearance. The skin was darker, the lips plumper, the eyes brown instead of pond-scum gray, but it was definitely her. The baseness of her nature seemed to seep from the paper itself. Piek/Mors had arrived on a Dutch passport – again, as with the de Bruijn document, issued in Amsterdam two years earlier. Even the date of issue was the same in each case.

'Any idea how Mors might have got out?' Parker asked.

'Not yet. She could still be in North America.'

'You don't sound convinced.'

'I'm keeping an open mind. We'll continue searching, but it would be a hell of a risk for her to take.'

'What if she had no choice?'

'You mean the gunshot wounds? Unless Hernández was lying, she had recuperated sufficiently to supervise the dumping of a decoy body. My feeling is she's gone. Spend enough money, and even someone like her could be spirited from the continent like she'd never existed.'

Parker thought about it and decided Ross might be correct. He wondered why Quayle hadn't taken the same route, instead opting to leave openly, if on a false passport: arrogance, maybe, or a lack of time to arrange an alternative route. Perhaps, in the end, he just wanted to get back to wherever it was he came from as quickly as possible, particularly now that he believed himself to be in possession of the missing pages he had traveled so far to find.

Parker replaced the documents in the folder, closed it, and pushed it back toward Ross.

'What are you going to do with all this?' he asked.

'Nothing, or next to nothing.'

Parker waited. He knew that they were at last getting to the real reason why Ross had brought him all the way to Arizona.

'Officially,' said Ross, 'I know a certain amount about Quayle and Mors, most of it gleaned from the law enforcement agencies in the jurisdictions in which they committed their crimes, and the rest from you. Unofficially, I know more: again, most of it from you. I can only act on the first body of knowledge, not the second.'

Parker understood something of the balancing act that Ross was attempting to pull off. Originally, Ross had been tasked with investigating the crimes of the Traveling Man, which had inevitably brought him into contact with Parker; but as Ross's inquiries progressed, it became apparent that the Traveling Man might have represented just one manifestation of a larger conspiracy. At the very least, the Traveling Man had come into contact with men and women who believed in the existence of realms beyond this one, and some of those individuals were committed to the search for what they termed the Buried God, a search governed and funded by a cadre known only as the Backers.

The nature of the Buried God was unclear – a religious icon of some kind, possibly; a fallen angel, perhaps; or something far worse – and whether it truly existed or not was largely irrelevant, at least as far as even the most sympathetic of Ross's superiors in the bureau were concerned. What mattered was that the Backers, and those working with them, were believed to be responsible for a litany of illegal acts, including corruption of institutions of the law, and of state and federal government; copious financial crimes; and multiple homicides. Ross had been tasked with identifying the Backers, a duty complicated by inadequate resources

– because there were those in the bureau's highest echelons who regarded all talk of Backers and Buried Gods as the stuff of fairy stories, and a drain on funds that could be better directed elsewhere – and the possibility that the reach of the Backers might extend to the FBI itself.

And now there was the matter of Quayle, because he, too, had links to the Backers. Earlier in the year, a man named Garrison Pryor had been tortured to death in his Boston apartment. Pryor, the head of an investment group thought to be a major conduit for the Backers' money, had been under investigation by the FBI's Financial Crimes Section, largely at Ross's instigation. Ross was of the opinion that just a little extra pressure might have resulted in Pryor turning federal witness, and revealing what he knew of the Backers. Before that pressure could be applied, Pryor was silenced, and footage from security cameras, as well as eyewitness statements, suggested that a woman resembling Pallida Mors had entered Pryor's apartment building shortly before his arrival home, and departed two hours later, having presumably butchered the financier in the interim. Why, Ross wondered, would Mors have killed Pryor, unless it was at the behest of the Backers? A favor returned, but for what?

So Ross had further justification for pursuing Quayle and his acolyte, but was officially reluctant to delve too deeply into their reasons for being in the United States to begin with. It was Parker who had informed Ross of Quayle's search for the missing vellum pages. Quayle had recovered two of those pages, but unbeknownst to him, Parker had managed to secure one more, found concealed in the spine of the book of fairy tales. So far, he had elected not to share this fact with the agent.

Ross had decided that Parker should try to find out as much as he could about the vellum inserts, and Quayle and Mors, while the FBI hunted for the two culprits in its own manner. Two parallel investigations: one official, one unofficial, with the latter funded by Parker's consultancy retainer from the bureau. Where possible, Ross would feed Parker information relevant to his inquiries, and in return would expect to be kept apprised of any progress – of which, so far, there had been little, or none that Parker was yet prepared to share. As already noted, trust was lacking in their relationship.

Which brought them back to the Westin, and two sandwiches, and a file containing identity pages from a selection of European passports.

'What do you want me to do?' said Parker.

'The passports appear to be genuine, but if you're right about Quayle, he's British, not Dutch.'

Quayle had specifically claimed to be English, and a lawyer. A law firm bearing that name had operated in London for centuries, but ceased to exist shortly after World War Two. It was assumed that Quayle had appropriated the name and the profession, one more identity to add to Haffner, De Bruijn, and however many others he might have accumulated.

'He said he was English, and sounded like he was,' said Parker. 'But there's obviously a Dutch connection.'

'Which we haven't yet managed to establish.'

'Can you see Quayle and Mors taking a trip to Amsterdam every time they need new passports?'

'One imagines there are easier ways to secure them.'

'A middleman.'

'Or middlewoman, gender being no impediment to fraudulent pursuits. My thought was that you might know someone with experience of such matters, someone who might have had occasion in the past to operate in Europe under a false identity.'

Louis.

'I'm not sure he's ever been to the Netherlands,' said Parker.

'Actually, he has.'

Ross knew more about Angel and Louis than either of those men might have wished, given the abundance of criminality in their backgrounds. This added another layer of complication, and obligation, to Parker's relationship with Ross.

'I'll ask.'

'I think you'll find him remarkably knowledgeable on the subject.'

'Do you want me to come back to you with what he says?'

'Only if he can't help, but I'd be surprised if that's the case.'

'And if he can?'

'Then he might like to return to the Low Countries, and make some further inquiries in person.'

'He prefers to travel first class.'

'Business.'

'He won't be happy.'

'Neither will the taxpayer,' said Ross, 'but all things are relative.'

XV

As this conversation was concluding, its subject was in the New York apartment he shared with the love – and, sometimes, bane – of his life. Louis was sitting with Angel, who was unable to sleep due to pins and needles in his fingers and toes, a side effect of chemotherapy. Earlier in the year, Angel had undergone the removal of part of his bowel, and although he had avoided a bag, if only narrowly, chemo was destined to be a regular part of his life for the foreseeable future, a development about which Angel remained volubly unhappy.

At least he had a future, as his partner liked to remind him. Angel was an unusual human being. He had always stood out from most of the crowd, in large part because any members of the crowd with an instinct for self-preservation would have taken a step or two away from Angel in order to avoid having their valuables stolen, but also due to a dress sense that tended toward – if one were feeling charitable – the individualistic. But Angel was also profoundly moral in his way, particularly since his decision to set aside larceny as a lifestyle choice, and was far less compromised in this regard than his partner.

Where he did not differ from most men was in his distrust of doctors, and his response to virtually any ailment had generally been to ignore it in the expectation that it would eventually get bored and leave his body, or to tackle it with the aid of whatever was on special that week at CVS. Unfortunately, tumors of the bowel rarely responded well to such courses of treatment, and Angel had finally been browbeaten into consulting an internist, with the result that he was now in possession of less of his own body than before. Rather than convince Angel of the error of his ways, this experience had simply hardened him in his attitude toward doctors. The quality of the medical profession, in Angel's view, had only deteriorated since the days when barbers performed surgery, because back then at least a man was assured of a decent haircut for his trouble.

'My fucking feet,' said Angel. 'I feel like I'm being tortured.'

He had woken up cold. That was part of the problem. Angel had never liked sleeping in a warm room, but he'd have to get used to it if he was to mitigate this particular torment. The nausea was less of a problem, because the medication helped, but then they were still learning how to cope with all this, he and Louis both. Otherwise, Angel appeared largely untraumatized by his diagnosis, surgery, and ongoing treatment. Louis had read about people being deeply affected emotionally and psychologically by their cancer, but Angel was not one of these, or so Louis believed. Perhaps it was because Angel had already suffered so much in the past – at the hands of abusers in childhood, and from the violence of other men in adulthood – that he was able to face this latest assault on his being with a degree of equanimity, pins and needles excepted. But he was quieter than before: not maudlin or depressed, just more introspective. Louis had registered this, at least.

A clue as to Angel's state of mind had come from the unlikely source of Paulie Fulci, who, along with Tony, his brother, had been employed by Louis as security, and occasional nursemaids, both during Angel's surgery and the initial period of his recuperation. Paulie had come across Angel with a box of marbles on his lap. The box, like the marbles themselves, looked old. Angel was moving the marbles one by one from the box to the blanket over his knees, then back again.

'What are you doing?' Paulie asked.

'Counting.'

'Marbles?'

'Days.'

Paulie had left him to it, but informed Louis of the exchange upon the latter's return to the apartment.

'What do you think he meant by "days"?' Paulie asked.

'I don't know,' Louis replied, although he had his suspicions.

'You know what I think?'

Paulie paused, waiting for Louis to reply, and thus give him permission to continue. Most men – most women, too – would have considered the question largely rhetorical, and plowed on to reveal the answer. Paulie Fulci's mind didn't operate that way, but then it wasn't clear how Paulie's mind operated, exactly. He and his brother had that much in common.

'No,' said Louis, when the silence became too much even for him to bear. 'What do you think?'

'I think maybe when you go through what he's been through, you start spending more time in the past. You do it because you're not so sure you got enough days left for a future.'

Louis looked very hard at Paulie.

'What?' said Paulie.

'Did you change your medication?'

'It's always changing.'

'Does it ever work?'

Paulie took some time to consider before replying.

'No, but these new pills make me feel different.'

Louis was interested now.

'Different how?'

Again, Paulie mused.

'I need to piss more often.'

At which point Louis stopped being interested.

When he had gone in to check on Angel, the box of marbles was nowhere to be seen, and Louis elected, for reasons he could not have explained, to leave unremarked the subject of their existence. He had not been aware Angel possessed such a collection, and could only conclude that it was some relic from childhood. If Angel did not see fit to mention it to him, then Louis was disinclined to pry. After all, both men had their secrets.

Music was playing softly: Egberto Gismonti's 'Ciranda Nordestina'. Louis had not chosen it, although it suited the mood and the hour; he had simply hit play on the system, and had not been disappointed.

Angel scratched absently at the PICC line in his arm, the other end of the catheter lodged somewhere near his heart. He seemed to be sleeping now. A further session of chemo was scheduled for the following day, after which they would leave the city for Maine, where Angel could gaze out on the waters of Casco Bay from the window of their Portland apartment.

Gismonti faded away, to be replaced by Steve Reich and the first part of 'Tehillim'. Angel shifted position in Louis's arms.

'Where do you walk, when you dream?' Louis asked.

But Angel did not answer, and Louis both felt and heard the depth and regularity of his breathing, and was glad.

It doesn't matter, thought Louis, *as long I am there.*

As long as I am where you are.

III

Trackway and Camp and City lost,
Salt Marsh where now is corn;
Old Wars, old Peace, old Arts that cease,
And so was England born . . .
Rudyard Kipling, *Puck of Pook's Hill*

XVI

Darkness to the west, then: darkness in Arizona, darkness in New York, for these are both western places to the European mind.

But darkness of another kind to the east.

This is Northumbria, spanning Durham, Yorkshire, and Northumberland, the northernmost county in England. Here was once the frontier, the last place, where, in the second century, the Romans built their vast fortifications to hold back the Scots and the Picts: first Hadrian's Wall, running from the banks of the Tyne in the east to the Solway Firth in the west; and later, in a fit of optimism – or arrogance – the more northerly Antonine Wall, from the Firth of Forth in the east to the Firth of Clyde in the west, before abandoning it in favor of a consolidation of the southern defenses. In time, the remains of the Antonine Wall will come to be referred to as the Devil's Dyke, but by then the Romans will be long gone, their fortresses already falling into ruin, leaving the blood to dry, and the land to bear their scars.

Because the land remembers.

So the Romans depart, and chaos descends. The Angles invade from Germania, battling the natives and one another, before eventually forging two kingdoms, Northumbria and Mercia, only to see them fall to the Norsemen in the ninth century, who will themselves be defeated by the kings of Wessex.

More blood, more scars.

In 927 AD, Northumbria becomes part of Athelstan's united England. In 1066 William the Conqueror lands with his Normans, and crushes the Northumbrian resistance to Norman rule. The Norman castles rise, but they, like the Romans and the Angles before, are forced to defend themselves against the Scots. They leave their dead at Alnwick and Redesdale, Tyndale and Otterburn.

The land has a taste for blood now.

More conflicts follow – the Wars of the Roses, the Rising in the North, the Civil War, the Jacobite rebellions – and the ground makes way for new bones, but the blood never really dries. Dig deep enough, expose the depths, and one might almost glimpse seams of red and white, like the strata of rock: blood and bone, over and over, the landscape infused by them, forever altered and forever changing.

Because the killing never stops.

So the sun rises on this Northumberland morning, but without the heat required to burn off the mist on the Hexhamshire Moors that lie between the Devil's Water to the east and the valleys of the River Allen to the west. Its light catches the spire of St Andrew's at nearby Corbridge, a church built in the seventh century with stone from Hadrian's Wall, for Corbridge was once Corstopitum, or Coria, the northernmost outpost of the Roman Empire.

These layers again; these old connections.

Sheep graze here, and in summer bog orchid flourishes. To the casual eye, the moors might seem beautiful, but there is a harshness to them that cannot be denied, and in this spot the line of the horizon to the west is disrupted by a series of ruined dwellings, barely more than a succession of jagged walls with half-recollected windows and doors, like rotten teeth in the dislocated jaw of the landscape. Perhaps, in more verdant surroundings, this settlement might have been reclaimed by nature, to be lost and ultimately forgotten amid woods and greenery, but on the moors it remains as exposed as the land itself. Raised in an age when the houses of many common folk were built to last only for a generation, it is strange that these dwellings should have survived, although upon closer examination their walls appear thicker than the norm, and more carefully aligned, with little reliance on timber and wattle-and-daub fillers for their construction. The windows are narrow, barely more than slits;

designed for defense, one might say. Odd, too, that the stones have not been scavenged for some other purpose, or that livestock, even in the most inclement of weather, does not seek shelter among the ruins.

This place was once home to a group of families who inter-married to such a degree that the original lines were difficult to identify even for those most intimately involved in their creation, and impossible for outsiders. For many years, they worshiped at St Andrew's, as required by law and the Church of England, although some of their fellow congregants whispered that they did so only under sufferance, and were paying lip service to a god in whom they did not truly believe. And this was true, although the families were careful to give no cause for further investigation of their faith, even if mute testament to its alien nature stood not far from their hamlet.

Because another church once gazed out over the Hexhamshire Moors, its stones at least as old as those of St Andrew's, its walls bearing carvings of faces with no connection to a Christian God, or to His Son and saints. Here the families would offer up their prayers behind closed doors, until the threat of imprisonment and torture by the agents of the Reformation temporarily persuaded them to do otherwise. These strictures gradually eased, and greater freedom of worship became permissible, but by then the Familists, as their sect came to be termed, had decided to make a fresh start in the New World. They took their beliefs with them, and their church, its stones stored as ballast in the ships that carried them to New England, where it was reconstructed by Familist masons in a township that would come to be named Prosperous, in the state of Maine, and there the Congregation of Adam Before Eve & Eve Before Adam would endure – indeed thrive – into the twenty-first century, until its destruction by forces loyal to the private detective Charlie Parker.

But that, like the past itself, is another country. To be clear: the remnants of this earlier Northumbrian hamlet are not haunted, or not in any conventional sense of the word. The Familists brought their ghosts to the New World, and their demons also, but they left behind poisoned ground, blighted by their beliefs and – yes – perhaps also by spilled blood, because the land, and their god, demanded it. Now the rising sun shines on these old buildings, on their long rooms and cattle byres, and on a deep well blocked with stones, as though to prevent, not the drawing of water, but the emergence of something from below, for this is the kingdom of the Laidley Worm, the Lambton Worm, the Sockburn Worm – monstrous creatures all – and it is better to be careful than regretful.

Sun on grass and rock; sun on water and stone; sun also on the carapaces of the first of the ground beetles as they begin to explore their new territory, this previously unsuspected domain; the pallor of the exterior, and the redness of the interior. There is less blood than might have been anticipated, but the beetles are not troubled: the flesh itself is of a sufficiency to draw the smaller invertebrates on which they feed, although time will be required for the rot to set in, and the greater insect feast it will bring.

But that time will not be given to them. A figure is approaching, stick in hand, dog by his side: a farmer, come to check on his sheep. His name is Douglas Hood, and he and his forebears are part of this heathland, as assuredly as the grass and stones. They have built on it, raised livestock upon it, and buried their dead in it, generation upon generation. Hood knows every furrow, every hill and decline. He rarely leaves the environs of his county – rarely moves out of sight of the moors – because this to him is a world choate. Its colors are near-infinite in their variety yet remarkable in their particularity, so his eye is immediately drawn to a green that is not of nature, and a mound that is not of this place. As he draws closer, he sees the early-morning dew upon the plastic, and the shape beneath, imperfectly concealed. He might be mistaken, though. He wants to be. In his selfishness, he does not wish his moors to be despoiled in such a fashion.

But he knows, senses it on some animal level, even before he takes a handkerchief from his pocket so as not to leave any marks, placing it over the fingers of his right hand as he pulls back the layers of plastic, revealing hair, and a hand, and the roundness of a female breast. Beside him, the dog whines, and he reaches out to calm her, because she is a good creature.

He rises, removes his cap, and offers a prayer, because he cannot think of what else to do for her.

For this young woman in an old land, waiting to be named.

XVII

Skal and Crist arrived on time for Parker's ride to the airport. It was a temperate morning, and likely to blossom into a pleasant day, although it would be more pleasant still, Parker thought, if he were greeting it in Maine, and not in Arizona.

'Someone sent us pizza, a bottle of champagne, and a six-pack of beer last night,' said Skal, as they pulled away from the hotel.

'Really?' said Parker.

'Yeah. We had to call to make sure there wasn't some mistake, but it seems it was all being billed to an account at the Westin.'

'Wow.'

'So, being federal agents, and noted for our investigative abilities, we dug a little deeper, and found that it was SAC Ross's room account.'

'What a guy,' said Parker.

'We thought,' said Crist, taking up the baton, 'that maybe we should check with him, just in case.'

'Uh-huh.'

'But then,' said Skal, 'we looked at the food, and the champagne, and the beer, and decided, like, you know . . .'

'Yeah,' said Crist. 'Like, you know.'

'I know,' said Parker. 'Like, maybe you might have embarrassed him by mentioning it, and so it was better if it just remained unacknowledged, to save his blushes.'

Crist and Skal looked at each other. Clearly this was a better explanation for their silence than whatever they'd concocted between them.

'That's it,' said Skal.

'Yes,' said Crist, 'that's it exactly.'

They continued driving, watching Phoenix drift by.

'I never drank champagne with just another man before,' said Crist.

'Me neither,' said Skal.

'Or not one sitting in a bed next to me,' said Crist.

'Watching Jimmy Kimmel,' said Skal.

'So that was kind of weird,' said Crist.

'Kind of,' agreed Skal.

Parker kept his eyes fixed on the landscape, and tried to think sad thoughts.

'The crystal glasses were a nice touch, though,' said Crist.

'Yeah,' said Skal. 'We kept one each.'

'As souvenirs,' said Crist.

Parker gave up on sad thoughts, moved on to tragic, and continued to monitor his reflection in the glass until he was sure his face was straight. He watched the browns and beiges as the land rolled by. He saw only an insufficiency of green.

'You sleep well?' Skal asked him.

'Not really.'

'Strange bed, huh?'

'Strange bed, strange room, strange city,' said Parker. 'If I was here for another night, I'd probably have slept okay.'

'Yeah, why is that?'

'It's just a theory, but I think the mind is wary on a first night in a new place. It doesn't know where the doors and windows are, and it isn't sure that it's safe to sleep for long, so it keeps you tossing and turning. But if you go back for a second night, the mind has its bearings, and so you sleep better.'

'I never thought about it like that,' said Skal.

'Me neither,' said Crist. 'But it sounds right.'

'And how did you sleep?' asked Parker.

'Pretty good,' said Skal.

'Me too,' said Crist. 'Although I woke up with a headache. I think maybe it was the bubbles.'

'Yeah,' said Skal. 'It must have been the bubbles.'

Parker returned to thinking tragic thoughts.

* * *

Phoenix Sky Harbor airport hadn't improved significantly since Parker's arrival the day before, although it hadn't deteriorated either, which was something. He said goodbye to Skal and Crist, and thought he might even miss them. He knew that Ross had asked for a 6.30 a.m. wake-up call, because they'd both booked calls at the same time the night before. He wondered how long it would take him to spot the additions to his bill. As it happened, Parker's phone began ringing just as he was getting on the plane, and the caller display showed Ross's name. He rejected the call, just as he did the three that followed. Finally, Ross resorted to text messaging. The message consisted of two words, the first of which was 'You', and the second of which was unbecoming of a senior federal agent. Parker was still smiling as he took his seat in first class next to an elderly woman who had a small dog in a carrying case by her feet.

'You have a good time in Phoenix?' she asked him.

'It started out badly,' said Parker, 'but improved toward the end.'

XVIII

The Hexhamshire Moors have been transformed. Hikers are being redirected away from the area in which the body was discovered, and a white tent now covers the spot: an alien object in a landscape rendered stranger still by the presence of the Northumbria Police crime scene investigators, all of whom are similarly clothed in white protective suits, their faces masked, their hands gloved. This has been a difficult location to access: the main road is someway distant, although a farm trail runs perpendicular to it, permitting the police vehicles to drive slightly closer to the body. The moors are also a Site of Special Scientific Interest, so additional care must be taken. Still, the first two stages of the police investigation – the visual inspection, and the photographic recording – have been completed, and the evidence recovery plan has been established. They can now proceed to the forensic examination itself, although any fingerprinting will be left until last so as not to contaminate the scene.

But bad weather is approaching. The investigators can see the clouds darkening to the east, the storm ready to roll in from the North Sea, so they curse it, and the believers among them offer a prayer to the heavens.

Crime scene investigators are foragers, gatherers. They scavenge evidence. This is fingertip work, eyes on the ground. Of the four elements, fire and water are the principal adversaries, although air, in the form of strong winds, is no friend either. Now two of those elements may be on their way, and the instinct is to rush, to salvage what they can before nature destroys it; but to rush is to err, and so they must proceed methodically, and hope.

What is already clear is that the woman was not killed where she lies, nor did she die with this plastic beneath her; there is too little blood on the material for wounds so deep. Yet how did she get here? They can see no sign of a vehicle's tracks, so someone must have carried her – no, dragged her, because it is the farmer, Hood, who points out some slight disturbance to the texture of the heath, northwest of where the body was discovered.

Hood has come back to witness the investigation, he and his dog. He returned to his home once the police had finished asking him questions. He did not enjoy the experience of being interrogated. He lives a solitary existence out here, except for the animals under his care. He has never married, has never even slept with a woman. He came close to doing both once, when he was a younger man, although he cannot say what caused him to retreat from her, except perhaps that he was not in love, and recognized the pain this absence would ultimately bring down upon both of them. He sees her sometimes, around the town. She has children and grandchildren now, but he has no regrets. There are times when he is lonely, but he believes this to be part of the order of things, because all men and women, married or otherwise, are sometimes lonely.

He knows that the police must have found him odd. He was nervous, and out of practice at speaking with outsiders. He was concerned that they might suspect him of killing the woman, and he supposes they must have, at least at the start. Perhaps some of them still do. He has no alibi, unless the dog counts. But if he had killed the girl, he would not have left her remains wrapped in plastic on these moors, his moors, before inviting the police to inspect his handiwork. He would have buried her deep, or dropped her weighted body in one of the mires.

He shivers, and feels a pang of revulsion at himself for even considering such an act. He is pragmatic about killing. He has shot foxes and vermin, slaughtered chickens and sheep, and even dispatched one of his own dogs when a ram broke its back, although he cried after, and was not shamed by it. But he prefers the vet to take care of his dogs when their time comes, soft bugger that he is.

Now he stands by the Familist ruins, watching the police go about their business. They have already examined these surroundings: he can see the footprints left by them, both among the stones and up and down the rise on which the remnants stand. He hopes the police find the evidence they require to solve the crime, or enough to dismiss him from their inquiries. He wants no cloud of suspicion over his head.

At this, he lifts his face to the sky, where the darkness to the northeast is already trailing tendrils of rain. It will be close, he thinks. If he were down among those men and women, he would tell them to work faster. He wonders if he should tell them anyway, but fears that it might only cause them to become more suspicious of him. If so, he should not be out here where they can see him, but he is genuinely curious. He has only ever encountered activity like this on the television, either as part of a news bulletin or in the course of a crime drama. He could probably have helped them, if they'd asked. After all, nobody knew these moors better than he.

He thinks again about the dead woman, and the manner of her abandonment. It makes no sense to him, no sense at all.

XIX

A car was waiting at George Bush Intercontinental in Houston to whisk Parker to the federal courthouse on Rusk Street, where he thought the judge looked happier to see him than before, or at least only slightly less unhappy. Either way, it counted as progress. In his absence – according to Tracey Ermenthal, who escorted him into the courtroom – his character had been dissected and weighed before being sewn back up again, having been deemed suitable for public display.

'I think Ross may have said something that helped,' said Ermenthal. 'Maybe he's not such a bad guy after all.'

Parker didn't contradict her, but settled instead for noncommittal.

'Yeah, maybe.'

The man who called himself José Hernández was dropped off at the Plaza de Benito Juárez in Nogales by a black 4WD bearing *estadounidense* plates. Hernández was the only Hispanic occupant, the others all being white males with weapons showing. Nobody paid them any attention, which is to say that everyone in the vicinity conspicuously avoided staring in their direction, even as the 4WD sped away, and Hernández dropped his US Border Patrol baseball cap in the nearest garbage can before attempting to lose himself in the bustle of the city.

Within minutes, he was being followed.

Within an hour, he was dead.

XX

Detective Inspector Nicola Priestman was the chief investigating officer on the Hexhamshire Moors case. She was forty-three years old, married with two kids, and resolutely practical in all matters. She read the occasional mystery novel, usually while lying by a pool in Italy for two weeks each summer, with a glass of something cold and alcoholic beside her, and could occasionally be persuaded to join her husband in watching a crime show on TV at the weekend, but most of their depictions of police work were puzzling to her. She was not haunted by her cases, or driven to fight injustice by some inner torment or past trauma, and did not drink to excess. She got on well with most of her colleagues, the requisite sexists and boors apart – and anyway, such dregs of the male sex were not unique to law enforcement. Priestman had her eye on a promotion to deputy chief inspector, mostly for the money. Only to her husband had she admitted her ambivalence about progressing further up the ranks. As a DI, she could still engage in hands-on investigation, even if her desire to do so made her untypical of her rank, which was viewed by many aspirants as a nice way to stay out of the rain. If she rose to DCI, she'd be supervising investigations, but mostly from behind a desk. Then again, it wasn't as though anyone was offering her the job on a plate. It would be a year or two yet. She had time to think.

Right now, though, she was thinking about the body on the moors, and Douglas Hood, who was watching the police from the ruins on the hill, his dog sitting at his feet.

Derek Hynes, regarded by some in the force as Priestman's pet detective sergeant, joined her. He was a large, untidy man with a large, tidy mind. He and Priestman had known each other for many years, and it always gave her pleasure and reassurance to have him by her side.

'Still up there, I see,' said Hynes.

'From what I hear,' said Priestman, 'he has a proprietorial interest in these moors.'

'He's welcome to them.'

'You're not a fan of nature in its wilder state?'

Hynes had been born and raised in Kenton, one of the rougher areas of Newcastle. He wasn't a fan of the great outdoors. Even parks made him uncomfortable.

'I slipped earlier and got shit on me trousers,' he said. 'Sheep shit, I think. Can't say for sure. I might have to ask forensics to check.'

Hynes seemed about to say more on the subject, but was distracted by movement on the hill.

'Hello,' he said, 'looks like Heathcliff is coming our way.'

Hood and his dog had left their post, and were walking in tandem toward the two officers. Both Priestman and Hynes had spoken with Hood earlier, and while they hadn't entirely dismissed him as a suspect, neither really fancied him for the killing of the girl, and for much the same reason that Hood himself had come up with: why murder someone, then wrap her up and report the body?

'Can we help you, Mr Hood?' Priestman said, as the man came within earshot.

He stopped when she spoke, and the dog instantly assumed a seated position. He had it well trained, she'd give him that. She had a dog at home, Spike, that seemed to take a perverse pleasure in doing the opposite of whatever it was told to do, and only sat when it was bored.

Hood seemed to be considering the question. He looked at the dog, as though seeking advice or direction from it. When none came, he went with his own instinct.

'No,' he said, 'but perhaps I can help you.'

'And how would that be?'

Hood's face assumed a look of profound sadness.

'I think,' he said, 'I might know where that young lass was killed.'

XXI

He sat in his apartment, a TV dinner fresh from the microwave slowly cooling before him – if 'fresh' was the right word for a pre-prepared meal loaded with additives, and recently irradiated; he didn't believe it was, and these details were important. The apartment was very neat. It didn't contain any books, newspapers, or magazines, and he didn't consume any music or films in non-digital formats. It was surprising how much clutter objects added to a home – although, again, he wondered if 'home' was the correct term for a series of interconnected boxes to which he had added little of his own personality in the three years he'd lived in them, beyond a series of perfectly preserved vintage Apple computers, arranged on glass shelves, that functioned as art pieces. He didn't see any reason to invest in anything more lavish. The apartment had come pre-furnished, while the photographs and prints on the walls had seemed perfectly acceptable to him when he moved in, and continued to be so. He didn't trust his own taste when it came to art – didn't really have much taste at all, to be honest.

Or hadn't until recently, because he recognized that the windows at Fairford were art.

The windows at Fairford were beautiful.

He had never really understood what people meant when they referred to art as 'speaking' to them. Oh, he gathered they were discussing some abstract process of connection, a stirring in response to a visual stimulus. He had just never experienced it for himself, or not until he visited St Mary's church at Fairford. Sellars had explained the history of its stained-glass windows to him. Sellars had told him of heaven and hell, and old gods.

Sellars had told him about the Atlas.

He shifted in his chair, causing his injured foot to slip from its cushion. He gasped. The real pain of the injury was mercifully dulled by the medication. He'd ditched the ibuprofen in favor of some prescription pills left over from a dental implant. Damn, though, that sudden movement had still smarted. He'd informed the doctor at the clinic that he'd taken a misstep, which was true, as far as it went. The doctor, some foreigner, didn't bother exploring the details of the accident any further. It wasn't as though it was a particularly interesting injury, but he also recognized that some aspect of his own character, or lack of one, dissuaded other men from engaging in lengthy conversations with him, professional discussions excepted. Males found him dull, and he cultivated that dullness. Oddly, he was better with women, although money might have played some part in his success with the opposite sex. But the more perceptive among both sexes (and their kind worried him, oh yes: you had to keep an eye out for those ones, and avoid them whenever you could) might also have felt a shiver of anxiety in his presence, like staring at the placid surface of a pond only to glimpse a creature old and ravenous briefly flick a fin in the shallows before returning to deeper water.

The girl had witnessed the revelation of that presence, at the end of her life.

On the television screen, a reporter was speaking from the Hexhamshire Moors. Behind her, the white forms of the investigating officers moved against the horizon, like ghosts drifting across the land. A drone shot followed, giving a larger picture of the scene, with the tent at its center, although the drone didn't hover directly above it, which was a shame. He supposed the police had given the news crews instructions to keep their distance, but he wished they hadn't. He was curious to look on the faces of those who would soon be hunting for him. He was good with faces. If they came for him, it might be the difference between being caught and having time to run.

Or would have been, had he not fractured his ankle out on those moors. Now he was more vulnerable, but not to an extent that concerned him. He was certain he'd left little evidence – although he wished the promised rain would come along and wash away anything that might help the police – and he was sure he hadn't been seen by anyone. Such risk. Such excitement. He hadn't felt his pulse race that way since –

Well, since ever.

At least he had someone with whom to discuss it, someone who understood the thrill: Sellars. He hoped Sellars wouldn't be too angry with him, because it hadn't gone as planned, not by a long shot. But he'd managed to kill the girl, which had to count for something. She'd have been found eventually, so what did it matter? A week, a month, what was the difference? Only the death itself was important. But he really didn't want Sellars to be upset, because he longed to do it again. He wanted to kill another one.

He felt the urge to call Sellars and tell him why he'd had to leave the girl on the moors, but he had been warned against making contact unless it was absolutely necessary. Eventually, Sellars would get back in touch, and he could make his apologies. Maybe they could even compare notes, once he was able to get around a little better.

For now, though, they needed the police to remain confused.

Two killers, like two heads, were better than one.

XXII

Priestman and Hynes, accompanied by one uniformed officer, Oakenfold, and a crime scene investigator called Suzy Grant, tramped across the moors in the footsteps of Hood and his dog. Hood was setting a fast pace, and Hynes in particular was struggling. Priestman had the sense to exercise regularly. She swam, ran a bit, and brought her own mutt for long walks at weekends. Hynes resented walking further than the front of a building to the door of a car, and vice versa. He had also yet to encounter a situation that could not be improved by a cup of tea and a cigarette.

'Tell me about these people,' Priestman asked Hood, as his dog darted off to send some birds skyward. She wasn't from Northumbria. She'd been born and raised in Surrey, in the southeast, and had only traveled north for the first time to go to university. She'd liked it enough to stay, and marry a Geordie, but she wasn't of this land, and would never be, not even if they buried her in it.

'The Familists,' said Hood. 'They were a sect – a cult, I suppose. Long time ago now. But they haven't been forgotten, not around here. Theirs was a god of nature: leaves and branches. Thorns, too, I imagine. Kept themselves to themselves, except on Sundays when they worshipped with the locals like good folk. You had to keep up appearances in those days, or questions would be asked. The authorities weren't above a bit of torture either, to keep people in line. After that, if you didn't learn your lesson, they put you to the torch.'

He took a breath, and frowned, perhaps surprised by his own loquacity.

'This was during the Reformation?' said Priestman.

'It was. Catholics didn't give two figs if you went to church or not, long as you stuck to the rules. Didn't even bother putting seats in chapels for the poor folk, the Catholics. Didn't matter to the priests and bishops if the commoners were present or not. Probably didn't matter to God either, what with all He had to be getting along with. It was the Reformers who cracked the whip for Sunday worship. Never know what people might get up to otherwise.'

'So the Familists did the clever thing and showed up like the rest?' said Priestman.

'They did, until they didn't have to pretend any more. Then they sodded off to America in 1703, and took their church with them. The Chapel of the Congregation of Adam Before Eve and Eve Before Adam, that was what they named it. All they left behind were rumors and ruins.'

Priestman smiled, despite the circumstances. 'Rumors and ruins': it was a nice turn of phrase. Funny, but now that Hood had found his tongue he couldn't seem to stop talking. She really thought he might be making up for lost time, like a man forced by exigency to eat a food he has previously considered disagreeable, only to discover that he has been mistaken in his assumptions, and so makes it a staple of his diet.

And he was no fool, this man.

'You mean rumors of killings?'

Hood had referred to these earlier, when the police had first asked him about the nature of the old buildings, although he hadn't elaborated.

'That's the story.'

'Sacrificial killings?'

'I don't know about that. There was no evidence for it, only hearsay, but it was said that the Familists weren't above murdering to protect themselves. They may have gone to church on Sundays, but they conducted their own worship in secret. The problem is that there are no secrets, not out here, doesn't matter how far into the moors you go to hide. Tales of hole-and-corner worship would have attracted attention: from the curious, from informers. I suppose some of them might have come out to snoop on the

Familists. If they did, it's likely they never found their way back again. Ended up drowned in mires, most of 'em.'

'Most?'

Hood's expression changed. He seemed about to say something more, then reconsidered.

'Most,' he echoed, and that was all.

THE WELL

THE HISTORY OF BRITISH ARCHAEOLOGY IS A CURIOUS
one. It probably begins with the monks at Glastonbury Abbey who,
upon uncovering some old bones while rebuilding their church after a
fire, concluded, somewhat erroneously, that they had discovered the
remains of King Arthur. They were followed – rather more successfully – over the centuries by men such as John Leland, the favored
antiquary of Henry VIII, and William Camden, the author of the
Britannica of 1586, and founder of the first society of British antiquaries in 1577. This institution became popular with lawyers, who
used it as a front to debate the flaws of the legal system, until James I
became aware of its potential for sedition and shut it down. It was
long rumored that one Josias Quayle, a minor figure in legal circles of
the time, was the man responsible for informing on the activities of
his colleagues, although this has never been proved.

After Camden came Robert Plot, the first Keeper of Oxford's
Ashmolean Museum in the seventeenth century; John Aubrey, who
credited druids with the creation of the kingdom's stone circles; and,
in the eighteenth century, William Stukeley, who pioneered the use
of excavation to study ancient sites – which earned archaeologists
the soubriquet 'barrow diggers' – and was a founder of a new
Society of Antiquaries in 1707. Finally, in the nineteenth century,
figures such as John Lubbock and Herbert Spencer helped to place
the study of the past on a more respectable and professional footing,
leading to the establishment of the first chairs of archaeology in
British universities.

But the greatest of them all – at least in my opinion, for I knew
him well – was Augustus Pitt Rivers, the first Inspector of Ancient
Monuments, and it was at his instigation that, in 1884, I led a field
club, a mix of amateurs and students of archaeology, to investigate
the site of the Familist settlement on the Hexhamshire Moors of

Northumberland. What follows is a faithful account of that dig, and the disappearance of Walter Hodges, a student.

May God have mercy on him, wherever he may rest.

It should be noted that archaeological digs are not without their complexities, and these are not limited to technical or physical challenges. Quite often, local superstitions attach themselves to ancient sites, leading to a reluctance among the populace to facilitate any examination or excavation. In truth, this kind of objection tends to be more common in the investigation of druidic constructs – and barrows, of course, due to a fear of disturbing the dead.

But in Hexhamshire we were surprised to find this antagonism extended to the foundational site of the *Familia Caritatis*, the Familists, given that they had only come into being in the 1580s, and had largely ceased to exist by the early part of the nineteenth century. We could only attribute such ill feeling to a misplaced conception of the sect that had become ingrained in the locals over the years, including a belief that the Familists had murdered to protect themselves from scrutiny or persecution. Northumberland lore held that among their victims were men and women from the surrounding villages of Corbridge, Bardon Mill, Haltwhistle, and Wylam. Suggestions that these unfortunate individuals might simply have gone astray on the moors, or been taken by some general class of blackguard, were met with skepticism, at best.

The result of this ill feeling was that our little group of five found it impossible to secure accommodations in any of the nearby communities, and resigned ourselves to spending our nights under canvas. Still, I regarded this as no great imposition, because I have always preferred to situate myself in the vicinity of a dig; or at least this was my penchant, before Hexhamshire.

Pitt Rivers's curiosity about the Familist site was linked to his belief that the sect's presence there had been but the latest in a series of settlements, and excavation might reveal evidence of earlier Roman and pre-Roman communities. I admit it was curious that Familists should have chosen such a remote, harsh location, one that would have left them vulnerable to the predations of border reivers and other outlaws, but it might well have been a consequence of their desire to worship their god of wood and leaf in secret, and without fear of being tortured or killed for their idolatry. Of course, the chapel they built is now in Maine, in the United States, and the town they founded there, called Prosperous, has apparently been as successful as its name suggests. Its inhabitants, though, are unwelcoming to outsiders, or so I have been informed, and prefer to leave their Familist roots unexplored.

Of the members of our group, Walter Hodges was the youngest at twenty, yet also potentially the most gifted. Pitt Rivers had virtually guaranteed him a post as one of his assistants should he achieve a First in his finals, which seemed a foregone conclusion to most. I was a little less enamored of Hodges. I felt his work was sometimes hurried, and he lacked the patience necessary to be a great archaeologist. Perhaps it would have come in time, but we shall never know. Goetz, the other student on what was intended to be this first dig of three, was one year behind Hodges, but one year older, and seemed to bear him some undefined ill will. Goetz was of Prussian descent, and distantly related to Bismarck himself, or so he claimed. Clement and Morgan, meanwhile, were banker and accountant respectively, and enthusiastic members of the fledgling Northumberland Geological, Archaeological, Botanical and Zoological Society, a range of interests which promised more breadth than depth to their scholarship.

We reached the Familist site shortly before noon on the first day, and set up our camp amid the ruins of the settlement. Although it was early April, and growing milder by the day, much of the Hexhamshire Moors are dreadfully exposed, and we believed we might be glad of the shelter provided by the walls. We were not mistaken, for barely had we raised canvas before a wind rose from the east, blowing in off the North Sea, and had we not enjoyed the protection of the ruins our tents might well have been on their way to Ireland before too long. We lit a fire, and made a pot of tea to warm ourselves before commencing our preliminary examination.

It was Hodges who discovered the well, much to Goetz's displeasure.

It lay beneath the floor of the largest structure on the site, which had probably once been home to the sect's leader, one Deakin Carr, a descendant of Christopher Vittell, the head of the principal Familist group in England, based in Balsam, Cambridgeshire. Carr had enjoyed a reputation for violence in his youth, and was briefly ostracized by his own people, who generally favored a lifestyle of tolerance and reflection, and objected to the bearing of arms. He returned to the embrace of the Familists after two or three years, and was adjudged to be a reformed character, yet it may be that something of the sect's unfavorable reputation in Northumberland can be attributed to Carr's earlier failings.

(But I digress, which is a flaw in my character, one that I have struggled, and failed, to address. It may be forgivable under these circumstances, representing a form of prevarication. I leave it for you to decide.)

The mouth of the well was approximately three feet in diameter, and had been disguised with scree and larger stones, including a single slab of slate wide enough to cover the hole entirely. Over this a thick layer of earth had been placed, one that had, by this time, grown a canopy of grass and weeds. How Hodges was alerted to the well's presence, I cannot say. Whatever my concerns about his temperament, he had an almost uncanny eye for a dig, and some small topographical or taxonomical distinction had clearly drawn his attention while Goetz and I were otherwise engaged in visiting the former location of the Familist chapel. Once he had revealed a section of the original floor, Hodges became convinced that other material had been added for the purposes of concealment, and managed to bring Clement and Morgan around to his way of thinking, for amateurs of their particular stripe are always seeking fame by uncovering something that serious archaeologists may have missed. By the time Goetz and I returned, half of the scree had been removed, and part of the well already lay revealed.

I was angry with Hodges; I am not afraid to admit it. His actions only served to confirm for me that Pitt Rivers's indulgence had exacerbated rather than curbed Hodges' worst instincts. Yet once I had recovered my temper, I found myself intrigued by the well. There was no mention of it in the existing records of the site; in fact, another well had been dug to the west of the settlement, one that was still in existence. It was unclear what reason the Familists might have had for digging a second, particularly inside a house.

The answer to this conundrum was provided by a closer perusal of the stones of the well itself, for they were older than those of the dwelling that surrounded them. Goetz speculated that the well might be of Roman origin, at which Hodges resorted to scoffing – not without some justification, it must be said, but it was still unbecoming to see him belittle Goetz in such a fashion. Nevertheless, Goetz should have known better: the stonework was too crude, and bore none of the precision of a Roman hand. No, this well had been dug long before the Romans came. Clement dropped a pebble into its depths, but we heard no sound, no splash. It was as though a hole had been bored to the center of the earth.

But by then it was growing dark, and any further consideration of the well would require daylight. We lit a fire for cooking, and ate ham tossed in the pan with hot jacket potatoes, followed by coffee and brandy. The food and drink eased some of the tensions between Hodges and Goetz, with the former apologizing for his earlier remarks, and Goetz appearing to accept. I had a quiet word with Hodges before we turned in for the night, admonishing him for his haste in acting without my consent, and reminding him of Pitt Rivers's likely displeasure should any damage be done to the site before its examination had even begun in earnest. The mention of Pitt Rivers in such a context seemed to have the desired effect, and brought the second apology of the night from Hodges. I retired to my tent believing a valuable lesson might have been learned.

The disposition of our encampment meant that we were situated in what was formerly the heart of the Familist settlement, and probably a communal meeting place. The walls of the old buildings provided perfect sanctuary from the wind, and, as stated earlier, I have a fondness for sleeping outdoors, even when my shelter is being tested by the elements, and tend to rest soundly as a consequence. I was surprised, therefore, to find myself coming awake during the night, and irritated to realize I had been roused from my slumbers by footsteps. I assumed it was one of our party attending to a call of nature, until I heard someone enter the building immediately to my right, the one housing the well. Whoever it was had no business stumbling around there in the dark, even if we had taken the precaution of replacing the slab over the mouth, just in case.

The moon shone brightly through the flap of my tent, but still I didn't care to investigate without the benefit of my lamp. Once I had lighted it, I crawled outside to establish the source of the disturbance, and was more disappointed than shocked to find it was Hodges who had woken me. He was standing by the well, his own lamp raised high before him.

'What are you doing?' I said, and was pleased to see him fairly leap into the air with shock.

'I heard noises,' he said, once he had recovered himself.

'Noises? What kind of noises?'

'From inside the well.'

I listened, but the only sound was the wind on the moors.

'You're imagining things.'

'No, I tell you I heard something.'

'It might have been an animal. A rat, perhaps.'

He looked at me, and I saw on his face the same expression that had accompanied his disparagement of Goetz.

'How could a rat climb up the inside of that well?' he said. 'And from where might it have climbed?'

He had a point: the interior of the well was not smooth, exactly, but even a rat would have struggled to find purchase. Anyway, that wasn't what I had meant; or at least, I don't believe it was.

'Not *in* the well, man – outside it, among the ruins.'

For the first time, Hodges appeared doubtful.

'But I could have sworn it was coming from under the slab,' he said.

'It's the wind. It plays tricks with sound.' I decided it was time to be conciliatory, not least because it was one thing to be wrapped up warm in my tent, and quite another to be standing in a roofless ruin on a northern night that had not yet fully shaken off the hand of winter. 'Come on, now, back to your tent. We'll take another look in the morning.'

I placed a hand on Hodges' elbow, and guided him out. I reminded myself that he was still barely more than a boy, one that might, with the correct tutelage, and some adjustment to his temperament, make a fine archaeologist. Once I was satisfied that he was safely back in his tent, and had advised him against any further nocturnal perambulations, I returned to my own Euklisia rug, and my rest.

Did I hear a sound before I slept, as of dry limbs scratching against stone?

No, I did not.

I swear it.

The next day we commenced a full and proper mapping of the two sites: the settlement itself, and the former setting of the Familist chapel. It was a fractious business, not helped by a soft, steady rain that began shortly before 10 a.m. and continued throughout the day.

Goetz's previous rapprochement with Hodges fell by the wayside, and the two young men bickered and fought until lunch, after which I deemed it prudent to separate them. Hodges I sent with Clement to secure milk and bread from one of the nearby farms. Curiously, our own supply had spoiled during the night, the milk turning to sour-smelling curds, and the bread becoming entirely moldy, even though both had been purchased fresh the previous day. Meanwhile Goetz and Morgan remained with me, and we made good progress in Hodges' absence, although Goetz's mood showed no signs of improvement, not even when he discovered an inscription carved on one of the stones cast aside during Hodges' attempted excavation of the well. It read 'Cave Veteris'.

'What does it mean?' said Morgan.

'"Beware Veteris",' said Goetz, which was probably about right. 'Who is Veteris?'

'A Celtic god,' I told him, 'but one mentioned only by the Romans garrisoned near this section of Hadrian's Wall. Sometimes it's written as "Veteris", at other times "Veteres", suggesting a god of multiple aspects – not unlike our own tripartite deity, one might say.'

Morgan blanched a little at the potential blasphemy, but did not voice an objection.

'They raised altars to it,' I continued. 'It was a cult.'

'I thought they had their own gods,' said Morgan.

'They did,' I said. 'But that doesn't mean they couldn't accept the existence of others.'

'And they worshipped this Veteris?'

'They made offerings to it, yes.'

'Why?'

I shrugged.

'Because,' I said, 'one can't be too careful.'

Clement and Hodges eventually returned with some milk, bread, and fresh eggs, although they'd been made to pay handsomely for their acquisitions, and even then were reduced almost to pleading before their money was accepted by the farmer, one Edwyn Hood, and his wife. We stored away the supplies, and I set Clement and Hodges to measuring the little cemetery to the north of the main site, and taking what rubbings they could from the stones, most of which were now concealed by grass. I estimated that we still had a couple of hours of daylight left, and the earlier absence of Hodges, and to a lesser degree Clement, had cost us valuable time. We would make up some of it while we could.

I was in the process of examining the brickwork of one of the houses, which bore more Roman lettering and was therefore either part of an older structure, or had been scavenged from elsewhere, when I heard a shout from the cemetery, and my name being called. Fearing some accident, I ran in that direction, Goetz and Morgan at my heels, only to find Hodges and Clement upright and apparently unharmed.

'A close call,' said Hodges.

I joined them, and saw what had occasioned the summons. Before me lay a partially open grave, with two halves of a flat stone, not dissimilar to that which now blocked the well, protruding from the hole, earth and grass still clinging to its surface.

'I felt it give beneath my step,' said Clement. 'I almost ended up in that hole.'

'Probably a fault in the stone,' said Morgan, who knew something of geology, as he peered at the exposed edges. 'Over the years water gets in. It freezes, thaws, and the flaw deepens.'

'Look inside the grave,' said Hodges.

I did. I could see bones, of course, because what else would one expect to see in a grave, but they were obscured by some dark cladding, almost like a web.

'What is that?' I asked.

Hodges had a lamp with him as part of his kit. He put a match to it, lay by the graveside, and lowered the lamp. By its glow we could see that the remains were entirely covered by a system of roots, yet they had not grown through the body but had instead wrapped themselves around it, as though swaddling the bones. Beneath the skeleton could be seen fragments of old wood, and another carcass, although this one was not similarly encumbered by nature's embrace.

'It's a woman,' said Hodges, pointing at the first corpse. 'See the rounded pelvis?'

I could, although it was barely visible through the vegetation.

'But where did the roots come from?' said Morgan. 'I can see no tree, no shrubs.'

He was correct. This part of the moors was bare of all but grass.

'Perhaps she was wrapped in them after she died,' said Clement.

'No,' said Hodges, who remained lying on the ground. 'They've definitely grown around her. No human hand did this.'

'And why put a stone over it?' said Goetz. 'Why not fill in the grave after the body was interred?'

'My God,' said Hodges.

He had dipped the light as low as it could reach, until the base of the lamp was almost touching the woman's bones, and we all saw them: the remnants of the bonds used to secure her hands and feet, and the thin leather strap between her teeth.

'She was restrained,' said Hodges. 'They buried her alive.'

Our meal that evening was a somber one, with little conversation and less bonhomie. We were all thinking of the dead woman, and the terrible manner of her passing. Not only had she been interred alive, but also those responsible had wanted her to die slowly. Had earth been piled on top of her, she would have suffocated; still an appalling death, but one that would have taken minutes at most, not days or weeks. And there was the issue of the roots or branches that enveloped her: they had grown around her, but appeared to have no source, unless the parent tree had died so long ago that these roots were the only evidence of its former existence. Even so, one might have expected to see a vestige of their connection to the soil, but there was none. Also, we could find no evidence of decay upon them. The fibers were strong, and a rich brown. Hodges had struggled to cut one with his knife.

Shortly before we retired to our tents, some passing remark of Hodges' caused Goetz to leap at him, and the latter landed a blow before Morgan and Clement managed to separate them. By now I had endured enough, for I could see no sign of relations between the two students improving under the present circumstances. I ordered both of them to return to Oxford first thing the next morning, where they would be given ample opportunity to explain their behavior to Pitt Rivers. In the meantime, Clement, Morgan, and I would remain on the moors to conclude our observations, as an example of how gentlemen and scientists – even those of the amateur persuasion – should behave themselves. We all repaired to our rest in varying degrees of ill temper, and after a time the night was still.

I opened my eyes. The noise, when it came, was unmistakably human. It was the sound of sobbing.

I ignited my lamp, and for the second night in a row departed my tent in darkness to investigate a disturbance. As before, it came from the ruin that housed the well. I stopped in the doorway. By the light of moon and lamp, I could see that the slab had been removed from the mouth of the well, and to my right a figure was crouched against the wall. It was Goetz.

'What are you doing out here?' I asked, but Goetz did not reply, and only continued to produce low, regular sobs, while his whole body shook. His gaze never left the well.

I moved closer to the hole, and saw a man's boot lying by the edge. It was dark brown, and made by Tricker's of London. Only one of our group wore such a boot: Hodges. Beside the boot was a broken lamp.

I rushed to Hodges' tent, calling his name, but just Clement and Morgan answered my call. Hodges' tent was empty. Together, all three of us returned to the well, and Goetz. I knelt before him.

'What happened? Goetz, where is Hodges?'

Goetz pointed at the well.

'*Die Wurzeln*,' he said. '*Die Wurzeln nahmen ihn.*'

'What's he saying?' asked Morgan.

I looked back at the well.

'He says the roots took him.'

I sent Morgan for the police at first light. We were all questioned, although Goetz would speak only German – I could not tell if this was a deliberate attempt at obstruction on his part, or a genuine result of shock; the police suspected it to be the former, and I the latter – and so I was forced to translate as best I could. He stuck to his story, which was that he had heard Hodges get up during the night. Some instinct, perhaps the lingering bad blood between them, had caused Goetz to go after him. When he arrived at the well, he found Hodges standing before it, the slab already removed from the hole and lying some three or four feet away, although it would have too heavy for Hodges to have shifted it so far alone.

'I heard something,' Hodges said to him, and then Goetz heard it too, or so he told us. It was a scratching, like nails or claws on a wall. It was coming from the well. He watched Hodges approach the hole, and lift his lamp. Hodges peered over the edge, and Goetz saw a dark tuberous length wrap itself around his right foot. Hodges tried to pull back, which was when his unlaced boot came off, and he fell to the ground. Before he could cry out, a second root coiled around his head, gagging him.

And then Hodges was gone.

They tried Manfred Goetz for the murder of Walter Hodges. He was found guilty, but avoided the gallows due to the intervention of some senior figures in the German government – it appeared he had not been lying about the Bismarck connection after all – aided by the fact that there was no body, and hence only circumstantial evidence of his guilt. He was sentenced to life imprisonment in Pentonville, but in the end lasted only a year before killing himself with a noose fashioned from bootlaces.

Did Goetz murder Walter Hodges? I do not know. All I can say is that I hope he did, pushing the younger man into the well, and Walter Hodges broke his neck when he eventually hit the bottom, or fractured his skull against the walls on the way down. I do not care to think about the other possibility. I do not want to believe that Goetz was telling the truth. I think of that woman's remains, bound by tree roots. I think of the warning on the stone.

I think of them all the time.

These impressions I shared only with Pitt Rivers in his study one night over brandy, not long after Goetz's death, and now I am committing this account to paper. What Pitt Rivers made of my version of the tale I cannot say, for he could be most taciturn when he chose, except that he suspended all further investigation of the Familist site on the Hexhamshire moors, a decision that has remained in force even after his passing. For many years, the Hodges family made a pilgrimage to the settlement on the anniversary of the boy's disappearance, and placed flowers by the well. I came to know Hodges' younger brother a little, after he went up to Cambridge. He told me the flowers would begin to die as soon as they were laid, and were withered entirely before the last of the prayers were said. Make of that what you will. As for me, I have lived for many years on a top-floor flat off Church Street, close to the university that I love. I chose the house because it has no garden.

Make of that, also, what you will.

XXIII

As they moved across the moors, Priestman noticed that Hynes had fallen behind, and paused to allow him to catch up.

'You're puffing like a steam train,' she said.

'I didn't sign up for a hike,' said Hynes. 'If I'd known, I'd have taken precautions.'

'What kind of precautions?'

'I wouldn't have come into work this morning.' He leaned over, his hands on his knees. 'Why would anyone choose to live out here?'

'I think it's beautiful,' said Priestman.

'Might be, if they put a roof on it.'

Hood had kept walking, and was about to crest a small hill, Oakenfold and Grant close behind.

'Hold on,' Hynes called out, before adding under his breath – or what was left of it – 'unless you want another body out here.'

'We don't have time to stop,' said Hood.

'And why is that?'

Hood pointed to the sky. The clouds looked darker, the sheets of rain closer. 'Wind's changed. It's going to bucket down before long.'

'Jesus,' said Hynes. 'As if things weren't bad enough.'

'You've got a coat,' said Priestman, 'and it's waterproof.'

'The coat may be, but I'm not.'

'God, you're a moaner.'

She returned to Hood and prevailed upon him to wait for her sergeant.

'Not far now,' said Hood.

'Thank Christ,' said Hynes, as he drew level.

Hood was not looking at him, but at a hollow in the earth.

'Christ won't want your thanks for this,' he said.

XXIV

Parker spent the best part of three hours in the witness box, much of it dodging barbs from the defense, before being permitted to go about his business. Tracey Ermenthal walked out with him, and they conducted a brief post-mortem on his testimony. The two accused had displayed no emotion as the recording of their conversation was played to the court, but its effect on the jury was obvious. One of the female members was crying by the end, and a couple of the males looked as though they wanted to tear the defendants apart.

'They're gone,' said Ermenthal. 'It's just a question of for how long.'

Parker had no pity for the two men, not after listening to them boast of what they'd done, but neither was he experiencing any sense of triumph, only a vague depression. It wasn't entirely due to the nature of the case, although that was part of it; mostly it was a consequence of exposure to the workings of the legal system. Anyone who spent time in a courtroom emerged with scars. The only variables were quantity and depth.

'You tell Moxie he has a favor to call in, if he ever needs it,' Ermenthal continued.

'Then I guarantee you'll be hearing from him. What about my favor?'

'Your favor?' Ermenthal began to laugh. 'Prosecutors in half-a-dozen states have a hard-on for you, and the US Attorney for the Southern District of New York thinks you should be arrested on sight if you ever set foot in his jurisdiction again. Your favor is that you're not in jail.'

She was still laughing as she walked away.

XXV

Priestman stood on the verge of a pit in the moors, like the aftermath of a meteor strike. The ground sloped down toward an uneven plateau at the center, accessed by a series of rough-hewn stone steps, now largely overgrown. The steps led to nothing, because the core was empty, but it had not always been so. Priestman could make out an order to the disturbance of the earth, a pattern to the growth of the grass. She felt profoundly discomposed, as though she were guilty of some form of trespass, and whatever had once occupied this place might take offense at her intrusion were it to return and find her there. She did not consider herself to be an overimaginative person. She had never liked dark fantasies or horror films. She didn't find them frightening; they just did nothing for her. But here and now, she thought she might have some inkling of what they did to others.

She finished pulling on her shoe covers, and raised the hood of her jacket so it covered her hair. Below, Hynes and Grant were squatting by a patch of ground. Although dusk was gathering, the shadows here were different from the rest.

'It's blood all right,' said Grant.

Priestman turned to Douglas Hood, who was standing nearby, the dog at his feet, its head on its front paws as it watched the activity with interest.

'Thank you,' she said, as she prepared to call in the discovery and get the rest of the CSIs moving.

'Better tell them to not to tarry,' said Hood. 'Won't be long before the rain comes to wash it away.'

She nodded, made the call, and descended to join the others.

XXVI

The federal government had booked a hotel room in Houston for Parker, but he decided he'd spent long enough in the west and southwest. There were no direct flights to Portland, and the ones with stopovers made him want to weep, so he caught the 4.30 p.m. United flight to Boston, and from there took a Concord bus north. The screens above the seats were showing a golfing movie, which he did his best to ignore. He could think of few things worse than actual golf, but watching a movie about it came a close second. Instead he kept his eyes on the road, and used the silence to consider Quayle.

He could, he supposed, have left the lawyer to rot in whatever dusty corner of Europe he had chosen for his fastness, there to while away his days until inevitable mortality solved the problem of his existence. Louis might not have liked it – Mors had hurt Louis, and Louis wanted to hurt her in return – but Parker had no personal stake in Quayle's continued liberty. On the other hand, if he were to intervene in cases that only affected him personally, he would essentially be washing his hands of moral responsibility, and become complicit in atrocities through inaction.

And Parker had an advantage: he possessed something that Quayle wanted very badly. Parker, after all, was one of only a handful of people to have been in contact with the original copy of *Grimm's Fairy Tales* sought by Quayle, the book into which three additional vellum pages had been sewn, fragments of an older work the nature of which Parker was still trying to establish. While he had been forced to surrender two of the vellum inserts during his last encounter with Quayle, the third was locked away in a safe deposit box. As yet, Quayle did not appear to know this, but it was possible he might soon begin to suspect. Most of those who had handled the pages were now dead, killed by Quayle and Mors. Only Parker, a book collector named Bob Johnston, and Leila Patton, a young woman in Indiana, remained alive, and Mors had already tried, unsuccessfully, to harm the latter. Parker did not want Mors making a second attempt should her employer decide that Patton might know something about the missing page. All of which meant that, at some point in the future, Quayle might return to the United States to resume his search. It would be best if he were dealt with before then.

The Dutch angle was interesting. Parker still believed Quayle to be English, but he obviously had contacts in the Netherlands. The dumping of the woman's body in Lagnier's junkyard suggested to Parker that the feds' inquiries had caused alarm over in Europe, with the result that a planned diversionary tactic had been employed in the form of the dead woman.

Now Ross wanted to use Louis to dig deeper. Parker decided that Louis's willingness or otherwise to travel to the Netherlands was unlikely to be an issue. If it offered Louis the chance to hunt Mors, he'd make the trip in a heartbeat. The only difficulties were the aftereffects of Louis's own injuries, and Angel's chemotherapy treatment. It resembled, Parker thought, the plot of a very violent soap opera.

The bus was largely empty. Parker counted only five other passengers, and they were all seated at the front. He was at the very back, so he didn't feel too bad about using his cell phone, although he kept his voice low both for reasons of courtesy and because he was about to ask Louis if he was prepared to take a transatlantic trip with the ultimate aim of ending two lives.

Louis picked up on the second ring.

'Where are you?' he asked.

'On a bus.'

'If you're broke, you can ask me for money. I won't give you none, but you can ask.'

'It's a long story, and involves a body.'

'Do I want to hear it?'

'I think you should. It concerns our English friends.'

119

Parker detected what might have been a growl from the other end of the phone.

'Are they back?'

'No – or not yet, but they entered the United States on Dutch passports, and at least one of them also left on a Dutch passport. A little bird suggested you might have contacts in the Netherlands, the kind that might be able to help.'

'Does this little bird have a name?'

'Ross.'

'That little bird knows more songs than I'd prefer. Someone should break its neck.'

'I'll admit he's hard to warm to. Is he right?'

'Yes.'

'You still have sources over there?'

'Good ones.'

'You interested in going back?'

'Maybe. When?'

'Soon.'

'I got shot.'

'I know.'

'In the groin.'

'And elsewhere.'

'Fuck elsewhere. A man's groin is, like, sacrosanct.'

'Yours especially.'

'You think you're just being funny, but it's the truth.'

'I believe you.'

Another pause, another growl.

'Angel has chemo.'

'I know that too.'

'He's resting now. I'll talk to him in the morning.'

'Okay.'

'Okay.'

Louis hung up. Parker stretched out his own injured leg. He'd busted his foot while jumping out a window during that final confrontation with Quayle and Mors. The damage was minor but – as the doctor had informed him – after fifty there really was no such thing as 'minor'.

He closed his eyes, if only to shut out the golfing movie, and eventually the bus reached Portland. He caught a cab to the airport, picked up his car from the parking garage, and drove to Scarborough.

Home.

XXVII

Sellars was woken by the alarm clock at 3 a.m., and instantly silenced it so as not to wake Lauren. She stirred in her slumber, and mumbled something, but he paid her no heed. She was used to his early starts after eight years of marriage, although she no longer minded when he spent nights away, not like she did when they first got together. Back then, she couldn't bear the emptiness on his side of the bed, said it made her feel sad: not only because she missed his presence, but also because it reminded her of how her life would be after he was gone. You know, when he was dead, like. He'd always thought it was an odd thing to say, but she was an odd one, Lauren. That might have been what attracted him to her, right from the start. She wasn't the same as the rest of the girls on the estate. They all had big mouths on them, and swarmed together like wasps. Lauren was quieter, always at the edges of groups, never the center. She liked it better there, she said. Made it easier to get away.

She was clever, too. She read all sorts of books. Had her own box at the local library, she read so many. The librarians just threw in anything they thought she might enjoy, along with whatever she asked for herself, but they still couldn't keep her satisfied. She'd never been bored, she said, not once, not while she had a book to read. She lived in them, and saw the world through their pages. That might have been part of the problem with their marriage. She'd had her head filled with all kinds of nonsense about love and romance, stuff that just wasn't true, couldn't be true, because no one was like that, not in real life, or no one they knew.

He got up, went to the bathroom, and dressed once he was done with his business. He'd been ill with a nasty tummy bug the day before, taking to his bed in the morning and moving between it and the toilet for the duration, but he felt a bit better now.

He looked in on Kelly and Louise. He was tempted to kiss them goodbye, but if he woke Louise he'd be the worst in the world. He contented himself with gazing on them for a while before closing the door, leaving just a little gap so Lauren would be able to hear if Louise cried out. Still in his stocking feet, he walked downstairs, put the kettle on, stuck some bread in the toaster, and turned on the television to BBC News, the sound barely above a whisper.

He saw the images from the moors.

He saw the police.

He saw a body being carried to a waiting ambulance.

'What did you do, Holmby?' he said. 'What the fuck did you do?'

XXVIII

Nicola Priestman sat in the corner of the dining room reserved as her home office space. She had a small desk, with a filing cabinet beside it. The family rarely used the room, except at Christmas or on those rare occasions when Priestman and her husband invited friends over for dinner, so most of the time she could leave it as messy as she liked. The kids knew better than to go near it, and her husband, too. She didn't have many rules, but that was one of them.

It was 6 a.m., and Priestman hadn't slept a lot the night before, but she was already dressed, and drinking coffee. The kids would be up soon, but Steve would take care of breakfast, make sure they didn't forget their lunches, and check that Robbie had his gym gear. She'd have a quick word with them before she left, but she'd be gone before they were.

Her laptop was open in front of her. She was trying to find out as much as she could about the Familists. There wasn't much, or not enough for her liking. In a strange way, she wished Hood had been wrong about where the girl was killed. The newspapers and the Internet crazies would be all over this sect stuff, and next thing they'd have idiots shouting about covens and devil worship, because nothing was guaranteed to bring out the fringe element more than talk of the occult. The investigators would have to live with it now, though.

Thanks to Hood's instincts, they'd been able to preserve the scene, although the press officer said he'd already had some environmental group complaining about damage to the moors. Priestman had wanted to get the site under cover before the rain came down, which meant she couldn't wait for the forensic team to trudge over with their gear. She'd authorized them to use their vehicles, and they'd left gouges on the landscape that could probably be seen from space. Even Hood hadn't been happy about it, although he'd kept his mouth shut. But she'd seen it on his face, as though she'd somehow disappointed him by betraying his trust in this way.

She rubbed the back of her neck, because it ached something awful. She would happily have accepted another few hours in bed, but she wasn't likely to enjoy any lie-ins for the foreseeable future. If she was lucky, she'd grab an early night to make up for it, but then she wouldn't see much of the kids. They understood why this sometimes happened, and Steve was very good about it as well, but it was one of the few aspects of her job that made her feel guilty. She knew the male officers didn't suffer familial guilt in the same way. It was a maternal thing. You couldn't fight it, so you just had to accept it. What couldn't be cured had to be endured, but women seemed to do a lot more enduring than men.

This brought her back to the body on the moors. They had a possible ID: Romana Moon, a teacher, originally from Arbroath in Scotland, but currently working at a primary school in Middlesbrough – or no longer working, Priestman thought. No longer working, breathing, sleeping, eating, yearning, loving. She'd missed two days at work, and on the afternoon of the second the principal sent someone round to check on her. When there was no reply, the principal called her parents in Scotland, and they notified the police. A day later, Romana's body had been found in Hexhamshire.

Priestman closed the window on the Familists and pulled up a map of the moors. Beyond the fact of her murder, the circumstances of Romana's death were troubling. Judging by the amount of blood found at the old chapel site, that was definitely where she'd met her end. Her hands had been bound behind her back, but they'd have to wait for the autopsy report to establish how long she'd been restrained; in other words, whether it was done far in advance of her murder, or closer to the end. This would, in turn, indicate whether she'd been transported to the location with the intention of killing her, or had perhaps been on the moors of her own volition, where she stumbled into the path of her murderer.

But if she just happened to be out there, perhaps on a solitary hike – unlikely, but possible – and was unfortunate enough to have encountered whoever killed her, then how did she get to Hexhamshire? Her car was still parked outside her flat in Acklam, so they'd have to check with public and private bus companies to see if any of their drivers could recall picking Romana up, or dropping her off in the vicinity of the moors. It was possible that she'd gone out there with someone she knew or had recently met, and the assignation had gone horribly wrong. They'd find out later that day if she'd been raped or otherwise sexually assaulted, which might give them some DNA with which to work. According to Romana's father and sister, who had already made a formal identification of the body, there was an ex-boyfriend, Simon Harris, in the background. He and Romana had broken up about three months earlier, at her instigation. Harris was due in for questioning later that day. Hynes was taking care of the arrangements. With his bluffness and hail-fellow-well-met demeanor, he had a way of putting people at their ease, but he was hard underneath, like a steel bar concealed in cotton wool.

Romana's sister had suggested that Romana might have begun seeing someone else since breaking up with Harris. She didn't know if it was serious, and Romana had been reluctant to share any details while the relationship was still in its nascent stages, but it was another avenue to explore. She also said that Romana wasn't the outdoor type, and, to her knowledge, didn't even own a pair of decent walking boots.

Which left the question of how Romana Moon had died at such an isolated spot. She might have been drugged, just enough to make her compliant, but they'd be waiting weeks for the toxicology report. Then there was the matter of the plastic sheeting, which was new, and of a type sold at any number of home improvement stores. If it had been brought out to the moors by Romana Moon's killer, then it was possible that he – or she, or even they, but Priestman decided to stick with 'he' for the time being – might have wrapped her in it and carried her over his shoulder, fireman style, to the chapel site, before –

Before killing her while she was naked – the blood pattern indicated that much – and then wrapping her in the plastic again to carry her away, which would have made no sense at all had it not been for the previous existence of the chapel. It was the setting that was important, lending further weight to a ritual aspect. Romana's killer wanted her life to end in that place, which meant he had no option but to transport her to the location.

But why not leave her there once he was done? The obvious explanation was that he didn't want her remains to be found: no body, no murder. So, he wraps her up again and begins to carry her, presumably to a vehicle on the road or farm track, but doesn't get that far, and instead leaves her out in the open, with not even a cursory effort at concealment.

Why?

Two possibilities: the first is that he was disturbed, maybe by another car, and panicked. While the police were still waiting for a more exact time of death, it was unlikely that Romana had been dead for more than eight hours when she was found by Hood, which meant she had been killed in darkness. That was unsurprising: no one was going to plan a ritual killing – and increasingly, as Priestman considered the evidence, it appeared to have been planned – and carry it out in daylight, even on an isolated moor. She was due to speak to the press at noon, and she'd issue an appeal for anyone driving through the area during the past, say, thirty-six hours to come forward, especially if they could remember a vehicle being parked on the main road near the old Familist settlement. In an ideal world, she'd have preferred not to mention the Familists at all, or not yet, but the media would find out about the connection soon enough, and the ruins were a landmark she could use to jog memories.

The other possibility was that, as Hood had suggested, the killer had fallen and injured himself while making his way back to the road, leaving him unable to carry the body any further. The ground was soft and uneven, and she and Hynes had slipped repeatedly while following Hood back from the site in the rain:

not badly, but enough to provoke bouts of swearing from Hynes. It would be even more difficult to negotiate the ground in darkness – and the killer might have been reluctant to use a powerful beam for fear of attracting attention. He was also carrying a body, so a headlamp might have been a more useful option. The CSIs were already back out on the moors, looking for trace evidence, although that blasted rain hadn't done them any favors. The farm track was part stone, and so far it hadn't yielded anything useful. They'd had more luck in the mud near the body, and at the murder scene, including a couple of clean boot prints that could be checked against the Forensic Science Service's imprint database, although the prints came from two or three different sources, any one of which might, or might not, have belonged to the killer, or killers.

But again, if the latter was the case, why dump the victim? If one of the perpetrators became injured, the other could probably have carried the remains for a while, unless the injury was so severe – a broken leg, perhaps – that the first man couldn't walk without assistance. Priestman would just have to wait and see what the CSIs discovered over the coming days. But whether a single killer, or multiple ones, the clever move would be to dispose of any footwear as soon as possible. And whoever killed Romana Moon *was* clever: not above risk-taking – because this murder, however well planned, had been fraught with danger – but smart enough not to have left Romana's clothing at the scene, thereby depriving the police of a great deal of potential DNA evidence.

She put her laptop in her bag, finished her coffee and went to say goodbye to her family.

XXIX

It was the boredom of the chemotherapy that got to Angel, the slow drip-drip-drip of the poison into his system as he sat in the hospital chair, the quantity of liquid in the bag never seeming to diminish, so that one minute felt like ten, one hour like a waking day, one morning like a week. He was stronger than anyone had suspected, himself included. His resilience had surprised them all, although a pharmacy's worth of medication certainly helped. But there was only so much a man could read, so much he could watch on the screen of an iPad, before he simply wished to be elsewhere, without the cannula in his arm, without the toxins, without the tiredness, without the weight loss, without the bruising, without the nausea, without the drip-drip-drip.

Without the cancer.

How many cycles now? Three? More?

How many to come? Too many.

Angel closed his eyes. At least he was home. He would not have to return to the hospital for a few weeks, to that damned chair, to the drip-drip-drip.

He dozed. When he opened his eyes, Louis was standing beside him.

'I brought you ice cream.'

'Thanks.'

Louis didn't inquire how he was feeling. Angel had asked him not to, because it was always some variation on weary or nauseous. If his condition suddenly deteriorated, Angel assured him, Louis would be the first to know. Likewise, Angel no longer asked after Louis's own injuries. The occasional wince at a missed step, and the muttered cussing when he sat down too heavily, or stood up too quickly, said it all.

'Parker is coming to visit,' said Louis.

'When?'

'In a couple of days.'

Angel looked unhappy.

'I thought we were going to head up to Portland. I want to get out of the city for a while.'

'Change of plan.'

'You could have consulted me first.'

'Happened too fast.'

'Is that why you bought me ice cream, because you felt bad about postponing our trip north?'

'No, I bought you ice cream because you got to eat, and ice cream is the only thing you don't complain about.'

Reluctantly, Angel accepted the carton of Ben & Jerry's Half Baked, and a spoon.

'They didn't have Strawberry Cheesecake?'

'No.'

'Where'd you go for it?'

'Doesn't matter where I went. You know, you sound like an old person.'

Angel ate a mouthful of the Half Baked.

'So we're definitely not going to Portland?'

'No, we're going to Amsterdam.'

Angel paused in the act of scooping out some more ice cream.

'If you feel up to it,' Louis added. 'I spoke to the internist. He said you'll have to be careful about infections on the plane, but you should be okay. We'll be traveling up front, so, you know, any contagions will probably be high-toned, and I have a list of doctors and clinics in case we need them.'

'Why are we going to Amsterdam?'

'Because the bitch that shot me travels on a Dutch passport, and the motherfucker that watched her shoot me also has a Dutch passport.'

'This from Parker?'

'From Ross, through Parker.'

Angel licked the spoon. He looked out the window at the city before him, at cars and people, at the remnants of the previous night's rain on the sidewalk, at life.

'You know,' said Angel, 'this is pretty good ice cream.'

XXX

The call came through as he was making his way gingerly from the bathroom to the kitchen. He didn't recognize the number, and almost let it go to voicemail before thinking better of it.

'Hello?'

'She was supposed to disappear, Holmby,' said Sellars.

No greetings, just an accusatory tone. Holmby felt aggrieved. After all, he'd broken his foot.

'I broke my foot,' he said, just to clarify the situation.

'What?' said Sellars.

'Actually, my ankle. The fibula. It's called a lateral malleolus fracture.'

'Why are you telling me this?'

'Because it happened on the moors. I slipped, and felt it go.'

'So?'

'I had to leave her. I couldn't walk *and* carry her.'

'Why were you carrying her to begin with?'

'Because I couldn't drive all the way up to where the chapel used to be. There's no road. I had to walk her up there, and when I was done, I had to carry her back.'

He waited for a reply. None came.

'Are you still there?' he asked.

'Yes.'

'It's not a problem.'

'If it wasn't a problem, do you think I'd be calling you?' He could hear Sellars breathing deeply, trying to calm himself. 'It's evidence. It leaves clues.'

'Then leave others.'

'What?' said Sellars.

'We knew this might happen. We weren't going to be able to

132

magic them away. Somewhere down the line, a second body would be found.'

'But not so soon.'

'It's happened now. Can't be helped. And I did what we agreed. I put one inside her, just as you were supposed to do with yours.'

'Like I did. No "supposed" about it.'

'So there we are.'

'But what about the next ones?'

'What about them?'

'I can take care of mine, but you can't do much with a broken ankle. Do you need surgery?'

'No, I was lucky. I don't even have a cast or a splint. They just strapped it up, and gave me cold packs and drugs, as well as one of those weird boots. I also have a crutch, but I don't want to use it unless I have to. Makes me feel like an invalid. But I'm supposed to rest the foot, and keep it elevated.'

'How long?'

'A couple of weeks.'

'That's bad, but it could be worse, I suppose.'

'Yeah.' He still felt guilty, which was a rare experience for him. 'I messed up. I'm sorry.'

Sellars relented in response. 'Could have happened to anyone.'

'Thanks. What will you do now?'

'I'll keep going. One more, then leave it for a while, or try to – if they'll let me.'

'They'll have to understand.'

'Will they?'

He thought about it. No, they probably wouldn't. Only Sellars had actually met the ones behind all this. Sellars had said it was better if he didn't, that he should keep his distance from them. He hadn't objected. He didn't like what he'd seen in Sellars's eyes when he spoke of them, the woman especially. Mors: Sellars didn't know if it was her real name, or one she'd adopted. Either way, it gave him the creeps.

'Bait the police,' he advised Sellars. 'It'll confuse them, and give us the space we need to do more. When I've recovered, I'll take care of two in a row.'

Another long silence. 'Maybe,' said Sellars, finally.

'How many will there be, by the end?'

'I don't know,' said Sellars. 'As many as are needed. We'll know when to stop.'

'How?'

'Because we'll be told. Because the world will have changed.'

'And what will the world be like after?'

'I don't know,' said Sellars, again. He hadn't thought that far ahead. 'I'll be in touch again soon. One last thing, Holmby.'

'Yes?'

'Did you find it hard?'

'Killing her?'

'Yes,' said Sellars.

He considered the question. He hadn't found it difficult to take the life of the Moon girl, but neither had he been aroused by the act. It was more like a practical exercise, a problem to be tackled and solved. It was better not to become emotional, because that led to mistakes. Then again, look at what had happened to him. All the calm in the world, and he'd still managed to crock himself while making his way back to the car – admittedly while carrying a body, but nevertheless.

He decided to be honest.

'I'd always wondered about it,' he said. 'I thought I'd like to try, because I was sure I had it in me.' Perhaps that's why he'd been chosen. They'd looked deep inside him, and glimpsed all his secret capacities. 'I'd killed animals, but killing Moon was easier. I felt sorry for the animals, but not for her. Physically, though, she was harder than any cat or dog. I had to test her flesh a couple of times before I figured out how it responded to the knife. I hurt her more than I would have liked. I'll do better next time.'

'I'm sure you will.'

'You'll tell them that, won't you?'

'Yes.'

'Because I really want to do it again.'

'I'll make sure they know.'

'Thank you,' he said. 'By the way, why the new number?'

'Just being careful. I picked up one of those weird SIMs, the cheap ones all the Pakis use. Go on now, put your foot up. You did good, all things considered.'

He frowned as Sellars ended the call. He didn't like racist talk. Mind you, it was funny that he should be so sensitive about it, given what they were leaving inside those dead women . . .

All this, everything he was doing, seemed to be the actions of another man, one that walked and talked like he did but existed on another plane, as though his darker reflection had stepped from a mirror and taken over this unfolding of his life. Even what he'd said about wondering what it might be like to kill a woman, about having the will and strength to do it, wasn't wholly true. It bore the same relation to reality as a seed might to an oak, or an embryo to a fully formed human being. Those thoughts had just been specks on his soul, dots on his conscience, and we all had bad thoughts sometimes, right? We all entertained fantasies that we'd never actually put into action. They were just . . . *there*. They intruded when you were least expecting them, and if you were in the right frame of mind you permitted them a little latitude just to see how they developed, and where they might end up. It wasn't wrong, because they weren't real. You weren't hurting anyone, except in your head.

But suppose one day you walked into an old church in Fairford, Gloucestershire, even though you had never been one for churches in the past. You'd heard that its windows were worth seeing, because your new friend from the Darknet had mentioned them during your conversations, and suggested you and he might like to meet at the church, get to know each other better; and suddenly there you were, standing on the cold stones, smelling the antiquity of the place, but you weren't alone, because waiting beneath the most famous of the windows was another man, slightly over-weight, with thinning hair; and you felt no unease about joining him, the two of you gazing up at the window together, not speaking, just looking; and then listening, because the voices came to you, and even though they spoke in a language you'd never heard before, still you understood what they were saying, what they wanted from you, because it was what you wanted for yourself, what you'd always wanted but never admitted.

'Do you hear them?' said the man next to you, and he was smiling, and suddenly you were smiling too.

Yes, you replied.

Yes, you told Sellars, *I hear them.*

XXXI

Parker had another reason for wanting to return to Portland as quickly as possible, aside from any dearth of affection for unfamiliar territories: Frank and Joan Wolfe, the parents of Rachel, his ex-partner, were driving from Vermont to Boston for an annual gathering of old friends at some fancy club, and had consented to a detour in order to drop off Parker's daughter, Sam, along the way, and pick her up again the following morning on the journey home.

They had entered into an odd conspiracy, he and Sam, one in which each acknowledged the other's singularity, yet agreed to leave it in large part unremarked. But Parker knew this: that his daughter spoke to her dead half-sister, Jennifer, and she in turn whispered to Sam of old gods. And what did Sam know of her father, and the part he was destined to play in some larger narrative? Well, that was less clear, but it was more than any child so young should have known.

Frank and Joan came by the house with Sam, although they did not linger. Relations between Parker and Frank had improved somewhat in recent times, largely as a result of a clearing-the-air talk back in Vermont the previous winter, and also because there was little scope for their relationship to deteriorate much further. Whatever the reason for the rapprochement, they remained formal rather than friendly with each other. They exchanged some comments on the weather, and the trees in Parker's yard, and the mileage Frank was getting out of his new Audi, and when those threads of civility began to fray, which didn't take long, the Wolfes got back in their car and headed south, off to mix with the great and the good of the Commonwealth.

'I like it when you and Grandpa talk,' said Sam, as her grandparents drove away.

137

'Yeah? I wish I could say the same.'

Sam wrinkled her nose in disapproval.

'I'm kidding,' said Parker. 'We just don't have a whole lot in common.'

'You have me.'

'There is that.'

'And Mom.'

'How is your mom?' said Parker, grasping the opportunity to steer the conversation onto safer ground.

'Good,' said Sam, but she was not to be so easily diverted. 'And Walter. You and Grandpa have Walter in common.' Walter was the family dog. He had once been Parker's dog, too, back when he, Rachel, and Sam had lived under the same roof. It was dumb, but mention of Walter always caused something to stick in Parker's throat, even after all this time. Damn dog. 'Which means you and Grandpa like lots of the same stuff.'

'You're right,' said Parker. 'He has a great deal to be thankful for.'

'Is that sarcasm?'

'Only if you think it is. So, how about ice cream? Or a nap?'

Sam wrinkled her nose.

'I think that's sarcasm, too,' she said.

They spent a great day together: a bike ride around Peaks Island, some shopping, and lunch at the Great Lost Bear, where Dave Evans and Cupcake Cathy ensured that Sam was treated like royalty, aided by the Fulci brothers, now returned from New York, who acted as her courtiers. The Fulcis even joined Sam in coloring some pictures provided by Dave, albeit with a disturbing intensity, and excessive use of black and red crayons.

'Jesus,' said Dave, as he watched – from a safe distance – the Fulcis concentrating on their artwork, 'they probably learned how to do that in therapy sessions at the mental institution.'

'You think it helped?' asked Parker.

'Not really. If Tony scribbles any harder, he'll go through the table. And what are they doing anyway? I gave them a picture of a unicorn to color, and now it looks like it's dying of gunshot wounds. They're not even staying inside the lines.'

The Fulcis were still trying to source suitable premises in Portland for their own bar, but so far two lease agreements had fallen through at the last minute. They were now considering opening a gym instead, as they were less interested in a serious investment than finding somewhere to loiter without concerned citizens calling the police. For now, there was always the Bear. Parker thought that, despite all his protests, Dave Evans felt sorry for the Fulcis; maybe not as sorry as Dave felt for himself for allowing them into his beloved bar to begin with, but a bit sorry.

'Sam's getting tall,' said Dave.

'Yeah.'

Parker felt the recurrent pang of any father often separated from his offspring, the sadness that comes from experiencing the child's progression to maturity in fits and starts rather than as a continuous process, or perhaps this was simply his own heightened awareness of their situation. He suspected that if, in years to come, he asked Rachel to look back on their daughter's childhood, she would wonder how the time could have passed so quickly, and how little of it she could seem to recall.

'She's a great kid,' said Dave. 'You're doing okay, you and Rachel.' He patted Parker lightly on back, as though sensing the direction of his thoughts.

The only pall over Sam's visit was cast that night, as they ate dinner at a window table in a restaurant on Congress Street. Four Massholes were occupying one of the adjacent booths: two guys and two girls, all in their early thirties. One of the guys was loud, even by Boston standards, and foul-mouthed – again, even by Boston standards.

'Why is that man using so many bad words?' asked Sam.

'Because he's from Boston,' said Parker.

'And why is he wearing a baseball cap indoors?'

Parker regarded men who wore any kind of cap or hat inside as blights on humanity, and was happy to have passed on this conviction to his daughter. He was still working on convincing her that grown men shouldn't wear shorts anywhere but on an athletic field, and was optimistic about an eventual result.

'Because he's from Boston,' he said.

'How do you know he's from Boston?'

'Because he's using so many bad words, and wearing a baseball cap indoors.'

'Oh. Okay.'

It was clear that Parker wasn't the only one who'd noticed, because one of the servers approached the Mass table to request that its occupants keep their voices down. The restaurant was casual, with great food, and its reputation inevitably drew all kinds. The volume of the Massholes' conversation decreased marginally as a result of the intervention, but the language didn't get any better. It wasn't that Parker was a prude, but Sam was still within earshot, and he wasn't the only person in the place with a kid.

'Do you need to go to the bathroom?' he said to Sam.

'No.'

'Are you sure? You should go, just in case.'

Sam regarded him thoughtfully.

'Do you want me to go to the bathroom so you can talk to that man?'

'Might do.'

'You should have said.'

Sam left for the bathroom, with one of the female servers keeping her company. Parker leaned over toward the party behind.

'Excuse me?' he said.

The guy in the baseball cap looked over at him.

'Yeah?'

'My daughter is concerned about your language.'

The guy laughed. He had very white teeth. In the event of a fire, the other diners could have used his dental work to guide them to safety through the smoke.

'Your daughter?'

'Yes. You see, I'm sensitive, and she worries about me. I mean, she's heard it all. You know what kids are like these days. But me, I lead a sheltered life, so maybe you could ease up on the swearing, for my sake.'

He laughed again, but his dining companions didn't. For whatever reason, possibly just more brain cells, they were able to perceive something in Parker that had passed their friend by.

'Fuck you,' he said.

'I thought you'd say that,' said Parker, 'so here's how it's going to play out. I'm going to keep asking you nicely to stop swearing – even if you're not swearing, but just in anticipation, because it won't take long for you to get around to it again – and eventually you're going to become so frustrated that one of two things will happen: either you'll give up on eating and leave, in which case you won't get to enjoy your entrée when it arrives; or you might take a swing at me with your best shot, except you look kind of slow, and I don't think your best shot is going to cut it, so someone will call the cops and, hey, still no entrée.'

'Let me guess,' he said. 'Next is where you threaten me.'

'Nope,' said Parker. 'This isn't Boston. We're subtler. I'm just going to go back to telling you not to swear, like this: Stop swearing. Stop swearing. Stop swearing. I may vary the tone to sound like your mom, or your grade school teacher, just to break the monotony. You know, go high, go low. I may even get my daughter to join in. Either way, you're not going to enjoy your meal here. I'd start thinking about alternative venues.'

At that moment, Sam returned.

'I was just explaining to the nice man how we're going to tell him to stop swearing, over and over, until he gets tired of it and leaves.'

Sam sat.

'Cool,' she said. 'Stop swearing. Wait, have we started?'

'We have now. Stop swearing.'

'Stop swearing,' said Sam.

'Stop swearing.'

'Stop swearing.'

'Stop swearing.'

'Stop swearing'

'Stop swearing . . .'

They were eating dessert. The restaurant was quieter now.

'He lasted longer than expected,' said Parker.

'I counted sixty before he gave in,' said Sam. 'But I might have missed some.'

She spooned a large glob of melting ice cream into her mouth.

'It was fun,' she concluded. 'I wish Mom had been here. She'd have joined in.'

Parker wasn't so sure about that.

'How about we keep this between us?' he suggested.

'But it's not like that time Uncle Louis threatened to shoot someone for using bad words in front of us.'

Parker had almost managed to blot that incident from his memory.

'That was certainly different. But I think your mom worries about us getting into trouble.'

Sam licked her spoon clean.

'Maybe you're right,' she said. 'It's probably better if she doesn't hear about stuff that would worry her.'

Her eyes flicked to her father, and the knowingness in them gave Parker a chill, but he said nothing.

And thus their conspiracy acquired another layer of complexity.

XXXII

The following morning, with Sam already safely on her way back to Vermont, Parker met Moxie Castin for a relatively late breakfast at Union in the old Portland Press Herald building, since the restaurant was close to the Superior Court at Newbury Street, where Moxie was destined to be tied up for most of the day. Moxie was wearing his serious lawyer wardrobe, which meant he'd dialed down the garishness of his tie, and found a suit that looked like it might once have fitted properly – not necessarily fitted Moxie, but fitted someone.

Since he didn't usually eat much before midday, Parker opted for just coffee and toast, while Moxie made a small concession to sensible dining by ordering the Light Hearted, a three-egg-white, vegetarian omelet, although he asked the server to hold the tofu because, as he put it, 'nobody actually likes tofu, and certainly not for breakfast.'

Parker generally tried to avoid morning meetings, or even talking to anyone for long before the time moved into double digits, but Moxie was heading out of town for a few days once his obligations at the courthouse had been fulfilled, and there was some housekeeping to be done after the Houston testimony. They got through it with a minimal amount of speech or effort from Parker, and moved on to the events in Arizona. Parker gave Moxie the condensed version, although he did mention the part about screwing Ross for beer, pizza, and champagne.

'The champagne flutes were a nice touch,' said Moxie. 'Pity about the flowers, though.'

'Next time.'

Moxie was familiar with most of Parker's business and legal affairs, and had issues with any number of them, but top of the list was the monthly consultancy retainer from the FBI. The news from Arizona made him even less happy about it, but this time there was no trace of good humor or indulgence in his response.

'MS-13?' said Moxie. 'And Ross was parading you in front of this Hernández?'

'Parading might be putting it kind of strongly.'

'But Hernández knew who you were?'

'Almost certainly.'

'You have to end this arrangement with Ross,' said Moxie. 'Now.'

'You're always telling me that.'

'Because it's the smart thing to do.'

'Smart or not, I don't consider it an option, not at the moment.'

'It's always an option. You think you're on the books somewhere in Federal Plaza? You're not. You're not even in the small print at the bottom of a stationery bill. You're a miscellaneous expense without an identifier, because that way you're deniable. You may be an open secret on Ross's floor, but that still doesn't mean you have any protection if, or when, it all goes to hell. I know you think you're using Ross in turn, and maybe you've been thrown a bone or two along the way, but all the risk is on your end.'

'I need Ross.'

'Why?'

'To find Quayle.' Among other things.

Moxie almost spat in disgust.

'Quayle? What, for Louis? Out of some misguided sense of duty? Tell me. I'd like to know.'

'Let me remind you that it was you who brought me into Quayle's orbit.'

'I hired you to look for a missing child, not embark on some transcontinental hunt for an apocalyptic fanatic.'

'Nevertheless.'

Moxie waved his hand wildly in the air for more coffee.

'You know,' he said, 'I'm starting to believe you might have incurred some form of brain damage the last time you were shot, and I'm speaking as a friend.'

Parker waited for him to calm down. Moxie didn't quite manage it, but his complexion gradually lightened from red to pink. The coffee arrived. When the server had departed, he resumed speaking.

'Ross is a member of the Colonial,' said Moxie. 'You know what that is?'

'It's a private club in Boston.'

'No, it's the *oldest* private club in Boston, older than the Union or the Algonquin. They've only been around since the second half of the nineteenth century, but the Colonial, or some version of it, has existed since the eighteenth.'

'And?'

'Nobody good is a member of the Colonial,' said Moxie. 'It's a society of predators. You know who was a member of the Colonial, until shortly before somebody excised a couple of his major organs in a bathtub? Garrison Pryor. That's how bad the Colonial Club is, and even Pryor's removal from its register of members represents only a marginal improvement in its moral quality, at least until someone worse is nominated in his place. Apparently, there's a scramble to fill the vacancy, so they're taking their time in choosing. My question is: if Ross is even on nodding terms with decency and morality, what the fuck is he doing in the company of people like that?'

Parker had no answer, beyond the fact of Ross's wealth.

'He has money.'

'He doesn't have money, not like the Colonials have money. He's not even close. More to the point, there are members of the Colonial who might not appreciate the presence of a senior federal agent on the premises. Some of them are so crooked they need to have their furniture specially made just so they can sit down, yet somehow Ross gets to practice shots in their billiard room and run a tab at their bar. Why? Because it's *their* billiard room, *their* bar, *their* club. Christ, it's *their* country! They make the rules, and Ross is colluding with them by breathing the same air.'

The restaurant host floated in their direction, looking alarmed, but Parker indicated that everything was okay, even if it wasn't. Moxie sat back, and took a deep breath.

'I'm advising you,' he said, 'as your lawyer, as your friend: tell Ross you're done. Let him take care of his own dirty work, because it is dirty. He's dirty.'

'I can't,' said Parker. 'It's gone too far for that.'

Moxie paid the check in cash, and stood to leave.

'You know the quotation, "should I wade no more/ Returning were as tedious as go o'er"?' he said.

'It's from *Macbeth*. I went to college, Moxie.'

'You did?' said Moxie, as he shrugged on his coat. 'Then maybe you should have paid more attention, because Macbeth was talking about wallowing in blood. And it didn't end well for him. Sometimes, it pays to turn back.'

With that, he went to ply his trade at the Superior Court.

Exit, thought Parker, *Moxie*.

XXXIII

Simon Harris, Romana Moon's ex-boyfriend, looked as though he'd been assembled from the abandoned parts of other human beings, and wore the kind of glasses that usually came free with another pair. His hair wasn't quite fair enough to be blond, but too red seriously to be considered as anything else. All in all, he screamed geek, which wasn't entirely unfortunate because, as he admitted to Priestman and Hynes, that was exactly what he was: he lectured in computer science at the University of Sunderland, and worked in game development in Middlesbrough on the side. Still, Priestman thought, with a better haircut, proper glasses, and a little more care for his clothing choices, he might have been considered handsome, in a pale way.

Harris hadn't consulted a solicitor. Objectively, Priestman might have regarded this as unwise in his position, but it made life easier for her. According to Hynes, Harris hadn't spoken a great deal in the car from the train station, although that didn't surprise Priestman. Guilty or not, few people felt inclined to chatter while sitting in the back of a police car with two big coppers looming in the front, even if one of them was DS Hynes at his most garrulous.

Harris's eyes were very red, and his nose was rubbed raw. He appeared to be in a state of some shock and grief; if he was acting, he was very good. But Priestman had questioned a lot of good actors in her time, none of them working on the stage, and she'd put her share of them behind bars. She could have left the questioning to Hynes and one of the detective constables, but the circumstances of Romana Moon's death were unusual.

'I loved her, you know,' said Harris.

'Then why did you two break up?' asked Hynes.

'Romana ended it. I didn't want to.'

'And why did she end it?'

'She said it just wasn't working, that she wanted some time to herself. But to be honest, I think I was just a bit dull for her.'

'Did Romana say that?'

'She didn't have to. I know I'm not the most exciting of blokes, and I haven't had much luck with women. I've only had a couple of relationships, and none of them lasted as long as Romana.'

'How long were you two together?' Priestman asked.

Harris sighed.

'About four months.'

'And that's your longest relationship?' said Hynes. He couldn't manage to keep the incredulity out of his voice, which Priestman thought was a bit unfair. She gave his shin a sharp tap under the table, and he bit his lip.

Harris glanced at each of them in turn, and sighed.

'I was lying when I said that I hadn't had much luck with women,' he said. 'Actually, I haven't had any luck at all.'

On the night Romana Moon was killed, Harris had attended the launch of a history of graphic novels at Forbidden Planet in Newcastle, after which he and a friend named Chris Cushing went for drinks at the Bigg Market, the city's main drag for boozing and carousing. Harris claimed to have lost track of the time, and stayed out so late that he missed the last train back to the apartment he shared with two others in Middlesbrough, so he ended up dossing on Cushing's couch. He had just got home that morning when he received a call from Romana's sister to say a body had been found, believed to be Romana's. Shortly after, he was contacted by Northumbria Police in the form of DS Hynes, and agreed to be interviewed at the force's headquarters in Wallsend.

'What does your friend Chris do?' asked Priestman.

'He's an artist,' said Harris. 'He draws graphic novels.'

'What kind?'

'Dark fantasy. He hasn't had anything published yet, but it's only a matter of time. He's very good.'

'What's he doing while he's waiting to be published?'

'He's on benefits.'

'Which means he's a government artist,' said Hynes. 'He draws the dole.'

But Harris didn't smile, and Hynes suddenly looked embarrassed. It happened sometimes, Priestman knew, in rooms and situations like this. For a moment, you forgot the dead.

Despite Harris's apparent alibi, Priestman wasn't entirely ruling him out just yet. The launch had concluded shortly after 8.30 p.m., and Newcastle was less than an hour's drive from the Hexhamshire Moors. It wasn't beyond the bounds of possibility that Harris – with Cushing to assist him, and provide an alibi – could have killed Romana Moon in the timeframe the ME had tentatively suggested. But as the questioning went on, it became clear that in the course of the evening Harris had talked to others who were at the launch, and later he and Cushing had stopped at a late-night takeaway for some soakage before returning to Cushing's parents' house. There was still a window of opportunity, but it was growing increasingly narrow. Harris was also willing to allow access to his iPhone, on which Google Maps was enabled, thereby providing a route guide to everywhere he'd been on the night in question – everywhere he'd been for the past month, in fact. Again, he could have left the phone with someone in Newcastle before leaving to kill Moon: Cushing, perhaps, if Harris went to Hexhamshire alone. They'd talk to Cushing later, Priestman decided, as well as any of the other named individuals with whom Harris had spoken at the Bigg Market, see what—

But then Harris came out with the clincher, and Priestman thought, *We should have asked him at the start. We really should have asked.*

Because Simon Harris couldn't drive.

And neither could Chris Cushing.

'Can you think of anyone who might have wanted to hurt Romana?' said Priestman.

'No,' said Harris.

'Anyone she might have argued with?'

'Only me, when we broke up, and that wasn't even really an argument.'

'Why not?'

'Because I wasn't angry. I was just sad.'

And Simon Harris started to cry.

IV

The thing from the churchyard
that was found with its hand missing
in the excavation
undertook on the north side
called
several times
wanted converse
about your assumptions . . .

Bill Griffiths, 'Decorating &
Insurance Factors'

XXXIV

The town of Deerhurst lies near the eastern bank of the Severn, and takes its name from the Old English words *dēor*, a wild animal, probably a deer, and *hyrst*, meaning a wooded hill. Like large parts of Gloucestershire, it is situated on land once granted by royal decree to the Catholic Church – nominally, at least, because land given by the king was exempt from taxes, and the local aristocracy were not above utilizing ecclesiastical connections to protect their wealth.

The area around Deerhurst had always been marshy, which meant it was prone to flooding, an issue that persists to this day. But in some ways, the challenges brought by the waters were Deerhurst's salvation. The threat of floods protected the village from exploitation, restricting its growth and development, and consequently Deerhurst retains a sense of isolation, even in the twenty-first century. A single road leads into the community, through low fields bordered by hedgerows, and visible in the distance as one draws near is the tower of a church. This is the Priory Church of St Mary the Virgin, the earliest parts of which date from the year 700 AD.

But down a laneway that runs past St Mary the Virgin, and through a set of floodgates, stands an odder structure, by name and nature: Odda's Chapel, discovered in the nineteenth century by the Reverend George Butterworth, the Vicar of Deerhurst. The chapel had been concealed for centuries under the plasterwork of an adjacent farmhouse, as though hiding from the modern world.

Odda's Chapel dates from the eleventh century, and is not as grand as St Mary's. Its yard is accessed via a small iron gate, and a larger opening in its walls permits entry to the chapel itself.

The interior is largely bare: cold stone, with evidence of what might have been a second floor beneath the roof, now long gone, and wooden supports for the ceiling. It is simple, and quiet.

Marcus Godwin knew Odda's Chapel better than most, just as he was familiar with every nook of the nearby St Mary's. He had lived in Deerhurst all his life, although he was no village recluse. He regularly haunted the British Library in London, and the Ashmolean in Oxford, particularly since his retirement a decade earlier, and the death of his wife shortly after. His pamphlets on Anglo-Saxon and Anglo-Norman Deerhurst were available for purchase from the unattended rack in St Mary's (*Price £3. Be Honest. And remember: God is Watching.*), and he had also written monographs on the famous windows at the similarly named St Mary's in Fairford, some thirty miles to the southeast. He was a regular contributor to, and attendee at, local history events throughout Gloucestershire, and was always willing to travel further afield if asked, although such invitations were rarer than he might have wished.

And yes, there were those who claimed he was just an old bore, and wondered what could possibly be left to say about these ancient buildings – or, perhaps, how much more they should have to hear about them from men like Marcus Godwin – but most regarded his as a gentle madness. He claimed to be descended from Earl Godwin, an Anglo-Saxon nobleman of considerable repute, although if this were true, Marcus's branch of the family had fallen on hard times, since his father and grandfather had both worked for the water company down at Frampton Cotterell, and Marcus himself had been a surveyor for the council. Not that these were jobs of which to be ashamed, mind, but they weren't the stuff of royalty.

Marcus was one of a number of villagers who kept an eye on St Mary the Virgin, and Odda's Chapel, because you never knew what mischief visitors might get up to. St Mary's possessed a famous Saxon baptismal font, ornate in its decoration, and some folks got a bit enthusiastic with their rubbing, although there was less of that now than there used to be. For the most part, they just took pictures with their phones, only to forget about them as soon as they left, at least until it came time to delete them in order to free up space for more photographs at which they'd never look, taken of things they otherwise wouldn't remember seeing. Marcus had a mobile, but it didn't have a camera or Twitter or any of that nonsense. It only made and accepted calls, like a telephone should.

Now, as the afternoon drew to a close, Marcus was sitting on a folding chair by the wall of Odda's Chapel, his back to the stone, and his face toward St Mary's. He could hear the lowing of cattle, and smell their spoor on the wind. Few visitors had ventured to the town that day. Threatened showers had yet to arrive, but the skies remained gray and cloudy, filtering the sunlight. Marcus didn't mind. He liked this time of day, when evening began its slow amble toward night. The village, hardly busy at the best of times, seemed to fall into quietude. He could hear the soft sounds of the world. If he lay on the ground, he might even be able to discern the beating of its heart. On the other hand, he probably wouldn't have been able to get up again, or not without help. He wasn't as nimble as he used to be.

On his lap lay a hardback copy of Richard Marks's *Stained Glass in England During the Middle Ages*. Marcus had purchased it with the intention of updating his own earlier work on the Fairford windows, perhaps with illustrations. His printer would give him a good deal on 500 copies, and with luck he might even cover his costs from sales to tourists before he died.

Except that he had started to reconsider the idea of returning to the book, just as he had begun to reexamine his attitude toward the church and its windows. He had noticed a change in the atmosphere of St Mary's, Fairford, during recent visits, one to which he was struggling to attribute a cause. Initially he thought it might have been a consequence of the deterioration in his own mental health. He had always suffered from a low-level melancholia that occasionally burgeoned into full-blown depression, and recently he'd sensed the black dog nipping at his heels. He wondered if his mood might be influencing his perception of his surroundings, because when last he visited St Mary's it had seemed

– well, *darker* was the only word he could find, as though the sun's radiance were struggling to be admitted through the church's windows, and through certain panes in particular.

He had first noticed it with the twelve small demons above Windows 25 and 26: the Persecutors' windows, as they were known, since they depicted the scourges of the Church. He thought their colors less vibrant than before, but the closer he looked, the more it seemed it was only the backgrounds that had grown fainter, making the images themselves appear more pronounced. A trick of the light, he had first assumed, yet upon subsequent visits, and at varying hours of the day, the impression remained. He had commented on it to one of the women who sometimes looked after the sale of books and souvenirs. She had joined him and remarked that, yes, perhaps from a certain angle they seemed a bit different, but she was no expert, and it might be that the windows just needed a good clean.

'Of course,' he replied. 'That must be it.'

But if that were the case, why should the demons be manifesting themselves more vividly?

'Or it might be the time of the year,' she added. 'It's been funny old weather, all dull and overcast. It's enough to drive a soul to the bottle.'

This was certainly true, Marcus thought, and yet . . .

The Persecutors' windows lay on the north side of the church, but there was a difference in tone also to the church's great glory: the West Window, depicting the Last Judgment. The reds of the fires of Hell now burned brighter, and their colors, previously limited to the two lower right panes and a portion of a third, gave the impression of bleeding more deeply into the surrounding work. No sunlight, however peculiar, could have the same effect on both north- and west-facing windows.

Marcus had gone outside, doing his best to examine the exterior of the glass from ground level, but it bore no particular blemish that might have explained the effect, no smudges or discoloration from pollution or windblown dirt and leaves. It was most curious, but when he raised the subject with others, including the vicar, they appeared less troubled by it than he, which was when he began to doubt the state of his psychological – indeed, physical – health, and began to read up on spots on the vision, strokes, and cancers of the brain.

But he also returned to his books, his little library of volumes on Gloucestershire history, its churches, and the creators of their windows – or one set of windows in particular, those at Fairford. The idea of revising his old pamphlet became an excuse for more esoteric researches, and all the time he found sleep harder to come by, and would lie awake at night and remember his wife, and think how lovely it would be to join her at last. He could go to his local GP, explain to him about his difficulties sleeping, and receive a prescription for some tablets that would solve the problem.

'Solve all your problems, if you took enough of them.'

The voice came to him when dark was deepest. Sometimes it sounded like his father, and at others his late wife, except that neither of them had ever used words like this voice used. Neither of them had ever called him such names – *'you sad old shit, you nasty, nosey old fucker'* – or warned him of what happened to frail men with too much time on their hands, too many hours to spend haunting churches, looking at windows, imagining shadows where there were none, when they should be minding their own business, reflecting on their uselessness, the burden they had become to themselves and others.

'Look at all those pills. Look at that length of rope. Look at that knife. Look at that shotgun. Take a sniff of that gas. Lovely gas . . .'

Depression, illness: could these be the cause of what he had seen, of these fantasies of self-destruction? Perhaps, but there was something more.

He had always felt a sense of peace in the church at Fairford, just as he did at St Mary's in Deerhurst. (Odda's Chapel was different. Although it was younger than either of those churches, it felt older, and its history was obscure, more open to conjecture.) Yet since he had begun to notice, or imagine, the changes to the Fairford panes, he had detected a growing ambivalence in himself, not only toward the windows but toward the interior of the church itself.

157

He could identify the moment when it had become most pronounced. It was about a week earlier, and he had stopped in Fairford shortly before the church was due to close for the day. Once again, he ended up moving between the windows, lost in contemplation of their colors.

And suddenly, he was alone.

Only a minute or two before, he had counted perhaps ten people sharing the space with him – visitors, and the volunteers by the door – and the low murmur of their conversations carried clearly to him, but now he noticed their speech had faded away, and when he looked around he was the building's sole occupant.

Which was when he heard the whispering.

Many years before, when Marcus was just a boy, he had attended school with a lad named Oliver Lewin, who came from a bad family: thieves, drunkards, and worse, who farmed remote land, if their stewardship of it could even be accorded such a name, and lived lives of near poverty. The Lewins were cruel to their animals, cruel to their neighbors, and cruel to one another. It was said that the father, Ambrose, had fathered bastards on two of his daughters, but the infants emerged stillborn and were buried in unmarked holes on the Lewin lands – or the Lewins claimed they were stillbirths, when it was more likely that the mites were smothered as soon as they emerged from the womb, especially if they were female.

The mother, Agnet, was a pathetic creature, a cousin to her husband, and no obstacle to his badness; perhaps even a facilitator of it, turning a blind eye and a deaf ear to his predations on his own children until, it was said, Ambrose began to notice the ripening of his youngest girl, the apple of her mother's eye, and Agnet – broken, silent, miserable Agnet – fed him a dish of death cap mushrooms, like some rural Claudius, sending him to join his bastards in the dirt. All this, too, in the middle of the twentieth century, but the country was different then – or perhaps, Marcus reflected, we only liked to tell ourselves as much, because he still perceived no shortage of abusers of women and children, except it was harder now to feed them poisoned mushrooms and get away with it.

But Marcus had permitted himself to become distracted. Oliver Lewin, Oliver Lewin . . .

Oliver was his father's son in appearance and appetite, but more warped still, because the cousins' blood had mixed badly in him. Families in Deerhurst – and Apperley, Walton Hill, even more distant Tewkesbury – warned their daughters to steer clear of him, and their sons too. Although only in his teens, Oliver Lewin was base matter.

He terrorized Marcus, who was no match for him, but did so in the most disturbing of ways: by befriending him, by trying to make Marcus his creature, by imposing his company upon him. After school, or on Saturdays as Marcus walked home from football, or on evenings when his mother sent him on errands, Oliver Lewin would appear by his side, materializing from woods, from the shadows of walls, even from open fields, as though emerging elemental from the earth itself.

And always, always, Oliver Lewin would tell Marcus Godwin of what he liked to do to his sisters when they were alone with him, and what he wished to do to convent girls and schoolmistresses, to young brides and old widows, and what he might do to Marcus, too, if he ever told on him, or shared with others the substance of their conversations together; an outpouring of filth, a testament to depravities committed and yet to be committed, every word pouring like sour milk into Marcus Godwin until he could take no more and puked his disgust into the dirt, only to free up more room for fresh perversions.

The whispering in St Mary's sounded to Marcus like the worst emissions from Oliver Lewin's mouth, and even though the words were spoken in another language, one with which Marcus was unfamiliar (one, he believed, that resembled no human tongue), still he grasped their import, and felt the exposure of his deepest self as surely as though he had been spatchcocked by a butcher's blade. The voices were many in one, and they knew: they knew how much he liked to hear Oliver Lewin's fantasies; how it was he who would wait for Oliver to appear, he who would loiter by tree and wall, hill and ditch, until Oliver arrived bearing the latest fruits of his imaginings; and how it was he who wanted to spend time with Oliver's sisters, and not only the older ones but the youngest, Margrett, the one that Ambrose Lewin died too soon to pluck. Oh, the things Marcus would do to Margrett as she wriggled and screamed, as he lifted her skirt, as he pushed her head down . . .

And it was then that the figures on the windows at Fairford began to move, lowering their faces to him, the persecutors and the persecuted, human and non-human alike; and the fires burned brighter, and the redness spread like blood across the West Window, subsuming saints and angels, the saved and the damned, and finally, God Himself.

'No!'

Marcus Godwin heard his own voice echo from the walls, and looked around to find that he was not alone, and the visitors remained, the volunteers too, and all were staring at him with expressions of shock. Before any of them could approach, before he had to contend with inquiries about his wellbeing, he was gone from St Mary's, gone from the churchyard, gone from Fairford, and had not returned since.

Because it wasn't true, the things he'd heard. He had spent his childhood trying and failing to avoid Oliver Lewin – his adulthood, too, until someone put an end to Oliver stabbing him to death in a remand cell while he waited to be tried for the rape of a student. Marcus was glad when he heard it. He never thought he would rejoice in the death of another human being, but Oliver Lewin proved the exception.

'I was never like him,' he said to the wind, to the dusk. 'I never wanted to do such things.'

Yet now he could no longer tell if this were true. Was there not some dreadful part of him that might have behaved in such a way, given the opportunity, and the assurance that he would never be caught or punished for it? I am human, said the philosopher, and nothing human is alien to me.

But I never even imagined inflicting such hurt on another person.

'*You did, in the church.*'

The voices said those things, not me.

'*But you pictured them in your mind. For a moment, you saw them. You saw yourself.*'

It was not I.

'*Believe that, if it helps. Lie to yourself, you beggar, you bore, you dying beast.*'

Marcus closed his eyes, and prayed softly to St Mary the Virgin, letting the wind carry his orisons to her.

Which was when he heard a sound from inside Odda's Chapel.

XXXV

Thanks to the early meeting with Moxie, Parker was able to catch the 10.25 a.m. United flight from Portland to Newark. He tried to read the *New York Times* on the plane, but an article on the ongoing tensions between the FBI and the White House brought him back to his conversation with Moxie. He wondered if Ross had returned to New York or was still down in Arizona. The former, he thought: Arizona was a feint, a distraction in the form of a young woman's body. Ross would now be waiting to hear from Parker about Louis's intentions. He probably already knew that Parker had booked a flight to New York. It would have been only a matter of pressing some buttons on a keyboard and accessing his credit card records. If Parker were to persist in his pursuit of Quayle, he would have to be more careful about covering his tracks, unless he wanted Ross monitoring his every move.

Alex, Louis's preferred livery driver, was waiting to collect Parker and take him to the Upper West Side building occupied by Angel, Louis, and Mrs Bondarchuk, their sole tenant who, along with her Pomeranians, functioned as the building's first line of surveillance and defense. Parker rarely liked staying in other people's homes, preferring the privacy of a hotel room, but Angel and Louis were different, and the former's illness caused Parker to want to make life as easy as possible for all concerned. Mrs Bondarchuk opened the door to him as he reached the first step, and gave him an all-enveloping hug, although he barely knew her. She smelled faintly, but not unpleasantly, of rum and cookies, and gratefully accepted a gift box of hand-dipped chocolates that he'd picked up from Dean's Sweets on Fore Street before leaving Portland.

Angel met him on the first landing.

'Good to see you up and about,' said Parker.

'It's cancer, not an amputation.'

'Still.'

Angel showed Parker to his room.

'I hear we're going to Amsterdam,' said Angel.

'Are you well enough?'

'I'm going, even if it kills me.'

'Let's hope it doesn't come to that. It might cast a shadow over the trip.'

'And after Amsterdam?'

'England.'

Angel reached out for the doorframe with his left hand, and leaned into it. He tried to make it seem casual, but Parker could see the tiredness on his face.

'They almost killed Louis last time,' said Angel.

'Yes.'

'In return, he wants to kill them. Twice over, if he can.'

'It's understandable.'

'But he's getting older. We both are. You are, too, but you've got more time.'

Parker waited.

'Ten years ago, even five, Mors would never have been able to take Louis down,' said Angel. 'No one could. Now, it's different. What I'm saying is, he can't watch your back the way he used to. He'll try, like I will, just as you'll watch ours, but he's in pain, and we'll be more vulnerable than before.'

'We'll find help. We always do.'

'You seem very sure of that.'

Parker took in the guest room. It was nicer than most hotel suites he'd stayed in, and contained reminders of Angel and Louis's presence, since each occasionally had cause to retreat to it. Neither ever took it personally if the other needed space for a while. He saw some of Louis's music, and artefacts from his heritage – Minié balls; a Charleston slave badge; and a travel guide for Afro-Americans from the 1940s, detailing hotels, restaurants, and gas stations where their custom would be accepted without violence or humiliation – along with small items of African and Asian art. Parker could recall the provenance of most, remembering an evening some years earlier during which Louis had explained the history of each.

Meanwhile, contained in a glass cabinet on one wall was a complete set of tools used by nineteenth-century burglars, the 'second-story' men: jimmies and heavy-chisels; the 'little alderman', a thin wedge of steel used to open safe doors; skeleton keys; drills and bits; cans of oil and powder; and a bottle of chloroform, to render an occupant unconscious, if required, by its application to a sponge, which would then be attached to a length of string on a stick and suspended over the person's bed from the window before the burglar entered the room. Angel, in his turn, had told Parker all this, carefully detailing the use of each item, handing them over so he could feel the weight, admire the craftsmanship.

These men were his friends, and more, much more.

But Quayle had to be found, whatever the risks.

'I have faith,' said Parker.

'In God?'

'No, in you, and in Louis. In all those like us.'

'There aren't many like us.'

'There are enough.'

Angel gave up using the door for support, and sat on the guest bed.

'Why is Quayle so important, aside from almost killing Louis?'

'Because of what he's trying to do,' said Parker.

'Which is?'

'He may be trying to bring about the end of the world.'

Angel took this in.

'Well,' he said at last, 'since you put it like that. So Quayle's a fantasist?'

'Probably, but a fantasist with ambition. The people he killed in Maine, in Indiana, they almost certainly weren't the first, which means they won't be the last, because he still doesn't have what he wants. I think Quayle has left a long line of bodies behind him. It's time that was stopped.'

Angel was watching Parker closely.

'But Quayle *is* different, isn't he? You believe that. I can see it in your face.'

'The more I find out about what he's looking for,' said Parker, 'the more he troubles me.'

But before he could elaborate, they heard the front door opening, and the yapping of assorted Pomeranians heralded the arrival of Louis.

'Bob Johnston will tell you more, over dinner,' said Parker. 'How's your appetite?'

'I tend to skip the appetizers, sometimes the entrées too.'

'You were getting kind of heavy, but no one wanted to say.'

Angel stood, and patted his belly.

'Every cloud . . .'

XXXVI

The autopsy on Romana Moon's remains was delayed due to administrative issues in which Priestman had no interest, over which she had no control, and about which she was not inclined to cause a fuss anyway. Sisterson, the pathologist, was doing her a favor by fast-tracking the autopsy – there was never a shortage of bodies to be examined – but there seemed to be little doubt about how Moon had died: she had suffered stab wounds to her torso, and her throat had been cut, so the only important questions that remained to be answered were left- or right-handed, and the length of the blade.

Priestman had been with Kevin Moon, Romana's father, and Romana's sister when they formally identified her body. Kevin Moon was a small man in his late forties, who worked as a site foreman for a construction company. He liked the TV series *Doctor Who* – liked it a lot – which was how his daughter had ended up with the name Romana, after one of the fourth Doctor's companions. Funny, Kevin Moon said, but Romana had never much cared for *Doctor Who*, except it wasn't funny at all, because he was talking about his dead child, while the surviving one held his hand. He'd left his wife at home, with friends and relatives.

'She didn't need to see her little girl that way,' Moon explained, as though any explanation was required, or the opposite were true of himself.

Priestman had made another run out to the moors that day to check on the CSIs, and the progress of the canvass, just in case anyone had noticed an unfamiliar vehicle on the night Romana died. In addition, a brace of officers, including a couple from West Tynedale who had been coopted into the team for their knowledge of the area, were also questioning residents and confirming their alibis, since it remained possible that Romana had been killed by someone living locally. The CSIs were doing their best, but there had been more rain, and privately they felt that they'd been lucky to get a tent over the two locations – killing site, and discovery – before it started bucketing down, because any other evidence had probably been washed away by now. They'd keep looking, though, because that was the job. You kept looking until there was nothing left to find.

And then you looked some more.

Finally, she'd taken the time to speak again with Douglas Hood, accompanied by Hynes. Hood still wasn't entirely off Priestman's radar – she had a natural distrust of people who seemed too helpful – but, as with the ex-boyfriend, Simon Harris, she didn't get a sense of Hood as a killer. Also, as Hynes pointed out, if Hood had killed Romana Moon, then he was going out of his way to aid the police in his own apprehension.

Hood's home was more comfortable than Priestman had expected. She'd been anticipating gray stone and unfinished furniture, as well as a pig in the kitchen; there were elements of the first two, but no sign of the latter. Hood lived in a centuries-old cottage that was almost cozy inside, in a very male way, dominated by a modern flat-screen television in the living room, and a surprising number of books, mostly paperbacks of seventies' espionage novels. They'd gone through the circumstances of his discovery of the body for a third time, and discussed Hood's movements on the night of the killing, which hadn't amounted to much at all, according to Hood, because he'd been in bed. Eventually, Priestman went with her instincts, which were that Hood was as straight as he appeared, and they spoke some more about the Familists.

'I still find it surprising that the memory of them has persisted for so long,' said Priestman.

They were drinking strong tea made by Hood from leaves, and served from a tin pot.

'Why?' said Hood. He sounded genuinely puzzled.

'Because they left here centuries ago.'

'They might have, but the damage was already done by then.'

'In what way?'

'Their presence changed the landscape. They scarred it. They built on it, and dug down into it. They murdered above ground, and buried the evidence below.'

'Are you saying the land remembers them?'

'Course it does. Nature remembers, and the land is part of nature. The Familists, they understood nature better than anyone, because their god was in it and of it. You think it was a coincidence that they chose Northumbria, and these moors, as the location for their church? I don't know of any other Familist chapels, except the one that was built here. Most of the Familists, they venerated in houses. They didn't go raising churches, except in this place.'

'Why?'

'Because this was once the heart of Christianity in Britain. Northumbria held the holy island of Lindisfarne, and Whitby Abbey, and gave the world Caedmon, the first Christian poet in Old English. But in those times, the influence of Christianity didn't extend much further than the monastery walls. Beyond them, the people believed in gods of the land, gods you could see and touch, because they were in the rivers, the trees, and the crops. That was the kind of god the Familists venerated, and so they set their church here, in the place where Christianity started, to remind folks of what had gone before, of what was sleeping in the soil.'

'Do you think the Familists have returned?' said Hynes.

Hood shrugged. 'I can't say if they have or not, only that it's of no consequence beyond the murder of that poor girl.'

'Why is that?'

Hood sipped his tea.

'Because whatever they worshiped never went away.'

The newspaper and television people were already running with the Familist angle. There'd been no hope of keeping it quiet, not really. Worse, though, it was all over the Internet, which, as Priestman feared, had drawn out the crackpots. According to Hynes, the press office had already logged a number of calls from people claiming to be druids.

'Did you know that druids are kind of the intellectual wing of paganism?' he said to Priestman, as she drove them back to Newcastle. She enjoyed driving. It helped her to marshal her thoughts.

Priestman admitted that she had not known this about druids. Hynes was eating a sandwich, so couldn't immediately elaborate, or not without spraying the contents of his mouth across the windshield. In Priestman's experience, Hynes was always eating, or thinking about eating. He probably dreamed of food when he slept.

'Not necessarily the ones who've been calling us, mind,' said Hynes, after he'd swallowed what he'd been chewing. He contemplated his sandwich for a moment, perhaps checking it for signs of sorcery. 'They're just mad.'

Hynes had spoken to Kevin Moon again after the police interview with Simon Harris, just to corroborate some details of what Harris had told them.

'Did he say anything more about Harris?' asked Priestman.

'Only that he liked him, and was sorry when it didn't work out between him and his daughter, but he said she'd always been one to know her own mind.'

'And she didn't mention arguments, or problems with Harris or any other men?'

'No.'

'What about the school?'

'Mainly female teachers. Gackowska and I will start talking to them first thing in the morning. The headmistress has organized a rota, so the classes can be supervised while the teachers are being interviewed.'

DC Lisa Gackowska was Hynes's latest protégée. She and Hynes operated well together.

'And the hospitals?'

'Already on it. Gackowska's been working the phones, pulling together lists from emergency units and walk-in clinics in Northumbria, Durham, Tyne & Wear, and Cumbria, as well as Scottish Borders, and Dumfries and Galloway: broken ankles, legs, serious sprains over the last thirty-six hours or so. I may be jumping the gun, but my guess is there'll be a lot.'

The moorlands gave way to civilization, and Priestman could see Hynes relaxing the closer they drew to concrete and cafés.

'He must have been watching her,' she said.

'He'd have to be a planner,' said Hynes, 'taking her out to a place like that to kill her. Still went wrong for him, though.'

He finished his sandwich, and carefully wiped the crumbs from his hands and clothing into the wrapper before folding it up and storing it away. Hynes was like that: fastidious. It was easy to underestimate him.

'She weighed about a hundred pounds soaking wet,' Hynes continued. 'She wouldn't have been able to put up much of a struggle, not against even a moderately strong man. Didn't do self-defense or weights, wasn't a runner, just a teacher. She might have started to tell on him once he started to carry her body back to his vehicle – I imagine killing someone takes it right out of you – but it wouldn't have bothered him too much if he was fit enough. I was wondering about the vehicle, too.'

'What about it?'

'It's hard to drive with an injury. Not impossible, just difficult.'

'Maybe an automatic?'

'Worth considering.'

'Or an accomplice.'

'Likewise.'

Again, Priestman made some mental notes.

'You should get some rest once we're back,' she told him.

'Says you.'

'I will.'

'You mean it?'

'Yes.'

And she did, so she had mixed feelings when Sisterson called her shortly after 6 p.m.: pleasant surprise at the fact that he had apparently completed the autopsy by close of business, but diluted by his first words.

'I think,' he said, 'you might want to come over here.'

* * *

Holmby was monitoring the news bulletins, flipping between the television and the Internet coverage on his phone, and stretching his leg in an effort to ease a cramp.

They'd had the body for long enough, he thought. By now, they must have found what he'd left for them inside Romana Moon.

He closed his eyes, and pictured the windows at Fairford.

Closed his eyes, and listened to the voices in the glass.

XXXVII

Marcus Godwin didn't dislike Odda's Chapel, not by any means. He wouldn't have been sitting with his back to its wall otherwise. It simply lacked the grandeur of St Mary's – both the Deerhurst and Fairford incarnations, although he had always found the former more welcoming, increasingly so following his unpleasant experiences in the latter.

Now he stood by the chapel gate, uncertain of what he'd heard, if he'd truly heard anything at all. He'd been frightening himself, sitting out here on his chair, thinking about Fairford, and dead Oliver Lewin. He certainly hadn't seen anyone go inside. He was by the gate all this time, and no cars were parked in the little yard off the lane. It was getting colder, too. He'd catch his death, if he weren't careful.

There! He heard it again: a kind of scratching, like a dog digging in the earth for a bone. Perhaps a fox had sneaked in there. You had to be prudent with those buggers. If you cornered one, it could give you a nasty bite.

He sniffed the air, and caught a taint upon it. Whatever was inside had dragged something along with it, something dead and rotten.

'Hello?' he said, just in case he had somehow missed a visitor, although he hadn't, he knew he hadn't. He was getting older, but he hadn't lost all his marbles.

Marcus opened the gate, and stepped into the chapel.

The regional team of consultant forensic pathologists operated out of Newcastle, and provided services for the Northumbria police as well as forces in Durham, Cleveland, and North Yorkshire. Craig Sisterson was the longest-serving by some considerable distance, but was due to retire before the end of the year. Priestman had met a few pathologists in her time, and they didn't really conform to a type, but had central casting been searching for a figure that screamed 'Pathologist!', then they could have done a lot worse than Sisterson. As Hynes once put it, 'If he lies down for too long, he'll be mistaken for a corpse himself.' Sisterson was attenuated and slightly yellowed, with long, delicate fingers and an expression of permanent disappointment with the world. It was said that he had been studying for the priesthood before throwing it all in to follow medicine – and a woman. She was a nun, so the whole business had probably involved the Vatican as well, all of which lent an element of transgression to Sisterson's general peculiarity.

'Do you want to look at her again?' he asked Priestman, once she had been admitted to his office. She would usually have sent Hynes or one of the other detective sergeants in her stead, but it wasn't often that Sisterson made this kind of request.

'Would it help?' she asked.

'Not particularly.'

'Then I'll pass, thank you.'

Sisterson shrugged, as if to say each to her own, but Priestman didn't know what she was missing. She noticed a thick cigar sticking out of the upper pocket of his jacket. It looked like something Winston Churchill might have waved in his fingers as he left 10 Downing Street. Now that she'd noticed it, she couldn't unnotice it. Sisterson followed the direction of her gaze.

'An early retirement gift,' he said. 'It's a shame I don't smoke.'

Priestman agreed that it was a shame.

'You don't know anyone who might enjoy it, do you?'

Priestman believed that DS Hynes might, but only if he wasn't told it had come from Sisterson. The cigar wasn't wrapped in plastic, and one never knew where Sisterson's hands might have been. Actually, one did, which was part of the problem.

'I'm afraid I don't.'

'Pity.'

He clasped his hands before him, the thumbs crossed.

'You'll have my written report in the morning, but the basics are as follows: stab wound to the right of the back, diagonally oriented, twenty-five inches below the top of the head, four inches from the front of the body; three to three-and-a-half inches in length, superiorly tapered wound. Cut a path through the skin and the subcutaneous tissue without penetrating the chest or abdominal wall. Superficial: my opinion is that it was the first blow struck.

'It was followed by a second transversely oriented stab wound to the left side of the back, thirty inches below the head and four inches to the front of the body, again involving the skin and subcutaneous tissue but not the chest or abdominal walls. Both ends of the wound tapered. Probably the second blow.'

He wanted to put her down before he cut her throat, thought Priestman, or maybe he believed it was easier to kill someone by stabbing her from behind than it actually was. The third possibility was that Romana Moon had been his first victim, and he had to work his way toward killing her. Whatever the reason for these injuries, they had only added to her pain.

'And then?' she asked.

'The fatal wound: a deep, obliquely placed, long-incised injury to the front side of the neck, starting below the left ear at the upper third of the neck, and deepening gradually with severance of the left carotid artery. The right-sided end of the injury was at the mid-third of the neck with a tail abrasion. No defense injuries. Lungs show aspiration of blood. Cause of death: severed throat. But you probably already knew that.'

'Still, nice to have it confirmed by an expert.'

Sisterson raised an eyebrow.

'Do I detect a note of sarcasm?'

'I don't think so.'

'Well, perhaps I should have it confirmed by an expert.'

'No shortage of experts in sarcasm around here. You said you had something to show me?'

Priestman wanted to go home to her kids. If she put her foot down, she might even be back in time to eat with them. She could call Steve, and ask him to delay dinner until she returned.

Sisterson produced a transparent sample bag from a drawer and placed it on the table before her.

'I found these lodged in the victim's throat,' he said.

Priestman picked up the bag and examined its contents without removing them. An already bad situation had just become much worse.

She was looking at a bloodied set of Muslim prayer beads.

Marcus Godwin stared at the shape in the corner of Odda's Chapel. It crouched naked by the wall, its body blackened like charred meat, stripes of pink and red visible where the skin had broken. It stank, and the little drain that ran along the side of the chapel was overflowing with its excretions, a mix of blood and whatever else it had voided. And then –

And then it wasn't there at all, and Marcus could see only shadow, and the beams of a dying sun, but he could still smell the presence in the chapel. Yet as he stepped back it manifested itself again, turning its head toward him, and he was minded of the twin beast heads that stood at each side of the inner porch door of St Mary's, Deerhurst, of the faces barely visible in its nave capitals, and of the tormentors in the windows at Fairford, because this was all and none of them.

Now the chapel around him was no longer old and bare but held a cross and an altar, and he inhaled incense and heard prayers being intoned, except no mass was being said because the chapel was empty of priests; and when Godwin looked behind him he saw a woman kneeling naked on the cold stones, a man standing behind her with a blade, and the man was whispering, '*You see it? You see it, don't you?*', and Godwin understood that this man and this woman were both here and elsewhere, modern and ancient, and as the blade began its work Godwin knew all that had come to pass before must surely come to pass again, was happening now as then, and would go on happening even after all trace of men had vanished, and nature had reclaimed their works and buried them.

The woman's blood overflowed the drain, soaking the earth, but by then Marcus was stumbling from Odda's Chapel, and the present reasserted itself like an image projected on gauze over a faded backdrop. His feet splashed in mud and floodwater.

175

He saw no one on the road, and no lights in the houses. He tried to call for help, but no words came. He heard only the wheezing of his own breath, and a soft splash from behind as something passed through the puddles, following in his footsteps, but he did not look back. He made for the church, striking the gate against the stone of the pillar as he went, only to hear that sound repeated moments later as his pursuer shadowed him. Marcus reached the church, but the door was locked because of the hour, and he pounded on the wood in the hope that someone might yet be inside, but there was no answer. In his despair, he risked a glance behind, and saw what was following him.

It was a girl of perhaps twelve or thirteen. She had dark-red hair, and wore a cream dress. Her face was familiar, but he struggled to place it. She reached out her right hand, and he almost extended his own in return until he noticed that all of her fingernails were gone, except for one that was filthy with dirt, the same dirt that was in her hair, her nostrils, and her ears, the same dirt that besmirched her shroud and her bare feet, and tumbled from her mouth in clumps as she spoke.

'Come,' said Margrett Lewin. 'I'm to let you play with me. Oliver told me so.'

Margrett Lewin, now long dead, drowned in a pond while still a child; drowned herself, if the stories were to be believed, rather than remain alive in a world that placed her at the mercy of men like her brother. But it was as though her skin was just a layer deep, because Marcus could glimpse what was inside her, the black and the red of it, and he backed away from her, fearing to let her out of his sight now that he had acknowledged her presence. He retreated down the stone stairs that led to the south wall of the ruined apse, Oliver Lewin's dead sister – or whatever had temporarily taken her form – keeping pace with him, but he missed the last step and landed painfully on his left side. A farmhouse stood at the back of the church, and he could see someone moving in its kitchen, but he had no strength left to make it across the yard to the door, and no breath to waste on cries for help. Instead he crawled toward the south wall, and he prayed as he went, even as he heard the gentle scuff of small bare feet descending the stairs behind him.

St Mary's, Deerhurst was noted for its antiquity, and its ornate font, but perhaps most of all the church was famous for the carving high on the exterior of the apse wall: the piece of Saxon sculpture known as the Deerhurst Angel, a stylized representation long exposed to wind and rain, yet beautiful even in its slow decay. It was beneath this relic that Marcus Godwin chose to lie, and face what was coming for him. He grabbed a handhold in the uneven stonework, and used it to raise himself to his knees. He pressed his forehead to the wall, and waited for the girl's touch, but it did not come.

He looked over his shoulder, but the girl was gone.

Marcus went limp, and let oblivion take him.

XXXVIII

Louis had booked a table at a seriously upscale Italian restaurant by Columbus Circle. They arrived early so he could order a cocktail, and express loud skepticism about the state of modern jazz within earshot of the patrons heading into that evening's performance at Lincoln Center.

'You don't even like jazz,' said Parker.

'It's my people's music,' said Louis, as he sipped his Old Fashioned. 'It's in our blood.'

'So you're all critics?'

'Can't take that away from us. It would be racist.'

The maître d' – it seemed impolite to describe him merely as a host, given the price of the food – came over to say that their table was ready, and lead them to a corner booth, although they were still waiting for one more of their party: Bob Johnston, the most curmudgeonly antiquarian book dealer in Portland, Maine – and possibly in the country – would be joining them at Parker's instigation. Johnston didn't like flying, and had insisted on taking the train down to New York. Parker didn't mind, even though the Amtrak ticket had cost more than his own flight. Johnston's expertise might yet lead them to Quayle.

'Does he still want to hire me to kill someone?' Louis asked.

Johnston was a clever man, and hugely knowledgeable about books, but his people skills left a lot to be desired.

'I find it's better not to raise the subject with him,' said Parker. 'I think his list of targets is potentially endless.'

'How can a book dealer build up so much resentment?' said Angel.

'He says people don't know how to treat books.'

'People don't know how to treat people.'

178

'Yeah, except people eventually die, no matter how you treat them. But if you look after books, they abide.'

'Please tell me he said that, not you.'

'It was Johnston, but he kind of has a point.'

At that moment the man himself appeared, carrying two cloth bags heavy with books. The bags, Parker knew, were of Johnston's own design, with waterproof exteriors and cushioned inner layers, because Johnston had described them to him at length back in Portland before Parker could find an excuse to flee. Johnston had made an effort for the occasion, and was dressed in cottons and tweeds of various greens and browns, like a college professor experimenting with rural camouflage. Parker introduced him to Angel, whom Johnston had not met before.

'And you remember Louis.'

Johnston did.

'Still have that money set aside, if you're interested in some work,' he said.

'I'm not,' said Louis.

Johnston hid his disappointment manfully.

'Well, if you hear of anyone who's in the market for a commission—'

'A contract,' Louis corrected him, not for the first time. Parker figured Johnston was doing it deliberately. He had a certain penchant for mischief.

'Sorry, a *contract*, you let me know.'

'Sure, if I don't shoot you first.'

'Ha-ha,' said Johnston mirthlessly. He took his seat and ordered a beer, but not before casting a final suspicious glance at Louis, just in case he might not be above following through on the threat before Johnston got to his entrée.

Parker gestured at the bags.

'Good hunting?'

'Not bad, but not as good as it used to be. The Gotham Book Mart is gone, the Carnegie, Seven Gables. You still got the Strand, and Argosy, but the rest are too upscale for me. You can't dig for treasure at Tiffany's.'

Parker empathized. He missed trawling record stores in

179

Manhattan; bookstores too, but at least bookstores still survived, for now. It saddened him to think that Portland, a city of 70,000 people, had nearly as many bookstores as Manhattan, and certainly more record stores. Most recently, Other Music had closed, joining all the record stores that had once filled St Mark's, back when Parker had briefly lived there after –

After Susan and Jennifer were killed, but let those thoughts go. This is not the time.

Now only Academy was left, over on 18th Street. There might have been one or two others of which Parker was no longer aware, and he knew that Brooklyn had some, but he rarely went over there now.

Susan and Jennifer again. This persistence of loss.

The server came to take their orders. Johnston glanced at the menu. After they'd given him some time to recover from the shock of the prices, and Parker confirmed that he was picking up the check, Johnston settled for the osso buco. They shared some appetizers, and eventually relaxed into conversations about the city, history, and culture, while carefully avoiding politics and religion, like gentlemen, until they came to the subject of Angel's ongoing recuperation.

'Not that it's any help to you, but I had cancer,' said Johnston. 'That was a few years back.'

'What kind?' asked Angel.

Johnston tapped his mouth and throat.

'It sucked balls,' he said, which was about as succinct as a man could get on the subject, even though it might have been open to misinterpretation under the circumstances.

'And now?'

'It's gone, and it hasn't come back. I figure it will, sometime, in some form, but it's been five years now, which isn't bad. I don't taste certain foods as well as before, but physically, that's about the extent of the damage.'

'And aside from physically?'

Johnston took a moment before replying.

'I know that it's in there somewhere, dormant, biding its time, and I don't want to go through that pain again. I hope something else takes me instead. The only time I ever regretted not getting married was during the radiation treatment. My sister came down from Houlton to look after me, God bless her, but I never felt more alone. It's good that you have someone that cares for you. It doesn't make it easier, but it sure doesn't make it harder.'

He finished his beer, and asked the waiter for another.

'Hey,' said Louis.

'Yes?' said Johnston.

'Folks at the next table look like they're having a good time. Maybe you should go over there, see what you can do about it.'

Silence reigned for four or five seconds, and then Johnston laughed. Parker had never seen him laugh before. He hadn't been certain that Johnston was capable of it.

'I might just do that, if they get too cheerful.'

Louis's mouth flickered a smile.

'I'll keep you posted,' he said.

And thus dinner passed pleasantly. Their plates were cleared, and they declined dessert, but Louis and Johnston agreed on a brandy. Now that they had come to some understanding of each other, they commenced talking quietly between themselves, seemingly about country musicians who had shot people. They dealt with Billy Joe Shaver, and moved on to Johnny Paycheck. Parker wondered if he had somehow created a two-headed monster, but kept this to himself.

The tables nearby emptied, increasing their privacy.

It was time.

'Tell us,' said Parker to Johnston, 'about the Atlas.'

XXXIX

Sellars gave up trying to sleep. He left Lauren lying unmoving beside him, her face barely visible under the blankets, her breathing deep. He put on his dressing gown and a pair of slippers, and went outside to smoke. He was supposed to be trying to give up. He told Lauren he was making a real effort, but didn't think she believed him. She had a nose. She could smell the smoke on his clothes. But a) he spent most of his working day around people who smoked, and it wasn't as though he could deal with them from inside a protective bubble; and b) she wasn't that bothered if he wanted to kill himself with cigarettes, so long as he didn't smoke anywhere in the house, or where the kids could see him. Out of sight, out of mind.

The police were all over Romana Moon's death, and the cult angle had set the media barking like overexcited dogs. All the fuss and attention would increase the pressure on the police to find her killer, when they shouldn't even have had a murder to solve; a disappearance, yes, but not a murder. If only Holmby hadn't slipped; if only he'd managed to get the body safely back to his car, because there weren't supposed to be any bodies, only blood and memories.

Fucking Holmby.

Yes, the Northumbrian site was always going to be among the most difficult because it was so isolated, and part of the journey to and from there would have to be taken on foot. But it was important to Sellars that one of the killings should take place there, and Mors had offered no objection. It probably suited her employer's ends: he wanted old sites of worship, and while the Familist shrine might not have stood for long in Hexhamshire, the god it venerated was more ancient than any Christian deity.

182

Sellars had offered to take care of it, but Mors warned that he was too close to this one. She, like Quayle, prized objectivity. Anyway, Holmby claimed to have found the perfect victim, and said he'd already started working on her. A roofie in her drink, he announced, and she'd be docile as a kitten; she might have been, but light as she was, she still tipped the scales at more than a kitten, and dead weight was hard to carry. Sellars knew that from experience. Despite Mors's objections, he and Holmby should have collaborated on the Northumbrian killing, just to be certain that Holmby was capable of finishing that first job. He had been, as it turned out, but had literally fallen at the final hurdle.

Now that Holmby was incapacitated, it made sense for Sellars to remain out of contact with him, because it wasn't as though Holmby could be of any help for the next few weeks. Sellars would continue alone, which suited him. In addition, if Holmby had been careless, and left DNA at the scene or on the body, then he, not Sellars, would be the one the police went after.

Sellars stopped puffing on the cigarette. It suddenly tasted bad. He stubbed it out against the outside wall of the kitchen, and flicked the butt over the neighbors' wall. The house next door was rented to a bunch of students, and they wouldn't notice another cigarette end in the yard.

He hadn't left a body to be found, but Holmby had. If Holmby had been inattentive enough to lose his footing on the moors, what else might he have failed to notice? If the police did manage to connect Holmby to Moon, what would Holmby do when they came knocking on his door? Would he brazen it out? Would he keep his mouth shut? Sellars and Holmby weren't friends. They'd never even met before they came together at Fairford. True, Sellars – aided by Mors, or whatever techie she was paying for the trouble – had tracked Holmby for months on the Darknet, where he liked to lurk. Holmby was adept at lurking, and knew his way around the Net in all its forms, but he left a trail, mainly at sites specializing in images of dead women – murdered, mostly, although he tended to shy away from the more sadistic material. Holmby wasn't interested in torture. He was a purist. He just wanted to know what it might be like to kill someone, preferably a woman. I2P, the Invisible Internet Project, had finally enabled Sellars to begin chatting securely with Holmby online, and the rest was easy. Now they were just two men, formerly strangers, currently acquaintances, who'd been tasked with killing an indefinite number of women – or males, if the opportunity arose, but females were easier, and more potent.

Two men serving old gods.

'What are you doing out here?'

He nearly jumped out of his skin. Lauren had come down the stairs, through the kitchen, and opened the back door, all without alerting him. Sellars thought that if the police ever did arrive to arrest him, they could probably do it with sirens blaring and a band playing, and he still wouldn't notice until they put the cuffs on him.

'Doing my best not to have a heart attack,' he said. 'You scared me half to death.'

Lauren folded her arms, and shivered.

'You didn't answer my question.'

'I couldn't sleep. I came out for some air.'

'You came out for a cigarette, too.'

'Wasn't me. That was one of the students next door. You'd think they'd know better, but they don't.'

'Liar,' she said, but didn't bother to fight about it. 'You're not sick, are you?'

'No, I'm not sick.'

'You're worried about something, though. You wouldn't be standing alone in the dead of night if you weren't.'

He had to throw her a bone. He didn't want her nosing about.

'Work stuff. I've been offered more hours, and I'm not sure that I want to take them. But if I don't agree, I could be in trouble.'

There was some truth to this. Additional shifts and longer hours were on offer because business was good, but they were not compulsory.

'Have they said that to you?'

'Not in so many words, but you know . . .'

She shrugged. 'We can always find ways to spend the extra money.'

'Yeah, but it'll mean I'll have to be away from home even more than I already am.'

She looked up at him then, and he felt a little part of himself break. He could see her sadness, and a future where he was no longer in her life, except for every second weekend when he arrived to pick up the kids so they could stay with him for a couple of nights, while he and Lauren exchanged awkward words on the doorstep.

But all she said was, 'We'll manage.'

She wrapped her gown tighter around her body, and the shiver returned.

'I'm going back to bed.'

'I'll be up in a minute.'

'Fine.'

She was almost in the kitchen when he spoke again.

'Lauren?'

'Yes?'

'There's no one else.'

The look flashed again, but fainter now. She was tired, tired of everything.

'I could understand it better if there was,' she said. 'Don't forget to lock the door.'

And she left him alone with the dark.

XL

Quayle was taking the night air – and also taking a chance by doing so, if only a small one. The modern building that towered over him still had lights on in some of its offices, but Quayle had spent time watching it before entering its environs, and detected no signs of activity, while no surveillance cameras monitored this area, so he would not be troubled by security. He had made sure of the positioning of the cameras many years earlier, before they were even installed. In his hand was the key to the partners' entrance, shiny and new since the most recent changing of the locks.

Where he stood had once been his cobblestoned courtyard, over-looked not by an edifice of glass but a trio of stoop-shouldered buildings, blackened by centuries of pollution and forever bathed in shadow, the disposition of the edifices being inimical to the best efforts of sunlight. From this location, he had monitored the changes in the city and his chosen profession, altering his own performance accordingly like an actor anticipating the reactions of his audience, so that the firm of Quayle might survive, even thrive, without suspicion.

Quayle could recall a time when lawyers were of a single breed, when barristers, or 'apprentices at law' as they were termed, dealt with their clients personally instead of through an intermediary attorney, just as attorneys might plead for their clients from the side bar of the court. But as the two professions of barrister and attorney – or later, 'solicitor' – grew more distinct, Quayle decided that his firm should follow the latter path; he was no great pleader of cases, and something in his character caused judges and juries to look askance at him, and penalize his clients accordingly. Also, a solicitor had a lower public profile than a barrister and, if he so desired, might be seen by none but his own clients. It also suited Quayle to be excluded from the social burden of the Inns of Court, even as the solicitors' own Inns of Chancery decayed, and to be beyond the reach of the discipline of the judiciary.

Finally, unlike barristers, solicitors could charge clients directly, and were not reliant on a legal colleague to pay them for their services. There was money in being a solicitor, if one went about it the right way: money in wills, in property. So it was that the firm of Quayle retreated into the umbrous regions of the profession, the business being handed down from one family member to another, always bearing the name of Quayle, and always boasting the distinctive profile of that line – to such a degree, it was said, that a man might struggle to distinguish this Quayle cousin from that uncle, or that brother from this nephew, so strong was their blood, as though they were all minor variations on a single theme. But since no two Quayles ever appeared to occupy the same room, or govern their firm during the same period, such opportunities for comparison never arose.

For the first time in many years, Quayle recalled Fawnsley, the last of his clerks, who had continued to serve the firm until well into his eighties. Fawnsley, with a pot of tea forever brewing beside him, thick as treacle; Fawnsley, with his foul soups of salvaged vegetables, the dregs of the market stalls; Fawnsley, with his pauper's sandwiches stuffed with unidentifiable meats already on the turn, even though Quayle paid him well enough. There was no Mrs Fawnsley, Fawnsley not being of 'the marrying kind', as the euphemism of the day went, although Quayle was convinced the clerk had never acted on his urges. It lent the man an additional patina of sadness, and frustrated desire.

Back in 1929, or perhaps 1930, a fellow solicitor had remarked to Quayle, more in sorrow than any great surprise, at Fawnsley having been glimpsed in the vicinity of Lady Malcolm's Servants' Ball, an infamous gathering of the city's working-class sodomites and other assorted degenerates.

'Did he participate in the festivities?' Quayle asked.

'My chap couldn't say. Said he was lingering outside. Might

have been considering joining in, I suppose. Just thought you should know.'

The news had merely confirmed what Quayle already suspected, but he said nothing of this to Fawnsley, not directly; it would have broken the man's heart for shame. Nevertheless, the following Friday he invited Fawnsley to join him in a small sherry as he was preparing to close up shop for the weekend, and in the gentlest and most roundabout of terms indicated that the firm of Quayle dealt in matters most private and delicate, and the guardians of those secrets – namely Fawnsley, and Quayle himself – must forever be vigilant in case they should inadvertently leave themselves open to intimidation or, perish the thought, blackmail.

He thought that Fawnsley might have paled slightly in response, although it was difficult to be certain given that the man spent most of his days in the tenebrous surroundings of the office. Whatever the case, there were no more reports of Fawnsley loitering at Lady Malcolm's, nor was he ever glimpsed in the environs of the city's molly houses. But Quayle, in whom unexpected traces of humanity occasionally flashed like small, primitive fish somehow surviving the slow contamination of their environment, would wonder, as the years went by, if he might not have fastened Fawnsley in his loneliness and celibacy by even this most circumspect of interventions.

Yet Fawnsley, too, had also been most tactful, in his way. If he suspected his employer of involvement in affairs that might charitably have been described as esoteric, but more accurately as deeply occult, he gave no indication of it; and Fawnsley always found some business that required his immediate absence from the practice whenever Quayle had visitors of a more arcane stripe, just so Quayle might have no fear of his listening at the keyhole.

It was after Fawnsley's death that Quayle decided to shutter the firm. The old man had been with him for too many years to be easily replaceable, and Quayle lacked the energy to commence training Fawnsley's successor, even had he found a clerk he could trust. The legal profession, too, had changed, or perhaps Quayle was suffering the inevitable lethargy and melancholia of the excessively long-lived, and had become fatally infected by nostalgia. He had witnessed the dissolution of Clifford's Inn, the last of the old Inns of Chancery, in 1903. The solicitors no longer required such premises for the purposes of education and accommodation, or for dining and the convening of moot courts, although Quayle had sensed some general sadness at the disposal of Clifford's, at this final severing of ties that went back to the settlement of the royal courts at Westminster in the fourteenth century. The loss was more profound for Quayle, who had also been present for the destruction of Thavie's Inn in 1769, the first to fall, and had therefore been cursed to witness both the beginning and conclusion of the disbandment.

Or perhaps he had only imagined such matters. After a time, it became difficult to distinguish between memory and dreaming.

Fawnsley was with him on the day Clifford's was sold. They had raised a glass to its memory.

'Most regrettable,' Fawnsley had said, shaking a dandruffed head. 'Most regrettable indeed.'

Years passed. More old buildings were razed, and new growth ascended from the city floor to take their place. Fawnsley became older, grayer, frailer, until finally he, too, was gone.

Most regrettable. Most regrettable indeed.

But by then Quayle had also secured the Atlas, if in an incomplete form. He had passed the years since in trying to gather the missing leaves. The search had left so many bodies in its wake as to be uncountable, and still their sum seemed destined to increase. There would be no end to them, not while the Atlas remained deficient.

He looked up at the windows of the old building. They still bore some of the original crown glass, cleaned and restored, but in the darkness behind, where there should have been only brick, he could detect signs of movement: a certain shimmering, like pools of water gently rippling, catching the artificial light from the offices beyond, and reflecting it, transformed, on the walls above.

And as he witnessed this display, Quayle was afraid.

XLI

Bob Johnston's cloth bags did not contain books alone, but also printed papers, copies of old photographs, and a series of single-word notes written in block capitals as *aides-mémoire*, all relating to the subject at hand. Johnston had been circumspect in his investigations, some of which had caused him to delve deeper into the world of the despised Internet than he might otherwise have cared to venture. Parker had warned him to be wary. Quayle was alert to signs of pursuit, and he was certainly not unique in his interest in the Atlas.

Johnston produced a photocopy of a bookplate bearing the letter 'D' twinned, and beneath the motif the single word 'London'. Parker recognized it from the copy of *Grimm's Fairy Tales* – later retrieved from the body in Arizona – that Quayle had traveled to the United States to find.

'The bookplate was the starting point,' said Johnston. 'And, in a way, the end.'

Dunwidge & Daughter, antiquarian booksellers: founded in Chelsea in 1775 by one Cardwell Dunwidge, and destroyed by fire in the 1920s – not that many mourned its passing, the loss of its stock apart; and even this, it was whispered, was better off burned. From the start, the business dealt only in occult volumes, a very specialized area of literary commerce often noted for the rarity of the items involved, and the anonymity of their buyers.

Unlike his competitors, principal among them being James Lackington, the crown prince of the London book trade at the end of the eighteenth century, Cardwell Dunwidge did not issue catalogs. He was familiar with the specific requirements of his clients, and frequently acquired books with the profits from their future sale already as good as in his pocket, but he was not above making speculative purchases. These he would collate into lists, copies of which were then handwritten by his clerks, and circulated to interested parties.

Because such books were rarely available in numerous copies, they retained a desirability for collectors that was only enhanced by their transgressive nature. Even those without a particular interest in the occult might be prepared to invest heavily in a book that was *sui generis*. On the other hand, some volumes were so 'specialized' that it was better to keep the fact of their existence less widely known, and limit the details of their sale to those individuals best positioned to appreciate their particular qualities without being overly troubled by issues of taste or morality. Auctions were held in which the bidders did not even set eyes on one another, but placed their bids from nearby clubs or coffee houses, the sums written on folded sheets of paper and brought to Dunwidge by a succession of illiterate urchins.

Lackington despised Dunwidge, as did Lackington's business partner, John Denis, who was responsible for convincing Lackington to include an occult section in their first catalog, issued in 1779. As a competitor, Dunwidge should barely have been worthy of their attention. Lackington's catalogs included tens of thousands of volumes, and they were selling close to 100,000 books a year. Dunwidge's sales, meanwhile, might have amounted to a thousand volumes in a good year, but were probably closer to six or seven hundred.

But what sales! More than £26 from the painter Richard Cosway for a Cabalistic manuscript attributed to the painter Rubens, and almost £160 from the same Cosway for a manuscript of emblems from the *Coronatio Naturae*, this when a farm laborer earned nine shillings a week, and so could work for seven years and still not be able to afford what Cosway had acquired after perhaps only a moment's pause to listen to his banker's wails.

So Dunwidge was their rival not only for inventory but also for customers, especially at the more select end of the market. Yet it was widely known that Dunwidge had debased appetites, and kept street children close for more than the purpose of transporting letters and bids. While this was no crime in the eyes of the law, Lackington, although somewhat lapsed from his Methodist faith, regarded Dunwidge as an abomination, and Denis agreed. Unfortunately, few of Dunwidge's clients had similar qualms, and some even shared his taste for pedophilia.

Denis, who was himself a collector of the occult, eventually severed ties with Lackington to set up his own firm. When he died in 1785, his son, also John, inherited both his father's business and his prejudices. Dunwidge remained a goad to him, and an affront to decency, but at least Denis was in good company, for rare was the bookseller in London who would openly admit to commerce with Cardwell Dunwidge.

Privately, though . . .

Well, that was another matter.

The Dunwidge family remained pariahs in the London book trade, but successful ones, a situation that persisted until the ascent to the Dunwidge throne of Eliza, sole scion of Wenham Dunwidge, at the turn of the twentieth century. She was cleverer than her progenitor, even at an early age, eventually achieving the notable distinction of having the fact of her existence appended to the company name, and the less welcome one of burning to death in the fire that had finally wiped the family business from the face of the world.

'What caused the fire?' Parker asked.

'It may have been started by a man called John Soter,' said Johnston. 'He was suspected of beating Eliza's father to death, and of killing a London book scout named Maggs. He was also believed to have murdered a prostitute named Sally Campion, as well as two street children.'

'Why?'

'That I can't tell you. Most of what I discovered came from the newspapers of the day, and even they weren't entirely clear on what might have caused Soter to commit his crimes. And Soter wasn't around to ask: he disappeared, believed to have fled to Europe, or even the United States. What I do know is that Soter was a private detective, hired to locate a missing book collector named Lionel Maulding, and also to locate a book: an atlas.'

'Who hired him?' Louis asked.

'That's where it gets really interesting,' said Johnston. 'Soter was working for a London lawyer named Atol Quayle.'

Quayle paused with the key in the lock of the door – or *one* of the keys, in *one* of the locks. Even after all this time, he was never less than scrupulous about the security of his stronghold. It seemed to him that he had heard a sound, as of a voice crying out in uneasy sleep: a formless utterance, without meaning but undeniably human. Such a yell was not unusual in the city at this time of night, but what disturbed Quayle was that it appeared to have emerged from somewhere in his own rooms. He completed the unlocking as quickly and quietly as he could, the dust of the tunnels still upon him, before hurrying up the stairs to his living quarters, where he faced one final door to unfasten. Even as he did so, he wondered if he might have misheard. If the doors were all secured, how could someone have gained access?

He entered his lair, and was bathed in preternatural light.

'Quayle?' said Parker. 'You're sure that was the name?'

'Atol Quayle,' Johnston confirmed. 'Lionel Maulding was one of his clients. Maulding was a recluse, but a wealthy one. His disappearance, like the Soter killings, made all the papers of the day. It was a hell of a mystery – still is, I suppose, if we're discussing it almost a century later.'

'That would make Atol Quayle –' Angel did the math, working it out on his fingers.

'You need to borrow a hand?' asked Louis.

'Hush, I'm counting . . . Maybe the great-grandfather of the man we're looking for?'

Parker guessed that their quarry was probably in his late sixties or early seventies, although it had been difficult to tell. He dyed his hair, dressed in well-cut clothes, and wore fashionable glasses, but in harsh light the wrinkles on his face were clear to see, and his eyes were those of a sick old man.

'Assuming ours didn't pull the Quayle identity from a hat,' said Louis. 'This is a guy with at least two passports in other names.'

'No, the choice of the Quayle name wasn't random,' said Parker. 'Whether it's real or not, it meant something to him, but my guess is he wasn't lying about it.'

'Sorry to rain on your parade,' Johnston interrupted, 'but there are no more Quayles. The firm was very old, but it ceased to exist after World War Two. No partners, except way back in the sixteenth century. The partner, Couvret, was a Huguenot refugee, who came to England to escape religious persecution in Europe.

'As for the law firm, the line of continuity is hard to trace. Sometimes it passed to a son or brother, at other times to a cousin or nephew, but it was always a Quayle, until this last one, Atol, closed up shop in 1946, and died shortly after. Here: I found a death notice from *The Times* of London, dated September, 1948.'

He pulled another sheet from his file, and handed it to Parker.

'"QUAYLE, Atol,"' Parker read, '"solicitor of the Inns of Chancery. Died London, after a short illness. Service private." Odd that it doesn't give a date of birth, or even the month he died.'

'No details about parents, either,' said Johnston, 'or qualifications, or his career. No surviving relatives, obviously, because there didn't appear to be any.'

'Then who placed the obituary?' said Parker.

'He might have arranged it himself, before he died. That would explain the absence of a date of death. He could have left instructions, possibly with another lawyer, to be followed to the letter.'

'What about Couvret?' Louis asked. 'Did he stay in the legal business? Maybe his descendants took care of Quayle's affairs, and vice versa.'

'That's a nice idea,' said Johnston, 'but Couvret died – violently murdered by persons unknown shortly before the end of the sixteenth century. There's a reference to the killing in William Herbert's *Antiquities of the Inns of Court and Chancery*, 1804, and Thomas Allen's *History and Antiquities of London, Southwark, and Parts Adjacent*, from 1839, although Allen seems to have drawn on Herbert's account, which makes his contribution largely redundant.'

Louis stared hard at Johnston.

'You seriously need to find a woman. Or a man. Just someone.'

'I have my books,' said Johnston, defensively.

'Any of them shaped like a woman?'

'No.'

'Well, there you are.'

'What happened to Quayle's offices?' Parker asked.

'He owned a number of properties, all adjacent. Some were destroyed in World War Two, but most of those that survived were later demolished, and the sites redeveloped. They're now mostly law offices, from what I can tell.'

'And who got the money?' said Angel.

'According to the terms of sale, it was paid into what's called an "interest in possession" trust, where the trustee is obliged to pass on all income from the trust as it arises. The trust was set up back in the nineteenth century, with the trustees in this case being a firm of London attorneys named Lockwood and Dodson. They could have been the ones who had Quayle's obituary published. The advantage of an interest in possession trust is that the trustees pay tax on the income before it's handed over to the beneficiary, so if it's set up right, the beneficiary doesn't have the tax authorities snooping around.'

'Is Lockwood and Dodson still in existence?' said Parker.

'Absolutely, although it's now Lockwood, Dodson and Fogg. The firm was responsible for the development of the site, and its offices now sit where Quayle's once did.'

'And who is the beneficiary of the trust?'

'I don't know. In Britain, trusts have to be registered with Revenue and Customs, the equivalent of the IRS, but as long as the taxes are paid, they could give a shit about the beneficiary. Like I said, if you establish the trust properly at the start, you ensure a certain amount of privacy. If money is still coming in from investments covered by the trust, then we've no way of finding out the ultimate destination.

'Most of the information I've shared with you was easily available online or in books, so I didn't have to dig too deeply. You warned me to be guarded in my inquiries, and I have, or I hope so: I don't want this Quayle, whoever he may really be, to come knocking on my door asking why I'm interested in his affairs. The dangerous stuff I leave up to you, although it strikes me that *all* of this is dangerous, so it may simply be a question of degree.'

Louis ordered another round of drinks. Parker opted for a final glass of red wine. Nobody was rushing to make them pay the check, not that the management would have been likely to move Louis on in any case, not even if the line stretched to the sidewalk. You knew you were in good company when the appetizers were comped.

'What about Soter?' said Parker.

'War veteran,' said Johnston. 'Suffered some form of trauma during the Battle of the Somme at a place called Delville Wood, which was about as bad a place as you could choose to be in 1916. He was shipped home in the aftermath, and spent time at Craiglockhart Hospital in Edinburgh, which was where they treated officers suffering from shellshock. While he was up there, his wife and children were killed in a bombing raid on London. The papers speculated that grief, combined with whatever he'd gone through in France, might have driven him insane. He was later arrested for bothering some general he blamed for the slaughter at Delville, but was released without charge. By then he was working as a private detective: mostly divorces, straying husbands, fraud cases, that kind of thing. He'd been in the same business before the war, which was when he came to Quayle's notice.'

'What was his background?'

'Not unlike your own: he was a police detective until 1912, part of the Criminal Investigation Division of the London Metropolitan Police.'

'Any clue as to why he left?'

'None.'

'I mean, did he jump or was he pushed?'

'Again, I don't know. All I can tell you is that he had a talent for finding people, which is strange.'

'Why do you say that?' asked Angel.

'Because,' said Johnston, 'he seemed so lost himself.'

* * *

Quayle's lodgings consisted of a dining room; a living-room-cum-library, in which he spent the majority of his waking hours; a kitchen; a bedroom; and a bathroom. The living and dining rooms were wood-paneled, and had remained largely unchanged since the nineteenth century, apart from the addition of marginally better lighting, a radio, and a record player. He accessed the Internet, if only occasionally, via a secure dongle provided by Mors. The bookshelves contained many legal tomes, both old and more modern, since Quayle, although long retired from the profession, enjoyed keeping up with developments; a great deal of classic eighteenth- and nineteenth-century fiction, along with a considerable collection of poetry and drama; and a valuable assemblage of occult volumes, some of them purchased in person from Lackington, Denis *père et fils*, and generations of Dunwidges, although even Quayle had kept Eliza Dunwidge at a distance. He was, he had often thought, rather glad that Soter had caused her, either accidentally or intentionally, to be burned alive.

A door was set in the shelves facing the entrance to Quayle's rooms. Had a stranger succeeded in opening it, he would have discovered only a blank wall, and an exploratory tap would have suggested a reassuring thickness. Then again, any stranger taking such liberties would very quickly have ended up dead. The ethereal light bathing Quayle's walls was leaking through the frame of this door. So, too, was the sound he had heard from the yard. It was a man's voice, one that Quayle had not heard in almost a century.

It was the voice of John Soter.

Soter, seated in a corner of The Ten Bells in Spitalfields, looks up from his copy of the Evening News, *and rumors of war with Germany, as his name is called.*

'Mr Soter? Mr John Soter?'

Standing before him is a man he does not recognize, although he knows the type: a functionary, running a master's errands. A cheap suit, growing worn at the elbows and cuffs, but clean and unwrinkled; old shoes, but well shined; ink on the fingertips of the right hand, and a corpse's pallor. A junior clerk, but not from a bank: the clothes are too sad, and the demeanor too cunning. A legal man: Soter has spent time with enough of them to be able to identify the breed by sight.

'That's right,' he says.

'My name is Fawnsley. My employer, Mr Atol Quayle – an esteemed figure in Chancery – would like to meet you.'

Soter checks his pocket watch. It is almost 8 p.m., and he has the thirst for another beer.

'Can't it wait until morning?'

'Mr Quayle would prefer you to join him immediately. It's a matter of some urgency – and delicacy. He instructed me to inform you that you would be paid generously for your time, regardless of whether you ultimately elected to accept his commission.'

Fawnsley, hat in hands, wringing the brim as though to relieve it of a weight of water.

He doesn't want to disappoint his employer, thinks Soter. And not just that, he's frightened of him. Atol Quayle: the name is unfamiliar to him, but then there are as many lawyers around Fleet Street and the Strand as there are rats by the river, or so it often seems.

'All right, I'll go with you,' says Soter.

After all, what else has he to do? Another pint to consume, more bad news to read, and screaming children and a tired wife waiting for him at home. These nights stretch on so as winter closes, the darkness accumulating, its weight growing heavier upon him.

'I have a taximeter car outside,' says Fawnsley, already moving toward the door.

Soter finishes his drink, folds his newspaper and picks up his coat and hat. Fawnsley pauses to make sure he's being followed, and for an instant Soter feels the strongest urge to remain where he is, and let this Quayle find someone else to do his dirty work – for at such an hour, dirty work is all it can be. But it's not just tiredness that causes him briefly to reconsider, or the warmth of the pub against the chill of the night. It is disquiet, such as a man might experience upon walking close to the edge of a precipice, *and knowing that only the choice of an instant stands between him and oblivion.*

   'Mr Soter?'

And then it passes.

'I'm coming,' says Soter.

And is damned.

Parker looked at the photograph of John Soter. It was formal in setting, with Soter seated against a neutral backdrop in a well-pressed sergeant's uniform. He was clean-shaven, but looked older than his years. According to Johnston, Soter was only twenty-five when the picture was taken, but Parker would not have been surprised had another decade been added to that age. Each preceding generation led a harder life than the last. The evidence was etched into their faces, and haunted their eyes.

'Is this an official photograph?' Parker asked.

'No,' said Johnston. 'The British military didn't take pictures of its soldiers. If men wanted a portrait, they had to pay for it themselves. Soter probably had that one made for his wife, and maybe a few close friends. After he disappeared, it was one of the photographs circulated to the public in an effort to trace him.'

'You said he was an officer,' said Louis, 'but he's wearing sergeant's stripes.'

'He earned a battlefield commission to second lieutenant after Festubert in 1915, and to lieutenant at Vimy Ridge in 1916. It made him, in the language of the time, a "temporary gentleman". Had he stayed in the service after the war, he might have been allowed to keep the rank of second lieutenant, although probably not. Then he was shipped home, and the point became moot.'

'Did he ever find Maulding, this man he was employed to look for?' asked Parker.

'No, Maulding remained missing. Reading between the lines, it was assumed that Soter might have murdered him as well, and hidden the body.'

'Why?'

'Money, possibly. Maulding was a wealthy man.'

'So he killed Maulding for his money, and all these others –

men, women, and children – because he was insane? That doesn't sound right.'

'You're the detective,' said Johnston. 'I don't have much more for you on Soter. He was last seen alive at the rail station at Maidensmere – that's in the Norfolk Broads, in the southeast of England. Lionel Maulding had a home there, Bromdun Hall. The newspaper reports suggest that Soter left a note at Bromdun Hall before he vanished. Its contents were never made public, but if it was a suicide note, he didn't supply a body to go with it.

'One last thing about Maulding, though: he was a book collector, with a particular interest in the occult. His nephew, a professional idler named Sebastian Forbes, was the sole beneficiary of his will, a couple of university libraries apart. Forbes put his uncle's entire collection up for sale after the executor of the estate succeeded in having Maulding declared legally dead for purposes of probate. The catalog caused a hell of a stir when it was issued.'

'Let me guess,' said Parker. 'The executor of the estate was Atol Quayle.'

'The very same.'

Parker regarded again the photograph of John Soter, and thought of Johnston's description of him: lost.

'It seems as though Soter was keeping bad company,' he said.

'Does that make him bad too?' asked Angel.

'If only by association,' said Louis. 'But all those people didn't kill themselves.'

'That doesn't mean Soter killed them,' said Parker.

'Do you feel sorry for him?' Johnston asked. 'I know I do. I've seen his service record. A lot of them were destroyed during a bombing raid in World War Two, but his survived because it had been set aside during the murder investigations. The Forty-Seventh Division earned over twenty-five hundred awards for bravery during World War One, and Soter received the Military Cross for his actions at Vimy Ridge, along with that second promotion. He was a brave man, but the war did something terrible to him, and the loss of his family finished the job.'

Johnston was keeping his gaze averted from Parker, who understood that perhaps Johnston wished he hadn't started speaking at all, not once he began to notice the increasing similarities between these two men: the first born before the turn of the last century, and the second seated beside him; separated by almost one hundred years, but united by their professions, by violence, and their experience of loss.

'Yes,' said Parker. 'I feel sorry for him too.'

Soter, becoming indispensable to Quayle, or believing himself to be so; and his wife warning him against this association, for she meets Quayle once, seemingly by accident, on the Strand. Quayle greets her, although they have never crossed paths before, and she will wonder at how he comes to recognize her, she who should only be to him another face in the crowd.

'*I didn't like him,*' *she tells her husband.* '*He had pitiless eyes.*'

'*He's a lawyer,*' *Soter replies.* '*They have their pity excised at birth.*'

'*But you didn't.*'

'*No. Then again, I'm no lawyer.*'

'*And if you take his money, must you be pitiless too? What is it you do for him, this Quayle?*'

I find people who don't want to be found, he thinks, and help others who would prefer to slip their moorings. I offer bribes to those who ought to remain quiet, for the sake of the reputations of their betters as well as their own good health, but if there's rough stuff needed to reinforce the message, I leave it to coarser men, and pretend to know nothing of what follows. I shadow husbands who are cheating on their wives, and record the dates and times of their assignations; and I shadow women sleeping with men other than their husbands, and who will suffer more for their failings because of their sex. I conduct background checks, often on individuals of no apparent interest to anyone, and by the end am no wiser as to why they should have attracted Quayle's attention to begin with, except to be certain it will do them only harm. Sometimes, he sends me to private libraries to peruse the shelves, with a list of titles to be on the watch for, even when the contents are not for sale. I tell myself that Quayle merely marks them in the event of some future auction, but I know better.

Little by little, I am selling my soul to him.

But 'Nothing of interest' is all he offers in reply to his wife's question.

'And how did he know who I was?' she asks.

Which is a more interesting question, and one Soter raises when next he is summoned to Quayle's presence.

'Would you expect me to hire a man for delicate work without first knowing something of his own circumstances?' Quayle answers, and Soter is not hypocritical enough to find this unreasonable. He only wonders to whom Quayle entrusted the task of investigating him, and decides that, if Quayle knew what his wife looked like, then the lawyer probably undertook the task himself.

'Now, I have another errand for you . . .'

Then the war comes, and every manner of dying. By the end of it, Soter is alone.

Alone, but for Atol Quayle.

They were now the last table in the restaurant. A few people remained at the bar, the crowd bolstered by an influx following the conclusion of the jazz performance, but still no one was pressing them to leave. On the contrary, the offer of another round on the house was made, although Parker and Angel politely declined, Parker having drunk more that night than he had in years, and Angel, having eaten little, being mindful of his intake.

'And the Atlas?' Parker said.

Because this, according to Johnston, was at the heart of it all, the prize sought by the man who had used the Quayle name only recently in the United States, despite the fact that the last true Quayle appeared to have died halfway through the preceding century.

'I didn't write down what I discovered about it,' said Johnston. 'There isn't enough material to justify the paper, and as with the business affairs of Atol Quayle, I was reluctant to draw too much attention to myself by asking the right questions of the wrong people. Mostly, I just lurked on odd forums, and relied on mentions in other books. But if I'm right, Quayle is looking for the *Atlas Regnorum Incogniturum*, also variously known as the Atlas of

Unknown Realms, or more commonly the Fractured Atlas. Depending on the source, it either doesn't exist, shouldn't exist, or exists simultaneously in a multiplicity of different forms. It's alleged to depict universes beyond, or alongside, our own, but also reflects this one.'

'To what purpose?' Louis asked. 'If these are imaginary universes—'

'Not "imaginary",' Johnston corrected. 'Unknown, or not proven to exist, which isn't the same thing. There's a whole branch of theoretical physics devoted to this: the idea that all possible pasts and futures are real, and each is represented by a universe, like lines diverging from a central axis before moving further and further away from the source, so they resemble the branches of an infinite tree. There's a universe where we didn't meet for dinner tonight, a universe where Angel accepted a glass of brandy on the house, a universe where you didn't ask that last question.'

'The question stands,' said Louis, 'so that's at least two universes in which I asked it and didn't get an answer: What's the purpose of the Atlas?'

'To allow one universe to flow into, and alter, the other.'

'Excuse me?'

'The best analogy I discovered is that of a pane of glass standing between two artists, each of them with a pen in hand. One draws what he sees on the glass, and the other draws what she sees. The pane is then flipped, and the reality on one side becomes the reality on the opposite side, but holding the form drawn on the glass. In other words, it looks almost the same, but isn't.

'And for now, that's pretty much all I have, except that the Atlas has some connection to the Netherlands. It might have been made there, because it was certainly discovered in Tilburg toward the end of the sixteenth century, although allusions to it long precede that discovery. In any case, there are more Dutch references to it than any other, and it ties in with the passports your FBI contact mentioned.'

No one said anything. In some other universe, four men were dismissing the idea of a book that could alter worlds, but in that universe two of those men had not glimpsed vellum pages from an unknown source disrupting the typography of a collection of fairy tales, and causing mutations to appear among its illustrations.

'You did well, Bob,' said Parker, finally.

'What now?' Johnston asked.

'We'll follow the two leads – the Netherlands, and London – until we find Quayle and Mors.'

'I'd like to go with you,' said Johnston. 'I have some money put by, and can pay my own way. There are libraries in England with source material that might be useful, and collectors that don't advertise their presence on the Internet. I have names, and contacts, but you don't. Also, I know about books, and whatever the truth of what's happening here, it comes down to a book. Finally, I've got nothing better to do. I'm an aging man, and I've never been outside the continental United States. I've only seen the world through the pages of books, but I figure it might be interesting to have a different point of comparison before I die.'

'Quayle and Mors are killers,' said Parker. 'If they're intelligent, which they are, they're expecting us to come after them, and they'll be prepared.'

'I understand,' said Johnston, 'and I'm not pretending for a moment that I'm not frightened by them, or disturbed by all that's been done in the name of the Atlas. But this is something I can do, and better than you or most anyone else I know. If Quayle has the Atlas, or most of it, then it stands to reason that if I can follow the book's trail, it will lead us to him. I've reached the limits of what I can achieve from a desk in Portland.'

'Man says he can pay his way,' said Angel. 'And we'll need beer money.'

'We're not taking his money,' said Parker.

'Killjoy,' said Angel.

Parker turned back to Johnston.

'I think you just talked your way into a trip,' he said. 'And we can cover your expenses. We have some federal funding.'

'Damn,' said Johnston, 'I knew I was right to cheat on my taxes.'

* * *

Soter, in the offices of the firm of Quayle, Sebastian Forbes slouched in a chair: this fop, this pauper with a millionaire's tastes, anticipating the death of his uncle so that he may wallow in dissipation.

'We should like you to find Mr Lionel Maulding and return him to the safe and loving embrace of his family,' says Quayle. 'That is a fair summation of the situation, is it not, Mr Forbes?'

And Forbes nods, like the idiot he is, because he does not know the truth of the situation, not as Quayle does. But neither does Soter, and nor will he ever, not even as he watches the Atlas burn, and glimpses the end of all things.

Bob Johnston took a cab back to his hotel near Penn Station, while Parker returned to his room at Angel and Louis's place. He was tired, and unused to drinking more than a glass or two of wine. He went to bed, but was woken in the dead hours by a man shouting, yet when he went to the window, he could see no one outside. He drank some water, and listened to the voice. It seemed to fade in and out, and Parker thought that it might have been coming from one of the neighboring buildings, although their residents and condo boards weren't the kind to tolerate noisy drunks, or not for long, not unless they were very wealthy noisy drunks. Under other circumstances, he might have gone to investigate, or called the cops, but he was too weary for the former, and Angel and Louis would not have appreciated the involvement of the latter.

Parker heard footsteps below, and Angel coughing. Moments later came the sound of someone moving in the kitchen. Parker went downstairs, and found Angel making hot milk.

'You okay?' Parker asked.

'Can't sleep. This helps, or maybe just making it helps. By the time it's ready, I'm usually tired again. You?'

'I heard someone shouting.'

'Yeah? I didn't hear anything.'

'It was pretty loud. I think I can still hear it.'

'Huh. Show me where.'

*   *   *

Quayle opened the door behind the library shelves, using a key that he kept always in the right pocket of his trousers. As he turned the key, the lock released, but it did so with the sound of many mechanisms, the echoes gradually fading until they fell beyond the realm of hearing.

Behind the door stood a wall – and no wall. Both were possible, and so both states existed. A naked man hung suspended against the void beyond: a mute Lionel Maulding, still enduring his torments almost a century after his disappearance, although Quayle had largely ceased to notice the blood, so familiar was he with the show. Quayle could not have said where Maulding was, precisely. He supposed that some might have called it Hell, had Hell existed, except that Maulding had done nothing to earn this punishment beyond hunting for, and finding, the Atlas. Planes of existence held spaces between them, and in one of those rifts Lionel Maulding now dwelt.

At least he was not alone: others hung with him, each representing a life that had come into contact with the Atlas – and frequently, by extension, with Quayle – and ended as a consequence. He could name them all, even after all this time, right back to his former partner, Couvret. But only one interested him at this moment, because only one had changed.

When last Quayle had looked on John Soter, he was pendent and unmoving, his eyes, nose, and ears sewn shut with catgut, his arms and legs restrained. Inside that body, Soter's trapped consciousness roamed Delville Wood and Vimy Ridge, or walked through the shell of a bombed-out terraced house in Stepney, searching for a wife and two children long gone from this world, their bodies reduced to fragments of flesh and bone by German Gotha bombers. Quayle had been hearing stories for decades about the figure of a man glimpsed wandering Stepney by night, dressed in an old suit, calling a woman's name. He thought it might be Soter, or some aspect of him, and wondered if a similar figure might have been seen at Delville, or Vimy. The ways of the Atlas were peculiar, even to Quayle.

Now Quayle stared at Soter – and Soter stared back at him. He had somehow torn the catgut from his mouth, shredding his lips in the process, and done the same with the threads through the lids of his eyes, so that he appeared to be weeping tears of blood.

'Here!' Soter cried. 'I'm here! Find me! Help me!'

As he spoke, the catgut tried to wind its way back through the holes in order to blind and silence him again, but he resisted by blinking his eyes and opening his mouth, and all the time he continued to shout – 'Help me!' – until finally the catgut over-whelmed him, and he was quiet once more.

'It's gone now,' said Parker, as he and Angel stood in the guest room.

'Someone's bad dream,' said Angel.

'Must have been. It sounded like he was calling for help.'

'If you hear it again, let me or Louis know.'

'I will.'

But the voice did not return, and eventually Parker slept.

THE PARTNER

HE SHOULD NEVER HAVE JOURNEYED TO ENGLAND,
Couvret thought. He should have stayed in the Netherlands, or
returned to France to die, there to be buried in the same land as his
wife and child, even if he should never have discovered the precise
location of their bodies. He was first told that they had fallen victim
to the red plague, but later discovered this not to be the case.
Marianne and Jeanne had died at the end of a sword, slaughtered by
those who were seeking Couvret himself, and in his absence were
forced to content themselves with his family. Of the exact circumstances of their end only their killers might speak, but Couvret could
guess the general, if not the specific: to be doubly penetrated, first by
rape, then a blade. Often in such cases the women were imprisoned,
and the girls sent to convents, where they might yet be saved by
immersion in the tenets of Catholicism. Marianne and Jeanne, he now
knew, had not been so fortunate.

London had seemed like sanctuary of a kind, as long as one
thought of it as salvation, and not enforced exile for life. There were
other Huguenots here, a small community of those who had lost so
much, but had already commenced building new lives in a foreign
land, resigned to their banishment. And what did it matter where they
lived and worshiped, they proclaimed, for was God not with them
wherever they went? And Couvret would nod in agreement, and give
thanks to a deity whose power and benignity he had begun to doubt.

Because if God was truly omnipotent, and had created all things,
then how could an abomination such as the Atlas exist, except by His
will?

The offer of a position with the lawyer Josias Quayle of London came
to Couvret while he was still in Amsterdam, where he was seeking
safe passage from the Continent. One Daem, a Frisian mercenary,

delivered the message to him at *het Teken van de Eik*, the Sign of the Oak, an inn Couvret had chosen more for security than comfort, a decision his bones had come to regret. Of Josias Quayle, Daem could tell Couvret little, except that he was one of many English Protestants that felt compelled to extend the hand of charity to their suffering Huguenot brothers and sisters. Daem urged Couvret not to reject Quayle's assistance, reminding him that he was a wanted man. As a spy and enforcer for the Protestant Henry of Navarre, Couvret had Catholic blood on his hands, and was rumored to have been involved in the murder of the virulently anti-Huguenot Henry I of Guise, and his brother, Louis Cardinal de Guise, in December 1588, a rumor that Daem repeated to Couvret at the Oak. Couvret had offered Daem no reply to the allegation, which the latter took as a tacit admission of guilt.

Yet Daem was not to be trusted. He would take money from any side, and it was not apparent whose gold was currently lending weight to his purse. Upon making inquiries – for although hunted, and cornered in a foreign city, he had lost none of his skills as an intelligencer – Couvret subsequently learned that Daem had come to Amsterdam on the trail of a clerk named Van Agteren. It was this same Van Agteren who had first told Couvret of the Fractured Atlas, although Couvret saw no reason to share with Daem his knowledge of the man.

Even had Couvret been disinclined to believe Van Agteren's account of a book that could seemingly alter its own contents, and reflect its environment in the manner of a mirror; even had he doubted Van Agteren's story of the death of his lover, torn apart by an unseen force linked to the Atlas; even had he not himself glimpsed a dark form, like a shadow granted independence of its source, in the vicinity of the Oak before Van Agteren's sudden departure, and later detected a similar presence below decks on the *Orcades* as it carried him to sanctuary in England, one that had left its mark in the form of the shredded primitive drapes on the berth opposite his own; still Couvret could have identified the malevolence of the Atlas as soon as he discovered it among his possessions during the crossing. Van Agteren, he knew, must have placed the book there in an effort to save himself from it, and by doing so had cursed Couvret.

In his rooms by Holborn, Couvret now recalled picking up the Atlas. He had sensed its otherness, and felt he was handling, not an inanimate object, but some living entity that pulsed faintly under the pressure of his palm; and this was before he opened the book and perceived the hold of the ship being replicated before him on a previously blank vellum page, as though some unseen hand were assiduously recording what had so suddenly been revealed to sight. As if this were not strange enough, Couvret's brief examination of the ink, or whatever other substance was being used to create the impression, indicated that it did not appear to be on the surface of the vellum but *within* it. Sometimes it manifested itself as strange writing, at others as unfamiliar constellations, or the lineaments of continents as yet unmapped.

And all the time, it pulsed warmly.

Van Agteren had tried to destroy this book, and failed. Faced with a similar challenge Couvret briefly considered throwing it overboard, but something lingered in the dark, and the damaged drapes were a reminder of its threatening and otherworldly physicality. Were Couvret to attempt harm to the Atlas, it would not be tolerated; of this he was certain. So Couvret concealed the book between the baseboards of an old Dutch chest, which he assumed to be part of the ship's cargo, if not its furnishings. He placed with it a Bible, in the hope that God might succeed where man had failed. As he disembarked, he did his best to put the Atlas from his mind, and in this way came to London, and entered the orbit of the lawyer Quayle.

Two days later, upon returning to his lodgings, Couvret found that persons unknown had delivered the old Dutch chest to his rooms. Hidden between the baseboards was the Atlas, but it was no longer wrapped in a muslin shirt, as he had left it, and the Bible was gone, although the base of the chest was sprinkled with ash and fragments of burned paper.

Couvret had lifted the Atlas. A drop of blood exploded on the cover and instantly vanished, as though absorbed by the deeper red of its bindings. Another fell, and a third, as Couvret felt the blood coursing down his face. He scrambled for the little sheet of polished metal that served as his mirror, and discovered he had begun to bleed from the eyes. Moments later, the pain commenced, and he understood that this was his punishment for trying to rid himself of the book. Couvret screamed, but no one came, even though the sounds must have been audible to many. His sight became obscured, but he managed to inch his way to his bed, where he lay until the pain passed, and was relieved not to find himself blind by the end of it.

'I'm sorry,' he said. 'I'm so sorry. I won't do it again.'

But he could not have said to whom he was speaking, beyond the Atlas itself.

Josias Quayle did not involve himself in criminal cases. He eschewed any such dealings, preferring to limit himself to matters pertaining to wills, the transfer of property, and business transactions of the most intractable and complex of natures – the more recondite and involved, the better. He kept only one clerk, named Kenge, who was as sparing with speech as a miser was with money, and acted as guardian of his master's door.

At first Couvret could not understand why Quayle should have seen fit to offer him more than temporary shelter, especially given the differences between the legal systems in France and England. But Quayle, he discovered, acted on behalf of English gentlemen with interests far beyond the shores of their own island. With the French political situation in such turmoil, Quayle was grateful to have someone with knowledge of its institutions, as well as business and familial connections that might be exploited to the benefit of his clients – and, indeed, Quayle himself, since what benefited the patron also profited the lawyer. Couvret might have been a Huguenot, and a fugitive, but he had spent many years moving among the wealthy and powerful, who are always seeking to secure, and improve, their position. For such individuals, the most fanatical of them excepted, a man's religious beliefs were less important than his usefulness and trustworthiness, to which the Jews could volubly attest. Profit knows no color, and no creed. Thanks to his network of confidantes – and aided by the growing unpopularity of the Catholic League in France, and the ascent of Henry of Navarre to the French throne in 1594 – Couvret made himself invaluable to the firm of Quayle, and within four years, having immersed himself in the English legal system, was adjudged fit to join the great brotherhood of English lawyers. He was simultaneously, and unexpectedly, made a partner in the firm of Quayle, an arrangement celebrated with a great feast in the Old Hall of Lincoln's Inn.

Yet even as the legal community of London toasted his success, Couvret was struggling to conceal his unhappiness. Quayle had requested seven years of service from him in return for the provision of sanctuary, an agreement never committed to paper yet one that Couvret, as a gentleman, had no intention of breaching. No one could say that Quayle had not behaved admirably, even generously, toward him. Couvret was now a partner, with comfortable quarters adjacent to the firm's offices. He had money, and respect. He was also engaged in the cautious circling of a widow named Thomasin Hockins, whose daughter, Christabell, was barely days older than Couvret's own Jeanne would have been, had she survived. He was, he would readily have admitted, the envy of many a man in London.

But Quayle had changed, or perhaps some aspect of his character, previously concealed, was now making itself apparent to his new partner. Couvret had long known that Quayle was not greatly loved in Chancery, being regarded as cold and unyielding even by the norms of his profession. This made him popular with his clients, the majority of whom were of a similar nature to the lawyer. But at the French Church on Threadneedle Street, and the Strangers' Church at Austin Friars, where Protestants from the Continent came to gather, worship, and exchange gossip, Couvret had long heard darker rumors of Quayle, principal among them being that he was a secret occultist.

Couvret initially dismissed these whispers as hearsay. By then he had been working with Quayle for almost two years, and had detected no indication of any such interests. Yet the seed of doubt was sown, and the rumors grew increasingly persistent. More than once was Couvret advised to sever his relationship with Quayle for fear that he might become tainted by association. Accusations of sorcery could not only undermine his position, but might lead him to torture and death.

Yet Couvret remained loyal to the man who had offered him sanctuary, and it never once occurred to him that Quayle might have an interest in securing the Atlas.

For the most part, Couvret had largely ceased to be troubled by the Atlas. It occasionally intruded on his thoughts, and sometimes on his dreams, but days, even weeks might go by without his reflecting upon the fact of its existence. After his first four months in London, he had entrusted it for safekeeping to one Gardiol, a Huguenot from Provence who kept a book stall at St Paul's, enjoining him only to keep it wrapped in its coverings, and never to admit to its presence in his home. Gardiol, who was aware of Couvret's past as an intelligencer, assumed it to be some record obtained in the course of this work, and decided it would be better if he remained ignorant of its contents. He stored it behind loose bricks in his cellar, along with certain political tracts that might well have seen him hanged, drawn and quartered for treason had they been discovered.

Thus the situation might have continued – the book hidden, the partnership achieved, marriage to a wealthy widow completing the picture – had not Quayle, as the lawyers drank their toast to the new partner, and the Old Hall echoed with chatter and laughter, leaned close to Couvret, and whispered in his right ear, 'What know you of an atlas . . . ?'

Gardiol poured a glass of *jenever* for himself, and one for Couvret. A candle, the sole illumination in the room, flickered on the table between them, itself the only surface not encumbered by books, papers, and vellum, along with assorted quills, inks, and waxes. Gardiol supplemented his income by law-writing – the copying or creation of legal documents – and Couvret encouraged Quayle to engage him for such tasks whenever possible. It was no great imposition, since all of Chancery declared Gardiol's work to be superior to that of any other, in every respect.

'You seem ill at ease, my friend,' said Gardiol.

'I think I was followed here,' said Couvret.

'By whom?'

'I don't know.' He took a sip of the *jenever*. 'I don't believe it was a man.'

'A woman, then.'

'Nor a woman either, nor cat nor dog.'

Couvret had not glimpsed the shadow in years, not since the *Orcades*. Now he had seen it three times in as many days, the first as he returned from the Old Hall through the winter darkness, Quayle's words still echoing, as surely as though the lawyer himself were continuing to whisper them from the shadows.

'What know you of an atlas?'

And Couvret had been so discomfited by Quayle's inquiry that he had answered wrongly, so very wrongly. He should have replied that he was familiar with many atlases, although he had never as yet owned one himself, their construction being a matter of great expertise and expense. Yet now that he was a partner, he might consider commissioning one, or perhaps just a print of his homeland, because he missed it still . . .

But instead he had answered, 'Nothing.'

And Quayle had known that he was lying.

Now, in Gardiol's rooms, Couvret confessed all to his friend. He gave him an account of the Atlas's discovery, and the deaths of Van Agteren's master, the scholar Schuyler, and of Schuyler's daughter, and Van Agteren's lover, Eliene, each a victim of the Atlas. He spoke to him of the events on the *Orcades*, and the chimerical presence he had felt both on the ship and, earlier, in Amsterdam. Finally, he informed him of Quayle's question in the Old Hall, and the reappearance of the shadow.

'This Van Agteren, you believed all he told you?' said Gardiol.

'Not at first. Later, I had no doubt.'

'Did you suspect him of murder?'

'Because of what befell his lover and her father? I did, and I have since established that others also suspected him of involvement in those deaths, because he was already being hunted when we met. We had that much in common. It was what drew him to me.'

'And what changed your mind about these matters?'

'The shadow. The Atlas.'

'The same book that you entrusted to me?'

'Yes, and I'm sorry for it.'

Gardiol refilled Couvret's glass; fear did little for a man's appetite, but much for his thirst.

'You know that I have long warned you about Quayle,' said Gardiol.

'You and others, although you accept his money readily enough.'

Gardiol took the sally in good spirit. 'I don't believe gold and silver take on the aspect of their possessors. Even if they did, it would cease upon any transfer of ownership.'

'That's expedient reasoning.'

'But necessary, if one is not to die in penury. And before you resume your sermonizing, let it be recorded that you have accepted more than gold from Quayle: you have bound yourself to him, and share his sins in the eyes of many.'

'In yours?'

'Not in mine. We have known each other too long for that, but you have exposed yourself to his humors. Quayle suffers from an excess of black and yellow biles, and such a combination of choler and melancholy promises only harm to those around him. It may be why he has never married.'

'He has a woman.'

'He has a whore,' Gardiol corrected.

Her name was Zenobia, although Couvret had cause to doubt it was her given name, and she had been sharing Quayle's bed for some months. Zenobia was small, dark, and barely nineteen. She appeared delicate enough to be snapped like a twig by a pair of moderately strong hands, but one of Couvret's sources claimed that, some years earlier, she had killed a merchant in Cheapside when he tried to rape her, and he may not have been the first man to suffer at her hands, or the last. She might even have been charged with murder in the Cheapside incident had it not been for Quayle's intervention. There were suggestions that Quayle had been grooming her since her child-hood – as ward, lover, and more.

'I don't believe she is a whore,' said Couvret, 'but if you feel compelled to suggest as much to her face, I'll make sure that your eulogy mentions all of your accomplishments.'

Gardiol retreated.

'What do you know of John Dee?' asked Gardiol.

'That he is, or was, the Queen's alchemist,' said Couvret, 'and if it was not for her protection, he might well have burned at the stake by now.'

'He will burn in the next world, if even half of what they say about him in this one is true. As it happens, two books of his were offered to me for sale not long ago.'

'I did not think Doctor Dee would part with his collection so easily.'

'He did not. While Dee was wandering in Europe, his library at Mortlake was vandalized, and many of his most prized books and instruments were stolen. This would have been in, oh, 1587 or 1588, I believe. The damage and the losses were only discovered upon his return, and he has been seeking the missing volumes ever since.'

'And why should this concern us?'

'The man who tried to sell them to me claimed they had been promised to him by one William Wentworth in the event of the latter's death.'

At this Couvret set aside his *jenever*. William Wentworth had formerly been among Quayle's familiars, until Couvret suggested it might be wiser to dispense with his services, Wentworth having a reputation for gross illegality that sat uneasily with the duties of a lawyer. Quayle had agreed, albeit with a show of reluctance, although Couvret thought he might secretly have been seeking an excuse to rid himself of this creature. Wentworth took his dismissal badly, although he did not live long enough to nurse a grudge. Within days, he was found poisoned in his room.

'Wentworth did not strike me as one inclined to make bequests of books,' said Couvret. 'He could neither read nor write.'

'And yet it seems he held in his garret part of Dee's collection.'

'How?'

'It is my conviction that your partner might have engaged Wentworth to ransack Dee's library.'

'Quayle? To what end?'

'Because Quayle was searching for a book.'

'And he thought Dee might have it?'

'Yes, or some other volumes in Dee's collection that might point the way to it.'

'But why steal so much? Why ransack Dee's accommodation?'

'To disguise the true purpose of the raid.'

Couvret contemplated this.

'Then what happened to the rest of the stolen volumes?'

'I expect Wentworth was told to dispose of them, probably by burning, or throwing them in the Thames,' said Gardiol. 'Naturally, being of a criminal disposition, he was disinclined to do so, or not without first secreting away a few trifles for his troubles. Why, I cannot say.'

'I can,' said Couvret, 'although it's only speculation. Wentworth may have been an illiterate, but he was envious of those who were lettered, and retained an odd fascination for books and manuscripts. I noticed the way he would stare at the contents of Quayle's shelves. In an odd way, he understood their value. I think it might have pleased him to have had some such volumes in his possession, even if their contents were destined to remain an enigma to him.'

The candle had grown markedly lower. Gardiol, being unwilling to plunge them into darkness, even temporarily, secured another, and lit it from the first.

'Poisoning is an unusual death for such a man,' he said.

'And poison is a woman's weapon,' said Couvret.

'I've heard it said that Wentworth and Zenobia might have been brother and sister.'

'Quayle once told me they were both bastards, but added nothing of a blood connection.'

'Which is not entirely to give the lie to the tale. Different brood mares, or so the gossips would have it, but the same sire.'

'No great love between them,' said Couvret, 'if one could poison the other.'

'None at all, one might say. Let us suppose that Quayle sent his consort to kill Wentworth, possibly in order to silence him for fear that bitterness at his treatment should loosen his tongue. What I do not understand is why Quayle should only now have begun to ask you about the Atlas. After all, you have been in his service for a number of years.'

'Because he had no reason to question me about it,' said Couvret. 'As far as he was concerned, I was a young lawyer, and nothing more.'

'He did not offer you employment because he already knew you had the book?'

Couvret shook his head. 'I now believe it was bad luck. Quayle has sometimes set me to tracing Huguenots during my time with him, often without sharing the reason for his interest. Most recently, these searches have centered on men who passed through the Lowlands. Now I know why: Quayle must have learned that Van Agteren came into contact with a Huguenot refugee in those lands, to whom he passed on the Atlas. It must have come as a shock to Quayle to discover only recently that he might have been sheltering that same Huguenot under his roof for so long.'

'But you never chose to mention your knowledge of Van Agteren to Quayle?'

'No. I can offer no reason other than that it seemed to me unwise.'

'In light of what you knew of Quayle's more cabbalistic interests?'

'Perhaps.'

'You are being disingenuous.'

'I was being careful.'

'And Quayle never spoke of Van Agteren to you?'

'No, or not until these last few days.'

'Because now he is certain that you are the very man he has been seeking.'

Couvret's skin felt clammy, and even the slight heat of the candle seemed to prickle. A hundred minor incidents over the previous months – a glance from Quayle here, a word there – started to make new sense.

'Yes,' said Couvret. 'I see it all.'

'And when he raised the subject with you, you gave yourself away.'

'I fear it is so.'

They both lapsed into silence.

'Tell me more of this shadow that haunts you,' said Gardiol.

Couvret tried to find the right words, but it was as difficult as describing smoke.

'It is taller than a man, although it has something of the aspect of one,' he said. 'The head is overly large, and distorted in shape, as though by some malformation of the skull. Yet –'

'Go on.'

'Yet sometimes I think its form is not consistent,' said Couvret. 'Once or twice I have caught sight of a pallor within, like a withered, gray child that has found a way to cloak itself in night. It makes no sense, I know, but what of this makes any sense?'

Gardiol reached across the table, and gripped Couvret's hands, a gesture of reassurance that served also to stop them from trembling.

'I should like to look upon this Atlas,' he said.

'No!' Couvret yanked back his hands. 'You must not.'

'Why? How can I help you if I'm speaking in ignorance of the subject?'

'Because the book is alive,' said Couvret. 'No, that's not right. Better to say that some consciousness has found a way to inhabit it, or use it as a window into our world. It sees, and then registers, its surroundings. Once it has done so, it seeks to replicate them in its pages. I have witnessed it done.'

'And what then?'

'I do not know, but the shadow and the book are linked. Were you to open the book, I fear you might bring whatever is following me down upon yourself. For the present, I alone am afflicted. I do not want company in my suffering.'

'Then why not simply surrender the Atlas to Quayle? It's clear that he wants it, and believes you may know of its whereabouts.'

'Do you think he would let me live, once I did so?'

Gardiol considered this.

'Possibly not,' he said. 'That was foolish of me.'

'But there is more.' Couvret reached beneath his shirt and withdrew a plain wooden cross, secured around his neck by a strip of leather. 'The Atlas is no instrument of God. I admit that its existence has sometimes caused me to doubt my faith, but never to abandon it entirely. Without faith, I am nothing. If I give the book to Quayle, I believe I may render myself complicit in some great evil, and be damned for it.'

'Then what will you do? You cannot destroy it. You told me so yourself.'

'Neither can it stay here, in these apartments. Quayle knows you and I are intimates, and that you are a man of learning. He will quickly realize that if I were to have entrusted the book to anyone, it would be to you.'

Gardiol rose.

'It's late,' he said, 'and tiredness will only cloud our judgment. Let us both sleep on the problem. We are wise fellows, and with two such heads, some solution must surely present itself.'

They embraced, and Couvret returned to his lodgings. He watched the dark as he walked, but the only shadow that trailed after him was his own.

Over the days that followed, Couvret did his best to act naturally around Quayle. He was aided by the fact that the firm was currently embroiled in a difficult and complex inheritance case, the legal costs for which were steadily consuming the very estate over which a rogues' gallery of relatives was fighting, with the consequence that all were likely to end their days in debt to the lawyers. But once or twice, as he worked on the latest sheaf of claims and counterclaims, Couvret caught Quayle contemplating him in a way that gave him to under-stand the subject of the Atlas had not been forgotten, nor his response to the broaching of the subject.

On the third night following his conversation with Gardiol, Couvret woke to find his dead wife in the room with him. A smell of rot had caused him to emerge from sleep, and when he opened his eyes, Marianne was standing at the end of his bed. She was withered, and a gray-green mold covered much of her face and torso. Her belly had been opened, and she was holding something small and red in her hands. She extended it toward him, so that he might know it for what it was.

'*I was pregnant when you left me,*' she said. '*I did not realize it then, but I was growing large with child by the time they came to find you. They asked me where you were hiding, but I could not tell them, so they each took a turn with me before cutting our baby from my womb. Look! Can you see? It was a boy, a little boy.*'

And as she spoke, the dead infant opened its mouth. It fixed its lips to what remained of her left breast, and she gave it suck.

'*We are in torment,*' she said, '*but it can be brought to an end.*'

Couvret did not want to enter into discourse with this phantom, but the word came despite this.

'How?'

'*Give them the book. Let it be made complete. If you ever loved me, permit it to be done.*'

Then she was no longer at the end of his bed, but by his side. She leaned down to plant a kiss upon his mouth, and Couvret woke in earnest this time, screaming and thrashing, dawn's light trickling through the drapes. He pushed the bed sheet aside, and felt wetness upon his hands.

He looked down, and saw that they were coated with mold.

That night, he returned at last to Gardiol's lodgings. He knocked, but received no answer. He tried the lock, and the door opened to his touch.

Gardiol was seated at the table in the center of the room, the candle before him long extinguished, his hands palm-down upon the wood. The floor – or the parts of it not covered by a litter of paper, and torn books – was slick with blood, and Gardiol's mouth was stuffed with crimson-stained papers. As Couvret drew nearer the body, he saw his old friend's hands had been impaled upon the table so that his finger-nails might be more easily removed, and between the mangled limbs lay his tongue and eyes. How he had finally died, Couvret could not at first tell, until he looked down and saw the redness staining Gardiol's hose at the groin, and what lay on the stool between his legs.

Couvret turned away, and was profoundly sick in the fireplace. Only when his stomach had nothing left to offer up did he return to the body. He composed himself, found a fresh candle, and commenced an examination of the scene. He did so carefully, his training as an *avocat* of the Paris Bar coming to the fore, since, unlike Quayle, he had always preferred criminal law. He had almost given up on finding anything of use when a slim object mired in the blood by Gardiol's left foot caught his eye. Couvret knelt, and removed from the gore a silver pin, of the kind used to fix one piece of a lady's wardrobe to another. Only the bottom half of the pin was bloody, indicating that it had fallen to the floor during, or soon after, Gardiol's murder. It meant a woman had been present when his friend died, and Couvret could guess her identity: Quayle's lover – no, in deference to Gardiol, Quayle's whore – Zenobia.

Couvret secured the door to Gardiol's chambers, and found the entrance to the cellar. It was cool, and unusually dry, which was why Gardiol kept many of his papers there. As in the room above, most of these now lay scattered on the ground, but the cellar wall appeared intact. Gardiol tested the bricks in the far-left corner, and they moved under the pressure, revealing three books wrapped in thick, oiled canvas to discourage the rats. The wires binding the largest of them remained intact; Gardiol had resisted the urge to view the book for himself, but then he had always been strong-willed – sufficient to endure torture and mutilation at the hands of Zenobia rather than give up the Atlas because, like Couvret, he was a man of faith.

But where was God while Gardiol's lifeblood was flowing from him? To this, Couvret had no answer.

He unwrapped the canvas, exposing the Atlas for the first time in years. He laid his hand upon it, and felt the familiar pulsing, but fainter than before, as of a sleeping animal. As Gardiol had suggested, Couvret had slept on the problem – at least before some simulacrum of his dead spouse had appeared to him, threatening to banish sleep forever. But it was not Marianne who had come to him, not truly. The eyes were not hers. Even in death they could not have changed so, becoming serpentine in their blank hunger. And if this had not been Marianne, then the fetus in her hands could not have been that of his unborn son.

Or so he told himself, because to believe otherwise was to risk going mad.

Couvret assembled before him some of the tools of Gardiol's trade – for a seller of books must also, of necessity, become a repairer, even a maker, of his stock – but mainly the sharpest of them, the blades.

The Atlas could not be destroyed, and it would not be lost.

But perhaps it could be taken apart.

Having first sent a message to Quayle advising him of the necessity of a brief absence on personal business, Couvret commenced his labors. He worked through the night, and all of the following day and the night after. The vellum was tough, and resisted the knives, while the pages were held together by threads stronger than catgut. At times, he discovered his fingers to be damp with moisture, as though the book were weeping some vital fluid during the process of its anatomization. After many hours of labor, he had succeeded only in removing a third of the pages, and these he commenced inserting into other volumes. His duties as Henry's spy had endowed him with certain talents in the art of concealment, and using these he now hid sections of the Atlas in the spines of other books; placed them against the pastedown endpapers before adding new layers to obscure the additions; or folded them into older manuscripts, which he then sealed with wax. When he became too exhausted, he slept, before waking again to continue. He ate what food was left in Gardiol's larder: some cheese and meats, and a little stale bread. His fingers bled, and a savage pain seized his skull. Eventually, he could go on no longer, for to remain in Gardiol's home was to risk discovery, and possibly arrest on a charge of murder.

Couvret gathered the fruits of his toil, and carried them upstairs. When they were all together, he put them on the cart that Gardiol used to sell his wares, and added to them as many more intact books from his friend's collection as the cart could hold. Only the Atlas, now much reduced, did he keep separate, returning it to its canvas and placing it in one of Gardiol's cloth satchels, which he slung over his shoulder.

Nearly two days had passed since his discovery of Gardiol's remains. The old man had started to decay, and flies buzzed around the corpse. Someone would soon come to investigate the smell, and it would be best for Couvret if he were long gone by then. He wheeled the cart into the street, and summoned one of the street children to him, ordering him to assemble a dozen of his peers. When they arrived, he shared between them what coins he had, and instructed them to take a handful of books and papers each, to be dispersed among the booksellers at St Paul's, and on Paternoster Row, but with no indication of their source. Others were to be left at the houses of the wealthy by the Thames, between Westminster and London. The boys took the books, as many as each could carry, and vanished into the warrens of the city.

At that instant, Couvret's eyes began to bleed, as the Atlas, already wounded by its disassembly, sensed its further dispersion. He staggered into the laneway by Gardiol's dwelling, bumping into a stranger along the way, who shouted after him in irritation, but Couvret kept moving. He fell to his knees in a puddle of water, and got back to his feet, but by now he was seeing the world through a veil of red. He heard his wife call his name, and knew that this time it was truly she, because the voice was full of love. He followed the sound of it, and smelled the river, but by now his whole body burned with pain, and his clothing was covered with pinpricks of blood as he hemorrhaged from every pore. Only then did he realize that he no longer had the Atlas. The strap of the satchel must have broken at some point, the Atlas falling with it, and he had failed to notice this in his agonies.

His vision darkened. He believed himself at last to be going blind, but could still make out the shapes of buildings and houses, and the bank of the river before him. Then all grew cold, and the darkness took on a new form, one reminiscent of a man but much larger, and topped by a deformed skull on which Couvret could perceive a pair of blunt horns. Within the shadow glowed a shape that might almost have been mistaken for that shape of a pale, deformed child.

Couvret heard his wife's voice telling him not to be afraid, although he could not help but be so. The darkness stretched out a finger to him, the member hardening to the consistency of bone as it pierced his chest and entered his body.

He called out to God, but God did not answer.

Couvret's heart was rent asunder as the pain of his old life was ended, and a new torment commenced.

XLII

The Northumbria investigation team gathered shortly after 8 a.m. to go through Sisterson's autopsy findings, and the actions for the day, including the ongoing effort to establish Romana Moon's movements in the days leading up to her death. Priestman left the best – or worst – until last, when she passed around the set of *misbaha*, which she now knew to be the correct term for Muslim prayer beads. Sisterson, having completed the *coup de théâtre* to his satisfaction, had given her a long disquisition on the *misbaha* before entrusting them to her care. He was, Priestman concluded, a very unusual man.

Most of those present recognized the *misbaha* for what they were, and anyone who didn't was quickly brought up to speed. It was left to Hynes to encapsulate the thoughts of everyone present.

'Shit,' he said. Which was also what the chief superintendent had said when Priestman told him about the beads, variations on the same word subsequently being offered by various DCIs and other senior officers. Two possibilities existed: either Romana Moon had been killed by a Muslim who wanted to signal a motive for the murder, or someone was trying to cause a great deal of religious, political, and social unrest.

'I spoke to Nabih before I came in,' said Priestman. Nabih Uddin was one of a handful of Muslim detectives on the force. He was not yet part of the Romana Moon investigation, but the discovery of the *misbaha* meant that was about to change. 'He said it was unlikely a devout Muslim would have left a set of beads in a woman's body, but he also suggested that a devout Muslim wouldn't have killed her to begin with.'

Hynes, who had dealt with the city's Muslim community in

the past, held the bag up to the light. A *misbaha* contained either thirty-three or ninety-nine beads. In the case of the latter, two additional beads separated the whole into units of thirty-three, enabling three prayers to be counted thirty-three times. The *misbaha* in the bag was the smaller set, and looked both cheap and relatively new to Hynes; he could detect no signs of wear and tear, or the discoloration that might have come from regular use.

'What are you thinking?' Priestman asked.

'They look fresh out of the box,' said Hynes. 'Perhaps he didn't want to use his own. Funny how sentimental people can be.'

One of the younger DCs frowned. Hynes's sense of humor was an acquired taste – if you were unlucky.

'Or,' Hynes continued, 'the killer, wanting to stir things up, just went into a shop and bought himself a set. Mind you, if our boy was smart, he'll just have found them on the Internet.'

But Priestman had learned never to underestimate the stupidity of criminals, which meant a canvass of sources for prayer beads would be required. This would be time-consuming. Newcastle upon Tyne alone had sixteen mosques, most of them around Elswick and Arthur's Hill to the northwest, along with God – or Allah – alone knew how many ancillary shops and services.

'I'm going to talk to Nabih later,' said Priestman. 'I'll see what he has on his plate, and what can be postponed or reassigned. Once he's up and running, we'll have him liaise with the neighborhood inspectors and their PCs on the ground to find out if anyone has been making more-than-usually hostile noises. But' – she paused to make sure she had their attention – 'the reason for the inquiry doesn't leave this room, not yet. Nabih knows, but he'll keep his mouth shut. If this gets out, we'll be dealing with fascists as well as religious lunatics. So: softly, softly. Am I clear?'

She waited for the muted chorus of agreement to die down. She trusted them to stay quiet because it wasn't hard to visualize a situation involving the local far-right activists – of whom there was no shortage – squaring off against the Muslim population, and even the overtime wasn't worth that.

'Right, then,' she said. 'Let's get started.'

Hynes was closest to the door. He was just about to open it and make a break for freedom when Nabih Uddin appeared, blocking his way. From the look on his face, Uddin wasn't the bearer of good news.

'What is it?' said Priestman.

Uddin pointed to the *misbaha* on her desk.

'Romana Moon,' he said. 'She wasn't the first.'

XLIII

Holmby limped around his kitchen, trying to put together his breakfast. He'd already spilled tea on the floor while hopping from the sink to the table, and decided that he really needed to have a think about the most efficient way to get around his apartment, or else he'd spend the day cleaning up after himself. He remained uncomfortable with the crutch, but he'd have to get used to it if he needed to go any distance. He didn't want to become a prisoner in his own home, reduced to spying on his neighbors like James Stewart in *Rear Window*.

In truth, he suspected he'd be mobile sooner than he'd suggested to Sellars. He ran a couple of times a week, and was familiar with his own rate of recovery from minor injuries. This one was more serious, but he remained certain he'd be moving well in a week or so. He had some meetings lined up, but could postpone the more distant of them, and Skype the important ones. Even with the BMW automatic, he didn't want to drive more than he had to, and trains were a nightmare at the best of times.

The local BBC reports had nothing fresh on the Romana Moon investigation, and neither had Sky News. He checked the newspaper stories on the Internet, but Romana had already been relegated to Other News, if she figured at all. Holmby experienced a sense of outrage on her behalf. What was the world coming to, he thought, when a young woman could be slaughtered like a pig out on the moors, and yet the media grew bored with her after just a few days? He was almost tempted to write a letter to the editors.

But as he sipped his tea, he also noticed that his memories of his time with Romana Moon were becoming less vivid and more distant, just like those reports. It was distressing. He didn't want to lose her too soon. She'd been his first, and these things were important, so he sat at his kitchen table and worked hard to recall her, bringing to mind every detail he could, working step-by-step from beginning to end. It helped, but he remained dissatisfied.

So instead, he began thinking about the next girl.

As it happened, Sellars had also decided not to work that day. He'd left home shortly after 7 a.m. as usual, but called in sick as soon as he found somewhere quiet to stop.

Sellars enjoyed his job. It wasn't like the usual courier and delivery nonsense, with too many drops to be made in too little time. Carenor was a specialist service: it looked after the transport of everything from fine art and gemstones to rare books and legal documents, and charged a premium as a guarantee of discretion and security. Many of its vehicles didn't even bear the company name, and its drivers were recruited for their intelligence as much as their skill behind the wheel. Carenor had one central hub, in Manchester, and two subsidiary operations in London and Glasgow, but drivers went wherever they were needed, so Sellars, although based in Manchester, might just as easily find himself driving to Cornwall or Inverness as Bradford or Sheffield, as well as to the Continent. He preferred the longer trips: the mileage and subsistence allowances were generous, and it gave him more time to sit in the van or truck and listen to the radio, follow an audiobook or, most recently, learn Spanish. He already had French from school, and a little German, just enough to get by. It was one of the reasons why Carenor gave him so many of the European runs, as few of the other drivers boasted much proficiency in other languages.

With the call made to the office, he inserted the new SIM into a used Nokia he'd picked up cheap at a CeX store, and drove to the M6. He wasn't in the mood for audiobooks, or *Como está?*, so he listened to Radio 3 along the way. It calmed his nerves, but not by much. The more he considered Holmby, the more problematical the man became. Finally, he stopped at the first motorway services with a Costa, where he ate a bacon roll and flicked through a discarded copy of the *Daily Mirror*, but mostly continued monitoring the news reports on his phone. Northumbria Police had scheduled a press conference on the Romana Moon killing for that morning, and shortly after 10 a.m. the first details began to seep onto the Internet. Sellars read them with a rising sense of dread. There was no mention of the prayer beads, which didn't surprise him – the police would sit on that for as long as they could – but an appeal was being issued to hospitals and clinics in Northumbria and the surrounding counties for information on anyone over the age of sixteen who might have been treated for a serious sprain, or a fracture of the ankle or leg, during the previous forty-eight hours.

Sellars hid his face in his hands, and closed his eyes. When he opened them again, two new messages had appeared on his phone.

The first was from Holmby, which he decided to ignore.

The second he didn't ignore, because the sender wouldn't have liked that.

No, not one little bit.

XLIV

D S Hynes and DC Lisa Gackowska were taking care of interviews at Larkin-Brook Academy, the school at which Romana
Moon had taught, having first given the nod to Cleveland Police
that they'd be on their patch. It was a dull, overcast morning to
be entering a moribund part of a city that routinely made lists
of the least favorable conurbations in which to live. Kids growing
up in Middlesbrough, Hynes reflected, could already feel the boot
of inequality pressing down on their necks by the time they started
to read and write, not helped by the fact that half the city's
schools were fucked anyway.

If Larkin-Brook Academy wasn't the worst of them, Hynes
remained content to leave the winner unvisited, even if it seemed
unlikely that Larkin-Brook could possibly expect much serious
competition. Its students scored, on average, half a grade lower
than their peers in exam results across the board, but performed
much better when it came to rates of teenage pregnancy and early
criminal behavior. The school was predominantly male, which
probably didn't help matters, Hynes being of the opinion that
young women generally exerted a moderating influence on teenage
boys, although any teenage girls at Larkin-Brook had their work
cut out, judging by the likely lads congregating in the schoolyard
as the two officers arrived. The school buildings themselves were
colored dirty beige trimmed with a dirtier white, and the grounds
had the unkempt appearance of wasteland.

'You think our car will still be in one piece when we finish?'
Gackowska asked. She was slim and blond, and looked like a
stiff breeze might carry her out to sea. If any breeze ever had the
temerity to do so, Hynes was pretty certain it would return
Gackowska to dry land pretty sharpish, while apologizing for

any inconvenience caused and promising not to do it again. Gackowska had a stillness about her that could be unnerving, which was why Hynes liked conducting interviews with her by his side. It drew out guilt the way a magnet attracted iron filings.

'That'd be getting off lightly,' said Hynes. 'We'll be lucky if it hasn't been nicked, or set on fire.'

'Who was Larkin-Brook?'

'No idea,' said Hynes, as he watched a lanky streak of piss with bad hair launch his schoolbag at the legs of some fleeing unfortunate, taking him down with pinpoint accuracy. 'It could be two people, in which case they can share the blame.'

He and Gackowska got out of the car. Someone made pig noises, and Hynes thought it might have been the school-bag-throwing streak of piss. Even if he wasn't the one, he had the look of a self-professed alpha about him, or what passed for it under the circumstances. Hynes made a beeline for him.

'All right?' said Hynes. 'Nice day for it.'

'Fuck off.'

The kid was playing to the crowd, and they were lapping it up. Hynes had made the right choice.

'What's your name?' said Hynes.

'I just told you: F—'

'Yeah, "Fuck off." I heard you the first time.'

The schoolbag was sitting at the boy's feet. Quick as a flash, Hynes picked it up and tossed it to Gackowska.

'Hey, you can't do that!'

'I just saw you assault another boy with that bag. It's evidence, Mr –'

'Clifton,' said Gackowska, reading out the name on a battered exercise book. 'Ryan Clifton.'

'There you go: Ryan Clifton, aka Fuck Off. Well, you see that car, Ryan Clifton?'

Hynes indicated the unmarked Skoda, and waited for a reply. It took a while in coming, because Clifton's demeanor had already changed. He was now clearly wishing he hadn't opened his mouth, or thrown the bag, or even got out of bed that morning. Eventually, he managed to summon a single syllable, but the effort cost him.

'Yeah.'

'Good,' said Hynes. 'It doesn't look like much, that car, but I like it a lot, and exactly the way it is. If something were to happen to it, no matter how minor, I'd take it very badly, very badly indeed. I'd feel compelled to find someone to blame, and because I'm a busy man, I wouldn't have time to look very far, if you catch my meaning. So, Ryan Clifton, I'm entrusting you with the wellbeing of this police vehicle. Consider it an introduction to civic responsibility. If there's even a dead leaf on it when we get back, I'll become such a part of your life you'll think you came out of the womb with me attached.'

Hynes took the bag from Gackowska and threw it back to Clifton.

'Have a nice day at school,' said Hynes. 'I hope it's fucking filled with learning.'

V

This oratory looks evil. With herbs overgrown
It fits well that fellow transformed into green
to follow here his devotions in the Devil's fashion.
Sir Gawain and the Green Knight
(trans. J.R.R. Tolkien)

XLV

Like so many of England's great cathedrals, Worcester had begun its existence as a Catholic place of worship: first, in the seventh century, as a priory, of which no trace could now be seen; then as a Benedictine monastery in the tenth century, of which the crypt and certain other elements persisted; until finally, in the sixteenth century, Henry VIII put his mark on it, and Worcester succumbed to the forces of the Reformation. Its age meant the cathedral reflected a variety of architectural styles, from its Gothic bays and medieval chantry, to the Norman crypt and Chapter House.

It was near the door to this Chapter House that Sellars now lingered. Most visitors to Worcester came to view the tomb of King John, but Sellars had little interest in old English kings. Instead, he was gazing upon a stone effigy in the cloisters: the image of a face surrounded by leaves and branches, the roots of which were lost in the figure's mouth and nostrils.

A Green Man.

The Green Man had first begun speaking to Sellars when he was still in his teens. He'd always been a quiet, solitary child, even before the IRA tried to kill his mum and him, and adolescence was hard. He started hearing voices when he was thirteen, but he didn't tell anyone about them. His mum and dad had separated when he was still barely able to walk, and his dad had dropped out of his life and gone to live in Australia, where he started a new family. He sent money back, but only sporadically, and never enough of it to make life any easier. His mum did her best for her son, and he'd loved her dearly, although she was never the same after the bomb went off. It did something to her nerves, and might also have done something to Sellars's own mind, although he tried not to dwell on this possibility. She became afraid to go into the city, and then afraid to go further than the shops at the end of their street, before becoming afraid even to leave her own home. By the time she had to be committed, Sellars was eighteen, and could look after himself.

But by then he'd also put a face to the voices he heard. His class had been taken on a trip to Worcester, where he'd stood before the Green Man, this symbol of pagan worship in a Christian church, a sop to the nature-spirit beliefs of the peasantry in an age when a good or bad crop was the difference between living and dying. There, before this ancient god, he listened as the babble in his head rose to a cacophony before being silenced forever, and what came after was one voice. He'd fallen to his knees before it, even as the other kids in the class pointed and laughed, although they stopped when blood began to pour from his nose and ears, and his eyes turned white as he collapsed unconscious on the stones. After that there'd been a detour to a hospital, and a diagnosis of ruptures to the eardrum and septum, the cause of which could not be determined. Sellars didn't care. All he knew was that he was no longer frightened, and the voice of a god now spoke to him.

In the years that followed, Sellars had more than once prostrated himself in the hollow once occupied by the Blessed Chapel of the Congregation of Adam Before Eve & Eve Before Adam on the Hexhamshire Moors, his face against the grass, listening as though for some exhalation deep in the earth from the same deity. He'd heard nothing, yet still experienced a feeling of religious ecstasy comparable, he imagined, to that enjoyed by pilgrims at the Church of the Nativity in Bethlehem, or the Church of the Holy Sepulchre in Jerusalem: a sense of walking in the footsteps of the sublime, and being at only one remove from one's god.

Then, some years back, he had taken Lauren to the United States. Lauren was already pregnant with Kelly at the time, but not so far gone that travel was in any way uncomfortable for her. She wanted to go to Florida, but Sellars convinced her that she'd enjoy New York more. He'd never been to America before, never mind New York, and had his own reasons for wanting to visit the northeast of the country, but he'd been right about the city. It was Lauren's kind of place, full of museums and art galleries, and so big and busy that she could lose herself in its flow and not be noticed as she took in everything. Sellars kept her company at some of the sights, although Lauren was happy to let him go to a bar, or the big clothing stores, while she wandered the Met, and MoMA, and the Cloisters. Afterward, she'd come back and tell him of what she'd seen, and he never got bored of listening to her, not once. Had he gone with her, he'd have lost the will to live after half an hour, but something of her enthusiasm communicated itself to him, and he saw these paintings, sculptures, and buildings through her eyes, and recreated them in new forms.

Sellars thought that he had never loved Lauren more than he did during their week in New York. When he caught glimpses of them reflected in shop windows, or the mirrors of bars, he saw the couple they might have been, and a future they might have enjoyed, but only if he were someone else. Perhaps that alternative version was out there, somewhere, in one of the parallel universes he had come to believe existed. He hoped so. It helped him to think there could be a variant of himself that was not beyond salvation.

When they were done with New York, they hired a car and headed north, stopping off in Boston for a few days before moving on to Maine. By a circuitous route, and with Vermont as a final destination, they came to a small town in central Maine, as though by accident rather than design, where they stopped for lunch. Sellars left Lauren reading a book in a coffee shop while he went and stretched his legs, just to have some time alone. She didn't mind. She knew his ways by then. Every day or two he needed some solitude, and she'd quickly learned not to take it personally. It was just in his nature. As long as she had a book, she was content to let him do as he pleased.

So Sellars gently abandoned her to a novel and a cappuccino, and walked to the end of the block. He spotted the truck parked by the corner. It had been described to him in an email he'd received before they left England, although he didn't go straight up to it and open the passenger door, but instead paused by the window so the driver could see his face. The man behind the wheel was dressed in jeans and an old brown suede jacket, with the hands of someone who wasn't afraid of manual labor, all cuts and calluses. He didn't look like any cleric Sellars had ever met before, but Americans, he had already realized, were different from other folk.

'Pastor Warraner?' he said.

'That's me. You must be Mr Sellars.' Warraner reached out one of those hard hands, and the two men shook. 'Welcome to Prosperous.'

XLVI

Hynes and Gackowska weren't getting very far with the teachers at Larkin-Brook. From what they were being told, Moon got along well with the other staff, and had no particular issues with any of the pupils, or none 'beyond the usual', as a woman named Elspeth Calley put it. Calley was in her early forties, and single. She'd informed them of this right from the start, Lord knows why, except that she seemed to be inviting the two detectives to inquire further, or suggest she might somehow be at fault for her un-attached status. Calley certainly had an edge to her, Hynes thought. She wasn't unattractive, but some combination of personal and professional circumstances had served to cut away at her from the inside, and the marks were starting to show through to the skin. Mind you, she was teaching at Larkin-Brook, and had been for fourteen years. That was enough to leave scars on anyone.

'What do you mean by "the usual"?' Gackowska asked.

'You've seen this place,' said Calley. 'It's hardly Eton. There isn't a teacher here who hasn't had some damage done to a car or bike, even a house: eggs thrown, a broken window, dog shit on the doorstep. And you don't even want to know what they write on the toilet walls.'

Her arms were folded, the fingers of her right hand tapping impatiently: a smoker.

'And how did Romana Moon cope with this?'

'Pretty well, actually. Larkin-Brook hadn't poisoned her yet. She was young, idealistic, probably thought she could save a handful of them. Someone buckled the wheel on her bike once, but mostly the little bastards seemed to like her. Mind you, the caretaker didn't tell her what he scrubbed off those toilet walls about her – male *and* female.'

239

'But he told you,' said Hynes.

Calley shot him a glare, and he decided she was less attractive than he'd first thought, possibly even a genuinely nasty piece of work, but no joy could come of alienating her.

'Sorry,' said Hynes. 'I didn't mean it to sound so accusatory.'

He did, and she knew it, but they reached an unspoken agreement to let it drop. They had the measure of each other now, or Calley believed she had it of Hynes, an erroneous view he intended to do his best not to correct.

'I get told a lot of things around here,' she said. 'It's one of the privileges of long service.'

Her right hand lifted involuntarily toward her mouth, the index and middle fingers poised, but she caught herself doing it just in time.

'We could stop for few minutes,' said Hynes, 'if you'd like a cigarette.'

'Is it that obvious?'

'Takes one to know one.'

'We're not supposed to smoke on school property,' she said. 'It sets a bad example for the pupils.'

Hynes couldn't imagine how that might be possible, short of burning the place to the ground, but he could tell from Calley's tone and expression that rarely a day went by without her disposing of a cigarette butt somewhere in the environs of Larkin-Brook.

'What are they going to do?' Hynes said. 'Arrest us?'

'You can always show them your badge.'

'Actually, it's a warrant card, but it must work because I haven't been nicked yet.'

Hynes stopped just short of tipping her a cheeky wink. He saw Gackowska stare at him, and shake her head slightly in wonderment and, perhaps, disgust. He ignored her. Sometimes a man had to turn on the charm.

'Well, as long as I have police protection,' said Calley, and this time Gackowska's sigh was audible.

Hynes and Calley stood to leave.

'You all right to stay here?' Hynes asked Gackowska.

'Fine,' she said, although she didn't sound it.

'They have a library in the corner,' said Hynes, as he drew his ciggies from his pocket in anticipation. 'You can always find something improving to read.'

XLVII

In the quiet of the cathedral, Sellars remembered Pastor Warraner – the unfamiliar cadences of the man's speech, the smell of wood and sweat that filled his truck – and his own gathering anticipation as they followed the road out of Prosperous until they came to a turn-off marked PRIVATE, secured with a lock and chain.

'We're not trying to hide it,' said Warraner, as he climbed back into the truck after removing the chain, 'or not exactly. Most people don't even know it's here, because we've tried to keep it out of the tourist guides. If someone wants to visit, they can ask, and I'll always do my best to accommodate them, as long as they have a valid reason for their interest. We get a couple of historians every year, either of religion or architecture, and the occasional student of folklore. They come, ask a few questions, take some pictures, and leave again.'

The second road passed through forest until it arrived at black iron railings that encompassed the town's original cemetery, now largely fallen out of use. A gate permitted access, but this, too, was locked. As before, Warraner went to open it, but Sellars barely noticed what he was doing. His attention was focused entirely on the small, primitive chapel that stood at the center of the cemetery. Its walls were of rough-hewn gray stone, with an oak door and narrow slit windows, while its orientation was western rather than the more usual eastern orientation of Christian houses of worship.

'Is it what you expected?' Warraner asked, and Sellars wanted to say yes, yes it was, because he had seen photographs, and read accounts of its transport from Northumbria to America as ballast, and how those blocks were stored until the Familists were ready to move them into the heart of Maine, there to rebuild their house of worship just as it once had been, only for the Familists to fade away, leaving the Blessed Chapel of the Congregation of Adam Before Eve & Eve Before Adam as the sole indication they had ever existed here at all.

Or so one version of the story went, because the Familists had never really vanished. Warraner, and the secret others in the town, were testament to that.

But the church was also not as Sellars had anticipated. Its very primitiveness communicated a sense of ancient power, an impression reinforced as Warraner finished unlocking the gate and invited Sellars to enter the churchyard, so that the carvings in the upper corners of the building became visible to Sellars as he advanced, as though emerging from the stones themselves: the Green Man, in all his glory, all his malevolence.

Then Sellars was inside the chapel, with its rows of hard benches, and its absence of any Christian decoration, only four more faces, one on each wall: the Green Man in spring, summer, autumn, and winter. Sellars turned circles before the altar, taking in each one in turn, over and over, until finally he asked Warraner if he might be permitted to lie on the floor.

'Of course. Do as you please.'

So Sellars stretched out on the stones, placed his right ear to the floor, and listened. The day was still, the church was silent, and Warraner was standing unmoving by the east wall. Sellars could hear his blood pumping, and the sound of his own breathing, but nothing else. He could feel his disappointment as a kind of heat behind his eyes, and a curdling in his stomach. He had traveled all this way, just to—

And then it came.

Elspeth Calley smoked Rothmans, which were a bit strong for Hynes, so he stuck to his own Silk Cut Purple. They talked about the school, and the weather. Calley asked Hynes how long he'd been married, and he told her that he and his wife had been married for fifteen years, but together for twenty. She inquired if he was happy, and he replied that he was, because it was the truth. He didn't think she was coming on to him, or not exactly. Were he single, and were Calley in the right frame of mind, she might have consented to meet him for a drink, or something more. Mostly, though, he believed that she was lonely, and unhappy, and was genuinely curious as to why others were not.

'So,' said Hynes, 'did everybody really like Romana Moon?'

'Yes, they did. Even I liked her, I suppose, and I don't have much affection for anyone.'

'You used to chat?'

'In the staffroom, mostly. Once or twice when some of us went out for drinks together.'

'I'd been told she didn't socialize a lot with the teachers outside school.'

'Not with the teachers, no.'

She let that dangle like a hook, to see if Hynes would bite, and he did.

'Are you saying she might have been friendly with students?'

'What do you mean by "friendly"?'

'What do *you* mean by it?'

Calley took a long drag on her cigarette, and scratched at her left calf with the toe of her right shoe. She had good legs, even if the same couldn't have been said for her heart.

'I heard you put Ryan Clifton in his place,' she remarked.

'I'm sure he's a decent kid,' said Hynes, 'deep down.'

'I'm sure he isn't. He has a friend, Karl Holmby. Karl's brighter than Clifton, which wouldn't be hard, and possesses what passes for charm around here, meaning the girl sometimes comes before he does. Karl left school last year with a couple of A levels. Romana helped him a lot. I think he wanted to do well in order to impress her, and he kept the rest of the pack at bay in return, so she had an easier ride thanks to him.'

She emphasized the word 'ride', just in case Hynes had failed to catch the innuendo.

'Was she sleeping with him?'

'I don't think so, or not back then. She wasn't a fool. She enjoyed teaching, and didn't want to risk being fired – or sent to prison. But there was something between them. She knew Karl liked her, and under other circumstances she might have been inclined to take it a step further. He certainly wanted it. You could smell it off him.'

Good Christ, thought Hynes.

'And then?'

'Karl left school, and Romana left her boyfriend.'

'But the two events weren't connected,' said Hynes. 'You said Holmby left school last year, but Romana was still seeing Simon Harris until earlier this year.'

'Well, somewhere along the way she and Karl got together.'

'How do you know? Did you see them?'

'No. It was something Ryan Clifton said to me.'

'Really?'

Hynes couldn't imagine Elspeth Calley giving Ryan Clifton the time of day. In fact, it was hard to conceive of her even being willing to teach him, assuming he could be taught.

'Clifton's a vile specimen. Your lot will have to deal with him down the line, I guarantee it. Funny, his mum is lovely, and we had his older sister a few years back, and she was no trouble at all. But Ryan Clifton is a dirty bugger, and cruel with it. He's been suspended a couple of times for vandalism and bullying, although he's cunning enough to have avoided expulsion so far.

'Anyway, I had a confrontation with him about a month ago: another assignment he'd failed to deliver, which expanded into a discussion of his general behavior. Before I knew it, he was shouting, and I was shouting back. I should have known better than to engage with him on that level, but I had a headache, it had been a worse day than usual, and all I wanted was to go home and pour myself a big glass of wine.

'Eventually I just told him to get out. I probably said some things I shouldn't have, such as how he was destined to end up on the dole, or in jail, but nothing that wasn't the truth. I was sick and tired of him, but also a bit scared. He's intimidating, and has a temper. I was relieved to see him storm off, but then he stopped at the door, and when he turned back it was as though he'd sloughed off all his anger, but what was left behind was so much worse, like the muck at the bottom of a pond after the water has drained away.'

She sucked again on her cigarette, but more nervously now.

'And he said: "It's okay, Miss Calley, I won't hold it against you. When I leave here, I'll come back and give you a good fucking, if you want, just like Karl fucked Miss Moon."'

'Those were his exact words?'

'Yes.'

'You believed he was telling the truth?' said Hynes.

'I did.'

'Why?'

'Because I'd seen the way Clifton had been looking at Romana during the year, and how she tried not to catch his eye. I couldn't figure out what was behind it, but when he said that, it made sense to me.'

'Karl Holmby might have lied to Clifton about the relationship,' said Hynes. 'It wouldn't be the first time a teenage boy made claims like that in order to look big in front of his mates.'

Calley stubbed out her cigarette against the wall, and dropped the butt down a drain.

'Clifton's attitude said different, or it did to me.'

'Did you raise the subject with Romana?'

'No.'

'Why?'

'We were colleagues, not friends. It wasn't my business, really, and it was only a suspicion.'

'Did you tell anyone else, or report what Clifton said to you in the classroom?'

'No. I didn't want to get Romana into trouble. Even if it wasn't true, it would have caused all kinds of difficulties for her.'

Hynes considered all she'd told him. He'd barely smoked his own cigarette, so intently had he been listening to Calley. He tapped off the dangling ash, took a last drag, and sent the butt the way of Calley's, since it wasn't like the school had seen fit to provide a bin for the disposal of illicit ciggies. He'd need addresses for Clifton and Holmby, but he didn't want to ask the school secretary because it would immediately get around that the police were asking about them. Neither did he entirely trust Elspeth Calley. He was thawing slightly toward her, mostly because she wasn't scared to appear awful, but he had learned long ago that – shock, horror – people sometimes shared information with the police for entirely self-serving reasons, and were not above sowing discontent out of vindictiveness, or a desire to settle old scores. Calley might have claimed to like Romana Moon, but this had to be put in the context of an individual who had already admitted to not being very fond of anyone at all.

'What's Karl Holmby doing now?' said Hynes.

'He's at Teesside University.'

'What's he studying?'

'I'd have to check. It's something scientific.'

'Do you have home addresses for the two boys?'

'I'm sure I do, somewhere,' she said, 'but you could just—' She paused, and he could see her thought processes following his own. 'You don't want to go through the school, right?'

'Not if I can avoid it.'

Hynes felt himself entering into a devil's pact with Calley, if only out of expediency. He was using her, but also playing into her hands. She clearly enjoyed gossip, and gossip was always about power. Neither did he hold out much hope for her keeping quiet about Karl Holmby. If Calley was willing to share her speculations with the police, she was also capable of spreading them more widely, if she hadn't already done so, whatever she might claim to the contrary. Still, a warning wouldn't hurt.

'I have to advise you not to share what you've just told me with anyone else,' he said, 'not until I've had a chance to talk to Holmby and Clifton. If rumors of a relationship were to get out, and affect the course of the investigation, you could find yourself in legal difficulties.'

It was rubbish, of course, and Calley probably intuited as much, but Hynes knew that few among the populace did not retain some fear of the law. In fact, the only people who didn't were criminals; the more bent they were, the less they were afraid.

'I won't say anything,' she said. She checked her watch. 'Is it okay if I go now? I have a free period next, and it's one thing giving up class time to talk to you, and another to give up my own.'

Hynes told her that she was welcome to do whatever she liked, but he had two more questions for her before she left.

'You said Ryan Clifton scared you, and that you weren't the only one frightened of him. Do you think he or Holmby might be capable of killing someone?'

'You mean, capable of killing Romana Moon?'

'Yes.'

Calley gave the question serious thought.

'Clifton could hurt a person, but deep down I suspect he's a coward, like all bullies, and he doesn't have the psycho-logical resilience required to hide his involvement in a murder. Even when he's pulled up for bad behavior at school, he can't disguise his guilt. Karl is different: there's real intelligence behind the charm, but also something rotten. Someday Clifton will end up behind bars, but it won't be for a great criminal enterprise. It'll be for thieving, or the consequences of a blow struck in anger, and you won't have to try hard to get a conviction. But if Karl Holmby ever finds himself in the dock, he'll make you work for your money, and whatever he's done will see him put away for a long time. Does that answer your first question?'

'It does, with interest,' said Hynes.

'And the second?'

'We're asking this of everyone, so please don't be offended by it.'

'I'm very difficult to offend.'

Hynes doubted this, but he let it pass.

'Where were you, and what were you doing, on the night Romana Moon died?'

Calley laughed.

'Am I a suspect?'

'I could be overly dramatic and tell you that everyone is a suspect,' said Hynes, 'but it would make me sound like a detec-tive in a film.'

He smiled, but Calley noticed that he was standing slightly in front of the door, so she couldn't slip by him if she did decide to take offense and attempt to storm off.

'I've never been a suspect before,' she said. 'It feels quite . . . *exotic.*'

Hynes was tired of her now, and also slightly ashamed at himself for the way he'd handled her, even if it had produced results. Gackowska wouldn't be happy at being excluded either, and if Calley did decide to prove difficult at some future date, the unorthodox nature of their discussion over cigarettes wouldn't reflect well on Hynes.

'Romana Moon's throat was cut,' he said. 'And that was after whoever killed her worked his – or her – way up to it by stabbing her twice in the upper body. She died in a lot of pain before her remains were dumped on a moor. That doesn't strike me as very exotic.'

If Calley reacted at all to this, it was only with disappointment, as though she'd expected more of Hynes.

'Now you do sound like a detective in a film,' she said. 'Was that supposed to make me feel bad?'

'It was a reminder of why we're here.'

'And we were getting on so well.' She took in the grim buildings around her, and the uneven, pitted playing fields. 'I hate this place. Romana would have ended up hating it, too. I wish she'd had the chance.'

The ambiguity of that final statement didn't pass Hynes by.

'As for where I was on the night she died,' said Calley, 'I was at home. I have the ground floor in a shared two-story house in Redcar. I own the property. It used to be my parents', and I inherited it when they died. A couple, Tom and Ione Newton, rent the top floor. Their daughter was ill the night before last – she's only little, and has a lung condition – and they had to take her to the hospital. That was shortly after eleven, I think, because I'd just watched a movie on Sky, which started at nine. When I heard the commotion on the stairs, I went out to see what was the matter, and spoke to the Newtons. I was wearing my dressing gown and slippers, because I always change into my nightclothes if I don't have to go out in the evening. I heard them come back shortly after two in the morning. I had to go to the loo anyway, so I stepped out to ask after their kid. I have telephone numbers for both of the Newtons, if you want to check with them.'

Hynes made a note of the names, and took the numbers from Calley as she read them out from her phone.

'I'm sorry,' she said, when she was done. 'I shouldn't have been so flippant. This is all unfamiliar to me.'

'I'd be surprised if it wasn't,' said Hynes. 'And we're grateful for your help.'

'I'll find the boys' addresses for you, and return with them.'

Hynes thanked Calley, and escorted her back inside. He watched her walk away, and tried to remember when last he'd met such an unhappy human being. A bell sounded, signaling the end of class, and he returned to the library before the corridors were swamped with kids. Inside, Gackowska was already halfway through a small Philip Pullman hardback entitled *Lyra's Oxford*.

'So,' she said, barely glancing up from its pages, 'when are you two moving in together?'

'Maybe when the missus passes away,' said Hynes. 'Well, her and every other woman on the planet.'

He shared with Gackowska all that Calley had told him, concluding with one final observation.

'She tended to refer to Ryan Clifton by his last name,' said Hynes, 'and just once or twice used his first name, but Holmby was either "Karl Holmby" or just "Karl".'

'You think she likes him?'

'Maybe enough to envy Romana Moon, whether Romana was really having an affair with Holmby or not.'

'I can't wait to meet him,' said Gackowska.

'Neither can I,' said Hynes, 'although perhaps for different reasons.'

He ducked just in time to avoid being hit by a flying copy of *Lyra's Oxford*.

XLVIII

At Worcester Cathedral, Sellars reached out a hand toward the carving of the Green Man, and time ceased to be of consequence. Then and now became one, so that he was both standing in an English cloister and lying on the cold stone of the Familist chapel in Prosperous, listening to faint disturbances from below ground. He thought that if one might have been permitted to hear the roots of a tree growing, the work of many years compressed into only a few moments, it would have sounded not unlike what he was hearing. He had a vision of a great dark tree concealed beneath the chapel, its branches forever reaching, seeking to devour.

'Do you hear it?' Warraner asked.

'Yes,' said Sellars, but the word caught in his throat, and he realized he was sobbing. He did not share all of the Familists' beliefs – and by then he had met Mors, and knew there were greater deities than his – but in this ancient place of worship, he had at last found confirmation of his faith.

'And do you see it?'

'I think so. If I close my eyes, I see branches, so many branches. Branches like roots.'

'And the fruit?'

This, too, Sellars discerned, because the limbs of the great tree were adorned with the withered remains of the dead: women and girls, for the most part, and some males, though only children. A tree must be fed, and great old trees have great old appetites. For centuries, Prosperous had survived, indeed flourished, by tending the tree, acquiescing to its needs, and so the dead became part of it, and decorated its boughs.

'Yes,' said Sellars. 'And it is beautiful.'

* * *

251

He would have stayed longer with Warraner had Lauren not been waiting for him. He might have spent days, even weeks, in Prosperous, and never tired of it. He had barely passed an hour in the chapel, yet already he was 'bowing down to the Green Man', to use Warraner's words.

'If you stayed, you'd be lost to it,' said Warraner as they left the church behind them, and Sellars thought he detected just a hint of regret to the pastor's voice.

'Are you lost to it?' Sellars asked.

'My family has always tended the chapel. It is our duty. We undertake it willingly, and we are not entirely alone. We have the board of selectmen to assist us, if needs be, and Morland, the chief of police, plays his part. At the same time, generations have lived and died in Prosperous without ever really understanding what it is that keeps their families in comfort and safety, or why they are so reluctant to leave the town for new lives elsewhere. It is the Green Man. We are his children, whether we know it or not. So, in answer to your question, we are all lost to it.'

Warraner dropped Sellars off at the same corner, and the visitor returned to his wife inexpressibly altered. She detected the change almost as soon as they got in the car and began driving west again.

'Is something wrong?' she asked, after fifteen minutes had passed in uneasy silence.

'No, I just liked Prosperous.'

'Do you want to move there?' she joked.

Sellars considered this for so long that Lauren began to grow concerned he might be giving serious consideration to the possibility. Had she asked him that question while they were in the coffee shop, or walking back to the car, he might have answered differently, but the more distance they put between themselves and Prosperous, the more its allure diminished.

'I don't think so,' he said at last. 'These small towns, they close in on you.'

Back in Worcester, back in the cathedral.

Prosperous was different now. Sellars wasn't privy to all of the details, but some falling out between the selectmen had ended in bloodshed, and a failed attempt to neutralize a private detective named Parker had resulted in the destruction of the shrine. Warraner was gone, and Morland, too. Sellars did not know what had become of the entity that dwelt in, and under, the chapel, but he supposed it to be no more. It must have been part of the building, its essence lodged deep in its stones, because it had traveled with the church when the blocks were transported across the Atlantic. Now that the building was only so much rubble, and those that had kept its spirit nourished were scattered or dead, the great tree below the ground had probably withered away and died.

But it was only a single manifestation of an older, greater life force, one that had its origin back in Northumberland. In Prosperous, Sellars had been mistaken in accepting it as a lesser deity, a being inferior to the Not-Gods. It was different from them, that was all; its reality was as much physical as spiritual, and its appetites and desires mirrored those of the men and women that worshiped it. It blessed the land, and those that worked the fields. It gave life to many, and asked only for the lives of a few in return.

Sellars wondered if, even as he left the chapel in Prosperous behind, Warraner was aware that the visitor had already fallen under its spell, just like the preacher himself. Perhaps that had been the Green Man's intention all along, ever since that first encounter at Worcester. It had called Sellars to Prosperous so that he might be convinced of the truth of its existence, and thus be transformed. The Green Man had chosen him and, in a voice like dry leaves a-rustling, had entrusted itself to his care.

Sellars left the carving to return to the main body of the cathedral, where he took a seat and waited. Some residue of the Old God, the God of crucified sons, of doves and saints, was present here, but it was faint, like the smell left by the dying in their final days, and so did not disturb him.

Finally, a woman took the seat beside him, the pungency of her odor subsuming all before it. He turned to look at her.

'What,' said Pallida Mors, 'went wrong?'

XLIX

Priestman spent an hour on the phone with detectives from the Kent and Essex Serious Crime Directorate, and the London Metropolitan Police, discussing Helen Wylie, the young Londoner whose remains had been discovered in the grounds of the Church of St Martin in Canterbury just over a week earlier. Wylie had been killed with a serrated knife, a single savage wound that had opened her vertically from her abdomen to her chest. But if neither the weapon nor the cause of death was identical to those in the Romana Moon case, the presence of *misbahas* linked both victims. Already Priestman had arranged for the ongoing exchange of all relevant information between the two forces, in addition to whatever was inputted to HOLMES2, the IT system used by UK police forces to collate information on serious incidents. For now, Priestman and her superiors concurred with the decision of Kent and Essex not to make public the detail of the *misbaha*. Priestman was also pleased to be remaining in overall control of the investigation in Northumbria, aided in part by two vacancies at detective chief inspector level. Effectively, she had been informed, she was now acting DCI, with the small print to be worked out later. Romana Moon was to be her primary focus, and everything else on her desk should be set aside or redistributed as she saw fit.

Unfortunately, Nabih Uddin had no good news for Priestman about the prayer beads found lodged in Romana Moon's throat. An initial check revealed that this particular example retailed for the grand sum of £2.99, and was available in three out of the five stores and mosques that Uddin and the Muslim officers assigned to him had visited so far that day. Similar beads were also sold through eBay and Amazon, although a single wholesaler

– TaroBass Limited, based in Walsall – was responsible for their distribution throughout the United Kingdom.

'I called TaroBass,' Uddin told Priestman, 'and spoke to Jahan Badi, their head of sales. He says that the beads are acrylic, and imported from Zhejiang, China. They cost just a few pence each to manufacture. He couldn't say for certain how many sets they sell each year, but he reckons it's in the low to mid-five figures.'

'Let's continue asking, just in case,' she said.

Priestman wasn't entirely surprised to learn that the beads were less than unique, but it was still disappointing. Examination of them had revealed no trace of fingerprints. They were waiting to find out if they contained any DNA other than Romana Moon's, but Priestman wasn't holding out much hope. In the meantime, she'd added a photograph of the *misbaha* found in Helen Wylie's mouth to the accumulating array of evidence. It looked more ornate than the Hexhamshire set, although Uddin expressed the opinion that the Canterbury *misbaha* still probably hadn't cost more than a fiver.

Priestman hated this. The beads were the worst kind of complicating factor, and, at some point, the fact of their existence would have to be revealed, if someone didn't leak it to the press first. With luck, the presence of the *misbahas* would only become public after they'd made an arrest, or during the trial. Either way, the police would be forced to weather a storm of criticism for not disclosing it earlier, but the ferocity would be greater if the killer turned out to be a Muslim.

And that possibility had to be considered. Hynes had already been in contact with Romana's parents and ex-boyfriend to establish whether Romana had Muslim friends, or even enemies, but none of them could think of any. He'd done his best to muddy the waters slightly by asking about Hindus, Buddhists, Sikhs, and Bahá'í as well, since they also used prayer beads, although Nabih had assured him that the kind found in Romana Moon's throat were definitely *misbaha* because of the number of orbs on the string. Obviously, Romana's family wanted to know why Hynes was asking about religious types, but he told them he wasn't at liberty to discuss procedural details at the present time, whatever that might mean. He'd also made it clear to the Moons, and to Simon Harris, that they were not to share with friends or others outside the immediate family any discussions with police on the progress of the investigation, for fear of jeopardizing it. All three assured Hynes that they'd remain silent, but Priestman still feared it wouldn't be long before a journalist or blogger learned that the police were investigating a possible Muslim connection.

Uddin went on his way, just in time for Priestman to take a call from Hynes himself.

'We might have something,' said Hynes, and told her of Elspeth Calley's suspicions about Romana Moon and Karl Holmby.

'What do you think?' said Priestman, when he'd finished speaking. 'You've met Ryan Clifton – and Elspeth Calley – while I haven't.'

'Calley's sour as a bag of lemons, but I don't see why she'd lie about what Clifton said to her. As for him, he's a little shit. If I stepped in him, I'd throw away my shoe. We're still at the school. Calley's going to give us addresses for Holmby and Clifton, but we still have a couple more interviews to do before we leave.'

The Holmby information was interesting, but tainted slightly by Hynes's sense that Elspeth Calley was ambivalent at best about Romana Moon.

'Do you think Calley was troubled enough to do something about it?' Priestman said.

'We'll check her alibi for the evening, but I'm pretty sure we won't find she's been lying. If Calley did want Romana Moon dead, she found someone else to do it for her. My gut feeling is that she limits her assassinations to character.'

Priestman finished making notes. 'We still need to establish if Romana might have argued with any of her Muslim students or their families,' she said.

'I didn't want to ask Calley directly,' said Hynes. 'She's too sharp. I kept it general, but if Romana did have any problems of that sort, I imagine Calley would have mentioned them. Still, there are a couple of Muslim teachers on the staff here. Might not hurt to have Nabih do a follow-up, just in case.'

Hynes promised to call Priestman back once he and Gackowska

were finished with the last of the school staff, but they agreed that Ryan Clifton and Karl Holmby would have to be interviewed separately but simultaneously, to prevent one from warning the other that the police were asking questions. Priestman was about to hang up when Hynes asked her to hold on for a moment, and she heard voices, one of them Hynes's, the other female and unfamiliar to her.

Hynes came back on the phone.

'That was Calley,' he said, 'with addresses for Ryan Clifton and Karl Holmby. She also confirmed Holmby's course of study at Teesside. You're going to love this. He's a first-year student of forensic science.'

L

Marcus Godwin wasn't found until four hours after he'd collapsed against the wall of St Mary's, Deerhurst, and then only because a resident of one of the neighboring houses chose to take a short-cut to the village by way of the cemetery. By the time he was discovered, it had been raining steadily for some time, and Godwin was very cold and wet. He was taken to Gloucester Royal Hospital, but he had only recently recovered from a bout of pneumonia, and exposure to the elements brought on a renewed attack. His condition deteriorated overnight and throughout the following day, to such an extent that his older daughter began sleeping in a chair by his bed, and his son traveled up from Cornwall, just in case the worst came to worst.

Godwin regained consciousness in dimness. He stayed very still for a few moments before glancing to his left, where his daughter lay dozing in her chair, a blanket over her body and a pillow at her head. He called her name, but his throat was dry and the word was barely audible, even to himself.

'Alyce,' he whispered. 'Alyce.'

She did not move, and Godwin returned his attention to the figure in the upper right-hand corner of the room. It resembled one of the Saxon beast heads from Deerhurst, carved from ancient stone yet now apparently emerging from the white-painted surroundings of his hospital suite. As he watched, another appeared in the opposite corner, and the paint on the walls began to blister and flake, falling to the floor like the sloughed flakes of an old skin. Revealed by the disintegration were rough-hewn blocks. As more paint vanished, further blocks began to show, and the temperature in the room fell so rapidly that Godwin could see his breath clouding before him.

Now the floor was buckling, the sheet tiles warping and melting to be replaced by flagstones, until finally no trace of the hospital remained – *yet it did, because he could still see it if he concentrated, but it was hard to keep it fixed in place, and so it faded in and out like a wavering in his consciousness* – and Godwin and his drowsing daughter were enclosed by the confines of a narrow chapel, illuminated by a light that seemed to come from within the walls themselves. He both felt and heard movement all around as tendrils of ivy emerged from the cracks between the blocks, interweaving to create faces from the greenery until the original stones were barely visible through it.

From the open mouth of one of the faces appeared a green tuber thick as a wine bottle, like a great tongue lolling. Further and further it extended, moving toward his daughter, bifurcating as it drew closer. When at last it reached her, one half moved over the chair to probe at her mouth while the other wound its way around her right leg, ascending over calf, knee, and thigh before vanishing beneath the folds of her skirt.

'Alyce,' said Godwin again, louder this time.

His daughter brushed at her mouth with her left hand, even as her lips parted, her jaws unlocked, and the Green Man entered her body from above and below. The chapel walls receded, the space increasing, and before Godwin a great stained-glass window arose, and its lower regions were filled with living creatures.

'"On the other side is Hell,"' Godwin rasped from memory, those hours spent with the works of Neale and Bigland, poring over their descriptions of medieval glass, and of one window in particular, '"in which is the great Devill . . ."'

This was not just any church, Marcus knew: this was St Mary's in Fairford.

He tried to get up, and all motion ceased. Suddenly he was conscious of a vastness above him, as of one who wakes to find himself on an isolated plain, surrounded by night. He looked up to see red veins opening amid the living blackness, as though some massive entity were pressing itself against the very fabric of the universe, seeking to force its way through. Marcus glimpsed teeth, and many eyes, and jointed limbs like the legs of a giant insect, before the entity appeared to coalesce and re-form, and the room was filled with the sound of great wings beating, until a countenance became visible, its lineaments almost human, its longing inexpressibly so, and its hatred beyond all understanding.

It was almost beautiful.

Marcus Godwin thought: *If this is God, I do not wish to die; and if I must die, do not cause me to wake again in His presence.*

He felt a fierce pain in his chest, and with it came a final understanding – *No, this is not God* – even as a second face appeared alongside the first.

Not God.

Not-Gods.

Marcus closed his eyes. He heard his daughter cry out as the alien noises of machines and monitors took the place of the beating of wings. Hands were on him now, and a beam of light shone into his eyes, but it was all in vain because he was leaving; he had done no harm in his life, and thus had no fear of judgment, only of the Not-Gods.

'"On the other side is Hell . . ."'

'Dad!'

'". . . in which is the Great Devill."'

'You have to step back, miss. We're—'

'They're in the windows.'

'Please, Daddy, don't go.'

'Tell them . . .'

'Miss!'

Marcus smelled the sea, and heard his dead wife speak his name.

'Tell them they're in the windows.'

Gone.

All gone.

In his London rooms, Quayle was privy to visions similar to those being witnessed by the dying Marcus Godwin, although he had no knowledge of the old man or the manner of his passing.

Because universes were in tumult.

Quayle felt oppressed by the weight of his own failure. It should have been for the Atlas to finish the reordering of the world, but the Atlas remained deficient, and so this world was deficient also. But what waited beyond its boundaries would wait no longer; blood spilled in foregone places might bridge the final gap, yet how many lives would it take? The discovery of the Moon girl's remains on the Hexhamshire Moors so soon after Wylie's death at Canterbury would establish a pattern, and the proximity of the body to the former site of the Familist chapel was also deeply unfortunate. Two dead, and already an error had been made. Mors would see what could be done about it.

But Quayle had not given up hope of finally restoring the Atlas, and had resumed his search for what appeared to be at least one missing page. He had returned to his primary sources, both the books on his shelves and those that resided in other libraries, and had engaged a trusted acolyte in similar work. Something must have been overlooked: a line mistranslated, a reference misinterpreted. They would locate the error, and proceed from there.

Yet Parker was coming.

Parker: Quayle wondered if the detective's relentlessness might also have communicated itself to others. In worlds beyond worlds, did the Not-Gods sense Parker's approach?

He shook off the notion. No, he would not countenance this. Parker was a man, and only that. He had been lucky so far, but all men ran out of luck in the end, because all men died.

As Quayle prepared to close the door behind the shelves, he saw the threads at Soter's mouth contort for a moment before tightening once more. Had he not known better, Quayle might almost have believed Soter had smiled.

LI

Despite Parker's reservations, it had been decided that Bob Johnston should travel ahead to London, if only by a few days, while Parker accompanied Angel and Louis to Amsterdam. In the past, Parker would have been happy to entrust the inquiries in the Netherlands to Angel and Louis alone, but – as Angel had pointed out to him – illness and injury respectively had left both men weaker than before. Nevertheless, he continued to worry about Johnston as well.

'I've spent my life working with old books,' said Johnston, when Parker broached the subject of his security. 'You'll only get under my feet.'

Parker had to admit there was some truth to this, and besides, he had no burning desire to sit around the great libraries of London while the book dealer lost himself in dusty volumes. On the other hand, Johnston would be asking questions about the Fractured Atlas, and doing so on Quayle's territory. Unless he was very careful, word of his efforts might get back to the lawyer.

'I'd feel happier if we had someone watching your back,' said Parker.

'But I'd feel unhappier,' said Johnston, 'and I have to tell you, I'm usually pretty unhappy at the best of times.'

Which put an end to the discussion.

Parker called Ross. As usual, the FBI man didn't sound pleased to hear from him, but Parker considered this to be Ross's default position on everyone, and so wasn't inclined to take it personally.

'We're about to get moving,' said Parker. 'You need to find some extra cash under the floorboards.'

'How much?'

Parker named a figure that, even allowing for business-class flights, and hotel rooms in which a man could stretch upon waking without banging his hands against the walls, was clearly considerably higher than Ross had been anticipating.

'That's not going to fly,' said Ross.

'Then neither are we.'

'Let's be serious. You want Quayle at least as much as I do.'

'And you want Louis to call in favors. In his world, favors come with a price attached.'

'Mors shot him. I would have thought that might be sufficient motivation to economize.'

'He's prepared to pay for his own bullets.'

'I'm going to pretend I didn't hear that.'

'Plus, as he and Angel get older, they prefer to travel in serious comfort. They're not big Red Roof Inn guys.'

'Yeah, about that fucking champagne delivery. I know that was your—'

Parker continued talking over him. It seemed like the safest option.

'Unless of course, you'd like us to knock on the door of the US Embassy in London, give them your name, and tell them you said it was okay if we slept in the basement.'

On reflection, Ross decided this would not be okay.

'Give me a couple of hours,' he said. 'I'll see what I can do.'

Ross met Conrad Holt, deputy director of the FBI, in one of the comfortably upholstered booths of the White Horse Tavern on Bridge Street in Lower Manhattan. Holt had ordered the lunch special: $10 for a cheeseburger deluxe with a draft beer, which, as anyone familiar with prices in the Financial District would confirm, was tantamount to giving the food and booze away for nothing.

'I think you should have ordered something stronger,' said Ross, as he took a seat.

'Are you ever the bearer of good news?'

'Rarely. If it was good news, we could have spoken in your office, and sent out a memo after.'

'They serve Paddy whiskey here for five bucks a shot' – Holt took a bite of cheeseburger – 'but I only drink it when I have a cold. Otherwise, I steer clear. You eating?'

'No.'

'Then talk, and I can eat while I listen.'

'It's about Parker,' said Ross. 'And Quayle.'

'Forgive me for not looking more startled.'

'I'd have struggled to forgive you if you were startled at all.'

Ross was engaged in a delicate balancing act when it came to his superior. Holt was one of only a few individuals familiar with Ross's arrangement with Parker, and probably the only one who didn't believe that Ross himself was crazy. This was because, years earlier, it was Holt who had detailed Ross to investigate the activities of the killer known as the Traveling Man, and clean up the shambles left behind.

But the more Ross had learned about Parker, the more apparent the private detective's strangeness became, while Parker's own investigations increasingly began to dovetail with matters that concerned Ross and Holt, in particular the activities of the Backers. Unlike Ross, Holt was not prepared to countenance any non-rational explanation for the Backers' efforts; he saw them only as a group of wealthy, corrupt individuals who were engaged in a criminal conspiracy to perpetuate their own power, a conspiracy that had infected any number of financial, political, and corporate entities. What they chose to believe in the privacy of their own homes was of no concern to Holt. He just wanted them stopped.

Now there was this whole Quayle business with which to contend, and a series of killings linked to a missing book. (Holt was mildly impressed to be encountering murders with a literary origin. It made a pleasantly cultured change to the norm, although he kept this opinion to himself.) If Ross was correct, Quayle was linked to the Backers through the death of Garrison Pryor, which appeared to have been carried out by Quayle's associate Mors, possibly in return for assistance received while she and her mentor were in the United States.

'Where are we on Quayle?' said Holt.

The FBI had no jurisdiction to make arrests on foreign soil, except where extraterritorial permission was granted by Congress, and then only with the consent of the host country. But the bureau retained agents and other personnel – known as 'legats' – in legal attaché offices situated in embassies and consulates, administered by the FBI's International Operations Division in Washington, D.C.

'The legats in London and The Hague have been in contact with national law enforcement and Interpol, but the consensus appears to be that the Quayle and Mors identities are entirely manufactured. Pallida Mors is a reference to "pale death" in Horace's *Carmina*, while the Quayle legal firm ceased to exist in the forties, and was followed soon after by the demise of Atol Quayle, seemingly the last of the line. Because of the Dutch passports used to enter and leave the Americas, the legats are continuing to focus on the Netherlands, but so far to no avail.'

'And you still think Parker can do better?'

'I believe so, with the help of his associates.'

Holt finished his burger, and pushed away the plate of fries.

'Now you really are putting me off the rest of my food,' said Holt. 'At least I got to enjoy my burger before you mentioned those two. Is that fucking Angel still wasting FBI time?'

Ross's office continued to be the recipient of anonymous missives concerning the supposed location of a network of secret FBI restrooms across the United States. The latest communication, received the previous month, had pinpointed the Barbed Wire Museum in La Crosse, Kansas; the Sasquatch Museum in Cherry Log, Georgia; and the Umbrella Cover Museum on Peaks Island, Maine as likely locations for these facilities. On this occasion, fifty key blanks of various designs had also been included, with a printed note advising that the sender did not wish to inconvenience the taxpayer, and expressing the hope that some of the blanks might be appropriate for the manufacture of the relevant restroom keys. The typed return address was *A Friend, c/o The Great Lost Bear, 540 Forest Avenue, Portland, ME 04101*. Holt had to be dissuaded from sending the blanks to be dusted for fingerprints.

'They'll require funds.' Ross named the figure given to him by Parker.

'Jesus Christ,' said Holt, 'we're not sending an entire delegation. It's only three guys.'

'Four.'

'Who's the fourth?'

'A book dealer.'

Holt opened his mouth to say something, but couldn't figure out what that should be, beyond taking the Lord's name in vain for a second time, and so closed it again without saying anything.

'Apparently,' said Ross, 'they prefer to travel in comfort.'

'Like kings, you mean.' Holt swallowed what was left of his beer. 'Just transfer the money. We're looking for foreign killers of American citizens: no oversight committee is going to object to the use of any and all means to bring them to justice. But if anyone asks, we were dealing with Parker alone, and resourcing him with strict guidelines on accountability, and assurances of his full cooperation with the legats.'

'I'll let him know.'

'Not that it'll make any fucking difference,' said Holt, as he dropped a ten and a five on the table, and pocketed the receipt.

'No,' Ross admitted, 'probably not.'

LII

Sellars drove home to Manchester, stopping only to fill up on fuel, and confirm with the office that he would be back at work the following day. His encounter with Mors had left him shaken, but she had that effect on people. At least he could rationalize his fear of her, because he knew what she was capable of doing. He'd seen her handiwork for himself.

Some years earlier, a Dutch investigator named Yvette Visser had begun taking an interest in certain shipments being made to and from the Continent, and in particular those arriving at, or originating from, a number of freeports in Switzerland, Spain, Luxembourg, Latvia, Lithuania, and Romania. 'Freeports' was the term most commonly used to describe free economic zones, designated areas in which customs duties and taxes were suspended. They varied in size from entire ports to individual warehouses within the precincts of international transportation hubs, and were – depending upon the view one took – either secure, convenient locations in which the uber-wealthy could store valuable physical assets, including wines, vintage cars, and fine art; or more-or-less lawless shelters that, at their most unscrupulous, facilitated tax evasion, money laundering, and the concealment of stolen goods. Thus it was possible for the owner of a Picasso stored in a freeport to sell the painting to a buyer, also allied to the freeport, without the painting ever leaving the building, or even the room in which it was housed, thereby avoiding capital gains or value-added taxes. And should the new owner elect to hang the latest acquisition on a wall in one of his or her many homes around the world, various shelf companies, as well as other freeports, could be used to move the painting through enough countries that its point of origin, and final destination, would be ascertainable only to God Himself.

A significant part of Carenor's business involved the discreet transportation of goods to and from some of these European freeports, which was how Sellars had initially become familiar with Mors – and, ultimately, Quayle. Sellars had since been responsible for transporting a number of valuable assets on their behalf, most often while engaged in legitimate or semi-legitimate business for Carenor.

All had been going smoothly until the arrival of Yvette Visser. She specialized in tracking stolen art, and was working for a consortium of lawyers based in New York, Paris, Berlin, and Amsterdam. This consortium was seeking to resolve claims for paintings misappropriated during the Nazi era, most of them from Jews but some also from private and public collections looted by Fat Hermann Goering and his stooges. As part of this investigation, Visser had begun sniffing around the smaller of the two Luxembourg freeports, known as the Enclave Lusur, a slightly awkward play on the French phrase *en lieu sûr*, meaning 'in a safe place'.

The Enclave, as it was known to those who availed themselves of its services, was situated behind high walls close to Findel airport, and competed for business with the larger Le Freeport. While Le Freeport was a purpose-built facility that had been opened in 2014 by Luxembourg's Grand Duke himself, the older Enclave was housed inside an old redbrick warehouse bearing the faded name of its former occupant, a failed shipping company. Unlike Le Freeport, it had commenced operations with no fuss at all, the duchy of Luxembourg having been quietly advised that it might be better to keep all public associations with the Enclave to a minimum. Its shareholders included Russians, Albanians, Nigerians – Nigeria being to freeports what Ronald McDonald was to fast food – along with the kind of minor royalty from Saudi Arabia and the United Arab Emirates whose names set off alarm bells in American and European intelligence agencies every time they boarded an international flight.

The Enclave's battered external walls concealed concrete

reinforced with steel, and a state-of-the-art security and fire prevention system, the latter based around the use of inert gas in place of water to prevent damage to items. More than two hundred cameras monitored the interior and exterior of the building, and only biometric confirmation permitted access to its strongrooms. All this meant that when Visser's inquiries finally led her to the gates of the Enclave, her months of hard work seemed destined to come to naught.

But Visser was resilient, and had funds to disperse as she saw fit, her employers being prepared to tolerate certain underhand methods to track thieves – though only, one understood, on a purely theoretical level. If Visser couldn't gain access to the Enclave's records or its vaults, she could follow the paper trail left by the shippers. She spoke to customs agents, both active and retired, in five European countries, and spread a little financial goodwill where required. By the time she was finished, she had compiled a shortlist of companies worthy of examination, and the names of local representatives and drivers who might be susceptible to pressure. Among these companies was Carenor, and one of those drivers was Christopher Sellars.

Sellars first learned of Visser from Dylan Lynskey, Carenor's CEO, during a routine staff briefing. Lynskey was a former military man who favored blazers and club ties, and liked to reminisce about his time in 'the Service', even though the closest he'd come to combat was chucking-out time in the bars of Larnaca as part of British Forces Cyprus. Standing before an image of Visser projected on a screen, Lynskey reminded his staff of the duty of confidentiality the company owed its clients (which was probably true); stressed that Visser's inquiries were part of a larger investigation, so were not specifically directed at Carenor (which was only partially true); and assured them that Carenor, with a reputation to protect, was scrupulous in its adherence to the law, as well as all national and international requirements governing tax and customs declarations, especially those pertaining to the transfer and ownership of works of art (which was certainly *not* true, if only because it would have made Carenor unique in the art world). If they were to be approached by Visser, Lynskey instructed, they should refuse to answer any questions, and immediately contact either him or Karyn Toner, Carenor's oleaginous legal advisor – although Lynskey omitted 'oleaginous', not least because he was sleeping with Toner behind his wife's back.

Sellars hadn't realized just how clever Visser was, and the extent of her researches, until she confronted him the next day at a Starbucks off the M6. Visser had obviously been following him – unless she just liked hanging around motorway services, which seemed unlikely – and this made Sellars very unhappy. He and Mors had met just hours earlier, and during that encounter he'd transferred into her care two small oils on canvas by the nineteenth-century French landscape artist Jean-Baptiste-Camille Corot, and a larger oil of Madame Helleu, the wife of the portraitist Paul César Helleu, painted by her husband in 1893. Together, the Corots were worth perhaps £100,000 or more, but the real prize was the Helleu, because earlier that year an inferior version of the same painting, with an upper estimate of €150,000, had fetched nearly €800,000 at Sotheby's in Paris. It seemed that Quayle was in need of operating funds, and strategic inquiries had unearthed a buyer for all three works, a Qatari businessman who desired some nineteenth-century works of a specific size and style for the bedroom of his mistress's apartment in Kensington, and was happy to cut a cash deal for a quick sale as long as he wasn't bothered by unnecessary paperwork. This suited Quayle entirely, as the three paintings had once formed part of the collection of a Jewish art dealer whose final resting place was an oven at Bergen-Belsen. During a trip to Le Freeport for Carenor, Sellars had taken a detour to the Enclave, supervised the removal of the paintings from one of Quayle's vaults, presented the requisite (and entirely falsified) documentation to the resident custom official, who knew better than to ask too many questions about attribution and valuations, and proceeded on his way, encountering no further difficulties until he reached London, and Mors.

Now here was Yvette Visser, pretty in a studious way, sliding into the seat across from him while kids played video games nearby, and detritus from fast-food outlets piled up on tables.

'Mr Sellars?'

He didn't reply, didn't even nod, just folded his newspaper, finished his coffee, and prepared to leave.

'So you know who I am,' said Visser. 'That's good. It will save time.'

She had a slow, singsong accent. He might even have found it attractive in another woman.

Sellars's jacket had caught on the arm of his chair. He was still trying to free it when Visser said, 'What were you doing at the Enclave yesterday?'

He thought about denying his presence there, but what would have been the point? She knew, otherwise she wouldn't be asking. She probably had photos, too. He remained standing, and stared down at her. If he was hoping to intimidate her, he was destined to be disappointed, because neither her smile nor her voice faltered in the slightest.

'I ask,' Visser continued, 'because Carenor filed paperwork only for Le Freeport, and your company has an official policy of not dealing with the Enclave, because it attracts the wrong sort of attention from the British authorities. But unofficially, who knows? So your presence at the Enclave means that you were engaging in questionable activities either on Carenor's behalf, or your own. I'm guessing the latter, and not for the first time.'

Sellars stopped fighting with his jacket. He now knew that Visser, or someone in her employ, had been watching him and was aware of Carenor's occasional commerce with the Enclave. Sellars was one of only two company drivers trusted with access to the facility, and with knowledge of the layers of obfuscation that enabled Enclave assets to be transferred through three separate business entities in Italy, Latvia, and Spain, all without leaving their temperature-controlled environments, before Carenor even touched them.

'It's understandable that you might want to earn a little extra money,' said Visser, 'although I'm not sure your company would approve. Look, why don't you sit down and hear me out? It won't take long. I have no desire to get you into any trouble with your employer. Perhaps we can even help each other. For example, I may be able to help you stay out of jail.'

271

Sellars resumed his seat.

'What do you want?' he said at last.

'An Americano, to begin,' she replied. 'After that, information.'

Sellars passed Liverpool, Mahler playing on the van's radio. When he was younger, he could never have imagined himself listening to classical music. It was all new wave hits for him, and anything with synthesizers. He still enjoyed the sounds of his youth, but they came tinged with sadness now. Odd how Mahler could leave him less depressed than early Depeche Mode. He had grown middle-aged, and hadn't even noticed it happening. He couldn't have imagined that either, back when he was a teenager.

We lose ourselves by degrees: our youth, our souls.

Listening to classical music. Being middle-aged.

Killing, and facilitating the killing of others.

But Visser was special. She was the first, the instant when Sellars progressed from making paintings disappear to making people vanish. Sellars had marked Visser, and death had come for her in the shape of Pallida Mors.

Sellars listened to Visser's pitch, or gave the appearance of doing so, but already she was fading from his world, her voice coming to him as though through dense fog, distorted and distanced by the elements. He could see himself in the mirror over her right shoulder. It enabled him to arrange his features in response to those fragments of her discourse that continued to register with him, permitting him to offer reasonable facsimiles of anger, regret, fear, and finally, reluctant acquiescence.

Yes, he told her, he could obtain copies of documents pertaining to Carenor's activities at Le Freeport, and a second, similar zone near Geneva. No, he did not have direct access to client records at the Enclave, but – and here Visser's eyes lit up as though a bulb had been switched on in her skull – he had made, strictly against company policy, copies of paperwork relating to specific Carenor customers, and particular assignments that had concerned him at the time. To be honest, he informed Visser, he had long feared a day like this might come, and he had a family to support.

He wasn't prepared to go to jail to protect Lynskey and the Carenor board. In fact, he went on, it was almost a relief to learn that these activities would soon be forced into the open. Did Visser know he was one-eighth Jewish, or maybe it was one-sixteenth? Didn't matter. Someone on his late father's side. Never knew him. Died before Sellars was born. Lovely man. Everyone said so.

And Visser nodded along, but he could tell she wasn't interested in some manufactured family history.

'When will you have those papers for me?' she asked, when she guessed he had finished justifying to himself his betrayal of his employers.

'A couple of days,' he said. 'I'll be in the office tomorrow. I'm supposed to log into the system within twenty-four hours of a delivery or collection to fill in all sorts of nonsense, but I have a bit of a backlog. We're old-fashioned that way. The big companies, they use handheld devices to speed up record keeping, but Lynskey is too cheap, or too careful, for that. If I have an excuse to be in the system, I can nose around.'

'What about the material you copied? Is that at your home?'

'Yes.'

'So why can't we get it now?'

'Because my wife is there, and I don't want her involved in any of this.'

Visser ceased to press him. So she had a heart, Sellars thought, although not much of one, as her next words confirmed.

'If you don't come through,' she said, 'I'll hang you out to dry: with your employers, with Revenue and Customs, maybe even with the police, depending on why you were visiting the Enclave, and on whose behalf.'

She let the last part hang, and Sellars was almost certain that she was referring to Mors. Sellars and Mors had met, as usual, in the basement car park of serviced offices in West London, and had departed in separate vehicles. The car park used cameras only at the entrance and exit lanes, so the transfer of the three paintings had not been filmed, which was not to say that it had not been witnessed. The basement had appeared empty of other people, but Sellars couldn't recall if another car had entered behind him, and he had left the car park immediately after Mors. Perhaps he should have waited longer, but he was in a hurry to get out of London before the afternoon traffic grew too heavy, and he hadn't been checking for surveillance or signs of pursuit. But however she had done it, Visser had connected Sellars to Mors. Visser wouldn't have been able to identify Mors – and Sellars wished her luck with trying to – but the Volvo V60 that Mors had used to move the paintings might be traceable: if not to her then to a rental company. And Visser was clearly good at what she did, because otherwise Sellars wouldn't have been contemplating her murder.

'There's no need to threaten me,' said Sellars, giving it some sulk. 'I told you I was in.'

'Good,' said Visser. 'If it helps your conscience, you're doing the right thing. This is looted artwork we're talking about, with Nazi fingerprints all over it. It deserves to be returned to the heirs of its rightful owners, or the institutions from which it was stolen.'

Sellars nodded along, and pocketed the card she gave him listing all her phone numbers, two of them handwritten. One, Sellars, noticed, was a London number: a hotel, possibly, or a short term apartment.

'My colleagues and I look forward to hearing from you,' she said – just to let him know that she wasn't working alone, he figured, in case he should get any ideas about attempting to intimidate her, or worse.

It won't matter to Mors, he thought.

And he was right: it didn't.

Sellars had watched Visser drive from the parking lot, taking a note of her car registration, and the fact that she was alone. He didn't use his own phone to call Mors, instead gathering enough coins for the public phone, having first ascertained that there were no cameras in the immediate vicinity. He passed on to Mors the description of Visser's car, along with its registration, her direction of travel, and the telephone numbers the investigator had provided.

And Visser had disappeared that evening.

The following morning, once Sellars had learned, via Mors, that Visser was no longer going to be a problem, he asked to meet with Dylan Lynskey in order to inform him of the attempted solicitation. Lynskey was initially annoyed that Sellars hadn't contacted the company immediately, but quickly calmed down once he realized that Visser's first attempt at inveigling her way into Carenor's records had been successfully repulsed. He congratulated Sellars on his honesty, and added that it wouldn't be forgotten when it came to his end-of-year bonus.

The police arrived the following day, accompanied by one of Visser's associates, a big Dutchman named Hendricksen, with Sellars's name at the top of their list. Sellars met them with Karyn Toner seated by his side, and under strict instructions not to answer any questions relating to freeports other than to confirm that Carenor's drivers were occasionally required to visit them, either to make deliveries or collect items for transportation. In the end, it was Hendricksen who brought up the Enclave, and Toner swatted him away with the usual platitudes about client confidentiality. She refused to acknowledge that Carenor did business with the Enclave, which suited Sellars just fine.

The two detectives with Hendricksen were named Hamill and Mount, and were attached to Scotland Yard's Art and Antiques Unit. Hamill, the woman, was in her fifties, and more like an academic than a detective, with a manner that couldn't have been more deceptively sweet if it had come wrapped in chocolate. Mount was younger, and had a noticeable underbite. Sellars ignored him from the start. Hamill, he decided, was the one to watch.

They went through his conversation with Visser, which required him to commit some smaller lies of omission to add to the larger one about the phone call.

'So Ms Visser did not make any allegations concerning your visits to the Enclave?' said Hamill.

'I can't answer questions about the Enclave.'

'Let me rephrase that one. Did she imply that you might be

engaged in the transport of goods independently of your duties to Carenor?'

Toner shot Sellars a puzzled look, but he chose not to register it.

'Is that a fancy way of saying "smuggling"?' said Sellars.

'Yes, I suppose it is.'

'Then, yes, Ms Visser did make that allegation, but I ignored it.'

'Why?'

'Because it wasn't true.'

Hendricksen intervened, although Hamill didn't appear happy about it. 'Then why would she make such an allegation?' he asked.

'I think she was trying to blackmail me.'

'Blackmail you?'

Hendricksen gave a little semi-laugh that made Sellars want to punch him in the face. Scoffing: that's what the Dutchman was doing, and Sellars experienced a surge of righteous indignation. Whatever else he was trying to get away with, Sellars wasn't dissembling about Visser trying to pressure him into revealing Carenor secrets. Frankly, he was glad that Mors had taken care of her. Yvette Visser, in his view, had been severely lacking in principles.

'She wanted me to access confidential records in our systems,' he said. 'She warned that if I didn't help her, she'd suggest to Carenor that I was working off the books, which would have been a lie.'

Hamill regained control, speaking before Hendricksen could open his mouth again. 'And you simply ignored this?'

'I didn't argue with her, if that's what you mean.'

'But if the allegations were untrue, why did you agree to provide her with the information she was seeking?'

'I just needed to get her off my back. I told her what she wanted to hear, then reported our meeting to Mr Lynskey first thing the next morning.'

'Why wait? Why not get in touch with him immediately?'

'Because it might have meant going into the office that evening to discuss it in person, and I wanted to go home. I have a family, and I don't see enough of them as it is. I was at Mr Lynskey's door at eight a.m. sharp the following morning, waiting for him before he even arrived at the office.'

'That was very laudable of you,' said Hamill, even if she didn't sound like she meant it. Sellars wondered if Mors could be persuaded to deal with her, too, and maybe the Dutchman into the bargain.

'What did you do after Ms Visser left the motorway services?' Hamill asked.

'I finished my coffee.'

'Is that all?'

'I went to the gents'.'

'Did you make any telephone calls?'

'Only to my wife, to tell her I might be delayed.'

Hamill pounced on this. 'Delayed? Why?'

'Because I'd been sitting listening to Ms Visser when I should already have been back on the road. I'd be heading into rush-hour traffic.'

'And you made no other calls?'

Sellars recalled the corridor outside the toilets. No cameras, or none that had the payphones in view.

'No.'

'Would you be willing to let us examine your mobile phone?'

Sellars looked to Toner.

'You don't have to do that,' she said. 'And since you haven't been arrested, the Police and Criminal Evidence Act doesn't apply. Your phone can't be seized.'

'That's not entirely true,' said Hamill. 'Under statute and common law, we can seize as evidence material that we reasonably suspect relates to the commission of an offence.'

'I think the key term here,' said Toner, 'is "reasonable suspicion", and you're so far from that, you couldn't see it from the top of a mountain.'

Hamill glowered at her, and Toner glowered back. Entertaining though all of this was, Sellars decided to put an end to it.

'You can look at my phone,' he said.

Toner began to object, but Sellars raised a hand to silence her. She was so shocked at his temerity that it actually worked. Hamill, meanwhile, appeared to be trying to figure out the catch.

'I've nothing to hide,' he continued, 'but it's got all my contact details on it, and a lot of numbers that I need for work.'

'You can back up everything before we take it,' said Mount.

'Do I get it back? It's a new iPhone.'

'In a couple of days, I should imagine.'

'I've got an old one at home somewhere. I'll just use that while I wait.'

One of the technical support geeks helped Sellars to back up the contents of his phone, Sellars claiming to be a bit of a Luddite when it came to anything more complicated than browsing the Internet. The police wrote out a receipt for the phone and went on their merry way, Hendricksen dragging his feet behind them, having clearly received fewer answers than he wanted, and fewer still that he believed. Once they were gone, Toner gave Sellars a flea in his ear for 'overstepping the mark', as she put it, before asking him if Visser's allegations about extracurricular activities had any basis in fact.

'None,' said Sellars.

Most of the favors he did for Mors and Quayle coincided with Carenor business, either at Le Freeport or the Enclave itself. As for the two or three exceptions to this, he remained certain that Quayle's business dealings with the Enclave were destined to remain as confidential as anyone else's, if not more so. Let Toner go snooping, if the mood took her. She'd find nothing.

And if by chance she did, Mors could always take care of her as well.

Eventually, Sellars's phone was returned to him. Hamill and Mount came by with it, along with some more questions, although they were essentially the same as the previous ones, but couched in different terms. In the hours after his meeting with Visser, Sellars's van – and his face – had been visible on motorway and other traffic cameras all the way from the services to the junction leading to his home. He could also account for his movements over the following forty-eight hours, by which time Visser had been reported missing. He might have been the last person to talk to her before she vanished, but whatever had befallen her, it had not come to pass at his hands.

Visser had sent an email to Hendricksen at 5 p.m. on the afternoon of her disappearance, probably from the side of the road, giving a short account of her meeting with Sellars. It was the last communication anyone ever received from her. When her car was found, parked on a residential street in Morden, South London, both her mobile phone and laptop were missing. They, like their owner, were never found.

For the next six months Sellars was on his best behavior, conscious that the police might well be monitoring him, and aware that his bosses at Carenor certainly were. He noticed that he was not sent to Le Freeport, or the Enclave, during this time, and all his runs were limited to the United Kingdom. Finally, though, he was assigned a Luxembourg pick-up – and by Dylan Lynskey in person, no less. This followed Karyn Toner's resignation from Carenor, which in turn coincided with the discovery by Lynskey's wife of her husband's extramarital indiscretions.

'Sorry about restricting your runs,' Lynskey told Sellars. 'It was Karyn's doing, not mine. Legal flim-flam. Watching our backs. You understand.'

Sellars did, especially when his understanding was aided by a cash payment from Lynskey.

But his abiding memory of that period, and the accompanying recognition of Mors's capacities, came from the days after his first interview by the police. He had taken care of a delivery of vintage wine to a property developer in Bromley, after which he made a detour to The Glades, the big shopping center nearby, where he parked next to a nondescript Toyota with tinted windows. Mors was waiting behind the wheel, and together they drove to a lock-up garage near Grove Park Cemetery. Inside was Yvette Visser: gagged, chained to a D-ring cemented into the floor, and looking very much the worse for wear. Mors had been feeding her, but not a lot. Mostly Mors had been narcotizing her to keep her subdued. Visser continued to look groggy even as Mors produced a little leather wallet filled with blades and other devices, and removed from it a scalpel, which she handed to Sellars.

'Finish her,' she said.

'Why me?'

'Because you were careless, and because we have to know that you're capable of it. We might need you to do it again someday.'

But it wasn't only that, Sellars knew. If he didn't do as Mors asked, she'd kill him. He was certain of it. He had to prove his loyalty, or else he and Visser would share the same fate. Sellars brought to mind his conversation with Visser, how she had been prepared to ruin him, to deprive him of his job, and his family of support, all because some greedy Jews wanted to get their hands on paintings that had once belonged to their grandparents and great-grandparents so they could sell them at a premium and feather their nests with the proceeds. To hell with her. To hell with them all.

Mors stepped behind Visser and lifted her head by the hair, exposing her throat.

'Do it,' said Mors.

The scalpel felt very light in Sellars's hand, but there was no denying its sharpness. It cut Visser's throat with the minimum of effort. Afterward, he and Mors wrapped the body in black plastic garbage bags, and hosed away the blood, before burying her in the cemetery, Mors having already located a recently dug grave that would easily accommodate another body.

Sellars hadn't greatly enjoyed killing Visser, but he'd done it, and without moaning about it later. Neither was he tormented by her murder, haunted by memories of the act, or any of that other nonsense one read about in books or saw in films. It had been necessary, that was all, and easier than he might have anticipated.

Plus, it made the ones that followed easier still.

But killing Visser had changed him, he couldn't doubt that. Lauren – so perceptive once again – had noticed something different about him as soon as he returned home that night, and it wasn't just the smell of the soap he'd used to wash away the blood from Visser's body and the dirt from the digging of her grave. It was a fundamental alteration to his state of being.

'Did anything bad happen today?' Lauren asked him, as he lay beside her in the dark.

'Why would you say that?' he replied, and instantly recognized it as the wrong answer. You never answered a question with another question. It was as good as an admission: of the truth of an implication made by another, or of one's own guilt.

'Because you seem distracted.'

'A woman got hurt,' he said, and he was surprised to hear himself speak. He had a momentary urge to clamp his hands over his mouth. 'There was a lot of blood.'

'Where? On the motorway?'

'No. On a side street.'

'Is she –?'

'I don't want to talk about it, love. Honest.'

And Lauren let it go, because that was her way, but it didn't mean she stopped thinking about it, because that, too, was her way. She added his response to others he had given, or would offer her in the future: about cash found in a shoebox in the shed (remiss of him, that was); about journeys that appeared to take longer than they should have; about how often, or how seldom, they made love. The distance between them had grown, until it became so great as to be beyond bridging.

Visser had done this, because the worst of it had commenced with her death.

Sellars took the exit for home, or what now passed for home. It wouldn't be that way for much longer, because something would have to change between Lauren and him. He'd have to find his place in an altered world, but so would everyone else. He wondered if most people would even notice when the Atlas had finished its work. There would be no breaking of seals, no signs in the sky. This world, Quayle said, would continue almost exactly as before, except for those who understood where, and how, to look. They would see shadows where no shadows should be, and forms shifting at the periphery of their vision. As for the rest, they would watch the rise of intolerance, and the subjugation of the weak by the powerful. They would witness inequality, despotism, and environmental ruination. They would be told by the ignorant and self-interested that this was in the natural order of things.

But in their hearts they would know better, and feel afraid.

LIII

Parker, Angel, and Louis traveled together to Amsterdam with KLM, on the grounds – as Louis argued – that only the desperate flew internationally on an American airline. It might have been unpatriotic, but he had a point; Parker couldn't recall having experienced a more comfortable flight, although it helped that the federal government was picking up the tab.

Two people were waiting for them, independent of each other, upon their arrival. The first was a driver, although the kind that looked like he might have learned his trade at the controls of a militarized vehicle, or possibly the wheel of a getaway car. He was in his late fifties, of medium height and heavy build. He wasn't holding a sign, but zeroed in on the three men as soon as they entered the arrivals hall. He ignored Parker and Angel, and spoke only to Louis.

'It's been a while,' he said.

His expression gave no clue as to whether he regarded this as a good or bad thing.

'It has,' said Louis.

With that the driver turned his back on them and headed for the exit without bothering to check if they were following.

'Well,' said Parker, 'that was a touching scene.'

'An old friend,' said Louis.

'Obviously. He seemed very emotional at being reunited with you.'

But before they could proceed, their path was blocked by a young woman with short red hair who barely came up to Parker's shoulder, but with whom he wouldn't have screwed for all the air miles in the world. She was lean the way hunting dogs were lean.

'Mr Parker?'

'Yes.'

'My name is Armitage. I'm one of the legats here in the Netherlands. SAC Ross informed us you were on your way.'

Which was the downside of spending government money, Parker thought. He hadn't shared their travel arrangements with Ross, but nonetheless wasn't shocked to find a federal welcoming committee at Schiphol. They could have hidden their tracks better, but Parker had decided that Ross was already aware of their destination, and the false trail should be laid after their arrival. There was no point in alerting him by attempting misdirection from the off.

Armitage took in Angel and Louis. She didn't appear concerned at their presence, merely interested, probably as a result of whatever background information Ross had seen fit to share with her. Angel nodded a greeting, while Louis found something more interesting in the distance to engage his attention. The chauffeur, meanwhile, was no longer anywhere to be seen.

'Agent Ross asked me to ensure that you got to your hotel safely,' said Armitage, 'and offer any assistance you might require.'

'You mean he ordered you to keep an eye on us,' said Parker.

Armitage didn't bother trying to deny it.

'He did tell me a great deal about you.'

'Anything good?' said Angel.

'We have excellent relations with the Dutch authorities,' said Armitage. 'We wouldn't want you to jeopardize them.'

'That would be a "No",' Parker informed Angel.

'I figured,' said Angel, 'once I managed to translate all that fancy diplomatic language.'

Parker returned his attention to Armitage.

'I think we have transportation already arranged, but we appreciate the offer.'

'And I'd appreciate it if you could tell me where you plan on staying while you're in the country.'

'I'm sure you would,' said Parker.

Armitage waited. To her credit, she remained unperturbed. If she knew their arrival time, she must also have been aware of the hotel bookings made on the same credit card. It was her attempt to test the waters, and she'd found them to be cold.

'I see,' she said, at last.

'I thought you might.'

Armitage proffered a business card, which Parker accepted.

'Feel free to get in touch,' she said, 'day or night.'

'I'm sorry,' said Parker, 'but I don't have any cards of my own with me.'

'Don't worry about it,' she said. 'I have your number. And I mean that in every sense.'

She didn't bother saying goodbye, but vanished into the crowd. Once she was out of sight, Louis zoned back in.

'Those reservations we made with Ross's money?' he said.

'Yes?'

'We're not going to use them.'

'I guessed as much,' said Parker. 'You have somewhere else in mind?'

'I did, from the start.'

'She'll follow us.'

Louis picked up his bag and started walking.

'She'll try.'

It was, Parker later decided, the most terrifying trip he'd ever taken in a motorized vehicle. He still hadn't learned the driver's name by the end of it, but he hoped with all his heart that he'd never again have to spend time in a car with him. They lost Armitage about five minutes out of the airport. She was in the front passenger seat of a silver Mercedes, being driven by a man slightly older than she was, and dressed more casually. Parker made him for a local, but he was no match for Louis's buddy, who drove like a man with fire licking at his tires. But if the motorway journey was bad, the city driving was worse, as trams, pedestrians, and any number of cyclists appeared only seconds from destruction. Parker looked to his right, and saw that Angel's eyes were firmly closed.

'You okay?' Parker asked.

'Just tell me when it's over.'

'You'll know when he stops.'

'That's no guarantee. If he stops hard enough, I'll just keep going. This belt won't save me.'

But eventually they came to a halt outside a canal house on Herengracht. It bore no name, so clearly wasn't a hotel. An elderly woman came to the door as the driver removed their bags from the trunk of the car. Angel and Parker watched as Louis approached her.

'You've changed,' she said.

'Older,' Louis replied.

'No, in other ways.'

Louis gestured toward Angel.

'Blame him,' he said, before reconsidering. 'Actually, blame both of them.'

The woman gripped Louis's right arm.

'He'll be pleased to see you.'

'You sure about that?'

'Yes. He was always very fond of you. And you are the last of them, the last of the Reapers . . .'

The building was divided into four self-contained apartments, the first-floor unit being occupied, at least temporarily, by the woman, with the other three seemingly vacant. The rooms were small but comfortable, and furnished with antiques that managed to impress without being oppressive. It had the feel of a safe house, a place of refuge. It contained no books, no magazines, no TV, and the only toiletries were travel-size containers of shampoo and shaving foam, disposable razors, and a single paper-wrapped bar of soap in each bathroom. A table on the first floor had been set for breakfast: fruit, bread, preserves, and cold meats. They had eaten on the plane, but Parker found room for some coffee and fruit.

The woman, whom Louis introduced as Anouk, drank her coffee while standing by the window, alternating her attention between her guests and the canal beyond. Music played low from a radio. Parker noticed that Anouk wore no rings on her fingers, but two hung from a chain around her neck: a pair of gold wedding bands, one thicker than the other. She caught the direction of his gaze.

'Eczema,' she said. 'I could never wear anything on my fingers, so I put my wedding ring on a chain instead. When my husband died, I added his to mine.'

Something in the way she mentioned her spouse, and the manner in which Louis paused ever so briefly while buttering his bread, led Parker to understand that this was difficult history. He did not pursue the subject. If Louis wanted to explain later, he would.

'How long will you stay?' Anouk asked.

'A few days,' said Louis.

She finished her coffee.

'Long enough,' she said. 'Always with you, just long enough.'

She placed her cup in the sink, and left without saying anything more.

'What now?' said Parker.

'We rest. Later, I'll go out. When I come back, I'll know more.'

Angel turned to Parker.

'Is it me, or did everyone just get more enigmatic since we landed?'

'It's the foreign air.'

'Well, I'm sure I'll be illuminated in good time.' He shot Louis a meaningful look before heading upstairs. The flight had exhausted him; he could barely keep his eyes open, and his face was ashen.

'Anything you want to tell me?' said Parker, once Angel had gone.

'Back in the day,' said Louis, 'I did some work here for a man named De Jaager.'

He didn't elaborate on what that work might have entailed. He didn't have to. After all, as Anouk had said, Louis was the last of the Reapers. He cut men down.

'The final contract, Timmerman, I did for free. It wasn't his real name, just what people called him. It means "the Timber Man". They all had nicknames back then: The Reverend, The Old Guy. Probably still do. Makes them feel important. Timmerman was a Bosnian Serb from Belgrade, linked to the Zemun clan.

The Serbs were running ecstasy and heroin from the Balkans through the Netherlands, then on to the rest of Europe. Timmerman did their wet work for them, and there was a lot of it. The Serbs and the Dutch have been involved in turf wars since the seventies, but it all got messier after the Balkans exploded. The Dutch were no longer just dealing with Serb gangsters; now they were facing down mass murderers.

'Timmerman earned his name by crucifying Muslims and Croats during the war – he didn't distinguish between men and women, apart from raping the women first – and brought his hobby with him when he came to the Netherlands. One of the first men he nailed to a wall after he got here was Jos, Anouk's husband. Jos was only a driver – no rough stuff – but the Zemuns wanted to send a message about the new dispensation, and he was a soft target. They left him to die in a warehouse in De Heining.'

Louis poured himself a little more coffee.

'So I found Timmerman, and I executed him. Paulus, the man who drove us here, is Jos and Anouk's nephew, and De Jaager is Anouk's brother-in-law. De Jaager is mostly a facilitator, not a criminal, although it's a subtle distinction. He puts the right people in touch with one another, and takes a commission.'

'Have I forced you to renew an acquaintance you'd prefer to have left dormant?' Parker asked.

'You've never forced me to do anything. I asked these people for their assistance, and they agreed to help. They could have refused, and no one would have held anything against anyone else. They're taking a chance, just as I am, maybe as we all are. The Zemuns haven't gone away, and they haven't forgotten Timmerman.'

'Do the Zemuns know about you?'

'They know Timmerman was killed by an outside contractor, and that's all. They've had a lot of time to ask questions, but I'd have heard if they were getting close.'

'Is De Jaager the one you're meeting later?'

'Yes.'

'But not here?'

'No. He never comes here. Even Anouk doesn't live in this place. No one does. It's a shelter, a neutral zone. We can spend a couple of nights here, but then we'll have to move.'

'What about weapons?'

Louis lifted his jacket. The butt of a little pistol poked from a discreet holster by his right side.

'My room only had toiletries,' said Parker.

'If you need something . . .'

'I'll ask.'

Louis stood. 'I'm going to rest for a couple of hours. You should do the same.'

Parker nodded. 'I'll head up shortly.'

He was left alone with only the music for company. He stood at the window and took in its framed view of Herengracht. He thought he might go for a walk later, find a place to get coffee or a glass of wine, and try to gauge the flow of the city. This was just his second trip to Europe, and while he had been in Amsterdam for only a few hours, already the United States seemed impossibly young. But he remained concerned for Bob Johnston, now alone in England.

Anouk appeared in the doorway.

'I'm sorry,' she said. 'I didn't mean to disturb you.'

'Not at all,' said Parker. 'I'm done, thank you.'

She touched the wedding rings on their chain.

'Did he tell you,' she asked, 'about this?'

'Yes.'

'I know about you, too.'

'Good,' said Parker.

'Yes,' said Anouk, as she began clearing away the remains of breakfast, 'I think maybe you are.'

LIV

Sometimes, Hynes thought, the gods of policing – or, more likely, the more potent deities of criminality – found ways to scupper the best laid plans of ordinary, decent coppers. First of all, Gackowska's car was involved in a collision at Gateshead, which delayed her arrival at the station by an hour, with the remains of her rear bumper poking up from the back seat when she did eventually appear, and her face a mask of fury. They'd planned to pick up Ryan Clifton at his home, before he headed off to school, but the accident put paid to that idea. Hynes and Gackowska instead drove straight to Larkin-Brook, only to discover that Clifton hadn't yet made an appearance. This wasn't an entirely unusual occurrence, according to the headmistress, although she didn't sound particularly heartbroken at the prospect of Clifton's absence. Hynes guessed that she probably had quite enough bastards to be getting along with, thanks very much, and one fewer would be a small but welcome mercy.

They then headed for the Clifton home in Heron Hill, which was among the oldest of the suburban estates built by the city council after World War One in order to tackle overcrowding and poor housing. For many years it had been one of the more desirable places to live for working-class families, with its tree-lined streets, and its gardens front and back, but it was a long time since anyone had clamored to be housed in Heron Hill. It was a black spot for dumping, with rubbish strewn over its neglected greens, and a nexus for every kind of anti-social activity imaginable: drug abuse, vehicle crime, criminal damage and arson, violence and sexual offenses, possession of weapons – and even, Hynes suspected, given the undeniable vigor, enthusiasm, and originality of its criminal element, some transgressions that had probably yet to be categorized. Any store in the area that stocked Lambert cigarettes, white cider, and lottery tickets was unlikely to struggle for business. As for how the estate had come by its name, Hynes could only speculate, but he guessed that no heron with even a rudimentary instinct for self-preservation had alighted there in many years.

Perhaps surprisingly, the Clifton residence was one of the better-maintained houses on its street, although it wasn't exactly up against stiff competition. The windows were clean, the grass was mown, and someone had even made an effort to grow some flowers in the beds. A white van stood in the drive, its rear doors secured by triple external bolts, with a raised metal security post embedded in the concrete to prevent the vehicle from being stolen.

The woman who answered the door carried the marks of tiredness and self-neglect that came from being part of the working poor. Her face had the wrinkles and lines of an older person, and her cheeks the gauntness of one who habitually went without. Her long hair was colored black from a bottle, and her face was too pale for her lipstick. Combined with heavy mascara and purple eye shadow, it lent her the appearance of someone who had gone ten rounds with the champ and emerged the loser. She was struggling to get her right arm into a coat while holding the door open with her left. Under the coat, she wore what looked like a store uniform. Her shoulders slumped as she saw the two police officers on her doorstep, marking them for what they were even before they displayed their warrant cards.

'What's he done now?' she asked.

'What's who done?' said Hynes.

'Ryan. Why else would you be here?'

'He hasn't done anything,' said Gackowska, 'not that we know of. We just wanted to speak with him. We thought he might be able to help us with some information. Are you his mother?'

'For my sins. I'm also late for work. And Ryan's at school, so you'd best look for him there.'

'He's not at school, unfortunately. We've already been and asked.'

Mrs Clifton's features contorted with frustration.

'There's nothing I can do about that now,' she said. 'I'll talk to him when he gets home.'

Hynes noted that she said 'I'll', not 'we'll.' It made him wonder about Ryan Clifton's father.

'What about his dad?' he asked.

'What about him?'

'Is he still around?'

Hynes had a momentary out-of-body experience as he both watched and heard himself say something he instantly regretted.

'Yes, he fucking is still around,' said Mrs Clifton. 'He's in bed, a-fucking-sleep, because he was working until all fucking hours last night. Show some respect, why don't you?'

Gackowska shot Hynes a look indicating that, should he have any more stupid questions he fancied asking, he might like to resist the urge until he was alone in front of a mirror.

'I'm sorry,' said Hynes, and he was. He'd arrived on the Cliftons' doorstep with a set of assumptions based on where they lived, and the character of their son. And, yes, ninety-five percent of the time he might have been correct, but that didn't make the underlying attitude any fairer. 'No offense meant.'

But the fire had gone out of Mrs Clifton almost as quickly as it had ignited. She didn't have the energy to spare for pointless anger.

'It doesn't matter,' she said, as she pulled the door closed behind her. 'I've heard worse.'

She bustled past them, and they followed.

'Perhaps we could give you a lift to work,' said Gackowska, 'to make up for it.'

'To ask questions about Ryan, more like.'

'That, too,' said Gackowska.

Mrs Clifton checked her watch, but there was a theatrical aspect to it. Hynes guessed that she was probably at least curious as to why the police wanted to speak to her son. Ryan Clifton might have been a nasty sod at times, but he was her nasty sod, and she was damned if she was going to let him be thrown to a pair of police wolves, not without good cause.

'I work in Hillstreet,' she said, naming one of the big shopping arcades in Middlesbrough city center. 'You can drop me off there.'

Hynes opened the back door of the car for her, and Gackowska took the passenger seat, although it was she who had driven from the station. Being the passenger would make it easier for her to engage with Mrs Clifton. While the woman was getting settled, Hynes made a quick call to Priestman, informing her of the situation. It wasn't a disaster by any means, despite the earlier delay. Ryan Clifton, being absent, had no knowledge of the police's interest in Karl Holmby, and they now had Clifton's mother in the back of the car, so she couldn't have alerted her son even if she wanted to – and so far, they saw no evidence of any such desire on her part. Had she wanted to warn Ryan of the police's interest in him, she could simply have declined the offer of a ride. Nevertheless Hynes promised Priestman – who was already on her way to the university to question Karl Holmby – that they'd hold on to Mrs Clifton for as long as they could.

'We might even take her for tea and a bun, to kill some time,' he said. 'She's already late for work anyway. We'll talk to her boss, just to make sure she doesn't get any aggravation, or lose pay. She works in a supermarket. I expect she'll be glad of the opportunity to skive off for an hour or two.'

Priestman agreed that keeping Mrs Clifton occupied was probably a good idea until they had eyes on Karl Holmby, and hung up. Hynes took a last look at Heron Hill. He smelled burning on the air. Someone was setting fire to refuse. He supposed it was better than dumping it, although he couldn't be certain. He climbed in the car to find Mrs Clifton glowering at him from the back seat.

'Would you like me to turn on the siren?' Hynes asked, as they pulled away from the curb.

'Fuck off.'

He thought she might have been smiling as she spoke, but it was hard to tell.

Priestman, accompanied by Nabih Uddin, had more luck with Karl Holmby. Since the boy was over eighteen, the police were under no obligation to inform an appropriate adult of their intention to interview him, and so were free to turn up at the Teesside University campus, take a seat outside the lecture theater, and watch Holmby file in as part of a coterie of young men and women. Uddin had obtained Holmby's photograph from his police proof-of-age card, and his appearance hadn't changed since the picture was taken. Priestman thought he was good-looking in a pretty way, and carried himself with a certain confidence, an absence of awkwardness. As much as his height – he was six feet tall, at least – this made him stand out from the crowd. It wasn't hard to see why he might have caught Romana Moon's eye.

The timetable for Holmby's course was available online, so they knew he had the rest of the day free after a morning exam. They might have approached him at home before he left for college, but they didn't want to disrupt his education unnecessarily, or tip off his family to any police interest. He would be easier to handle alone. Priestman could have left the Holmby questioning to Uddin and another officer – it wasn't as though she didn't have enough on her plate – but based on what Hynes had learned about him, she was keen to talk to the boy herself. And if nothing else, she had learned the virtue of patience during her years on the force. It was impossible to commit murder without leaving evidence, however minor, and one piece inevitably led to another. They would find Romana Moon's killer. They just needed a break, and Karl Holmby might provide it.

She made some calls while they waited, as did Uddin. He was still working on the prayer beads, and with the help of the neighborhood inspectors, and PCs on the ground, had collated a list of some of the more vociferously misogynistic members of the local Muslim communities, who were currently in the process of being interviewed. In addition, he had also obtained descriptions of a handful of white males whom storeowners recalled purchasing *misbahas*, along with some names. The individuals in question were converts to Islam, but so far all had alibis for the night of Romana Moon's death. The descriptions of the remaining men were so generic as to be almost useless.

Uddin remained skeptical that the killings were the work of a Muslim, and was leaning toward the theory that someone in the white community was trying to foment unrest. Like other forces, Northumbria had a Prevent team tasked with working closely with communities to identify those at risk of radicalization, but a good part of the team's time and resources were being eaten up in monitoring potential right-wing activists, particularly in the poorer parts of south Durham, including some of the former mining towns. Back in 2010, a truck driver from Burnopfield, a member of a group called the Aryan Strike Force, had been jailed for ten years for making ricin, a potent toxin, in his kitchen, and the northeast accounted for almost a quarter of right-wing referrals under the Prevent program. Killing a white girl, and trying to frame a Muslim for the crime, might have been regarded as a serious escalation, were it not for the fact the Burnopfield trucker had enough ricin in his home to kill nine people.

The exam finished shortly after eleven, with Holmby being one of the first out the door. He saw them coming, and, like Ryan Clifton's mother earlier, didn't need a uniform or warrant card to identify them. He seemed to lose some of his height along with a little of his confidence, as though one were a function of the other.

'Karl?' said Priestman. 'My name is DI Priestman, and I'd like to talk to you about Romana Moon.'

She didn't get any further, because Karl Holmby's face crumpled and, like Simon Harris before him, he started to cry over the dead woman.

LV

Hynes and Gackowska took Mrs Clifton to The Teahouse on Grange Road. By the time they reached their destination, she had given Gackowska permission to call her Tina, but when Hynes did the same, she swore at him again. Hynes, being built of stern stuff, elected not to take it personally. He ordered tea and scones for three, and made sure to keep the receipt, adding by hand the quid he'd thrown in the tip jar. He'd never get that quid back, of course, but it was the principle of the thing.

Tina Clifton called her workplace in their presence, informing her boss that she'd be late, and explaining why. Gackowska then took the phone, and stressed that Tina Clifton was in no trouble of any kind, but was proving hugely helpful with information pertaining to an ongoing investigation. She also added that Tina was the kind of employee the store should be happy to have, and a credit to the whole team, which Hynes thought was overegging the pudding, but seemed to please Clifton.

Once they were settled, he decided to stay quiet and let Gackowska do the heavy lifting. They learned that Tina Clifton had two children, of whom Ryan was the younger. The daughter, Becca, was in Australia, and unlikely to be returning any time soon.

'I'm glad,' said Tina Clifton. 'I miss her a lot, but she's better off out there.'

Hynes wasn't about to argue. He'd never been to Australia, but couldn't imagine there were many parts of it less appealing than Heron Hill.

'And Ryan?' said Gackowska.

If it were possible for someone to weep briefly on the inside but remain dry-eyed without, Clifton managed it. A lifetime of memories crossed her face in an instant.

296

'Ryan's not so bad, or not as bad as they say,' she said.

'"They"?'

'Oh, you know: the teachers at his school, the guidance counselors. They don't hold out much hope for him. They don't even like him very much.' The tremor in her voice was barely detectable, and she conquered it quickly. 'He's dyslexic, which doesn't help, and he's angry, but they're all angry at that age, I suppose. I know I was. Still am, probably, but it's worse for boys. My Becca was a monster all the way through to her late teens – Jesus, the fights we had – but I could see the woman in her, even then. Ryan, though, he's still a kid, and behaves like one. He and his dad go at it hammer and tongs. Sometimes I think the best thing for Ryan would be to join his sister in Australia, even if it was only to work in a bar for a year, or pick fruit, or whatever it is you do over there if you've got no skills. I'm afraid his dad might kill him otherwise.'

She caught the frown on Hynes's face.

'I'm only joking,' she said.

'Is there physical violence between them?' Gackowska asked.

'What do you think?'

They dropped the subject.

'Ryan has been in trouble with us in the past,' said Gackowska.

It was all relatively minor – criminal damage, trespassing, possession of cannabis resin, a controlled substance, although not with intent to supply – but they were familiar with the pattern, and how it could escalate.

'That hardly makes him special in Heron Hill,' said Clifton. 'And you're asking me a lot of questions, but you still haven't told me why you turned up on my doorstep this morning, unless it was just my turn to be fed scones by the taxpayer.'

Hynes decided to take the baton from Gackowska at this next stage of their little relay.

'What can you tell us about Ryan's friends?'

'Any friend in particular? Come on, out with it.'

'Karl Holmby.'

'I don't think Ryan and Karl see much of each other anymore.'

Hynes got the impression that she considered this a positive development.

'But they used to?'

'Yes, when they were at school together.'

'Even though Ryan was a year behind Karl?'

'He wasn't always. Ryan got held back two years ago, but he and Karl are the same age. Born in the same month, as it happens. They've known each other all their lives.'

'So what changed things between them?'

'University, for a start. Karl has a new set of friends, while Ryan is still hanging around with a lot of the same people from school. But . . .'

She paused. Hynes and Gackowska gave her time.

'I don't even know why I'm telling you this,' said Clifton.

'Because you don't know us,' said Gackowska. 'It's not like we're teachers, or other parents at the school.'

'You're police. I know that much.'

'We're not trying to make life any harder for your son than it already is. It's Karl Holmby we're curious about.'

'So why aren't you talking to *his* mum?'

'We may well do that.'

'Or Karl himself?'

They didn't answer, and her face changed as she saw the light. Tina Clifton, thought Hynes, was about as far from stupid as you could get. He hadn't met her husband, so could only assume it was his genes that were dominant in their son. 'Oh, I get it now. You came to pick up Ryan so he couldn't warn Karl, and right now mirror images of you two are looking for Karl, or already have him.'

'Not quite mirror images,' said Hynes. 'I'm better-looking than the other bloke.'

'God help him,' said Clifton.

Hynes looked hurt. 'I bought you a scone.'

'It'll take more than that to turn me blind. And what's Karl done to make you lot interested in him?'

'We'd rather not say for now,' said Gackowska. She had decided that Hynes appeared recently to have contracted some form of flirtation virus. If necessary, she'd forcibly inoculate him by banging his head against a wall. 'It may be nothing at all.'

'Or maybe it's Romana Moon,' said Clifton.

See, Hynes wanted to pronounce, *smart as a shiny new button, this one.* He took a moment to check the surrounding tables, just in case someone might be paying attention to them, but the nearest was unoccupied, and he doubted their voices would carry any further.

'Why would you say that?' Gackowska asked.

'Because why else would four coppers be tracking two kids from Larkin-Brook?'

'And suppose it was about Romana Moon?' said Hynes softly. 'What would you say then?'

'I'd say that my boy, for all his faults, would never hurt a woman, and if you're trying to suggest otherwise, then maybe I should phone a lawyer.'

'We've no reason to believe that Ryan had anything to do with the murder of Romana Moon,' said Gackowska.

'And Karl Holmby?'

Neither of the two officers replied. It was deliberate on their part, just like Gackowska's use of the word 'murder'. Let Tina Clifton think what she wanted. What was important was that she understood the seriousness of the crime under investigation.

'Fucking hell,' said Clifton.

'Did Ryan and Karl have some kind of falling out?' said Gackowska.

It took a while for Clifton to answer. Hynes knew what she was doing: replaying the lives of her son and his friend, wondering if she might have failed to spot something foul in Karl Holmby – and perhaps, despite any protestations to the contrary, in her own son.

'No, or if they did, it was before what happened to that poor woman. Karl just moved on, leaving Ryan behind, but he was always going to do that. Ryan couldn't see it, but I could. Karl's brighter than Ryan, more ambitious, but it's also just the kind of person he is. He uses people, and when they've served their purpose, he throws them away. He can be charming, but I never really trusted him. He wasn't just clever: he was too clever.'

'Did Karl or Ryan ever mention Romana Moon to you?' said Gackowska.

'She taught both of them, so her name would come up on occasion. Ryan certainly spoke about her. I don't remember Karl doing it – well, except one time, in our kitchen, when he and Ryan were laughing together about something that happened in the schoolyard involving her, and Karl made a remark I didn't much like.'

'Do you remember what it was?'

'Not exactly. It was some smutty innuendo. Miss Moon sometimes rode a bike into school, if the weather was nice, and Karl started talking about riding her, or her riding him, and cocks instead of saddles. I told him to keep his mouth shut, and not to talk about any woman that way. I doubt it did much good in the long run, but it kept both of them quiet for a while.'

'When was this?'

'Oh, probably at the start of Karl's final year in school.'

'And that's the only time you heard them speak about her?'

Clifton's expression altered, and they watched as she tried to pin down a memory.

'No, there was another incident, now that you come to mention it. I suppose I put it down to Karl becoming more mature, or the influence of university life on him. It was one of the last times he and Ryan were together at the house, so it would have been, oh, just before last Christmas. They were in the living room, and I was in the hall. Can't remember what I was doing. Tidying, probably. I spend my life cleaning up after Ryan and his dad. Ryan and Karl were watching some film on TV, and Ryan must have been commenting on one of the actresses, because he said her tits – his word – were nearly as good as Miss Moon's. I was too tired to say anything about it, at least not then, but Karl did it for me. He told Ryan to keep his fucking mouth shut, and watch what he said in future. I think he gave Ryan a thump for good measure, because I heard Ryan cry out. At the time I just thought, you know, good on Karl, but I don't think I really registered how angry he sounded.'

She regarded the two listening officers.

'Was there something going on between Romana and Karl?' she asked.

'We don't know,' said Hynes.

'But you think there might have been.'

'If there was, would Karl have discussed it with Ryan?'

'Maybe, but Ryan wouldn't have joked about her breasts if he'd known. He'd have more sense than to do that.'

Elspeth Calley suspected that the affair between Karl Holmby and Romana Moon, if it was a reality, had begun after Holmby had left Larkin-Brook. The change in Holmby's attitude toward Moon, noted by Tina Clifton, seemed to support this.

'Is there anything else you can tell us that might be helpful?' Gackowska asked.

'No, I don't think so.'

'Did you ever meet Romana Moon?'

'Of course: at parent-teacher meetings, and once when Ryan was in trouble for fighting in class, or after class, or before class. Ryan's always in hot water over this or that. Sometimes, I think he always will be.'

'I spoke to him, you know,' said Hynes.

'Did you? When?'

'Yesterday, at the school. I told him to mind my car.'

'And did he?'

'It was still there when I got back, complete with wheels, so he must have done. If you want me to, I could have a word with him again. I could take him for a coffee, maybe buy him a scone.'

'Ha! Do you really think that would work with my Ryan?'

'I don't know. It worked with his mum.'

He could see the words 'Fuck off' forming on her lips again, but they didn't come. Instead she said, 'Let me think about it.'

Hynes scribbled his number on a page from his notebook, and handed it to her.

'Don't go sharing that with all your single friends,' he said.

This time, she did tell him to fuck off.

And she was definitely smiling.

LVI

Like Hynes, Nabih Uddin was currently out of pocket, although only for three cups of tea. He had already decided that he didn't like Karl Holmby enough to buy him anything more substantial, and he thought Priestman might be similarly unenthused, mainly because she was being unusually friendly. In Uddin's experience, the apparent pleasantness of Priestman's manner was frequently inversely proportional to the depth of her dislike, and she was currently all smiles.

Holmby had recovered his composure pretty quickly. In Uddin's view, what they'd seen had amounted only to a simulacrum of the act of crying, since it hadn't been accompanied by actual tears.

'Because of what happened to Miss Moon,' he said, when they asked him why he'd become so upset.

He sipped his tea, cradling the cup as though for warmth. Uddin noticed that he slurped as he drank, which was another reason to dislike him, Uddin being very particular about manners. The world, in his view, didn't need any more unnecessary noise.

'Were you expecting us to contact you?' said Priestman.

'Not me personally, but I assume you're speaking to everyone who knew her.'

'We're not, as it happens. Our list is still quite short, for now.'

Holmby looked puzzled. 'So why me?'

'How well did you know Romana Moon?'

Priestman was still radiating goodwill, but Uddin could see that Holmby was beginning to doubt her sincerity. He wondered how long it would take for him to start putting up the shutters. Not very long at all, as it turned out.

'Uh, maybe I should call someone,' he said.

'Such as?'

'A solicitor.'

'Why would you want to do that? Have you done something wrong?'

'No.'

'Well, then. You're not under arrest: we just want to talk to you. If you prefer, we can take you to a police station, and you can be formally questioned there. I have to warn you, though, that if you request legal advice, it can take up to thirty-six hours before it's made available. In the meantime, you'll have to sit in a cell. We'll inform your mum as a courtesy, of course, even though you're no longer a minor, but you might be happier not to have her involved. I would be, if I were you.'

Uddin didn't know if Holmby's degree studies in forensics touched on his legal rights. He hoped they didn't. The police had nothing with which to charge him, and no reason to hold him for questioning. If he got up and walked away, they'd just have to finish their tea alone.

But Holmby didn't walk away. He was a sharp boy, yet the operative word here wasn't 'sharp' but 'boy'. He was just a teenager, and as such had all of a teenager's arrogance and insecurity, which was like building a house on shifting sands. Uddin could see that he was curious, and maybe Holmby thought he was clever enough to joust with them without giving too much away. On the other hand, if he had been having an affair with Romana Moon, he must already have guessed the reason for their interest in him, especially after being informed by Priestman that they weren't simply working their way alphabetically through a list of past and present pupils at Larkin-Brook. This puzzled Uddin, because – unless Holmby was practiced at dissimulation, even to a sociopathic degree, which admittedly wasn't beyond the bounds of possibility given what had been done to Romana Moon – he appeared genuinely confused.

'Okay,' said Holmby at last. 'I'll talk to you.'

'Thank you,' said Priestman. 'We'll try to be as quick as we can. How well did you know Romana Moon?'

'Well enough.'

'What does that mean?'

'She helped me with my studies. I needed three A levels to get into the course here: two Bs and a C, but that was the minimum. She taught biology, and I got my B thanks to her, but she also tutored me in mathematics, because Mr Bowen had cancer and couldn't do it. I don't think he'd have offered anyway, even if he'd been well. He's not that kind.'

'Did Miss Moon give similar help to any other pupils?'

'No, I don't think so.'

'Which is it: no, she didn't, or you don't think she did?'

Uddin caught the anger in Holmby's eyes; a fleeting glimpse of what lay beneath, but quickly veiled. Holmby didn't like being challenged in this way, particularly by a woman; didn't like it one bit. Uddin glanced at Priestman, and suspected her smile was a bit more genuine. She'd seen it, too.

Come out, come out, wherever you are . . .

'No, she didn't,' said Holmby, with some force.

'You were special, were you?'

'Have you been to Larkin-Brook?' said Holmby.

'No, but my colleagues have paid a visit.'

'Pity they didn't tell you what it's like.'

'And what is it like?'

'It's a shithole. I was the only one in our year going for a course that required three good A levels. So, yeah: in answer to your question, maybe I was special. I wanted to get into university. I wanted to study forensics. Most of all, I wanted a qualification that would eventually get me out of Middlesbrough. Happy?'

'Happy for you. Why did you want to study forensics?'

'I've always been keen on it, ever since I started watching *CSI* and *Bones* with my mum. Those shows are bullshit – there's better stuff on Netflix, real stuff – but the science behind them is the thing. I wanted to know more.'

'So you were a bit of an expert before you even started studying the subject?'

It seemed to Uddin that Holmby almost physically recoiled from the trap.

'I wouldn't say that.'

'Sorry, it just appeared that was what you were saying.'

Holmby pushed his cup away, still half-full. The gloves were off now.

'Do you think I hurt Miss Moon?'

'She wasn't hurt. She was butchered.'

'I didn't do it. I wouldn't do something like that to anyone, but especially not to her.'

'Because you liked her?'

'Yes.'

'And she helped you with your studies?'

'Yes.'

'Is that all?'

'What do you mean? Isn't that enough?'

'I don't know. Would you have said that you and Miss Moon were friends?'

'Yeah, we were friendly.'

'That's not the same thing.'

'Isn't it?'

Uddin had to give Holmby credit: he wasn't easily rattled, and even when he took a knock, he recovered his poise with ease. He had something of the boxer about him, dancing, dodging blows.

'Not in my experience,' said Priestman. 'I find that people sometimes confuse my being friendly with wanting to be their friend.'

Holmby thought about this. 'I suppose that's true.'

'So, which one were you and Miss Moon: friendly, or friends?'

'I think we were friends.'

'Anything more than that?'

Holmby eyed them both carefully before fixing his attention on Uddin.

'Doesn't say much, does he?'

'He's the watchful type. He spots all kinds of things, like when someone doesn't want to answer a question. That makes him anxious.'

Uddin's face remained entirely neutral.

'How can you tell?' said Holmby.

'I'll admit the change is subtle. Back to Miss Moon. Were you two anything more than friends?'

'What does that mean?'

Priestman stopped writing. Uddin noticed that Holmby had started out trying to read her notes upside down, but gave up when he couldn't interpret Priestman's shorthand. She could touch-type as well, spoke three languages, and had a near-photographic memory. Privately, Nabih Uddin regarded Priestman's combined abilities as tantamount to sorcery.

'Karl,' she said, 'I'm now wondering if you actually really want to see the inside of a holding cell after all. You're studying forensics at university, so I find it hard to believe you're stupid. But just in case you somehow lucked your way in here, and are too frightened to admit you don't understand all the long words, I'll clarify my question. I'm asking if the relationship between you and Miss Moon ever went further than friendship – and be careful how you answer.'

'Why would you ask me that?'

Uddin couldn't tell if Holmby was shocked, or just pretending to be. On reflection, he thought it might be a little of both.

'Have I offended your delicate sensibilities?' said Priestman.

'She was my teacher.'

'Have you ever read a tabloid newspaper? If you haven't, you'd be surprised at what goes on in the world.'

'We were friends. She helped me. She—'

'Yes, we got all that first time round. Spare us the echo. What interests me are rumors of a relationship between you and Romana Moon.'

Holmby was goggling like a fish, but Uddin could also see him calculating his response.

'I think he's about to lie,' said Uddin.

'Really?' Priestman didn't take her eyes from Holmby.

'Yes, although he may also have been lying already. I get that vibe from him.'

'See?' said Priestman to Holmby. 'Told you he was watchful.'

'Anyway, I'm bored with him now,' Uddin continued, 'and I don't want any more tea. Let's take him in.'

'Wait!' said Holmby. 'I haven't had a chance to answer yet.'

'It's hardly worth hearing if you're just going to tell lies,' said Priestman.

'I haven't been telling lies, honest.'

'And I hate it,' said Uddin, 'when people append words like "honest", or "honestly", or "to be straight with you" to their statements. It gets my goat.'

He was no longer even bothering to look at Holmby. Uddin's face, thought Priestman, bore an expression of intense existential sadness, as though he had already heard too many lies in his life, yet Karl Holmby seemed intent on disappointing him further by adding at least one more untruth to his burden.

'I didn't sleep with Miss Moon, if that's what you mean,' said Holmby. 'I just said I did.'

'Said it to whom?' asked Priestman.

'Ryan.'

'Ryan Clifton?'

'Yes.'

'And why would you do that?'

Holmby shrugged. He couldn't meet her eyes, so kept his own fixed on the table.

'Dunno.'

'Dunno isn't good enough. Try again.'

'I thought it would be funny.'

'Funny to say that you'd slept with your ex-teacher?'

'And cool. Because she was older and, you know, good-looking.'

'Is that all?'

Holmby's face had already turned red, but it darkened further.

'No.' His voice was small.

'Go on.'

'I tried to, you know . . .'

'No, I don't.'

'I tried to kiss her once, at her flat. I *did* kiss her, but she pushed me away. She told me not to be silly.'

'When was this?'

'After I got my results. I went to her flat to tell her. She invited me in, asked if I wanted a coffee. She was really pleased. I hugged her, and she hugged me back, although not as hard, and that was when – when I did it.'

'But she rejected you.'

'Yes.'

'Was she nice about it?'

A shrug, which suggested the encounter hadn't just been awkward, but something more.

'How did it make you feel, when she did that?'

'I was ashamed.'

'Were you angry?'

'I suppose.'

'What did you do then?'

'I left.'

'Left?'

'I ran out, and—'

Holmby swallowed. He was still staring at the table, but Uddin could see that his face was red, and his eyes were watering, although whether from grief or remembered humiliation remained unclear.

'Go on. You've come this far. We may as well hear it all.'

'I called her a name.'

'What name?'

'I called her a cock-teaser.' The tears were in full flow now. 'I felt bad after, but I didn't know how to say I was sorry.'

'So instead you told Ryan Clifton that you'd slept with her?'

'Yes.'

'And he believed you?'

'Yes.'

'That was a strange way to show you were sorry for what happened.'

'I was still angry, too.'

'With Miss Moon?'

'And with myself – mostly with myself.' He looked up now. 'I wasn't angry enough to hurt her, though. I really liked her. I wouldn't be here if she hadn't helped me. I was planning to go to her funeral, bring some flowers. I was going to say sorry then. I thought it would be my last chance.'

Priestman sat back. She told herself that Karl Holmby was still just a boy, with all of a boy's capacity for selfishness and mindless malevolence, but if one of her sons ever behaved as badly as Holmby, she'd string him up by the balls.

'Karl, I have to ask you where you were on the night Romana Moon was killed.'

Holmby answered without hesitation.

'I was at home.'

'You seem very sure of that.'

'I had an exam the next day, which is how I know, and I haven't been going out much these past few weeks. I want to do well here, so I don't have time to mess about. Even if I hadn't been studying, I'd still have remembered where I was when I heard she died, and what I was doing when it might have happened.'

'Can someone confirm you were home?'

'My mum. She was with me.'

'Do you drive, Karl?'

'No. I mean, I've been behind the wheel of some of my mates' cars, and I know how to drive, but I don't have a full license. I'm going to work during the summer to pay for lessons, and pick up some old banger on the cheap. Either way, I figure a license would be a good thing to have.'

Priestman had resumed recording everything he said in her careful shorthand. Holmby watched her write.

'What is that?'

'It's a version of Pitman shorthand.'

'Must be useful.'

'It is. Who told you about Romana Moon's death?'

'Ryan did. He heard about it at school, and texted me.'

'And how did you react?'

'I saw the message as I was waiting for the bus home. I called him, just to be sure he wasn't joking.'

'Is that the kind of thing Ryan Clifton would joke about?'

'You never know with Ryan, but he swore he was telling the truth. I called my mum to check, and she said she'd heard it, too.'

'What did you do then?'

'I went back into college, and sat in the one of the toilet stalls.'

'Why?'

'I think I was in shock. I cried. I didn't want anyone to see me do it. I waited until the bathroom was empty before I came out to wash my face. After that, I went home.'

'Did you speak to anyone about Romana's death?'

'Lots of people. It was all anyone was talking about. I mean, it was on the news. I've never known anyone who was murdered before.'

Priestman put her pen away. She had more questions, but she sensed that Holmby was largely telling the truth – 'largely', because no one ever told the truth, not entirely. Still, the boy hadn't shied away from the poverty of his own behavior, and his shame did not appear counterfeit.

'Walk with me, Karl,' she said, and nodded at Uddin to suggest he should remain where he was. Uddin didn't move. He knew what Priestman was doing: checking to see if Holmby was carrying an injury to his leg, or even his back. If he were, it would be possible for him to hide it for short periods, but not if he walked on it for a while. Uddin kept an eye on them as they headed outside, but could as yet detect no sign of a limp from Holmby.

Uddin sat at the table, three cups before him, like a sidewalk huckster waiting for pigeons to dupe, and – in common with Priestman – wondered what Karl Holmby was hiding from them.

LVII

Hynes and Gackowska eventually found Ryan Clifton in Middlesbrough's Albert Park. Tina Clifton had suggested they try there, once they'd promised not to make any trouble for her son if they did track him down. He was sitting by the lake, a pad on his knee, sketching boats. So absorbed was he in his work that he didn't notice Gackowska approaching from his left, and didn't become aware of Hynes until the DS's shadow fell across him.

'Not bad,' said Hynes.

Clifton looked over his shoulder, saw who was speaking, and made as though to run, but Hynes clamped his right arm before he could rise, and held him down with his left hand.

'If you try to get away, I'll make your life a misery,' said Hynes. 'Really, I will. I've had lots of practice. But if you listen, and answer a few questions, I'll let you get back to your drawing. Who knows, I might even be inclined to smooth some ruffled feathers back at Larkin-Brook, save you a truancy report.'

'Why would you do that?' said Clifton. Hynes could feel that the boy remained ready to flee at the first opportunity. He didn't fancy trying to chase him around the park. It would be undignified. He considered cuffing him to the bench, but decided to save that as a last resort.

'Because deep down I'm a nice person. Everybody says so. Isn't that right, Detective Constable?'

Gackowska had joined them now, and was standing poised in case Clifton somehow managed to break free.

'No,' she said, 'they don't.'

'All right, so I lied, but I might be prepared to make an exception for you, Ryan. How about we buy you a cup of tea? We've

311

just had one, mind, but there's always room for another, and if there isn't, I can make room – though we don't need to go into the details of how I might do that, not unless you really want to.'

Ryan Clifton didn't look as though he wanted to discuss the functioning of DS Hynes's waterworks, sensible lad.

'What do you want to talk to me about?' he asked.

Hynes's smile faded.

'The murder of Romana Moon.'

Priestman didn't get much more out of Karl Holmby, beyond confirming that he didn't appear to be suffering from any obvious injury. Then again, they might have been mistaken in ascribing the dumping of Romana Moon's corpse to a possible fall. Even if her killer had injured himself, he could just as easily have sprained a wrist, or busted a rib. It was all supposition for the time being.

Karl Holmby lived alone with his mother. Claire Holmby worked in a care home, making 'shit money', according to her son. Her ex-husband, Clement Holmby, had done time at H.M. Prison Northumberland, and other institutions, on firearms charges, and possession of cocaine, amphetamine, and heroin with intent to supply. He was a rotten piece of work, by all accounts, including his own son's, but the last anyone had heard of him, he was living with a slapper in Sutton Coldfield. Karl had an older brother up in Newcastle, whom he saw occasionally, but they weren't very close. Karl also confirmed the drift away from the company of Ryan Clifton. He had college friends now, and Ryan didn't fit in with them – not that Karl had made any great effort to introduce Ryan to the group, preferring instead to keep his new life separate from the old.

'How does Ryan feel about that?' Priestman asked.

'I don't know. He's okay with it, I think. We don't talk about it much. Don't talk much at all anymore.'

Four different answers to the question, only the last two of which might have been true. Priestman let it go.

'We're going to have to ask your mum to corroborate what

you've told us about your being home on the night Romana Moon was murdered. We'll put it in the context of a general questioning of everyone who might have had contact with Romana, so your mum won't have to know about the lies you were spreading.'

Holmby nodded, but didn't say anything. Priestman stopped walking.

'Look at me, Karl.'

He did.

'If we find out you haven't been honest with us, I'll arrest you for obstructing the progress of a murder inquiry, and I'll make sure that your academic career comes to a permanent, grinding halt. Do you understand?'

'Yes.'

'Do you have anything else you want to say?'

'No.'

'Okay, then. We'll contact your mum later today. You could help us by sharing her phone number.'

Holmby recited it by heart, and Priestman added it to her notebook.

'We'll be in touch,' she said.

Holmby took in the campus, its buildings, and his fellow students, as though with new eyes, perhaps because of how close he might be to having it taken from him.

'Do you think you'll find whoever killed Miss Moon?' he asked.

'We're trying.'

'A quarter of all murders in the United Kingdom remain unsolved. Did you know that?'

'I might have read it somewhere.'

'It was in one of the Sunday newspapers, a few years back. I found the figures when I was researching an essay. Forty-two out of forty-four police forces in England and Wales provided data for the survey. You know which ones didn't?'

Priestman didn't answer, but let him talk.

'Staffordshire and Northumbria. So your force was one of only two that didn't release figures about their success with murder investigations. Why was that?'

'I don't know.'

Holmby shifted his bag on his right shoulder.

'I'm sorry you're the ones investigating Miss Moon's death,' he said. 'I think she deserves better.'

And he walked away.

The mention of Romana Moon seemed to have quashed any desire to run on Ryan Clifton's part, although this didn't cause him to make his way to Albert Park's coffee house with any noticeable degree of eagerness. Hynes didn't blame him. Unless Clifton was a complete idiot, he had probably figured out by now that his friendship with Karl Holmby had brought the police down on him. Hynes suspected that, if given the chance, Clifton would probably start out by lying in a misguided effort to protect his friend. Hynes didn't have the time or patience to tolerate any efforts at deception. After all, there was only so much tea a man could drink. With that in mind, he left Clifton at a table under Gackowska's watchful eye, ordered tea for three, a chunk of rocky road for Clifton – then, after a brief moment of doubt, a slice of lemon drizzle cake for himself – before setting them down on the table and announcing, 'We know your pal Karl Holmby claimed to be having sex with Romana Moon. If you try to deny it, I'll do my best to make sure you complete your education in prison. By the way, the piece of rocky road is yours. I don't like chocolate. Never have.'

Gackowska looked at the tray.

'What about the lemon drizzle?'

'That's mine.'

'Didn't you get me anything?'

'I hear you're watching your figure.'

'You're sharing that lemon drizzle.'

Hynes's shoulders slumped.

'Fine. I brought a knife, just in case you decided to be difficult.'

He cut the cake in two. Gackowska picked up the larger slice before Hynes could even put down the knife.

'I hope you die single,' he said.

'So do I,' said Gackowska. 'I won't have to share lemon drizzle with anyone.'

Clifton still hadn't touched his rocky road, so Hynes pushed the plate closer to him.

'Eat up, son. You're going to need your strength if you plan on annoying me more than you already have.'

Clifton reached for his cake.

'So,' said Hynes. 'Karl Holmby and Romana Moon: do tell.'

Sellars was at home when the call came through to his burner phone.

He had already chosen the next girl. He'd found her on a prostitution website: young – barely out of her teens, if that; council flat, with reviews that suggested she was working without a pimp, trying to earn some extra money in the evenings. One of the punters mentioned a crying baby, which had quite put him off his stride, so he'd docked her a star. Sellars made a note of the baby, and wondered if there was a way to take both of them. Two for the price of one: he could dispose of the girl at one site, and the infant at another. He'd never contemplated killing a child before, but what kind of life would it have if its mother was already working on her back? He'd be doing the poor mite a favor by putting it out of its misery.

Sometimes, Sellars marveled at how far he'd fallen.

But now his phone was ringing: Holmby. Maybe he'd sprinkled holy water on himself, and his ankle had miraculously healed.

'This had better be good news,' said Sellars.

But it wasn't.

All credit to Ryan Clifton: being the target of police questioning hadn't affected his appetite. He wolfed down the rocky road, crumbs and all. If the plate had been remotely edible, he'd probably have given that a try as well. In addition, any residual loyalty he might have felt toward Karl Holmby had rapidly dissipated under pressure. This was largely down to Gackowska, who – thanks to what they'd learned from Tina Clifton – pushed the right buttons when it came to exploiting the boy's bitterness at his friend's elevation to the ranks of university life. Ryan Clifton's sense of grievance ran deep and raw, and Hynes knew that whatever affection might have remained between the two boys was likely to be destroyed by all Clifton chose to share with them that day.

Hynes felt sorry for Ryan Clifton, and his mum. It made him determined to do what he could for both of them, although the realistic part of him understood that Clifton was probably doomed. He already looked too big and old for his school uniform, and his natural belligerence bubbled barely below the surface, making it a wonder that his skin didn't pop with rage; and while his willingness to sell his friend down the river was undeniably useful to the investigation into the killing of Romana Moon, it spoke volumes about the shallowness of his character.

'He told me he did it with her twice,' said Clifton. 'Once on her couch, and then again a couple of days later, in her bed.'

'Did you believe him?' said Gackowska.

'Not at first. I told him he was full of shit, that he'd been watching too much porn on his phone.'

'What made you change your mind?'

'A few things.'

'Such as?'

Clifton discovered one last crumb that he'd missed, hiding on the underside of his plate, and wetted a finger in order to consume it.

'He had a pair of her knickers. Said she gave them to him – as a souvenir, like.'

Hynes watched a duck take off from the lake beyond the window, heading for more congenial surroundings. He knew how it felt.

'What made you think they were Romana Moon's?'

'We'd seen her bend over in class, and sometimes she had to stretch to write on the board. If you dropped a pen, you could look up her skirt. She always wore the same kind of underwear: the colors changed, but they all had a little white frill on them, like the ones Karl showed me. And—'

He stopped.

'Go on,' said Gackowska.

'They'd been worn, like.'

'Christ,' said Hynes.

'She asked,' said Clifton.

'I did,' said Gackowska, 'and I appreciate your answering so honestly.' She said this without gagging, which impressed Hynes. 'What else made you think Karl might be telling the truth?'

'He said Miss Moon had a scar on her belly, just above her – you know . . .'

Thankfully, he left the rest to their imaginations. Hynes didn't react, but the autopsy report on Romana Moon had mentioned an appendectomy scar.

'Is there any other way that Karl might have known about the scar?' said Gackowska.

'What do you mean?'

'Did Miss Moon take physical education classes at the school, or supervise sports? Did she swim?'

'No, I don't think so.'

'We found a gym membership card among her possessions. Was Karl a gym member?'

'No, Karl doesn't like sport. He looks the part, but he was always picked last for everything.'

Hynes stepped in.

'Ryan, we talked to your mum this morning.'

Clifton didn't look happy to hear this. 'Why'd you do that?'

'We went looking for you at school, but you'd decided to take the day off. Your house was the next natural stop. She's a nice lady, your mum. Cares about you a lot.'

Clifton didn't contradict this.

'She'll tell my dad that I skipped school.'

The way he said it caused Hynes to wince.

'No, she won't.'

'How do you know?'

'Because,' repeated Hynes, 'she cares about you. We made a deal with her: if you helped us, we wouldn't cause any problems for you – or her. She'll keep your dad out of it.'

'I am helping you,' said Clifton. 'Aren't I?'

Jesus, thought Hynes, *he's pleading. What's going on with him and his dad?*

'Yes,' said Gackowska, 'you are.'

Her reply cleared a little of the boy's fear, if only to send it scurrying back to the shadows.

'When we spoke to your mum,' said Gackowska, 'she mentioned overhearing an argument between you and Ryan over a remark you made about Miss Moon. Do you remember that?'

'Yeah.'

'Was that before or after Karl told you he'd slept with her?'

Clifton didn't rush to answer.

'Before,' he said finally.

'And did he tell you that he started sleeping with her before or after he left school?'

'After.'

'She'd been helping him with his studies, though?'

'Yeah.'

'Did Karl have feelings for her, even then?'

'Maybe. He stopped joking about her.'

'But you're certain that the relationship, if it did happen, didn't commence until after he left school?'

'That's right.'

'Do you know why their relationship might have come to an end?'

'Karl said Miss Moon was scared about losing her job if anyone found out she was fucking an ex-pupil. Karl said he understood. Anyway, he'd had her by then. Time to move on, you know? He said she asked him not to tell. Made him swear.'

'But he told you.'

'Yeah, but I'm his best friend, or I was,' Clifton said, sadly. 'He used to tell me everything.'

Gackowska exchanged a glance with Hynes, like a soldier about to step into a minefield.

'Were you envious of him, Ryan?'

'Envious?'

'Because he'd slept with Miss Moon.'

Clifton registered genuine bewilderment. 'No. Why would I have wanted to sleep with her?'

'She was very pretty.'

'She was old – nearly thirty.'

Despite the circumstances, Hynes had to bite his lip as

Gackowska – thirty-two, and with only a cat to warm her bed
– did her best to keep her face from falling.

'Well, thirty's not that old,' she said.

'Kind of is,' said Clifton.

Hynes decided to take over, if only to give Gackowska time
to compose herself.

'Ryan, we've been asking this of a lot of people, and we're
going to be asking it of a lot more, so don't feel that you're being
singled out, understand?'

Clifton eyed him suspiciously. When someone told you that
you weren't being picked on, you usually were.

'What is it?'

'Can you tell us where you were on the night Romana Moon
died?'

Clifton thought about the question.

'I don't remember. Out somewhere, probably.'

'Could you be more specific?'

'Not really.'

'You can't, or you won't?'

'I can't. I'm out most nights. If not, I'm in my room.'

'Any idea which one it might have been on that night?'

'Depends.'

'On what?'

'On whether my dad was working late. If he was on nights, I
was home. If he wasn't, I was out.'

'What's he on this week?'

'Nights, but it varies.'

'Please make an effort to find the right answer before I die of
old age.'

Clifton did.

'He was on days all last week,' he said at last, 'so I'd have
been out.'

'Where would you have gone?'

'The arcade, I suppose, the one at the back of Caddow's pool
hall. Terry lets me play for free if I help him clean up. Sometimes
I look after things if he wants to nip out for a smoke, or if he's
busy. He's all right, is Terry.'

'So Terry's the owner?'

'Yeah, Terry Caddow. He's all right.'

It seemed that Terry was, conclusively, all right.

'Would he remember your being there?'

'Might do. Wait a minute.' Clifton counted on his fingers, and his face brightened. 'It was the night a bloke ripped the baize on one of the tables. He was trying for some fancy shot, and tore a strip from it. Terry threw him out, and he had to get someone in the next morning to fix the table. They found Miss Moon's body that morning. I know, because I was talking about it with Terry, while he was showing me the new baize. Terry'll back me up. He'll tell you I was there.'

Clifton sat back, smiling.

'Because Terry's all right,' said Hynes.

'Yeah!' said Clifton, then frowned. 'Do you know Terry?'

Hynes and Gackowska left Ryan Clifton to his own devices in Albert Park. It didn't seem worth sticking him in the back of the car and dropping him off at school. Let him sketch trees and ducks. He'd be a lot happier.

'What do you think?' said Gackowska.

'We'll talk to Terry, who's all right,' said Hynes, 'but I don't believe Ryan Picasso back there is lying about anything. I can't see the point.'

He took out his phone and called Priestman to let her know they'd found Clifton, and to share with her what they'd learned.

'Karl Holmby told us that he didn't sleep with Romana Moon,' said Priestman. 'He claimed to have made the story up to impress Clifton, and maybe as revenge on Romana for rejecting him.'

'Well, Ryan Clifton says that Holmby showed him a pair of Romana's used knickers, and told her about the scar on her stomach. I haven't met Karl Holmby, but even without that, I'd be inclined to give Clifton the benefit of the doubt.'

Hynes could almost hear Priestman coming to the boil. He thought the phone was starting to grow hot in his hand.

'We'll bring Holmby in,' said Priestman. 'Even if he has an alibi for the night in question, that little bastard lied to me about Romana.'

'Do you still have eyes on him?' asked Hynes.

'No, we're on our way back to Newcastle.'

'Gackowska and I can pick him up. Where'd you leave him?'

'At the uni, but last I saw, he was heading off campus.'

Priestman gave him Holmby's address before hanging up, still in a rage, leaving Hynes to explain the situation to Gackowska. They got in the car, Gackowska driving.

'You're right, you know,' said Hynes, as they pulled away.

'About what?'

'Thirty's not that old.'

'No, it's not.'

He waited a heartbeat.

'Now thirty-*two* . . .'

LVIII

Louis made his way on foot to the Rijksmuseum. Despite the afternoon heat, he wore a black wool jacket and vest over an open-necked white shirt, and gray trousers. The vest was just loose enough to hide the shape of the little pistol tucked into the waistband holster. The gun would be awkward to reach, but Louis had no desire to make it more accessible only to find himself staring down the barrels of weapons wielded by twitchy Dutch anti-terrorist police.

He had made a promise to himself never to return to Amsterdam, yet here he was. He could not deny the beauty of the city, but had never warmed to it. The killing of Timmerman had provided the justification required to turn his back on this place. Louis prided himself on his dispassion, or used to until he and Angel were drawn irrevocably into Parker's orbit, but he had enjoyed ridding the world of Timmerman. The hit was quick – two shots to the chest as Louis closed on him in the underground car park, followed by a double-tap to the head – but it remained one of the few occasions on which Louis would have been more than content to let the target suffer. In an ideal world, he'd have crucified Timmerman, pulled up a chair, poured a glass of Malbec, and watched him fade away, but even allowing for the Serb's modus operandi, the similarities to Jos's murder might have caused difficulties for those left behind.

As for the Zemuns, Louis knew that they would have neither forgiven nor forgotten the death of one of their enforcers, even if they would probably have been forced to deal with Timmerman themselves, in time. Men of his stripe were rarely astute enough to rise to a position of authority sufficient to ensure their own safety, however relative. Shifting allegiances eventually made uneasy bedfellows of former enemies, and sacrifices were required to salve old wounds. The world would never run short of sadists, and so its Timmermans – particularly as they aged, and accrued bad karma – occasionally had to be thrown to the lions as a gesture of good faith. But the time and place of that oblation was for their masters to determine, and not for outsiders to decide. Unendorsed killings and unavenged deaths were bad for morale, and undermined the integrity of the whole. After all, why should men like the Zemuns be feared if they could not even protect their own? Thus it was that the Zemuns would continue to trail silken strands linking Timmerman's husk to themselves in the hope that, someday, one of those filaments might twitch.

Louis arrived at the Rijksmuseum an hour before closing, its halls already growing quieter. When last he was in Amsterdam, the main building had been shuttered for renovations that would ultimately take almost a decade to complete. Under other circumstances, Louis might have dawdled longer in the museum's restored halls, but instead he made his way directly to the great Night Watch Room, where visitors clustered at one end before the massive Rembrandt that gave the space its name.

The man he had come to meet was at the other end of the chamber, far from the crowd, the only figure seated before a huge altarpiece. De Jaager had barely changed in the ten years since Louis had last seen him. His white hair and tanned features were fractionally thinner, and his clothing hung marginally looser on his body, but otherwise time was being gentle with him. He looked to be in his early sixties, but was closer to eighty. When he turned his face to Louis, his eyes were those of a bright, curious child.

'My old friend,' he said, shaking Louis's hand. 'Come, sit with me.'

Louis sat, and together they took in the altarpiece.

'Beautiful, isn't it?' said De Jaager.

'What am I looking at?'

'*The Last Judgment* by Lucas van Leyden. He was barely into his thirties when he began it in 1526, and wouldn't live to see forty. This is only the second time in half a millennium that the altarpiece has been permitted to leave Leiden. We are safeguarding it for the Museum de Lakenhal while it undergoes repairs. I thought you might find it interesting. See, the good people are congregating to Christ's right, while the sinners are being fed into the mouth of Hell on his left. Hell is always to the left of Christ. As a left-handed person myself, I find this invidious.'

Louis had to give credit to van Leyden for his visual imagination. Hell's mouth was that of a huge serpent, lit by fires from deep within, while various demons tormented naked sinners before consigning them to the flames. He saw one with a face for a groin, a tongue poking like an engorged phallus from its mouth, and another that—

He leaned forward, before standing so he could more closely examine the altarpiece. He was not mistaken: one of the demons appeared to be a Green Man.

'What is it?' said De Jaager.

'I've seen something like this before.'

'Where?'

'In a chapel in Maine, before the building was destroyed.'

'What happened to it?'

'I blew it up.'

'Well, I trust you'll restrain your more extreme critical impulses here.'

'I'll do my best.'

Louis resumed his seat.

'I must admit I'm surprised by your return,' said De Jaager. 'The Zemuns turned out to be fonder of Timmerman than anyone could have imagined. They asked some awkward questions following his demise.'

'Of you?'

'Of everyone.'

'Yet you appear to have weathered the storm.'

'Fortunately, others chose to take credit for the killing: a previously unknown offshoot of Al-Qaeda, which was harboring some residual bitterness about the Muslim blood on Timmerman's hands. It didn't seem worth going to the trouble of contradicting them. Consequently, the Zemuns believe the outside contractor to have been Muslim, possibly Sudanese.'

'Glad it worked out so well.'

'As are we all. I just thought you might like to know that the Zemuns are unlikely to connect your presence here to what happened a decade ago. You can probably dispense with the gun.'

'I didn't think it showed.'

'It doesn't, but I hardly expected you to go out underdressed, and I supplied it for you in the first place. How is Angel?'

'Recovering, slowly.'

'But sufficient to travel safely?'

'Yes.'

'That's good. It shows resilience. I always liked him, you know. He is one of the better Angels.'

And De Jaager smiled briefly at his own joke.

'The man with you,' he continued, 'this Parker, is more problematical. I believe there was some difficulty at the airport.'

'Armitage: one of the local FBI legats.'

'She's well regarded. Hers is not attention I would invite.'

'That makes two of us.'

'Yet you indicated that the information I received came from the FBI.'

'Through unofficial channels.'

'You lead a complicated life. Be careful you don't trip on its entanglements.'

Together they contemplated the altarpiece silently, until Louis asked, 'Did you choose the Rijksmuseum just so you could show this to me?'

'Not for this alone. Let's walk.'

The old man stood, and he and Louis made their way from the hall, De Jaager pausing occasionally before paintings as the inclination took him, until they came at last to the gallery overlooking the reading room of the Cuypers Library, one of the world's great collections of art history. From where they stood, they could look down on its lines of desks, most of which were now unoccupied, apart from a pair of young women reading alone in one corner, and an elderly man who appeared to have deliberately positioned himself as far from them as possible. He was hunched over an enormous volume that almost exceeded the span of his arms, and further smaller books stood piled around, a fortress of paper and print. His gray hair was long, and tinged with yellow. Although the library was warm, the scholar had dispensed only with his ragged black overcoat, which hung on the back of his chair, while retaining multiple layers of cardigans, vests, and sweaters. Up close, Louis knew, he would smell unwashed.

'Who is he?' asked Louis.

'Cornelie Gruner. He's a book dealer, although that hardly does justice to the scope of his endeavors. He lives above an old bar called *het Teken van de Eik* – the Sign of the Oak – and keeps a bookselling business beside it, but the doors are rarely open, and the lights rarely lit. It may not look like it, but he has money. He owns the building occupied by the Oak, and the adjoining one housing his bookstore. He's usually in the latter, hiding like a rat among its contents, and answers the bell when the mood strikes him. The rest of the time, he's either in his rooms above the bar, or haunting the city's more esteemed libraries. Lately, he's been spending a lot of time here, and at the Ritman, which specializes in Hermetic manuscripts. He's also been scouring the archives of the Scheepvart Museum, which houses one of the largest collections of maritime records in the world, and those of the Ets Haim, the old Jewish library. It's quite a remarkable burst of activity by his reclusive standards.'

Gruner emitted a series of coughs, like old bones rattling in a box.

'He sounds unwell,' said Louis.

'If he is, he hasn't consulted any physician known to us. I suspect he sleeps in those clothes, and bathes only at Christmas, whether he needs to or not. He stinks of piss and perspiration, has never married – perhaps unsurprisingly – and appears to be entirely asexual. He maintains a handful of associates, most of them book dealers like himself, but none he would call a friend. Gruner is, by all accounts, a brilliant man. He has doctoral qualifications in law and the physical sciences, although he has never practiced in either field. He's also an occultist, and a forger.'

'What kind of forgery?'

'Documents, mostly, both historical and more modern. There were rumors he had misled some private collectors, and a number of American universities, with fake leaves from medieval manuscripts. One of the collectors, a Finn named Koskinen, kicked up a public fuss, and threatened to sue.'

'What happened?'

'Koskinen died. He burned to death in a fire at his home in Vaasa a few years ago, along with his collection.'

'Accidental?'

'A misplaced cigar, but the Finns remain anxious to trace a female suspect caught by a neighbor's security camera leaving the house shortly before the conflagration commenced. The image was poor, but she had silver hair, which caused the Finns to suspect she might be an older woman. Also, some documents and volumes thought to have been in Koskinen's collection were subsequently put up for sale through very select channels.'

'Was Gruner one of those channels?'

'He was. Curious, is it not, that an object of your search should answer to the description of the woman captured on camera in Vaasa?'

Mors. The woman certainly got around.

'Any other reason to believe Gruner might be the link I'm seeking?'

'The combination of occultism and passports in this instance is quite distinctive. In the good old days, Gruner maintained a steady trade in forged Dutch, Belgian, and German passports, as well as driving licenses, national identity cards, and whatever else the discerning international criminal might require. His clientele was high end, because he charged a considerable premium. Gruner had access to blanks through contacts at the relevant bureaus, and he paid those contacts well. The result was not only quality papers, but also entries on the relevant national databases, which meant Gruner's documents stood up to official scrutiny. After that, it was simply a question of renewing the originals when the time came, and so the forgeries became genuine articles, like painted lead transmuted to gold.

'It's more difficult now, of course, as biometrics have rendered some of Gruner's skills largely redundant. Even the more active national security agencies struggle to maintain an up-to-date collection of unsullied papers for their operatives, and woe betide anyone who burns a useful identity without good cause. Anyhow, Gruner has made his money, and no longer needs to take such risks. He can indulge his love of books and art, if love is what it truly is.'

'Art?'

'I can't attest to the truth of this from personal experience, but his rooms above the Oak are reputed to contain some fine paintings. Nothing after the end of the eighteenth century, and most from the sixteenth and seventeenth centuries, but tastefully curated. Even the walls of the bar are not unadorned, although the display is mostly for effect; the paintings are all damaged, or from the schools of minor figures. They add to the atmosphere, if you like that kind of thing.'

Louis picked up on something more than a critic's disdain in De Jaager's voice.

'Any other reason why you're not a regular patron of the Oak, the artwork apart?'

'That old man, for one – I don't want to put money in his purse – but the Oak is also not a place I care to visit. There's a reason why a bar so old, one that dates back to the sixteenth century, isn't on tourist maps, or mentioned in every guide to the city. It's almost as though Gruner has deliberately contrived to have it excluded, or has managed to mask its presence so that it passes virtually unnoticed by citizens and strangers alike.

'If one chooses to enter, it seems quite acceptable, in an unremarkable way, like any of a dozen older bars in this city I could name off the top of my head. But then one orders a drink, and sits, and something odd happens. The chair no longer feels so comfortable, and one perceives it to be the wrong height for the table. Whatever one is drinking – beer, wine, or the house-made *jenever* – starts to taste wrong: stale, bitter, whatever it might be. The light becomes bothersome: too bright or too dim. I have heard people complain of a low, insistent buzzing, as though insects – bees, or more likely wasps, because there is malevolence to the sound – are swarming nearby. And if one perseveres, one experiences a rising nausea, until one is forced back onto the street, into the fresh air, and perhaps one resolves never to darken the door of the Oak again, because it has quite enough darkness of its own on which to thrive.'

Louis listened to all of this without interruption.

'So who drinks there?' he asked, when De Jaager finished speaking. 'Because that is one fucked up business model.'

'Not if one of its purposes is, or was, to launder money.'

'A big black hole in the shape of a bar.'

'Exactly.'

'Was all the money Gruner's?'

'He was known to take on temporary partners.'

'Who became disappointed investors.'

'Yet remained sanguine about their losses.'

Below, Gruner began putting away his papers and pens as the closure of the library was signaled.

'Do you have any idea what he's researching?' said Louis.

'We have friends in each library, so we know exactly what he's requested in every case.'

De Jaager reached into an inside pocket of his coat, and removed a single sheet of white paper.

'This list is accurate up to yesterday, and includes publicly available books that didn't require him to file a formal request. As soon as the Rijksmuseum closes, we'll be given details of whatever is currently occupying him, and I'll ensure the titles are passed on to you. For now, though, I can tell you that at the Scheepvart he sought records relating to the manifest, crew, and passengers of a British vessel named the *Orcades*, which plied the route from Amsterdam to London during the late sixteenth century. At the Rijksmuseum, and at the Ritman and Ets Haim, he has displayed an interest in old maps and atlases, as well as in late medieval Dutch craftsmen who specialized in the creation of stained glass, both here and in England.'

At that moment Gruner, as though somehow realizing he was the subject of interest and speculation, stared up at the observation gallery upon which they were standing. Neither man reacted, and a good ten seconds passed before Gruner looked away to resume packing his belongings into a worn leather satchel.

'Does he know you?' Louis asked.

'Only as I know him: distantly. But he is now aware of our regard.'

'Let him wonder. We'll be talking to him presently.'

A museum guard appeared and began speaking forcefully to them in Dutch, but his manner changed as soon as he recognized De Jaager, becoming more deferential, until he left them alone once more. By then Gruner was making his way from the library, a cloth bag under his right arm. One of the young women seated in the far corner of the room followed soon after, leaving the other to walk to the librarian's desk and speak quietly with him for a few moments. A piece of paper changed hands, the girl slipping it into her jacket pocket as she, too, headed for the door. She glanced up as she passed below Louis and De Jaager, and the latter responded with a nod and a smile.

'They look like teenagers,' said Louis.

'But aren't, which is precisely the point.'

'And Gruner doesn't suspect?'

'He has a low opinion of women – of most of humanity, really, but of women in particular. To Gruner, they register only slightly below *zwarte mensen* like you.'

'Doesn't like the colored folk?'

'I fear they will ring the bell of his bookshop in vain.'

'You think he might make an exception for me?'

De Jaager took Louis's arm, and guided him toward the stairs.

'I suspect,' he said, 'that a great many people make an exception where you are concerned.'

VI

It is not what they built. It is what they knocked down.
It is not the houses. It is the spaces in between the houses.
It is not the streets that exist. It is the streets that no longer
   exist.
It is not your memories which haunt you.

James Fenton, 'German Requiem'

LIX

B ob Johnston had never set foot outside the continental United States during the previous sixty-eight years of his existence. It was not a matter of any great shame to him. Ever since early childhood, when he had first discovered reading, he had viewed the world through the prism of words; because of his library, he had entire universes at his fingertips.

But thanks to those same books, Johnston was wise enough to understand that life had, perhaps, disappointed him, or he had disappointed life; he was not entirely certain which statement offered the more substantial truth. He had been too cautious in love, and loneliness was the price he had paid for it. He had grown insular and misanthropic, compounding a solitude that was not always a burden, yet at times was undeniably so. He had discovered worlds in books, but books were not the world entire, and it had taken only a few hours in London to confirm this for him, like a suspicion long hidden but conspicuously ignored for fear of the regrets it might unleash. Now, as he walked Charing Cross Road, a bag already hanging heavy with his purchases from each shoulder, he felt both sorrow at his own foolishness, and joy that this realization had not come too late.

He should have been wearied after his flight, but was not; he had slept soundly on his aircraft bed, while marveling at the comforts that could be acquired using other people's money. Parker had presented him with an envelope of sterling before the trip, the majority of which Johnston had deposited in his hotel room safe, the rest being distributed evenly across various pockets, along with forty pounds in his left shoe, just in case he was mugged. He made sure to get a receipt for any expenses he incurred, including a cab ride and a day travel ticket on the

333

London Underground, because he did not wish Parker to think him a spendthrift. He had taken particular advantage of federal funds in only one regard. Upon his arrival at Heathrow, he had been greeted by a driver bearing his name on a card. The driver informed Johnston that he was at his disposal.

'How far is Fairford, Gloucestershire from here?' said Johnston.

The driver checked his phone. 'About an hour and a half, if that.'

So Johnston asked to be driven to Fairford.

The existence of the church of St Mary's at Fairford owes much to a wealthy Catholic clothier named John Tame, whose remains now rest in a marble tomb in its Lady Chapel. Tame, concerned for the wellbeing of his soul after his death, and fearing he was destined for the tribulations of Purgatory, if not somewhere worse, decided to buy his way into Paradise by building a great monument of stone and glass to God. There had been a church in Fairford since the eleventh century at least, although nothing of that first structure now remains. With Tame's support – and after his death in 1500, that of his son, Edmund – a great restoration project commenced, of which the crowning glory was the installation of a complete set of stained-glass windows between the years 1500 and 1515. The windows tell a story to be read by worshipers, one that proceeds in order from the birth of the Virgin Mary to the final Ascension of Christ.

Yet the circumstances of their creation remain a mystery. The records are incomplete, in part due to a lack of interest in pictorial art for the early period of the windows' existence, but also because of the Reformation, which led to the destruction of much religious art from the middle of the sixteenth century. Portions of the Fairford windows may even have been removed to save them from ruination, although the evidence is contradictory, and later their panes, along with the paintings on the church walls, were covered with whitewash to obscure them.

So it was that legends arose about the windows, including that John Tame had seized a ship bound for Rome, and upon finding it laden with painted glass, decided to build a church to house it, a tale given the lie by the proportions of the panes, which were clearly designed to fit the church, not vice versa; and that the windows were at least partly the design of Albrecht Dürer, one of the greatest German artists of the age, which remains unproven. What is certain, though, is that they were the work of many craftsmen, Dutch artisans among them, probably supervised by King Henry VIII's glazier, Barnard Flower, himself a native of the Netherlands; and they are the greatest medieval windows in England.

Bob Johnston stood before the West Window, and the Last Judgment. He had seen so many versions of it on screens, and examined so many pictures in books, that it should have been somewhat unremarkable to him, but it was not. Instead he could only marvel at its detail, at the use of color and the care taken in the presentation of the figures, human, divine, and diabolical alike. Some of the windows, damaged in the great storm of 1703, had been imperfectly reassembled from fragments, lending them the appearance of a modernist collage, but most remained startlingly intact.

Yet even as he took them in, he was conscious of a growing perception of being observed, like a specimen under a microscope or – and he could not think how this image had presented itself to him, only that he wished it had not – of a living body on a slab, about to be explored by the instruments of vivisectionists. Strangest of all, while the saints and angels, even Christ himself, bore expressions of serenity, even vacancy, the demonic representations were more alive, more vibrant, and often seemed to be staring directly and intently at him.

Johnston might have put this down to his own knowledge of the Atlas, and its connection to these windows, had it not also been for a feeling of restriction, as though the walls and ceiling of the church were closing in on him; or the play of light on the panes before him, which cast Christ and the saved in shadow while giving added illumination to the depiction of Hell; and a tickling in his mouth and throat that, within the space of a minute, became a burning, so that he was once again in the cancer ward, once again enduring radiation therapy, once again weeping, and wishing to die.

He was being corrupted by this place, by Fairford, the dormant cancer cells in his body reawakening at the instigation of the images in the glass, because they knew about him, knew why he was here, and would deal with his curiosity by turning his body against him, leaving him to rot from the inside out, all because he couldn't mind his own business, because he was foolish enough to believe that he might still be able to reclaim some value, some purpose, from his existence—

Then he was outside, standing amid the gravestones of the cemetery, heaving great sobbing breaths, and he could not recall the leaving of the church, only that it was now behind him, and the burning sensation had passed. The driver was standing by the limousine, smoking a cigarette, and the sun was shining upon all.

Johnston stumbled away from St Mary's, and did not look back.

But he had no more uncertainty.

This was the place.

LX

Cornelie Gruner walked slowly toward the heart of the city, traversing each canal without looking back, seemingly watching only for the endless phalanxes of cyclists that made negotiating Amsterdam on foot such a perilous business. He had registered the presence of the two young women in the Rijksmuseum library; even with his failing eyesight, one of them had been familiar to him from the Ets Haim a few days earlier. He might have dismissed this as mere coincidence – after all, he had found fertile soil to till in both institutions, so it was not beyond the bounds of possibility that others might also have – but he possessed a researcher's acuity, and so had taken note of the titles on her desk on each occasion, the first time out of simple curiosity, but the second, at the Rijksmuseum, out of something more akin to concern. He had found no point of correspondence between the works being consulted by the girl in the two institutions: the selected volumes were notable only for their randomness.

Now the appearance of De Jaager had confirmed to Gruner that he was indeed under observation, because De Jaager did not take a casual interest in anyone. The question was, at whose behest was he operating? De Jaager was a broker and facilitator. If he was monitoring Gruner, someone was paying him to do so. The *zwarte* who had been with De Jaager at the Rijksmuseum, though, was unfamiliar to the book dealer, and did not resemble the natives of the old Dutch colonies who formed the majority of Amsterdam's black population, infesting the Bijlmer district to the southeast. Gruner might have regarded black as inferior to white – in general terms if not the specific, as he was grudgingly prepared to concede that some exceptional specimens managed to overcome the natural deficiencies of their race – but he was not so blindly prejudiced as to perceive them as indistinguishable.

He crossed Singel, and chose his favored route through the Oudezijds Achterburgwal by way of the Book Passage. Gruner took his time examining the stock on display, although he didn't expect to uncover any treasures. Still, it troubled him to discover one of the girls from the Rijksmuseum perusing battered paperbacks and old vinyl records in which she clearly had little interest, while her companion went ahead, presumably to pick up Gruner when he finally elected to emerge on the other side. He saw no sign of De Jaager, or the black man; it appeared they were content to let children do their work for them.

Gruner wondered how long De Jaager had been keeping tabs on him. Yes, he had noticed the young women in just two libraries, and could not recall their faces from elsewhere, but this did not mean De Jaager had not assigned others to watch him, or that the surveillance did not extend to monitoring Gruner's requests for books or documents. He was forced to accept that De Jaager might now possess more information about his research than was desirable, which meant that certain parties would need to be informed of De Jaager's interest.

The girl in the passage had her back to Gruner as she flicked through a box of old prints, but she was watching his reflection in a pane of glass. She wore a summer dress that ended just above the knee, and favored battered sneakers over shoes – just in case, Gruner supposed, she had to move quickly in pursuit of her quarry, although given his age, and the parlous state of his knees, she could have attached a ball and chain to one of her ankles and still have been in no danger of losing him.

The situation was delicate, and complicated. While Gruner had an obligation to share the fact of the surveillance, he could not risk action being taken against De Jaager as a result. Only the young underestimated the old: over the years, De Jaager had served the interests of many men, both honest and crooked, but always behaving with the same integrity toward both. If they failed to adhere to similar standards, De Jaager simply declined to aid them again, regardless of the money on offer. He was, therefore, not entirely mercenary in his dealings, which meant he had accumulated markers to be called in when required. He was liked and respected, contributing, in his way, to the smooth running of the city. There would be consequences if De Jaager or any of his people were harmed. Gruner did not like to think of what might transpire if Quayle dispatched Mors to investigate De Jaager further in order to force him to reveal the identity of his client.

As though in response to these concerns, Gruner's attention was arrested by a copy of De Forel's 1975 facsimile edition of the *Fabrica* of Andreas Vesalius, in very good condition, the boards undamaged and the binding strong. Gruner never ceased to be impressed by the efforts of these pioneers of anatomical drawing – not only by the beauty and accuracy of their compositions, but the lengths to which they went to secure bodies for their explorations, and the conditions under which they were forced to work: the filth, the blood, the stench. He stopped at one particularly striking plate of a woman, her interiority revealed from her throat to her reproductive organs, and held up the book so that the plate and De Jaager's young woman were side by side in his view, as though she, reflected in the glass, were also being exposed to this intimate gaze.

'How much?' he asked the owner of the stall, a widow named Bock. He had bought from her in the past, and found her to be optimistic in her valuations. She now named a price that was at least a third more than the book was worth, and was surprised when he did not quibble.

'Would you like me to wrap it for you, *mijnheer*?' she asked.

'No, *mevrouw*, but it is a gift for someone – a surprise. I would be grateful if you could provide me with a card upon which to write a greeting.'

Bock obliged with a cheap photographic image of the Flower Market, and watched as Gruner wrote on the blank side in his meticulous hand. When he was done, he added it to the page in the book depicting the anatomized woman, and returned the whole to Bock.

'One last favor,' he said. 'I should like you to present the book to the young lady in the red summer dress, with my compliments.'

Mevrouw Bock could not help but fix him with a look that suggested there was no fool like an old fool, particularly one that looked and smelled as Gruner did, but a sale was a sale, and the passage had been quiet that day.

'Now?' she asked.

'As quickly as possible.'

'As you wish, *mijnheer.*'

Gruner moved on the next stall. He watched as Bock approached the girl, presented her with the book, and pointed to him. The girl looked surprised, and Gruner gave her a small, formal bow before continuing on his way. As he turned left at the end of the passage, he saw that the girl was no longer following him, but had remained where she was. In one hand she held the book, in the other the card on which Gruner had written two words.

Voorzichtig zijn.

Beware.

LXI

B ob Johnston dropped the bags of books at his hotel, and took the opportunity to use the restroom, his bladder having been sorely tested by the combination of unfamiliar exercise and a pot of English breakfast tea. (And who could have guessed, after decades of bags dropped into disposable containers, filled with water heated to a temperature appropriate only for coffee, that tea could taste so good? Johnston had been so overcome by the experience that his purchases now included, in addition to books, a sturdy red teapot, and a tin box of tea leaves.) Parker had put him up at Hazlitt's in Soho, and it gave Johnston no small pleasure to be domiciled in a building with such august literary associations.

He was still shaken by his experience at St Mary's, to such a degree that he took time to examine his mouth and throat in the bathroom mirror, aided by a small Maglite, expecting to glimpse lesions appearing from the tender tissue. But he saw only the flesh of an aging man, a dupe whose imagination could be played upon by images in glass.

No, he thought, *it's more than that. The only thing worse than believing in the truth of the Atlas is* not *to believe.*

With his bladder blessedly empty, and a bag folded into a pocket – just in case, because one never knew when a book might call one's name – Johnston consulted his map of the London Underground. He traced his intended route, and headed for the evocatively – and not inaptly – named World's End.

The building at World's End, Chelsea, formerly occupied by Dunwidge & Daughter, Booksellers, still stood, although it was now a private home that had been in the ownership of the same family since the 1930s. The dwelling, part of a terrace of fine redbrick houses, bore no trace of the fire that had consumed Eliza Dunwidge, the titular daughter, along with most of the firm's stock of occult volumes. Eliza's father had also died that same night, both possibly by the same hand: that of the notorious killer, John Soter.

The more Johnston explored Soter's history, the harder he found it to accept that Soter could have killed men, women, and children in a concentrated spree caused, if contemporary reports were to be believed, by psychological damage incurred while fighting the Germans in France. With the assistance of an amateur British military historian named Billy McLean – a man so reclusive he made Johnston seem positively gregarious by comparison – he had obtained all extant copies of Soter's medical records from Craiglockhart Hospital. These indicated that, in the opinion of the psychiatrists dealing with him, the profound trauma from which Soter suffered was a combination both of his experiences on the Western Front and the loss of his family to a German bombing raid. Yet Soter exhibited no signs of anger, and staff had never been given cause to restrain him for violent behavior. He displayed only courtesy and solicitude toward the nurses responsible for his day-to-day care, and was unfailingly polite to all visitors, although he was found to be unable to refrain from weeping if given the opportunity to converse with the very young.

Was it possible that, following his discharge from the hospital, Soter's condition had deteriorated to such an extent as to cause him, either through rage or delusion, to kill two children, a boy and a girl, in addition to a prostitute, and at least three others, including the Dunwidges? Johnston had no expertise in these matters, and so could not offer an opinion that would have held up in a court of law. All he could say was that John Soter did not seem like such a man.

Johnston climbed the steps of the house, and rang the bell. He had been in touch with the owner by email, notifying her of his interest in the fire that had once reduced the property to a shell, and was pleasantly surprised to find her willing to admit him to her home. The door was opened by a cheerful, elegant woman in her fifties, who introduced herself as Rosanna Bellingham – 'the matriarch', as she described herself, the patriarch, Norman, having been deceased for some years, following thirty years of marriage that had left her with 'five children, and many happy memories'. All this Johnston learned while he was still in the process of taking off his coat, which overwhelmed him slightly. He said that he was glad to hear their union had been joyful, and Bellingham asked him if he happened to be married. He replied that he had never been so fortunate, and suddenly found the widow appraising him in a new way, like one who has ventured out for a walk with no intention of buying a car, only to have her eye unexpectedly caught by a vintage model. To be honest, it made Johnston nervous.

Bellingham led him to a country-style kitchen, where she offered him his choice of tea, coffee, or 'something stronger', adding that she always enjoyed 'a small one' at this time of the evening. Since it was already growing dark, Johnston opined that something stronger might well be in order. Bellingham poured two glasses of gin that did considerable damage to their parent bottle, added splashes of tonic that did not, dropped in a couple of cubes of ice by hand, along with a slice of lemon, and presented Johnston with the finished product.

'If that's a small one,' said Johnston, 'what does a large one look like?'

Rosanna Bellingham tapped the bottle. 'It saves the trouble of washing a glass.'

Johnston tried to decide if she was joking or not. It concerned him that she probably wasn't. He took a sip of his drink, and decided to wait a while before taking another in the hope that the ice might yet dilute the contents sufficiently to enable him to stand up again without immediately falling over.

'I'm grateful to you for allowing me to visit,' he said.

'You weren't expecting me to agree, were you?'

'No, I wasn't.'

Rosanna tested her own drink. Johnston heard the ice clink against the side of the glass, and noticed for the first time that the woman's hand was shaking slightly. He might have put it down to nerves, or even, given the generosity of her pour, incipient alcoholism, but she didn't have the look of someone with a problem, or not one that involved liquor. Her eyes were clear, and her face had none of the bloating and blurring that Johnston associated with those who drank to excess.

'If you'd approached me even two or three months ago with a similar request,' she said, 'I'd probably have ignored your email, or sent a polite refusal.'

'May I ask what has changed?'

'This house has changed,' she said.

'In what way?'

'You'll think me foolish.'

'I can assure you I won't.'

And he meant it: Johnston had touched fragments of the Fractured Atlas, had seen how they altered the pages of the book in which they were concealed. This world, he now knew, was stranger than he could ever have imagined.

Rosanna Bellingham seemed to accept that he was telling the truth.

'I think something has returned to this place,' she said. 'I think it's being haunted.'

LXII

Louis returned to the safe house to discover Parker waiting in the kitchen, his suitcase by his feet. Angel sat at the table, drinking coffee. He looked better for a few hours of rest. Anouk was preparing something in a pot for supper. Whatever it was, it was heavy with paprika.

'Change of plan?' said Louis.

'You and Angel have this in hand,' said Parker. 'These are your people, so I suspect you always had. I'm going to London. Join me when you're done.'

'Johnston?'

'Call it caution. I think I was wrong to let him go on ahead without us. I've been feeling that way since we got off the plane at Schiphol.'

Louis shared with Parker what he had learned about Cornelie Gruner from De Jaager, and the three men agreed among them a plan of action to investigate the activities of the former.

'I'm sorry I won't get to meet him,' said Parker, as Paulus pulled up outside to take him back the airport – at, Parker hoped, a speed that wouldn't leave his eyeballs pressed into his brain like raisins in dough.

'Gruner, or De Jaager?'

'On reflection, both.'

'I'll pass on your regards to De Jaager – and Gruner, although maybe not in the same way.'

'You step carefully.'

'Always do.'

'Except, it seems, when you're getting shot,' said Anouk, without diverting her attention from the stove.

'Yes,' Louis admitted. 'Except then.'

LXIII

B ob Johnston and Rosanna Bellingham stood in the living room of the latter's home, which was situated on the second floor, at the same level as the front door and hallway, and overlooked the currently empty street.

'Eliza Dunwidge died there,' said Bellingham, pointing to the fireplace. 'Her charred remains were found lying half-in, half-out of the hearth. The fire consumed everything on this level, and most of what's above, so my grandparents purchased little more than a shell. Only the basement survived intact.'

'Do you think John Soter had anything to do with Eliza's death?'

'That's what the papers suggested at the time. My grandparents kept an album of press clippings about it. My grandfather had a ghoulish aspect, and rather relished the notoriety the case brought to his property. I've set the album aside. You can take it with you, if you wish. It's up to you whether you want to return it. Any attachment I had to it has vanished. The newspapers speculated that Soter might have fled abroad in the aftermath, or killed himself out on the Norfolk Broads.'

Just as Soter didn't strike Johnston as a deranged killer, neither did he seem likely to have taken his own life on the Broads. A man that could survive the carnage of the Somme, and the loss of his wife and children, was not one to despair easily.

'Have you heard of a lawyer named Atol Quayle?' he asked.

'It rings a bell. Wasn't he John Soter's occasional employer? Why do you ask?'

'I'm just wondering if anyone by that name has ever tried to contact you.'

'No. I doubt the firm still exists – or does it?'

'It doesn't seem to,' said Johnston, 'but someone out there is continuing to use the name. He claims to be a retired English lawyer, when he's not killing people.'

'You didn't mention that in your original email.'

'I didn't want to alarm you.'

'Or were you worried that the mention of killings might have caused me to keep my door closed to you?'

Johnston conceded the point, helped by the absence of any apparent bitterness on Bellingham's part at this lacuna.

'I must say,' she added, 'that you don't behave like a book scholar. You're more like a private detective.'

'I've been keeping company with one,' said Johnston. 'His name is Parker. I think some of his habits may be rubbing off on me, which I find disconcerting.'

He tried the gin again, but suddenly found the taste to be off. He sniffed the air. It smelled of the lilies in the vase by the window, and some kind of subtle scent that he traced to a candle burning in an antique lantern by a second fireplace in the dining room, yet a more pungent odor was underlying both. It reminded him of pork ribs on a barbecue, but not the kind one might care to eat, as though the meat had been spoiled before it was placed over the coals, and no one had noticed until it started to char.

'You smell it, don't you?' said Bellingham.

Johnston saw no point in denial.

'What is it?'

Bellingham took a step away from the fireplace, and said, 'It's her.'

LXIV

The Principal Backer sat in one of the Colonial Club's smaller meeting rooms, his attention mostly fixed on the screen by the far wall. A younger relative of one of the senior members – a grandson, or perhaps a nephew; the Principal Backer was not entirely sure which, and didn't care much either way – had written a book on the actor Charlie Chaplin. The member's peers, or those who were sufficiently bored, or desirous of remaining in his good graces, had convened to listen to a presentation, and attend a screening of one of Chaplin's films.

The Principal Backer was not particularly close to the member in question, a semi-retired investment banker named Reesen. It was rumored in the Colonial that Reesen's forebears had changed their name from Rosenfeld back in the early nineteenth century, some fifty years before the family began to acquire the wealth that would ultimately elevate it to a position of authority and influence in the Commonwealth. A surname like Rosenfeld would have been sufficient to deny one membership of the Colonial until relatively recently, the club not being notable for the welcome it offered to Semites, Negroes, Hispanics, or Orientals, not unless they were scrubbing pots or cleaning toilets. Times had changed since then, some vestiges of progressive thinking having infiltrated even the hidebound environs of the Colonial, although one would still not have required more than two hands to count those members that were not white Protestants.

Reesen interested the Principal Backer. He was a liberal by the club's standards – liberal even by the standards of most of his own family – and supported causes of which many other members would not have approved, but maintained a relatively low profile within the Colonial itself. He generally dined and drank alone, and had shown no inclination to be nominated to the Central Committee – a body monolithic in its avowed resistance to change – instead being content to regard it from afar with a degree of amused contempt. The Principal Backer was curious, therefore, to see who might feel compelled to support this latest literary venture by Reesen's relative. He was surprised by some of those in attendance, and the apparent friendliness, even familiarity, with which they greeted a host whose beliefs differed radically from their own. It added to the Principal Backer's understanding of the complex currents of influence and obligation lying beneath the club's facade.

The short film itself was mildly amusing, although the Principal Backer struggled with silent comedy. It struck him that Chaplin, a communist sympathizer, would have been blackballed by the Colonial had he applied for membership, and those in the audience who were laughing loudest at the antics of the Little Tramp, and responding with damp-eyed emotion to the more sentimental moments, were the same men who would step over him if he were discovered lying on the street.

One of the club's porters discreetly entered the room, located the Principal Backer, and informed him that Miriam, his niece, had left a message requesting that he call her. This required the Principal Backer to leave the presentation, since members were permitted to use cell phones only in the courtyard garden. Even had a member wished to break this rule, he (the Colonial, like most such establishments, being a predominantly male domain) would have been prevented from doing so by the building's security shielding, which blocked all such signals. The Principal Backer entered the courtyard, discovered it to be empty, and dialed the relevant number, even though he had no niece named Miriam, no nieces at all.

'What is it?' he said, once the call was answered.

The voice of Armitage competed with the noise of Amsterdam's traffic.

'We lost them on the way from the airport,' she said. 'They've gone to ground.'

'That's unfortunate,' said the Principal Backer, his tone indicating that this news was significantly more troubling than the word suggested.

'It seems that one of them may be familiar with a local fixer named De Jaager,' said Armitage. 'The driver that picked them up at the airport was one of De Jaager's people. I've noticed him around. The Dutch security services keep tabs on De Jaager, just to see what he might be up to, and I requested a status report. They're under the impression that De Jaager may recently have begun shadowing a book dealer named Cornelie Gruner.'

'What do you know about this Gruner?'

'I'm working on acquiring that information now. I thought you might prefer if I went through backdoor sources.'

'Send it on as soon as you have it,' said the Principal Backer. 'And thank you.'

He hung up, and returned to the meeting room. The film had come to an end, and the author was now signing copies of the book for those in attendance, his blood-patron having purchased enough copies for all. The Principal Backer took one, and even asked for it to be dedicated, although he had no intention of ever reading it.

After all, it was important to maintain appearances, and keep one's mask in place.

LXV

Cornelie Gruner stopped for dinner and a carafe of wine at a bar on the Rembrandtplein. He was curious to see if the young women were continuing to stalk him, and was gratified to discover they were not. Neither could he find any sign of De Jaager, or the black man who had been with him at the Rijksmuseum, and no one else appeared to be taking any particular notice of him as he ate. Nonetheless, De Jaager's surveillance remained impolite on principle. He knew where Gruner lived and worked, and a gentleman would have made his inquiries in person. Gruner would have declined to answer, of course, but the courtesy would have been appreciated.

Gruner bit into his bread, crumbs falling from it to be lost in the filthy strata of his clothing, where they would join in the ongoing slow molder of fabric and flesh. He regarded the fading light, and began to eat more quickly. Gruner no longer liked to be on the streets after dark, and made sure that the door to his rooms above the Oak was always locked behind him by nightfall. If he were forced by unusual circumstances to work late in his bookshop, a connecting door opened into a short, low hallway, to which only he retained access, and thus to the rear of the bar.

Because Cornelie Gruner was frightened.

The old bookseller had long worked with occult materials, including rare grimoires and manuscripts. He had even sold such works to the Vatican itself, back in the days when that institution remained committed to sourcing volumes for the Black Shelves of the Archivo Segreto Vaticano, housed in the sixteenth-century Tower of the Winds: fifty miles of rare and curious books and documents, including the Papal Bulls excommunicating Martin Luther, the account of the trials of the Knights Templar in Chinon in 1308, and the records of Galileo's trial before the Inquisition in 1633. Gruner's efforts had involved finding, or replacing, some of the Archive's collection missing since Napoleon Bonaparte ordered it to be relocated to Paris as part of his desire to consolidate all European knowledge at the heart of his empire.

Even now, Gruner regarded his efforts to replenish the Archives as the crowning glory of his life as a bibliophile. Between 1810 and 1813, Napoleon's convoys had transported more than three thousand crates of papers, containing over 100,000 individual items, on poor roads from Rome to Turin, crossing the Mont Cesis pass into France before proceeding to the Archive's new home in the Hotel Soubise. The majority arrived safely, but a flood washed away the contents of two wagons at Borgo San Donnino, and more items were lost when crates fell from a wagon at Susa. Further depletions occurred following Napoleon's return from Elba, and his final defeat at Waterloo. Books and documents were mislaid, stolen, or destroyed, and the Vatican's quibbling over the cost of the Archive's return resulted in rare items being removed from carts to lighten the load. The Archive that left Rome in 3,249 crates was sent back in 2,450; more than a quarter of the original collection would never again be seen in Rome.

And among those missing items were eight pages of the *Atlas Regnorum Incognitorum*, the Atlas of Unknown Realms, also known as the Fractured Atlas.

Gruner finished his food, and threw back what was left of his wine. He felt the evening grow colder, even through his many layers, but few others showed signs of being troubled by this perceived fall in temperature. At Vijzelstraat, a shape broke the waters of Herengracht before submerging again. Gruner detected a presence in the murk, as though a statue or carving in its depths had briefly been made visible. He saw features distorted by weeds, and a tongue that resembled the inverted trunk of a young tree, its roots protruding from between the figure's lips so that they splayed over its face. A sightseeing boat passed by, churning the waters, and by the time it had passed, the image was gone.

Gruner had tracked down five of the Atlas's missing pages. It took him almost three decades to do so, involving the expenditure of a great deal of effort and money. When the pages were finally in his possession, he passed them not to the Vatican, but to the lawyer Atol Quayle. It was not just a matter of price, even if Quayle was willing to pay more for them than the Vatican, which had a habit of pleading penury when it came to market values. Neither was his decision to aid Quayle entirely a consequence of Gruner's fear of the lawyer's vengeance, although by the time Gruner had obtained the final leaves, Mors had entered Quayle's service, which did, admittedly, help to focus Gruner's mind on making the correct decision. No, Gruner loved books, and the pages of the Fractured Atlas belonged together. What was important was the integrity of the volume. Gruner knew enough about the history of the Atlas to recognize its importance to occultists of a specific stripe, and had learned more during the many years in which he had known, and assisted, Quayle. Only gradually had he come to understand the queerness of the lawyer himself, but by then it was too late for him to disengage himself from this strangest of clients.

Finally, he had touched the pages of the Atlas, and his understanding was complete. He watched as they turned from blank vellum to representations of the room in which he sat; to maps of continents that did not exist, nor had ever existed, on this earth; and to images of faces that seemed to gaze out from the leaves as though through glass. By then he wished he had worn gloves before handling the book, but the damage was done. The Atlas had infected him, and he would never be the same again.

Gruner gathered his change from the table, and added the coins to the little purse he kept in the deepest recesses of his coat, anchored to his belt by a chain that ran through a small hole in a pocket. The waiter didn't bother to thank him for his custom. In his many years of eating at the restaurant, Gruner had yet to order an additional drink, or leave anything resembling a tip, even by the undemanding standards of Dutch service, which required no more effort than rounding up the bill to the nearest euro or two. Gruner picked up his bag, and looked around him once more, but this time he was not concerned about De Jaager or his acolytes. The light was dying even faster than he had anticipated, and he divined the imminent thickening of shadows. The vision in the water was a warning to him that he should seek some well-lit place, there to sequester himself until dawn, lest he be forced to glimpse something far worse.

The Atlas was close to completion – Quayle had told him so – and as its consummation drew nearer, so its influence on this world increased. Fissures were opening, holes punched between one reality and another. Few perceived them, but Gruner could, because he had been in contact with pages from the Atlas. Now he no longer slept as well as before, and feared the dark.

He shuffled along the banks of the canal, his head down. The first of the visitations had come to him only weeks earlier, causing him to worry that he might be suffering some form of breakdown, or incubating a tumor in the brain. He began experiencing visions reminiscent of the horrors in the Last Judgments of Hieronymus Bosch, Hans Memling, Fra Angelico, and, most particularly, Lucas van Leyden, whose altarpiece was currently residing in the very museum Gruner had so recently vacated. Some of these nightmares seemed to have stepped directly from the artworks in question, and a few were hybrids – a head by one painter, a body by another – but most bore no resemblance to anything he had ever seen, and appeared to be conjured solely from his own subconscious.

It took Gruner only a few days to realize that the emergence of the waking nightmares had coincided with the latest communication from Quayle, requesting his assistance in rechecking previous sources for errors: any references that might have been missed, any mistranslations or misinterpretations pointing to the existence of further pages missing from the Atlas. It was as though contact with the lawyer had activated some contamination buried deep in Gruner's system, in the form of those atoms transferred from the Atlas to his fingers years earlier. He, like Quayle, was now of the Atlas, and the Atlas was of him.

On the third night of his researches, as he worked late and alone above the Oak, the building sealed and otherwise empty, Gruner heard someone trying to gain access to his quarters through the locked door. He detected a hissing from without, and footsteps on the floorboards – then moving up the wall, and across the ceiling, as though whatever was outside were capable of crawling like a lizard or spider. The following morning, he discovered deep scratches in the wood around the handle and hinges of the door, and marks on the plaster of the walls and ceiling of the hall: sharp indentations, as of claws or chitinous limbs. Deeply unsettled, Gruner called Quayle in London.

'What is happening?' he asked.

And Quayle replied, 'The beginning of the end.'

LXVI

Rosanna Bellingham took up position in the open doorway of the living room, perhaps in case she felt the need to retire to the safety of the hall. Bob Johnston stayed where he was, being reluctant to cede space to something he could not see and that, as yet, posed no threat to him.

Until he'd become involved with the Atlas, Johnston had never experienced anything remotely resembling an encounter with the otherworldly, and regarded those who made such claims as either fraudulent or soft in the head. Oddly, he continued to maintain that position, but was prepared to make an exception for himself because he knew he was neither fraud nor lunatic.

The air hadn't grown colder, the furniture hadn't started to move about of its own volition, and nothing was making woo-woo noises in his ear, but Johnston would not have attempted to deny that the atmosphere in the room had changed, and the smell of burned meat was now stronger than before. And while he was not about to flee, neither was he particularly inclined to venture closer to the fireplace. He did reach out a hand, though, like a man testing for a static charge. The analogy was not inapt, because the hairs on his right arm slowly stood on end. With as much dignity as he could muster, he withdrew the hand as quickly as possible.

'Does it . . . do anything?' he asked. He noticed that he had instinctively lowered his voice, which seemed unnecessary, but this was alien territory for him. Also, his question implied an acceptance of some form of agency, which caused him to become irritated at himself.

'No,' said Bellingham, 'but sometimes the stink gets worse. It permeates the house, and it's impossible to stay inside. I've started to eat out more, for obvious reasons.'

Johnston was surprised to hear that she could muster any appetite at all.

'How do you sleep?' he said.

'Pills, when booze won't suffice. It may sound peculiar, but one almost begins to get used to it. Most of the time I find it more annoying than anything else. I just wish it would stop.'

'Have you consulted anyone?'

'You mean a priest? I'm not religious.'

'And this hasn't caused you to reconsider?' He had to admire her commitment to agnosticism, if not outright atheism, in the face of apparent evidence of life beyond the grave.

'I don't believe this has anything to do with religion,' said Bellingham. 'And when I said this house was haunted, I didn't mean by a ghost.'

Johnston tried his best not to look confused.

'I may not entirely be following you,' he said.

Bellingham used her glass to gesture at the fireplace.

'Whatever that is, it's not some remnant of a person returned to visit its former home. It's not a spectral presence, with a consciousness, or a purpose. That's the stuff of stories. I think it's more like a bubble of memory that has suddenly burst, releasing all the stale air inside. It was always there. It was just that no one was aware of it until now.'

Johnston considered this to be an interesting, if flawed, approach to rationalizing the problem.

'If you're right,' he said, 'it should fade away in time.'

'That's easy for you to say, but how long will it take? Have you ever had a rat die under your floorboards?'

He admitted that he had, and it was not a pleasant experience – or a short one.

'Well,' said Bellingham, 'there you are.'

Johnston was prepared to buy into a certain amount of what Bellingham was suggesting, but not the entirety of it. The presence in the room might only have been a manifestation of a memory given sensory form, but there was badness to it – and it wasn't just the smell, even as he tried to ignore all he knew about the particulate nature of odors, and therefore whatever he might be inhaling as long as he remained in proximity to it. No, whatever this was, it was malevolent in its intent.

'Do you think it's her?'

'Eliza? I told you: it's not a person, or the ghost of one. It's memory, a persistence – but yes, I'll accept that it may be some remnant of her; it's *her* persistence, as though time has become tangled, and we're smelling something from long ago.'

Seeing it too, Johnston thought, because the area around the fireplace was warped ever so slightly, like an image viewed through a smear on glass.

'Then what's caused it?' he said.

'I don't know.'

'Have you changed anything: knocked down a wall, maybe?'

'Or held a séance, or sacrificed a goat in the basement? Isn't that how it works in films?'

Johnston acknowledged the obviousness of his question with a grimace.

'Have you ever held a séance?' he asked. 'Just wondering.'

'No, and I'm not about to start now. Perhaps it's all down to the same business that led you here.'

The Atlas: that, at least, made some kind of sense. Soter had been searching for Lionel Maulding, and Maulding had been seeking the Atlas, which led both of them to Eliza Dunwidge, a dealer in occult volumes. Now Quayle – either a descendant of Soter's original employer, or someone with an odd sense of historical humor – was also hunting for the Atlas, which meant poking around in the past.

And *pop*: a bubble had burst.

'Have you seen enough?' Bellingham asked.

'I haven't really seen anything at all,' said Johnston, 'but I've smelled a sufficiency.'

He followed Bellingham from the room, and waited as she closed the door behind them. This cut off the worst of the odor, although more than a hint of it remained in the hallway. They returned to the kitchen, where Bellingham retrieved a plastic carrier bag from the shelf and placed it before Johnston. Inside was a thin photo album: black cover, black pages, like a memorial volume.

'My grandfather's collection of murder memorabilia,' said Bellingham.

Johnston flicked through it, finding newspaper clippings, old photographs of the house in which they now sat, both before and after the fire, and a few charred pieces of stationery from Dunwidge & Daughter, including invoices, compliment slips, and a letter signed by Eliza Dunwidge to a collector in Warwick, itemizing new acquisitions that might be of interest to him. The handwriting was ornate, the language equally so. This, thought Johnston, was an educated, intelligent woman; an odd one, and with esoteric fascinations that bordered on the satanic, but undeniably interesting. He would have been curious to meet her. In a way, given that his skin and clothing were sullied by their exposure to whatever was in the living room, he supposed he already had.

He found the picture of Soter with which he was familiar, and beside it one of Eliza Dunwidge with an older man, whom he guessed to be her father. Whatever Eliza's intellectual gifts, they had not been matched by any similar degree of pulchritude. She was unpleasantly plain, like cheap wallpaper.

Johnston moved on, then paused. Before him lay two halves of the same story from the *Daily Graphic*, an illustrated journal with which he was unfamiliar, pasted on adjoining pages. It consisted of reports on a number of legal matters, including two murder trials, a handful of larcenies, and an interesting case of blackmail that might otherwise have absorbed Johnston's attention had it not been for the illustrations above the next-to-last story, which marked the passing of a year since the last sighting of the 'suspected murderer, John Sotere'. The first illustration was a version of Soter's photograph from the previous page, but drawn in profile, while the second was of a man depicted full face, his features familiar to Johnston, but only from a passport photograph taken almost a century later. He had not come across these *Daily Graphic* pages in his researches because, just as Soter's name had been misspelled, so also had the second man's. He was referred to as 'Mr Atol Quail, Lawyer'.

Johnston looked closer. The similarity was remarkable.

'Someone you know?' asked Rosanna Bellingham.

She came around the table to join him, leaning in to view the pages. He caught her scent, and felt one of her breasts against his back. He tried to recall the last time a woman's breast had rested against his back, but it was so long ago as to be lost to him.

'Not personally.'

His voice sounded odd, so he cleared his throat in the hope that this might help restore it to normality.

'Lionel Maulding's lawyer, right?' she said. 'Unlikely you'd be acquainted with him, really. He's long dead.'

'Yes,' said Johnston, 'he must be.'

'You don't sound convinced.'

'Says the woman with a ghost in her living room.'

'I told you: it's not a ghost.'

'Semantics.'

'It's my living room. I'll decide what is and isn't a ghost. What about him?'

She tapped an index finger against the drawing of Quayle. Johnston half-expected it to flinch in response, and was grateful when it didn't.

'Definitely not a ghost,' said Johnston. 'But now I know that the man we're looking for comes from the same bloodline.'

He closed the album, and returned it to the carrier bag. He would take a longer, more detailed look at it later.

'What will you do when you find him?' Bellingham asked. 'Call the police?'

Johnston thought of Parker, and of Angel and Louis.

'Only,' said Johnston, 'if he's lucky.'

VII

Out of the ash
I rise with my red hair
And I eat men like air.
                    Sylvia Plath, 'Lady Lazarus'

LXVII

Cornelie Gruner made it back to his roost just as the rain began to fall. He had managed to reach the buildings he owned without being disturbed by any more visions, visitations, or whatever one chose to call them. Damn Quayle. Damn his Atlas. Damn them all.

The moisture made Gruner's hands slippery. He fumbled for his keys.

He found the correct one, and inserted it into the keyhole.

Angel had struggled to gain entry to Cornelie Gruner's rooms, but not because the security or the locks were particularly sophisticated – quite the opposite, in fact. He'd slipped past the bartender easily enough, the man being more concerned with watching a football game on his iPad than worrying about customers, and made his way up the stairs without encountering anyone else along the way. According to what De Jaager had told Louis, Gruner occupied the entirety of the top floor, accessed via a single door with two locks. The first was a simple Yale, which Angel took care of easily enough, but his problems began with the second, which had a keyhole reminiscent of those found in medieval cathedrals, and a mechanism to match: stiff and unyielding, like the most austere of clerics. At one point, Angel began to despair of ever getting the door open, a feeling not helped by his own physical and mental weakness. He hadn't been forced to concentrate on a lock for months, and the effort brought on sweating, nausea, and a filthy headache. When he finally heard the tumblers click, he almost wept with relief and satisfaction. The antique mirror at the end of the hall, surrounded by an ornate gold frame, reflected his feelings back at him.

Gruner's quarters consisted of a large living area, a bedroom, a bathroom, and a small, galley-style kitchen that smelled of boiled vegetables. Access to each room was via a narrow channel that wound through canyons of books and papers, the lowest of which came up to Angel's waist, and the highest to his chest. They grew taller as they neared the oak banker's desk that formed the centerpiece of the accommodations, like the foothills on the approach to some great mountain. He was at once gratified and disappointed to find everything entirely free of dust: gratified because it meant that he would leave no trace as he searched, but disappointed because it offered no clue as to what might most recently have been occupying Gruner's attention, beyond whatever lay on the desk. Also, if Gruner had a safe hidden behind some of those books, it would be a bitch to find.

Angel started with the desk itself. He stepped back, took a small digital camera from a pocket of his jacket, and photographed everything, first from a distance, then as a series of separate, closer images. It was an old habit. The best robberies were those that took a while to notice, and the longer the gap between the theft and the reporting of it, the more time available to dispose of the proceeds. Equally, it required a certain degree of care and skill to toss a room without making it look like it had been tossed. Finally, Angel wanted to record as many of the titles as possible. He had no idea what books might be important, but De Jaager would know, or maybe crazy Bob Johnston.

When he was done, he checked the position of the chair on the floor, and saw that it had worn four deep holes in the fabric of the old rug on which it stood. He sat down slowly, doing his best not to disturb the chair's position. He placed his gloved hands flat on the rectangular leather space that constituted Gruner's entire work area, the rest of the desk being a smaller simulacrum of the book-canyon floor, and breathed deeply in the hope that it might help to clear some of the remaining nausea. There was no point in going to considerable lengths to conceal the fact of his intrusion only to spoil it all by throwing up on the man's possessions.

But for the first time in many months, perhaps even since he had received the original cancer diagnosis, Angel was happy. He had dealt with the lock. He had gained access to Gruner's chambers. He was more or less upright, physically if not morally. He had a purpose. He was still useful.

He was alive.

When he was certain that the dizziness had passed, he set to work. Proceeding from left to right, he began sorting through the papers on the desk, opening manila folders and box files – Gruner's preferred methods of storage, if the desk and surrounding shelves were anything to go by – in order to examine their contents. The thick drapes were already drawn when he entered the apartment, which made things easier; he didn't have to worry about lamplight alerting any interested parties passing on the street below.

Angel had expected most of the handwritten notes to be in Dutch, but Gruner worked principally in English. Either he was assembling material to be read by someone outside the Netherlands, or he just preferred it that way. Then again, everyone Angel had met so far in Amsterdam seemed to speak better English than he did, so maybe it wasn't too surprising.

It didn't take Angel long to find the first reference to the Atlas, contained on the second page of five separate leaves of closely written script. Gruner's handwriting was so small as to resemble ants on the paper, and Angel struggled to make sense of it, even with his spectacles on. He settled for photographing the contents of each file before restoring it to its rightful place and moving on to the next. He continued in this way for half an hour, until he came to a folder marked 'Carenor'. Inside was a sheaf of lined pages detailing payments and dates going back to the previous decade, entered in Gruner's hand but using different colored inks over the years, and marked either *Verzameling* or *Levering*. A quick Google search revealed that the former was the Dutch word for 'Collection', which meant that the latter was probably 'Delivery', but Angel sought a translation anyway, just to be sure. Finally, he came to a more recent addition that obviously represented some form of crosschecking of those earlier entries.

Angel googled Carenor, and found the company website. So Gruner was in the habit of using a British courier firm specializing in the transportation of delicate or valuable objects, particularly art. This made some sense, given the various paintings on the walls of his rooms, and in the bar below, but why did the file not contain any formal documentation from Carenor? It suggested that services were being supplied off the company's books, but why then employ a seemingly respectable courier to begin with – unless Carenor wasn't respectable, despite appearances to the contrary in the form of a classy website, and testimonials from galleries and institutions of which even the notably philistine Angel had heard.

He looked again at the list of dates and payments, the latter representing monies paid or received. They were large sums for a courier company: none lower than €4,000, while some were considerably greater. Carenor seemingly charged a premium for its services, and Gruner was also being paid well for his own. Angel didn't know what a clean passport might cost, but another quick search provided him with an answer: maybe €3,000 for a Dutch version on the Darknet, and €2,000 for a German. The Darknet had made such items easier to acquire, which might have suppressed the price in recent years. But what if one didn't want to work through unknown agents, or preferred the kind of guarantee of quality that came from using a man like Cornelie Gruner, and the security of transportation assured by a firm like Carenor, either officially or unofficially?

Angel placed the two lists side by side, and had just finished photographing each in turn when he heard a noise at the door.

Cornelie Gruner stepped into his old bookshop, which was as much a home to him as his rooms above the Oak, if not more so. He locked the door, hung his coat on a stand, and shuffled to the little toilet next to the register, where he relieved himself of the wine he had drunk. He felt safe in this place, with the blinds drawn on the main window and the bolts thrown on the front door. Just to be certain, he created a gap between blind and glass using a finger and thumb, and checked the street to left and right. There was still no sign of De Jaager's women – or, mercifully, of anything worse.

Gruner was tired, and considered taking a nap in his chair, but wanted to verify one or two details from the day's efforts. The works he required were in the back room of the store, which functioned as an extension of his personal library. He opened the door, and smelled an unfamiliar perfume before his eyes found the source.

'Welcome, *mijnheer* Gruner,' said the woman. 'Please sit.'

And Gruner did, because she was holding a gun, and it was aimed at him.

LXVIII

Angel had been a thief for most of his life. He had not always been a good thief, although he had definitely improved as the years went by. One skill he had cultivated was the ability to listen and work at the same time, so that a portion of his attention was always fixed on unseen stairways and doors, alert to the possible return of a residence's rightful occupant. The stairs leading from the Oak to Gruner's chambers had felt old and solid beneath his feet, but Angel had still kept to the side nearest the wall, where the wood was less likely to creak. He, though, had reason to want to ascend unnoticed. If this was Gruner returning home, he had no cause to mask his approach, not unless Angel's presence had somehow been detected, which seemed unlikely: he'd been working undisturbed for some time now, and Gruner's rooms appeared devoid of any form of electronic surveillance or motion sensors. More importantly, De Jaager had assigned people to follow Gruner, and give ample warning to Angel should the old book dealer head for home, but no message had come through to his cell phone. Either De Jaager's employees had lost Gruner – and it didn't say much for their abilities if an elderly man could get away from them – or someone else was trying to gain entry.

The light from the lamp extended little further than the perimeter of the desk itself, so Angel didn't think it could be seen from under the door. He killed it as a precaution, and the room was instantly plunged into almost total darkness. To alleviate the gloom, he leaned back and opened the drapes a crack, enough to permit the streetlamp beyond to offer some illumination. If he had to move quickly, he didn't want to break an ankle, or anything else, by falling over a pile of books.

He waited for the sound of a key turning, but it did not come. Instead he heard what sounded like scratching at the wood and lock. Did Gruner have a cat? Angel hadn't seen a litter tray or food bowl, and he'd been through the entire apartment. He listened for any hint of an animal's cry, but heard nothing resembling one. The scratching grew more persistent, and the door moved in its frame as whatever was outside placed its full weight against it. If this was a cat, Angel thought, it was the kind kept in zoos, and fed on hunks of raw meat. A dog? If so, why wasn't it barking?

The scratching reached such a crescendo that he heard splinters of wood bouncing off the floor outside before the racket ceased, leaving only silence. Angel stood. Very slowly, and very quietly, he navigated his way toward the door, stopping when just a few feet away. He picked up no sound of retreating steps from outside, which meant that a presence still remained in the hall. He stared at the door, aware that, on the other side, a living entity was staring back.

He reached out a hand – just as, in a living room in London, Bob Johnston made a similar motion toward a Victorian fireplace before thinking better of it. The sound of music drifted up to Angel from the street below, and he heard a girl shout something in Dutch, and laugh. The wood felt warm to Angel's touch, and he caught the faintest smell of burning, like a match that had briefly ignited before being snuffed out.

Angel waited. His illness and subsequent recuperation had taken a great deal from him – confidence, strength, and a length of intestine – but it had also endowed him with more patience than before, and a comfort with stillness that he had previously lacked. One minute went by, then two. After five, he heard movement from one of the lower floors as someone ascended the stairs. He tensed, but then a door opened in a room directly beneath him, and bottles clinked as a case of alcohol was removed from storage.

Another skill that Angel had acquired over the years was the knowledge of when to leave a property. Most prison sentences resulted from people staying in the wrong place for too long, and at that moment Angel intuited it would be a very good idea to depart Gruner's chambers as quickly as possible. The rear of the property overlooked a small yard, accessed from the top floor by a narrow set of external stairs. He could use this stairway to leave, but would then have to find a way back to the street. It wouldn't necessarily be difficult, but he might attract attention from neighbors on the way down, and he still needed to get to the hallway to do it, because the only access to the stairs was via the window.

Angel swore. Nothing in this life, he thought, was ever simple.

He lowered himself to his knees before leaning down to peer beneath the bottom of the door. A bare bulb in the ceiling provided the hallway's sole illumination, but there was enough light for Angel to see that it was clear of feet, or paws. He also glimpsed fragments of wood on the floor. From his jacket pocket, he removed one of the pistols supplied by De Jaager. It didn't have a suppressor, so he'd have to move fast to avoid being arrested or shot by Dutch law enforcement if he were forced to use it.

The door on the floor below slammed shut, and there came the sound of a crate of bottles being set down. The footsteps recommenced, but this time they were climbing to the top level, and Gruner's rooms. They reached the hall, and a man's voice called '*Hallo?*' Angel held his breath as the steps approached Gruner's door, and the same voice said '*Wat de hel?*', which Angel didn't need Google to help him translate. He heard a foot brushing against the splinters of wood on the floor, and then a knocking at the door.

'*Mijnheer* Gruner?'

The door handle turned, making Angel glad that he'd locked it again after gaining entry. Finally, the voice said '*fock*' loudly, and headed back down the stairs. Angel heard the box of bottles being lifted, and knew that the man would certainly return to the top floor soon, probably with a brush and pan to clean up the mess before Gruner got back, unless he called the police to report an attempted break-in. Angel decided to take his chance. He stepped into the hall, pulling the door closed behind him. He caught his reflection in the gilt mirror on the far wall, his features distorted by oxidization, so that he seemed to be moving through shadow and fog.

He opened the window, climbed onto the outside stairs, and descended. Rain started to fall, which helped conceal his presence. He had to pause once on the way down, when a man in a bartender's white shirt and black pants – although not the same one he had passed earlier – appeared inside with a sweeping brush. Angel waited until the bartender was out of both sight and earshot, and continued to the yard, where two doors faced him: one with a light behind it, leading to the restrooms of the bar, and the other the entrance to the adjoining building, where Gruner kept his bookshop. Under different circumstances, Angel might have been tempted to explore the latter, but he'd endured more than enough stress for one night, and his headache had returned with a vengeance.

He tried the door to the bar, and was relieved to find it open. He entered the men's restroom, and washed his face with cold water before exiting. The bartender from earlier glanced at him with mild curiosity, as though trying to figure out where Angel had come from, or just how long he'd spent in the restroom, and what that might mean when it came time to clean it. Angel simply nodded a goodnight, and walked down to Singel. He saw a figure illuminated in a nearby car as the engine started: De Jaager's driver, ready to whisk them away.

'Any problems?' asked Louis, as Angel got into the back seat beside him.

'I think someone might have tried to get in while I was there, but they went away again.' Which seemed like the simplest explanation for what had occurred.

'Not Gruner,' said Louis. 'He's being followed, so we'd have been informed.'

'When are you planning to speak with him?'

'Maybe tomorrow, after you tell me what you found in his rooms.'

'I can do better than that,' said Angel. 'I'll show you, once I hook up my camera to a laptop.'

Only as they reached De Jaager's safe house did it strike Angel that the mirror in Gruner's hall had been clear when he entered the old man's rooms, yet tarnished when he emerged.

Tarnished – or polluted.

But he chose to leave this unremarked.

LXIX

Cornelie Gruner regarded the woman before him as she skimmed idly through one of the books on his desk, bending the pages hard enough to leave marks. He disliked seeing a book mishandled, even under such circumstances as these. When she licked her fingers to turn the pages, he was forced to intervene.

'You should be more careful with that,' he said.

'Why, is it valuable?'

Gruner thought this was the kind of question only an uncouth individual would ask, but then, judging by her accent, the woman was American. In his experience, Americans had a tendency to confuse price and value, equating the latter solely with the former. She had also so far failed to introduce herself, which he regarded as compounding her rudeness.

'It belonged to a man named Maggs,' he said. 'The overwriting in it is said to be the work of a *djinni*.'

The book was a copy of Molitor's *Tractatus De Lamiis*, originally published in 1489, although the edition currently being abused by the woman dated from 1561, with a contemporaneous binding, which was most unusual; the other copies Gruner had seen were all rebound in the seventeenth or eighteenth centuries. Such an edition was worth about €3,000 to the right collector, but Gruner would never have parted with this one, although to the inexpert eye it appeared to have been sorely disfigured. The original Latin text was virtually unreadable, obscured as it was by script in another, older language.

'And what is a *djinni*?' said the woman. She sounded bored.

'A spirit, or demon, from Islamic mythology.'

'You mean a genie, like in *Aladdin*?' She was laughing now. 'You're telling me that a genie wrote in this?'

'So Maggs said.'

'Did you believe him?'

'Unfortunately, he died before I was born, but I have spoken with a man who claimed to have met him. He said that Maggs's entire torso and lower body were covered in a similar script, like a living book. Maggs claimed that the *djinni* used one of its fingernails as a nib, its blood for ink, and Maggs's skin for vellum.' Gruner paused for effect, before adding, 'As a consequence, I tend to wear gloves when I handle that volume.'

The woman closed the *Tractatus*, and set it aside. While she tried to appear unconcerned, Gruner noticed that she rubbed her right hand clean against the leg of her trouser suit, and her lips moved as though to rid her mouth of some nasty taste.

'You're a very odd man,' she said.

'And you have the advantage of me,' he replied, 'as I know nothing of you.'

'My name is Armitage.'

'And what do you do, *missen* Armitage – aside from intimidating old men in their places of business?'

'I am a federal agent of the United States government, stationed as a legal attaché at our embassy in The Hague.'

'The FBI? I was not aware that the bureau had jurisdiction overseas.'

'Congress has given us extraterritorial jurisdiction to protect US citizens and US interests abroad.'

Armitage rattled off the reply like a candidate responding to a particularly unchallenging test question. Gruner found her to be somewhat arrogant.

'Fascinating,' he said, almost managing to sound as though he meant it. 'Do you have identification?'

Armitage produced her badge and ID, and slid it across the desk to Gruner. He examined it critically.

'When even fakes are so convincing,' he remarked, 'how can one be certain of what is real?'

'Oh, you're being too modest. I hear you're quite the expert on falsification.'

So that was it: a fishing expedition. Let Armitage dangle her line. She would catch no fish here.

'FBI shields are outside my area of competence.'

'I guess you'll just have to take my word for it, then.'

'You do seem most sincere.' He returned the black leather case to her. 'And how do I impinge upon American interests in the Netherlands, Agent Armitage?'

'By your assistance of Atol Quayle in his hunt for the Fractured Atlas.'

Gruner did not immediately respond to the allegation, neither to confirm nor deny the truth of it. He was unfamiliar with the general behavior of US federal agents, but he did not believe they brandished their weapons without cause. If Armitage was indeed a federal agent, and Gruner had no particular reason to doubt her, she was behaving in a most unusual manner.

'The Fractured Atlas is a myth,' he said at last, 'and Atol Quayle is long dead.'

'Or long-lived,' said Armitage. 'It depends on whom one asks.'

For the first time since she had identified herself, Gruner began to feel actively worried by the woman.

'Was he the one who claimed to have met Maggs?' Armitage continued. 'I can't think of anyone else that might have.' She ran a finger along the spines of the books on Gruner's desk. 'Is the Atlas mentioned in all of these?'

Gruner saw no advantage to lying.

'Some of them.'

'Quayle thought he'd traced the final pages, didn't he? He believed the Atlas was complete, but he was wrong. Now, with your help, he's trying to figure out what he might have missed.'

'I'm afraid you have your stories confused,' said Gruner, 'which is not unusual when it comes to the Atlas. Myths tend to accrue obscuring layers, and the Fractured Atlas may be one of the greatest myths of all. The lawyer Atol Quayle was among those who devoted many years of their lives to the search for it, but without success. That hunt goes on, though, and I am not ashamed to admit I am among the seekers. After all, it's not illegal.'

'But why devote all that effort to what you claim is a legend?'

'Because every great myth has a truth at its heart. I would like to know the truth behind the Fractured Atlas.'

Armitage, who had been holding the gun casually for a while, now leveled it at Gruner with more purpose. No one had ever pointed a gun at him before. He was not finding it an edifying experience.

'Mr Gruner, where is Atol Quayle?'

'Dead.'

'Try again.'

'Undead. Is that what you'd prefer me to say?'

'Are you trying to be funny?'

'I'm trying to bring this conversation to a satisfactory conclusion for both of us.'

'That will require honesty.'

'Are you really an agent of the FBI?'

'Yes.'

'But I sense that you may not be here in an official capacity.'

'No.'

Gruner took a deep breath. He smelled himself. He'd grown so used to his own odor that he no longer noticed it very often, except perhaps in summer. It came to him now, though. He thought his fear might be accentuating it.

'Quayle is in London. I have not met him in many years. He does not like to travel.'

'Yet you have supplied him with passports.'

'I assume that even he sometimes has cause to move across borders, however reluctantly.'

'How do you contact him? How do you supply his needs?'

'Through a courier.'

'Carenor.'

Gruner shrugged in place of a verbal acknowledgement.

'You already seem to know so much,' he said, 'that I wonder why you're bothering to question me at all.'

'I'm just confirming details. I didn't really expect you to be helpful.'

'Then what next? Are you going to shoot me?'

He was smiling as he said it. He thought it might help: two reasonable people, laughing at the absurdity of such a thing.

'Yes,' said Armitage.

She stood, and Gruner shrank back in his chair.

'Your gun will make a noise,' he said. 'People will come. *My* people.'

'Your people are bartenders and waiters.'

A heartbeat.

'Mors is not.'

'Is she here? I don't see her.'

'If you harm me, she will find you.'

'Don't flatter yourself. You're just a bookseller.'

'If I'm just a bookseller, why kill me?'

'To stop Quayle from completing the Atlas.'

'You don't understand: the Atlas *wants* to be completed, if not by Quayle, then another. It will find a way.'

'But not through you.'

Gruner noticed that Armitage was holding a book in her left hand. The boards had been torn from it, leaving only the pages themselves, hundreds of them. He could not see the frontispiece, and so could not identify the work, but the vandalizing of it pained him, even now, at the very end of his life.

In a single quick movement, Armitage struck Gruner hard on the head with the butt of her pistol before thrusting the book at his chest. She placed the muzzle of the gun against its pages, and pulled the trigger once, because once would be enough. The sound was no louder than a heavy volume being dropped on a table. Gruner, she thought, should have known better.

Armitage lifted away both gun and book, the latter now further defaced by a hole. A second hole had been torn in Gruner's many layers of clothing, from which blood was spouting. The old man's eyelids fluttered. He tried to speak, but only more blood bubbled from his lips. She listened, but nobody came to investigate the shot.

While Gruner sat dying, Armitage cleaned down the surfaces she had touched, and placed in a bag the remnants of the book she had used to suppress the sound of the gunshot. After the slightest of hesitations, she added to it the copy of the *Tractatus*, because she noticed that some of the oils from her fingers had transferred themselves to the pages of the book, in one case leaving an almost perfect fingerprint. She checked the street before leaving, and found it to be empty, but still she waited a few moments after opening the door slightly, just to ensure that no one was about to emerge from the Oak. Thankfully, its door was closed against the rain, and she was able to depart unobserved.

Armitage walked quickly to her car, opened the trunk, and dropped the bag containing the two books on top of the body revealed within. She hadn't intended to kill De Jaager's girl, but the young woman had been watching Gruner's property, and Armitage had been forced to take action. She'd just hit her a little too hard, that was all, but driving from Amsterdam with a dead girl in the trunk of her car wasn't an option. This stretch of canal was quiet and dark enough for her needs, and Armitage had deliberately reversed into the parking space with such an eventuality in mind. It was the work of seconds to dump the girl in the water, minus her identity card: Eva Meertens, twenty-three years of age, now sinking into the murk, although she'd rise to the surface again soon enough. Armitage was tempted to throw the books in with her, but decided against it. She'd probably burn them instead.

Just to be safe.

LXX

Parker's flight to London City Airport took barely an hour, and the time difference meant that he arrived in London just five minutes after leaving Amsterdam. He checked into his hotel, left a message for the absent Bob Johnston, and was walking the streets of the city by 9.30 p.m.

And so, while the body of Eva Meertens descended slowly into dark waters, Parker moved through High Holborn and Chancery Lane, following paths previously taken by Quayle and his legal forebears. Thanks to Johnston, Parker was familiar with the long history of the firm of Quayle, but he remained unable to establish how the current bearer of that name fitted into the lineage, if at all. The Atol Quayle who had died in London in 1948 left no children, or none that he was publicly prepared to acknowledge, and Johnston had discovered no trace of brothers, sisters, nieces, or nephews – not even cousins, however distant. Atol Quayle appeared to be that rarity: an entirely solitary man.

Stranger yet, Johnston had encountered difficulties in establishing the precise nature of the processes through which the firm was passed from one Quayle to the next, despite inquiries to the Law Society. True, Johnston had unearthed references to this Quayle having studied in Cape Town, or that Quayle earning certain qualifications in Bombay, but it proved impossible to determine if this were actually true, the records in many cases being incomplete, or the firms at which apprenticeships were reputedly served, and training received, having long since ceased to exist. Even at the time, determining the bona fides of any of the Quayles would have been difficult. Either those institutions and individuals responsible for their education and legal apprenticeships were remarkably unlucky, many – in the case of the

379

former – having been the victims of fires and floods that destroyed records, or – in the case of the latter – succumbing to the inevitability of mortality; or generations of Quayles had covered their tracks by claiming personal and professional histories that could not easily be verified.

But why go to all that trouble? Parker did not hold the legal profession in very high esteem – he made an exception for Moxie Castin, and one or two other lawyers, although only reluctantly, and with the expectation that they must eventually disappoint him – but he thought an imposter would surely have been exposed by his lack of knowledge. Then again, Parker had read *Bleak House*, in which Dickens displayed an opinion of lawyers that was even lower than his own, and if the novel's depiction of the nineteenth-century legal system was even remotely accurate, someone with a sufficient degree of arrogance and cant, and a modicum of legal knowledge, could conceivably have hidden himself away amid its arcane machinery.

But would generations of frauds have managed to ensure the kind of longevity, and therefore success, that the firm of Quayle had enjoyed in London? It seemed unlikely. It was just one more oddity to add to a growing collection linked to the Quayle name.

Even though Parker was close to the heart of London, he passed comparatively few people on these streets. It seemed that this area only truly came alive when the courts were in session, and at the close of day the lawyers abandoned it, ascending from the whole filthy business into cleaner reaches, their black robes fluttering behind them like the wings of crows. But by walking this city that was foreign to him, Parker was attempting to render it less alien, and familiarize himself with aspects of a case that had roots buried deep in the past. By circuitous ways he came to Whitechapel, and found the address at which the book scout, Maggs, had been killed, allegedly by John Soter, near to which the body of the bookseller Wenham Dunwidge, father of Eliza, was also discovered; and the bar where the prostitute named Sally Campion was last seen drinking before she, too, seemingly became one of Soter's victims. What had been a tenement in Maggs's time was now a block of expensive apartments, but the bar retained its identity, if not its former reputation as a staging post for hookers, and traded on its connections to Jack the Ripper, who had selected one of his victims from its clientele. Parker found no mention of John Soter in the framed reproductions of newspapers that decorated the pub's walls, only the Ripper. He thought the proprietors were missing a trick.

Finally, he returned to the legal byways of the city, and the offices of Lockwood, Dodson & Fogg, formerly the site of Quayle's firm. The structure was fairly anonymous when viewed from the front: a glorified glass box, with a modicum of decorative work at rooftop level. Parker had sourced a satellite image of the area, but zooming in on the LDF building hadn't revealed very much, other than a small outdoor area at the rear, and what looked like parts of an older structure, possibly retained for historical reasons, standing slightly apart from its modern neighbor.

Two security guards sat behind a desk in the main lobby, which, with its uncomfortable furniture and bad abstract art, appeared to have been designed to discourage dawdling by visitors. A total of five businesses were listed as tenants, but three of them, according to Johnston, were subsidiaries of LDF itself, which had developed the property. The final tenant was a financial management company, of which Emily Lockwood and Carolyn Dodson, Parker knew, were both directors. Of the third partner, Giles Fogg, Johnston had found little mention. Further digging revealed that Fogg was terminally ill, and unlikely to survive the year. Parker wondered if the partnership would have to order new stationery.

One of the guards was watching Parker as he examined the nameplates beside the revolving doors. The guard didn't bother getting up from his chair to establish the reason for the interest, but didn't look away either. Parker wasn't concerned. He'd be visiting LDF in person soon enough, and when that happened, he could make any formal introductions required. In the meantime, he kept his face angled slightly from the camera above the door. He had no idea if questions about Quayle would be welcomed by LDF, but didn't see any reason to spoil the surprise.

He made one full circuit of the property, but the value of the effort was limited by the fact that this was one of the few office buildings he'd seen in which all the lights weren't burning, despite the absence of anyone working inside. Parker could never quite figure out why someone wasn't employed just to turn off the lights at night in big offices, or why they weren't retrofitted for motion activation if security was one of the concerns. LDF, as owners of their own block, appeared more inclined to cut down on unnecessary costs, although it did lend the premises a brooding aspect, a handful of lit rooms excepted. The courtyard was hidden behind a high wall, and the older construction at the rear, or the part of it visible to Parker, appeared appropriately antiquated. If the LDF building was essentially a modern glass box, this other edifice was an archaic brick one.

Parker left LDF, and found a bar called Ye Old Cheshire Cheese. So far, he hadn't managed to do anything that made him feel like a tourist in London, and drinking somewhere with 'Ye Olde' in its name seemed to fit the bill, and more. He entered the small chamber to the right of the main entrance, and ordered a glass of red wine.

He had just taken a seat when his cell phone rang, and Bob Johnston's number appeared on the display. Parker, Louis, Angel, and Johnston were all in possession of a clean set of burner phones for communications among the four of them – cheap Nokias that, unlike smartphones, would be difficult to trace, as long as they were careful about their use. Parker also had a second burner, the number of which he had shared with Rachel and with Moxie Castin, to whom Parker's professional calls were being redirected in his absence.

Parker stepped outside to talk.

'All okay?' he asked.

'I'm back at the hotel, and I saw your message,' said Johnston. 'I think I may have poisoned myself with gin.'

'You know, there are other ways to embrace the spirit of London,' said Parker. 'You could get on a tour bus, or buy a T-shirt.'

'I'll take that under advisement. I wasn't expecting to see you for a few days.'

'Amsterdam didn't appeal.'

'That's an untruth. I bet you came on my account.'

'Maybe I was missing you some. So, what did you find out before you succumbed to Mother's Ruin?'

'I visited the former home of Dunwidge & Daughter. The current owner, Rosanna Bellingham, thinks it may be haunted.'

'What do you think?'

'I think it smells as though someone burned to death in it.'

'Someone did.'

'Yes, Eliza Dunwidge, almost a century ago. Unless Rosanna Bellingham is in the habit of incinerating corpses, there's no reason why it should still stink of charred flesh.'

'Badness lingers.'

'That's what Rosanna suggested, even if the smell has only recently become obvious. She gave me an album of cuttings relating to the history of the house. I'm looking through it now.'

'Anything interesting?'

'Lots, but that's not the same as being relevant. I found an illustration of Atol Quayle in an old newspaper.'

'And?'

'It looks much like the man in the passport pictures: not an exact likeness, even allowing for the difference between a sketch and a photograph, but enough to suggest a family resemblance.'

'I'll take a look in the morning.'

'Good, because I'm going to swallow two aspirin and go to bed. Where are you?'

'Outside a bar.'

'Find out anything?'

'That it's more comfortable inside.'

'I'll take that as a "no", then. See you in the morning.'

Johnston hung up, and Parker returned to his chair. He was reading a book on crime and punishment in London, one of a number he had gathered in an effort to understand the world that had produced, and sustained, Quayle's legal firm. Most of it was profoundly depressing. William Calcraft, one of the City of London's most famous nineteenth-century hangmen, and apparently an otherwise mild-mannered individual, had enjoyed jumping on the backs of prisoners as they disappeared through the trapdoor of the gallows, riding them like ponies as they transitioned from this world to the next.

John Soter was mentioned briefly in the book, mainly because his alleged murder of the prostitute Sally Campion had occurred in the vicinity of Miller's Court in Spitalfields, where Mary Jane Kelly, the Ripper's final victim, had died. In fact, the book scout Maggs, another of Soter's supposed victims, had also once lived in Miller's Court, and died at Princelet Street, not far away from it. According to the book, Maggs's body had been severely mutilated: his eyes were burned out, and reports suggested that Soter had attacked his mouth with a sharpened piece of wood, probably post-mortem. Campion, meanwhile, had been eviscerated, and Wenham Dunwidge was so badly beaten that his skull had collapsed.

Maggs, Campion, and Dunwidge: all murdered on one of the Ripper's former hunting grounds, and all brutalized, but in markedly different ways. Parker reflected on what Johnston had told him about the smell in Rosanna Bellingham's home. Badness lingered, and if blood penetrated deep enough into wood, the stain became near permanent. The past gave substance to the present, and all old places were storehouses of memory: the more ancient the site, the greater the accumulation, and bygone atrocities called to new. Parker had witnessed it in his own life, in the desecration of the house in which his wife and first child had died, and so knew this to be true.

John Soter: the more Parker learned about him, the harder it became to balance Johnston's description of a former soldier who was courteous and kind to women, and wept when an infant reminded him of his own lost family, with the image of one who could tear apart men, women, and children. Because here was the most disturbing part: whatever the truth about the adults, there appeared to be little doubt that Soter had killed a young boy and girl, shooting both. A Luger pistol, kept by Soter since the war, was found after his disappearance, and the bullets used on the children had almost certainly come from the same weapon. Soter had also been seen in the area a short time earlier. The dead boy and girl were never identified, and their bodies lay unclaimed for months before eventually being buried in paupers' graves. According to Johnston's researches, the corpses were dumped by Soter behind bins of rotting meat, the contents of which had been treated with some combination of acid and lye that leaked over the bodies, disfiguring their faces beyond recognition, and damaging their remains so badly that a proper autopsy was never performed. The pathologist did conclude that the children had suffered from a bone disorder, 'possibly rickets', that caused grave deformities to their limbs. It was a wonder, the pathologist noted, that they had even been able to stand upright.

Parker finished his wine, put the book away, and headed into the night. He considered walking back to Soho, but he was tired, and the darkness now seemed oppressive to him after the comfort of the bar. He hailed a cab, and asked the driver to take him to Hazlitt's. The unfamiliar city passed like a series of slides framed by the window, but he barely noticed it.

It was to the detail of the boy and girl killed by Soter to which Parker kept returning. Earlier that year, he had briefly glimpsed a child with deformed limbs, this one on the streets of Portland, while following a man linked to Quayle. The sighting had been only momentary, but it had stayed with Parker: a pale creature, more like an emaciated bird than anything else, its limbs misshapen, its leg and elbow joints bent at unnatural angles. He had not seen it since, and for this he remained thankful.

In Johnston's reports, he had found its echo.

LXXI

Karl Holmby sat in his brother's apartment in Newcastle, a bottle of Becks in hand. By now Karl had drunk four beers, and was starting to feel the effect. He was half-watching one of the *Alien* movies, and wondering when Gary would return from whatever was so important that he'd had to leave in such a hurry, even on his crutch, assuring Karl that he'd be back before he knew it, and they'd talk more then.

Karl hadn't known that Gary had injured himself. Gary claimed to have slipped on wet cobblestones. It didn't mean anything, not even if the police were speculating that whoever was responsible for dumping Romana Moon's body on the moors might have done so only after incurring an injury. Lots of people slipped and injured themselves, every day, or so Karl told himself.

Gary Holmby's apartment was part of a new development on the Quayside, standing across the Tyne from the BALTIC Centre for Contemporary Art, which was housed in one of the old mills that once flourished along the river. Karl had only been inside the BALTIC on one occasion, and that was with Ryan Clifton. They'd traveled to Newcastle for a concert, and Karl had expected them to kill the time beforehand by mooching around the shops, or maybe finding somewhere in the Bigg Market that would serve them a few beers without kicking up a fuss about ID, but instead Ryan had suggested visiting the BALTIC.

Karl assumed Ryan was joking at first. He knew his friend liked to draw, and even painted a bit, but he'd never associated Ryan Clifton with the frequenting of actual galleries, not unless he was hoping to nick something from the gift shop. It made Karl reconsider what Ryan might have been doing on those days when he didn't bother turning up for school. Karl had always supposed Ryan was playing pool, or sneaking into movies, or just doing nothing at all, which for Ryan was still preferable to learning. Instead, it seemed he might have been frequenting the Heritage in Middlesbrough, or the Institute of Modern Art. Funny how you could think you knew someone only to have him surprise you with a left hook personality-wise. The BALTIC hadn't been so bad, either. At least it was free to enter, and when Karl eventually got bored, which didn't take long, he sat outside and had a smoke while looking at the girls, the city, the river, and the apartment block on the other side of the water, the one in which his brother had recently acquired a nice two-bed with a balcony, and a parking space for his BMW.

Gary was older than Karl by seven years, and the younger brother had spent much of his early adolescence despising his senior. It wasn't just the difference in their ages, but also their personalities. Gary had always been a bit of a loner, and preferred spending time on his computer to socializing with actual living, breathing human beings his own age. All Karl's friends thought Gary Holmby was weird, and Karl had tended to agree with them. The fact that a lot of clever adults, particularly female ones, liked Gary only caused Karl to dislike him more, even though Karl shared his brother's ability to mix easily with his elders.

But then Gary became the first male on their street – and the first person in the extended Holmby clan – to progress to university. It emerged that all those hours spent alone in his bedroom, staring at a screen and tapping on a keyboard, had helped make Gary some kind of genius when it came to stuff like symmetric cyphers and encryption algorithms. He started earning serious money almost as soon as he left college, with three big-name companies fighting to recruit him. Gary ended up working for two of them, one after the other, until he had bled them for all the information and experience he required. Since then, Gary had been operating as a freelance consultant, with an hourly rate that was more than their mum took home at the end of a full week at the call center.

The brothers had grown closer after Gary left home, despite what Karl had told the police, distance lending him a different perspective on his sibling. It was Gary who had encouraged Karl to consider university; Gary who promised to help him out with a weekly allowance if he got a place on a good course; Gary who told him that he didn't have to be like all the rest, that he could be anything he chose to be; Gary who assured him that it wasn't about becoming better than everyone else, because he was already better than them. He had ambition. He was good-looking. He was clever. Karl had all the advantages. He now needed to put them to good use.

By then it was clear to Karl that his brother wasn't some stereotypical computer nerd, either. He dressed well, drove a fifty-grand car, and was never short of female company. Women didn't just like him, but were actively attracted to him. He had money in his wallet, which always helped. He listened. Females old and young fluttered around him like moths.

And then he hurt them.

Not physically, or at least Karl didn't think so. Gary just enjoyed the thrill of the chase, of luring women into bed before dumping them. It was a game to him, and the smarter or better-looking the woman, the more pleasure Gary derived from drawing her in, and throwing her back into the sea when he was done. Karl thought it might be a form of revenge on all those girls who had rejected Gary when he was a teenager, before he had the cash to afford nice clothes and a fancy car. That was the way women were, Gary would inform his brother. They were conniving, always looking for the advantage. You had to teach them their place, because they'd kick you in the balls otherwise.

When Miss Moon had rejected Karl – first giggling at him and then, as he grew more insistent, becoming angry, before screaming at him to leave – it was to Gary that he decided to turn, because he knew Gary would understand. Karl had taken the train to Newcastle, drinking a couple of cans of cheap lager on the journey, thereby adding alcohol to his cocktail of shame and rage. He'd started blubbering as soon as he got to Gary's apartment, after which Gary gave Karl a few more beers, and offered him a bed in the spare room.

Karl was pretty certain it was his brother who had proposed picking up Miss Moon, and fucking her every which way before laughing in her face, just as she'd laughed at Karl. He might even have suggested posting pictures of her on some of those revenge porn websites – they were rancid as anything – just to compound her humiliation. But by the next morning Karl had forgotten most of the conversation, distracted as he was by his hangover, and his continuing sense of mortification at his behavior. God, he'd even stolen a pair of Miss Moon's knickers, just to impress Ryan Clifton . . .

Many months later, Gary had sent a picture of Miss Moon to Karl's phone. She was in a bar, looking away from the camera, unaware that she was being photographed. Under the image, Gary had written:

SHE'S SMILING NOW. SHE WON'T BE SMILING SOON! #REVENGEISADISHBESTSERVEDCOLD

Karl panicked. He could barely remember what he'd said months before in the apartment, or what actions he and Gary might have discussed. Anyway, it had just been a way for Karl to let off steam. He hadn't been serious. It had been stupid of him to come on to her to begin with. Most of all, he didn't want his brother to have sex with Miss Moon, because he didn't want Gary to have what he couldn't.

(SHE HAS A SCAR ON HER BELLY, RIGHT ABOVE HER PUSSY. #HAHAHA)

PLEASE LET IT GO, Karl texted back, and heard nothing more about it. His brother always did have a weird sense of humor. Gary went to Europe for two cybersecurity conferences, grabbing a weekend for himself in Berlin along the way, and suddenly Karl was into revision for his first-year exams. He didn't ask Gary again about Miss Moon. He didn't want to make him angry, because Gary had a temper. He assumed his brother had done as he asked.

Until Romana Moon's body turned up on the Hexhamshire Moors.

And the police came calling.

LXXII

Sellars had no trouble making the appointment with the young hooker. The phone he used to contact her was a fresh one that he'd bought at a market stall, and the SIM came from another Asian corner store. The shop had a security camera, but Sellars wasn't overly concerned. Even if, by some miracle, the police traced the card back to the store, he figured that the owners wiped the camera footage on a regular basis, as long as nothing untoward had occurred in their little retail empire. Jesus, they were so old they probably still relied on a VHS tape, and wound it back each night.

The girl lived in a block of council flats, which made everything easier for Sellars: no entry camera, just a buzzer, and then a lift that stank like council lifts everywhere, which meant a mix of fast food and human waste. When she opened the door, she appeared even younger than on her Internet profile. The flat smelled of baby, and the living area held a crib and a playpen, but he couldn't hear or see the infant, and the place only had one bedroom.

'You got a kid?' he asked, which seemed like a question with an obvious answer, under the circumstances, but still, he had to ask, if only for the sake of appearances.

'My friend's watching her.'

Her voice was very soft, and didn't sound like it belonged to someone who should be living in a dump like this. A small shelf beside the television was crammed with books, some of them clearly university texts. Sellars was starting to build up a picture now: a student; pregnancy; estrangement from her parents; a need for money. Better and better. It made it unlikely that she knew many people in the block, apart from whoever was looking after the child: a neighbor, or a neighbor's daughter, who'd be paid for babysitting out of the evening's proceeds.

Or wouldn't, in this case.

Sellars's only regret was the absence of the baby. He'd planned for it, and Mors had been excited to learn that the girl he'd selected was also a young mother, or as excited as Mors ever got about anything. She'd even given him a second syringe with the correct dosage for a child, and instructions on exactly how much to inject in three-month increments from a newborn to two years of age. The girl herself would receive a standard dose: just enough to make her docile, but not so much that Sellars would have to carry her to the car.

In the end, he didn't even bother taking off his shoes. He was on top of her as soon as she showed him into the bedroom, and injected her on the floor. He'd grown adept at keeping their mouths shut without being bitten – you only made that mistake once – and knelt on her back until she grew drowsy.

'Why'd you do that?' she asked, slurring her words.

'I didn't want you worrying.'

''Bout what?'

'About anything at all.'

She was having trouble keeping her mouth moist. The drug did that, Sellars had noticed. Eventually, she accumulated enough spittle to croak the word 'Baby.'

'Boy or girl?' he asked, as he helped her up.

'Girl.'

'Little girl. That's nice.'

He found a coat, and managed to get her arms into the sleeves before buttoning it up. She wasn't fighting him, but she wasn't cooperating either. Sellars was concerned that Mors might have misjudged the dose, or maybe the girl was more resilient than she appeared. He pulled her toward him as they got to the door, one arm around her shoulders, the other working at the lock.

'No,' she said, and tried to move away, but he had her now. He forced her against the wall, and topped her up with the second syringe, the one intended for her baby. It did the trick. Within a minute she was pretty much asleep on her feet, but now he *was* forced almost to carry her out. Thankfully, the hallway was empty as they shuffled to the lift. An old woman entered on the fifth floor, and rode down with them, but Sellars held the girl close, whispering to her as though to a lover. The old woman kept her gaze averted from them, for reasons of prudery or privacy, and did not look back as she exited.

Sellars got the girl outside, and put her in the back of the unmarked Carenor van: plain white, with a set of plates stolen from a similar model he'd found parked at Newcastle Airport. He laid her under some tarpaulin, closed the doors, and headed for the M6. It was just as well he'd given her the second dose, he thought. They had a long way to go, and it wouldn't have done for her to start kicking up. He'd selected the site on the basis of the following day's job: a pick-up in north London at sparrowfart the next morning. He'd told his wife that he planned to find a cheap bed and breakfast on the outskirts, to save himself having to get up at three in the morning, and informed the company of the same thing. He was covered.

Sellars was bound for the Sinodun Hills of Oxfordshire, and in particular the Wittenham Clumps, twin copses of beech trees that marked the site of an Iron Age fort at Dorchester-on-Thames. The girl wouldn't be the first sacrifice accepted by that ground, so her bones would have company.

Sellars heard her cry out softly from behind him.

He thought she might have been calling a child's name.

Gary Holmby was fretting.

He'd contacted Sellars as soon as Karl called him to say that the police were asking questions about Romana Moon. Sellars had told Gary to invite Karl up to Newcastle, and keep him there for a couple of days. For now, Sellars said, it was important to calm Karl down, and make sure he said nothing to the police about any possible connection between his brother and Romana. Sellars assured Gary that the matter was in hand, and the police would very shortly be presented with a new set of distractions.

But then the police had called Gary – his mum had surrendered his number to them, under protest – wanting to know if his brother had been in touch, because Karl had dropped off the radar. Gary denied it, of course. What was he going to say: that Karl was on his way up to Newcastle because he was afraid Gary might have stabbed a woman to death on the moors, and he needed to look him in the eye when he asked about it in order to be certain of the truth? Yeah, and maybe the police would like to come around and arrest Gary now, save him the trouble of making his own supper. He could have tea and toast at the station while he signed the confession. Hynes, the detective who called, had requested that Gary get in touch if Karl made an appearance, and Gary assured him that he would. He and Karl would have to talk to the police eventually, of course, but not before they got their stories straight. Karl would also have to phone his mum to let her know he was okay. She didn't worry much when he stayed out overnight, especially not since he'd entered university, but the police would have contacted her as well. Karl already had five missed calls from her, as well as three more from a number he didn't recognize. Gary guessed that was probably a police number, possibly even the same copper who had spoken with him. Karl had a bunch of voice messages as well, but Gary told him not to listen to them, and to turn his phone off until the morning.

Karl hadn't needed much encouragement to stay in Newcastle for a couple of days. It was a weekend, and he only had one more exam the following week. Gary gave him a free run at the pay-per-view movies, and whatever else he might want to watch. Tomorrow he'd take Karl somewhere flash for dinner, and they'd head to a nightclub after. Karl being under twenty-one wouldn't be a problem, not with the goodwill Gary had earned over the years. Gary would find them a couple of girls, and they'd bring them back to the apartment. Karl wasn't a virgin, but he'd never been with a proper woman. Gary would fix that.

But the immediate challenge was convincing his brother that Gary wasn't responsible for Romana Moon's death, and hadn't even seen her since Karl asked him to stay away from her. Gary knew he should have found another girl on whom to lose his killing cherry, but Romana was convenient, and good-looking, and she'd made his brother feel like shit on a shoe. Gary had been careful to ensure that she didn't know his real name, or too many details of what he did for a living. He didn't even allow her to take any pictures with her phone – either of the two of them, or him alone. He told her he was tired of all this social media nonsense, thought it put too much pressure on a relationship from the start, and remarked how nobody seemed to believe anything was real anymore until they'd captured it on their phone. He also worked in cyber-security, he said – a glancing moment of contact with the truth, but not enough to pose a danger to him – and understood how vulnerable these new technologies rendered us.

He knew she'd google him, though, and would be suspicious if nothing came up with his name attached, regardless of how much he professed to want to distance himself from the demands of an electronic existence. It hadn't taken him long to establish an online identity, one that chimed with the information he'd shared with her: a website for a nebulous business consultancy, backed up by references to the company in articles and reports either manufactured by him from standard templates, or presented in the form of summaries, and inserted into locked or subscription-only sites.

After his second date with Romana, he offered to give her some advice on her own use of the Internet, and she'd brought along her laptop and phone, as requested. This enabled him to discover her passwords and access codes, and establish that she didn't use the Cloud to back up her information, which would make it simpler to erase any digital footprints once he'd killed her. Unfortunately, he'd held on to both her phone and her laptop after her death, which meant that he still had them when Karl called to say the police had been asking questions.

It had been stupid of Gary to keep Romana's stuff. Mostly he'd just been waiting until his ankle didn't hurt quite so much before getting rid of it, but there was a part of him that also liked the idea of having a few souvenirs of the event. He particularly liked the laptop. She'd kept a lot of photos on it, some fairly intimate – she had body issues, it seemed – and a great deal of music, most of it rubbish, but important to her, and therefore a facet of her personality. He'd started deleting the music, tune by tune, as though progressively removing all remaining traces of her from the world, just as he'd excised her physical presence. He was doing the same with the pictures, with the exception of the naked and semi-naked shots. It reminded him of the power he'd felt as he took her life on the moor.

His first task, therefore, once his brother was safely situated on the sofa with a beer in hand, was to dispose at last of the phone and laptop. The phone would be easy – drop a bit here as he walked around, and another there – but the laptop would be more difficult. After considering the problem, he'd returned it to its hiding place in his bedroom closet. If he was going to dump it, he needed to erase everything on it first, and he didn't have time to do that, not with Karl in the apartment, and not before he'd had a chance to store elsewhere the photos he wanted to keep.

But he also wanted to call Sellars, and let him know that he had Karl. So he'd left his brother in front of the TV, unburdened himself of Moon's phone, and made contact with Sellars, all while trying to ignore the pain in his ankle. Along the way he bought some tequila, fresh limes, a bag of tortilla chips, and a tub of salsa. He'd make a jug of margaritas, and try to put Karl's mind at rest. Karl wanted to be convinced, which helped. They'd already briefly discussed the murder, so Gary knew how his brother's mind was working.

'*You didn't hurt her, did you?*'

'*Cross my heart, I didn't hurt her. I never even spoke to her, because you told me not to.*'

'*You're sure?*'

'*Course I'm sure.*'

'*What about the scar?*'

'*What scar?*'

'*The one on her belly, the one you told me about.*'

'*She was wearing a cropped top. I saw it when she stood up to go to the bar. You could see it in the photo I sent you. That doesn't mean you can go mentioning it to the police, though.*'

'*I'm not stupid.*'

'*I know you're not. I'm just saying. They'd twist it, and make us both look bad. They might even try to pin it on us.*'

'*Shit.*'

'*Yeah. Why'd you have to say you slept with her anyway? That's where all this trouble started. That's why the police are asking questions.*'

'*I don't know. Just because.*'

'*Doesn't matter. What's done is done.*'

'*Swear you didn't hurt her, Gary. Swear it.*'

'*Jesus, Karl. I didn't hurt her – I swear. Happy?*'

But Karl wasn't, not yet. Gary would work on him.

It would all be sorted by morning.

Sellars gave the Holmbys only the barest of thoughts as he drove. He didn't know Gary Holmby well enough to care if anything happened to him, and he didn't know his brother Karl at all. Sellars had offered to take care of the whole mess. He felt partly responsible, since he was the one who'd found Gary to begin with, but Mors was adamant that there should be no further association between Sellars and Gary Holmby. The girl was the priority – the girl, and the Wittenham Clumps – not the Holmbys.

Sellars wondered what Mors planned to do with them.

Whatever it was, it wouldn't be pleasant.

LXXIII

Hynes spoke with Priestman one last time before bed. Karl Holmby had vanished, which was worrying. They'd tried his friends and family, but he hadn't reached out to any of them, or so they all claimed. Priestman remained convinced that Holmby was lying to them, but she wasn't sure about what, exactly. She also believed – through instinct, female intuition, call it what you will – that he hadn't slept with Romana Moon, and they knew he couldn't have killed her, because his alibi was solid. He'd surface soon, though; he was just a kid, not an international criminal. He didn't even own a passport. They'd pick him up over the next day or two, but in the meantime Hynes informed Priestman of his intention to speak in person with Holmby's brother Gary, probably early the following morning. According to the Holmbys' mother, who was reluctant even to confirm her own name to the forces of law and order, the two brothers had grown tighter in recent years, which seemed to contradict what Karl had told Priestman about their relationship. Even if Karl wasn't with Gary, the older Holmby boy might be able to shed some light on the younger's personality and behavior.

'You think we're making any progress?' Hynes asked Priestman. 'Because it doesn't feel that way to me.'

'We're closer than we were,' she replied. 'Small steps.'

Hynes said goodnight.

Small steps? Baby steps. Barely steps at all.

He went to bed, but couldn't sleep.

It was wrong, all wrong.

LXXIV

Karl Holmby wasn't enjoying this last beer. It might have been because it was one of those fancy American IPAs his brother enjoyed drinking, but that tasted of soap to him. Then again, he hadn't been able to enjoy much of anything since the police came to question him.

If he were being honest with himself, he might have admitted to living in a state of disassociation since the moment he'd learned of Miss Moon's death. Her murder had drained the color from Karl's world, rendering all experience into shades of gray. It would show in his final exam results, he was sure. He'd done well in his earlier assessments, but his overall performance would now take a hit.

He put down the beer, and curled up on the couch. He wanted his mum. He should go home to her and confess everything. She might be angry with him for a while, but she'd understand. He hadn't done anything wrong, apart from shooting his mouth off to Ryan Clifton about fucking Miss Moon – well, lying about fucking Miss Moon, which made it two things he'd done wrong.

Three, if you included telling Gary about her.

Four, if you added enabling Gary to kill her.

The beer fug vanished. He knew Gary had killed her. He'd known ever since her body had turned up on the moors. He'd just blinded himself to the fact, still hoping to be proved wrong, because the reality was too horrible to face. But that was just foolishness. It was what little kids did: turn their back on reality. No, Gary had killed her, clear as the nose on Karl's face. Gary might have been the super-intelligent one in the family, but Karl had always been able to see through him, right down to the rot within. Gary's flaw was arrogance, like a lot of the serial killers

398

Karl had read about over the years. In the end, ego was their downfall. Gary was certain he could lie to his younger brother and be believed, because he was smarter than Karl – smarter than anyone else he knew. His wealth and success proved this.

Serial killer.

Karl sat up. He hadn't even considered the possibility that Miss Moon might not have been Gary's first victim – or if she was the first, that he might have enjoyed killing her enough to continue with others.

The time for confessing all to his mum had passed; whatever he had to say, he'd tell it to the police, even if he had no proof, only suspicions. Yes, Gary had given him a sense of his own potential. Without him, Karl would never have made it to university. He also admired Gary, although his admiration was tinged with envy at the life Gary had made for himself. But he didn't love Gary. He never had. By turning his brother over to the police, Karl's conscience wouldn't be so troubled that he'd endure a lifetime of guilt as a consequence. He didn't think his mum would blame him for it either, not if Gary had killed a woman. Even if she did, Karl would live with the burden. And if he was wrong – if, if, if – and Gary hadn't killed Miss Moon, then he would live with that guilt, too.

Here was the truth: Gary might have killed Miss Moon, but if he had, then Karl was also responsible for what had befallen her, because he'd given Gary the idea of humiliating and hurting her. Until Karl had gone whining to Gary, Miss Moon had been only an abstract concept to his brother: some do-gooder who was offering extra tuition to a working-class kid in order to assuage whatever liberal, middle-class guilt she had carried into her professional life, and perhaps indulge her savior complex along the way. If Karl benefited from her largesse, that was all to the good, but Gary had no real interest in her, just as he had little or no interest in anyone who couldn't pay, benefit, entertain, or pleasure him. *Miss* Moon was an abstraction, a kind of Platonic ideal of the teacher, but by turning to Gary in his hour of need, Karl had given concrete form to *Romana* Moon, and planted the idea that his brother might like to play with her.

And Gary had played with her, leaving her ruined and bloodied on the moors.

The intercom chimed. Karl ignored it, but it rang again, more insistently this time, the caller keeping a finger on the bell. He checked the screen, and saw a woman wearing a cap. He pressed the answer button.

'Hello?'

'Pizza delivery for Holmby.'

'I didn't order pizza,' said Karl.

'A Mr Gary Holmby did, for two. Delivery to be accepted by a Mr Karl Holmby if he wasn't present, according to the note.'

'I don't have any money.'

'It's on his account, tip included.'

Gary had suggested that he might bring back some late-night food, but Karl couldn't figure out why his brother hadn't simply collected it himself. Then again, maybe Gary was now too grand to queue for takeaway pizza, which it wouldn't have surprised Karl to learn.

He buzzed the woman up, and heard the doorbell ring shortly after. Karl glanced through the peephole. The same woman was standing outside, two pizza boxes in her arms – although not in one of those insulated bags, which was odd – but the hallway was otherwise empty.

Karl opened the door, and the woman thrust the boxes at him. Her face was very pale, almost translucent, like the flesh of some deep-sea fish, the kind that hunted with luminous lures. Her irises were a milky gray. The pizza boxes were light, and radiated no heat. Old grease stains speckled the cardboard, which smelled bad, really bad, and—

Suddenly, Karl realized it was the woman who stank, and he wanted to get as far away from her as possible, even before he spotted the gun that the boxes had concealed. He tried to close the door, but she was strong and fast, and was inside before the boxes falling from his hands had even made it to the floor. The butt of the gun broke his nose, and he fell hard, his eyes squeezing shut in pain. He heard the door close, and smelled the woman drawing closer. He opened his eyes again. Her left hand was poised to strike, and a second later he felt the stab of a needle entering his neck. He lashed out, catching her shoulder, and she struck his nose once more.

Which was when Karl Holmby blacked out.

VIII

Dire portents appeared over Northumbria and sorely
frightened the people.

Anonymous, *Anglo-Saxon Chronicles*

LXXV

In his cottage on the Hexhamshire Moors, Douglas Hood was trying to calm his dog.

'Hush now, Jess, there's a good girl.'

But the dog would not be quieted. She turned circles by the front door before racing to the back, where she stood with her hackles raised, staring at the wall, growling low in her throat. Hood went to the window and looked out, but could see nothing beyond his own yard by the light cast from the kitchen.

He had lived too long on this land to underestimate the oddness of it. Once, on an autumn evening with only the barest of mists upon the ground, he and Jess had stood on a rise listening to the sound of men marching in military step, the tramp of their boots muffled and irregular, fading in and out like a radio signal, as though separated as much by time as distance; and the dog had inclined her head as orders were shouted in a foreign tongue, and they heard the rattle of buckles, and armor, and weaponry. Finally, a man cried out – a single, piercing expression of agony – before all was silent.

And when Hood and Jess went out early the next morning to check on the sheep, the dog began digging at a declivity in the soft ground, and upon joining her Hood saw the rusted metal of a helmet half-buried in the earth, and the pitted blade of a sword, and fragments of old brown bones. The researchers from the university came to claim it all, and later declared them to be the remains of a Roman legionary, with grievous wounds to his right femur, and his right arm missing below the elbow. A mark to the left part of his ribcage suggested the insertion of a thin blade beneath the armpit; a mercy killing, to put him out of his pain. An analysis of isotopes in his teeth revealed that he'd come from northern Spain, which meant he was some poor bastard Vardullian, probably garrisoned at the Roman fort of Vindolanda to the south. They'd buried him, but hadn't marked his grave, and he'd been stripped of anything of value before being put in the ground: a strange business for a strange place.

Hood was invited to attend when the artefacts were put on display at the Great North Museum as part of a new exhibition on life in the legions, but he did not reply to the letter. After all, it was not the first time he had seen or heard older presences on the moors, and he doubted it would be the last. But he also felt a sense of culpability for having informed the authorities about the soldier's bones. In retrospect, he should have called Jess away, and covered up the remains again, leaving them where they lay, 'as ashes under Uricon', to quote his beloved Housman. (The breadth of Hood's reading and learning might have surprised some. After all, there was only so much television a man could watch.) The legionary was part of the moors, and they were his rightful resting place, not some glass case in a museum – or later, a storage box in a basement. It should not have mattered, of course: the soldier was long dead, and logic dictated that any concerns he might once have had about the grave he would ultimately occupy, if any grave at all, had come to an end when the issue of mortality moved from abstract to concrete. Rationality, though, was an incomplete response to the intricate nature of this world, and the past and present were not so distinct as some cared to believe: the unveiling of the soldier's bones by the shifting landscape was proof of this, a physical manifestation of the ancient revealed to the gaze of the modern, yet buried on moors so old as to make a mockery of cities, armies, and the fleeting aspirations of men.

Now, in his kitchen, Hood killed the lights, that he might better see what lay beyond the glass. He closed his eyes so they would adjust more quickly to the dark – although he did so with some reluctance, as though unwilling to cede even a moment's inattention to whatever might be moving in the night – and when he opened them once more, the yard came into clearer focus. He could make out the shapes of plants and shrubs, and the wall, centuries old, marking the boundary of his garden. Jess was sniffing at the jamb of the door, and he saw her wrinkle her nose at some scent she had picked up. She started to move again, staying close to the interior walls, pausing only to growl at whatever was outside. It appeared to be circling the cottage, but Hood could hear no animal sounds, nor detect the footfalls of man. The only noise that came to him was the faintest of rustlings, low to the ground, but it might just have been the wind testing leaf and branch.

Hood stepped away from the window. This was his dwelling, his redoubt, and whatever was out there had no business intruding upon it. His shotgun stood in the hall closet, and would take only moments to load. He used it for hunting rabbits, mostly, although he had once shot a dog that was worrying his sheep, before leaving the corpse by the side of the road in case its owner came looking for it, because it was one thing to kill a man's dog and another to leave him wondering at its fate. He'd felt sorry for the dog; it had only been acting according to instinct. Its owner was the one at fault, and therefore bore the blame for the fate of his animal.

The memory of the dead dog led him to Jess. If he went outside, he'd have to permit her to come with him; she might hurt herself otherwise in trying to get out, because however frightened or disturbed she might be, she would not wish to leave him unprotected. And although Hood remained no wiser as to the nature of the presence beyond his walls, still it set jangling something primitive in his blood, an atavistic warning beacon embedded deep in his genes.

Hood was instantly propelled back to the firesides of his childhood, where old men and women recounted tales of the Ettins, the lost giants who built the Devil's Causeway from Corbridge to Berwick; and the Redcaps, who took the form of old men but were baser beings beneath, and dyed the fabric of their hats in the blood of those they killed. He thought of the braags and the gyests: shape-shifters, entities without a fixed physicality, seeking to lure the unwary onto marshy ground, where roots and weeds would coil around bellies and legs to pull them under, so that they, like certain shot dogs, would never be found, leaving their loved ones without a grave at which to mourn. The stories shared about these creatures had real force, for they held a truth at their heart: not only about the lethality of marshes and moors, but the nature of the uncanny. Names and forms had to be ascribed to the threats from beyond – vampire, werewolf, gyest, worm – because the worst of them had no form at all, instead electing to inhabit elements of this world as they saw fit: tree, earth; disease, cancer; water, mire; a standing stone, an old church; a man, a woman; root, branch . . .

In his kitchen, it seemed to Hood that the voices of these older folk, now long silenced, spoke to him again, sharing tales that were more than myths, and truths disguised as lies. Their words became a litany, the testimony of a congregation united in the face of the threat posed by an older god, a deity of leaf and bough. In that moment, Hood saw another version of himself open the door and step into the dark. He watched tendrils move swiftly across the soft ground to envelop Jess, slowly squeezing the life from her. He felt branches burst from his own body, roots pouring forth from his nose and mouth, as he became one at last with the Green Man.

'Jess!' he called, and so forceful was his command that she came to him instantly and sat by his side. He took her by the collar and dragged her to the empty fireplace in the living room, where he attached one end of her leash to her collar, and the other to an iron ring set in the stone of the hearth. He brought a cushion for her to lie on before kneeling to add wood and paper to the grate, because he always kept a store of it ready, the weather in these northeastern regions being unpredictable and testing. He struck a match and put it to the paper, and did not rise again until the flames caught, and the first of the wood began to burn. When all was done, he wrapped himself in a blanket and took to his favorite chair, the dog now settled at his feet, still watchful, and thus they waited for dawn to break, sometimes dozing, sometimes listening, Hood rousing himself only when the fire needed to be replenished.

Because all wood fears the flame.

LXXVI

Gary Holmby returned to his apartment to find the television turned off, and the living room illuminated only by the moon and the distant lights from across the river. A peculiar smell hung in the air, like spoiled food. It was one he associated with Karl's bedroom in the middle part of his teens, before his brother discovered that girls preferred boys who didn't stink excessively of their own hormones.

He called Karl's name, but received no reply. Two pizza boxes lay open on the dining table, but both were empty, with not even a crust to be seen. Could his brother have asked a friend to join him, perhaps that deadbeat Ryan Clifton? But Gary doubted that Ryan could have made it to Newcastle so quickly, not unless the two of them had already hatched a plan to meet up before Karl headed north.

He saw that his bedroom door was open, yet he knew he'd closed it before leaving the apartment. The bedside lamp was burning, but he'd left it that way. As he drew nearer, he saw a pair of booted feet on what remained of the mattress, followed by the rest of his brother, lying on his side facing the door, his eyes half-open, and his nose and mouth covered in blood. More blood stained the pillow, and he'd vomited on the floor.

Around the bed, the room had been torn apart: closets and drawers emptied; clothes piled in one corner, bed sheets in another; the contents of Gary's private bathroom ransacked and broken on the tiled floor. In the midst of the wreckage stood Romana Moon's laptop, displayed on a chair like the centerpiece of some conceptual art installation.

It was to Gary Holmby's credit that, in the final moments of his life, his main concern was for his brother, even as the darkness behind the bedroom door came alive, and that rancid smell intensified; even as he turned to witness the face of a drowning victim emerge from the shadows, and heard a grating voice speak his name as though in disappointment; even as he registered the gun, and its tumorous suppressor; even as the bullet tore its way into his chest, sending him sprawling onto the bed, so that his head lay for an instant against the warmth of his brother's body, and he felt Karl's fingers tentatively touch his face; even as he began to slide away – from the bed, from Karl, from family, from life; even as the woman stood over him, this time leveling the muzzle at his face; even—

Mors stepped back. On the bed, Karl Holmby was mumbling something that might have been a plea, or a summoning of his dead brother. Mors contemplated Karl. It would be easier to kill him now and leave him where he lay, but that struck her as a waste. She had a better use for him. She waited until she was certain the suppressor was cool before removing it to be stored in one of her pockets. She found a satchel, into which she placed Romana Moon's laptop, then returned to the bathroom and doused a towel with water. She washed Karl's face clean of blood, and examined him critically. His face had swollen, and his eyes would be black by morning – except she didn't think he was going to live that long.

Mors got Karl to his feet, first moving him to the other side of the bed in case he stumbled over his brother's remains. He made no attempt to fight her as she led him from the room, thanks to a combination of shock and sedative. Gary Holmby's car keys lay on the sideboard in the living room. Mors pocketed them, restored the pizza delivery cap to her head, and opened the door. They were only two apartments away from the lift, and the hallway stood empty, but still she raised the hood on Karl's tracksuit top as she walked him out. Together they waited for the lift to arrive, Karl swaying slightly like a drunk.

When they reached the garage level, Mors pressed the key fob to identify Gary's car, and opened the boot. Even through the stupor of the sedative, Karl now seemed to understand the danger he was in. He tried to brace himself against the body of the BMW, but Mors twisted his right arm behind his back in order to force him into the space. Once he was lying inside, she gave him the last of the sedative. She didn't want him causing her any further problems.

The release button for the garage door was fitted to the BMW's inside roof, and her own car was waiting on a side street about a minute's drive away. She parked so that the two vehicles stood rear to rear, and simply shifted Karl Holmby from one to the other.

Then, while Sellars drove south with his burden, she headed west with hers.

To Beltingham.

To the yews.

LXXVII

Hynes was woken by his phone shortly after 6 a.m. His wife muttered something beside him, from which he picked up at least two swear words, one of which she'd previously upbraided him for using, which didn't seem entirely fair. What's sauce for the goose . . .

Hynes hit the answer button, because it was Priestman's name on the caller display, but he didn't begin talking until he was out of the bedroom.

'Boss,' he said,

'We have trouble,' said Priestman. 'And we're about to have a whole lot more.'

Parker was also awake early, which didn't suit him at all, but his body clock remained screwed up by the transatlantic flight. He decided he could only spend so long staring at the bedroom ceiling, so he showered and dressed before making his way reluctantly downstairs, where he encountered Bob Johnston by the reception desk, a book in hand. Johnston looked disturbingly fresh for the hour, and full of enthusiasm at the prospect of a new day in a new city.

'Good morning,' said Johnston.

'Go away,' said Parker.

'I'll just let you find your mojo, will I?'

'Go away,' Parker repeated, this time with feeling.

Johnston departed for the hotel's breakfast room, humming happily to himself, the brightness of his mood undimmed. Parker headed for the street. If everyone else staying in the hotel turned out to be a morning person like Bob Johnston – hell, if even one other person was that way – Parker might have to cause an incident. He found a convenience store on Old Compton Street, bought the international *New York Times* and the *Guardian*, and took a seat in a coffee shop on Berwick Street called My Place, complete with an old 1960s Gaggia coffee machine and an ambience of quiet calm. If it didn't make him feel any happier at being up and dressed before 8 a.m., at least he was now somewhere that wouldn't make him any unhappier.

Parker ordered an Americano with a side of sourdough toast, and watched London gather pace. When his food arrived, he began reading the *New York Times* from cover to cover. Parker hadn't ventured abroad as much as he might have wished, but he had learned that one of the great pleasures for a traveler was to read a newspaper from home while staying in a foreign place. He didn't even turn to the *Guardian* until his second cup of coffee was long finished, and My Place had begun to fill up. On the inner pages of the paper, he came upon a story about the discovery of a young woman's body on some moors in Northumberland, and an account of the ongoing investigation into her murder. Only when he reached the fourth paragraph did he find a reference to the Familists, and the police's belief that the victim, Romana Moon, had been killed on the site formerly occupied by their church, the same church that Parker had almost died investigating, and the rubble of which was still being discovered by hikers in Maine woodland, thanks to the dispersive effects of high explosive.

Parker read the story twice before paying his bill and returning to the hotel, where he opened his computer and spent a further hour finding out all he could about Romana Moon's death. When he was done, he booked a British Airways flight from London Heathrow to Newcastle for that afternoon, and called Bob Johnston's room.

'You in a better mood now?' Johnston asked.

'Not so much,' said Parker, and told him of what he had read.

'You really feel the need to head up there?'

'I do.'

'You have other places to check out: maybe the church at Fairford, or the lawyers' offices . . .'

413

'The lawyers won't be back in their office until Monday, and that church isn't going anywhere.'

Johnston was quiet for a time.

'The church is important,' he said at last. 'Somehow it's crucial to the Atlas.'

'You've seen it, and I trust your judgment.'

'You should see it, too.'

'I will, when I'm ready. Finish your research here first. Without it, I won't even know what I'm looking at when I get to Fairford, never mind what I'm looking for.'

Johnston's plan for the day was to spend time at the British Library, and possibly also at the Senate House Library, which housed the book collection of the University of London. He had obtained a pass for the Senate House as a visiting researcher, and was particularly interested in examining the papers of Florence Farr, an actress, mystic, and Chief Adept of the occult order known as The Golden Dawn. Johnston had discovered that Farr, who died in 1917, was a close associate of Eliza Dunwidge, and Farr's papers reputedly contained references to the Fractured Atlas. Parker had originally intended to accompany him, if only to keep a watchful eye.

'When will you return?' asked Johnston.

'Sometime tomorrow, I hope.'

'Well, okay – I guess.'

Parker couldn't figure out when Johnston had taken charge of their investigation. He assumed a memo had been sent, but he must have missed it.

'Well, thanks,' said Parker, as he hung up the phone. 'I guess.'

Hynes watched Priestman stalk the floor, her shouts echoing from the walls while various officers tried to keep their heads down for fear of catching her eye, and thus inadvertently becoming a target of her rage. Hynes had seen her lose her temper before, but never on such a scale. Someone, somewhere would soon wish they had never been born.

'How did this happen?' she said. 'How the *fuck* did this happen?'

What had happened was this: a report had appeared on a

far-right website claiming that Muslim prayer beads had been discovered in the mouth of the murder victim Romana Moon, and the police were deliberately keeping this detail from the public – not for operational reasons, but as part of an ongoing institutional policy of protecting minority offenders in order to avoid accusations of racism. Under ordinary circumstances, such a story, given its source, would probably have been dismissed by all but the most rabid neo-fascists, except that the website had printed a picture of what appeared to be a *misbaha* lodged in a woman's throat.

Hynes currently had the site open in front of him. All he could say for certain was that the picture looked real enough.

'Are we sure it's Romana?' he asked.

'We've compared the images of the teeth with her remains,' said Priestman. 'We're almost certain it's her.'

Hynes examined the photograph more closely. It had been taken with a high definition camera using a flash, so the image was very clear. Nevertheless, Hynes enlarged it on Priestman's computer, leaning in so his nose was almost touching the screen.

'That blood is fresh,' he said.

'What?'

'Look at her nostrils, and her upper lip. I don't think the blood on them has dried yet.'

'Meaning?'

Hynes admired, even adored, Priestman. She was the best copper he'd ever worked under. Sometimes, though, frustration was capable of blinding her.

'Meaning,' he said, 'I think her killer took that picture.'

LXXVIII

Douglas Hood stood in the morning light, surveying the wreckage of his garden.

Every plant and bloom inside the boundary wall was dead, as though each had been touched by some great frost, while all without remained intact. Even the grass on his lawn was blackened, and the air smelled of decay.

Hood looked to the south, as though to discern in the distance the lineaments of a chapel miraculously restored, rising from a hollow in the moor.

They put blood in the soil, he thought. *They put blood in the soil, and something that should be dead has now come back to life.*

LXXIX

Louis and Angel slept late, and were woken by Anouk. She arrived carrying a tray containing a pot of coffee, which she placed on a low table by the window before opening the drapes.

'He wants to see you,' she said.

'When?' said Louis.

'As soon as you've dressed.'

'Here?'

'No, Paulus will come for you.'

'Is there a problem?'

'There may be. Eva Meertens is missing.'

Paulus picked them up within the hour and drove them to Café Hoppe on Spui, where De Jaager was sitting at the back of the old cask-lined bar, an empty cup in front of him. As soon as they were seated, a bartender pulled across a heavy drape to give them some privacy, and brought three fresh cups of coffee, along with a platter of cheese, ham, bread, and boiled eggs, before making himself scarce.

'Eat,' said De Jaager.

Louis picked at the food. Angel did not; the nausea was strong that morning, and he ached deep inside.

'Anouk told us that Eva is missing,' said Louis.

De Jaager took a sip of coffee.

'She's not missing any longer,' he replied. 'She's dead. They pulled her body from a canal not half an hour ago.'

Louis finished a piece of bread and ham before speaking again.

'Any signs of injury?'

'To the head.'

'Accidental?'

417

'Possible, but unlikely.'

'When was she last seen?'

'Shortly before your friend entered Cornelie Gruner's apartments. She and Liesl separated at that point. Liesl's mother is ill, and she had to return home to take care of her. She should have stayed with Eva, but –'

De Jaager shrugged.

'Does Liesl know?' said Angel.

'Not yet. I've only just found out myself. I'll ask Anouk to tell her, and stay with her for a while. The girl will blame herself for what has happened.'

'And who do you blame?' said Louis.

'Not you, if that's what you're wondering, even though I'm not ruling out a connection to your presence here. And I don't believe this is Gruner's handiwork. He's not a killer.'

'Do you think someone might be protecting Gruner?'

'From what?'

'Unwanted attention.'

'You're the threat. The logical step would be to kill you.'

'Actually,' Angel suggested, 'if someone is afraid of Gruner revealing what he knows, then the logical step would be to kill Gruner.'

Louis and De Jaager stared at him.

'Just saying,' Angel added.

De Jaager took out a cell phone. 'It had crossed my mind to speak with Gruner. This shadowing shit must come to an end now.'

'What if he doesn't want to talk to us?' said Louis.

'Then I'll start burning his precious books in front of him, one by one, until he changes his mind. If he doesn't, I'll progress to burning parts of him. One of my people is dead. This is not how things are done here, not when it comes to mine.'

De Jaager selected a name from his Contacts list.

'*Paulus*,' he said, '*breng me mijnheer Gruner.*'

The website responsible for publishing the picture of Romana Moon was run by a man named Harry Stoller. He had been a peripheral figure in far-right circles for decades, mostly because he was an appalling human being, even by the standards of racists and fascists, and therefore struggled to find anyone willing to be publicly associated with him. The rise of social media had transformed Stoller's existence, enabling him to disseminate hate speech without requiring him to show his face – which was a good thing all round, because the only thing more rotten than the condition of Harry Stoller's soul was the state of the rest of him.

Stoller claimed to have almost half a million subscribers to his YouTube channel, and many multiples of that number in viewers of his Facebook videos and tweets. He hated everyone who wasn't white, and most people who weren't white and British, but he also hated lots of white people too, a surprising number of them fellow travelers on the far-right bandwagon who were either too cautious for him, or too extreme; too intellectual, or too stupid; too liberal, or too reactionary; or who, basically, just weren't Harry Stoller. He operated out of a council flat in Bradford, which he shared with his sister, Lottie, although some of his opponents liked to suggest that his 'sister' was just Harry dressed in drag. Objective analysis, though, had concluded that there really was a sister, and she and Harry might even be sleeping together, if only because no one else would sleep with either of them.

Hynes received a crash course in Harry Stoller from Nabih Uddin on the drive southwest from Newcastle to Bradford. Priestman had prevailed upon West Yorkshire Police to allow her people to handle Stoller; no one needed the complicating factor of another force in an already difficult investigation, but under-cover officers from West Yorkshire were keeping a discreet eye on Stoller's flat until Hynes and Uddin arrived.

Assigning Uddin to the task of confronting Stoller probably represented a deliberate act of provocation on Priestman's part, and was unlikely to make Stoller any more likely to cooperate willingly, but Hynes didn't really care. He fully expected Stoller to be difficult. In fact, he was hoping for it.

'We have plenty of racists of our own here in Northumbria,'

said Hynes. 'I don't see why someone had to send those pictures all the way to Yorkshire.'

'Stoller has an audience,' said Uddin. 'Whoever took the photos wants to play to the biggest crowd possible.'

'But bloody Harry Stoller, of all people. That even a murderer should stoop so low.' Hynes shook his head in sorrow. 'Why doesn't the local council just throw him out on his ear?'

'Because he's well resourced, and the council isn't,' said Uddin, who was driving. They'd been forced to make a quick detour to the on-call magistrate in order to secure a warrant to search Stoller's premises, and now Uddin was intent on making up for lost time. He had a heavier foot than Hynes. At the rate he was going, Hynes guessed Uddin would get them to Bradford in less than two hours.

'Whenever the council tries to make a move against him,' Uddin continued, 'Stoller unleashes his lawyers, but not before letting his followers know that the authorities are trying to shut him down. Cue thousands of nuisance emails, phone calls, even attempted denial-of-service attacks. It's easier just to leave him be.'

'Lawyers cost money,' said Hynes. 'Stoller's an unemployed racist living in a council flat with one of the Ugly Sisters. How come he's on Perry Mason's books?'

'Stoller has money. He's clever enough to keep it hidden, but he has it.'

'How?'

'Subscriptions, advertising. He makes money from YouTube: you look at one of his films about how the Holocaust never happened, someone tries to sell you a bar of soap, and Stoller gets a cut.'

'Yeah, but come on,' said Hynes. 'How many people in Britain really care what someone like Harry Stoller thinks?'

'Enough. After the United States, Britain is the biggest source of traffic to far-right websites. But only about twenty percent of Stoller's audience is British anyway. The rest come from all over. It's like that old Coca-Cola advert, the one about teaching the world to sing, except with more racists in the chorus line.'

Hynes felt profoundly depressed. It wasn't that he didn't have prejudices: he did, loads of them, largely against idiots. Stupidity, he knew, did not recognize boundaries of color or creed. But he had come to believe that, like driving a car, people should have to pass a test before being allowed access to the Internet. Most would fail, because Hynes intended to set the test himself.

'Nabih, how do you know all this?'

'I'm a Muslim born to Pakistani parents,' said Uddin. 'Men like Stoller hate me on principle, so it makes sense to keep myself informed.'

Hynes watched an elderly woman in a Toyota move rapidly into the slow lane to avoid them. He offered her a wave of apology, and she gave him the finger in return, which was no kind of example to be setting the youth of today.

'You know,' said Hynes, 'according to Priestman, you were ordered to come on this run.'

Uddin looked surprised.

'Really? Because I offered.'

He smiled. Hynes smiled back.

'I'm shocked to hear that,' said Hynes. 'Shocked.'

Priestman had a headache, the kind no pills could cure.

The Northumbria police's media center was already inundated with calls about the Stoller photo from newspapers, television, and other outlets not generally renowned for their outright fascism. For now, the official line was that the provenance of the photo was still being established, and a statement would follow shortly. It would buy them some time, but only a few hours, by which point Hynes and Uddin should have managed to doorstep Stoller, assuming he hadn't gone to ground. It was crucial to establish how he might have come by the picture, and work back up the chain in the hope it might give them a lead on Romana's killer, but Priestman knew the chances of a direct link were slim. If Stoller had received the image electronically, the best she could hope for would be an IP address, which would give them the originating location, and perhaps even a computer name. It seemed unlikely, though, that the sender would not have covered his tracks.

The only piece of good luck to come their way was that, so

far, only Romana Moon's name had been mentioned in connection with a *misbaha*. Helen Wylie, the victim found at Canterbury, had not been referenced. But if Hynes was right – and further analysis of the image confirmed that he probably was – then Romana had been photographed by her killer shortly before or after her death, which gave rise to a high probability that a similar picture existed of Helen Wylie. If so, it could only be a matter of time before it, too, was published.

Priestman had just finished speaking with one of the press officers when Gackowska called to inform her that Karl Holmby had not returned home the previous night, and still had not been in touch with his mother. His brother's phone, meanwhile, was going straight to voicemail.

'Have you tried Ryan Clifton?' Priestman asked.

'He says he doesn't know where Karl is.'

'Do you believe him?'

'Yes, oddly. He thinks Karl might be angry with him for shooting his mouth off about Romana Moon. He feels bad about that. I don't think Ryan Clifton has so many friends that he can afford to lose one.'

'Did he have any idea where Karl might have gone?'

'He doesn't think Karl has a girlfriend, so that's one avenue ruled out. He gave us a couple of other names. We're checking them now.'

'What about Mrs Holmby?'

'She continues to show no great love for the police. I have to say that I quite like her, even if she isn't being particularly helpful. She's brought up two kids to make something of themselves, despite the early influence of her ex-husband, and she worked hard to do it. I think she's worried about Karl, but not enough to help us find him.'

'And her ex, our old friend Clement Holmby?'

'We're put out feelers for him, just in case. He's no longer with the slapper from Sutton Coldfield, because she's been locked up for arson. Claire Holmby told us that she doesn't know where he is. She said she hoped he was dead, but she didn't think God was that good.'

'What next?'

'Garner and I are on our way to Gary Holmby's residence.'

Rory Garner was another of Hynes's protégés. His expenses already had a touch of the fanciful about them, which was Hynes all over.

'Well, call me as soon as you have anything,' said Priestman.

'Will do. Any word from Nabih and Hynes?'

Priestman checked her watch.

'No, but they should be in Bradford by now.'

'I wish I was with them,' said Gackowska, 'just to see Harry Stoller's face when Nabih knocks on his door.'

Catching sight of Harry Stoller's face was proving difficult for Hynes and Uddin.

'I've told you already: he's not here,' said a female voice from the other side of the door. The door was reinforced with steel, and the windows to either side of it were covered by wire mesh. Hynes might have ascribed this to Stoller's chosen vocation – a piece of faded graffiti on the wall read NAZI SCUM OUT – but most of the other flats in the complex were similarly protected.

'I don't care,' said Hynes. 'I have a warrant to search these premises. And by the way, I know your brother's in there.'

'How do you know he's in here?'

'Because he never fucking goes out.'

Hynes looked to Uddin for confirmation of this fact. Uddin nodded. 'He never does fucking go out,' he said. 'Everyone says.'

'What if I don't open up?' said the woman.

'I'll have you arrested.'

'Can't arrest me if I don't open up.'

There was a kind of logic to this, but only insofar as it applied to a door that was still on its hinges, and Hynes let her know as much. He discerned some mumbling, and then an exchange of words between the woman and what sounded like a man, before chains began to rattle, bolts were pulled back, and keys turned in locks. It was like hearing the Tower of London open for business. Eventually, the door was thrown wide, revealing a hallway that was surprisingly clean and uncluttered, and smelled of cheap air freshener; and a woman of indeterminate age, her hair an explosion of gray tangles, her face an accumulation of swellings and protuberances assembled into a rough approximation of human features, finished off by two perfect blue eyes that appeared to have been stolen from the corpse of a model for high-end lenses. Most of her body was hidden by a long yellow housecoat that had given many years of stout service, and now just wanted to be put out of its misery.

This, then, was Lottie Stoller.

'Show me the warrant thing,' she said.

Hynes showed her the warrant thing. She read it without the aid of spectacles, high-end or otherwise.

'Well?' called a voice from deep inside the flat.

'Looks real,' she shouted back.

'Better let them in, I suppose.'

Lottie Stoller peered at Nabih Uddin.

'One of them's a—' She gave some consideration to the correct term to use, and spent a few seconds distinguishing between the word in her head and the word that should, for the sake of avoiding arrest, emerge from her mouth, before finally settling for 'an Asian.'

The male voice swore in response, but said nothing more.

Lottie led Hynes and Uddin to what had once been the larger of two bedrooms, but had since been transformed into what was clearly the nerve center of Harry Stoller's little factory of hate. Two walls were fitted with floor-to-ceiling shelves containing books, pamphlets, box files, binders, and an array of beautifully painted model tanks and soldiers, all of them World War Two German. (It never failed to puzzle Hynes that the most virulent of Little Englander racists seemed to retain an unhealthy fascination with the very regime a whole generation of their forebears had risked their lives to defeat.) A desk at the window bore two huge computer screens, one of which displayed a series of windows showing news feeds and videos, the sound turned down to a low babble of conflicting voices, while the second screen contained a series of conversations Stoller was having with media outlets, fellow bloggers, and assorted lunatics. The picture of what was, in all likelihood, Romana Moon's bloodied mouth had pride of place in the top right-hand corner, taking up a full quarter of the screen.

Sitting at the desk was a man of medium height, dressed incongruously in a shiny blue suit cut in a style that had gone out of fashion back when people still paid for clothing in weekly installments, and a red, white, and blue tie wide enough to cover most of the stains on the white shirt beneath. His long gray hair was slicked back, and he was clean-shaven, with the unfortunate result that more of his face was exposed to view. Harry Stoller looked like a depilated bat: small dark eyes, an upturned nose, and a mouth that, even in repose, bared sharp yellow teeth. Hynes and Uddin identified themselves, and displayed their warrant cards, but Stoller barely glanced at them, so absorbed was he by his online activities.

'He's dressed nice because he thinks he's going to be on television,' said his sister. Her voice dripped with so much contempt, it was a wonder the carpet wasn't awash. 'The BBC are going to call, give him his own show on Saturday nights, just because someone sent him a picture of a dead girl.'

'Why don't you go and do something useful?' said Stoller. 'You two want a cup of tea?'

Hynes accepted the offer, but Uddin didn't. He wouldn't have put it past Lottie Stoller to spit in his cup.

'Looks like you're being kept busy,' said Hynes.

'Never been busier,' said Stoller. 'A young white girl killed by Muslims, who marked their handiwork by sticking prayer beads in her mouth: what do you think's going to happen now? The fuse has been lit. By this time tomorrow, there'll be mosques burning, and about fucking time.'

Neither of the two detectives was interested in getting into a debate with Stoller – they were here only to find out how he'd come to be in possession of the photograph – but Hynes couldn't help but fear that he was probably right, and they would soon be looking at fires, broken glass, beatings, and worse.

'How did you get the photo?' said Uddin, as Lottie Stoller brought Hynes a mug of tea. He thanked her, but she left the room without acknowledging him, although she did cast a cold eye on Uddin. Hynes doubted that any non-white person had ever previously been permitted to cross the threshold of the flat.

'It was emailed to me.'

'From?'

'A Gmail account composed of random numbers and letters.'

'And what made you think it was a genuine picture of Romana Moon?' said Hynes.

Stoller grinned.

'Because,' he replied, 'it wasn't the only one.'

LXXX

Sam sat in her bedroom's rocking chair, an open book on her lap now ignored. Lazy sunlight shone through her window, its pane a combination of stained panels at the edges and a clear panel at the center. It was the colored glass that had caught her attention. There were patterns on it that she could not recall seeing before, as though previously unnoticed flaws in the material had suddenly been made apparent by the angle of the sun's rays.

She set the book down, and walked to the window. The voice of her half-sister spoke from the room behind.

don't touch it

Sam hated it when Jennifer sneaked up on her like this. She could see Jennifer's reflection in the glass, her blond hair hanging long over her shoulders, concern on her face. This was Jennifer as she was on the other side, but had Sam turned around, she would have seen her as the Traveling Man had left her on this one: blinded, bloodied, faceless.

Dead.

'Why not?'

look closer

Sam did, and discovered that the patterns were not random. They formed figures, and faces. They were nightmares given substance. And further back, Sam detected a shimmering, as of twin suns concealed by mist and cloud.

'They're in the glass,' she said.

yes

'Does our father understand this?'

i don't know

'Why not?'

it's harder for me to see him while he's across the water
'I'll ask Mom if I can speak to him. I'll tell him.'
good
'But why can't I touch it?'
because they'll sense you if you do
'Who will?'
you know who
Sam caught the glow of the suns, like bright eyes staring back at her.

'Yes,' she said, 'I think I do.'

LXXXI

Angel and Louis sat with De Jaager, waiting for Cornelie Gruner to be brought to them.

'The one you're looking for,' said De Jaager, 'Quayle.'

'Yes?' said Louis.

'Could he have killed Eva?'

'He has a woman called Mors who does that kind of work for him. It's possible that he might have sent her here, but Gruner probably only became aware of us late yesterday, so Mors would have been forced to move fast. Even then, why kill Eva?'

'Maybe because she was watching Gruner, and whoever killed her didn't want to be seen,' said Angel.

'But seen doing what?' De Jaager asked.

His cell phone rang. He checked the display.

'It's Paulus,' he told them.

He took the call, and received the answer to his question.

Hynes was standing outside the Stollers' flat, speaking on the phone to Priestman.

'Stoller received ten photographs,' he said. 'If there was ever any doubt about the identity of the woman in the first picture, it's gone now. It's definitely Romana.'

Stoller possessed pictures of Romana on her back, her arms and legs splayed in a crucifixion pose; a close-up of her face; a side profile, in which, a single bloodstain apart, she might have been mistaken for a sleeping woman; four images of the wounds to her body; and finally, two of the *misbaha* at the very back of her throat.

'So why didn't he post them all?' asked Priestman.

'The sender advised him not to. Stoller was given instructions to post the picture with the *misbaha* first, and then wait.'

'For what?'

'For us to come along and ask him about it.'

'Seriously?'

'Seriously. After that, he was free to post the rest. If he did as he was told, he was promised more pictures.'

'Of Romana?'

'The sender didn't say.'

'He can't post those other photos. The situation is bad enough as it is.'

'We're working on that.'

'Seize everything if you have to. Empty his flat of anything with a screen.'

'I don't think that'll do much good. You've heard of the Cloud, boss? Very popular, the Cloud. Stoller can simply access his material from another machine.'

'Then arrest Stoller.'

'We could do that,' said Hynes, but his tone made it clear that he didn't think this was the best of ideas. He waited for Priestman to follow the logic.

'He's our point of contact with whoever took those pictures,' she said, eventually.

'Yes. And Stoller may be unpleasant, but he's not stupid. If he posts the worst of those images, he'll be open to accusations of exploiting the death of a young white woman even more than he already has, and of possible collusion with her murderer. At least, I've made it clear to him that this is how we'll paint it when we talk to the media. He and his sister will be burned out of their flat, and Nabih and I will be out here selling bags of popcorn for the show.'

'And is Stoller willing to cooperate?'

'Up to a point. He's prepared to give us enough information to help trace the email back to its source, and in return we're supposed to acclaim him as the great British patriot that he is. We'll also allow him to use one more image online, the least explicit of them, without kicking up a fuss.'

There was silence while Priestman contemplated the deal. They could tell Stoller to go to hell, but that would entail spending hours emptying his flat of its electronics, and days trying to gain access to the information they required, because Stoller would surely lock it down, assuming he didn't simply delete it all out of spite.

'What do you know about tracing a Gmail message?' she said.

'Only what Nabih and Stoller have told me. They're getting along surprisingly well, incidentally, which is either heartening or worrying, depending on your perspective. With some assistance from Google and the service provider, we can determine the location from which the email was sent, and even the computer that was used to send it, because Google places identifiers in the browser of any device that accesses its services. Obviously, we won't know who sent it, but we'll know everything else, and it'll be enough to get us a warrant.'

A group of older teenagers had gathered by the stairs to the left of the Stollers' flat. One of them was doing circles on a BMX bike, and eyeing Hynes's phone with obvious intent. Hynes reached into his pocket to display his warrant card.

'I'll have that and all,' said the boy.

They were on the fourth floor. Hynes wondered if the boy's bike could fly.

'Does Nabih understand enough about computers not to have Stoller pull the wool over his eyes?' said Priestman.

Uddin wasn't one of the constabulary's forensic experts, but only because he didn't want to spend the rest of his career indoors, damaging his eyesight.

'I think Nabih should have been a spy, so probably.'

'All right,' said Priestman. 'Tell Stoller we'll allow it.'

'But we won't, will we?'

'Of course we won't. As soon as you have what you need, I want Stoller rendered harmless. Don't forget that you're on West Yorkshire's patch, though. They'll want to be there once you stop playing nice. They have some scores to settle with Harry Stoller.'

'Are they near?'

'If you stand on your toes, I reckon you should be able to see them.'

The warrant allowed the police to seize all computers and

431

associated media in the flat, and Uddin was familiar with the requirements for the preservation and logging into custody of that kind of equipment. They had tamperproof tags and clear bags in the car, but they'd need something bigger to accommodate the entire contents of Stoller's office. It wouldn't hurt to include West Yorkshire, Hynes thought, once Uddin started packing things up. They might even be willing to help with a bag or two, because the lifts weren't working.

'Stoller's place looks like you could launch satellites from it,' said Hynes. 'All that stuff won't fit in the back of the car.'

'Consider a van on its way.'

'And I can't carry stuff. I have a bad back, so we'll need willing bodies.'

'Noted.'

She ended the call, and Hynes stored his phone safely in his pocket.

'Did Adolf Hitler do something wrong?' shouted the boy on the bike, indicating Stoller's flat.

'He invaded Poland,' said Hynes.

'Bastard,' said the boy, although whether he was referring to Stoller, Hitler, or Hynes himself, the detective could not say.

Hynes was about to go back into the flat when he heard Uddin call his name, and had just closed the door when Uddin added:

'We've got another email.'

LXXXII

Angel and Louis sat in the back of Paulus's car, with De Jaager in the front passenger seat. They were driving out of Amsterdam toward the Belgian border, and ultimately Brussels, from where Angel and Louis would fly to London. Anouk had packed their bags as soon as she was informed of Gruner's death, and Paulus had collected them before picking up the three men from Café Hoppe.

'It seems you were right,' De Jaager told Angel. 'The smart move *was* to kill Gruner.'

'And Eva was in the way,' said Louis. 'I'm sorry for bringing harm to one of your people.'

'I told you already,' said De Jaager. 'The blame lies not with you but with whoever killed her. But Gruner might have contacted someone in the city once he realized he was being followed, and that call could have led to his death as well as Eva's. Perhaps he had even been forewarned you might come, and recognized you at the Rijksmuseum.'

De Jaager believed it to be unwise for Angel and Louis to stay in the city any longer. It wasn't just that both Gruner and Eva were dead: the Dutch police would already be asking questions of the staff at the Oak, and Angel had been on the premises the previous night. He might not have been seen emerging from Gruner's apartments, but he had certainly been noticed by at least one of the bartenders, and could have aroused his suspicions. De Jaager wasn't certain how crooked Gruner's staff might be, but if they were working for him then they were probably just crooked enough, and under no illusions about their employer's sanctity, or lack thereof. It would be better, therefore, if Angel and Louis departed Amsterdam with all possible speed, and also avoided leaving for the United Kingdom via a Dutch transport hub, just in case.

Louis watched old Amsterdam become new as they passed into the suburbs. Could Quayle and Mors, or someone aligned with them, really have moved so quickly to silence Gruner? But who else knew that Angel and Louis were in the Netherlands? Only Ross, and the local feds, represented by Armitage. Louis was no cheerleader for the FBI, but even he had to admit that the bureau wasn't in the habit of dumping the bodies of young women in canals, or murdering elderly book dealers.

City turned to countryside, flat but not featureless, an otherworldly landscape to him. Europe had always made Louis feel like an interloper, an arriviste, with its Babel of tongues and a history with which he had no connection beyond the fact that, centuries earlier, someone from this continent had forced his ancestors into slavery.

To his right, Angel appeared to be dozing. The radio was tuned to a Dutch channel, NPO1, which De Jaager was monitoring for developments, translating anything interesting for Louis's benefit. Commentators were speculating on a possible link between the deaths of Gruner and Eva Meertens, if only because the police had refused to rule it out. Louis thought this might be the reason why De Jaager had decided to accompany them as far as the Dutch border: contacts worked both ways, and there might well be those in the Dutch security services who were aware that Eva Meertens had sometimes worked for the old man. Being out of the city would give De Jaager time to think, and enable him to establish all he could about the circumstances of Eva's death before he was faced with any awkward questions from the authorities. Louis noticed that De Jaager was rejecting all but a handful of the many calls he was receiving.

De Jaager caught his eye in the mirror.

'Anouk will be sorry not to have been able to say goodbye,' said De Jaager. 'She was always fond of you, as am I, but I do not think you will be returning here. At least, I would advise against it.' He checked the screen on his phone. 'Did Angel damage the door of Gruner's apartment while entering?'

'No, that's not his style.'

Angel opened his eyes upon hearing his name.

'Someone tried to force a way inside while I was there,' he said.

'Why didn't you mention it before now?' said De Jaager.

'It didn't seem important. It might have been, if whoever it was had got in, but that didn't happen.'

'The police,' De Jaager continued, reading the message on his screen, 'believe that whoever killed Gruner may also have tried to gain access to his private rooms. That's unfortunate for Angel.' He turned to Paulus. 'More haste, I think.'

Paulus accelerated. Louis took out his phone, and called Parker.

'We're coming to join you today,' said Louis.

'That was sooner than expected.'

'Well, we wore out our welcome sooner than expected. I'll explain when we see you.'

It had been agreed between them that Louis and Angel would stay near Parker and Bob Johnston, but not at the same hotel, so rooms had been reserved for them at the Soho, ready to accommodate them whenever they chose to arrive.

'I'll let Bob know,' said Parker. 'I won't be there to greet you personally.'

'Where are you going?'

'North. I'll explain when I see you.'

'Touché,' said Louis, and hung up. He tried to stretch out. His wounds were troubling him.

Angel closed his eyes again. The rest of the journey passed in silence; only a sign marked the divide between the Netherlands and Belgium.

And at a truck stop in Meer, just over the border, a man was waiting: De Jaager's last service to them, and to a missing woman who had not been forgotten.

LXXXIII

Hynes stood behind Harry Stoller, examining the images on the screen. Hynes couldn't help noticing that Stoller had begun to salivate excessively. When he spoke, his spittle flecked the keyboard and the display, and he had resorted to wiping his mouth at regular intervals with a cloth handkerchief.

There was no doubt they were looking at pictures of a different woman. Her dark hair bore a faint blue tint, and was cut in a bob. Her build was heavier than Romana Moon's, but only because Romana had been so slight. She was unclothed except for purple underwear, and it was clear that her throat had been cut. A red *misbaha* dangled from her open mouth.

'Same sender,' said Stoller, indicating the email address. 'Same prayer beads. Same Muslim bastard. We'll drive them into the sea for this, you mark my words.'

The email contained only the images of the dead woman. This time, no additional instructions regarding their use had been included.

'Why would a Muslim killer send photos of a dead white girl to a man like you?' Hynes asked.

'What?' said Stoller.

'You heard me.'

'Who knows how those animals think?'

Stoller seemed to have forgotten that Nabih Uddin was one of 'those animals', or perhaps he had fallen back on baiting him after the initial détente. But so excited was Stoller by what he was seeing, and the possibilities for mayhem it presented, that Hynes suspected he had ceased to pay much attention at all to Uddin, who had quietly gone about placing a USB stick in Stoller's second, linked computer, and was copying the email information for Priestman.

'My view,' Stoller continued, 'is that they want a war of race and religion more than we do. If that's the case, we'll give it to them.'

He cracked his knuckles hard, and his fingers moved back toward the keyboard, ready to fire the next round of virtual shots in the escalating conflict. Uddin checked the screen, and nodded once to Hynes, who pulled Stoller's chair back from his desk before stepping swiftly in front of him and slipping a cuff on his right wrist.

'Up you come,' he said, lifting Stoller none too gently by the collar of his shirt. Hynes heard fabric rip, but by then he was already turning Stoller around.

'Put your left hand behind your back,' Hynes instructed.

'You can't do this,' said Stoller. 'I've done nothing wrong!'

'Other hand,' said Hynes.

'No. Absolutely not.'

Hynes forced Stoller to the floor, and with Uddin's assistance got him cuffed.

'It's for your own good,' Hynes told Stoller. 'That evidence has to be preserved, and I wouldn't want you to get in trouble for pressing the wrong button.'

'People have a right to know about the second victim,' said Stoller. 'You can't hide the truth from them.'

Hynes leaned in close to Stoller's ear.

'Listen to me,' he said. 'That woman is someone's daughter, someone's sister, someone's wife. If you think I'm going to let you post pictures of her corpse online just so you can make a name for yourself, you're beyond salvation.'

'Lottie,' Stoller cried, 'call the lawyers!'

His sister came running to the door. She tried to get in, but Uddin blocked her.

'Please go to the living room and sit down,' he told her.

'Fuck you, you brown bastard. I won't have you ordering me around in my own home.'

Seconds later, Lottie Stoller was also in cuffs, but she continued to shout and swear, adding her voice to her brother's. They were both moved to the living room, still bellowing, with Uddin to keep an eye on them. Hynes thought about gagging them, but was convinced he was in enough trouble already.

He called Priestman again.

'You'd best send the cavalry,' he said, but there was no levity to his tone, not with pictures of two dead women on the screen before him.

'It's coming. What about Stoller?'

'Cuffed – for his own protection, of course, and the preservation of evidence. The sister, too.'

'Leave Nabih to take care of everything. Tell him to get the train back, or cadge a lift. I want you here.'

Hynes heard sirens approaching.

'It's all about to go to hell, isn't it?' he said.

'You mean it hasn't already?' said Priestman, and hung up.

Hynes went to the window. On Bradford, a city that was a quarter Muslim, the sun still shone.

For now.

LXXXIV

The sun was also shining on the Joost truck stop at Meer in Belgium, not far from the Dutch border. De Jaager ordered three beers, and a coffee for Paulus. The air smelled of diesel and freshly mown grass. A waitress brought four plates of French fries, which they ate outside while watching a steady stream of trucks pass along the highway.

De Jaager was receiving more updates on Eva Meertens and Cornelie Gruner. Meertens had been dead when she went in the water, which meant the police were now ruling out the possibility that her death had been accidental. The blow to her head, although severe, probably hadn't killed her immediately. With treatment, she might have survived. Gruner, on the other hand, had been shot through the heart, but appeared to have suffered no other injury beyond a single blow to the head. Either torture had not been required to find out what he knew, or his killer had no interest in interrogation, and was concerned only with silencing him.

'What will you tell the police when you return?' Louis asked De Jaager.

'About Eva? I haven't decided. But it was foolish of me to meet you at the Rijksmuseum: an old man's taste for the dramatic. We were seen together, and the museum's security footage will confirm our presence there, along with that of Eva and Gruner. The police will want to know who you are, and it won't take them long to trace your presence in Amsterdam back to your arrival at Schiphol, which means they'll have Angel on camera as well, and probably Paulus. If someone at *de Eik* should give a description of Angel that matches whatever is on the airport footage, well, I will have even more explaining to do. It pains me to say it, but you might be advised to seek the assistance of your FBI contact in New York to confirm your bona fides.'

Louis couldn't picture Ross riding willingly to their rescue. It didn't matter that they hadn't done anything wrong – well, beyond a little breaking and entering. Ross would want to maintain deniability for as long as possible, and it wasn't as though he and Angel had any official status. They didn't even own Junior G-Man badges.

'We might have to wait for the situation to deteriorate before calling in that favor,' said Louis.

'If it deteriorates any further,' said De Jaager, 'he'll be testifying at your trial.'

The discussion was curtailed by the approach of a large blond man, dressed in a dark suit that, given his build, Louis guessed must have been made to measure. If he wasn't ex-military, he'd watched a lot of movies to get the walk right, and he didn't appear to be armed. He nodded at Paulus, and greeted De Jaager by name, but omitted any honorific, and did not offer to shake hands.

'This is *mijnheer* Hendricksen,' said De Jaager, emphasizing the title, as though to point out the other's failure to extend a similar courtesy to him, even if he seemed otherwise untroubled by it. 'He is notoriously unrefined.'

'And you are a crook,' said Hendricksen, before adding 'by inclination and association.'

His Dutch accent was very thick. He pulled up a chair, and joined them.

'*Mijnheer* Hendricksen,' De Jaager continued, 'is also prone to moral judgments, and a lack of respect for his elders. Were I in a better mood, I might be inclined to joust with him. But not today.'

Hendricksen waited for an explanation. It came from Paulus.

'The girl pulled from the canal this morning,' he said.

'One of yours?' said Hendricksen.

'Yes,' said De Jaager.

'Was she working for you when she died?'

'She was watching Cornelie Gruner.'

Hendricksen absorbed this information before turning his attention to Angel and Louis.

'And where do these two fit in?'

'They were also interested in Gruner.'

'Cornelie Gruner was an old man who didn't bathe enough, and ought to have been haunting houses for a living. Why should I be concerned about what happened to him?'

'You're here, aren't you?' said De Jaager.

'Because you told me I might learn something to my advantage, and I believed you. You may be a crook, but you're not a liar.'

Louis decided that either Hendricksen had history with De Jaager, or else he was predisposed to being difficult with everyone.

'Carenor,' said Louis.

That did the trick. Hendricksen reacted to the name, before displaying irritation at having given away his interest so easily.

'Where are you from?' said Hendricksen.

'Lots of places,' said Louis.

'You're American. That's only one place.'

'If you say so.'

De Jaager nibbled on a French fry, his eyes moving between the two men. He was still too troubled by the death of Eva Meertens to enjoy watching Hendricksen and Louis spar, but at least it seemed to be providing him with a measure of distraction. He tapped Hendricksen lightly on the left arm.

'Why don't you tell my friend here what you know about Carenor?' he said.

'And in return?' asked Hendricksen.

'He may help you discover what happened to Yvette Visser.'

LXXXV

Hynes was back in Priestman's office. He'd have taken a seat, but didn't trust himself to be able to get up again if he did. In fact, he was eyeing the underside of Priestman's desk and wondering if he should just crawl beneath it and remain there until the world stopped falling down around his ears.

First of all, he'd wasted his time trying to keep Harry Stoller from pasting any more pictures of dead women on the Internet. It seemed as though every media outlet in the country, along with every racist, Islamophobe, and conspiracy theorist with access to a computer or smartphone, had by now received the images – either directly from the same source as Stoller, or forwarded by someone else further along the chain. The genie was well and truly out of the bottle, and it didn't matter that one of the murdered women had yet to be officially identified, and her relatives informed. The Internet would take care of that.

They had a tentative name for the second woman: Kathy Hicks, 24, a shop assistant; originally from Sussex, but living in Bristol – or now, more accurately, not living at all – and reported missing two weeks earlier. They still didn't have any sign of a body, though, just pictures of Hicks with prayer beads in her mouth. MUSLIM SERIAL KILLER PRAYS ON WHITE GIRLS was the misspelt headline on one of the websites Hynes had already seen, but there were worse headlines out there, and fouler to come. Already, windows were being broken in mosques, and the house of an imam in Brentford had been set on fire. Reports were coming in of confrontations between gangs of white youths and young Muslims. In Stoke, detectives were investigating the alleged gang rape of a woman wearing a hijab. Soon, Hynes knew, someone would be killed as a direct result of those photographs unless the police got a handle on what was happening.

He put those thoughts out of his head for now, because Priestman was on the phone to the tech team, nodding, writing – 'Yes, yes, I get it.' – and Hynes dearly wanted to move behind her so he could read what she was scribbling.

'Yes. Well done.'

She hung up.

'And?' said Hynes.

'The pictures of Romana Moon were sent late last night from her own laptop,' said Priestman. 'We've confirmed her private IP address.'

'Christ.'

Priestman was already on her feet, and making for the door.

'That's not the half of it,' she continued. 'They were sent from Gary Holmby's apartment complex. Call Gackowska and tell her to lock it down. You join her as fast as you can, and bring bodies with you. Nobody enters or leaves that building until I arrive with a warrant, you hear?'

'Yes, boss.'

'Bloody Karl Holmby,' said Priestman, as he followed her from the office. 'I knew he was a liar.'

On the computer screen in his rooms, Quayle watched scenes of fire and broken glass; of men and women screaming obscenities at those of a different color and religion to themselves, and those others screaming back; of a policeman being carried from the entrance to a mosque, blood streaming from a wound in his head; of women once alive, and now alive no longer; of hate, violence, and loss. Before him lay the Atlas. Continents formed and disintegrated on its pages, potential new worlds being revealed for an instant before turning to ash. He felt the barriers between universes weaken further, yet still they would not break.

And Parker was near: if Quayle could not sense his presence, the Pale Child could. From the corner of Quayle's chambers, it whispered his name, over and over.

A warning.

An imprecation.

'Let him come,' said Quayle to the dark, to the Child. 'Let him come, and we will add him to the pyre.'

Hendricksen took the first pull on his beer. He'd decided to order one about halfway through the telling of his story, but it sat untouched until he was done. He had unburdened himself to these men – two of them strangers, and the third barely more than that – for no reason other than a word: Carenor.

'Does Sellars have a criminal record?' Louis asked.

'Other than tickets for speeding and parking, no,' said Hendricksen. 'He's clean, or seems to be.'

'Except nobody clean does business with the Enclave,' said De Jaager.

'Being the pick-up and delivery man doesn't make you dirty,' said Angel.

'Ignorance is no defense in law,' said Hendricksen. 'Carenor, by the nature of its business, must be aware of the Enclave's reputation, and the likelihood of illegality in any transaction in which it might be involved. The company simply chooses to play the odds. I think Sellars does, too – or did, before Visser and I became interested.'

'And then Visser disappeared,' said Louis.

'Yes.'

'Do you feel accountable?'

Hendricksen met his eye.

'Are you going to tell me I shouldn't?'

'I don't know you. I'm not going to tell you to do anything at all.'

'Then yes, I do feel accountable. I was the senior investigator. I should have reined her in.'

'Doesn't sound to me like she was the kind of woman anyone reined in.'

Hendricksen gave a small, sad smile.

'Nevertheless, I should have tried.'

'Do you think Sellars killed her?' said Angel.

'No. He could account for his movements from the time he

and Visser met at the service station to the moment we became aware she was missing. He had multiple witnesses, not just his wife, and made phone calls from his home number. He also worked overtime at Carenor during that period.'

'He was making himself visible,' said Louis.

'I believe so. He was manufacturing an alibi, so that when Visser disappeared he would not be suspected of any involvement.'

'Hard to prove a suspicion like that.'

'Impossible, one might say.'

'And there was no other case in which you were involved that might have put Visser in danger?'

'No. All our resources were focused on tracing missing artworks. We'd been working on almost nothing else for eighteen months. And you know, while a certain amount of money might have been involved, and the reputations of some institutions placed at minor risk, none of it would be worth killing for. The art world is riddled with fraud, theft, and double-dealing. It's so crooked that I struggle to enter most modern galleries without wanting to piss on the floor, and whatever love I might once have had for art in anything but the theoretical sense has largely vanished. Many of the most elite galleries and auction houses regard scandals, court cases, and the occasional confiscation of stolen works as part of the cost of doing business. They're irritants, but no more than that.'

'Could someone at the Enclave have targeted Visser?' asked Angel.

'That's not how the Enclave operates,' said Hendricksen. 'You have to understand how much money is represented by the assets it stores: we're not talking billions of euros, but tens of billions. The Enclave is untouchable. It doesn't have to kill people. It doesn't have to make them disappear. It's so far beyond the reach of an agency like ours that any investigations we might pursue would have zero impact upon it, and any trouble its clients might find themselves in with the authorities, tax or otherwise, would remain exactly that: their trouble, not the Enclave's. No, whatever befell Visser occurred because we were looking too closely at Carenor, not the Enclave, and Sellars is the key.'

'But you couldn't pin anything on him?' said Angel.

'No.'

'Are your inquiries ongoing?' Louis asked.

'We continue to work to trace missing art, just as we continue to monitor Carenor, or as much as we can with limited time and resources.'

'What about Sellars?'

'Unofficially, and without informing the British police, we tried to keep tabs on him for a while, but he didn't leave the country again for many months, and when he did return to the Continent, he stayed well away from the Enclave.'

Louis wished Parker were around to ask these questions; he was better at figuring out the angles. Louis and Angel were not private investigators, but career criminals. In another existence, Angel was stealing from the Enclave, and Louis was shooting anyone who objected. In this one, they served Parker. As Angel once remarked, something had gone horribly right with their lifestyle.

'De Jaager said that you had connections to Maine,' said Hendricksen.

'That's right,' said Angel.

'May I ask what they might be?'

'We own some property there.'

'Is that all?'

'No. We sometimes work with – or for – a man named Parker. He's a private detective, based in Portland.'

'Is Parker the reason you're here?'

'That's right. Why?'

'Because, a few years ago, we traced payments from certain sales of looted art to a private bank in Bangor, Maine. These were the proceeds of paintings swindled from wealthy Jews imprisoned at a camp called Lubsko during World War Two. The prisoners surrendered the works in return for promises that their lives would be spared. They were killed shortly after, of course.'

'Uh-huh,' said Louis, noncommittally.

'We made no progress with the bank, naturally.'

'Naturally.'

'In fact, we'd despaired of ever establishing the ultimate destination of those funds, until someone uncovered a nest of ancient Germans, living off the last of their stolen wealth in the comfort and security of the northeastern United States.'

'No shit?'

'No shit at all. That someone's name, if I recall, was Parker.'

'It would be.'

'The same Parker whose interests you're currently serving?'

'If there are two of him, we're all in more trouble than we thought.'

'Interesting,' said Hendricksen. 'At least one of those involved with this conspiracy suffered an unpleasant demise. Shot at long range, but not, it seems, by Parker.'

'Uh-huh,' said Louis, again.

'Although it was nothing more than the individual in question deserved.'

'Ain't that a relief?'

Hendricksen regarded Louis with fresh eyes, and extended a hand.

'I apologize for any earlier impoliteness on my part,' he said. They shook.

'No apology necessary,' said Louis.

Hendricksen shared a similar handshake with Angel, and said, 'Yvette Visser was not only my colleague, but also my friend. She left behind a partner and a young son. This is very personal to me.'

'No chance she ran away to make a new life for herself?' said Angel.

'None.'

'Had to ask.'

'I know, just as I know she's dead.'

No one said anything more for a time. The five men watched more trucks and cars pass through a dull landscape close to a border that barely existed. Eventually they returned to the business at hand, but with a new impetus. They were now all on the same side.

'So why would Gruner be using Sellars?' said Angel.

'Or vice versa,' said Louis.

'Because Gruner collected art.'

'And forged passports.'

'Wouldn't want to entrust forged documents to just anyone.'

'But Gruner also bought and sold old books.'

'Occult books.'

'Which the parties involved might have been reluctant to entrust to the mail.'

'Or even to a courier they didn't know.'

'If he bought and sold occult books, he must have been aware of the Atlas.'

'Which means he knew Quayle.'

'And Gruner also provided false passports.'

'Dutch passports.'

'Like Quayle's.'

'Which, once again, a man might prefer not to leave open to the possibility of interception.'

'Hello, Mr Sellars.'

'Who happens to be moving back and forth between England and the Continent on behalf of Carenor.'

'A seemingly respectable company.'

'Maybe even an actual respectable company.'

'But unlikely.'

'Agreed.'

Hendricksen finished his beer.

'Do you two do this often?' he asked.

'Do what?' asked Angel.

'The *Koot en Bie* act.'

'The what?'

'Dutch comedians. A double act.'

'Oh,' said Angel. He had no idea what Dutch comedy might be like, and was pretty sure he didn't want to find out. 'Only when it might be annoying to other people.'

'Can you send us what you have on Sellars and Carenor?' Louis asked Hendricksen.

'It's on my laptop, back in the car. Why don't you let me take you and your friend to the airport? It will save Paulus a trip, and allow *mijnheer* De Jaager to return to Amsterdam and concentrate on investigating the death of Eva Meertens in his own way.'

Louis and Angel had no objection. They said goodbye to De Jaager amid exhaust fumes and the growls of big rigs, and turned toward Brussels. Before they left the parking lot, Hendricksen emailed a series of files to a dropbox, to be accessed by Louis at his convenience. Louis would share the details with Parker later.

The three men spoke a little on the journey, but were mostly quiet. There was no awkwardness, though, because that was not the kind of men they were.

Hendricksen drove. Angel returned to dozing.

And Louis thought of Quayle, and Pallida Mors, and tried to work out which of them he wanted to kill more. The latter, he decided: not just because she'd put two bullets in him; not even because of the depth of her corruption, and the bodies she had left in her wake, perhaps Eva Meertens's among them; but because of what she represented. She was Pale Death, and he was her opposite. Just as Parker was coming for Quayle, he was coming for Mors.

And he, the last of the Reapers, would cut her down.

LXXXVI

Priestman had wanted to be present when the police entered Gary Holmby's apartment. In retrospect, Hynes thought, she should probably have waited outside, because he certainly wished he had. The body lay on the bed, already buzzing with flies. All the windows in the apartment were closed, and the heating was on high, so it was oppressively warm. Decomposition commences with death, although it usually takes close to twenty-four hours before the odor becomes particularly noticeable, let alone unpleasant. In the swelter of the apartment, Gary Holmby had begun to smell bad.

'What do you think?' Priestman asked, as Hynes stepped outside for a breath of fresh air, and to rustle up some Vicks VapoRub from the CSI team.

'The room temperature has botched things up a bit in terms of a time of death, and he's bled a lot, so I wouldn't be making guesses based on lividity,' said Hynes. 'But he's stiff as a board, so he's been dead for twelve hours at least, I'd say. Which means he hasn't been emailing images of dead women, not unless they have the Internet wherever he's gone.'

'No sign of a laptop?'

'Only his own, so far. Romana Moon owned a PC, but it looks like Gary Holmby was an Apple guy all the way. The bedroom had been turned over before we got there, though. Whoever killed Gary could have taken the laptop with them, if emails were still being sent from it earlier today. I can't see anyone wanting to hang around in the apartment, not without a mask.'

'The second set of emails didn't come from here,' said Priestman. 'They came from a Starbucks in Kingston Park.' Kingston Park was a northern suburb of Newcastle.

'Cameras?'

'We're looking, but there's a big Tesco supermarket nearby. Someone could have sat in the car park and piggybacked on the Starbucks Wi-Fi. We're accessing the security footage to see if we can come up with a list of vehicles.'

The VapoRub was produced, and Hynes gave his upper lip and nostrils a good smear. He was already suited and booted in full barrier clothing. Priestman would leave the scene to him and the CSI team. Examining a dead man's home wasn't her job. Gackowska, meanwhile, was already on her way to the Holmby residence in Middlesbrough, and had been tasked with supervising the search for Karl Holmby.

'There are empty beer bottles inside,' said Hynes, 'and pizza boxes, but no signs of crusts or crumbs, which is odd. No receipt either. If they were delivered to the building, there should be a delivery docket somewhere nearby, but we haven't found one yet. We'll contact the pizza company, see what it has on its records. We also have an unopened bottle of tequila, some limes, and a bag of nachos in a bag on the hall table, along with a credit card receipt in Holmby's wallet from shortly after ten last night, courtesy of a fancy convenience store within walking distance of here.'

'So he probably had company,' said Priestman. 'His brother?'

'We've only just begun canvassing the other residents, but we already have a woman down the hall who remembers seeing someone who might have been Karl Holmby arrive late yesterday afternoon.'

It was possible that Karl could have acquired a gun, or even found one belonging to Gary in the apartment, but why use it to kill his brother? If Karl had sent the emails, what was he doing with Moon's PC? He had an alibi for the night she died – multiple alibis, in fact. He couldn't have murdered her, yet somehow her computer had ended up in Gary Holmby's flat. Could Gary have murdered Romana Moon, only to have his brother find out and kill him in revenge? But then why disseminate pictures of her mutilated body, along with images of what appeared to be a second victim, Kathy Hicks, to media outlets both respectable and otherwise?

Meanwhile, violence continued to spread because of those pictures. Priestman had already been in touch with the Avon & Somerset Police to agree a joint approach, since they had been looking into the disappearance of Hicks, which meant that three separate forces were now involved in the investigation, given Essex & Kent's jurisdiction over the Helen Wylie killing. Already it had been decided to reveal the fact of the discovery of another *misbaha* at the scene of the Wylie killing, and to do so within the hour. Better that the police should tell the public than to have it appear on another anti-Muslim website. They could attribute to 'operational requirements' their failure to share this detail before now, and hope the excuse flew.

Another press conference was scheduled for early the following morning, to be chaired jointly by representatives of the three police forces. Their principal aim, in association with police around the country, would be to get the situation under control, and prevent any further bloodshed or damage to property. *Good luck with that*, Priestman thought. Someone, it seemed, wanted to start a religious and racial conflagration, and was doing a very good job of it so far, but she didn't believe it was Karl Holmby. She wasn't ruling him out as a suspect in the shooting of his brother, but the emailing of the photographs didn't make sense to her. Could Karl be working with someone else, someone older and less scrupulous than he?

Then again, perhaps Karl Holmby was much brighter than she'd suspected, and had led them on a merry dance so far. In a way, she hoped this might be true, because the other possibility was that Karl wasn't half as smart as he thought he was. If he hadn't killed his brother, then he could have crossed paths with whoever had, and that seemed unlikely to bode well for Karl.

Daylight was continuing its slow dissolution into night, and Priestman was exhausted. She knew Hynes and Gackowska must be tired as well. Priestman wished she could tell them to go home and get some rest, but she wanted Hynes as her eyes in Gary Holmby's apartment, and Gackowska was among those engaged in the search for his brother, which also meant being entrusted with the death knock for the Holmbys' mother. For that alone,

Priestman would secure an extra day's leave for Gackowska, once all this was over. She told Hynes to stay in touch, and call her with an update before he left, regardless of the hour. She then got in touch with Gackowska, who was working through a list of Karl Holmby's friends and associates as part of the ongoing effort to trace him.

'How is their mother?' Priestman asked.

'She threw us out of the house before she could shed a tear. It's full of the kind of men and women who make a virtue out of not helping the police.'

'Do you think she'll tell us if she hears from Karl?'

'Maybe. She's not stupid, just one of the angriest women I've ever met.'

And she was now mourning her older son, which wouldn't make her any less angry. Priestman thanked Gackowska, gave her the same instructions she'd given Hynes, and hung up. Her car was back at Wallsend, so she bummed a ride from a uniform. She was almost at the station when she swore, causing the officer to glance at her anxiously.

'Everything all right, ma'am?'

'No, but never mind.'

She had just remembered that the Moon family would be arriving on Monday to claim their daughter's body from the mortuary. She couldn't be present, but she thought someone from the force should be.

She'd make it happen. It was the best she could do.

LXXXVII

Parker's flight north was delayed, before being cancelled due to a technical problem with the aircraft. He and his fellow passengers were rebooked on a later flight, which meant he didn't get into Newcastle until 7 p.m. He picked up a rental car at the airport, but saw no point in trying to negotiate the moors in the dark, so instead secured a room at the Malmaison on the city's Quayside. A fog had descended, and he got lost in it on his way from the airport. He eventually crossed a bridge over the Tyne to enter the city, but the fog was by then so thick that he couldn't see the river below, or even the end of the bridge itself. He found it deeply unsettling, and was grateful to at last reach the streets. As he drove to the hotel, he noticed a lot of police activity at one of the big apartment blocks nearby. When he got to his room, he turned on the local news, and learned of the Holmby brothers – one missing, one dead – but the names meant nothing to him, not then.

Parker ordered room service, staring down at the dark river while he ate. His phone rang as he finished. Just a handful of people back home had the numbers he was using while abroad. All had been told to keep them private, and to call only if absolutely necessary. Now the display was showing Rachel Wolfe's name. Relations between Parker and Sam's mother had reached their nadir the previous fall, when Rachel had begun proceedings to restrict Parker's access to his daughter. She'd elected to take that step following Sam's brief, terrifying abduction by a man being hunted by her father. However painful it might have been for him, Parker was willing to agree to her terms, but something had changed Rachel's mind. He hadn't asked her what it was. She would tell him in her own time – perhaps. For the present, he was just relieved that he could continue to see his daughter without restriction.

'Rachel?'

'I hope you don't mind me calling. I remember what you said about this number.'

'Is something wrong?'

'Sam wanted to speak to you, that's all. I think she's missing you.'

'Sure, put her on.'

'Where are you?'

'The northeast of England.'

'Are you okay?'

'So far.'

'Good. Stay that way. Here's Sam.'

A rustling, then 'Hello?'

Parker felt the particular piercing combination of joy and sorrow that came only from hearing the voice of his child while separated from her by a great distance.

'Hello, bear,' he said.

She liked it when he called her that. He wasn't sure why. She would usually have responded in kind, but not this time, instead launching straight into tales of school, friends, her grandparents, and her mom – all, it seemed, without pausing even once for breath. Parker listened contentedly until the tone of her voice changed, and he knew that Rachel must have moved out of earshot.

'Daddy, Jennifer asked me to tell you something, and I agreed.'

In an instant, the texture of his surroundings appeared to alter, their shadows growing deeper. All sound was deadened, and the blackness of the river beyond the glass became like liquid night. He saw faces in the fog.

'What did she say?'

'That you have to be careful, that they're in the glass of the church. They're not just pictures. They're real. Do you understand, Daddy? Because I'm not sure that I do. Jennifer says they're in the glass. And they're real.'

AN INCIDENT AT FAIRFORD, 1703

❖

From the Reverend Edward Shipman of Fairford to the writer Mr Daniel Defoe, in response to his newspaper advertisement seeking first-hand accounts of the Great Storm of 1703, later published as part of The Storm (1704).

Honoured Sir, – In obedience to your request I have here sent you a particular account of the damages sustained in our parish by the late violent storm; and because that of our church is the most material which I have to impart to you, I shall therefore begin with it. It is the fineness of our church which magnifies our present loss, for in the whole it is a large and noble struc-ture, composed within and without of ashler curiously wrought, and consisting of a stately roof in the middle, and two isles running a considerable length from one end of it to the other, makes a very beautiful figure. It is also adorned with 28 admired and celebrated windows, which, for the variety and fineness of the painted glass that was in them, do justly attract the eyes of all curious travellers to inspect and behold them; nor is it more famous for its glass, than newly renowned for the beauty of its seats and paving, both being chiefly the noble gift of that pious and worthy gentleman Andrew Barker, Esq., the late deceased lord of the manor. So that all things considered, it does equal, at least, if not exceed, any parochial church in England. Now that part of it which most of all felt the fury of the winds was a large middle west window, in dimension about 15 foot wide, and 25 foot high, it represents the general judg-ment, and is so fine a piece of art, that 1500*l* has formerly been bidden for it, a price, though very tempting, yet were the parishioners so just and honest as to refuse it. The upper part of this window, just above the place where our Saviour's picture is drawn sitting on a rainbow, and the earth his footstool, is entirely ruined, and both sides are so shattered and torn, especially the left, that upon a general computation, a fourth part at least, is blown down and destroyed. The like fate has another, west window on the left side of the former, in dimension about 10 foot broad, and 15 foot high, sustained; the upper half of which is totally broke, excepting one stone munnel. Now if these were but ordinary glass, we might quickly compute what our repairs would cost, but we the more lament our misfortune herein, because the paint of these two as of all the other windows in our church, is stained through the body of the glass; so that if that be true which is generally said, that this art is lost, than have we an irretrievable loss. There are other damages about our church, which, though not so great as the former, do yet as much testify how strong and boisterous the winds were, for they unbedded 3 sheets of lead upon the uppermost roof, and rolled them up like so much paper. Over the church porch, a large pinnacle and two battlements were blown down upon the leads of it, but resting there, and their fall being short, these will be repaired with little cost . . .

I have nothing more to add, unless it be the fall of several trees and ricks of hay amongst us, but these being so common everywhere, and not very many in number here, I shall conclude this tedious scribble, and subscribe myself,

Sir, Your Most Obedient And Humble Servant,
Edw. Shipman, Vicar.
Fairford, Gloucest January, 1704.

SHIPMAN SET ASIDE HIS QUILL, AND RUBBED HIS EYES. Behind him, his wife placed her hands upon his shoulders.

'You are doing the right thing, husband,' she said.

This was the second version of the letter he had written. The first was already consigned to the flames.

'But it is not a true account of all that took place,' he replied. 'I fear I have lied by omission.'

'Yet can you explain those events?'

'No, I cannot.'

'And would you be believed, even if you could?'

'I do not know.'

'They would think you mad, or possessed.'

Shipman knew she was correct, but it did not make this concealment of the truth any easier to bear.

'I have begun to think that we should leave this place,' he said, 'and seek another living.'

She kissed his pate tenderly.

'Your will is my will, but you now know more about this church than any man alive.'

'I know more, but understand in a lower degree.'

'Would you bequeath these problems to another, to one less capable of coping with them?'

'It is my wish, at this moment, for you think me stronger than I am.'

'But is it what God would will?'

Shipman stood, and embraced her.

'I fear,' he whispered, 'that God's will may have found some opposition here.'

The Reverend Edward Shipman had never been inclined to despair, not even before he found his vocation. He trusted in God, and God was hope, yet as he stared at the wreckage of his church, and the destruction wrought on its beautiful windows by the recent storm, he could not help but weep. The windows had survived the depredations of the Roundhead army in the previous century when William Oldysworth, hearing of the troops' march to Circencester, had ordered the removal and concealment of the larger panes. In doing so, some of the glass had been damaged, and the restoration work that followed was, of necessity, poorer than the original; but better that than no windows at all, and for this alone Oldysworth had earned his seat by the Lord's right hand.

It was said that the great Albrecht Dürer himself had designed the stained-glass artwork, although Shipman had been unable to establish the truth of this assertion, and anyway, he regarded their human authorship as irrelevant in the main. They were the work of God Himself, acting through the hands of men – and now that same God, acting through nature, had left them in ruins, or so attested the more dolorous of worshipers, who regarded the visitation as proof of the disobedience of humanity, and its ongoing rush toward damnation.

But Shipman was reluctant to ascribe to God every misfortune incurred by man, even if he kept this opinion largely to himself. The Lord had created the world, and every creature in it, but this did not make Him responsible for each dog bite, bee sting, or spoiled jug of milk; and if this were true, then neither did He choose deliberately to visit storms, famines, and pestilences upon his greatest creation. God had made the world, then left it to function according to His design while He watched how man might respond, and in what manner he might deal with its turbulences.

So Shipman did not lose faith, but recovered his strength to lead his flock in the clearing of the debris, and the long, costly process of restoration to come. He spent that first day supervising the removal of the broken glass, excepting those parts sufficiently large as to prove salvageable, and which might be returned to the West Window at some point in the future. He ordered the fallen battlements lowered from the porch, and set three men to covering the hole in the roof that had resulted from the lost lead. It was hard, dusty work – and bloody with it, thanks to glass shards, wood splinters, and fragments of sharp stone – but many hands meant it progressed faster than anticipated, and by day's end the floor of the church was clear of detritus, and no longer exposed to the elements; the roof was whole once more; and wood had been fixed to the West Window to prevent the wind from blowing in, thereby securing the glass against further damage. In the evening dark, Shipman knelt before the West Window, and gave thanks to God.

As he was getting to his feet, and contemplating the benefits of a good scrub and a hot meal, he heard a sound from the porch. It seemed to him that it might be a dog, because it was not footsteps he discerned but the scratching of claws on the stone. He waited for the animal to leave, but instead it commenced an abrasion of the door, tearing at the wood as though to force a way into the church.

Shipman had no patience for any further damage to St Mary's, and rushed to send the beast on its way, with a swift kick in the arse for its troubles. Yet he could see the door shaking in the frame, and began to fear that this was no ordinary hound; if so, then to aim a kick at such a monster would be to risk losing his boot to its jaws, along with the foot it contained.

He had almost reached the door when the scratching stopped, only for it to be replaced by another sound, because Shipman now clearly heard the claws working at the wall, moving up the wall of the porch and onto the roof. A bird, then? But what bird could cause a heavy oak door almost to bend inward with the force of its blows?

The impact of talon on stone continued, shifting from the porch roof to the main wall of the church. Shipman paused to raise another prayer to the Lord, opened the door, and stepped outside.

His first thought was that the evening was darker than it had any right to be, given the hour. He looked to the sky and saw heavy clouds so low they seemed to brush the church spire. It was these clouds that had cast the church and its surrounds into shadow. Now Shipman backed out of the porch, the better to see what was ascending the north wall. At first, he could distinguish nothing at all due to the pall over the town, but slowly he picked out a shape against the brick-work. It looked like a child, but no boy or girl could have scaled such sheer walls unaided.

'Ho!' said Shipman. 'Ho there! Come down.'

The figure responded to the call, but in no human fashion. Instead it scuttled sideways like a lizard and thus proceeded across the exterior of the church. Its skin was entirely black, but of a hue that seemed to absorb all light, so that it resembled a hole torn in the fabric of the world, revealing only void beyond. Shipman thought he could discern horns on its head, and a short, pointed tail.

The presence looked down, and was suddenly familiar to him.

On the north wall of the church, above the stained-glass representations of the persecutors of the faith, was a series of smaller windows, each inhabited by the image of a demon. One of these was a horned figure with black skin and white eyes. It was those same eyes that now regarded Shipman.

So shocked was the reverend gentleman that he failed to notice further movement on the exterior, but it did not take him long to register. It was as though in becoming aware of the one presence, he became aware of the many, the way a man who spots one ant will quickly find his vision accommodating itself to the comings and goings of the entire nest. Shipman's church was alive with creeping, scrambling silhouettes, some familiar from the windows of his church, others too strange for any glass, but all without relation to any creatures found in nature.

And in the churchyard stood one more: it was larger than the rest, with a greatly distorted skull, and sickly illumination seemed to shine from the core of its being. Within the light, Shipman thought he could perceive a broken, malformed child, pale and naked, its limbs misshapen, its head at once fetal and birdlike.

Beyond the churchyard was the town. Shipman could see people walking its streets, could even see the windows of his own home, his wife moving through the rooms behind, but none looked his way, and he noticed that the gloom cast by the clouds had not extended to the rest of Fairford, and appeared confined to the church and its environs. He tried to call for help, but the words emerged muffled and indistinct. He was alone.

At that moment, something impacted him with great force on the back of the head, and all consciousness was lost to him.

Shipman awoke in his own bed, to which he had been carried on a pallet by a group of parishioners who had come across their shepherd's prostrate figure as they returned from the fields. It appeared he had been struck by a piece of masonry that had fallen from the damaged church, although it was not clear how it had managed to land on the unfortunate cleric's head, so far was he found from the chapel, and it was concluded that the stonework must have taken a bounce along the way, imbuing it with the velocity and trajectory required to cause him harm.

An examination of Shipman by the local bonesetter revealed that no lasting damage had been done, and the skull was unbroken. The wound, which had bled profusely, was stitched up, leaving Shipman miserable and in pain. He was prevailed upon to accept some laudanum, which rendered him unconscious for the night, and the best part of the day that followed. When he woke, he spoke only with his wife of what he had seen, expecting her to be immediately dismissive, and to ascribe his words to the aftereffects of the laudanum. Instead she told him that she had woken the previous night to a scratching at the glass, and upon looking out had glimpsed a shape climbing the wall into the churchyard, before it was lost to the shadows of the gravestones.

'I think that same entity threw the stone at my head,' said Shipman. 'I believe it wanted to knock my brains out.'

'Yet what was it, husband?'

But Shipman only closed his eyes, and waited for her to leave.

Two days after his accident, Shipman finally felt well enough to rise from his bed. He returned to the church, and found that work had already commenced on repairing the damaged windows, if only with clear sheet-glass. He also examined the door of the church, and discovered that a piece of wood had been fixed to its base.

'What is this?' he asked.

'We think a dog might have tried to get in,' said one of the laborers. 'The splinters were so bad that we had no choice but to cover it up as best we could, for now.'

Shipman said nothing. He went inside, and inspected the work. All of the holes in the windows had now been covered, save one: high on the north wall, two men were fixing a crack in the glass above the depiction of Annas, the very window that contained the image of the beast Shipman had seen climbing the wall of the church. He noticed that one of the workers had a bandaged hand, and could offer only limited assistance to his fellow on the scaffolding.

'What happened to you?' Shipman called up.

'I caught it on the glass, Mr Shipman,' came the reply. 'Can't think how. We've had a job with this one, and no mistake.'

His colleague grunted. 'You'd almost say it didn't want to be fixed,' he said. 'We'll see it done, though.'

And they did, although both men would later say that they suffered more injuries, more cuts, scrapes, and splinters, in the repairing of the single fissure in that window than they did in all the rest of the works combined.

The restoration of the church would be a long slow process, aided by donations of time, skill – and money, because the laborer must be paid. Not a day went by during those first weeks without Shipman being obliged to show visitors around St Mary's, explaining to them the history of the windows, and how the damaged panes might be returned to something of their former grandeur, in the hope of receiving some contribution in return for his efforts. He guided lords and their ladies, commoners and professional men, and rarely did they leave without making an offering. But he also received gifts from those who did not trouble him for his time, and who had not even visited the church, or not to his knowledge. One of the most generous had come from Jonas Quayle of London, a lawyer – a notoriously tight-fisted profession, which made the donation all the more surprising.

Yet in those same days and weeks Shipman heard whispers, and began to connect a series of peculiar incidents: the farmer's wife whose entire flock of chickens was ripped apart as though by a fox, except that all of the heads were missing, only later to be discovered in a pile by the exterior of the church's north wall; the blacksmith who lost the use of his left hand when he was distracted – or so he claimed – by a horned creature with dark skin and white eyes that seemed drawn to the flames of his furnace; and of two children who saw what they believed to be a naked, deformed figure kneeling by a pond to drink, only for it to grasp one of them by the arm and drag her beneath the surface, where she drowned, leaving the survivor to tell the tale. There were other accounts, too, but some Shipman dismissed as the usual strange lore of village life. Only those that resonated with his personal experience, or described sightings with some correspondence to the windows of the church, troubled him, and would continue to do so to the grave.

But so also would he grow increasingly interested in the history of the glaziers who had created the stained glass, and the tales of their presence passed down through generations of villagers at Fairford: how they had been troubled by nightmares that left two of them in Bedlam, and caused one to kill another in error, having mistaken him for an image in the windows come to life; of the designs rejected by Barnard Flower, and consigned to the fire, because he believed no one would worship in any church that contained them, or no devotee of a Christian bent; and of the glaziers from Tilburg, five in all, who shared the same dream of a buried book that called to them from the depths of the earth.

And sometimes Shipman would think back to those final excised lines from his letter to Defoe, and wonder if he should have left them in, even at a cost to his reputation, or his living.

'It is my opinion that, in shattering the glass of our church, nature briefly gave license to roam to that which should have been contained; and by repairing the damage, order was restored to this place. But how, or why, the images should have assumed such physical forms, I cannot say . . .'

IX

Besides I find this tree hath never been
Like other fruit trees, walled or hedged in,
But in the highway standing many a year,
It never yet was robbed, as I could hear.
The reason is apparent to our eyes,
That what it bears, are dead commodities . . .
                John Taylor, 'The Description of Tyburn'

LXXXVIII

A trio of yews dominates the churchyard of St Cuthbert's in Beltingham, Northumberland. To the south and southwest respectively stand a male and female pairing of at least four centuries in age – and perhaps even older than this, for the main body of St Cuthbert's dates back to the fifteenth century, and it is not unlikely that the two yews might have been planted at the same time as the church was raised.

Yet parts of St Cuthbert's are more ancient still, because structural elements have been dated to 1260, and to the east can be seen the broken shaft of a seventh-century Saxon cross, indicating that this place has been sacred to Christians for almost a millennium and a half, although if an early Saxon church ever existed in the same spot (and this remains in dispute), it has long since vanished, its wooden walls reclaimed by the earth. Most likely, though, the cross was the only symbol of their belief that the Saxons erected there.

They were being most careful.

Look closer at this cross, and regard its plinths: they are the remains of a Roman altar from the same site, which means that this ground has seen devotion since at least the second century, when the Romans first invaded. With barely a glance, we have moved from centuries of veneration to millennia.

Old, so very old.

But why this place? Perhaps it is because Beltingham sits only a few miles from what was oft considered the geographical center of the British mainland at Haltwhistle; is, in fact, the parent parish of the region, and was in all likelihood a center of Druidic worship centuries before the Romans nailed Christ to the cross.

Not Haltwhistle, but Beltingham.

And there is more to come.

Let us return to the yews in the churchyard. The yew is a sacred tree, linked to death, burial, and rebirth in early Nordic, Celtic, and Anglo-Saxon traditions. In ancient Greece, it is associated with the underworld, providing a gateway from this world to the next. It was no great stretch for Christianity to adapt these beliefs to the concept of resurrection, and just as the early church repurposed pagan sites for the veneration of the One True God, so also did it lay claim to the yew, protecting and nurturing it, so that even as the wild yews vanished from the land, the church yews flourished.

But what of the third yew at St Cuthbert's? It is a male tree, standing to the north. The trunk is split and twisted, lending it the aspect of a suffering martyr, an impression reinforced by a slight redness to the bark, as though stained long ago by blood. This seemingly tormented creature, its branches cobwebbed, its exterior flaking like skin, is actually in the process of regenerating: the trunk is hollow, the interior heartwood and sapwood rotting away while a new cloak of bark forms around it. In a century or so, the tree will look completely different.

This male yew was already old when St Cuthbert's was being built in the fifteenth century; old, even, when the thirteenth-century stones were being put in place. It has sheltered Christians from the storm for at least 900 years, but probably much longer, and may well be the scion of a predecessor that towered over pagans in its time, when this place had no walls and gods showed no mercy. After all, the Fortingall yew to the north, which sits at the center of the Scottish east-west axis, is 2,000 years old, at the lowest estimate.

Such power in the earth; such memories.

All these dead.

All this blood.

Karenza Lumley had spent her teenage years despising her given name – due in no small part to the tendency of packs of young men and women to nip and tear at any signs of difference or individuality – and her adulthood cherishing its distinctiveness.

Her mother's people were originally from Cornwall, and Karenza's name was derived from 'car', the Cornish word for love. How her ancestors had ended up traveling from the southwest corner of the country to the northeast was unclear, but family lore suggested it was a matter of the heart, which probably meant an unanticipated pregnancy outside the bonds of marriage, back when such mishaps brought serious consequences for all involved.

Karenza was a sensible bluestocking, a retired schoolmistress who voted Conservative, and approved of Britain giving two fingers to the European Union. She would never have expressed it in those terms, of course, some variation on 'damn' being the crudest epithet permitted to pass her lips, and the idea of raising a non-Churchillian – indeed, non-metaphorical – two fingers to anyone being anathema to her. She loved her country, and she loved this little church. It was said that the remains of St Cuthbert had been hidden nearby to save them from the Vikings, and something of his spirit continued to imbue the church and its surroundings with a sense of tranquility. Karenza didn't know if this was true, and it didn't concern her greatly either way. Like her Christianity, her views on such matters were entirely practical: this was a peaceful place, and if St Cuthbert was responsible for its grace, then more power to the lingering effects of his old bones. If St Cuthbert had nothing to do with it, his absence didn't detract from the fact of its calm.

Karenza had never married. She had never particularly felt the need for male – or, God forbid, female – companionship of a sexual kind when she was younger, and the absence of any such desire had only deepened in the intervening years. While aware that autumn romances were not uncommon, she held out little expectation of any alteration to the pattern of her life at this late stage, and would have welcomed it even less. There were committees to be chaired, and jams to be sold; pews to be polished, and floors to be swept; prayers to be said, and hymns to be sung, because apparently God liked that sort of thing, and it was good for the lungs. Was Karenza ever lonely? Not that she would have admitted, but in recent years, as her limbs began to ache more deeply, and her energy levels started to flag more noticeably, she had become aware of a certain emptiness, a dearth that was almost physical. When she tried to picture it in an effort to understand its nature, she was drawn again and again to the image of a vase that had never been filled with flowers: a plain object, not entirely unpretty, gathering dust, paperclips, and discarded coins, whereas it might once have been permitted to sit in sunlight, all stem-green and blossom-red, thereby discovering that this was a purpose to be preferred.

St Cuthbert's was open daily to visitors from April to September, and otherwise at weekends. Most pilgrims were respectful, others less so, but all left some trace of their passing, even if only in the form of dirty footprints, and the occasional forgotten National Trust leaflet or piece of discarded litter. It was Karenza's habit, therefore, to enter the churchyard via the lychgate each evening – or sometimes, if she was feeling tired, to arrive early in the morning, as on this day – to clean and tidy, and check for any signs of new damage.

She commenced a single circuit of the exterior, silently greeting each of the yews in turn. Karenza found nothing odd in this. These evergreens were living creatures, and the sacredness – or sanctity, spirituality, call it what you will – of the site was partly their doing; of that much, Karenza had no doubt, her matter-of-fact Anglicanism easily accommodating this dash of pantheism.

She proceeded to the rear of the church, to pay her respects to the oldest of the yews. A murder of crows had gathered nearby, alternately alighting on the tilted gravestones before rising again to circle the tree without passing above it or coming to rest on its branches, as though attracted by the yew even as it repelled their attentions through the force of its great, time-earned will. It was not unusual to see birds behaving in this way around the yews of St Cuthbert's, although Karenza could not recall ever glimpsing so many acting in unison.

Karenza might have loved the trees, and found their presence a source of reassurance and continuity in a world that had long been moving too quickly for her liking, but she was also wary of them, for the common yew was among the most poisonous plants to be found in the English landscape. Every part was lethal, save the pulp surrounding the seed, and any animal foolish enough to feed on it was likely to be seriously sickened, if not killed. In a curious twist, dead yew branches were even more dangerous than the limbs of the living organism, revenant discards seeking vengeance for their severance.

Karenza drew closer to the tree. The morning light deepened the redness of the bark in spots, like the shadows of clouds fixed upon it. She picked up movement on the scaly bark, and a low, insistent buzzing. Masses of flies were stuck to the red sap oozing from the trunk, except the yew had been dry only the previous day, and rarely leached so copiously – not like the old yew at St Brynach's in Nevern, said to weep in mourning for the crucified Christ, which was a leap of faith too far even for Karenza. Yet this was not the pink of the sap at St Brynach's, or of other yews she had seen, but a vivid scarlet, the natural color of the fluid seemingly intensified by some new element.

Higher up, Karenza glimpsed a whiteness, although it was not uniform. Like the trunk, it was streaked with shadow. She moved so near to the tree that she could smell its essence, and hear the movement of its branches, could almost feel the slow progress of its regeneration, the inverse of her own gradual, inexorable decline.

A man was lodged in the hollow heart of the yew, his naked body banded with blood, his flesh torn where the wood had scourged him as his legs were forced into the recess, so that the tree appeared almost to be consuming him. His arms were draped over the iron rods holding in place the branches of the ancient organism, and his head lay against his right shoulder, exposing the long, jagged incision at his throat. His eyes had been scoured from their sockets, as though whoever was responsible for his death had wished him to stumble blindly into the underworld. Flies swarmed furiously around him, already laying their eggs in his concavities, so that the cavern of his mouth was near black with them.

And the yew, recognizing neither the supremacy of Christian over pagan, nor man over beast, held Karl Holmby in its grip, and accepted his sacrifice.

LXXXIX

In the reading room of the British Library, quieter at the weekend than on other days, Bob Johnston worked his way through the latest series of books he'd requested. Some were held off-site, so he'd been forced to wait a day for them to be delivered. Now, though, he was immersed in their contents, aided by Latin and Dutch dictionaries, and the Internet, courtesy of his battered old laptop. His mood was light. He'd had coffee with Rosanna Bellingham that morning, and she'd kissed him goodbye when they were done; just a peck on the cheek, but close enough to his mouth that the corner of her lips touched his. He thought it might have been intentional.

Hoped it might.

Johnston returned to tales of blood, glass, and atlases.

And unbeknownst to him, moved closer to the time of his torment.

XC

Hynes had started to wonder if he'd ever see his bed again, and if he'd still have a wife to share it when he got there. At the very least, she'd probably have changed the locks.

He'd slept in an empty cell at the station the night before, too tired even to contemplate getting behind the wheel of his car, and concerned at waking Charlotte, his wife, by thumping in late just to grab a few hours between the sheets. He'd texted her before turning off the light, and tried calling that morning, but Charlotte hadn't answered, which made him angry because he was bone weary, hungry, and currently looking at the naked body of a boy jammed into the hollow of an old yew tree. He didn't need her being in a strop with him on top of all that.

Then, just as he was simmering nicely, Charlotte called him back. She'd been out buying the ingredients for a chicken korma, she told him, which she planned to prepare and leave in a pot on the stove, because she knew he liked a homemade curry. He could heat it up when he got home, whenever that might be. She hadn't been able to get to her phone in time when he called, but was glad to hear from him because she'd been worried, what with all the trouble she'd seen on the television.

Hynes's vision grew blurred. He was forced to turn away from the body, the tree, and the CSI team, even as the final touches were being put to the tarp that concealed Karl Holmby's remains from view.

'Can you hear me?' Charlotte asked. 'Hello?'

'Yes,' said Hynes. He was struggling to speak. A chicken korma: amazing the things that got to you. 'I'm still here.'

'I thought we'd been cut off.'

'So did I,' although he meant it another way, one he couldn't

473

have explained except to say that after twenty-four hours filled with rage, cruelty, and violent death, he had felt estranged from normality, from all that was good and kind, as though he had crossed from this world into a more vicious realm; and it had seemed impossible to him that his wife could be part of such an existence, let alone navigate its depths in order to find him, and speak with him once more.

'What's happening?' she said. 'Where are you now?'

'Beltingham. We've found Karl Holmby. He's dead.'

The local morning news reports were already naming the body found in an apartment in Newcastle the previous day as that of Gary Holmby. Before the day was done, they'd be naming his brother too. Hynes didn't share with his wife the precise nature of the boy's death. That would be made public in time, and she didn't need to know, not right now. Sacrificed to a tree: whoever was tasked with filling out the CID10 form on the killing would go down in police history.

'Oh no,' said Charlotte. 'Their poor mother.'

'Yeah.'

Gackowska was back with Mrs Holmby. The hard men and women continued to surround the house, but this time Gackowska had been admitted without difficulty, and permitted to stay. Clement Holmby, the estranged father of the two young men, had shown up intoxicated shortly after midday, only to be forcibly removed half an hour later. He was currently in custody at Heron Hill, where he was sobering up in a cell prior to being interviewed, just in case he had anything worthwhile to share.

Hynes saw one of the CSI team beckoning to him.

'I have to go,' he said.

'So will you be home tonight?'

'I hope so,' he said, and not just because his back ached after a night in a cell. 'That korma won't eat itself.'

'I'll wait up for you.'

'You don't have to do that. I don't know what time I'll be back.'

'Doesn't matter. I can always snooze on the couch if you're late.'

He told her he loved her, and she told him that of course he did, and not to be daft, and he felt a little better about the world when he hung up.

He returned to the entrance to the tarpaulin, still wearing his protective clothing and booties, and joined the small group gathered around the deputy pathologist, Lerner. She would replace Sisterson when he retired, which was good news all round, Lerner being reasonably accomplished when it came to civil conversation – remarkably so, when compared with her boss. Also present, along with the members of the CSI team, were the vicar, who'd been forced to cancel the services for the day and send his parishioners elsewhere; and a local tree surgeon named Maxham. Lerner took Hynes aside for a moment, and spoke quietly to him. She was nearly as tall as he, so Hynes experienced the rare pleasure of not having to lean down in order to hear someone speaking softly.

'The body is lodged pretty firmly in that hollow,' she said. 'He wasn't a heavy lad, but it would still have taken some effort to hoist him up there, and force him into the heart of the tree. Climbing it wouldn't be too difficult, though. Lots of handholds.'

'Are we talking two people?'

'Possibly, although I can see what might be rope marks under his arms, so I'd hazard a guess that he might have had a loop slung around him before being pulled up. Hard to tell for certain, though, and there are multiple abrasions to contend with, but one strong person could have been able to do that.'

'Anything else?'

'He was already dead by then. We've got blood at the north base of the trunk, a lot of it. I think his throat was cut there, and he was allowed to exsanguinate before being moved again. He was then positioned over the hollow of the trunk, and pressed into the gap.'

'Pressed how?'

'Both clavicles appear fractured, and there's extensive damage to the ribs, sternum, and scapulae, along with all of the tearing I mentioned a moment ago. His neck is also broken, as is his nose, although that may have occurred prior to death. I'd say someone stamped repeatedly on his sides and shoulders from above to get him in there. I can also see what appear to be stab wounds to the torso, but I'll need a proper examination to be sure.'

Hynes was already considering the possibilities for evidence recovery. They'd be looking for fragments of clothing from the killer, and pieces of shoe rubber or leather, maybe even blood or tissue in case he – or she, because one couldn't go making assumptions – had suffered injuries while stamping on Karl Holmby. They might get full or partial tread marks from his skin. Also, the killer must have held on for balance to the branches or their metal supports. It was unlikely that prints could be obtained from the wood; they'd try, but they might have more luck finding hair, tissue, or fibers. All this would have to be done before Holmby's body was removed, which raised the question of how the extraction was to be achieved. He and Lerner returned to the main group, and listened as Giordano, the head of the CSI team, addressed the problem.

'The yew is at least nine hundred years old,' said Giordano, 'but probably much older. There's no sense in damaging it more than we have to. Mr Maxham here has been working on these trees for decades, and says the hollow is mostly old decaying wood, so he can cut into it without doing any harm to the yew. He's confident he can create enough space for us to lift out the body, but he can't do that until CSI has finished its work.'

'How soon will that be?' asked Hynes.

'We're stretched,' said Giordano, 'because we're working both this scene and the brother's apartment, but we'll manage. At least the tree's not high, so we can access it with ladders, and Mr Maxham has offered us the use of his equipment as well. With luck, we'll be ready to take him out by late this afternoon.'

That would be good, Hynes thought. It was turning into a warm day, and he didn't suppose Maxham had much experience of cutting around corpses that were beginning to smell. He called Priestman – he was contemplating buying another phone and leaving the connection between them open permanently, just to save him the trouble of hitting the redial button all the time –

and brought her up to speed, but even as he did, he realized that they were now even further away than before from understanding what was happening.

Priestman wasn't familiar with Beltingham, so it was left to Hynes to describe the narrow, winding road that led to St Cuthbert's, and the handful of houses by the lychgate that gave entry to the churchyard. The lychgate had a security camera, but it faced toward the church, not the little green that represented the heart of Beltingham, and the footage from it revealed no sign of anyone coming or going since late the previous afternoon, not until the arrival of Karenza Lumley that morning.

'Which means?' said Priestman.

'Karl Holmby was taken to the churchyard from the north, through the woods. It wouldn't have been easy, but the other option would have been to enter through the lychgate, and either disable the camera or risk being seen. We have officers working the woods now, and looking for points of entry. Whoever brought Karl here must have parked somewhere nearby. They didn't walk all the way from Newcastle.'

'Did Karl have prayer beads in his mouth?' Priestman asked.

'No, or not that we've found. They might have fallen out while he was being stamped on, or they could be stuck deep in his throat. None on Gary Holmby's body either. Why?'

'Just a thought. Romana Moon was killed at the Familist spot, and now Karl Holmby, who knew her, is murdered at one of the county's oldest sites of worship, both with their throats cut.'

'But Gary Holmby was shot,' Hynes pointed out.

'Still, they're connected, along with Helen Wylie, who was left at Canterbury, another holy site, and Kathy Hicks, wherever her body may be.'

Priestman let Hynes go. Extra manpower had been drafted in so the canvass of the area could start, in the hope that someone might have noticed an unfamiliar vehicle in the vicinity of St Cuthbert's, or seen strangers acting suspiciously.

Or anything; anything at all.

XCI

Since the discovery of Romana Moon's body on the moor, Douglas Hood had made a point of spending time walking the land during daylight hours in order to monitor more closely those who might pass through it. He would have done so even if the detective, Priestman, had not requested it of him, but the fact that she had entrusted him with the task gave a sense of mission to what might otherwise have been another manifestation of his own anger at the despoliation of this place.

Further fuel was added to Hood's rage – and sorrow, too, because rarely did an hour go by without his brooding on Romana's final moments, and her family's ongoing grief – by the small but steady stream of visitors drawn to Hexhamshire by voyeurism, and the smaller but equally steady group lured there by a possible link between the murder and the long departed Familists. Hood had already sent packing two lunatics in white robes, the speed of their departure accelerated by the implied threat of the shotgun hanging loosely over his right arm, and Jess's bared fangs. The Lord alone knew what kind of idiots the most recent news reports might attract, with their talk of Muslim prayer beads and religious slaughter. Hood was already tired of images of bullet-headed bullies in tight shirts screaming obscenities at frightened women in veils, and of young men of different skin colors fighting running battles. If a Muslim was responsible for the killings, Hood thought, then to hell with him, and let the law have its way with a vengeance. But equally, he had no time for fascists. Let them try to rally their troops by the old Familist plot, on this land that he and his forebears had tended for so long, land that his kin had fought to protect from their kind during the last war, and he'd shoot them, and take his chances with the courts later.

But if he was determined to patrol these reaches by daylight, he was less willing to walk them at night, not after recent events. He had pulled up all the withered bushes and shrubs in his garden, and set them alight instead of adding them to the compost heap, for fear that whatever had poisoned them might find a way to taint the land still further were it to be reintroduced. In addition, Hood was determined that Jess shouldn't go out after dark, or no further than the light from the porch extended, and then only at the end of her leash. To her credit, the dog now showed no particular inclination to roam, not once the sun had gone down. No fool was Jess.

As though sensing she was in his thoughts, the dog nudged at his hand. They were not far from where the Familist chapel once stood, but it was time to be getting home. He patted her, and she nudged him again before turning toward the site and waiting for him to follow.

'No, girl,' he said. 'I hear the teapot calling.'

Jess remained where she was, only briefly inclining her head in the direction of the old place of worship while yipping once. Hood knew her every sound and action, and could gauge her moods and desires from them. Someone was over by the church site. Jess could smell them.

Hood immediately tensed. He had his shotgun with him, but he was tired, and wanted only to return to his home, his chair, and the football. But the measure of a man was the degree to which he was prepared to inconvenience himself for what was right; he had accepted a duty of care, and it would only rankle if he chose to neglect it. Anyway, it might just be hikers taking a breath at the hollow – and a detour from the usual public rights of way, it had to be said – or the latest of the general murder tourists and nosey-parkers.

He followed Jess, and saw her tail begin to wag. So this was not fear on her part, or the recognition of an intruder on her territory, but closer to pleasurable anticipation. The dog raced on, pausing occasionally to make sure Hood was following, until they came at last to the slight incline that acted as the boundary of the hollow. Hood looked down to see a man standing at the

479

very center of the site, his hands by his sides, the wind catching the tail of a short black overcoat that ended just above his knees. He was perhaps slightly above average height, his hair graying, and if he was carrying any middle-age fat, it was well hidden. He glanced up as Hood appeared, but did not seem troubled by the sight of a stranger carrying a shotgun. Either he was familiar with the ways of the land, or he was familiar with guns.

But those eyes . . .

Hood had witnessed his share of grief and loss, and seen his quota of rage too, but had never encountered such a perfect synthesis of all three, this quintessence, in one being. He felt as though he were intruding on some intensely private moment of communion with pain, and his first instinct was to retreat and leave the visitor in peace. Here was no gawker, no dabbler in mysticism and the esoteric; here was one who had suffered greatly, and whose connection to this place was somehow as intimate as Hood's own. All this Hood understood in a single moment, and later he would wonder at the clarity and speed of his insight.

And the site itself was altered; this, too, Hood recognized. Weeds had emerged from the soil, and the grass was blackened in places. The very air smelled bad – not of rot, but of a sweetness that verged on the sickly. Jess had also detected the change in her environment. She hesitated on the rise, and spun in a single anxious circle. Then, before Hood could stop her, she raced toward the man in the hollow. For a few seconds, Hood feared she might be about to attack, confused by this assault on her senses, but her tail continued to wag. She slowed as she drew near him, and made the final approach more slowly, her tail still moving, her ears back slightly. Like many border collies, Jess was generally wary of strangers, and tended to keep her distance even when her master did not. Hood could not recall her ever displaying such open affection toward a stranger before. He noticed that she stayed close to the man's right leg, and even as he stroked her head, she continued to regard suspiciously the ground around her – not sniffing, just watching, the way she sometimes did when she feared a wasp or bee might be hiding in the undergrowth.

Hood walked down to join them, minding his step as he went. The damage to the grass was similar to that which had been visited on his own garden, although the weeds were unfamiliar to him. Their leaves were large and heavy, and green with yellow undersides, reminding him uncomfortably of amphibian bodies.

The stranger nodded. The ferocity of his emotions, glimpsed by Hood in that single brief flash, had already been concealed. Had Hood not come upon him so unexpectedly, he might never have been permitted to glimpse it at all.

'You have a fine dog,' said the stranger.

'But willful,' said Hood, 'when it takes her. I believe it's a female trait.'

The man smiled, but it was little more than a reflex action.

'Is this your property?' he asked, and Hood now heard the American accent.

'Some of it. Around here, it's a complicated business. Parts of the moor are owned by the Ministry, parts by the National Trust. My land abuts this site, and I have grazing rights, but my sheep don't trouble it.'

Hood swatted at an insect. There were a lot of bugs, attracted by the new growth. The man ignored them, and allowed his gaze to move on to the ruins of the settlement further north, visible on the next rise against the setting of the sun.

'Is that where they lived?'

'Who?' said Hood.

'The Familists.'

'Are they what drew you here?'

'What else might bring a person to this place?'

'Curiosity, if you watch the news.'

'The woman who died?'

'That's right.'

Some seconds of contemplation, while he continued to pat the dog, then: 'I guess you have a point. I wouldn't be here if I hadn't read about her, but she's not the reason I came.'

'Then what is, if you don't mind me asking again?'

The stranger continued to stare at the jagged remains of the Familists' village.

481

'Those people tried to kill me,' he said. 'They succeeded, in a sense, but I came back.'

Hood thought he knew him then. He had read the reports on the Internet: an old church blown to rubble; a town half-razed by fire; wealthy, self-interested men and women, driven to murder by petty jealousy, isolationism, and the desire to dictate the way their community should be organized. Running alongside, or beneath, the official version of events was a shadow narrative that some might have been inclined to dismiss as fantasy – rumors of disappearances, and killings unrelated to competition for seats on local councils – had the bodies of two missing young women not been discovered in unmarked graves in the local cemetery. They might not have been found at all had it not been for the explosion that destroyed the church and its environs, disrupting the soil, and questions still remained about how the girls had come to be buried so deep, and in such narrow fissures, almost as though they had not been interred but instead dragged into the earth from below.

'Who are you?' said Hood, because he wanted to be certain.

'My name,' said the stranger, 'is Parker.'

And any last doubts were dispelled.

XCII

Sellars and Mors met in the outdoor car park of a mall off the M1, one of those semicircles of retail hell that Sellars usually did his utmost to avoid, but that Mors favored for their anonymity. The news bulletins were dominated by reports of religious and racial tensions, to which the mystery surrounding the killing of the Holmby brothers had only added – especially the nature of Karl Holmby's death, and the placement of his body. Sellars had to give Mors credit: she had a flair for the macabre. In addition, the police were now chasing their tails trying to establish a connection between Romana Moon, the Holmbys, Helen Wylie, and Kathy Hicks. They wouldn't find one, not beyond the theoretical. Sellars had killed Hicks before Gary Holmby had even chosen Romana Moon, and her body was now safely hidden in Walsingham, in the southeast of England.

And Gary Holmby was also dead, which was almost certainly for the best. Once again, Sellars was forced to admit that he could perhaps have chosen a better accomplice, because Holmby had caused them no end of trouble, although, in Sellars's defense, recruiting someone willing to kill young women was hardly an exact science. Oddly, Holmby had also held on to Romana Moon's laptop for unknown reasons of his own, but Mors had recovered it before killing him, and used it to cause further confusion. A pity she hadn't added some prayer beads to the remains of the brothers while she was about it, but never mind: the absence of *misbahas* would be at least as troubling to the police as their presence might have been, and he understood the reasoning behind her decision. Aside from adding another layer of complexity and obfuscation, it would allow Mors and Sellars to limit that particular detail to female victims, which would help to stoke the fires of intolerance currently burning across the country.

And they had at least one body in reserve: the little doxie that Sellars had killed amid the Wittenham Clumps before burying her nearby, a red *misbaha* wrapped around her tongue. Funny, he still didn't even know her real name.

Sellars hadn't stayed long at the Clumps, and he'd buried her in a shallower hole than he might have preferred. It was the first time that he'd really understood the power of the locales selected by Mors and Quayle for the killings. He'd felt the weight of the past pressing upon him as he dug on Castle Hill, and could have sworn he heard voices and smelled wood smoke, even though he was alone and no fires burned nearby. He was conscious of presences, and shifting forms, and wondered if, on the other side of some partition grown momentarily insubstantial, men and women from a distant time were regarding an umbrous figure digging a grave.

But he didn't mention this to Mors as they watched potted plants being stored in the trunks of cars, and families eating fast food in the sunlight. He was sure she wouldn't have been surprised at what he'd experienced, but he didn't want her to think he was troubled by it.

'How many more?' he asked.

'I don't know.'

'That's what you always say.'

'Because it's the truth.'

The window on Sellars's side was open, and he kept his head turned toward it like a dog on a long journey, breathing the fresh air instead of Mors's body odor. He'd done some reading on the subject, and was surprised to discover how many of those who survived attacks by serial killers mentioned a scent exuded by their assailants, a chemical expression of their moral corruption. He wondered if his wife now detected a similar stink coming from him. He suspected she might. She'd mentioned something the last time they'd made love, shortly after he'd cut Kathy Hicks's throat, something that had bothered him. She'd asked if he was feeling poorly, and he saw her trying to breathe through her mouth as he moved on her, her face averted and her eyes closed, but not in anything approaching ecstasy. Not that they'd ever be making love again: she'd told him that morning about her meeting with a solicitor, because she wanted a divorce.

He'd been expecting it, of course, but the announcement still stunned him. Perversely, as soon as it was out of her mouth, he found himself determined to do all he could to prevent the dissolution of their marriage. It seemed that Lauren knew more about him than he'd thought. She'd found some emails on his laptop from a few years back, and she'd also kept one of his old phones. He thought he'd lost it, but she'd had it all along, holding it in reserve until the time came when she decided to use its text messages against him. They'd been going through a rough patch after Louise's birth, and he'd slept with a couple of women while he was on the road. He'd managed to get it out of his system pretty quickly, though, which made the impending separation all the more frustrating. Lauren was leaving him because of past failings, when he was so much better now. He actually had little interest in sex at all, and would have been content just to tick along with her, doing it a couple of times a month but otherwise cohabiting companionably, making sure the kids were looked after. Okay, so he had progressed from sleeping with women to killing them, but no man was perfect.

He stifled a giggle, and Mors looked at him curiously.

All gone now, or that was what Lauren thought. But he had a surprise for her, one she certainly wouldn't see coming.

'Quayle feels the world changing,' said Mors. 'We're close.'

Sellars recalled again the shades at the Wittenham Clumps, and knew she was right.

'Have you chosen the next one?' Mors asked.

'I think so,' said Sellars.

'When will you take her?'

'I'm not going to.'

Mors looked puzzled.

'Why not?'

'I can't. You'll have to do it.'

'And why is that?'

'Because I want the next one to be my wife.'

XCIII

Angel and Louis made it to Heathrow without incident, and the driver sent by Parker was waiting for them with a sign showing names that, while matching those on their passports, bore no relation to their actual identities. Angel was thankful for the pick-up. He and Louis had spent a couple of hopeless minutes at the baggage claim trying to make some sense of the available escape routes from an airport that resembled interconnected circles of hell.

'Didn't these people once have an empire?' Angel asked Louis, as they gave up on the map.

'So the story goes.'

'Maybe they still do, and no one can figure out how to get to it.'

The journey to their hotel took about an hour, and Louis immediately made some calls once they were safely checked in. He and Angel were now sitting in a corner of a bar in Balham, South London, regarding a middle-aged man robotically feed coins into a slot machine with more flashing lights than a Christmas tree. Sometimes he won. Mostly, he lost. When he eventually ran out of coins, he would walk to the bar, hand over a bill in return for change, and start again. His blank expression never altered, regardless of the result. Angel, who regarded gamblers as halfwits at the best of times, found the whole spectacle profoundly depressing. A pair of televisions displayed a soccer match that no one was watching, and the carpet smelled of stale beer and fresh urine. Angel had drunk in some dumps over the years, but even dive bars had character. This was less a dive than a morass, a vacuum with a name over its door. They'd ordered drinks, but only to maintain the pretense of custom. If

Angel had known how bad this place would be, he'd have brought along his own glass, and maybe some coveralls for his clothing.

A newcomer entered, ordered a soda – for which, they noticed, he didn't pay – and approached their table. He was in his early fifties, with dark curly hair flecked with gray, and the kind of eyes that would always betray amusement, even – or especially – if they were watching someone being tortured. Had Angel come across this man drowning, he'd have thrown him a concrete block and waited for the bubbles to stop. A blue canvas bag was slung over one shoulder. It looked very old. Drawn on it in black ink were the logos of various bands: Stiff Little Fingers, The Jam, The Clash, Rudi, The Undertones.

'You must be the Americans,' he said, placing the bag at his feet. His voice held the hint of an accent so soft that Angel might have mistaken it for Scottish instead of Irish were it not for their reason for being in this drinking hole, 'hole' being the operative word.

'How did you guess?' asked Louis.

'You're too well dressed to be natives. Well, you are. Your friend is just too differently dressed. No offense meant,' he added to Angel.

'Fuck you,' said Angel.

He smoothed his shirt defensively. Everything Angel wore matched, just not necessarily with anything else he happened to be wearing at the time.

'You know,' said Louis, 'when someone says "No offense meant", you can take it that offense was meant; and if the other party replies "None taken", it means they're offended.'

'That's very enlightening. What if the other party replies "Fuck you"?'

'Well, that just means "Fuck you."'

The new arrival shifted in his chair, but it was the only sign he gave of any displeasure at the exchange. His amused look remained unchanged throughout, which confirmed to Angel that painted glass spheres might just as easily have been lodged in his sockets for all his capacity to communicate real emotion.

'Kirwan says hello, by the way,' he informed them.

'I don't know anyone called Kirwan,' said Louis.

'He told me you'd say that. I suppose it makes you legit.'

'And what makes you legit?'

'What I have in this bag. My name's Danny.'

'I don't recall asking,' said Louis.

'Pleased to meet you anyway.'

Danny offered a hand. It wasn't accepted. He inspected it, wiped it on his jeans, and tried again. After letting it hang in the air for a few seconds longer, he took it back.

'You're being very unfriendly,' he said.

'That's because we're not here to make friends.'

'You're going the right way about it, then.'

'We've had a lot of practice.'

Danny sighed, and sipped his soda.

'Are we done with the niceties?' said Louis.

'Nearly, I suppose. You got a discount on these, you know.'

'Uh-huh?'

'Yeah. Since it was Americans that sold them to us in the first place, it seemed only fair. We have plenty more where they came from.'

'You're very talkative, aren't you?' said Louis.

'I don't like long silences. They remind me of the grave.'

A phone rang twice in Danny's pocket, stopped, and rang twice again. He made no effort to answer it, but instead stooped to pick up his bag. He struggled with it for a moment, as though it appeared to be caught on the leg of his chair, but he got there eventually. As he stood, Angel felt something strike his ankle.

'Goodbye, now,' said Danny. 'If you get into any trouble, be sure to call someone else.'

He walked into the sunlight, sucking some of the light from the day in the process.

Angel looked down. Another blue canvas bag, smaller and newer than the first, lay at his feet. Nobody else in the bar seemed interested in what they were doing, but that didn't mean anything. Angel wondered which of the scattered denizens was also working for the man named Kirwan. In a movie, it would have been the guy playing the slot machine, in which case he would have been in line for an Oscar, so engrossed did he seem in losing money.

'You were unfriendly, even by your standards,' said Angel.

'I don't like his kind.'

'Then maybe we should have dealt with someone else.'

'Time was pressing, but I'll be sure to bathe later.'

When they left, the canvas bag was still on the floor, emptied of its contents. Seconds later, the bartender picked up the bag. He dropped it in a bucket of bleach and water before returning to making change for the slot machine, and waiting in vain for a better class of clientele.

XCIV

* * *

Parker and Hood walked together to the latter's cottage, Jess at their heels. A wind blew over the moors, making Parker glad of his coat. His rental car was parked on the road below, far from the path he had taken to the Familist site, but Hood promised to give him a ride back to it in his Land Rover when they were done.

They made one detour on the way to the cottage, because Parker wanted to see whence the Familists had come. He was surprised by how much of the original settlement survived. The houses were roofless, and most of them were single-room dwellings in which families would have lived next to livestock, so only the outer walls remained, yet they appeared remarkably resilient. One or two of the stones were defaced by graffiti, but there was no garbage, no broken glass or discarded beer cans, nothing to suggest that this was a place that attracted visitors, or none that stayed for long.

'Folks don't come up here much,' said Hood, when Parker remarked upon it. 'Even the hikers give it a wide berth.'

'Why?'

'Legends. Tales of disappearances. And it feels wrong. Gets in your bones if you hang around. There was evil in the Familists, and they didn't take all of it with them when they went to America. You saw the weeds at the old church hollow, and the blackening of the grass. I'll show you what's left of my garden as well. That's not normal.'

'Has it happened before?'

'Not in my lifetime. It's recent. Something's changed – or returned.'

'What do you think has caused it?'

Hood didn't hesitate. 'The killing of that young woman.'

* * *

The Theosophical Society – from the Greek words 'Theos', meaning a god, and 'Sophia', meaning wisdom – was founded in New York City in 1875 as a non-sectarian body with the aim of encouraging the study of comparative religion, philosophy, and science, and the investigation of what was believed to be the ancient, hidden wisdom underlying all the world's major religions, whether they chose to recognize it or not. The Theosophists regarded this world as an illusion, and were convinced that through the development of a higher intuition, the interior or invisible world might be perceived.

Whether Quayle subscribed to any of these beliefs was immaterial, and since the Theosophists greatly valued tolerance as part of their desire for universal brotherhood, he was unlikely ever to be challenged on the subject. What mattered to him was that the society's London headquarters in Gloucester Place held one of the finest collections of esoteric and occult books in Europe, from which members could borrow in person or by mail. Quayle had no time to wait for the librarian to hunt down and send out the volumes he sought, and so had elected to visit the library in person. In any case, he required sight of only three books, and the references he wished to crosscheck would take up less than an hour of his time. While the library was usually closed on Sundays, a phone call had been enough to assure Quayle that someone would be present to admit him, provided he did not plan to tarry.

Unfortunately, upon his arrival he found that all three of the required volumes had recently been checked out by a visiting subscriber, and the librarian politely declined to share the identity of this individual with him, although, if the need was urgent, he did offer to pass on Quayle's contact details to the subscriber in question, or else the library could inform him as soon as the books were returned. Neither option suited, so he left the society in a bad mood, if not yet overly apprehensive. The absence of the works he required was probably a coincidence, and nothing more.

London, as it was wont to do in summer, even in the season's early weeks, was holding in the heat as assuredly as if the city were trapped under glass, and the air was heavy with humidity. This did not trouble Quayle, who was always cold, but as the temperature of the city rose, so too did that of its citizenry. As he walked to Marylebone Road to hail a cab, he heard shouts from the vicinity of the Old Marylebone Town Hall, and witnessed a scuffle involving two older men, one wearing a Sikh turban and the other a luminous tabard. Quayle couldn't make out all that was passing between them, but it was clear that the man in the tabard, who was white, had mistaken the Sikh for a 'Muslim bastard', and the subsequent exchange of words had escalated to blows. A crowd had gathered around them, but no one seemed inclined to intervene. Instead they egged on the antagonists according to their sympathies, or in order to ensure that the entertainment did not conclude too soon. A policeman arriving to break up the scuffle had to fight his way through the onlookers, and a chorus of jeers accompanied his separation of the two men.

Similar scenes were being played out in cities and towns across the land, and the hostilities had even spread to the Continent, where ultra-right-wing nationalists were using the killings in Britain to take preemptive action against Muslims in their own countries, along with any other immigrants unfortunate enough to cross their paths. It didn't matter that religious leaders and politicians were calling for calm, or rational voices were pointing out that, beyond the presence of the *misbaha* on the victims' bodies, there was no evidence of the crimes having been committed by a Muslim, and the prayer beads might well be an attempt to incite precisely the very discord currently being witnessed. Ears were blocked to reason, and eyes closed. The Atlas, now so close to completion, was altering the topography of the world at an accelerating rate.

Unseen by all but Quayle, the Pale Child crouched at a street corner, stretching out a hand at random to touch those that passed. Quayle saw its fingers brush against the belly of a pregnant woman, and watched her stumble before regaining her balance. She walked on, rubbing her stretched skin at the place where the Pale Child had marked her.

Quayle wondered if she had felt the infant die in her womb.

A cab stopped, and he directed the driver to take him to Fleet Street. He had endured enough of the city and its people. He needed seclusion, and his books. Yet the incident at the Theosophical library began to trouble him.

Why those volumes? he thought. *Why now?*

Parker had expected Hood's home to be some version of Cold Comfort Farm, but discovered instead the congenial dwelling of a man who tolerated inclemency while out on the moors, but saw no reason to endure further hardship inside his own four walls. Those same walls were decorated with landscape scenes, and various prints of dogs and horses, while the furniture, for the most part, was old but well maintained. Only a large screen television, a satellite box, and a Roberts satellite radio would have appeared out of place a century earlier. The cottage itself was unusual in its design, constructed as it was with thick walls, small windows, and a low ceiling on the ground floor, with even smaller slit windows on the level above. Hood explained that it was one of the last bastles built on the moor, a bastle being a stone farmhouse designed for defense, and dating originally from the seventeenth century, when disputes between border families often descended into bloodshed.

'So you live in a fortress,' said Parker.

'And glad I am of it,' said Hood.

He boiled a kettle and warmed the teapot, before adding leaves and water. He stood the pot on a metal stand and left the tea to brew while he dug out a tin box that contained a thick slab of fruit cake, and took from the refrigerator a square of deep yellow butter that didn't look to Parker like it had come wrapped in any paper with a brand name. He cut Parker a slice of cake, and offered him the butter.

'I don't use it, thanks.'

For the first time since they'd met, Hood looked actively shocked.

'Don't Americans use butter?'

'Not this American.'

'What do you put on your bread?'

'Nothing.'

'You're joking.'

'I'm not.'

Hood regarded Parker with new puzzlement.

'Why would a man choose to eat his bread dry?'

He made it sound less like an inquiry about food, and more an existential problem to be addressed. It made Parker feel as though he had missed a life lesson.

Parker shrugged. 'I've been that way ever since I was a kid.'

'I suppose you don't take sugar in your tea, either.'

'As it happens, I don't.'

Hood shook his head at the queerness of some folk.

'You might as well be in jail,' he said.

'You're not the first person to suggest that.'

Hood poured the tea.

'If I'd known what you were like,' he said glumly, 'I'd have used tea bags.'

XCV

The Wittenham Clumps, formed from chalk and standing high above the River Thames in Oxfordshire, have been a locus of power and worship since the Ice Age. The tallest of them, at almost 400 feet, is Round Hill, but the most important is Castle Hill, which was the site of a hill fort from the Bronze Age to the Iron Age – one that, at its apogee, was protected by concentric levels of wall, ditch, and stockade. But by 300 BC, the fortress lay abandoned, and no cause for its desertion was ever established. The only clue came in the form of a burial pit in which was discovered the huddled body of a man, and upon him, separated by a fine layer of earth, the dismembered remains of a woman. Iron Age settlers did not bury their dead in this manner. These, it seems, were sacrifices, but they had not been sufficient, and so the Clumps were left to old gods, their names long forgotten.

Now, more than two thousand years later, a vixen dug amid the beeches on Castle Hill, her paws scattering fine showers of earth as she sought methodically for the source of the scent that had lured her here. At last, her claws struck softer stuff.

The vixen lowered her head, and began to feed.

XCVI

Hood lit a fire. The cottage was cool, but not so much as to call for a blaze.

'Force of habit,' Hood explained. 'I always find an empty grate depressing. And anyway—'

Parker waited, but Hood did not go on.

'And?' he prompted.

Hood stabbed at the pile of wood with a poker, sending a small shower of sparks flying.

'All green things fear fire,' he finished.

They drank the last of the tea, and Hood recounted for Parker his discovery of Romana Moon's body, and the events that followed. He spoke also of the Familists, and what he knew of their history, even though they were long departed from this island, they and their chapel decorated with images of the Green Man; gone to the New World, gone to Maine, there to thrive until they drew the wrong man to them, this man, the one sitting opposite, whom they tried to kill – *did* kill – but who was restored to life by the actions of surgeons or the will of God, depending on what one chose to believe.

'You're certain they're all gone from the area?' Parker asked.

'Why would they hide themselves now?' said Hood. 'We no longer burn heretics at the stake.'

'Then what's happening here?' said Parker. 'Why did Romana Moon die on these moors?'

'Are you a gardening man?' Hood asked.

'I have a garden.'

'That's not the same thing, as I'm sure you know.'

'Then no, I wouldn't claim to be a gardener.'

'There are seeds that can lie dormant for long periods, waiting for rain. Over in Israel, they planted a two-thousand-year-old seed found in the ruins of a fortress called Masada, and it grew into a Judean date palm that had been extinct since five hundred AD. The Russians dug up seeds from a squirrel burrow, and germinated a campion that had died out thirty-two *thousand* years earlier. Maybe the Familists left behind a seed, a little part of their green god hibernating under the ground, and now someone has put blood in the earth to wake it.'

'But not a Familist, not if you're right about them.'

'Old places have power,' said Hood, 'and this is a very old place. Beltingham's another, not far from here.'

'Where they found the body of the boy?' Parker had heard something about it on the car radio.

'Sacrificed to a yew tree.'

'Is that what you think was done to him?'

'What else would it be?'

'There's nothing to suggest a link between the crimes.'

'You're not keeping up with events. They're saying Romana Moon taught that boy in school, so they're connected all right. Someone killed his brother, too, over in Newcastle. Then there's Helen Wylie, and the Hicks girl, both left, like Romana, with beads in their mouths. They haven't found Hicks yet, but my guess is she was murdered somewhere with a history of worship, and maybe also of trouble and ruin, though her body may lie elsewhere.'

'Why do you say that?'

'Because whoever killed Romana moved her from the chapel site after she was dead. He didn't want it known that she'd died there. He was trying to hide the fact.'

'Then why leave the dead boy in the yew?'

'You're the detective. I'm just a simple farmer.'

Parker let that one go. He looked at his watch. It was time to leave, but he had one more thing to do, one service he could perform for Hood, and for all these people. It had come to him as he stood amid the ruins of the settlement, whispered in a voice that sounded like that of his dead daughter, but faint, as though heard from afar.

'Can we take a detour to the hollow on the way back to my car?' he said.

Hood didn't look overjoyed at the prospect. 'Why would you want to do that?'

'Humor me.'

Hood stood, the dog rising with him, and found the keys to his Land Rover.

'Nothing humorous about it,' he said.

Sellars sat at the kitchen table with his wife and daughters, eating pasta and listening to one of the new digital stations the girls liked because they played dance music, the kind he couldn't have identified even if someone placed a gun to his head. His wife knew all those songs: it was another point of separation between them, another factor distancing him from his women-folk, three against one. He suspected it was deliberate on Lauren's part.

The children recognized that something had changed between their parents, although they had yet to be informed of the cause. Lauren had agreed to wait a couple of days before telling the kids about the separation. Now that the subject had been raised and discussed, and a path forward seemingly agreed, some of the tension had gone out of her, and she was more relaxed than she had been in months, even years. She laughed with the girls, and was polite with her soon-to-be ex-husband. She could afford to be magnanimous because she would shortly be getting what she wanted: to keep the house, which had always felt more like hers anyway; to have the girls to herself, apart from a weekend or two a month, and perhaps a couple of evenings here and there, depending on how generous she and the court decided to be; and to rid herself of the burden of him, and therefore also to be freed from the suspicions that had tormented her for so long. Once a respectable amount of time had passed, she'd take another man to her bed, the bed in which she and Sellars had conceived their two beautiful daughters. She'd probably even keep the mattress. It was only a year old, and mattresses were expensive.

Lauren made a joke, and Kelly smiled along with it, but Louise didn't. She was the more sensitive of the girls, even though she was the younger, and hadn't yet learned to hide her emotions as well as her sister. Kelly was her mother's daughter, but Louise was more like her father. She glanced at him now as she sucked the tagliatelle from her fork, and his heart hurt. How could Lauren ever have imagined that he'd just walk away from these girls to become some absentee father who would have to ask permission to visit when he started missing them too much; who wouldn't be with them when they opened their gifts on Christmas morning; who would no longer be able to look in on them when he got home, no matter how late, because he needed to be sure they were safe in their beds before he could close his eyes; who would eventually be forced to play second fiddle to someone called Steve, Bobby, Ricky, or whatever other fucker Lauren was already lining up as his replacement. He saw how the men looked at her in the pub when they thought he wasn't paying attention. Lauren was an attractive woman, head and shoulders above any of the others in their local. They'd be sniffing around her like the dogs they were before he'd even had a chance to collect the last of his belongings from the house and move them to whatever rotten little rental he could afford with the money left to him after the settlement.

His hand had closed so tightly on his fork that his knuckles were white. He willed himself to relax. It wasn't going to happen, none of it. Mors would take care of it, and when it was over, he would be left to raise the girls alone. He would no longer be free to take on overnight pick-ups and deliveries, or dawn-to-dusk runs, which might mean finding another job, but he didn't mind. The most important thing to him was his daughters and their happiness. He still hadn't decided if it would be better for them if their mother's remains were found, so that her fate would be known, or if Lauren should simply vanish entirely. He was leaning toward the former; it would be harder for them at first, but at least they wouldn't always be seeking her face in a crowd. Eventually he might drive them to the Hexhamshire Moors, and they'd lie on the ground together, all three of them, and listen to the Green Man growing big and strong beneath the earth.

Fingers touched his, and Lauren said, 'You all right?'

He resisted the urge to pull his hand away. 'I'm fine. Why?'

'You've been sitting there for ages with the same forkful of pasta hanging in front of your face. I thought you might have turned to stone.'

Kelly giggled. Even Lauren smiled properly.

'Like Mr Tumnus,' said Louise, and Kelly giggled harder. Lauren joined in, and soon all three of them were laughing at him.

He couldn't remember who Mr Tumnus was, until Kelly said, 'Daddy's a faun,' and then he understood: half-man, half-beast, with horns on his head and cloven hooves for feet.

Yes, he thought, *that's Daddy all right.*

Hood parked by the side of a dirt road, one that ran perpendicular to the public path, and told Parker they'd have to walk the rest of the way. Hood wouldn't traverse the moors in his Land Rover without good reason, he said, because of the damage it caused to the ground, but neither did he wish to get stuck in mud, not in the dark, and not so near the Familist site. He didn't seem to regard walking over the moors as a much more appealing option, but at least some light remained in the sky for the present, although clouds were already gathering, and rain would soon start to fall.

'It won't matter,' said Parker. 'We'll be done by then.'

Hood took a small spade from the bed of the Land Rover and handed it to Parker. He kept Jess on her leash because he didn't want her taking off, although she showed no inclination to do so, and kept careful pace with the two men.

Eventually they reached the incline, and stared into the hollow. It was now almost entirely filled with weeds. They seemed to Hood to be moving slightly, even though the wind had died down.

'That's not possible,' he said. 'They can't have grown so fast.'

Parker didn't reply, but descended, trampling the weeds as he went. Hood remained where he was, because Jess had gone as far as she was willing. She lay on the ground, her head between her front paws, and watched silently as Parker used his right foot to clear a space of greenery before beginning to dig. Hood felt the impact of the spade through the soles of his feet, and the sound it made was closer to a blade cleaving flesh than steel on soil.

Parker struck a second time, and Hood noticed a black substance bubbling like oil from the gash. It smelled sharply of decay. Parker continued to work until he had cut a single sod, which he then set aside. Finally, he removed an object from around his neck. Hood saw that it was an old cross on a piece of leather cord. Gently, reverently, Parker placed the cross in the hole, restored the sod, and tamped the ground to hide any evidence of interference, just as the first drops of rain arrived. He then picked up the spade and rejoined Hood. Jess rose to her feet to greet him, her tail wagging.

'That was a cross you put in the hole,' said Hood.

'Byzantine,' Parker said. 'An old cross for an old place.'

'Was it precious?'

'It was to me.'

Hood almost asked him why he had buried it in the ground if this was so, but stopped himself just in time. The preciousness was the point. This, too, was a sacrifice, but of a different ilk to Romana Moon's.

Parker walked on, the spade over his right shoulder. Hood remained standing where he was, beside that damned hollow. He could still make out the Familist settlement on the hill. Someone should have razed it to the ground long ago, and filled in the hollow as well. Once Hood was certain the police were finished with this place, he would talk with some folk to see what might be done – but quietly, mind: he didn't want Historic England or the Ancient Monuments Society to catch wind of it. It would be better for all if the ruins just vanished quietly overnight.

Jess tugged at the leash, and Hood freed her. He was no longer concerned for her, and felt no jealousy as she joined the other man, this stranger, walking beside him in mute escort. They reached the Land Rover, the rain descending steady yet unheeded upon them, and Jess barked her farewell when they returned Parker at last to his own vehicle and watched him drive away.

He would not return, Hood knew, but the land could rest quietly now.

XCVII

Sisterson autopsied Gary Holmby's body that same evening, while Lerner took care of the younger brother, Karl. The tree surgeon had proved to be as good as his word, managing to pare back the interior of the yew with minimal damage to Karl's corpse, and none whatsoever to the living parts of the tree. He had also refused to invoice the police for his services. He said he wasn't inclined to profit from a boy's death.

The Gary Holmby autopsy produced a surprise. He'd been shot at close range with a 9mm bullet that lodged in the wall of the apartment after exiting his brain, but he also had a fractured right ankle, and the injury was very recent. It might have been a coincidence, but that seemed unlikely.

Karl Holmby's examination was more challenging. In common with Romana Moon, he had received stab wounds to the torso in addition to having his throat cut, although with a different knife. Sisterson had estimated that a blade of about eight inches in length was used in the Moon killing, while Lerner found that Karl had been stabbed with a shorter blade. More importantly, Lerner opined that Holmby's stab wounds were both pre- and post-mortem, while Moon's had all been inflicted prior to her death. The Holmby incisions were also more precise, and none were suggestive of hesitation wounds.

'What's your conclusion?' Priestman asked, as she spoke with Lerner over the phone.

'Whoever killed Karl Holmby was making a token effort to replicate the Moon killing, but not with any great exactitude.'

'Almost as though they didn't much care whether we decided it was the work of the same person.'

'That's not for me to say, but I can tell you that having checked

504

Dr Sisterson's notes, and consulted with him, Romana Moon and Karl Holmby did not die by the same hand. They both died on their knees, but the angle of the wounds alone would suggest that Romana Moon's killer was six inches taller than Karl Holmby's.'

Priestman resisted the urge to place her forehead on her desk and close her eyes for a while, maybe for the rest of the day, or even her life. Two killers: one for Romana Moon, and the other for the Holmbys? Could the Holmby murders have been committed in revenge for Romana Moon's death? Karl Holmby had told Ryan Clifton that he and Romana Moon were intimate, and Clifton had been indiscreet enough to communicate this information to Elspeth Calley, and possibly others as well. But Karl had an alibi for the night of Romana's murder, and neither of the brothers had been named as a suspect in her killing, so there was nothing to point an avenger in their direction.

Neither of the brothers. Karl might have had an alibi, but what of Gary? Romana had told her sister that she'd begun seeing someone, but declined to share further details while the relationship remained in its early stages. Could Gary Holmby have been Romana Moon's new boyfriend before possibly becoming her killer? But if Romana had rejected the younger sibling's advances, why accept those of the older, unless she was deliberately trying to complicate her life, or wound the already slighted Karl still further.

Priestman was jumping ahead. They needed to trawl the Holmbys' lives, and particularly their electronic communications, but so far their phones and laptops remained missing, presumably taken by whomever was responsible for their deaths. And if they had been killed because of what happened to Romana, then the Moon family, and their associates, could be under suspicion, although how they might have come to consider the Holmbys complicit in their daughter's murder remained unclear.

Priestman was anxious to secure the toxicology report on Karl Holmby. The report on Romana Moon had been fast-tracked, so they now knew Romana had been dosed with benzodiazepine in order to keep her acquiescent as she was led to her death. Karl

Holmby was a tall, healthy young man. If his killer had managed to transport him from his brother's apartment to Beltingham, then either that individual had an accomplice, or Karl was rendered unconscious or semi-conscious for the journey. Priestman guessed the latter, just to save someone the trouble of carrying him, which would risk drawing unwanted attention. Give him just enough sedative, and Karl could have been walked with just a modicum of support. If Karl was also found to have benzodiazepine in his system, well—

She thanked Lerner, hung up, and tried to think.

Hynes was back at Gary Holmby's apartment building, figuring out the stages of a journey that had taken Karl Holmby from his college in Middlesbrough to a yew tree in Beltingham. There was no camera in the building's elevator, but the surveillance footage from the garage revealed Gary Holmby's BMW being driven out shortly before 11 p.m. Unfortunately, the camera pointed toward the street, not into the garage, so they could only see the back of the driver's head, which was also concealed by a cap. Hynes thought it looked like the kind that might be worn by a pizza delivery driver. If so, where was the driver's own vehicle, because they also had footage of a similarly becapped individual holding pizza boxes while using the buzzer to gain access to Gary Holmby's apartment about an hour earlier. The caller had kept his – or her – head down while entering, the clothing being sufficiently baggy and nondescript to leave the gender to guesswork.

That was the word used by the building's supervisor – 'nondescript' – as he showed the camera footage to Hynes. When Hynes remarked upon it, the supervisor admitted he was studying for a BA in English Literature with the Open University because he didn't want to be a glorified caretaker all his life. Hynes reckoned the supervisor was in his sixties, and while applauding his drive to improve himself, was concerned that he might have left it a little late in life to be contemplating a new career. But Hynes hoped he was wrong, because right now he was wondering about a change of career himself, given the state of his current one, and the associated mushrooming of bodies that he found depressing in the extreme. If Hynes had to retrain, he'd be in sight of sixty before he was properly equipped to do anything else. It struck him as just too much effort, and therefore he should stick with the law in the hope that, somewhere down the line, he might become proficient in it. He chose not to share these thoughts with Priestman as he updated her on the situation. He knew she had enough on her plate. At least he'd managed to sleep in his own bed the night before, if not for very long. He'd advised his wife to take a picture of him before he left, just so she'd have something to remember him by.

'We've contacted every restaurant and takeaway offering pizza deliveries in the area,' Hynes told Priestman, 'along with Deliveroo and the other delivery services, but no luck. I think those boxes were empty when they arrived, which means that was no delivery driver. We found blood and vomit in the trunk of the BMW, and I'm guessing it's Karl Holmby's. The blood type matches, but we should know for certain by tomorrow.'

Priestman asked one or two more questions, thanked him, and hung up. Hynes knew that his report was just one of dozens Priestman was collating, adding them to the overall picture in the hope that, if they filled in enough gaps, they'd at last have some idea of what they were looking at.

He checked his watch. He'd promised to represent Priestman later that morning, when Kevin Moon came to collect his daughter's remains, and city traffic could be tricky. He was about to press the call button for the lift when one of the CSI team summoned him from the doorway of the apartment.

'What is it?' said Hynes.

'Got something,' said the investigator.

In his right hand he held a bag.

And in the bag was a knife.

XCVIII

K evin Moon sat alone in the waiting room of the mortuary. He'd been given a cup of tea, and a nice woman from the bereavement service had dropped by to make sure he was comfortable and had everything he needed. The Anglican chaplain had also offered to sit with him, but Kevin didn't want to be around strangers. If he couldn't be with his family, he'd rather be alone.

His wife should have been here beside him, but he'd come down to breakfast that morning to find Doreen still in her dressing gown, crying on the kitchen floor with one of their dogs in her arms. She wasn't hysterical. She wasn't even sobbing. She just seemed to be shedding an endless stream of tears, and was incapable of speech, as though she'd lapsed into some form of catatonia. Kevin managed to get her into a chair before calling the local doctor. Like most GPs these days, he didn't usually offer house calls, but he made an exception in their case. Doreen was suffering from an acute stress response, the doctor said – delayed shock, although Kevin could have diagnosed that himself, for fuck's sake, and he hadn't spent seven years in medical school. The doctor told him that the attack could last anywhere from a few minutes to a couple of days, and the best thing was to get Doreen back to bed, and make sure someone kept an eye on her. He gave her a shot to help her rest, and wrote out a prescription for a course of sedatives.

'How strong are they?' Kevin asked.

'They'll just take some of the edge off.'

'She'll know what's happening, though, won't she? She won't be a zombie?'

'No, she'll be lucid.'

'Because she wouldn't want it all to be a blank. She'll want to remember saying goodbye to Romana.'

The doctor made sympathetic noises, and went on his way. A neighbor arrived to stay with Doreen, and said she'd arrange for a steady stream of friends to keep her company while Kevin was gone. They'd have been there for her anyway, she said, and would be for as long as Doreen needed them. Kevin doubted that – eventually they'd drift away whether his wife needed them or not, because life went on, didn't it? – but he nodded politely. What else could he do?

A couple of Kevin's friends had offered to accompany him to the mortuary, but he turned them down. He drove to Newcastle in solitude, in a silent car. He thought about Romana all the way, but didn't cry. He'd never been what you'd call the emotional kind. He wished that he were, because he could feel it building up inside him, this great flood of pain and grief. He felt the urge to pull over by the side of the road, find a quiet spot, and scream until he tasted blood in his mouth.

But he didn't, of course, because what good would it do, a grown man shouting at the sky while his daughter lay alone on a gurney, waiting for her dad to join the undertakers in order to bring her home for the last time? Instead he drove on, and tried to recall as much about Romana as he could, carefully storing away each memory so he'd be able to find them again in the awful years to come.

Eventually he arrived in Newcastle, and the GPS directed him to the mortuary because he couldn't remember the route from the last visit, when he'd been forced to look down on a bloodless face and tell the police that yes, this was his daughter, even though it wasn't really, not any longer. Now here he was, back in the waiting room, with the obligatory cup of tea, and the absence, and the yearning that would stay with him always and never be sated, not until he was himself put in the ground and could start searching for his little girl on the other side.

Kevin's older daughter, Hayley, lived in Hartlepool, south of Newcastle. She'd promised to be with him by noon, but there'd been some problem with one of the kids, and then the car wouldn't start. What with one thing and another, she now wouldn't arrive until close to one, long after the two undertakers. They wouldn't mind waiting, though; they had the awful patience of those who routinely dealt with the bereaved and their dead.

Kevin grew tired of watching his tea grow cold, and stepped outside to stretch his legs. He envied those who smoked: it gave them something to do with their hands, and an excuse to hang around the entrances to buildings. Someone standing by a door for any length of time without a cigarette just looked awkward, odd, or up to no good. Not wishing to appear any of these things, he thrust his hands into his pockets and strode slowly forward and back, forward and back, going nowhere in particular, to no end, with nothing to see.

A man was walking toward the entrance to the mortuary. He wore a short black overcoat, and Kevin sensed his interest in him. He had something of the policeman about his aspect. It was in the bearing, and the eyes.

'Mr Moon?' he said.

'That's right. Do I know you?'

'We haven't met. My name is Parker.'

He didn't offer a handshake. Even if he had, Kevin wouldn't have been close enough to accept it. Parker remained standing by the door, giving Kevin whatever space he might require.

'Are you with the police?' Kevin asked, even as he picked up the accent. He doubted Northumbria Police recruited from the Americas.

'No. I'm a detective, but not that kind. Private.'

Kevin had been advised to be wary of propositions from outside agencies, although he hadn't expected one to materialize so soon. Hynes, the big DS, had told him to expect mediums, psychics, diviners, and God knows what other kinds of charlatans to offer their assistance in the search for his daughter's killer. Many wouldn't ask for money, Hynes said; they just wanted to be involved. Some might even be sincere, but that wouldn't make them any saner. Hynes had also mentioned private investigators, and stressed the family should keep its distance from them, and be especially wary of those that made direct approaches. If any of them did raise their heads, Hynes said, the Moons should give him a call, and he'd take care of it.

'The police are looking after things,' said Kevin. 'We don't need anyone else.'

'That's not why I'm here,' said Parker.

'If you've come to offer your sympathies, I appreciate it, honest I do, but I'm waiting to bring my daughter's remains back home. It's difficult, and private. You understand?'

'Yes,' said Parker. 'I apologize for intruding on your grief.'

He had already begun to turn away when Kevin Moon spoke again.

'Wait,' he said. It had taken him a moment to realize that he'd looked into this man Parker's eyes and recognized them, because they so resembled his own. 'Who did you lose?'

'A wife. And a daughter.'

'How old was she, your daughter?'

'Four.'

Kevin swallowed. 'Was it –?'

'Murder? Yes.'

'Did they find the one responsible?'

'No, I found him.'

'What did you do to him?'

'I killed him. He left me no choice.'

Kevin Moon felt that he had strayed from the gloaming into a deeper tenebrosity. A voice that sounded like his own, but spoke from anomalous processes, assumed his part in the conversation.

'Would it have ended differently if he had?'

'You mean, would I have spared him?' A moment passed. 'I like to think so, but maybe I'm lying to myself.'

'I'm sorry for your loss.'

'And I for yours.'

'Is that why you came here?'

'In part, because I understand your pain, or some complexion of it. I didn't expect to meet you, or talk with you. I just wanted to pay my respects from a distance.'

'How did you know I'd be here?'

'Yesterday I was with Douglas Hood, the farmer who found

511

Romana's body. The police have stayed in touch with him, and one of them mentioned to him that your daughter would be returned to you this morning.'

'Are you a friend of Hood's?'

'I'd never met him before yesterday.'

'Do you know something that might help the police find whoever killed my daughter?'

'No, or not yet.'

'Then why were you on the moors?'

'Because not long ago, the descendants of the people who once lived and worshiped there tried to have me killed.'

Kevin Moon now knew more about the Familists than he ever could have wished. He'd read about them on the Internet while trying to understand how his daughter should have come to breathe her last in such a desolate place.

'Were you the one that blew up their church?'

'No, I was otherwise occupied at the time. Some friends took care of the church on my behalf.'

'They knew what they were doing.' Moon had seen photographs of the crater they'd left behind. It looked like a bomb had been dropped there. 'Do you think a Familist murdered Romana?'

'Perhaps.'

'Have you spoken to the police about it?'

'No.'

'Will you?'

'Yes, once I know more.'

Moon took in passing cars, and passing people. He took in life, and was reminded that his daughter had none of it.

'I should tell them you were here.'

'You should.'

'You won't hinder them, will you? The police, I mean. Whatever you're doing, it won't get in their way? It won't make it harder for them to find whoever killed my daughter?'

'No.'

Moon nodded. His throat was tightening, so he had to force out the words that came next.

512

'What happens?' he said.

'When?'

'Later. After.' He gestured at the building behind him, and the body within. He gestured at time, and the dead days to come. He gestured at loss, grief, and guilt. He gestured at the ghost of a girl.

'You set aside that part of her,' said Parker. 'You lay it in the ground, or place it in an alcove in a wall, and try to hold on to what's left. Nothing is ever the same again, but it's tolerable, after a while. You'll find time passes differently for you. It becomes sluggish. Joy is rare. The temptation is to suffer and grieve alone, to cut yourself off from others. For some, it's the only way, and it kills them in the end. They die inside, but they don't know they're dead. Better to learn to live with the pain. If you can, work to ease the pain of those around you. Try to decrease the sum of their grief. It will make it easier for you as well. Not by much, but it will enable you to go on.'

Kevin saw a car approach.

'My other daughter's here,' he said.

'I'll go.'

'Thank you for coming, and for talking.'

'Sure.'

'I—'

Parker waited.

'Could you have done anything to save them?' said Kevin.

'I once believed I could, but I was wrong. Had I been there, I'd have died alongside them. For a while, I thought that might have been preferable, but not anymore.'

'I find myself wondering if there was something I might have done to save Romana,' said Kevin. 'I keep trying to discover if there was a mistake I made, way, way back, that caused her to take that path, the one that led to the moor, or if there was something I could have said, some advice I could have given her, that would have helped her when . . .' He still couldn't bring himself to say the words, and so settled for 'when she found herself out there.'

'There isn't anything,' said Parker. 'Someone else made the

decisions that led to her death, not you or your daughter. Were you close?'

'She was my Romana, always was. Couldn't do a thing wrong in my eyes. Used to drive her mother mad.'

'Then it was you she thought of at the end. You were there with her. She didn't die alone.'

The car pulled up, and a woman who resembled an older, fuller version of Romana Moon got out.

'Dad?'

Kevin hugged his daughter, and held her close. As he did so, something broke inside him. He buried his face in her hair, and stayed that way until he had recovered himself.

When Kevin eased himself from her embrace to introduce her to the detective, Parker was gone.

Hynes arrived just as Kevin Moon and his daughter separated. He had also failed to notice Parker's departure, although he had registered the presence of the stranger in conversation with Moon while searching for somewhere to park.

'A friend of yours?' he asked Moon, as they entered the building.

'No,' said Moon, 'not a friend, but maybe something more.'

And he told Hynes of the private investigator.

XCIX

The British Library was the largest such repository in the world, if judged by catalogued items. Its name was redolent of a certain antiquity, but it had only been in existence since 1973, when it was established to combine collections from a variety of sources, including the British Museum and the old India Office. These collections were entrusted to the new institution only to be scattered to the four winds once again, since the British Library in its nascent form was spread over a number of distinct sites, including buildings in Holborn, Aldwych, and Blackfriars, most of them ill-suited to the storage and preservation of rare maps, documents, and books. It was not until 1982 that work commenced on a permanent home for the Library on London's Euston Road, and another fifteen years would pass before it finally opened its doors to the reading public. But many older patrons retained a greater fondness for the original Reading Room at the British Museum, with its tiered shelves of old volumes, and iconic domed ceiling.

Quayle was not among them. The collation into one central archive of documents from so many sources had expedited his search for the missing pages of the Atlas. Consequently, he had made more progress in the previous two decades than he had since the incomplete volume had first come into his possession in the 1920s. His most recent researches at the Library had left him only a few steps behind the late but unlamented Vernay, the sorry individual who had originally managed to lose the book of fairy tales containing what Quayle had mistakenly believed to be the final, concealed pages of the Atlas. Quayle was now convinced that his error lay in sources held either at the Theosophical Society or, more likely, the British Library.

The Library retained about forty-five percent of its stock in London, with the rest kept in storage in Yorkshire. Each day, a van made the journey back and forth between the two locations according to the demands of readers. Thankfully, the documents and books required by Quayle all dated from before 1800, some even from medieval times, which meant they were held on site in London: martyrologies, books of hours, early maps of the New World, even a thirteenth-century plan of waterworks from Waltham Abbey. In the past, he had been careful not to order too many of these works at once out of concern that a pattern might be noted, since the Library retained a record of all requests submitted by readers. True, he was not registered under his own name, but he had no desire to attract attention to his efforts. Consequently his researches were slow but steady, and sometimes months, even years, passed between requests to view essential materials. Meanwhile, Quayle would order items that had no connection to the Atlas, or books that had previously proven to be dead ends or false trails, in order to put others off the scent. But now he had run out of patience and time. He was so near the end, so near to closing his eyes and embracing oblivion, but the hunters were circling, and he had to remain ahead of them.

Quayle arrived at the Library shortly after lunch, and submitted to the mandatory search of his bag. It contained only *The Times*, his notebooks, and some pencils, ink being forbidden in the reading rooms. He found a terminal, and from memory began entering his requests: a twelfth-century martyrology from the priory of Christ Church, Canterbury; a mid-thirteenth-century book of hours, to which two later owners, Mysterys Felys and Christopher Colston, had added coded references to the Atlas; a set of geomancy diagrams from 1490, probably intended for Henry VII; and an early medical dissertation from the Dutch university of Leiden, part of an assemblage of vellum documents curated by the physician and naturalist Sir Hans Sloane, whose collection was bequeathed to Britain following his death in 1753 at the remarkable age of ninety-two, albeit in return for the then no less remarkable sum of £20,000, to be paid to his executors. Sloane was of particular interest to Quayle because he had acquired part of the monumental library of Cardinal Filippo Antonio Gualterio, papal nuncio to the court of King Louis XIV of France at the beginning of the eighteenth century. Gualterio's collection contained two pages of the Atlas, concealed in the bindings of separate natural history volumes. Quayle did not believe this to be a coincidence, and was convinced that Sloane had been aware of the Atlas's existence.

Somewhere in the library, a child was crying, and a party of tourists was gazing at the book collection of King George III stored in a vast multistory glass case in the foyer, the only physical indicator of the building's purpose, since no other volumes were visible to visitors without access to the reading rooms.

The martyrology, the first item sought by Quayle, came up as being in use. So, too, did the book of hours, and the geomancy diagrams. Only the medical dissertations were available. Quayle might have accepted the absence of one source as unfortunate, but not three. He logged out of the system, and began to hunt.

The British Library contained more than 1,200 desks scattered across eleven reading rooms, but the age of the documents sought by Quayle meant they would have been delivered to the Manuscripts Room, probably by hand. Whoever was examining them would be found there. Quayle showed his pass, and entered. He proceeded directly to a reference shelf, and removed one book, then another, taking his time. He found an empty desk at the back of the room, laid down the books, and sat. He detected no sign of any interest in his presence. After a few minutes, he stood and made his way along the rows, his keen eyes taking in the volumes and papers on each desk.

In the fourth row sat a man in his late sixties or early seventies, poring over the geomancy diagrams. Beside him were the book of hours, and the martyrology, along with a yellow legal pad on which he was making notes. He was lost in his work, and did not notice Quayle return to the far desk, collect his satchel and reference works, and relocate to a space closer to his quarry. There Quayle remained, and did not move until the other man rose, probably to go to the bathroom, leaving his books and papers behind. When he was gone, Quayle rose and strolled past the desk. Each volume requested by a visitor to the library contained a slip with the reader's name upon it. Poking from the pages of the martyrology was a slip bearing the name 'Bob Johnston'.

Quayle returned to his spot, and waited for Johnston to return. He ordered the medical dissertations to pass the time. They arrived within the hour, the library being quiet, and Quayle worked his way through them. The references to the Atlas were concealed in the form of a Vigenere Cypher based on the Dutch words *verloren ziel*, or 'lost soul', and soon Quayle, too, was immersed in his task, but not to the extent of ignoring Johnston.

Who are you? Quayle wondered.

Who. Are. You?

C

Parker made it to Newcastle Airport just in time to get on his flight to Heathrow. He caught the Express into central London, and took a taxi to Hazlitt's. The driver, softened into cooperation by the promise of a decent tip, waited while he ditched his bag, before driving him to Chancery Lane.

'What do you think of this serial killer business, then?' the driver asked, as they approached Trafalgar Square. 'Muslim bloke, they reckon.'

Parker looked at his boots, which still bore traces of Hexhamshire mud. No Muslim had killed Romana Moon on those moors. And if she wasn't the victim of a Muslim killer, then neither was Kathy Hicks, the woman whose body was still being displayed on Internet sites for all to see; nor Helen Wylie, murdered at Canterbury, and whose connection to the other killings had only recently been revealed by police; nor Eleanor Hegarty, a student from Bury, whose remains, gnawed by an animal, had just been found at somewhere called the Wittenham Clumps, also with a *misbaha* in her mouth.

'Who are "they"?' said Parker.

'The police,' said the taxi driver. 'Everyone.'

'Then everyone is wrong.'

'Yeah?'

'Yes.'

The driver looked at him in the rearview mirror.

'You with the police?'

Parker wondered how long it would be before someone from the murder team found a means to get in touch with him. He'd wait to find out, because he had no intention of making the first approach. He had already given them the scent by speaking to Kevin Moon. Let them work their way toward him.

'No.'

'Do you know something they don't?'

'Nothing worth knowing.'

'Well, then.' The driver, having thus dismissed Parker's opinion as worthless, turned on to the Strand. 'I won't have them in my cab.'

'Who?'

'Muslims. Not since Seven-Seven.'

July 7th, 2005 – 7/7 – had witnessed a series of coordinated suicide attacks on London's transport system by four young Muslims, resulting in the deaths of fifty-six people, including the bombers themselves. Parker thought it odd that the bombings should later have been named in an echo of 9/11, as though the tragedy required the connection in order to render it more significant. It struck him as strangely competitive.

'You can let me out here,' said Parker.

'Not at Chancery Lane yet, mate.'

'I'll walk the rest of the way. The fresh air will do me good.'

Parker added five pounds to the total on the meter, and placed it on the cash tray. After all, a promise was a promise. The driver shrugged, and pulled over.

'This is summer in London, mate: there is no fresh air. But please yourself.'

Parker got out, and started to walk. Near the Roman Baths on Strand Lane, a woman was handing out copies of the *Evening Standard*. Pictures of the dead women dominated the front page, with Eleanor Hegarty's larger than the rest. Already her private life was being dissected just as assuredly as her body, the word 'prostitute' figuring more frequently than 'student'.

This city seemed to be closing in on Parker. He wanted to be back in Maine. He did not belong here. Yet he carried what had once been Familist soil on his boots, and the scars left by the Familists' hired killers on his body.

He might not belong in this place, but he was meant to be here.

Now was the time for the hunt to begin in earnest.

Now was the time to bait the trap.

* * *

Sellars lay on his bathroom floor, knees to his chest, arms curled around his shoulders in grief. The girls were at school, and Lauren was at work, so there was no one to hear his sobs.

He had felt it during the night, a dying deep within himself. He had thought it a nightmare, until he woke to the pain.

The Green Man was no more. His god was extinct.

He called in sick to work once again, and heard the skepticism in his manager's voice. Questions would be asked, but he did not care, not now. Let it all come to an end. Let the Atlas be made complete. He would do whatever was required to hasten it.

But first, he would find whoever had killed his god.

Parker entered the lobby of Lockwood, Dodson & Fogg. It smelled of vanilla, and the floors were very clean. Behind the reception desk sat a trio of conservatively dressed women – one older, two younger – and a security guard. None of them made an effort to appear particularly welcoming, but then Parker didn't look like the kind of person who might be bringing business to the firm, or not the kind it desired.

Parker approached the senior receptionist, since it was likely that the other two were subordinates who would defer to her anyway. The woman was particularly stony-faced. Her make-up appeared to have been applied by a team of laborers on a break from plastering walls.

'I'd like to see Ms Lockwood,' said Parker.

'Do you have an appointment?'

'No.'

'As one of the senior partners, Ms Lockwood is very busy. Her diary is filled weeks in advance.'

'Well, I guess Ms Dodson will have to do, then. I'd have given Mr Fogg as my third choice if he wasn't indisposed, but my guess is he was just making up the numbers for the gender quota anyway. This place strikes me as a bastion of female leadership. Which is a good thing,' he added. 'Obviously.'

'May I inquire as to your business?'

'I'm sorry, but that's private.'

'Then I'm afraid we can't help you. I'll have to ask you to

leave, and make an appointment in writing, or through our switchboard.'

'Darn it,' said Parker. 'I've come a long way.'

'I'm sorry to hear that,' the receptionist lied.

'Maybe I could just take a seat and wait, in case a slot opens up in someone's schedule?'

'I don't think that will be possible.'

The security guard got to his feet, but didn't move from behind the safety of his desk. Maybe he was trying not to escalate the situation unless absolutely necessary, in the hope that the interloper might leave of his own volition, but it also struck Parker that while the guard might well be as soft as he seemed, he might also be smarter than he looked. Whatever game was being played, he wanted some understanding of the rules before becoming involved.

Parker took out his ID. He figured he'd stirred them up enough.

'How about this? I'm a licensed private investigator, based out of Portland, Maine, looking into the circumstances surrounding at least seven murders, along with one kidnapping and an attempted abduction. Now, I'd really like to speak with one of the senior partners.'

Parker wouldn't have believed that the receptionist's face could have hardened any further, but somehow it did.

'And what has it got to do with this firm?' she said.

Parker gave her a cobra smile.

'Because this is the last known address of the man responsible.'

He stepped back from the desk, and removed his jacket. The lobby was cool, but not quite cool enough for the weather.

'I'm going to take a seat over there while you make some calls,' he said. 'Take your time, but coffee would be good. Cream, no sugar.'

Parker sat at a table facing the desk. He picked up a copy of *The Times.*

After a few moments, he took out a pen and began tackling the crossword.

CI

Hynes arrived at Priestman's office carrying sandwiches and soup from Mister Woods Coffee, and a couple of Americanos that could be heated up in the microwave. He knew Priestman probably wouldn't have eaten, and she liked the coffee from Mister Woods, even reheated, and minus the possible apostrophe, which always bothered her.

'Sisterson says the dimensions of the knife found at Gary Holmby's apartment match the wounds to Romana Moon's body,' said Priestman, as she dipped her sandwich in her soup.

'Lab results?'

'We'll have to wait for the blood, but we got clean prints from the handle. I'm waiting for confirmation, but the initial examination suggests they're Gary Holmby's.'

'Jesus.'

'Exactly.'

They went over the implications together, as much in an effort to clarify details in their own minds as anything else. If Gary Holmby had killed Romana Moon, then he'd kept her laptop as a souvenir, and possibly the knife as well. Holmby didn't appear to be a convert to Islam; they weren't ruling it out for now, but it seemed unlikely, which meant the *misbaha* was meant to throw the police off the scent, sow religious hatred, or both. They'd have to establish if he'd ever given any indication of a bias against Muslims, or expressed any far-right sympathies, but for now they had a means of defusing some of the escalating tension on the country's streets. Ordinarily, Priestman wouldn't have been rushing to make public the results of the forensic examination until they had definite information about the blood on the blade, but these were far from ordinary circumstances.

On the other hand, until they found Kathy Hicks's body, they wouldn't be able to establish if the same weapon had been used on her. They'd already been in touch with Essex in an effort to find out if Hicks might have known Holmby, or Romana Moon, since *misbahas* had been placed in both women. Then there was Eleanor Hegarty, whose death was also linked to the others by the presence of a *misbaha*. She, too, had been stabbed, and her throat cut. Sisterson had requested, and received, electronic copies of the autopsy results, and Priestman expected to hear from him at any moment about the nature of her wounds. The blood of any one of those women might be on the knife found in Holmby's apartment – or the blood of none at all.

But who had killed Gary Holmby? If his brother was responsible, how did he obtain the gun, and where was it now? More to the point, who had subsequently killed Karl, and why?

And if Gary Holmby was responsible for murdering all three women, he had somehow bounced from Kent, where Helen Wylie had been killed; to Bristol, where he abducted Kathy Hicks and transported her to a location as yet unknown for her murder and burial; thence to Hexhamshire, possibly by way of Middlesbrough, if that's where he had first abducted Romana Moon; and finally to Bury, where Eleanor Hegarty had been living, before traveling south to the Wittenham Clumps in Oxfordshire, where her body had been found.

Which didn't seem likely at all, not in such a short space of time. And while Priestman was no expert on serial killers, she knew they were mostly territorial. Gary Holmby didn't fit the nomadic profile. He sometimes traveled for work purposes, but from what they had learned so far, these were generally high-end trips, often abroad. They involved stays in fancy hotels, but rarely for longer than was required for Holmby to complete his business. When he wasn't flitting between airports and hotels, Holmby was holed up in his apartment, in a small office that the techs were still in the process of examining. Finally, they had already established that Gary Holmby had been out of the country when Helen Wylie disappeared. While he might have killed Romana Moon, he hadn't killed Wylie.

'You know what I think?' said Hynes. He finished his soup, and went to work on his sandwich. He wasn't one for eating both at the same time.

'What?'

'I think someone is fucking with us,' said Hynes. 'Multiple someones.'

CII

Parker knew that Lockwood, Dodson & Fogg had a number of options when it came to dealing with his unwelcome presence in their lobby. The first was to ignore him in the hope that he might give up and leave, but Parker could have referred them to any number of people who had underestimated his ability to remain where he wasn't wanted. The second was to attempt a forcible ejection, either by their own security team – which probably wasn't up to the task – or by the police, who probably were. That, Parker thought, would be the American way. The third option, which was also the most sensible, and probably the most British, was to treat him civilly, find out what the problem was, and get rid of him as quickly as possible afterward.

Naturally enough, the latter path was the one LDF ultimately decided to follow, albeit with a certain amount of reluctance on the part of the senior receptionist, who personally took it upon herself to escort Parker into the beating heart of the building with minimal conversation and maximum disdain, like the housekeeper at Her Ladyship's mansion being forced to lead a plumber to a blocked toilet. It was a miracle she hadn't directed him to a tradesman's entrance at the back. Parker was just relieved not to have to sit for any longer in the lobby chairs. He'd been correct about their purpose, but had underestimated just how uncomfortable they really were. The coffee wasn't great, either.

Eventually Parker was led to the door of a very large, very modern office, with floor-to-ceiling windows overlooking the city, and air conditioning that was set just right. The woman who rose to greet him was in her early forties, with dark-brown hair pulled back in a bun. Her features were slightly too sharp to be considered beautiful, and her eyes were too intelligent to care. She was dressed in a gray business suit over a white shirt, and flat black shoes. Standing, she was about three inches taller than Parker. In heels, she would have left him feeling like her pet monkey.

'Mr Parker? Welcome. I'm Emily Lockwood.'

They shook hands. Her nails were very short, and she wore both wedding and engagement rings. The diamond on the latter was small enough not to appear vulgar but large enough not to seem cheap, and was surrounded by lots of smaller friends in case it got lonely. She returned to her desk, and directed him to a chair opposite. It appeared to have been designed by the same person responsible for the lobby furniture, but on a day when he was feeling less angry at the world. Sitting in it was closer to penance than actual torture. Parker wasn't offered more coffee, which was a further relief.

'It's quite the lineage your firm boasts,' said Parker. 'More than a hundred and fifty years have passed since it was founded, and I'm still talking to a Lockwood.'

'Did you think the names were just for show, and we would be owned by Russians?'

'Have they made an offer?'

'The Russians aren't really interested in acquiring law firms, but they do keep us busy. I gather you expressed a preference for speaking to a female partner. How very progressive of you.'

'Not really. It was two against one, so I thought I'd pick the winning side. And last I heard, Mr Fogg had taken a backseat.'

'Mr Fogg is terminally ill.'

'Yes.'

'Aren't you supposed to tell me how sorry you are to hear that?'

'I've never met him. It would be insincere.'

'Or polite.'

'Are we being polite?'

'I think so. You've been admitted to my office, haven't you?'

'I can't help but feel that it's under sufferance, although I had to some spend time in one of your lobby chairs, so we're both suffering, I guess.'

Emily Lockwood abandoned the etiquette lesson. 'I understand you're investigating a number of serious crimes,' she said. 'In what capacity?'

'Private.' He saw no reason to mention the ongoing federal consultancy retainer. He'd pull it out of the hat if required, although he didn't believe it would count for much on this side of the Atlantic.

'Are you working on behalf of a client?'

'No.'

'That seems unusual.'

'One of my friends was shot and injured in the course of this investigation. For that reason, I've decided to take it personally. Oh, and I hurt my foot jumping from a window.'

Lockwood tried to figure out if Parker was joking. He gave her no clue.

'I looked you up,' said Lockwood. 'You lead an interesting life, if one not without its misfortunes. I suppose you must be weary of people expressing sympathy for your loss after all this time, but still, one feels it should be acknowledged. I have a daughter of my own. I can't even conceive of what you must have gone through – what you're still going through.'

Parker tried to understand what kind of person would classify the murder of a man's wife and young child as a 'misfortune', and therefore what might count as a tragedy in Lockwood's world, but he managed a nod in recognition of the sentiment.

'See?' said Lockwood. 'That was politeness.' She checked the time on her phone, and made sure that he noticed her doing it. 'You mentioned some connection between your investigation and our offices.'

Parker gave her the abridged version of what had happened in Maine and Indiana, and the murders committed, or believed to have been committed, by Quayle and his acolyte, although he left out how the trail had taken him to the Mexican border, and the Netherlands, before England. Thanks to the wonders of the Internet, Lockwood already knew some, but not all, of what he had told her. She had not, she said, been familiar with the Quayle connection until a general inquiry had reached the firm from a federal legat named Canton, working out of the US embassy in

London. LDF had been unable to help him, beyond confirming that the firm of Quayle had ceased to exist in the 1940s.

'Just because this man used the name Quayle, and claimed to be a lawyer,' said Lockwood, 'does not mean the identity was real, or the claim true.'

'No,' admitted Parker, 'but I'm curious as to why he chose that particular name. Also, the man we're hunting bears some resemblance to an earlier Quayle: Atol, the last of his line, or so it seemed until this one showed up. Unless I'm mistaken, LDF owns this building, and the land on which it stands, which was formerly the location of the firm of Quayle. I'm interested in how that came about, and who benefited from the sale.'

Lockwood tapped a short message on her phone, and watched it vanish into the ether.

'The situation is more complex than you make it sound,' she said. 'Following the death of Atol Quayle, my grandfather acquired various properties formerly owned by the firm of Quayle, under an agreement made between my great-grandfather and some great-uncle of Atol's in the eighteen-nineties. I believe a lot of money might have changed hands at the time of the original agreement as a form of deposit. Perhaps Atol Quayle's predecessor required funds urgently, but I can't say for certain as the parties involved are obviously long dead. Since then, many of those properties have been sold and resold multiple times, including this one, which is now owned by a holding company in the Channel Islands, a legal entity entirely separate from LDF. This is London, Mr Parker: concepts such as ownership of property are complicated, and fluid.'

'In my experience,' said Parker, 'concepts like complexity and fluidity are useful for disguising illegality.'

Lockwood didn't disagree.

'London is awash with dirty money,' she said, 'literally billions in assets. We're a global center for money laundering, and the property market is the conduit of choice.'

'Including law offices?'

She laughed. 'Including law offices – but not this one.'

'You would say that.'

She stopped laughing, but the smile remained, like a light left on in a house after burglars have made off with all the valuables.

'So where did the money from the original sale go?' Parker continued.

'I can't say how much was left once the deposit was deducted, but whatever remained was presumably placed in the trust established under the primary agreement.'

'Which LDF administers.'

'My, you have been busy. I'd have to check, as we administer a great many trusts, but that's probably correct, given the familial and property history.'

'And who is the beneficiary of the trust?'

'I can't tell you that.'

'Why?'

'Because it would be a breach of our duty to the trustee – or trustees,' she added. 'Atol Quayle may have left instructions that any income should be directed to charities, or distant relatives and their descendants, on an anonymous basis until the trust is entirely depleted. That's often what happens in these cases.'

'But if Quayle is dead, why should it matter what you tell me? He's not going to file a complaint.'

'That's not how the law works, Mr Parker, or not here. But then, your history would suggest that your view of how the law works is largely a matter of your own interpretation and convenience.'

'Ouch,' said Parker.

Lockwood got to her feet. 'I'm sorry, but I have another appointment that has already been postponed for too long in order to facilitate this conversation. I wish you every success in your investigation.'

Parker remained seated. He'd discovered from experience that it was harder to give someone the bum's rush if he wasn't standing.

'I have one last question. What's in the old building on the far side of your courtyard?'

'How do you know about that?'

'Google maps. Those satellites see everything.'

'They're part of the original offices of the firm of Quayle, or certainly the incarnation dating from the late eighteenth or early nineteenth century. The premises were badly damaged during the Blitz, which might have precipitated Atol Quayle's retirement, but we decided to retain most of what remained as a monument to the legal history of the site. It's called – with accuracy, if not originality – the Old Firm.'

'What's inside?'

'Nothing. It's a façade, hiding an empty shell. If it wasn't protected by metal and reinforced glass, it would probably crumble to the ground.'

'Would it be possible to take a look?'

'Not without a hard hat, a signed waiver, and a wrecking ball. It's entirely sealed.'

Lockwood had opened the office door, and was waiting for Parker to leave. Short of chaining himself to the furniture, he couldn't delay his departure any longer.

'I'm staying at Hazlitt's,' he said, 'just in case you reconsider.'

'Did you think he might be hiding in there,' said Lockwood, as he passed, 'your elusive Mr Quayle?'

'Stranger things have happened,' said Parker.

'Only to you,' she replied. 'Goodbye.'

The door was closed in his face, and two security men were waiting to escort him back to the lobby. The first looked like he'd been on the receiving end of too many beatings, and the other looked like the one who'd inflicted most of them. Both had a good line in surliness. No one even glanced in his direction as he left, but he waved to the camera overlooking the main door.

After all, it seemed polite.

X

I kill where I please because it is all mine.
There is no sophistry in my body:
My manners are tearing off heads –

Ted Hughes, 'Hawk Roosting'

CIII

Bob Johnston packed away his legal pad and pencils, and returned his research materials to the librarian in the Manuscripts Room. With Vernay's acquisition of the volume of fairy tales as a starting point, he had been working backward, using his contacts in the trade to establish the provenance of the book. He had finally traced it to a bookstore named Antiquariat Gerhardt Falkenrath in Cologne, Germany.

The Falkenraths had been in the book business since the late eighteenth century. The founder, Uwe Falkenrath, had been careful to situate his business in Munz, on the left bank of the Rhine by Cologne's city walls. He made this decision because Munz was then under the jurisdiction of the archbishop elector of Cologne, who was relatively tolerant of the book trade, and also happened to be based in Bonn, eighteen miles away. The *Freistadt* of Cologne itself, on the other hand, was infested with clergy in the 1700s – 2,000 of them in a city of 40,000, earning Cologne the title of the 'German Rome' – and books of which they disapproved, which meant most books, were promptly put to the torch. Uwe Falkenrath had more reason than most to be wary of the church authorities, since he trafficked not only in works of an obscene or seditious nature, but also in occult volumes that, in a less enlightened age, might have resulted in Uwe being immolated on a pyre alongside his own wares.

His descendants had followed resolutely in Uwe's footsteps, growing more discreet as their literary specializations became increasingly esoteric. Antiquariat Gerhardt Falkenrath did not advertise its vendibles, and until recently its website had consisted solely of a name, an email address, and an invitation to inquire about areas of interest – 'until recently', because Antiquariat

Gerhardt Falkenrath was now no more. In what the city's eighteenth-century ecclesiastical rulers might well have regarded as a manifestation of delayed divine justice, the premises had burned down some weeks previously, turning to a blackened mass not only all its stock but also Gerhardt Falkenrath himself, who had been secured to a chair with wire before being left to incinerate with his merchandise.

From his sources, Johnston learned that Falkenrath and Cornelie Gruner had been in competition for decades – not for customers, but for particular rare books. Each had his own patrons, and rarely did a collector give business to both vendors, or not openly. This was particularly true at the higher, more arcane end of the market, where animosities and rivalries ran deep. While few of Johnston's contacts knew of the search for the Fractured Atlas, and those who did were generally unwilling even to speak of it, one collector, a wealthy Oslo salmon heir who was too young, too fanatical, or too foolish to be circumspect, had suggested to Johnston that Falkenrath's murder was a punishment for selling the Rackham book to the wrong buyer. Vernay might have been one of Falkenrath's established clients, the collector claimed, but Falkenrath should have known that more serious bidders were circling – more serious in both their finances and their intentions.

'Such as?' Johnston had asked.

'I don't know. Someone in London, I heard.'

'Heard from whom?'

'Cornelie Gruner.'

And now Gruner was also dead.

Today's work had involved more general research: an effort to reach a greater understanding of the Atlas itself through those who had sought it in the past, using Vernay and his interests as tools to unpick the locks. If Vernay's principal obsession was the Atlas, it stood to reason that the books he had ordered, and the references in his notes, were related to it.

When, in the aftermath of the Quayle killings, the FBI eventually accessed Vernay's home in Covington, Kentucky, it became immediately clear that someone had attempted to divest it of anything relevant to their inquiries, including the person of Vernay himself. (Most of his remains had yet to be discovered, although part of his jawbone had turned up by the Licking River, carried in the mouth of a hungry dog.)

Vernay's computer was missing, as were a number of his files, judging by the gaps in his office shelves. Some of these had been burned in a pile in the hallway, possibly in an effort to destroy the entire house – another example of fire being used to hide tracks in matters relating to the Atlas – but the blaze hadn't spread because insufficient accelerant had been used. The damage was still extensive, but Ross had passed details of most of what had been salvaged to Parker, who in turn had given them to Johnston. Aided by his own network, Johnston was now making more headway than the FBI had managed.

He left the library, but did not hail a cab. London passed by too quickly that way, and Johnston wanted to savor the city while he had the chance. Now that his appetite for travel had been stimulated, he had the urge to visit Paris, Rome, Barcelona, Berlin – all the great European cities, perhaps accompanied by Rosanna Bellingham, if things continued to work out between them. He had some money saved, and his own book collection was worth a low six-figure sum. He'd always intended to sell it someday, or so he'd told himself, even as it grew and grew. He loved those books, but was not sentimental about them. What mattered was that he had cherished and, in many cases, restored them. He had kept them safe, and ensured their continuance in this world. When he died, the collection would be dispersed, and he would have no control over this scattering. At least if he took care of the sale himself, he could be certain that the best items went to the right homes. Some he would keep, of course, because they were too precious to him to sell. And if he lived long enough, well, he would have new spaces on his shelves to be filled, and another treasury to assemble.

So he walked back to Soho, in the shadows of great buildings, in the shadows of history.

In the abiding shadow of Quayle.

CIV

Emily Lockwood resumed her seat, and informed her secretary that she did not wish to be disturbed. From her desk she accessed the security system, and used its cameras to monitor Parker's progress through the building. She was relieved to see him leave, and not only because of the nature of his questions. She found him unrefined.

A door opened in the wall behind her, and Pallida Mors entered the room. She stood silently behind the lawyer, watching as Parker waved to the camera before departing.

'You handled him well,' said Mors.

Lockwood did not react to the smell of Mors's breath, or the musk of her. Displaying an aversion to it angered Mors, and it was better not to do that. Unlike Sellars, Lockwood had given up wondering at the cause of the fetor. All she knew was that it was unnatural, and therefore its origins were best left unexplored.

'I would have preferred not to have handled him at all,' said Lockwood. 'I don't even understand why he bothered. He learned nothing he didn't already know, or nothing worth knowing.'

Mors kept her eyes on the screen, until Parker fell under the eye of the final external camera and was swept away by the city's tide.

'He wants us to know he's here. He's putting himself in harm's way.'

'Why would he do that?'

'He's hoping to draw us out.'

This was more than Lockwood wanted to hear. Even having Mors in the main building put the reputation of the firm at risk, which was why the woman rarely visited – and when she did, she entered and departed through the partners' door, unseen by

538

cameras or secretaries. While Lockwood maintained a pretense of knowing nothing of Mors's proclivities, she was aware of more of them than was conducive to consistently peaceful sleep. Now this man Parker was hunting Mors and Quayle, and had traced them to the firm's door. Were Mors to be seen in the vicinity of the building, the oddness of her appearance registering with some minor employee or visiting client . . .

'I don't want to know about it,' said Lockwood. 'I took a risk just notifying you of his presence, and allowing you to listen in on our conversation.'

As discreetly as she could, Lockwood removed a paper tissue from her drawer and wiped her nose. The tissue was heavily scented with eucalyptus.

'Are you ill?' Mors asked.

'A summer cold,' Lockwood lied. She reached for another tissue, in the hope that two might be more effective than one. God, the woman stank. It was even worse than Lockwood remembered.

'Allow me to help you,' said Mors.

She grasped a handful of tissues in her right hand, and jammed them hard against Lockwood's nose while gripping a handful of the lawyer's hair in her left. Lockwood had never before endured actual physical contact with Mors. Her skin was very cold and dry, like the integument of a dead reptile, and made Lockwood's lips and cheeks itch. Her fingernails were sharp, and dug into the tender tissue of Lockwood's nostrils, so that she drew in the essence of Mors with every breath, and tasted her on her tongue. She tried not to gag, but suddenly the face of Mors was close to her own, her voice whispering in her ear.

'Pay attention, bitch: you'll listen when I say, and you'll do whatever you're told. Remember where the money that built this firm came from, and the source of your own generous annual dividend, because I don't think you've even come close to earning it yet. We have an agreement, but perhaps you need to be reminded of its terms.'

Mors tossed aside the wad of tissues, but continued to grip Lockwood's head as she leaned down to kiss her, forcing the lawyer's jaws wide, her tongue invading her body, her lungs pumping great gusts of rank breath into her mouth, her teeth gnawing at lips and gums. Lockwood tried to scratch at her with her right hand, but Mors caught it easily while keeping the left pinned. Lockwood spasmed, her cheeks puffing, but Mors kept her mouth fixed, even as the lawyer began to purge her stomach of its contents. Only then did Mors step back, spitting out whatever had passed between them before wiping away the rest, while Lockwood fell to her knees and continued to retch on the carpet until only bile emerged.

'You'll need to get that cleaned,' said Mors. 'I'll be in touch soon.'

She exited the same way she had entered, leaving Lockwood alone with her regrets.

CV

Walsingham – or more accurately Little Walsingham, as two villages share the name, although Walsingham will do for our purposes – is reached by way of narrow, hedge-lined byways that are more lanes than roads. They lead to a settlement by the River Stiffkey that is still dotted with timber-framed medieval buildings, as well as the Georgian pubs and houses of a later era, all surrounding the Common Place, the square at the heart of the community. The village's prettiness alone would make it distinctive, but it is rendered more unusual still by various stores selling religious trinkets: statuary, candlesticks, and ornate thuribles; icons, plates, and images of the Virgin Mary. Such idolatry speaks less of a village in a predominantly Protestant England and more of a bastion of European Catholicism. The clue lies in the names above the windows – Pilgrim Shop, The Shrine Shop – for this was once the holiest site in England, a place of pilgrimage to rank with Jerusalem itself.

The manner in which this came about is peculiar, even by the standards of certain strains of religious devotion. It seems that, in 1061, Richeldis de Faverches, a wealthy noblewoman, had a vision in which she was transported to the home of the Virgin Mary in Nazareth, ordered to take note of its dimensions, and construct a replica in a specific location in Walsingham, which she duly did. Unfortunately, the house was built on the wrong site, but by divine intervention was moved overnight to the correct one. As word of this miracle spread, people began journeying to Walsingham to view what was literally a Holy House, and by the middle of the twelfth century the Augustinians had erected the Priory of the Annunciation of the Blessed Virgin Mary. The fourteenth century saw the construction of a church around

Richeldis's original structure in order to protect it both from the elements and the attentions of increasing numbers of pilgrims; but the Reformation led to the destruction of the Holy House and the priory, and these days it is to the Slipper Chapel, a mile from the town, that Catholic pilgrims come, walking barefoot from the village along what is known as the Holy Mile. Ruins are now all that remain of the priory, dominated by a single vast wall enclosing the east window.

And so the priory endures.

All quiet here, the streets and lanes empty, the leaves on the branches barely astir. All quiet at the Slipper Chapel, all quiet in the village. Later, people will remark upon it: how their dogs and cats seemed reluctant to venture beyond the door that day; how those animals already outside began to seek shelter, the cattle gathering in herds under trees, as though fearful of a storm; how Walsingham, unknowing, held its breath in anticipation of a moment of revelation.

The sun was low as Bobby Coppinger set up his camera to frame the east window, a copse of trees behind it marking the site of the Well Garden. He was standing close to the former location of the Holy House, a spot he had chosen quite deliberately in order to make the connection between what was gone and what remained. He had always been a spiritual man, if not a regular churchgoer, although more so since the death of his only daughter, Bernice, a year earlier. Her passing – an embolism while traveling to work, sitting on a bus surrounded by strangers – had driven a wedge between Coppinger and his wife, or perhaps widened a pre-existing fracture in their relationship. They now seldom spoke, and when they did, it was only about mundane matters, so that each mourned alone. Their estrangement was made worse by the fact that Bobby had taken early retirement just a few months before Bernice's death. Enforced proximity was rendering the marital situation increasingly intolerable.

Coppinger couldn't say why he had begun taking pictures of ecclesiastical ruins. He'd long held an interest in photography, and had owned a succession of moderately decent cameras over the years, but had never devoted himself to a single subject before. He was lately finding a beauty in absence, a grandeur in decay, but he was also experiencing a renewal of his childhood Catholicism. Curiously, he felt closer to God amid ruination, and no intact church, however magnificent, imbued him with the sense of peace and sanctity he found in gazing upon the vestiges of older constructions. (This was another reason for his alienation from his wife: she could not understand why he continued to turn to God after He had taken their daughter from them, and he could not explain it to her, except to say that, without his faith, he would have nothing.)

Even though he had spent most of his adult life in Norwich, barely an hour to the south, this was Coppinger's first visit to Walsingham; and while he was familiar with the east window from pictures, he had been taken aback by the physical reality. The ruin appeared to him less a window than a gateway, a great open door framed by turrets, a physical symbol of the journey from this world to the next. And yet, from another angle, it resembled a mouth, the jagged remnants of the window frames like tiny sharp teeth, a machine for the consumption of lives and souls.

Coppinger peered through the viewfinder, ready at last to take his first shot. He was using a twenty-year-old Nikon because he had no truck with digital cameras, not for this work. The pleasure for him lay not only in preparing, judging, and photographing, but also in the process of developing the final image. He had installed blackout blinds in his shed, which functioned as his darkroom as well as his den. He loved the moment when the image began to appear on the photographic paper, blankness turning to shades of black and gray, what was hidden slowly becoming observable.

His finger was about to press the button when a smudge appeared on the lens, just at ground level between the two turrets. An insect of some kind, Coppinger thought, and flicked a hand at it while remaining crouched, but the obstruction did not disappear. Dirt, then; he took a brush and cloth from his bag and examined the lens, but could see no mark. Still, he cleaned it carefully before resuming his position.

The stain remained, but its shape had altered. It now bore the lineaments of a human being: a young woman wearing a short coat or dress, her features obscured by the sun – her every facet, in fact, seeming more shadow than substance. Somehow, she had wandered into the frame without his noticing, and now stood at the entrance to the Well Garden. While it wasn't as though he had some exclusive license to photograph the priory, and a person could walk where she pleased, Coppinger did want to get at least one or two good shots before the light began to fade. He took his eye from the viewfinder, the first polite word already forming on his lips –

The girl was gone. The window was empty. He was once again alone among the ruins.

Yet when he returned to the viewfinder, she was there. Not a girl, exactly, but the semblance of one, her profile indistinct like a silhouette imperfectly cut from dark paper, or a drawing that has blurred at the edges as the ink begins to spread. But when he looked directly at the window, he could see no one.

Coppinger had no explanation for what was occurring. He did not believe in ghosts, and trusted only that he would be reunited with his daughter in another life, not this one. What he did next was, in a way, entirely logical, while simultaneously making no sense at all. He removed the camera from its tripod, held it before his face with the ruin framed in the viewfinder, and started walking forward. The image of the girl remained visible to him, although it did not grow any clearer, and he still could not discern her features.

In a story, he thought, this would be Bernice, come to visit him a final time, letting him know that he was right to have hope. But the part of him that had held her and loved her in life, and continued to cherish her memory, knew that this was not his daughter. It was not even some last remnant of her conjured from his memories. It was entirely another.

As he drew closer, Coppinger experienced a growing disquiet, one he could not attribute solely to the apparent presence of a specter in his camera lens. Rather, it was the apprehension one feels upon walking too close to rocks that the tide threatens to engulf at any moment. His hearing became less distinct, and he endured a chill both sudden and painful in his fingertips, his ears, and at the end of his nose. He felt a weight encompass him, and the world grew dark, until all he could see was the image in the viewfinder. Still, he did not turn back. The girl was calling to him: not with words, but with pain. It was her cold he felt, her compression, her darkness. She was not his daughter, but she was someone's daughter. She was a child in trouble, and Coppinger would have been less of a father to his own child, however lost to him she might be, were he to turn away from the sufferings of another.

At last he stood in the shadow of the east window. He lowered his camera. The stonework no longer framed trees and hills, but was instead filled with stars. One by one they died as he watched, some flickering to nothingness, others flowering in incendiary bursts before vanishing forever. As the stars went out, Coppinger detected movement in the void, as though a path were being cleared of light so that something monstrous could advance unrevealed until the final moment – monstrous, yet beautiful; this, too, he sensed. He could look upon it, if he chose. All he had to do was wait.

And against the last stars in the universe, the girl stood silhouetted.

close your eyes

Even in his fear, Coppinger did as she asked. He closed his eyes, and waited for the encroaching darkness to smother his own light, but it did not. The chill left his fingers, the pressure upon him eased, and when he opened his eyes he was just a man alone in a field, standing before all that was left of an old priory.

But no, not entirely alone: in the remains of the Well Garden, he thought he could still see the shape of the girl, although he could not be certain that it was not just the dappled play of light and shade, because a fresh breeze had arisen to caress the branches. He stepped through the arch without thinking, and was relieved to find himself safely on the other side, not drifting through a vacuum in the face of an encroaching tenebrosity.

He reached the garden. The girl was both present and gone.

Absent the shadow of her, but the body extant, or some vestige of it. Coppinger stood by one of the smaller wells that gave the garden its name. Its iron cover was secured with loops of green wire, but moved easily with a nudge of his foot. Coppinger squatted, and peered at the water below. He could see by the marks on the wall that the level had fallen recently. Thin, blond strands of weed floated on the surface, a pale presence suspended beneath them.

The body of Kathy Hicks had been revealed at last.

CVI

Quayle and Mors sat in the former's chambers, those nebulous regions that had not been graced by natural light for so long. Quayle was picking at the carcass of a roast chicken, brought to him by Mors. He was using only his fingers, and grease gleamed upon them in the candlelight. Beside his plate stood a bottle of Meursault, and a half-filled glass.

'So, Parker is here at last,' said Quayle. 'It's almost a relief.'

'He will not have come alone.'

'No, I don't believe so.' Quayle now knew of Bob Johnston's connection to Maine, but he doubted that Parker had arrived in London accompanied only by a book dealer. There would be others.

'Did Parker, or one of his people, execute Gruner in Amsterdam?' asked Mors.

'I doubt it. They may be killers, but not of unarmed booksellers.'

Mors looked puzzled. 'Then who did? Perhaps someone who wanted to prevent Gruner from telling tales?'

'But that would be us, and unless I'm gravely in error, we didn't murder him. No, Gruner was silenced not to stop him from helping Parker, but to stop him from helping us. It was an effort to avert the restoration of the Atlas.'

The Backers, thought Mors, *seeking to protect themselves. Why spend generations amassing wealth and power, only to see it vanish with the Atlas's completion?*

'What will you do?' she asked.

'Nothing. The Backers can't prevent what's coming. They can't even delay it. Killing Gruner was like the crazed sting of a dying wasp.'

And even if Quayle were wrong, Mors would take care of the

Backers in her own time, and her own way. She especially liked the idea of anatomizing the Principal Backer limb by limb, organ by organ.

'Parker is the main threat,' said Quayle. 'Without him, the others will falter. But—'

Mors waited. She thought she could hear the muffled cries of a man from deep in the heart of Quayle's refuge, as of one immured there. She had never seen what lay behind these walls, but Quayle had told her of it in some of their more intimate moments together. She wished she could witness it just once, those men and women trapped like flies, sequestered from time and space, from living and dying.

'We should probably kill them all,' Quayle concluded.

Mors was pleased. She owed the Negro for the gunshot wound she had suffered in Maine. She would pay him back for it, with interest.

'When?'

'Very soon. Let me think on it.'

'Lockwood is worried,' said Mors. 'She's afraid Parker will return.'

'Why?'

'Because he was curious about this place.'

She spread her arms to indicate the rooms in which they stood, insulated by old brick walls, protected by a thick sheet of glass, and lodged in the courtyard of Lockwood, Dodson & Fogg.

Quayle, hiding in plain sight.

'Then perhaps,' he said, 'we should invite him to visit.'

Douglas Hood returned from the moors with Jess at his heels. The previous night, he'd enjoyed his first peaceful rest since the discovery of Romana Moon's body. He had slept through without dreaming or waking, and even the morning light on the land appeared different to him when he rose, as though he were seeing the moors anew. At lunchtime, he met with three other landowners at the Dipton Mill Inn, and over a plowman's lunch, followed by syrup sponge and custard as a treat, an agreement was reached that the time had come to rid the moors of the last vestiges of the Familists. The memory of them had blighted the land for long enough. After the deliberations had concluded, Hood bought some shrubs to bring color and life back to his garden: cape figwort for the western wall, and hibiscus, hydrangea, and Michaelmas daisies. He'd plant them over the next day or two, and they'd flower between now and October.

Hood turned on the light in the kitchen, and set the kettle to boil. Beside him, Jess growled. Her hackles were raised as she stared into the living room. She barked once, and a man's voice spoke.

'Leave the dog outside if you don't want it killed.'

He was standing by the stairs, where he could clearly see both Hood and Jess. Hood did not recognize him. He held a pistol in his right hand, less like a handgun than the kind of weapon vets used to tranquilize animals.

'Who are you?'

'My name is Sellars.'

'What do you want?'

'First, the dog. I won't warn you again.'

Hood grabbed Jess by the collar and dragged her to the door. As he opened it, Sellars said, 'Don't try to run. It won't do you any good.'

'I won't,' said Hood, and he didn't. He put Jess into the yard, and closed the door. Instantly, she commenced scratching at the wood.

'Come here,' said Sellars. 'Take a seat.'

Hood entered the living room, and sat on the harder of the two chairs by the fire, facing the intruder. He wondered how the man had reached the farm, because he had seen no sign of a vehicle nearby. Perhaps he had walked all the way from the road, but why?

'I saw you on the news,' said Sellars. 'You were the one that found the girl.'

Hood hadn't spoken to the reporters and the TV people, but they'd filmed him nonetheless, even if it was only to capture him declining to comment before walking away. He'd watched himself on the screen, and thought he looked older and odder than he really was.

'Yes,' he said, 'I found her.'

'I probably should have taken care of her myself,' said Sellars. 'If I had, none of this would have happened. I wouldn't be here, and you'd still be safe.'

As the sum of his years increased, Hood had sometimes considered how he might die. He hoped it would be out here, in sight of his beloved moors, perhaps on the very land itself. He'd always feared cancer, or dementia, the kind of death that stole away body or mind, piece by piece. He would start to weaken, and a doctor would come, or some do-gooder from social services, to declare him incapable of looking after himself any longer. He would be consigned to a hospice or care home, without the company of Jess, or whatever dog might follow in her stead should he live so long.

Now he realized that this speculation was about to become reality, and he was to be granted his wish: he would die in his home on the moors. It was like one of those old folk tales, the kind in which a man makes a deal with the devil and gets what he wants in return, but not how he might have wished it to be. The devil twists the bargain, because that's what the devil does.

The Pattersons, his nearest neighbors, would take in Jess, he knew. She wouldn't be destroyed. That was some consolation.

A hissing came from the stove.

'Kettle's boiling over,' he said.

'Let it.'

Hood could hear Jess whining, and the scratching at the door grew more urgent. Hood willed her to run away. She wasn't the kind to attack someone, although he had no doubt that she would have done so had he been under threat, but he didn't want this Sellars to reconsider, and shoot her out of fear. Jess was a good dog. They'd all been good dogs, every one.

'They're saying on the television that a man named Holmby killed Romana Moon,' said Hood.

'He did.'

'On your orders?'

'I don't give orders. I only encouraged him.'

'Is that what you do: "encourage" other men to murder women?'

'He was the first, but I've cut a few throats myself in my time, and I'll probably cut more before I'm done with this life. Maybe I'll cut yours. I've never done a bloke before.'

'Not even Karl Holmby?'

'Not even him. That was someone else. You're lucky you'll never meet her. She's a bad one. She has a soft spot for animals, though. Doesn't like to see them hurt. Call it a sentimental streak. That's why your dog will live.'

Hood looked around him, taking in his home for the last time. He'd been born under this roof, an only child, and it was proper that the same spot should mark both his beginning and his end, but still he was frightened, and sad, and strangely weary. The latter emotion surprised him, being almost narcotic in its profundity. He had always been stubborn, and a fighter in his way, but if he tried to fight now, he'd be shot. He was going to die anyway, admittedly, but if he stayed where he was, he might at least find out why.

'You still haven't told me what you want,' he said.

'I want to know,' said Sellars, 'who killed my god.'

CVII

Priestman wrapped up the late briefing just as it was growing dark. The meeting, which included representatives of the other forces involved in the investigation, had been long: two hours of analysis and discussion of forensic reports, interview transcripts, statements, photographs, and video footage from each of the jurisdictions. The rapidity with which they were accumulating information was both heartening and daunting. Under ordinary circumstances, questions would have been raised about forces burning through their budgets in order to get faster results, but the Home Office had made it clear that any exceptional expenses incurred in this inquiry would be covered, and without caviling about overtime, manpower, or the use of multiple private laboratories.

And the investigators were making headway: in addition to the fractured ankle, Gary Holmby's height corresponded to that of Romana Moon's killer, based on the angle of the wounds, and his prints were the only ones on the knife. But Gary Holmby was now dead. If he had killed Romana Moon, someone had either avenged her death, or was clearing up loose ends.

Already, the 'Misbaha Murders', as the tabloid press was referring to them, had resulted in a first retaliatory killing: a Muslim named Zahid Sulemani, beaten to death in Newport, Wales by a gang of youths, the youngest of whom was only thirteen. Zahid himself was just seventeen. The reports of Muslims coming together to protect their communities, and clashing with bands of white males, were becoming almost routine. The revelation that the knife used to kill Romana Moon had been found in the apartment of Gary Holmby, a white Anglo-Saxon, had done little to stem the violence, with right-wing extremists accusing the police of fabricating evidence in order to protect Muslims and hide the truth. The confirmation that his fingerprints were those on the murder weapon wouldn't do much to change their minds.

But Gary Holmby, Gary Holmby . . .

The deeper they dug, the clearer it became that he could not have been working alone. His phone might have been missing, but the police had obtained details of his movements from Google through location tracking, and from the phone company through triangulation. Gary Holmby had clearly loved his iPhone, because he kept it with him constantly, but Google showed the phone in the apartment block on the night Romana Moon was killed. Holmby, they decided, had probably left it there deliberately so as not to be tracked, or even as part of the creation of an alibi.

But the tracking and triangulation, combined with witness statements, also revealed that Gary Holmby had been nowhere near Bury when Eleanor Hegarty was abducted; nor had he visited the Wittenham Clumps during the period in which she had probably been interred; and they had already established that he was on the Continent when Helen Wylie vanished, and in Glasgow when Kathy Hicks disappeared from Bristol, at the other end of the United Kingdom. They had him in the center of Middlesbrough in the weeks before Romana Moon died, though, which was something, although a check of the tracking on her phone did not show her and Holmby in close proximity on any occasion during that time.

Which meant that Gary Holmby was the prime suspect for Romana Moon's murder, but not for any of the others. If that was the case, he had been in collusion with at least one other person, each of them marking kills with a *misbaha*. It was now a question of establishing the points of contact between Holmby and this unknown other, but Holmby's emails were all on his laptop, leaving them only with his Gmail account, which he appeared to use solely for mundane communications. They were working their way through the messages, but if Holmby had been using Gmail to stay in touch with another killer, he had hidden it well.

Similarly, they were checking the call and text records for his phone, but if he had been wise enough to leave it at home when he killed Moon, he would not have used it to call an accomplice. The likelihood was that he had another phone, a cheap burner. Romana Moon's phone records revealed a number of calls made to someone identified only as 'Matt' on her contacts list. Matt had been added just a few weeks before she died, and the number corresponded to a Lycamobile SIM card bought in Durham shortly before the contact began. Durham was just over twenty miles from Newcastle, and Gary Holmby's tracking showed that he had been in Durham on the day the SIM was purchased, even if the new SIM had not been activated until three days later, which was also when Romana Moon's calls to Matt had begun. Confirmation was received from Lycamobile that the Matt number had only ever been used to call Romana Moon's phone, and the only calls received by it had come from her.

They had also ruled out the Moon family as suspects in the Holmby murders. The Moons had seemed an unlikely prospect to begin with. Kevin Moon had been at home in Scotland when the Holmbys were being killed, but was perfectly willing to share his movements with police, along with details of all calls made since the death of his daughter. He even admitted to knowing some rough lads in the building trade, but not the kind rough enough to shoot one man before lodging his brother's corpse in a tree.

Despite the absence of any signs of religious belief in Gary Holmby's life, let alone Muslim radicalization, the *misbaha* angle still could not entirely be ignored, and officers were continuing to interview known radicals about their activities, as well as those inside and outside the Muslim community with an interest in monitoring such individuals. Unbeknownst to his superiors, Nabih Uddin had even met privately with a man calling himself Abdul Hasib, 'Slave of the Reckoner', who was the subject of enough Counter Terrorist Command warning notices to wallpaper a house. Abdul Hasib had been a bad Durham boy in his youth – drinking, pot-smoking, and womanizing – before deciding that what God really wanted him to do was watch beheading videos, and brainwash young British extremists into fighting in Syria and

Afghanistan. He was also suspected of involvement in a plot to explode a fertilizer bomb near Birmingham's Bull Ring.

Abdul Hasib knew every Muslim hatemonger north of London, mainly because he liked to keep an eye on the competition, and informed Uddin that none of them was putting *misbahas* in murdered white women, because, he said, that would be *fusuq* – perversity, or evil doing – although he was referring only to the misuse of the *misbaha*, and not to the killings themselves, with which he had no particular problem, being quite content to reap the benefits in the form of increased hostilities between Muslims and unbelievers, and a consequent upsurge in recruits. In that way, Uddin thought Abdul Hasib had more in common with Harry Stoller than either would have cared to admit.

This, then, was the current state of play: Northumbria Police working on Romana Moon, and the Holmbys; Avon & Somerset searching for the body of Kathy Hicks; Kent continuing to investigate Helen Wylie's death; and Thames Valley tackling the killing of Eleanor Hegarty, whose movements in the days before her disappearance Greater Manchester Police were also helping to map, while also investigating her activities as a prostitute. Hegarty had been using a cheap burner phone for this darker corner of her life, and an Android for the rest. The police had the numbers for both – the burner from her online advertising, and the Android from her pay-as-you-go receipts – but not the phones themselves, and were currently trying to trace the callers to both, but mainly to the burner. Unfortunately, half of them had come from over-the-counter SIMs, and therefore unregistered numbers. Of the remaining callers contacted so far, all had alibis for the night of Eleanor's disappearance.

The Misbaha Murders, therefore, were directly tying up resources in at least five police forces around the country, and indirectly affecting every one of the forty other territorial police areas in the United Kingdom because of associated violence and unrest. If, as Hynes had said, the police were being manipulated, it was with an unprecedented level of success.

When the meeting concluded, Hynes took Gackowska for a drink. Priestman declined to join them, but this wasn't unusual, and they didn't hold it against her. Hynes and Gackowska knocked some ideas around, but none amounted to much. Both of them wanted a break from it all anyway, so Hynes listened sympathetically to various tales of woe from Gackowska's love life, and thought, not for the first time, that if he hadn't been happily married to Charlotte, he and Gackowska might have made a good match, despite the difference in their ages, until he remembered that marriages between police generally ended up in the divorce courts. Actually, marriages between police and just about anyone often ended up in the divorce courts. Still, one had to persevere.

They were just leaving when Hynes's phone rang: Priestman.

'I don't want to take it,' he told Gackowska.

'It might be good news.'

'And it might be Father Christmas, calling about that train set he forgot to bring when I was seven.'

'Oh, how lovely,' said Gackowska. 'I hope that's it.'

Hynes answered the phone, listened, thanked Priestman, and hung up.

'They've found Kathy Hicks,' he said.

CVIII

The call came through to Parker's hotel room just as he was emerging from the shower. He didn't recognize the number, but the area code indicated that the call was coming from London. When he picked up, a woman's voice asked him to hold for Emily Lockwood.

'I've decided to allow you to view the Old Firm,' said Lockwood, when she came on the line. Her voice sounded hoarse, as though she'd recently endured a coughing fit.

'Can I ask what caused your change of heart?'

'It's nothing to do with my heart,' she said. 'If I don't let you see it, you'll think we're hiding something. If I allow you to examine the building for yourself, your suspicions can be laid to rest, and you will, with luck, go about your business and find other people to bother.'

'That's usually how it works,' said Parker. 'Persistence, persistence, persistence. When can we do this?'

'We can have someone show you around tomorrow. How about two o'clock?'

'Two is fine. I appreciate your help.'

'Unwillingly given. Tell me something, Mr Parker: is it true that you've been shot?'

'Yes.'

'How often?'

'Twice, allowing for multiple injuries the second time.'

'Only twice?' she said, and hung up.

Everyone, Parker reflected, was a comedian.

The body of Kathy Hicks had been weighed down with stones from the walls of the Well Garden, including three or four placed

557

in a sack and tied around her waist. Her throat had been cut, but the *misbaha* was missing, at least at first. It was subsequently found in the mud at the bottom of the well, probably having become dislodged from her mouth when the body was dropped in the water.

It had been one of the more challenging killings for Sellars. The ruins of the priory stood at the edge of Walsingham, but close to the Common Place. The estate of which they were a part was hidden from view by buildings and high walls, but the main gate was always locked, and visitors entered via a door at the Common Place. Sellars had been forced to half carry the drugged girl down to the river bank opposite the wall of the estate, and enter from under the bridge. Mors had dropped them off, and waited nearby while Sellars took care of Hicks. He'd scouted out the ground the previous week, and thought that dumping the body in one of the wells might save him the trouble, and risk, of digging a grave. He hadn't reckoned on the water level falling, or the keen eyesight of some amateur photographer.

Leaving the site, flecks of Kathy Hicks's blood on his hands, Sellars had glanced back at ruins.

And the east window of the priory had been filled with unfamiliar stars.

Quayle was preparing to leave the Old Firm for the last time. A calfskin case stood open on his bed, containing all he would need for the coming days and weeks – for the rest of his life, in fact. Soon he would depart this place, and shortly thereafter he would sleep without dreaming, never to wake again. The end was close. The Pale Child had told him so.

Behind the walls, John Soter was screaming.

Mors took the call from Sellars. Dispensing with a greeting, Sellars said, 'Did you know Parker was here, in England?'

Sellars had remained in touch with the last of the Familists after the destruction of the church at Prosperous, and the accompanying extirpation of the spirit that dwelt within and beneath the old kirk. They told him what they suspected: that the devastation was revenge for their abortive attempt to kill Parker, and the consequences for the town – fire, death, and the abandonment of land and homes by families that had lived there for generations – confirmed that nothing of their god had survived. Sellars had urged them to try again, but they demurred. The church was gone, half of Prosperous lay in ruins, and even if this incarnation of their god were somehow to be reborn, its maturation would come too late. Generations would live out their lives, and centuries would pass, before the god's roots began to spread once more. What good was that to them?

But Sellars had faith. He still believed. The Green Man had spoken to him, and made him its apostle. The original seed of it lay dormant beneath the Hexhamshire Moors. It needed only a little moisture.

A little life.

So he had directed Holmby to give Romana Moon to it. He believed in the Not-Gods, but he venerated the Green Man. As the blood left Romana Moon, it had passed into the seed of the deity beneath the ground, and woken it from its slumber. Within hours, Sellars had seen in his dreams the first shoots emerging, and heard the song of rebirth.

And then Parker had come. The farmer, Hood, told Sellars of what the detective had done: an old cross buried in the ground, and after that the descent of the rain, hiding all traces of disturbance. Hood claimed not to have seen the actual committal of the cross. He turned away, he said, in case someone like Sellars should follow, seeking to undo what Parker had achieved. Sellars didn't believe Hood, but it was of no consequence. The god was dead. Had Parker been present in the farmhouse at that moment, Sellars would have torn him apart with his bare hands. In Parker's absence, Sellars had to be content with Hood. He'd tried to make it last, but his rage was too great. At least Hood's pain had been commensurate with it, however briefly.

But now Sellars wanted Parker.

'We knew only that he would come eventually,' Mors told him. 'We could not say when.'

'That wasn't what I asked.'

'He has only lately shown himself in London.'

'He has been to the moor,' said Sellars. 'He has killed my god.'

Sellars's voice caught in grief. Who knew how much DNA he'd left at Hood's cottage, along with footprints in the dirt, and tire tracks in the mud? The police would soon be looking for him, but he didn't care. He'd take his own life before they got to him, but only after he'd avenged his god.

'What do you want me to do?' said Mors.

'Help me to find Parker. Help me to kill him.'

And Mors saw the circle begin to close.

XI

Lo! thy dread Empire, Chaos! is restor'd;
Light dies before thy uncreating word:
Thy hand, great Anarch! lets the curtain fall;
And universal Darkness buries All.

Alexander Pope, 'The Dunciad'

CIX

Parker, Angel, Louis, and Bob Johnston met for dinner at Hawksmoor in Spitalfields. As requested, they were shown to a booth, and left Louis to order the wine.

'An apt choice,' said Johnston to Louis, who had decided on the venue. 'A steakhouse named after a noted architect and occultist.'

Louis stared hard at Johnston.

'I picked this place,' he said, once he'd determined that Johnston wasn't kidding, 'because I heard the steaks were good. You start using a crystal ball to make dinner reservations, and you'll be eating alone.'

From Johnston, Parker had received a history lesson on Nicholas Hawksmoor while walking to the restaurant. Born in 1661, Hawksmoor's fame was based on the six churches he had designed for the city of London as part of the Fifty New Churches Act of 1711, along with two others built in collaboration with another surveyor, John James. Hawksmoor's architectural creations were curious, involving pyramids and obelisks, as well as a sacred geometry derived from the Old Testament Book of Numbers which lent very particular alignments to these places of worship. St Mary Woolnoth, one of Hawksmoor's churches, stood 2,000 cubits from another of his designs, the masterpiece of Christ Church, Spitalfields, which in turn lay 2,000 cubits from Wellclose Square, long a hotbed of occultism.

Two thousand cubits, Johnston explained, or about two-thirds of a mile, was the distance from the Mount of Olives to Jerusalem, and the furthest a Jew was permitted to walk on the Sabbath. The rebuilding of London after the Great Fire, masterminded by another occultist architect, Christopher Wren, was based on this measurement, and Hawksmoor, who clerked for Wren, worked from it in turn. According to some observers, the disposition of Hawksmoor's churches could, if examined correctly, be seen as points on triangles and pentacles mapped over the city of London, like power generators on a great occult grid.

All of which would have been of only passing interest to Parker, had Johnston not added: 'In his youth, Hawksmoor trained as a clerk with a Justice Mellust in Yorkshire. I found only one reference to Mellust, in a history of the London rare book trade. In 1673, Mellust was sued in the Court of Chancery for the return of a copy of the *Disquisitionum magicarum libri sex*, a sixteenth-century treatise on magic written by a Jesuit scholar named Martin del Río, which Mellust was alleged to have obtained under false pretenses from the estate of a Yorkshire wool merchant named Paxton. The copy of the *Disquisitionum* was del Río's own, from the Jesuit college at Leuven in the Low Countries, and annotated in his hand, including a lengthy essay on the Fractured Atlas, possibly intended for a later edition.

'The litigant was Geoffrey Paxton, the son of the deceased. Paxton was almost illiterate, a dissolute and a drunk, with no interest in books of any kind. The gossip of the time suggested he had been encouraged to take the case by a wealthy collector, someone who didn't want his desire for the book to be made public, and was funded accordingly. Paxton was found dead at an inn two days after the resolution of the case in favor of the defendant, murdered for what was assumed to be the contents of his purse, although his killers took their time with him, and left him with his balls in his mouth. Guess which London law firm represented Mellust?'

'Quayle,' said Parker.

'In the form of one Creighton Quayle,' Johnston confirmed. 'Would you like the last piece of the puzzle?'

'Go on.'

'The *Disquisitionum* was the only volume Mellust bought from the Paxton collection, and there is no record of him purchasing, or even attempting to acquire, another book in his lifetime. It seems that Mellust, like Paxton, wasn't a big reader.'

'Except Mellust, unlike Paxton, didn't end up castrated.'

'Because he secured the book, even if someone else took the loss badly enough to sue him over the circumstances of its acquisition.'

'And the firm of Quayle represented Mellust in the case . . .'

'. . . because Mellust acted as a front for the firm in obtaining the *Disquisitionum*,' Johnston finished. 'Why Mellust chose to do so is another question. Perhaps some men enjoy the whiff of brimstone by association.'

Given Louis's response to his earlier comment about Hawksmoor, Johnston elected not to repeat that particular lecture at the restaurant. Everyone ordered steak, since it seemed foolish not to, and shared bread and ribs to start. Once the wine had arrived, Johnston took out his notes and updated them on the progress of his researches, which included collating, at Parker's request, media reports on the killing of Romana Moon on the Hexhamshire Moors, and the murders connected to it by the presence of *misbaha* – or, in the case of Gary and Karl Holmby, by suspicion of involvement in at least one of the killings.

'What links the body dumps are their antiquity,' said Johnston. 'They've all been places of worship – and, in some cases, sacrifice – for a long, long time.'

'But why not Fairford?' Parker asked Johnston. 'We know its church is connected to the Atlas, so why not stage a killing there?'

'I don't know,' said Johnston. 'But you haven't seen those stained-glass windows, and I have. The images on them have been intruding on my dreams. And . . .'

His face pantomimed his inner feelings, as he debated continuing.

'Go on,' said Parker. 'How much stranger can it get?'

'There is a word – *paneel*, or sometimes *panelen* in the plural – that recurs in Dutch texts related to the Atlas. It has always been translated as "panel", as in the illustrative panels of a book, usually in reference to the final page of the Atlas, the *laatste pagina*, but it also means "pane", as in a pane of glass. The original translation came from Couvret, the Huguenot who was Quayle's partner for a time, and probably died because of it.

565

Couvret is the one believed to have transported the Atlas to England, before hiding it when he realized just how dangerous it was. What if the mistranslation was part of Couvret's effort at concealment? What if *panelen* doesn't refer to paper, but glass, and Fairford is the last place? What if, in the end, everything comes down to that old church?'

'But why wouldn't others have spotted this?' asked Louis. 'Why not Quayle?'

'Because Quayle hasn't seen what Parker and I have seen,' said Johnston. 'He didn't get to glimpse the figures that haunt the pages of the Rackham book, the ones resembling images from the windows at Fairford. Perhaps he just doesn't know, or hasn't realized how significant they are.'

Johnston put his papers away, and made up for lost ground with his wine.

'I think you're right,' said Parker. He thought of Sam's phone call, one daughter passing on a message from another: *Jennifer says they're in the glass.* 'It comes down to Fairford, or it will, in the end.'

When they'd all spent too much time thinking in silence, Parker told them of his visit with Emily Lockwood, and the subsequent call offering him access to the Old Firm.

'Do you really think he might still be in there?' said Angel.

'It doesn't seem likely, but it can't hurt to take a look.'

Their steaks arrived. As Johnston cut into his – it was cooked so blue that he had to skewer it with his fork to prevent it from making a break for freedom – he said, 'That's not why you want to see it.'

Parker tasted his own steak. It was very good: maybe not New York good, but still pretty darned fine, and served with a lot less attitude. Parker had largely given up on Manhattan restaurants that made out like they were doing him a favor by taking his money.

'Really?' he said, neutrally.

'You want to go there,' said Johnston, 'because you believe the Quayle you're hunting may be the same Quayle who hired John Soter to find Lionel Maulding.' He was concentrating intently on his food, so did not look up from the plate as he continued. 'And he is.'

'That would make him kind of old,' said Angel. He was picking at his food, having ordered only the smallest of cuts. 'The AARP could use him as a poster boy for active aging.'

Johnston waved his knife in the air as he chewed, indicating that he wanted to swallow before he replied.

'Don't choke,' said Parker. 'It would spoil the evening.'

Johnston got the mouthful down.

'Not only is he that Quayle,' he said, 'but he's the same man who represented clients in the mid nineteenth century, and the eighteenth, and – since we're on a roll – probably the seventeenth and late sixteenth centuries as well.'

'And you figure this how?' said Louis. 'Through the same psychic that picks your restaurants?'

'Handwriting,' said Johnston, resolutely refusing to rise to the bait.

'What?'

Johnston took a sip of water.

'Lawyers leave a paper trail,' he said. 'It's in the nature of the profession, and solicitors like Quayle leave behind more paper than barristers. They deal with a lot of mundane business that doesn't require the involvement of courts – wills, transfers of ownership, trusts, business agreements – and copies of all those documents have to be stored somewhere.

'So, using some of Special Agent Ross's money – actually my own, but in the certain knowledge that it will be repaid from funds – I engaged a pair of impoverished English law graduates to go poking around the records of the Law Society, and the four Inns of Court, along with the National Archives, county record offices, diocesan record offices, and the Old Bailey, for criminal proceedings. They were told to look for any cases or disputes that might have involved the firm of Quayle, with a particular emphasis on matters relating to the acquisition of valuable books.

'In the end, they found less than I might have anticipated from a business that had been in existence for so long – if Quayle was using his offices to hunt for the Atlas, he did so very warily – but they still came up with a sizable sheaf of material. Most of them were uninteresting, even by the standards of legal papers. It's almost as though Quayle deliberately chose to specialize in the dullest aspects of the law – wills, administering estates, probate, property – in order to keep a low profile. But even he had to sign his name occasionally, or scribble a note.'

Johnston reached into his ever-present bag, and produced a fresh bundle of papers.

'Take a look.'

They did. Parker started out by trying to understand the contents of the documents themselves, but that made his eyes glaze over, so he stopped. Instead he took in a series of wills, property agreements, handwritten amendments to drafts, occasional letters to barristers, and signatures – many, many signatures. The earliest were ornate, in the manner of the times, and the style altered as the years progressed, but gradually a pattern became discernible. Sometimes obvious deviations occurred, as though the signatory had become aware that consistency over such long periods, and between supposedly different individuals, might invite investigation, but eventually even these fell by the wayside, probably at the start of the nineteenth century. After that, until the closure of the firm of Quayle in the 1940s, the signature appeared to be written in the hand of the same person. A graphologist might have begged to differ, and any graphoanalytical testimony either supporting or contradicting the theory wouldn't have stood up in court anyway, not without a mass of other corroborating evidence, but to the layman's eye, Atol Quayle had been signing his name, or variations upon it, for a very long time.

If Johnston expected Louis to take issue with his conclusions, he was destined to be disappointed. Speculating on an occult underpinning for Louis's choice of restaurant was one thing – he took his dining selections too seriously to leave them up to scrivening, or any other form of supernatural intervention – but Louis, through Parker, had seen too much to dismiss singularity without first giving consideration to it. He had experienced the strangeness of Quayle and Mors at close quarters, taking two bullets for his trouble. He also knew about the pages from the

Atlas, and the manner in which they had altered and distorted the book in which they were concealed.

'This doesn't change anything,' said Louis. 'We still need to find Quayle, no matter how old he is.'

'Sellars,' said Parker. 'We break him, and we get to Quayle.'

Thanks to Johnston's research efforts, aided by some of Parker's online contacts, they had secured employment records for Christopher Sellars and his wife, along with a home address, landline and cell phone numbers, and a copy of his Sellars's license. If Parker had asked Ross for help, he could probably also have obtained bank and credit card records, but for now he still preferred to keep the feds at arm's length. He'd have to contact Ross soon, though, if only to maintain some pretense of keeping him in the loop, and had already bought another SIM card for that purpose. Soon he'd have so many SIMs and burners, he'd have to start labeling them to avoid confusion.

Following Sellars, though, would entail Angel and Louis leaving London for Manchester, and might not yield any results. If Sellars was working with Quayle via Carenor, then he understood the value of caution. The confirmation they sought might only be found in his bank records, or on his phone. Perhaps Parker would have to involve Ross after all.

Their server offered them dessert, but none of them had an appetite for it. They walked together back to Soho, but first detoured to take in Hawksmoor's Christ Church. Its design was more reminiscent of a temple than a chapel, its tower as much obelisk as steeple, and its dimensions peculiarly top heavy, so that when looked upon from below, the whole structure appeared on the verge of tumbling down. It was, Parker supposed, breathtaking, yet he did not believe that the spirit of any god of love or pity had ever resided in its environs. Whatever Hawksmoor might have built it to honor, it was not any deity Parker recognized.

Just across from Christ Church, in Miller's Court, Marie Kelly – 'Black Mary' – had been found naked in her bed on the morning of November 9th, 1888, her breasts removed, and her abdomen emptied of its organs. Her uterus and kidneys were placed under her head, her intestines laid to the right of her body, her spleen to the left, and her liver lodged between her feet. Her face was so badly mutilated as to render her unidentifiable. She was assumed to be the final victim of Jack the Ripper, although there were those who dissented, pointing out that she was much younger than the previous victims, and the damage to her body bore no trace of the surgical skill associated with the other killings, none of which would have been of interest or consolation to Marie Kelly while she was being butchered in the shadow of Hawksmoor's greatest creation.

And even here, the echo of Quayle's name persisted, for Hawksmoor, in his capacity as Mellust's clerk, must have encountered his employer's attorney. Mellust, potentially a dabbler in the occult, had both served, and been served by, Creighton Quayle, an adept in those arts. Decades later, with Mellust long dead, Hawksmoor had embarked on his great project: the building of six strange churches, each informed by knowledge and fascinations that were far from Christian. Parker was sure that, if one looked hard enough, some evidence of Quayle's influence on Hawksmoor might have been discovered. For now, though, it seemed to Parker that the very air of London was infused with Quayle's essence. He was part of its hidden history.

This was his city.

Black Mary's Death Song

MAGGS: OLD MAGGSY THE BOOK SCOUT, FOREVER
haunting barrows and shelves, sniffing his way through miles of books
like a pig truffling in a forest. They all knew him, the dealers on
Charing Cross Road, and in Piccadilly. If Maggs wanted it, there must
be money in it, and if he was willing to pay even close to what they were
asking, then they'd missed a trick, because Maggs never missed any
tricks at all. He had his routines, did Maggs, and if he didn't show up
on the appointed day each week, they would wonder if he might be
ailing for something, or more likely on the scent of better pickings,
because there could be no other reasons for his absence, mortality
excepted, and Maggs was immortal. He would tell them so, if he had a
glass or two under his belt, for Maggs never drank more than a couple,
and then only small beer. Needed to keep a clear head, did Maggs.
Couldn't be too careful. Old Maggsy knew what was out there. Seen the
worst of it, he had. Seen things that would turn your hair white.

They believed him, too, for the most part, although not because of
anything to do with his hair. Admittedly Maggsy's hair *was* white,
although it didn't happen overnight, Maggs being no Marie
Antoinette. But those who knew him best could see it in his eyes when
he emerged from one brief – and, as has been established, entirely
uncharacteristic – period of seclusion. He'd changed, had Maggs. He
wasn't the same man at all, mentally or physically. Didn't need to be a
doctor to make that diagnosis.

And that was before he displayed for them his skin.

'Show them to us, Maggsy,' they'd say, when they were in their
cups. 'Show us your markings. Give us a flash of your tattoos.'

And always came the same reply.

'They're not tattoos,' said Maggs, 'not in any sense you'd understand. Wrote on me, he did. Wrote on me without even a
by-your-leave. Turned me into a book. Poisoned me.'

'Who did? Who poisoned you, Maggsy?'

They'd be sniggering, too, the more ignorant of them, the ones who didn't know Maggs as he used to be. A man entirely without imagination was Maggs. Never one for novels. Loved books, though, all books. Loved the sight and the feel and the smell of them, loved being surrounded by them, loved buying and selling them, but read only treatises on art, science, history, and philosophy. An educated man, in his way. Came from nothing – less than nothing, because the poor always enter this life with their account in deficit, and leave it in much the same way – but learned his letters, and put them to good use. With a better start, and some minor adaptations of character, he might have found a position more befitting his talents. But Maggs was what he was, and what he was not was a liar.

Which was what made the story of the markings so peculiar, because Maggsy claimed that he had discovered a book – although he couldn't recall how, exactly, seeing as he hadn't bought it, and would swear never to have laid eyes on it until he pulled it from a box of other volumes he'd acquired, each one picked and plucked by his own fair hand, but not this particular fruit – and over the course of a number of nights, this book, written in some unknown script, transferred its contents to all the other books on Maggsy's shelves. He returned one afternoon to find that every one of them had been over-written, despoiling everything he owned, and virtually reducing him to penury in the process.

But that wasn't the end, or even the worst of it, not by any means.

So sometimes, if the mood of the room was right, Maggs would display for certain eyes the markings on his body. Faded they were, with a violet tinge to them, although Maggs claimed they had never looked fresh, not even when they were first formed, but always appeared old. They covered his entire torso, line after line of them, and seemed to represent some form of language, although none that any man could read. The exception to this was one recurring set of symbols in Arabic, which a sailor with some knowledge of the region translated for Maggs as *djinni*. It was not a word that Maggs cared to hear spoken aloud, and I have to confess to being ignorant of its meaning, until the sailor told me that *djinn* were mythical beings, being something akin to demons for the Muslim.

I should stress that at this time I did not know Maggs very well.

As a bibliophile of sorts myself, when funds permitted, I was familiar with his reputation, and had indeed put some money his way in return for welcome additions to my own small collection, but we were no more than business acquaintances. But I had always found him to be a plain dealer, and while he never knowingly undervalued a book, neither did he ever set out to gouge a customer, and remained always open to negotiation, up to a point. This is important for what is to follow: you must understand and accept the fact of Maggs's honesty. Otherwise, whatever I have to share will be without meaning or value.

But let us return to the nature of the markings on Maggs's body. Like many others, I took them to be tattoos at first, despite their bearer's claims to the contrary, and could only imagine the hours that had gone into their creation, and the pain it must have caused. Yet later, as I came to comprehend him better, Maggs told me that the devices had all been added to his skin in one night, and for much of that time he had been unconscious, and therefore unaware of what was happening to him. But even then, he was disinclined to elaborate, and I could only surmise that some narcoleptic stupor had caused him to become sedated, although I still struggled to believe that any human hand could have so adorned Maggs's torso between sunset and sunrise.

It was only toward the end of his life that Maggs shared with me the truth, and it will hardly come as a surprise to learn that I was, at first, reluctant to accept it. Maggs, by his own description, had been rendered accursed. The book that found its way into his collection was more tomb than tome, but whatever was interred within it was far from dead: trapped in its pages was a *djinni*, and Maggs, in a moment of unintentional carelessness, had liberated this entity from its confinement.

I laughed when he told me this; of course I did. Who would not have laughed? This was the stuff of Burton and *The Book of the Thousand Nights and a Night*, not the conversation of rational men. It was only when Maggs mentioned that it was the bookseller and occultist Eliza Dunwidge herself who had confirmed the essence of his predicament that my laughter ceased. Eliza Dunwidge did not joke about such matters. Eliza Dunwidge did not joke about anything.

'What can I do?' Maggs asked her, but it seemed that there was nothing to be done, nothing at all, beyond suffer, and pray, although Maggs was not the praying kind.

At least he did not have long to wait.

The *djinni* came for Maggs. He woke to its touch, but by then its work was almost complete. A thing of old flesh it was, a being of discards and ruination, smelling of blood and rot, the miasma of the abattoir. Even after all those years, Maggs struggled to describe it in detail, although never did a waking hour pass for him without some recollection of that night. He spoke of a cloak of brawn, like diseased tripe, and small dark eyes set above the remnants of a sliced-off nose, such as one might have glimpsed in more primitive times, when the removal of the nasal pyramid was considered appropriate punishment for panderers and adulterers. He confessed, though, that the *djinni* was also strangely formless and indistinct, and he might have taken it for some product of his own imaginings were it not for the damage inflicted by it.

But what Maggs never had trouble bringing to mind was the nib used to mutilate him. It was itself part of the *djinni*, for one of the entity's limbs ended not in a hand but a single narrow, chitinous extremity, and this the *djinni* dipped into a wound in its own flesh in order to inscribe its message upon Maggs's skin. At this point, Maggs said, he lapsed back into merciful unconsciousness, and when he woke again the *djinni* was gone, but not before leaving him with a permanent dermal reminder of its former presence in his life.

But even these aspects of the case – the undeniable strangeness of the brandings, the involvement of Eliza Dunwidge, Maggs's deserved reputation for a kind of essential probity – would not have been sufficient to convince me of the truth of the tale were it not for one additional factor: the writing on his skin was not fixed in form. It altered. The arrangement of the words varied over time, as though some ongoing narrative were being projected onto Maggs's body, morphing as one plate was exchanged for the next, and the lamplight permitted to shine through. Maggs said that he could sometimes feel the letters moving, like insects crawling beneath his skin. I saw it for myself, or rather I witnessed the results of this constant rearrangement, having memorized one section below the collarbone at Maggs's request only to find it written anew a week later.

Maggs had not lied. He was cursed.

No, he was *doubly* cursed.

Because in the week before he died, Maggs finally told me of the murder of Mary Jane Kelly; of the woman named Dea Tacita.

And of the lawyer, Quayle.

This is what we have been leading up to. This is the story.

Of Black Mary, as they called her on the streets, all that need be known is that she was a tall girl, and buxom, but with features not yet reduced to coarseness by whoredom. Had she lived longer, she would have seen her looks fade rapidly, not helped by what Maggs described as a tendency to overindulge in cheap liquor. She lived in Miller's Court with a market porter named Barnett, with whom she shared a single room consisting of a bed, a table, and three chairs, so at least they could claim the luxury of one surplus item of furniture between them. Black Mary and Barnett had a falling-out in the days before her death, but it was not sufficient to remove him entirely from her affections, such as they were, and he continued to enjoy the run of her body until the night of her death.

And God have mercy, what a death she met.

By then, Maggs was also living in Miller's Court. He was a much younger man, this being 1888: barely nineteen, and working in Billingsgate Fish Market, which was how he had become familiar with Barnett, who was also employed there for a time, and thus with Black Mary. In fact, it was she who informed Maggs that a room had recently become vacant at Miller's Court, after its occupant was called to a pressing appointment with God, hastened on his way by the actions of an ax wielded by a rival in love. Maggs, who was one of six men sharing two beds in a tenement within sight and smell of the market, and competing for even this meager comfort with a multitude of assorted vermin, leaped at the opportunity to seek a modicum of comfort and privacy, even if it was in the worst street in London.

But Maggs was unusual in knowing his numbers and letters, and was popular among his fellow porters due to his ability to read aloud the contents of various newspapers and periodicals. He had also, thanks to an accident of fate, become aware of the value residing in certain old volumes. John McCarthy, the landlord of Miller's Court and many of the surrounding slums – as well as being a pimp and racketeer of note – was disposing of the possessions of one of his deceased tenants, among which were various books and papers, of which Maggs, in passing, helped himself to an armful. His growing love of books was out of all proportion to the size of his own library, and so he had taken to scavenging volumes where he could. Unfortunately, most of this latest crop were in Latin, and therefore beyond his ken, but he judged their bindings to be sound, and even, in some cases, remarkably fine. On a whim, he brought the cream of them to Sotheran's of Piccadilly. An hour later, once it had been established that he was no thief, Maggs emerged from the premises with more money in his pockets than he could have earned in many months of Billingsgate toil, with the promise of greater quantities to come should his keen eye chance upon similar treasures. His career as a book scout had begun.

For now, though, he was still resident at Miller's Court on Dorset Street, a thoroughfare that even the Peelers avoided, and one notorious for accommodating criminals of every sort. His newfound wealth he entrusted to the parish priest at St James's of Spanish Place, whom he knew to be honest, until such time as he could find more suitable, and less dangerous, living quarters. By night he lay awake and listened to the whores and their clients, and sometimes he would hear Black Mary sing, and would marvel that a woman so abused could still find the strength in herself to incant such melodies; or perhaps they were all that kept her sane. He did not know, and he could never bring himself to ask.

On the night of November 9th, 1888, Maggs listened to Black Mary sing 'A Violet I Plucked From Mother's Grave When A Boy'. Earlier he had brought her a piece of cod from Billingsgate, salvaged from the castoffs, and she had cooked it with some potatoes. He could have saved it for himself, but she needed it more than he, and now she was singing. He went to his window that he might hear her better, and saw a woman in the yard below, standing still as a statue. Maggs paid her no mind, because women came and went in Miller's Court at all hours of the day and night, and he took it that this one had paused merely to listen to the song. Maggs went to his bed, and the sound of Black Mary's voice lulled him to sleep.

When he woke the next morning, Black Mary lay butchered in her bed.

This is how she is remembered: as Mary Jane Kelly, and Marie Jeanette; as Ginger, and Black Mary; as an Irish whore, but with little badness to her; as an educated, lettered woman who had fallen on hard times, or an illiterate who required Barnett to read aloud to her the stories from the newspapers; and as the final victim of Jack the Ripper. Only some of these assertions can be true, but one is entirely false, and that is the final statement. I know this because Maggs told me so, and Maggs never lied.

It was Thomas Bowyer who found Black Mary's body, when he came to collect the rent for John McCarthy – to collect it, but more likely to evict Black Mary when she did not have the means to pay, for by then she was almost thirty shillings in arrears. He glimpsed the corpse through the window, and summoned the Metropolitan Police. Because of the extent of the mutilation, and the general fear of the Ripper that was prevalent at the time, Miller's Court was quickly poisoned with police: Sergeant Badham, who had helped to transport the body of Annie Chapman, the Ripper's second victim, from Hanbury Street earlier that same year; Chief Inspector Abberline of Scotland Yard, who was responsible for leading the team of detectives hunting the Ripper; the Irishman Anderson, who was an Assistant Commissioner; Edmund Reid, the famous aeronaut and head of the Criminal Investigation Division at Whitechapel; and Superintendent Thomas Arnold of H Division, who had fought in the Crimean War, and of whom it was whispered that he loved Semites more than his own kind.

Every inhabitant of Miller's Court was questioned, but Maggs, like the rest, could tell the police little. He had heard Black Mary singing shortly after midnight, and noticed a woman in the yard at about this time, but could offer nothing more.

'A woman?' said Superintendent Arnold. 'Are you sure?'

'As sure as a man can be,' said Maggs.

'Did you see her face?'

'No, for it was dark.'

'But a woman?'

'Yes, I would swear to it.'

Superintendent Arnold did not speak again, but Maggs thought he appeared troubled. Later, before he left the scene, Arnold knocked on the door of Maggs's room to confirm what had been said earlier: a woman, standing still, listening to Black Mary's death song.

Now we come to the meat of it.

Two days later, a curious incident occurred. Maggs was returning from Billingsgate to his room, a lightness to his step since he had just

577

that evening secured better lodgings nearby, Black Mary's murder having drained Miller's Court of any appeal it might previously have enjoyed as a place of residence. Maggs was stopped by McCarthy, the landlord, who said that a gentleman and lady wished to meet with him. McCarthy spoke nervously, and was politer to Maggs than was usual for such a coarse man. He led Maggs to an empty tenement room, where there waited, as promised, a couple who had no more business being in Miller's Court than the Queen herself. The man was much the older of the two, and, judging by his garb, either lawyer or undertaker. The woman was dressed entirely in gray, and remarkably beautiful, although hers was a cold beauty, as though her features were carved from ice.

The man held in his hands a book, and Maggs recognized it as one of the batch of volumes he had sold to Sotheran's. Maggs was instantly concerned: McCarthy had not objected to his salvaging of the books, but what if they had been acquired illegally by their previous owner? Ignorance was no defense in the eyes of the law should Maggs be found to have colluded, however unwittingly, in the passing of stolen goods.

The lawyer – for that was indeed what he was – introduced himself as Mr Bennett Quayle, and his companion as Miss Dea Tacita. He informed Maggs that he had recently purchased the volume in question from Sotheran's, and was curious as to how Maggs had come by it, since it was one that he had long sought. Maggs briefly explained the circumstances of the book's discovery, and the lawyer inquired if Maggs might be willing to accompany him and his companion to the tenement in question – in return for a small payment, of course. Maggs readily agreed, and guided them along Dorset Street, this supervision being necessary in order for the gentleman and lady to avoid being sullied by various forms of filth, both animate and inanimate. But when they reached their destination new tenants were already in residence, and the possessions of the previous unfortunate had long been scattered to the four winds.

The lawyer could not hide his disappointment at this news, for it emerged that the book was but one of four linked volumes, and the value of the complete set was considerable. Maggs suggested that the pair find a seat at the Barley Mow, and take a glass to keep out the cold while he made some inquiries. For the next two hours, Maggs scoured Dorset Street and its environs, questioning and searching, bribing and cajoling, until finally he returned to the Barley Mow with the three missing volumes in his possession, and presented them to the lawyer Quayle. This time, his reward was more than a year's wages at Billingsgate, and Maggs would never set foot in the market again.

At the time of his dying, he probably regretted this decision.

Quayle and the woman named Dea Tacita – who had spoken not one word since Maggs was introduced to her – accompanied Maggs back to Miller's Court, despite his willingness to hail for them a hansom cab by the Mow. The notes handed to him by Quayle felt conspicuous even in his pocket, and he was only glad that the lawyer had passed them to him unnoticed by any of the sharp eyes in the bar, or else he would very rapidly have joined Black Mary in whatever part of the next world she was currently occupying. As Maggs's wealth increased, so too had his shame at his lodgings. He was more conscious of the sights, sounds, and smells than ever before, even though it was only weeks since he had shared a verminous crib with half-a-dozen others. The presence of Quayle and the woman only increased this embarrassment.

And yet.

From the moment he first met her, Maggs had noted the disturbing state of Miss Tacita's clothing. It was filthy – perhaps not by the standards of the denizens of Miller's Court, but certainly by those of a lady, or one who aspired to the standards of such. Examined from close quarters, her gray blouse revealed itself to be stained and torn, the hem of her skirt was tattered and caked with the mire of the streets, and the insides of her cuffs were shiny with dirt. She wore perfume, but not a sufficiency of it. She smelled to Maggs like a disinterred corpse.

'I understand you were acquainted with the latest victim of the Ripper,' said Quayle, as they stood in the yard of Miller's Court, not one foot from where Maggs had seen the silent, stationary woman – a woman, he thought, of whom Miss Dea Tacita reminded him uncomfortably.

'Some say she was no victim of the Ripper,' said Maggs, and instantly regretted his words, although he could not have said why.

'And why is that?' said Quayle, before adding 'Speak,' when Maggs's reluctance to continue became too obvious to ignore.

'It's Superintendent Arnold's view, not mine.'

The Superintendent had returned to Miller's Court repeatedly since the discovery of Black Mary's body. Had he been a ghost, it might have been said that he was haunting the place. Once more he had arrived at Maggs's door, and this time had accepted the offer of a glass to warm his cockles.

'What is this view, exactly?' said Quayle.

'That the wounds to Black Mary's body were different from those found on the other women.'

'Different, how?'

'More extreme.'

'And what else?'

'That she was younger than the rest. That she was killed in her bed and not on the street.'

Close behind Maggs, Miss Dea Tacita began to hum a tune, one familiar to Maggs.

'Is that the sum total of the superintendent's suspicions?' said Quayle.

Now, I have said before that Maggs was no liar. A Catholic was Maggs, and one that went regularly to confession, a sacrament he did not take lightly. But on this occasion, he lied, and when he confessed it to the priest, and was asked for details of the nature of the lie, he declined to give them, and his penance was increased by three decades of the rosary as a consequence of his recalcitrant nature.

Because what Arnold had told Maggs, after a second glass loosened his tongue, was that he thought a woman might have killed Black Mary. According to Arnold, some said that Black Mary might once have been the mistress of a wealthy man, an individual of considerable reputation, one who had groomed her since childhood, and on whom she had turned her back upon recognizing the depths of his nature. Black Mary had hidden herself from him among the dregs of the city, becoming one with them, her tongue gradually loosening over the years, so that sometimes, when in her cups, she would speak of her 'Grand Mister'. Perhaps, Arnold opined, this gentleman had tracked her to Miller's Court, and sent someone to silence her.

Quayle repeated the question.

'I asked you,' he said, 'if that was the total of Arnold's suspicions?'

'Yes,' said Maggs, while inches from his back, so close that he could feel the heat of her breath, Miss Dea Tacita quietly sang, in a voice far poorer than Black Mary's, the song entitled 'A Violet I Plucked from Mother's Grave When A Boy'.

'Do you see that church?' said Quayle, and pointed to the spire of Christ Church, like a blade seeking to gut the heavens.

'Yes, sir.'

'Do you know who designed it?'

'Yes, sir. It is some of Nicholas Hawksmoor's work.'

'What can you tell me of him?'

'Only what I've read.'

'Which is?'

'That he was an occultist.'

'Oh,' said Quayle, 'he was much more than that. I knew him—'

He caught himself then, did the lawyer, or so Maggs thought.

'Or rather, should I say,' Quayle continued, 'I know of him. His churches are sacrificial spaces, but then are not all churches, given the nature of the oblation they commemorate?'

'I couldn't say,' Maggs replied. Miss Dea Tacita was toying with the lapel of his jacket, as though testing the quality of the material, smiling at him as she did so. She had loosened the collar of her blouse, and lamplight from a window caught her exposed, and unwashed, skin. Maggs saw the blood on it, and wondered how much more might be apparent beneath the rest of her clothing. Whoever slaughtered Black Mary must have been ensanguined in the aftermath; better to have removed as much of one's outer clothing as possible before commencing with such butchery.

'A wise man wouldn't,' said Quayle. 'Are you a wise man, Maggs?'

'I hope so, sir.'

'I hope so, too.'

Quayle handed him an envelope.

'This contains a list of books I should very much like to acquire, along with some suggestions as to the collections in which they might be found, and an advance on your expenses. I have no time to scour, and perhaps I lack the necessary talents. In you, I believe, I may have discovered an adept.'

After only a moment's hesitation, Maggs accepted the envelope, and was damned.

But had he done otherwise, he would have been dead.

He told me so, and I believed him.

All this I learned in the days before Maggs's death. By then he had become entangled beyond extraction with Eliza Dunwidge and her father, as well as with another Quayle, Atol, some descendant or distant cousin of the late Bennett Quayle, although the similarity between the two was quite remarkable, or so Maggs would sometimes remark as his life neared its conclusion, speaking in a way that suggested he was sharing less than he knew, but more than was wise.

He was a tormented man in those last days, was Maggs. He had allowed himself to be used, perhaps from that very first night in Miller's Court when he accepted the list of books from Bennett Quayle – or Atol Quayle, because sometimes Maggs used those two names interchangeably, as though they were one and the same.

But recently, Maggs confessed, he had made a terrible error. He had agreed to look for a very particular book, he said, an atlas.

No, *the* Atlas.

Was this his final mistake? It was not.

His last mistake, I suspect, was to have found it.

CX

Parker and Bob Johnston said goodnight to Angel and Louis in Soho before walking back to Hazlitt's together. Johnston was slightly drunk; not stumbling, or slurring his words, but seemingly with enough alcohol in his system to loosen his inhibitions. He spoke of his family, and his youth – he had served in the US Army, which Parker had not known – and Rosanna Bellingham, the woman who now lived in the building once occupied by the Dunwidges, a house possibly still inhabited by some trace of one of them. It seemed that Bellingham and Johnston were in contact, and had arranged to meet for dinner later the following evening.

'You're coming out of your shell,' said Parker. 'Next thing, you'll start being nice to your customers.'

Johnston let that one pass.

'I've spent too much time alone,' he said. 'Wasted years.'

He stopped suddenly, and placed a hand on Parker's arm.

'You know, I worry about you,' he said.

'Do you?'

'You're like a character in a movie, or a dime store novel – and god knows, I've read my share of them. Troubled. Solitary. In pain. But why do you choose to be companionless? I know why I did: because I was an asshole. You, though, you're not an asshole, and you shouldn't be without someone. This life passes so quickly. It's as though I woke up one morning, and I was old. Didn't matter how I felt, or even whether I looked good or bad for my age. The numbers didn't lie. I was an old guy, living alone in a bookstore, and I couldn't remember the last time I'd been touched by a woman who wasn't related to me by blood. That's just wrong.'

Johnston's hold on Parker's arm tightened, and, in that instant, he seemed to sober up.

'I know what you've been through,' he said. 'I know your wife died.'

Yes, she did, but she returned, or something of her did, something hostile and marred, just like whatever it is that waits in Rosanna Bellingham's home.

'And your daughter.'

Jennifer, who walks through moonlight to visit me, and speaks with her half-sister of worlds beyond this one.

'Still, it's not good to be so alone.'

But I'm not alone – which may, I admit, be part of the problem, because how can a man begin again when all that has gone before somehow persists? How can he endure, and not go mad, except by accepting the reality of his situation?

'I'll bear it in mind,' said Parker.

Johnston released his grip.

'What the hell do I know?' he said. 'I'm trying to date a woman who lives with ghosts.'

And Parker smiled at him.

'Don't we all?'

CXI

Parker decided to wait until a reasonable hour before calling Ross. The viewing of Christ Church, even if only its exterior, had unsettled him, its oddness skewing his perception of the city of which it was a part.

After some thought, he decided that Angel and Louis should hold off on targeting Sellars, at least until Parker had spoken with Ross. Meanwhile, Bob Johnston's tame law students had been instructed to investigate the origins of the trust established to administer the funds from the sale of the Quayle properties. Johnston was convinced that paperwork was the key to finding Quayle: somewhere, somehow, money was changing hands – Quayle could not have remained concealed for so long without it – and in the modern age, money left a trail. Johnston planned to meet the students for an early lunch later that day at the Jamaica Wine House in St Michael's Alley, a bar the book dealer had long wished to visit. The Jampot, as it was known, occupied a nineteenth-century building, but had been in existence since the middle of the seventeenth century, when it became the city's first coffee house. Anyone who could afford the penny admission could enter, drink, mingle, bargain, and gossip. In another age, and another life, Johnston admitted to Parker, he would happily have occupied a corner of a place like the Jampot.

'I think,' Johnston said, as he prepared to leave Hazlitt's for the day, 'that I was born in the wrong era.'

'Doesn't everyone feel that way, once in a while?' Parker asked.

'Maybe, but I feel that way all the time.'

They were standing together at the door of the hotel, watching London reveal itself to them. The smell of the air, the texture of the light, the faces of the natives, all were different here. Parker was experiencing it at one remove, as a visitor, yet if he stepped onto the street, and moved with its flow, no one would recognize him as a stranger, a foreign man with a foreign mind. Parker's grandfather, who had never warmed to urban life, and regarded even Portland, then a city of fewer than 60,000 souls, as a concrete jungle, once told him that all cities were the same, but he was wrong. All *great* cities were utterly distinct from one another.

Johnston hitched his satchel to his shoulder. 'Walk with me, would you? I'd like to see somewhere green.'

Parker fell into step beside him, and they strolled together to Soho Square Gardens, where they settled on a bench with a view of King Charles II's centuries-old statue.

'I kept working last night, after we got back from the restaurant,' said Johnston.

'And?'

'We know Quayle is trying to complete the Atlas. He believes that when it's finally unified, it will become the world: whatever is mapped in its pages, whatever version of the universe it represents, will become reality. But it may be that the Atlas has always been influencing this world. It's a pollutant. In a sense, it's trying to create the environment most conducive to its own needs, or the needs of whatever created the Atlas to begin with.

'Think of a fracture in a rock face, or even a whole series of fractures, being widened over time, mostly through natural processes, but maybe also by something trapped behind that's patiently chipping away. Gradually, and inevitably, one of the fractures will grow wide enough to allow that presence to escape, but the process could be accelerated by the intervention of another agency, someone assisting from the other side. Quayle is that agent. The more of the Atlas that's found, the faster the fracture widens. Find the last pages, and you blow a hole between realities.

'But Quayle's problem is that he can't entirely restore the Atlas. He thought he'd traced the last pages, however many there may be, but we found one of them first, and he doesn't know we have it, although by now he may be starting to suspect. So, he could either try to force us to hand it over – which would be dangerous, and time-consuming, and might involve returning to the United States, which he wouldn't want to do – or find another way to make the opening.

'And that's the context in which these *misbaha* killings make sense. Reading up on Hawksmoor helped me to understand: the theory that his churches are focal points, generators. They're similar to the murder sites. They're loci of power, most of them from long before the coming of any Christian god. Quayle is picking places where the barriers between worlds are thin, because they've been weakened by the potency of the belief systems that give meaning to those places. He's using blood to make up for the missing pages, and he's going to keep on killing, or convince others to do the killing for him, until he gets the result he wants.'

That couldn't go on indefinitely, Parker knew. With every victim that was uncovered, the likelihood of apprehension grew, because every corpse, every grave, left clues. The *misbahas* were designed to confuse, an added distraction in the event of bodies being found. Quayle was no fool: he had anticipated problems, and calculated the risks. He was close to achieving his goal. He was dealing with hazards, not uncertainties. How many more bodies would it take: Three? Two?

One?

'We should talk to the police,' said Johnston, 'but I doubt they'd believe a word we have to tell them. And of course, I might be completely mistaken about everything, but I don't think I am. This is the only explanation that makes sense, even if on most levels it makes no sense at all. But I saw the pages of the Atlas with my own eyes. I saw what it could do.'

'We both did,' said Parker. 'I'm going to talk to Ross. He may have some ideas on how to handle the police.'

Parker called Ross shortly before noon, which meant 7 a.m. on the East Coast. He knew that Ross was an early riser, having endured the occasional call from him at absurd hours of the morning. As usual, Ross deftly hid his delight at hearing from him. Parker thought that he could have been calling with the numbers for the following week's Powerball Jackpot, obtained through experiments in time travel, and Ross would still have sounded kind of pissed.

'Where are you?' said Ross.

'London.'

'Where in London?'

'I can't say for sure. I'm struggling to find my bearings.'

Ross took a moment to dredge for patience.

'What have you found out?'

Parker told him. It didn't amount to much, especially not when set against Ross's genetic predisposition against wild shows of enthusiasm. Ross did agree to look into Sellars's finances, and – at Parker's instigation – any payments to Sellars that might have come from Lockwood, Dodson & Fogg, or financial institutions connected to the law firm. It was a long shot, but Parker wasn't paying Ross by the hour.

'These killings,' said Ross, 'you're sure they're connected to the Atlas?'

'Bob seems to think so.'

'Bob is a bookseller, not a detective.'

'Bob is a born researcher, which makes him a good investigator.'

Parker was about to raise the issue of the British police when Ross preempted him.

'Have you had any contact with the law over there?'

'No, but the police will be aware by now that an American private investigator has been asking questions. Romana Moon's father would have informed them. I'm surprised they haven't already come knocking on my door.'

'You're hard to find.'

'Not that hard. If you don't know where I'm staying by now, you should probably find another line of work.'

'I should have found another line of work a long time ago.'

'You're stuck with it now,' said Parker. 'I think Bob is right about everything, but we don't have nearly enough to be able to convince a team of British detectives. They'll need to hear it from you as well. In the end, it doesn't matter if the Atlas exists or not. It doesn't matter if Quayle is deluded, the black sheep of his family, or someone who just liked the sound of the name. The problem never changes: what matters isn't the truth or falsity of the belief, but the consequences of it. The police will have to be made to understand that. A group of teenagers blew up buses and underground trains in this city out of some misguided religious lunacy, so it's not as though the concept will be alien.'

'Okay,' said Ross, 'when the time comes, I'll talk to them.'

'Thank you.'

'And you left a fucking mess behind in Amsterdam. Try not to do the same in London.'

'We didn't leave any mess in Amsterdam,' said Parker. 'That was someone else's work. Why don't you talk to Armitage, the legat? She was supposed to be your eyes and ears.'

'I would,' said Ross, 'if I could find her.'

CXII

Armitage was in trouble. She couldn't define precisely the kind of trouble, because she'd never experienced anything like it before, but it was definitely trouble, and she was undeniably in it.

Firstly, she was ill. Her temperature was higher than normal, and she was experiencing uncomfortable hot flushes at all hours of the day and night. She was only thirty-three, so it was unlikely that this was the sudden onset of premature menopause. Her mouth tasted bitter, which was affecting her enjoyment of food, because it altered everything that passed her lips. Her tongue was discolored, more purple than red, and if she scraped her finger across its surface, a yellowish substance accumulated under the nail. She was experiencing pinprick aches all over her body, especially when she tried to sleep. She would wake to them, as though bugs were biting her, following which the sensation would ease for a time. Gradually, she would doze off again, only for the pain to recommence.

She had stripped the sheets and taken them to the Laundromat, just in case something nasty had taken up occupancy in her bed, but it hadn't helped. Following consultations with her neighbors, who were enduring no similar difficulties, she got rid of her mattress, even though it was only a couple of years old, and engaged the services of a fumigator. She was now the proud owner of an expensive new mattress, along with box-fresh sheets and pillows, and the less proud owner of an apartment that smelled faintly of poison.

And still, she was not sleeping.

Her doctor could find nothing wrong with her. If an infestation of bugs was responsible, then the culprits were leaving no evidence on her skin beyond the scratches caused by her own nails. The doctor took samples of blood and urine to be sent off for tests, but it would be at least a week before the results came back. She was given a topical cream to use at night, tablets to help knock her out, and told to take a couple of days off work.

Armitage wasn't the kind to seek sick leave – she could have lost a leg in an accident, and would somehow have found a way to struggle to the office with a tourniquet on the stump – but the lack of sleep had left her fractious, and struggling to concentrate at work. She was making mistakes, and missing details. Her errors had already been noticed, and she had endured an awkward meeting with her superiors at which she was forced to admit to suffering from some as yet undiagnosed ailment. They were sympathetic, but she knew what they were thinking: stress. It would go in her file, and questions would be raised about her ability to function under pressure, because The Hague wasn't the most difficult of postings. If she were showing signs of laboring after just a couple of years in one of the duller European cities, how would she deal with Tel Aviv, Kabul, or even Mexico?

And, you know, maybe it *was* stress of some kind. She'd been required to dispose of Cornelie Gruner and Eva Meertens in the space of one night, and she wasn't some kind of psychopath. She'd only killed once before for the Backers, and that was before she'd even entered the Academy. Also, it had involved only the pouring of a phial of colorless liquid into a glass of vodka, and monitoring the effects once the drink was consumed, which was very different from shooting an old man in a chair, and fatally injuring a young woman before dumping her body in a canal. A place in the Academy had been her reward for that first killing, and influence was applied to ensure she ended up in the legat program, which was where the Backers wanted her, even if the reasons for this had never been explained. She hadn't even enjoyed much further contact with the Backers, rare requests for information apart, before the Principal Backer sought her help with neutralizing Gruner.

So perhaps it wasn't surprising that her body should be manifesting physical symptoms of psychological turmoil – it might have been stranger were it not – but it was still important that she recover as quickly as possible. If this meant taking it easy for a few days in the hope that the symptoms vanished of their own accord, so be it. Alternatively, the medical tests might reveal a larger issue that could then be addressed. What mattered was getting back on track, for the sake of her career and her general wellbeing, both short and long term; short in the sense of her current predicament, and long in relation to the Backers. If she couldn't be of use to them, they wouldn't aid her rise through the ranks of the bureau. She'd end up pushing papers in a backwater until she retired.

The problem with resting was that she should ideally have been doing it in her apartment, but she couldn't be at ease there. The smell of the chemicals used during the fumigation process seemed to be growing stronger rather than vanishing entirely within twenty-four hours, as she'd been assured it would, and opening windows didn't help. She couldn't settle on her chairs or her couch, and she realized that she had become frightened of her bed. Even in a narcotically induced sleep, she was suffering nightmares that remained disturbingly clear in her mind when she woke, visions in which the discarded organs on a slaughterhouse floor came together to form a hooded figure, a being composed of dead flesh. *Fucking Cornelie Gruner and his fairy tales*, she thought, *sowing bad seeds in my imagination before he died.* She'd resorted to spending hours in coffee shops watching crap on her iPad until it grew late enough for her to return home and swallow a pill, only crawling into bed once the drug began to take effect.

Her apartment was at the top of a quiet building in The Hague. She could have chosen to live in Amsterdam, since it suited the embassy to have some staff with quarters elsewhere in the Netherlands, but she preferred The Hague, and not only because it was the center of political activity, and the second city of the United Nations. Amsterdam struck her as a teenage town, too quick to chase easy fixes, while The Hague was more adult, more relaxed.

She was just finishing a coffee at Restaurant Deluca in De Passage when her private cell phone rang: the Principal Backer.

She had been avoiding him. If her sickness was stress-induced, then he was responsible, but there was nothing she could do for him in her present condition. She'd messaged him to explain that she was ill, and would be taking a few days off to recover. His persistence irritated her, yet if she continued to ignore him it would cause problems down the line, so she decided to answer the call.

'Yes?' she said.

'Am I disturbing you?'

'I was having coffee.'

'Because you sound annoyed.'

'Not annoyed: tired, and unwell. I left a message.'

'Which I received.'

'Good.'

'I simply wanted to check on your situation.'

'I'm getting better, I think.'

'That wasn't what I meant.'

Armitage silently swore at the phone. She should have known better.

'Tell me,' said the Principal Backer, 'have you discovered the cause of your ailment?'

'No.'

'Let's hope it passes quickly, for your sake.'

The ambiguity was so undisguised, it was all that Armitage could do not to call him on it. In the end, wisdom, and an instinct for self-preservation, prevailed.

'The police have no leads on the deaths of Gruner or Meertens,' she said instead, 'and no questions are being asked by other parties, by which I mean there's no sign of Mors or Quayle.'

'A pity. I thought he might have sent Mors to investigate.'

'And then?'

'We could have killed her.'

'Who do you mean by "we"?'

She heard the Principal Backer laugh.

'Not you, in case you're worrying. You're no match for Quayle's ice maiden, but neither are you being particularly useful by drinking coffee in expensive arcades.'

De Passage had been built in 1882. Its facades were stone, and its ceilings high-vaulted and made of glass. Armitage looked around. The arcade was busy, with any number of people talking on cell phones. None appeared to be paying her any attention, but then she was herself an agent, and knew how to monitor a subject without being spotted. Was the Principal Backer having her followed?

'How did you know where I was?'

'A lucky guess. If I were you, and seeking some escape in your city of residence, I wouldn't be drinking coffee near the Binnenhof or the Plein – too many politicians – and I wouldn't be at the Grote Markt, because it would mean adding tourists to the mix. No, I would look for solace elsewhere, and Deluca would be my choice. Am I correct?'

'Yes,' she said, but still did not know whether to believe the explanation. 'Is that all?'

'No, it's not all,' said the Principal Backer. 'Gruner is gone, but Quayle remains. If Parker can't stop him, the burden of doing so will fall back on us, and you'll have your part to play. When you return to work, we'll feed you some information that will restore you to the good graces of your superiors. In the meantime, enjoy your coffee, and I hear the Mango Scorpino is very good.'

'Wait!'

To her surprise, Armitage felt her eyes grow hot at the injustice of her treatment at the hands of the Principal Backer. She had killed for him, and this dismissal was less than she deserved.

'I found out something,' she said. 'About De Jaager, and Parker's friend, the one called Louis.'

'What is it?'

'I think Louis may have killed a Bosnian Serb named Timmerman at De Jaager's instigation. Timmerman was an enforcer for the Zemun crime syndicate. The Zemuns believe he was murdered by Muslims in revenge for atrocities Timmerman committed in the Balkans, but they're mistaken.'

'You're sure?'

'Do I have to be?'

'What are you suggesting?'

'That we tell the Zemuns about Louis.'

'To what end?'

'His death, and maybe that of his confederates, too.'

'Parker?'

'Why not?'

She could hear the Principal Backer breathing, weighing the pros and cons.

'All right, but only after the hunt for Quayle has ended. Well done. There is hope for you yet.'

He hung up. Armitage paid the check, and returned to her apartment. She detected no signs of surveillance along the way, even though she made sudden stops and reverses, and used reflective surfaces to watch those behind her. Only when she was safely behind her own door did she relax, but the feeling lasted only seconds.

Someone had been in her apartment. All her books were scattered on the floor, although everything else appeared undisturbed. She listened, and could hear no signs of movement, but remained on her guard while she checked that no intruder remained on the premises. A cursory inspection revealed that nothing had been stolen: her laptop was sitting in plain sight on the dining table, and an assortment of currencies that she kept in her bedside locker was untouched, as was her jewelry. By the time she had finished examining the scene in more detail, she had come to the conclusion that only her books had been tampered with, as though someone had been searching for a document believed to be concealed among them.

The smell in her apartment was also noticeably more pungent – less of chemicals, more of rot – and strongest nearest the books. Armitage was on the verge of calling the embassy, as any such incursion had to be reported to her superiors before the police were informed, when she noticed the damage to one of the volumes that lay open on the floor. It was *Master of the Senate*, the third part of Robert A. Caro's biography of Lyndon Johnson. The book had been vandalized by being overwritten in purple ink, in an alphabet Armitage did not recognize but a script that was almost familiar. At first, she thought the graffiti was limited to only a few pages, but as she flicked through the book, she saw that every page had been defaced. She picked up a second book, a novel, and found the same blighting of its contents. A third, a fourth: every one of her books bore similar markings, but one recurred more than any other, and seemed to be in a different alphabet that she thought might be Arabic.

الجن

And in the midst of the havoc lay a bookmark that was not her own. It was made of blue leather embossed with gold lettering, and bore the name *Antiquariaat Cornelie Gruner*. The underside was stained with dried blood.

Armitage sat against the wall, thinking, and did not move for a long time. When she finally did so, it was to return the books to the shelves, because she could not think of what else to do with them, but not before taking a picture of the Arabic word with her phone. The bookmark she cut into pieces, doused with lighter fuel, and set alight.

She did not call the embassy. She did not call the police.

And that night, she did not sleep at all.

CXIII

Priestman was staring at the printouts in disbelief, watched by Hynes and Gackowska. Hynes couldn't help but feel a hint of amusement, even amid the blood and bodies. You had to take your pleasures where you could, however small they might be.

'My god,' said Priestman, 'this man is a vigilante.'

'Or an avenging angel,' said Gackowska.

Priestman peered at her in a manner that could only have been more disapproving had it also involved rapping Gackowska across the knuckles with a ruler. Gackowska, though, wasn't easily intimidated, not even by her superiors. It was one of the many qualities Hynes admired in her. He liked to think he was partly responsible.

'Depends on how you look at it,' Gackowska added, doubling down, which caused even Hynes to bite his lip in mild apprehension.

'He's a *killer*,' said Priestman, with considerable emphasis. 'He should be in jail.'

'It's interesting that he isn't,' said Hynes, seeking to steer the conversation in a marginally less fraught direction.

'And why do you think that is?'

'Good luck?' Hynes suggested. 'Bribery?'

Priestman's eyes narrowed, which was always a bad sign. Hynes decided he'd had his fun.

'Or because it suits the higher-ups to have him roaming free,' he offered instead.

'He's not just roaming free,' said Priestman, 'he's roaming here. Do we have any idea where exactly he is?'

'None,' said Hynes. 'Yet.'

Hynes had already been in touch with the Home Office, but

the private investigator named Charlie Parker had entered the United Kingdom as a tourist, and had therefore not been required to supply evidence of the address at which he would be staying. Clearly, he was not a tourist in any meaningful sense, which raised the possibility of deportation if required, although it would be hard to prove he was actively in breach of immigration law.

'At least we know why he was interested in Romana Moon's death,' said Priestman. 'We need to talk to him.'

'In case he has anything useful to offer?'

'And to advise him that this isn't the United States, or more particularly the Wild West. Kevin Moon told you that Parker claimed to have spoken with Douglas Hood?'

'Yes.'

'Then someone should talk to Mr Hood as well, just in case Parker shared anything useful with him.'

'I tried,' said Hynes. 'Hood isn't answering his phone.'

'Mobile?'

'Home. He doesn't own a mobile.'

'I don't blame him, bastard things. If Parker did tell Hood anything useful, I'm sure he would have called us. Might still be worth sending a PC to talk to him, though, just in case. Nabih can always bring someone up to speed. What about Manchester, and Christopher Sellars?'

'We'll be on our way as soon as you've finished with us,' said Hynes.

A woman named Jan Watts had come forward to say that, a month earlier, she'd seen Gary Holmby at the Trinity Square center in Gateshead in the company of a courier named Christopher Sellars. Watts and Sellars had enjoyed a relationship some years before, when she was working in Liverpool. It ended when she discovered that Sellars was married with two young children. Watts had taken the deception badly, and left the city for a new job in Newcastle. She'd noticed a Carenor van parked at the mall, which reminded her of Sellars, and minutes later spotted him drinking coffee with another man whom she now knew to be the late Gary Holmby.

'It seems thin,' said Priestman. 'I recognize that we've been given a certain amount of latitude with our budget for this investigation, but I'm not sure it extends to funding day trips to Manchester to follow hunches.'

Hynes met her eye. Like Gackowska, he was no pushover, and sometimes you had to go with your gut.

'Respectfully, I disagree. Gary Holmby's taste in art extended to the kind of stuff that comes free when you buy a cheap frame, and he collected old computers, not Old Masters. Carenor, on the other hand, specializes in high-end art transport and storage, and when I called them, they had no record of a client named Holmby. Neither was Sellars supposed to be stopping off in Newcastle that day: the schedule had him in Edinburgh early in the morning to pick up ten small sculptures, which had to be moved to a temporary exhibition at gallery in Leeds by close of business. Admittedly, the quickest route from Edinburgh to Leeds is the A1 south, which puts him within shouting distance of Newcastle, but what's he doing coming off the motorway and entering the city? If he needed to stop for a cup of coffee and a sandwich, he could get them along the way. And even if Sellars was in Newcastle for something related to the art business, why meet up with a man who didn't appear to have any interest in art?'

'Maybe Holmby and Sellars were just friends,' said Priestman.

'How? We can find no school connection, no work ties, nothing.'

'Any signs that Holmby might have been gay, or bi? If so, he and Sellars could have hooked up online.'

'None,' said Gackowska. 'From what we know of Holmby, he went through the eligible female population of Newcastle like a dose of salts, which doesn't mean he wasn't open to experimentation, I suppose. And Sellars is married, although that doesn't mean much either, these days.'

Gackowska, Hynes thought, could be distinctly moralistic when the mood struck her. Meanwhile, Priestman was wavering, so he moved in for the kill.

'Sellars has access to trucks and vans,' said Hynes, 'and a reason for traveling around the country. There was a limit to what I was prepared to ask Carenor about his movements, particularly over the phone. So, we go over there, take a look at the driver rosters for the last month or so, and see what we can find.'

'And what if Carenor won't give you access to them?' said Priestman. 'You don't have enough for a warrant.'

'I can be persuasive,' said Hynes.

'He can,' said Gackowska. 'Sometimes even charming.'

Priestman looked from one to the other suspiciously.

'If I thought for one moment that there was something going on between you two . . .'

'Yuck,' said Gackowska.

Hynes held up his right hand. 'I'm a married man.' He scowled at Gackowska. 'But "yuck" is a bit strong.'

'Sorry, heat of the moment,' said Gackowska. 'I think I got sick in my mouth, though.'

'Have you finished?' said Priestman.

'Yes,' said Hynes.

'Yes,' said Gackowska.

'Regardless of what we get from Carenor,' said Hynes, 'we'll talk to Sellars, and try to establish the nature of his relationship with Gary Holmby. Never hurts to shake the tree.'

'Actually,' said Priestman, 'it sometimes does. That's how people get hit on the head by coconuts. Where's Sellars today?'

'Manchester,' said Hynes. 'Carenor doesn't only transport art – it would go broke if it did – so its drivers do more general courier work as well. Sellars is rostered for the local area, but only for a half-day, so he isn't due to begin making collections until after two o'clock, and probably won't be back at base until close to seven. That gives us some time to go through the paperwork, and have a conversation with his boss. If necessary, we can ask for Sellars to be called back early so we can have a chat with him.'

'Any chance he might be forewarned by someone at Carenor?'

'There's always that possibility, but I don't think it's likely,' said Gackowska. 'After a bit of to-ing and fro-ing with secretaries, I was put through to Carenor's CEO, Dylan Lynskey. I made it clear that anyone hindering us could be in a lot of trouble. Lynskey was the one who checked the schedule for the day Sellars and

Gary Holmby were seen together in Newcastle. I could be wrong, but I got the feeling that it wasn't the first time he'd fielded questions about Christopher Sellars.'

'Why?'

'He gave a sigh when he heard the name.'

'Anything on Sellars from CRO?'

The Criminal Records Office was no longer officially known by that title, but its initials had survived, largely because most police retained an instinctive suspicion of change – an instinctive suspicion of everything, really, which was why they were police.

'No club number,' said Hynes. 'He's been a good boy, or a careful one.'

Priestman took all this in. She trusted Hynes. He wasn't averse to putting in the hours, and didn't allow drudgework to cloud his eye for detail, but he was also clever and imaginative, and the years were sharpening him rather than rendering him duller. That he preferred to hide many of his better qualities, and indulge his worse ones, was a source of puzzlement and frustration to her, as was his apparent lack of any obvious ambition. Hynes was that rare beast: the man who had found his perfect role in life, and saw no reason to alter it. Gackowska, like some of the others mentored by Hynes, would go on to greater things, and he would regard her ascent with pride, although Priestman thought he might miss Gackowska more than the rest. He had a fondness for her – a blind man could see that – even if Priestman believed he wasn't foolish enough to imagine it could become anything more. At least, she hoped he wasn't.

'All right, get going – but I'm not signing off on any hotels, so you'd better work fast. What car are you using?'

'Thought I'd take my own,' said Hynes, already making for the door. 'The job ones all smell funny.'

But Priestman was too canny for that game.

'Don't you dare put in a claim for mileage.'

Hynes reacted as though he'd been shot. 'No mileage?'

'No mileage, not if there's a perfectly good job car you can use.'

Hynes shook his head in sorrow. 'Penny pinching. We'll be asking people to arrest themselves next.'

'Hardly worth making the trip if you can't milk the system,' added Gackowska.

'When this is all over,' Priestman told her, 'you and I need to have a long talk.'

But Hynes had already rallied. It was hard to keep a good man down.

'We'll make it up from receipts thrown away at motorway services,' he reassured Gackowska, as they vanished from Priestman's sight. 'Spread them over a month or two. Nobody ever checks the dates . . .'

Their voices faded, leaving Priestman to think in silence. If Sellars was bent, Hynes would know, and Gackowska too, because Hynes had trained her well, and made her better than she already was. And if something came out of it – a lead, an arrest – Gackowska would benefit more than Hynes. She was already in line for promotion, and another year would see her make DS. After that, she'd be on her way: DI, DCI, onwards and upwards. How would she look back on her mentor then? Hynes, with his pockets full of receipts, some more dubious than others, and his perpetual willingness to accept free meals and drinks at his regular ponce-holes, as the old guard liked to refer to the bars and coffee shops on their patch that occasionally saw fit to reward weary police with something for their efforts. Hynes wasn't greedy, accepted only what was offered, and didn't bear grudges. Most of the time, he paid anyway.

But Gackowska, as Priestman knew from her sources, paid all the time.

Gackowska would reject Hynes in the end, Priestman decided. When inevitably forced to do so, Gackowska would make him the Falstaff to her Hal. She would turn her back on him, because to do otherwise would endanger her own career. She would nod at him in the canteen, or exchange brief words with him in court, but no more than that, and in the aftermath only those closest to Hynes would be able to spot the flash of hurt in his eyes.

Priestman gathered her notes. She willed Hynes to be right. She willed Sellars to be the one.

* * *

Armitage received the call from a friend in the State Department's Bureau of Near Eastern Affairs while she was applying hydrocortisone to the fingers of her right hand, where the itching was worst. This whole decline in her health had begun with Gruner's death. She feared she might have contracted an infection from that filthy man.

Armitage and the State Department guy had dated when she was in training, and sometimes hooked up when she returned home on leave. He was smart, which she liked, and ambitious. It would never be more than a casual thing between them, which they both understood, but each saw in the other a kindred spirit, and a possible ally for the future. For now, he was useful to Armitage because he spoke Arabic.

'Can I ask where you found that word?' he asked her.

'No.'

He laughed. 'Doesn't matter, just curious. It's not terrorist-related, or nothing that sets bells ringing. It's Arabic for sure, but the reference is mythological.'

'What do you mean?'

'That word,' he said, 'is *djinni*.'

CXIV

Parker was met in the lobby of Lockwood, Dodson & Fogg by the lesser of the two goons who had escorted him from the building on his previous visit. The guard hadn't gained any further communication skills; if anything, he was even more sullen than before. Once Parker obtained a visitor's pass, the guard shepherded him through the first floor of offices, past a mostly empty canteen, and into the currently unoccupied outdoor plaza.

Now that he could view it properly, it was clear to Parker that the remains of the Old Firm did not extend fully across the space but extruded into it, leaving a gap of a few feet at either side. Some restoration work had obviously been done in the past, although it was hard to say how long ago; repointing was visible on parts of the exterior brickwork, but the roof tiles looked old, and a massive sheet of reinforced glass protected the exterior. As with the back of the building, the windows on two of the remaining three sides were bricked up, but four of those facing LDF remained uncovered. Paintings of rooms stood behind each, lending a *trompe l'oeil* aspect to the interior. The lower panes revealed a lawyer's chambers, unoccupied, and a waiting area with a fireplace and a clerk's desk. The upper, from what Parker could make out, depicted two aspects of a considerable library. It was eerily effective. As he drew closer, he noticed that the windows were not the originals. This side had once been a blank wall, into which the windows had subsequently been set. The whole exercise was a strange combination of preservation and cosmetic alteration.

From the right of the Old Firm appeared a man in his sixties, dressed in a custodian's overalls. His dark skin bore a thin sheen of sweat, and he was holding a bunch of keys in his left hand.

'This is Glenmore,' said the guard, the first words he had spoken to Parker since his arrival. 'He'll show you around.'

The guard took a seat at one of the tables dotted across the plaza before removing his cell phone from his pocket and swiping through images on its screen – probably films of kittens drowning, or children weeping as their toys were placed out of reach.

Parker extended a hand toward the custodian.

'Mr Glenmore,' he said. 'My name is Charlie Parker.'

Glenmore held up his right hand in apology. 'I'm dirty,' he said. 'It's a mess in there.'

But when Parker's hand was not withdrawn, he relented and shook it.

'Glenmore is my first name,' he said, 'so just Glenmore is fine.'

'It's unusual.'

'Not where I come from.'

Parker noticed that Glenmore was staring intently at him. He had no idea why.

'Which is?'

'Jamaica originally. Lot of people called Glenmore there.'

'There's a Glenmore Avenue in Jamaica, Queens,' said Parker, 'except I don't think that Jamaica is named after your island. If I remember correctly, it's something to do with beavers.'

If Glenmore the custodian found this fascinating, he did a good job of hiding it. Parker could hardly blame him.

'Huh,' said Glenmore, before allowing a short, awkward silence to elapse. 'Well, you want to look inside the Old Firm?'

'If you wouldn't mind.'

'Not a problem. Won't take long, though. Not much to look at, and you're going to get dirty like me.'

A camera was fixed to the brickwork by the top left-hand window. Parker wondered if Emily Lockwood was keeping an eye on him.

'I've come this far,' he said. 'No point in turning back now.'

He followed Glenmore to an open steel door set into the western wall, and entered a dusty hallway lit by a pair of low-hanging bulbs. A flight of stairs extended upward, ending at a small gallery that ran behind the windows to the left, and another brick wall to the right. A series of metal struts had been added to support the stairs and the gallery from beneath. The rest of the space was occupied by small gardening implements, tools, brushes, paint tins, and assorted wooden boxes. In one corner stood a table, a chair, a transistor radio, and an electric kettle, along with a mug, a box of tea bags, and a plastic container with a sandwich and an apple inside. This was clearly Glenmore's personal space. It was very quiet, the glass and brick combining to smother most noise, even with the door ajar.

Parker tested the internal walls with his fist before trying the first two steps of the stairs. They creaked under his feet, but felt solid enough.

'I wouldn't advise it,' said Glenmore.

'Have you climbed them lately?'

He didn't receive a reply, and turned to look at Glenmore, who frowned at him.

'Did you say something?' said Glenmore.

'I asked if you'd been up these stairs lately.'

'Yes, but I try to avoid it.'

'Still, you've survived this long.'

'Yes.'

'Well, then. Any other advice?'

'Don't fall.'

'That's helpful.'

Parker reached the top without incident, although the second-to-last step protested loudly under pressure. The brickwork to his right was of a different shade to the rest. It looked as though a second wall had been raised over the original, probably in the latter half of the last century after the firm of Quayle finally closed its doors. But he was no expert on construction, so it seemed wise to check.

'When was this new wall put up?' he called down to Glenmore. Again, he received no immediate reply, and began to understand. He descended the stairs, and stood before the custodian. Glemore's hearing aids were tiny, and colored dark to match his skin, while his hair hid the hooks holding them in place behind his ears. Yet even with them, Parker knew that Glenmore remained very deaf, and relied on lip reading to supplement the little he could hear.

He repeated his question about the wall.

'It was before my time,' said Glenmore.

'When did you start working for the firm?'

'Nineteen-ninety.'

Which didn't help Parker much.

'I think there used to be more buildings adjoining this one, but they were damaged in the war,' said Glenmore. 'When I came here, the outer wall had holes in it, and was starting to crumble. Ms Lockwood's father ordered the restoration, and the holes were made into windows. Mr Lockwood is dead now.'

'And what lies behind the inner wall?'

'The old rooms, I suppose, but there is no way to get to them.' He pointed to the steel door. 'This is the only way to enter or leave.'

'You're sure?'

'No other doors, and no proper windows.'

'I notice you wear hearing aids,' said Parker. Ordinarily, he would have avoided mentioning it, but it was important.

'Yes.'

'How well do you hear with them?'

'I hear okay.'

Glenmore sounded defensive, and Parker didn't blame him.

'If sounds came from behind those walls, would you notice?'

Glenmore glanced at the external structures of the old offices, as if to check that they had not undergone some alteration since last he looked.

'No,' he said, 'but what might make a sound in there, except rats?'

CXV

On the screen of his laptop, using the live feed from the security cameras on the outer wall, Quayle monitored Parker's movements. He had lost sight of the two men once they entered the building, but could hear them speaking via the two tiny microphones embedded in the mortar. Even had the microphones not been available to him, Quayle would have been aware of the proximity of others: the walls, though thick, did not entirely block out sound at such close quarters.

Which was why Quayle was keeping very still, because Parker was listening for him.

How persistent this man was, how unyielding: to have come so far in pursuit, and now to be so near. Parker suspected these walls hid something, and thought it might even be Quayle himself. Had he been permitted, the investigator might well have taken a sledgehammer to the bricks until he forced his way through.

Quayle breathed deeply of the air in his covert. The ventilation was, of necessity, modest – most of it came from gaps between the walls and roof, along with a series of small, discreet vents – and so the atmosphere remained consistently musty. It smelled of old food, the aging of paper, and a generic slow decay that might, in large part, have been a product of Quayle's own decline, the olfactory evidence of his half-life. He had been here for so long, but soon he would be gone. If Parker or some other agent did eventually manage to breach the walls, they would find only a furnished mausoleum without its occupant, a tomb without a pharaoh.

Quayle stroked the head of the man seated next to him in an oak chair, a piece of furniture so massive that its feet had remained in permanent contact with the floor since the moment of its delivery, it being easier to push than attempt to lift. The man's arms and legs were restrained. Heavy tape around his neck and forehead secured his head to the back of the chair, and kept his mouth sealed shut.

Bob Johnston could hear Parker. He was potentially as close to rescue as Quayle was to capture; a single incautious noise, and Parker might have detected their presence. But Quayle was not about to give himself away, and Johnston was incapable of doing so.

Johnston had been lifted from the western side of Gordon Square Garden as he made his way to the British Library. Even in a city as large as London, it was surprising how easily one could find oneself isolated and vulnerable. Johnston had learned this to his cost, although even had anyone witnessed his abduction, it might not have registered as untoward: a man walking; a woman with silver hair approaching from behind; a tap on the shoulder; an embrace, albeit one in which the man is a surprised, even reluctant, participant; a car pulling up alongside; the woman aiding the man in entering it so that he does not stumble, because he is the older party, and slightly unsteady on his feet, even if he had seemed fine just moments before.

Johnston had experienced the journey as though in a dream state. The initial sting of the needle had given way to heaviness in his eyelids and limbs. He had not lost consciousness, but could remember only fragments. He recalled the car drawing to a halt, and his being placed in a wheelchair, a blanket over his knees, before being pushed across cobblestones. He remembered entering an old building, and being yanked to his feet. There was a low, narrow tunnel, and people on either side of him, a man and a woman. His toes dragged along the dusty floor as he was carried along, and the lights his captors wore on their heads bobbed so that the very shadows appeared alive. The woman smelled bad, like death itself, and even though he had never met her before, he knew her for who she was: Mors.

Then stairs, and old rooms, comfortably furnished.

And Quayle.

Two fingers on Johnston's left hand had been crushed with

pliers, the knuckles expertly broken on each, and he was deaf in one ear where Mors had punctured his eardrum with an awl. All this damage had been inflicted upon him before he was even asked a question. Whether it was done as punishment for his temerity in joining the hunt, a taster of what would follow should he endeavor to remain silent, or out of pure sadism, Johnston could not have said, but he believed it might have been some combination of all three. Only when the gag of balled cloth was removed from his mouth did the interrogation begin in earnest, Mors standing over him, the awl poised above his right eye, the point half an inch from the pupil, while Quayle asked the questions. Johnston answered them, with no effort at dissembling. Like all those who love books and reading, he had a particular dread of blindness. It did not matter that the threat, even the likelihood, of death hung over him. Perhaps foolishly, Johnston held on to the hope that he might yet be rescued, but even were it not to be, he did not want to be sightless at the end.

Finally, Mors had departed, leaving only Quayle and the other man. Quayle used his name in addressing him: Sellars. Johnston now knew that Louis and Angel had been correct, and Christopher Sellars was the channel between Quayle and the late Cornelie Gruner.

Sellars had lurched toward the screen when Parker first appeared, his hatred so potent that it altered the musk of him. And when he could not reach Parker, he found another outlet for his rage: he slid a finger into Johnston's ruptured ear, and probed at the ruined drum until Johnston thought he would pass out from the pain.

The throbbing in Johnston's left hand was relentless, but it was as nothing compared to the agony of the damage to his ear, now compounded by Sellars's cruelty. It was as though the awl were still present, pushing deeper and deeper into his brain. One side of his head felt heavier than the other; were it not for the tape holding it in place, he was certain he would have been unable to hold it erect.

He could still hear Parker's voice. Once again, he tried to scream, but it was to no avail. Quayle took in his distress with interest, until finally the sounds of conversation from the other side of the wall grew fainter, and Parker and the custodian appeared once more on the screen, talking together in the court-yard, their words beyond the power of the microphones to pick up.

Johnston cried, and Quayle used a thumb to wipe away his tears.

CXVI

The security guard had put away his phone, but paid Parker and Glenmore no heed as they approached, his attention now focused on a sparrow pecking at crumbs on the table. The bird was so familiar with its surroundings, and the humans that passed through them, as to be nearly tame. It bobbed within inches of the man's right hand, which shot out with a speed that surprised Parker, catching the bird. Parker could see its head peeping from the hollow of the fist. The man slipped his thumb beneath the sparrow's beak, and with a flick of his nail broke its neck. Glenmore's expression was unreadable as he watched the tiny body being cast into a flowerbed.

'A woman used to come here,' he said to Parker. 'I had not seen her in many months, but she returned two days ago.'

'What was she like?'

'All white outside – her hair, her skin, even her eyes – and all dead inside.'

Mors.

'What was she doing?'

He shrugged. 'Checking.'

'Checking what?'

'This place.' He tapped one of the old bricks. 'Maybe you.'

'Does she have a name?'

'She uses many names. They think I don't hear at all, but I hear more than they know, and I got no troubles with my eyesight.'

'What names?'

'Sorrell, Cobbold, Dyson, North. And I have seen her, away from here.'

'Where?'

'Smithfield. St Bart's.'

612

'I don't know what that is.'

'It is a church, very old. My home is near Smithfield meat market. She smells of it, I think – of bad meat.'

'You think she lives nearby?'

Glenmore nodded.

'By the church. Maybe even under the church.'

'*Under* the church?'

Glenmore made a sound that might have been a laugh.

'Could be I'm joking,' he said. 'Could be. But you look up those names, and could be I'm not. If we're done, I ought to get back to work.'

Parker thanked him, but Glenmore was already walking away, and so Parker did not know if he heard. The guard stood as Parker approached.

'Why did you kill that bird?' said Parker.

'What bird?' the guard answered.

Parker perceived no trace of dissimulation in his face. Some men were so lost, even to themselves, that cruelty became normative, no longer worthy of even the dullest firing of their synapses, and passed without record from the annals of their existence; and when at last their damnation was confirmed to them, they would register only blankness at the judgment, and confusion as they burned.

Parker looked up at the windows of the LDF building. Emily Lockwood stared down at him, and then was gone.

'Never mind,' said Parker. 'I'm ready to leave.'

CXVII

G lenmore sat at his table in the dimness of the Old Firm. Usually, he turned the radio up loud for company – he could still discern rhythms, and found comfort in those of music – but not now, not today.

His hands were trembling, and he felt sick to his soul.

The steel door opened wider, and a figure appeared in the gap. It was only the second time that he had ever been alone in Emily Lockwood's presence, beyond the occasional passing encounter in a corridor or the plaza. The first was the previous day, when she had reminded him of how precarious was his family's position in this country. The government was cracking down on immigrants, she reminded him. He had come to Britain as a boy, had he not, brought from Jamaica by his father and mother? They must be very old by now. It would be unfortunate if their right to live in Britain were to be questioned. If they were unable to prove continuous residency, they could lose their benefits, and their entitlement to healthcare. They might even be deported. It was happening all around, every day.

And what about his job? The building sourced janitorial staff from an outside agency, so some might have viewed Glenmore as surplus to requirements. Because of the confidential nature of much of LDF's business, the partners preferred that it should employ its own custodian with access to otherwise restricted areas, but Lockwood was under pressure to make savings. She would do everything she could to safeguard his position, but . . .

'All went well?' said Lockwood.

'Yes, ma'am.'

'And you told him exactly what I instructed you to say?'

'Yes, ma'am.'

And not all of it was even a lie. He did live by the market, and had seen in his neighborhood the woman who went by many names, but only once, the night before, when she came to stand under the streetlight by his flat, so that he might perceive her more clearly and know she was there, if not yet the reason for her presence. He had somehow found the courage to go down to the street, although he could not have said why, beyond some vague notion that this woman wished to communicate a message to him. But the woman was gone, and if she had left any tidings, they took the form only of the threat she represented, and the smell of dead things that she left behind.

'Why don't you go home early today? You've worked hard.' Emily Lockwood took a step closer, to be certain that he could see the expression on her face, and understand the import of what she said next. 'Spend some time with your family.'

He stared at the table. When he looked up again, she was gone. Glenmore walked to the entrance, checked that the courtyard was empty, and closed the door. It had no internal lock, but lodged firmly in the frame when shut, and only he had the knack of opening it easily. He adjusted the volume on his hearing aids so it was at its highest level before climbing the stairs that led to nowhere, and so familiar was he with them that they made no sound as he ascended.

In the beginning, Glenmore had attributed to rodents the occasional noises from the other side of the wall, just as he had told the American, but the movement of rats did not sound like footsteps, nor did rats listen to music late at night, or engage in conversations in the voices of a man and a woman, one who sounded very much like Ms Sorrell, or Cobbold, or whatever she chose to call herself when she crawled from whatever hollow she inhabited, as lightless a dwelling as the sealed rooms behind the walls.

But it was none of Glenmore's business, and he had long ago elected not to mention it to his employers, and Ms Lockwood in particular, in large part because he was no 'foofool', the word his mother still used to describe a stupid person in the patois of her homeland. Either Ms Lockwood did not know of a presence in the Old Firm, in which case she, too, was a foofool; or she did know, and maybe others did too, so no good could come from revealing to them that he had become aware of signs of habitation in a supposedly dead place. Glenmore had been hired because they believed him to be almost entirely deaf, which he was, but with an ear pressed to the wall, and his hearing aids turned up full, he could hear a little.

He could hear enough.

Now he listened, but all was quiet.

The pale woman frightened him. It was not just spoiled meat of which she reeked – or if it was, it was not a consequence of any proximity to a butcher's market, but from the ongoing festering of her own innards. A 'duppy', his mother would have called her: a bad spirit inhabiting a body that was rotting from the infestation. But with whom would a duppy speak, except the devil himself?

Glenmore gathered his belongings, and departed, yet he did not go straight home. Instead he crossed to Lincoln's Inn, and took a seat by the kitchen at Old Buildings, the odors of the day's lunch offerings persisting in the warm air. He had glimpsed the duppy here too, entering the chambers from Old Square when all was quiet, believing herself unobserved. Old Buildings was aptly named: some of its structures dated from early in the sixteenth century, and it had survived the Blitz intact, like most of Lincoln's Inn. Glenmore had been told by one of the junior clerks at Old Buildings that cellars ran beneath it, some used for storage, others cut off by centuries of renovation and collapses.

'But anyone who knows the full extent of them is long dead,' the clerk had said. 'Long, long dead.'

Yet from the top of Old Buildings, Glenmore knew, one could see the offices of LDF, and the Old Firm standing between. Whatever moved through the Old Firm had to leave sometime, and the duppy had to be able to gain access to commune with her devil. Somewhere under Old Buildings, there existed a tunnel.

Glenmore had been raised in the Church of God, and each Sunday he traveled north with his family to the Community Church of God in Tottenham, there to listen to the words of the pastor. Glenmore had been baptized by total immersion, adhered to the ordinances of foot washing and communion, and believed that the moral image of God was revealed in the actions of good men.

Glenmore knew that Ms Lockwood wanted Parker to go to St Bart's, wanted him to look for the duppy, but Glenmore did not believe he would have to look hard, because the duppy, or some familiar dispatched at her behest, would be waiting for him.

Yet Glenmore had a wife, two grown-up children, and two aged parents, all of whom lived with him in a three-bedroom council flat that would still have been too small with half as many occupants. He had built a life in this country, and now some of those in the British government, men and women who had never worked as hard as he, who had never cleaned another man's excrement from a bowl or been called 'nigger' or 'wog', wanted to deprive him of it, and return him to a land that was his in name only. Ms Lockwood had promised to protect him, just as long as he did as he was told, and said what she wanted him to say.

And just in case he was tempted to falter, and ignore her wishes, there was the duppy, who had shone like unsheathed steel beneath the streetlight outside his flat, and stank of dying, to remind him that losing one's livelihood and losing one's life were not the same thing.

People suffered all the time, and died badly. Many called on God to save them at the end, but if God heard their pleas, He chose not to answer. Maybe the pastor was wrong. Maybe God was imperfect, and men, by acting in their own interests, were reflecting only the reality of His nature.

Glenmore was old, and had married later in life than he might have wished. He did not always understand his children, or his wife, even when he could hear what they were saying. (And the truth was that he sometimes turned off his hearing aids just so he could not.) His bones hurt, and he had not visited a doctor in years for fear of what he might learn. If the duppy came, he would not be able to protect his family from her.

Glenmore sat in the fading sunlight, and wished he were a wiser man.

CXVIII

Hynes and Gackowska reached Manchester without incident. They stopped for a coffee along the way, but Gackowska was pleased – and not a little relieved – to note that Hynes did not scour the surrounding tables for stray receipts he could claim as his own. They listened to the Beatles for most of the journey, and Hynes explained to Gackowska why *Abbey Road* was the band's best record, and how *Sgt Pepper's* wasn't really a concept album, no matter what anyone claimed to the contrary. Then he had to explain to Gackowska what a concept album was, and a B-side, until pretty soon he felt about a hundred years old and was tempted to check himself into a nursing home.

Carenor's main depot was located in an industrial park not far from the Etihad Stadium, and differed from the neighboring businesses only in the degree of security that had to be negotiated in order to enter, and the presence of temperature-controlled vaults in the warehouses, which were pointed out to them as they were escorted to the main building. They were offered coffee, which they declined, and the use of the bathrooms, which they accepted, before being shown to Dylan Lynskey's office.

Lynskey was dressed in a blue-and-white striped shirt with a wide white collar, and a pink tie that Hynes wouldn't have worn as a bet. A navy suit jacket dangled from a coat hanger on the back of the office door, and the walls were mostly decorated with the kind of artwork that Hynes suspected was just expensive enough to impress a certain type of visitor, but not expensive enough to excite anyone who actually knew anything about art. Since Hynes didn't fall into either category, he didn't care much either way, with the exception of a small framed sketch that he thought might have been a Lowry. He didn't want to ask, though, just in case it wasn't, and he made himself look stupid as a consequence.

Everything about Lynskey was slick, and he was on the defensive from the off, reminding them that Carenor was a high-end operation, noted for its probity and discretion, and had never been found guilty of any illegality. This, as Hynes and Gackowska well knew, differed from actively avoiding illegal behavior, or not being accused of it; and the more Lynskey spoke, the clearer it became that only a guilty man would be so concerned about stressing his innocence. Gackowska had done some research before they left the northeast, and in between listening to Beatles tracks, and Hynes's complaints about the depths of the younger generation's ignorance, she had enlightened him about the avarice, mendacity, and down-right crookedness of much of the art world. By the time they got to Manchester, Hynes was ready to arrest anyone in possession of a paintbrush and an easel.

Lynskey went through Sellars's employment record, noting that he traveled not only around Britain, but also abroad, and his handling of consignments was always scrupulous. During the fifteen years he had worked for the company, he had not been responsible for a single breakage, or even minor damage.

'Does he work alone?' asked Hynes.

'Some jobs require a two-person crew, but rarely more than that,' said Lynskey. 'On those occasions, a driver might be assigned a partner, but for the most part we use single-operator vehicles. That's fairly typical of the courier business, even in our niche.'

'Does he get on with everyone?'

'Not even Christ got along with everyone,' said Lynskey, which was a fair point.

'In general.'

'In general, yes. I'm curious as to what all this is about, by the way. Is Mr Sellars suspected of some crime?'

Lynskey might have been oleaginous, but he wasn't dim. Hynes knew that he'd probably googled Gary Holmby's name after their initial phone conversation, if he hadn't immediately recalled it from the news reports, but there was no point in rushing to confirm his suspicions.

'This is linked to an ongoing investigation,' said Gackowska, 'but we're really just trying to eliminate people from our inquiries. It means a lot of dead ends, but it has to be done.'

Lynskey smiled at her. She might have been delivering boiler-plate, but she was easy on the eye. His wedding ring flashed briefly in the sunlight and he blinked hard, as though his absent wife had somehow detected his interest in another woman and found a way to traverse time and space in order to remind him of his obligations. His smile faded.

Hynes and Gackowska listened to a brief history of the company, and further claims of probity, before deciding to cut to the chase.

'Has Mr Sellars ever been in trouble with the police?' said Hynes.

'Outside the company? I couldn't possibly say. He's had one or two speeding fines over the years, which hardly makes him unique among couriers. They're always racing against the clock, but he's never been in danger of losing his license.'

'And within the company?'

Lynskey shifted in his chair.

'Not so much "trouble", no.'

'But?'

Lynskey's discomfort increased. Either he was inordinately fond – or wary – of Sellars, and disliked being put in a position where he might have to betray confidences, or whatever he was being asked to reveal didn't just reflect badly on his employee.

'We had a problem, about three years ago.'

'What kind of problem?'

'A potentially embarrassing one. The seemingly endless search for artworks looted by the Nazis created some backwash that landed on our doorstep. A Dutch investigator named Yvette Visser believed that Carenor, either knowingly or inadvertently, might have been responsible for transporting certain disputed pieces across international borders.'

'And was she right?'

'No proof was ever offered, so I would dispute it.'

Hynes tried to figure out exactly what this might mean, but parked the problem for later consideration after his confusion grew too great.

'What happened?' he asked.

'Visser came to England, and promptly disappeared.'

'"Promptly?"' said Gackowska.

It was an odd choice of word, but Lynskey simply shrugged.

'Promptly,' he confirmed. 'I think she'd only been in the country for a few days before she vanished.'

'And how does Sellars fit into this?'

'Well,' said Lynskey, 'he was the last person to see her alive.'

CXIX

Parker returned to Hazlitt's to find an envelope on his bed, with his name written on the front in Bob Johnston's handwriting. He opened it to discover a copy of *Selected Poems* by John Dryden, in the Penguin edition. Earlier in the week, Johnston had informed Parker that Dryden had once lived only minutes from Hazlitt's, only for Parker to confess that he'd never heard of the poet. Johnston had done his best to hide his distress, but it had been a struggle. On the title page, he had written:

> *'The Souls of Friends, like Kings in Progress are . . .'*
> *Thank you, my friend, for this journey.*
> *Bob.*

*   *   *

Bob Johnston was alone. Mors was long gone, and now Sellars also. The latter had left soon after Parker, taking with him the stink of testosterone, and the turmoil of his rage.

Johnston remained bound and gagged. He had been given nothing to eat or drink since his abduction, and Quayle had not spoken a word to him after Sellars's departure. Since his surroundings were deprived of natural light, or a clock, Johnston had no idea of the hour. His nostrils kept blocking, making it difficult to breathe. At times he had come close enough to suffocation, or so it felt, that only the greatest effort of will had prevented him from panicking, or blacking out.

Quayle was elsewhere, although Johnston could hear sounds of movement from one of the nearby rooms, even if they were rendered strange by the damage to his ear; and while Quayle's living quarters were cramped and opaque, and should have been claustrophobic, Johnston was experiencing, by contrast, a sensation closer to agoraphobia, as though the space he occupied were merely an adjunct to a greater volume that was just barely concealed, an anteroom to a monumental hall so vast that were it to be revealed, its walls and ceiling, perhaps even the floor itself, would be lost to darkness. Perhaps, he suspected, he was experiencing some premonition of his own death.

The room was very warm, and smelled of burning, although the fireplace was empty and cold. For how long, Johnston wondered, had Quayle been occupying this space, or some version of it? It seemed impossible that it could be centuries, but even brief exposure had convinced Johnston that Quayle was beyond any conception of normality. Yet that he was insane seemed certain; no one could hide behind these windowless walls and not go mad, and no man could live so long without losing his reason.

Quayle reappeared, and added two small books to a pile on his desk. He seemed be engaged in some winnowing of his library, separating the grain from the chaff. He spoke without turning toward Johnston.

'We're almost at the end,' said Quayle, but he seemed to be talking as much to the shadows as to Johnston. 'I'll have done what I agreed to do, and soon my part will be over. I don't know what will happen to me after. Perhaps I'll just crumble to dust.'

Now he looked at Johnston, and grinned, but his eyes were pools of desolation. Quayle, he saw, was frightened; it came of striking bargains with forces that had a habit of reneging on their side of the deal, or finding ways to manipulate language as easily as men's souls. But Quayle was a lawyer, and familiar with raveling and unraveling tangled threads of legalese. He had probably convinced himself that the agreement was ironclad, and could not be turned against him. What had he been promised in return for his services? Longevity and prosperity, probably, or some variation on the same, because that was what most men sought. The rest – women, power – would follow naturally.

And he had received long life, longer than he could ever have wished for, or imagined possible, so that it had, in the end, become an intolerable burden; and prosperity, but with nothing on which to spend his wealth beyond the search for an artefact that would bring his own existence to a conclusion, until he was reduced to hiding from the world in a windowless box, a taste of the final resting place to come. For female company, he had Mors; as power, the infliction of misery. The bargain had probably not been to his liking after all, Johnston thought.

Quayle checked the feed from the cameras, and confirmed that the courtyard was unoccupied. The custodian, Glenmore, had locked up the Old Firm before leaving, and the canteen in the main building was shuttered and dark. Smoking was forbidden within its precincts, and so anyone desiring a cigarette would have to go elsewhere for the pleasure. No one would be coming near the Old Firm again until morning.

Quayle picked up a sharp letter opener and stepped behind Johnston, who was more conscious than ever of his exposed neck. But Quayle used the blade only to sever the tape holding Johnston's head and neck in place. He also pulled aside the tape sealing Johnston's mouth, but did not remove it entirely, just in case someone did come and he was forced to muzzle him again. A glass of water was produced, then a second. Johnston drank both down before Quayle fed him cold chicken with his fingers.

'I need the bathroom,' said Johnston, when he was finished.

'That won't be possible.'

'I have to pee. This isn't some trick.'

'I know it isn't, but smell yourself. I think the damage has already been done, don't you?'

And so another humiliation was added to the sum of Johnston's pain and misery for that day. It would not be the last; of that much, Johnston was sure.

'What now?' he said.

'For you?'

'I guess. And for everything.'

'It ends. For you, for everything. You should have stayed in America, with your own books. You should not have followed a man like Parker here, to inquire into the nature of mine. But curiously, you've helped me.'

'What do you mean?'

Quayle stopped what he was doing.

'Your notes,' he said. 'Your researches. After all these years, your scholarship enabled me to discover why the Atlas was incomplete, and perhaps might have remained so. That it should all come down to one Dutch word, *panelen*, and a deliberate mistranslation by Couvret so many years ago.'

Quayle seemed both baffled and amused by his own blindness.

'*De panelen zijn de laatste pagina,*' he said. 'Not the "panels" are the last page, but the "panes". I had always wondered why so many of the figures that haunt the Atlas, including the ones known to manifest themselves in the Rackham illustrations, resembled those depicted in the windows at Fairford, and especially their representation of the Last Judgment. What was the reason for it? Yes, some of the Fairford glaziers traveled from the Low Countries, where the Atlas was discovered again at the end of the sixteenth century, after being lost for so long. It was possible that, as it lay hidden in the ground, its influence infected some among these men, who came from generations of artisans. It found expression in their glasswork, just as I expect its visions haunted their nightmares, and the nightmares of their fathers, and their grandfathers, and all those who had spent their lives with the Atlas buried beneath their feet. It was simply one more manifestation of the Atlas's power, or so I thought.

'But what if it was more than that? What if the Atlas was waiting beneath the ground, and sensed that it would soon be found? It was *already* incomplete when it was first recovered, and Couvret, when he brought it to England, commenced a process of further dispersal, before hiding entirely what was left, all to keep it from me. And he succeeded, for a time: centuries passed until Maulding, aided by the Dunwidges and Maggs, secured the bulk of it. But the Atlas's consummation was never meant to come about through vellum alone.'

Almost without his noticing, Quayle had moved closer to Johnston as he spoke, so that he was now once again standing over the American.

'I think,' said Quayle, 'that at the beginning of the sixteenth century, the Atlas created its own final illustration, distinct from the book itself, and it did so in glass, through the hands of men.'

He placed his hands on Johnston's cheeks, like a priest praying over a penitent.

'The window is the last page,' Quayle whispered into Johnston's good ear. 'The window is the Apocalypse.'

His hands moved, his thumbs now searching his captive's face.

'I'm glad you came,' said Quayle. 'I had need of fresh eyes.'

CXX

G ackowska and Hynes were still in Dylan Lynskey's office, working their way through Christopher Sellars's movements in recent weeks. Lynskey had explained to them, in as much detail as he could recall, the circumstances surrounding the visit of the Dutch investigator Hendricksen, and the two detectives from Scotland Yard's Antiques Unit, Hamill and Mount. Hynes hadn't even known that there was an Antiques Unit at Scotland Yard. He thought he might apply. It sounded like an easy number that would involve drinking copious amounts of tea, so he was already overqualified.

Carenor used GPS tracking on its fleet, with a geo-fence facility that alerted the company when a driver left a designated area. The system also stored a full history of the route taken by each vehicle, which could be replicated on a series of onscreen maps. Unfortunately, as Lynskey admitted, the system was only checked when a problem arose, such as when a vehicle was delayed – or in a worst-case scenario, went missing – or if concerns were expressed about how efficiently a driver might be spending his working hours. Since Carenor's employees were carefully vetted, and many had been with the company for years, such checks were rarely necessary. In addition, none of its fleet had ever been stolen, although attempts had been made to break into them on occasion, people being what they were.

When Hynes and Gackowska accessed Sellars's route records via Lynskey's computer, they found gaps. Not all of them corresponded directly with women going missing, but some did. In addition, they discovered routes recorded on the system that bore no relation to where Sellars was supposed to have been on certain given days, despite the fact that he had clearly made deliveries, or received consignments, on his scheduled routes. In one case, the system showed him as being in Cardiff at the precise moment that he was picking up two paintings from a gallery in Glasgow, because the gallery owner had signed off on the pick-up time.

'Maybe there was a problem with the device,' said Lynskey, 'or the system.'

'Is there a way you can find out?' said Hynes.

'I can call the monitoring company and ask, I suppose.'

'Would Sellars always have used the same van?'

'The drivers have their own preferences and peculiarities when it comes to the fleet, but no, that wouldn't be possible.'

'Can you take a look at the records of the other drivers, and see if any of them have encountered similar problems during that period?'

'Certainly.'

They left him to it. Hynes used the excuse of a cigarette break to invite Gackowska to step outside, so they could speak without being overheard.

'Well?' said Hynes.

'If he was using the same vehicle all the time, I could buy the dodgy sat nav theory,' said Gackowska. 'But unless he's Magneto, I think Sellars has been blocking the signal.'

'I think so, too. He could be using a jammer, but brass mesh, or a lead-lined bag like the ones that protect camera film from X-rays, would do the job just as well.'

'Or a Faraday pouch,' said Gackowska. 'They shield phone signals, so they'd do the same for sat nav. What I don't understand is how the system showed Sellars as being in Wales when he was clearly in Scotland, unless he paid someone to do his rounds for him.'

'Let's play a game of "Ask Nabih",' said Hynes. 'He loves that. Lives for it, does Nabih.'

He took out his phone and called Nabih Uddin, who picked up on the second ring.

'A question, Nabih. How does a GPS unit show a vehicle sitting in Cardiff when it was actually in Glasgow at the time?'

'A spoofer,' said Uddin, without even pausing to think.

'A what?'

'A GPS spoofer. It broadcasts a fake signal that overrides the real one. Alternatively, it can rebroadcast genuine signals stored earlier to fool the receiver. The Fraud Unit found a spoofer on a truck just a couple of months back. A memo was circulated about it.'

'Incredible,' said Hynes.

'What?' said Gackowska.

'Nabih reads memos. Who knew?'

He hung up before Uddin could start swearing, and relayed to Gackowska what he had learned.

'There you go,' he said. 'A jammer and a spoofer.'

'If he's our bloke.'

'He's Chummy, mark my words.'

Chummy: Hynes was so old school, Gackowska reflected, he probably still secretly thought of himself as a Peeler.

Hynes checked his watch. 'Maybe it's time we asked Lynskey to summon Sellars, so we can have a little heart-to-heart with him. In the meantime, why don't you call Scotland Yard and get Hamill or Mount on the phone, see what they have to say about this Visser business?'

He left Gackowska to make the call, and returned to Lynskey's office.

Gackowska spent twenty minutes speaking about Christopher Sellars with DS Joanne Hamill of the Met's Art and Antiques Unit. By the end of the conversation, she had taken six pages of notes about freeports, and particularly the one known as the Enclave; about misappropriated artworks; about allegations of blackmail by Sellars against Visser; and about the doggedness of Visser's colleague, Hendricksen, who continued to contact Hamill on a regular basis to inquire about progress on the Visser investigation, of which there was none.

It seemed also that in the months following Visser's disappearance, Sellars had made allegations of harassment against Hendricksen, based on phone calls from Hendricksen to his landline and mobile, and sightings of the Dutchman near Sellars's home and place of work. No charges were pressed, but Hamill had been forced to advise Hendricksen to keep his distance, although she was pretty certain that he continued to keep track of Sellars's movements.

'He liked Sellars for it,' Hamill told Gackowska.

'What about you?'

'Sellars was certainly the last known person to see Visser alive, but we have her on the way to London while he was at home in Manchester and, unless he's capable of bilocation, I can't see how he could have harmed her in the timeframe we've established.'

'How tight is the window?'

'We've narrowed it to a couple of hours, but even allowing for a considerable margin of error, Sellars is still in the clear.'

'What about Lynskey, the Carenor CEO? Were Visser's allegations embarrassing enough for his company to justify having her killed?'

'From what I've learned about the art world in this job, it's virtually without shame, so the answer is almost certainly "No." Hendricksen supplied us with a lot of information indicating that Carenor, probably on behalf of some of its clients, maintains regular contact with the Enclave. If Hendricksen is to be believed, and I don't doubt him, the only reason anyone uses the Enclave is to avoid the attentions of the law, the taxman, or the rightful owners of stolen property. Hendricksen thinks that Sellars might have been picking up a little extra money on the side by smuggling, but Carenor isn't blameless either. If you do business with the Enclave, then you're not just flirting with illegality: you're taking it to bed and making it breakfast in the morning.'

'How much of this would stand up in court?'

'Almost none.'

'And Sellars hasn't come to your attention since then?'

'No. How good is he looking for those murdered women?'

'It's too early to say. We want to talk to him, and examine the sat nav on the vehicles he's been using.'

'All I can tell you for sure is that he didn't kill Yvette Visser, but . . .'

'But?'

631

'That doesn't mean he couldn't have found someone else to do it for him.'

Hynes and Lynskey were discussing Carenor's GPS when Gackowska returned. From a cursory examination, it appeared no other drivers had been affected by similar problems, at least not when it came to gaps in the online records.

'But we'd have to do a full crosscheck to be certain,' Lynskey added.

Hynes was already considering how much of this information they'd require in the event of an arrest and possible prosecution. All of it, he imagined. Obviously, they'd need their own digital forensics investigators to examine the equipment and records as well, but it wouldn't hurt to have Carenor set the ball rolling.

'Can you put someone on it?' he said.

'It'll be time-consuming,' said Lynskey.

'Anything worth doing usually is,' said Hynes.

Lynskey worried at his bottom lip with his teeth.

'Did you want to say something?' said Hynes.

'This is about the dead women, isn't it?' said Lynskey. 'The ones with the beads in their mouths.'

Hynes no longer saw any reason to dissemble. They needed Lynskey.

'Yes,' he said.

'I thought so.'

'And?'

'We'll help in whatever way we can.'

'Can the system tell us where Sellars is now?'

Lynskey confirmed with an assistant the number of the vehicle assigned to Sellars the previous day. Sellars's first two pick-ups weren't far from his home, and it hadn't made sense to drag him all the way into the yard just to have him drive back the same way. Another van had towed Sellars's assigned vehicle to his house late the night before, and left it parked outside.

'That's odd,' said Lynskey.

'What is?' said Hynes.

'The system's telling me the van is still at Sellars's home. It hasn't moved since last night. He should have been on the road for hours by now.'

'Why don't you call him, see what he says.'

Lynskey looked up the number, and made the call.

'It's gone to voicemail,' he said.

'We can contact the Spoc,' said Gackowska, 'and ask for a location on Sellars's phone.'

Spocs, or 'special points of contact', were officers responsible for liaising with phone companies, and processing requests by police for communications data. While such requests were supposed to be accompanied by paperwork – a lot of paperwork – and could take days to work their way through the system, it was possible to obtain the information rapidly in the event of an emergency, and file the documentation later.

'Or we could just go and knock on his front door,' said Hynes. 'If he's not there, we'll send out the dogs.'

Which sounded like a plan. Before they left, Hynes made sure that Lynskey had contact details for both him and Gackowska. If Lynskey heard from Sellars, he was to establish his whereabouts, and either get him to stay where he was, or come back to Carenor, before contacting one of them immediately. Hynes also reminded him of the importance of keeping his mouth shut about their inquiries.

Lynskey understood, and made no objection.

'You know,' he said, 'I never really liked him anyway.'

CXXI

Parker walked the streets of London, largely heedless of his direction, or seemingly so. Had the legat Armitage been permitted sight of him, she might have discerned a pattern in what, to an untrained eye, were random actions: backtracking, pausing by glass, slipping through Underground stations, all in an effort to determine if he were being followed, and by whom.

Perhaps he was mistaken, and the Old Firm was a deserted shell, its inhabitant long since vanished.

Perhaps, but he sensed a shadow.

He continued to circle, slowly closing on St Bart's.

In Amsterdam, De Jaager had attended the funerals of both Eva Meertens and Cornelie Gruner. The former, unsurprisingly, was a sad affair, De Jaager's personal sorrow rendered deeper by his sense of responsibility for what had occurred. He could have avoided the service altogether, he knew, but elected instead to torment himself still further. At least there were no grieving parents with whom to contend, Meertens having been an orphan since her teens, a consequence of being born to a mother and father who had made consistently poor life choices – drugs, and petty crime – that ultimately led to their premature demise. By taking Eva under his wing, De Jaager had hoped to ensure a different outcome for their daughter. Instead, he appeared merely to have hastened her end.

Gruner's last bow was a more sparsely attended affair, and untroubled by any excessive displays of grief. It took place at the Westgaarde Crematorium, which always reminded De Jaager of an upscale business park. Its interior was bright and modern, and its furniture colorful in a restrained manner; the facility might just as easily have accommodated a conference of thrusting dotcom visionaries as a congregation of mourners. Those who gathered to send Gruner on his way were largely elderly, and mostly male. They were present more to gossip, and speculate on possible reasons for Gruner's murder – his general unpleasantness being high among them – and the future of his book collection, than pay anything approaching their last respects.

De Jaager's people watched them all, just as they had monitored those attending the service for Eva Meertens. Identities were established, and backgrounds checked, but to little avail. No one arrived for either ceremony parading obvious guilt, De Jaager possibly excepted, and the two events had few attendees in common, again with the exception of De Jaager, and an assortment of undercover Dutch detectives engaged in a similar exercise.

De Jaager's sources had indicated to him that the investigators were as baffled by the two murders as he was. Meanwhile, his friends in the National Police Corps were aware that Meertens had been one of De Jaager's protégés, and was working for him at the time of her murder. They also knew that De Jaager had been shadowing Gruner. He wasn't a suspect – they knew De Jaager too well for that – but they were curious to know why Gruner should have been the focus of his attentions. This, in turn, had aroused their interest in Louis, who had been present with De Jaager at the Rijksmuseum on the day Gruner was killed. De Jaager informed them that he had simply been showing his guest around the museum, and had no knowledge of his current whereabouts, said guest having since moved on. The NPC continued to pressure him for further details, but softly: De Jaager's reputation as an honest broker protected him for the present. The only blessing was that, when shown an image of Angel from Schiphol Airport, none of the bartenders at the Oak connected him with any customer seen on the premises during the night in question. Perhaps they were telling the truth, in which case darkness and rain had come to Angel's rescue; or, more likely, they were lying as a matter of self-preservation, taking the view that whatever had befallen Gruner might also easily befall them should they cooperate with the police investigation. Moral corruption, De Jaager knew, was quite contagious.

Yet De Jaager also had powers that the police did not possess. The Dutch might have been one of the most law-abiding peoples in the world, but this was not to say that all were equally open to assisting the law with its inquiries – as the staff at the Oak proved – however justified those same inquiries might appear by any objective analysis. In addition, De Jaager had quietly made it known that a reward was on offer for information enabling his people to lay hands on Eva's killer before the police.

The whispers started, and De Jaager listened.

A car recalled; not all the numbers and letters on the license plate remembered, but some. A woman, small, and possibly with reddish hair, noticed in the vicinity of Gruner's place of business. A similar sighting – perhaps, just perhaps – near Lijnbaansgracht. Slowly, they were putting the pieces together, and De Jaager, the hunter, was sharpening his knives. He had been fond of Eva.

He would skin her killer alive.

Rosanna Bellingham sat in Rules of Covent Garden, a glass of wine almost empty before her. Rules was London's oldest restaurant, once the haunt of Dickens, Thackeray, and H.G. Wells. She knew Bob Johnston would appreciate its literary antecedents, and dining there might introduce him to the joys of steak & kidney suet pudding, and steamed sponge with custard.

Except Johnston was now an hour late for their early dinner, and their table had been given away. The maître d' assured her that every effort would be made to secure another once her guest arrived, but Rosanna was starting to feel annoyed. She had not yet progressed to being concerned, although that might follow. For now, she tried Hazlitt's for a second time, only to hear the phone in Johnston's room ring out again. On this occasion she left a message with the front desk, asking that it be passed to Mr Johnston should he return. She supposed he might have become caught up in his researches, and failed to notice the time, or else have forgotten entirely about their meeting. If the latter were subsequently revealed to be the case, she thought, Bob

Johnston could take his sorry self back to the United States, books and all, without ever glimpsing her face again. She had her pride.

The bartender approached.

'Would Madame like another glass of wine?'

She looked at her glass. What was the other option: return home to a ghost?

'Why not?' she said. 'And would you happen to have a newspaper?'

XII

Deflores: Yes, and the while I coupled with your mate
    At barly-break; now we are left in hell.
Vermandero: We are all there, it circumscribes us here.
              Thomas Middleton, *The Changeling*

CXXII

Gackowska and Hynes stood outside the door of the Sellars home on Heaton Street in Prestwich, listening to the sound of a child crying inside. It sounded like a little girl. The two officers weren't yet concerned enough to begin breaking down doors – if the police reacted like that to every crying child, half the doors in the country would be off their hinges – but there was an edge to the sobbing that Hynes didn't like.

The house was semi-detached, with a garage to one side in addition to an empty driveway at the front. A child's scooter lay abandoned by one of the flowerbeds. As Lynskey had indicated, the unmarked Carenor van sat at the curb.

Hynes tried the doorbell again, and through the frosted glass saw a figure quickly descending the stairs. The door opened, revealing a woman standing before them. Perhaps unsurprisingly, given the sound of crying, she looked harried.

'Yes?' she said.

Hynes and Gackowska showed her their warrant cards. She gave them a quick glance, and softened slightly.

'Mrs Sellars?' said Hynes.

She nodded.

'I'm sorry it took me so long to come down,' she said. 'One of the girls took a fall. I've warned them about playing too roughly.'

'Is she okay?' said Gackowska.

'She has a bump on her head, but she'll be fine.'

'We were hoping to speak with your husband.'

'He's not here.'

'Do you know where he is?'

'He's supposed to be at work.'

'Well, we noticed that his vehicle is parked outside.'

'I was wondering about that as well. I've tried calling him, but he's not answering his phone.'

The crying hadn't stopped, and was now being punctuated by wails of 'Mummy!' Hynes picked up an odd smell. He associated it with households in which cleanliness had been relegated to a luxury, and used dishes were left to grow mold in sinks. Sometimes it was a consequence of poverty and neglect, but equally he'd noticed it in homes where life was just temporarily getting on top of someone, perhaps because of a new addition to the family. But from what he knew about Sellars, his girls were no longer infants.

'Look,' said Hynes, 'do you mind if we come in for a moment?'

The woman opened the door wider, and stepped aside to admit them.

'You're welcome to join us,' she said.

Which was an odd way to put it, Hynes thought. The sour smell grew stronger as he passed, and he realized it was coming from her. She needed to give her clothes a good wash, in his view, and maybe her body along with them. Jesus, she was pale, with hair resembling filaments of steel, and eyes more white than blue, like bleached water.

'Maybe you could introduce us to the kids,' said Gackowska, as the door closed behind them.

'I'm sure,' said Mors, 'they'd like that very much.'

CXXIII

The Priory Church of St Bartholomew the Great – or St Bart's, as it is generally known to Londoners – dates back to 1123, although half of the original structure was destroyed in the sixteenth century, leaving an interesting combination of Norman, later Middle Ages, and Tudor architecture. St Bart's has survived the Dissolution of the Monasteries during the Reformation, the Great Fire of London, and the German Blitz, making it not only the oldest parish church in the city, but also a unique one.

Yet there is blood in the ground here, too, and not all of it shed by animals at the meat market nearby. Smithfield was long the favored site for the execution of heretics, who were burned at the Smithfield Stake in their hundreds, while swindlers and forgers – for coining was High Treason – would be taken there to be placed in vats of oil and boiled to death, or simply set to roasting on the woodpile.

In 1783, the city's gallows was moved to Newgate prison, just south of Smithfield, and its sacrifices were buried beneath the flagstones of Birdcage Walk. And busy was the Newgate tree in those early years: more than five hundred men and woman set to dancing from it before the end of the eighteenth century alone, which meant more than five hundred bodies sent to rot under the flags. The squalor of the gallows further infected a district already filthy with the blood and shit of cattle, their entrails clogging the drains as they were slaughtered and gutted. The air smelled rank, and typhus was rife within the prison walls. Each year, more necks were broken, more bodies laid down. Six hundred, seven hundred, a thousand, eleven hundred, the total slowing until, finally, George Woolfe brought it all to an end in 1902, when his was the last neck to snap.

And St Bart's watched over all, and watches still.

Parker approached St Bart's, and entered through the west door. The desk was unattended, and when he peered into the nave, he could see no sign of a guide or caretaker. He left the admission fee in coin, and entered. The interior smelled musty, and there was a darkness and intimacy to its spaces, a sense of deep antiquity alien to any North American house of worship. He felt himself to have been mistaken in coming here – not because of any threat, but the opposite: for a few moments, he experienced a sense of peace, almost of consolation. To his left stood a covered grand piano, and an area for private prayer and reflection. He passed both, and moved into the heart of the church.

A door closed, the sound so soft as to be barely noticeable. He waited, but no other visitor appeared.

He moved along the pews, pausing to examine the engraved stones in the floor marking the graves of those buried beneath: Dyson and Leafe, Rags and Tornell, North and Sorrell and Cobbold, among them the names used by Mors, if Glenmore was to be believed. She had been here. She had walked these aisles.

High on the southern wall, he thought he saw movement behind the glass of the oriel window, a kind of enclosed stone gallery built for the prior, that he might check on his monks from a place of concealment, but it could simply have been the play of light. The murk of the church seemed to thicken. Footsteps sounded either above or behind Parker, the stone of the walls and floors making the source difficult to establish. He headed back down the aisle to the door, his own steps quickening –

And stopped.

He had not been mistaken. They had meant for him to come here. This was where they planned to kill him.

A naked figure, unnaturally bright, stood high on a stool. Parker had barely noticed it upon entering, taking it to be simply another religious icon, albeit one of more than usual luminosity. Now he realized how wrong he had been.

St Bartholomew, the martyr, in gilded bronze.

St Bartholomew, a pair of shears in his raised right hand, and draped over his right arm, his own flayed skin.

St Bartholomew, a smear of blood on his shining cheeks, because the sockets of the statue were no longer hollow, and instead held two corporeal eyes.

For an instant, Parker was once again in a kitchen in Brooklyn, staring at the ruined, excoriated remains of his wife and child. He was outside a Louisiana shack, where a man named Tee Jean Aguillard had been turned into a human *écorché*, grasping a flap of his own skin to reveal the redness of his interiority. He was inside that same shack, looking down on Tee Jean's mother, Tante Marie, split from sternum to groin. All the work of the Traveling Man, all the creations of one who would have seen beauty in this statue. Quayle had chosen well the location of the trap. He had wanted Parker to see this before he died.

'Remind you of anyone?'

Parker turned. The man before him, whom Parker had glimpsed once or twice on the way to the church, was of average height and build, his face neither particularly handsome nor repellent, his thinning hair a nondescript brown. Only the weapon in his hands rendered him remarkable. This, too, was familiar to Parker. He had seen a similar armament in the hands of the Traveling Man: a tranquilizer pistol, loaded with an aluminum-bodied syringe. The needle would hurt when it struck – Parker could remember that much about the experience – but the pain would be much less than what would follow. Hanging from the man's belt was a small, sharp knife, the kind used to skin animals.

'Who are you?' said Parker.

'My name is Sellars. You killed my god.'

'And what god was that?'

'The Green Man.'

'You're a Familist?'

'I am the last Familist. Our church lies in ruins, and our god is no more. All because of you.'

'Your god was a dead tree.'

'If so, they hung your Christ from one of his limbs.'

645

'And now you've been sent by Quayle to do his dirty work.'

'Quayle wants you to die here. I'm happy to oblige. He's one step away from completing his work, but a drop more blood won't hurt. Did you see the eyes in the statue?'

'Yes.'

'Did you recognize them?'

'No.'

'They're your friend's eyes. They're Johnston's eyes. You killed him. By bringing him here, you led him to his death.'

Parker took the blow without reacting. He breathed deeply, until he could trust himself to speak again. He forced Bob Johnston from his mind. Grief wouldn't help, not now.

'How many others did you kill?' he said. 'All those women left with beads in their mouths?'

'Some of them.'

'Why?'

'Because in serving other gods, I also served my own. Now I'm going to send you to meet them. You're going to die like your whore wife and your whore child, butchered and flayed.'

'I don't think so.'

Sellars leveled the pistol.

'The doors are locked,' he said. 'No one can get in. No one is coming to save you.'

'I know,' said Parker. 'That's because they're already here.'

Gackowska dug her fingers into a gap in the floorboards, and used it to drag herself nearer the front door. Her right hand was clutched against her side, but the wound kept bleeding, and vital fluids streamed in her wake.

She glanced into the living room; its door, closed on their arrival, now stood open. The body of a woman lay sprawled against the fireplace. Her white blouse bore a mark like an Oriental poppy: dark at the center, and a lighter red beyond. Upstairs, the children had stopped crying. The pale woman had gone to see to them, just after she'd shot Hynes in the neck and chest, and Gackowska in the back and head. Gackowska had looked into the muzzle of the gun, and everything had gone black. When the light returned, her skull was filled with pain beyond description, and she was blind in one eye.

But somehow, she was still alive.

She shifted her grip, her fingers seeking for new purchase. One of her nails snapped, and the immediacy of the pain shocked her, even amid the greater suffering, but she did not pause. She found her grip, bent her arm, and inched forward. She could see the front door. Soon, she'd be able to touch it.

She'd had to crawl through Hynes's blood to get this far, pushing past his body to get to the hall. It was he who had spotted the plastic gloves behind a flowerpot, the material speckled faintly with red; he who had quickly sent a text to Nabih Uddin as the woman led them to the kitchen, requesting a copy of Lauren Sellars's photograph from her driving license; he who had tapped his own wedding ring to alert Gackowska to the absence of a similar ring on the woman's finger; and he who had died for his cleverness, when the woman spun, gun suddenly in hand, and fired, killing him almost instantly before turning the weapon on Gackowska.

She heard sounds from above her head, and redoubled her efforts. Three or four more feet, and she would be at the door. After that would come the challenge of standing, but she'd made it this far with two bullets in her, and in agony unlike any she had ever imagined . . .

So Gackowska didn't stop reaching for the door, not even when the feet of the pale woman appeared beside her, and a voice whispered, 'Now, where are you going?'; and not even when she dragged her back to the kitchen through her own blood. Gackowska stopped reaching only when the pale woman placed the warm tip of the suppressor against the back of her head, and pulled the trigger of the pistol.

Only then.

Sellars reacted to the noise behind him. He turned to see two men approaching from the west side of the chapel, the first tall and black, the second shorter and of indeterminate ethnic origin, with the demeanor of a homeless person. In their hands they carried not guns, but heavy church candlesticks. They wanted him alive, Sellars realized; he was no use to them dead, because a dead man couldn't lead them to Quayle. Between the two men, crouching by one of the pews, Sellars glimpsed a young woman whom he took to be the church attendant. She was talking on a phone, probably to the police. He'd been surprised to discover the desk abandoned when he'd followed Parker into the church. Now he knew why.

Sellars backed away, moving the muzzle of the pistol between Parker and the others – for all the good it would do, one dart for three men – until finally he came to the altar, and could retreat no further.

'It's over,' said Parker.

'Is it?'

'You have a blade, and an air pistol with a single tranquilizer. Quayle should have armed you better, because soon you won't have either of those weapons. One way of losing them will hurt, and the other won't. You should choose the easier way.'

'And then?'

'You tell us what you know, and the police, too. You show us where to find the body of our friend. You take us to Quayle.'

Through the walls came the sound of the first sirens.

'I don't think so,' said Sellars. 'But you're right: it's all over. By tomorrow, this world will have changed. In the meantime, I believe there's a third option.'

And Parker understood.

'Don't do it,' he said, too late.

Sellars raised the pistol, pressed it hard against his left ear, and shot the aluminum syringe into his brain.

CXXIV

Parker sat in the interview room, a cup of coffee cooling beside him. Angel and Louis were elsewhere in the City of London Police station on Bishopsgate. Parker wasn't sure why they had been taken to this particular location, and he didn't care. He was thinking of Bob Johnston. They should have protected him. One of them should have been with him at all times. Parker should have made sure of it.

As for the confrontation with Sellars, Parker and the others had done nothing wrong, beyond Parker using himself as bait. He had picked up on Sellars's pursuit of him near Lincoln's Inn, and remained on foot for fear of losing him. He kept his cell phone link to Angel open all the time, the microphone lead hooked to the lapel of his jacket. His initial thought was that Sellars was following him to make sure he was headed to St Bart's, where Mors would be waiting to take him. But Sellars had been the sole threat: when Angel and Louis arrived at the church minutes ahead of Parker, they discovered it to be empty apart from Dora Coyne, the young woman behind the admissions desk. It had taken them a minute to persuade Coyne that trouble might be on its way, and it would be better for her if she were not at her post when it arrived, but they now had her as an independent witness to all that had transpired.

Parker – speaking also on behalf of Angel and Louis – declined to answer any questions until the US embassy in London had been informed of their situation. He identified himself as a licensed private investigator from the United States, and a paid consultant to the Federal Bureau of Investigation. He also threw in Ross's name for good measure, and suggested that the embassy be asked to send a legal attaché as a matter of urgency. He was then left to wait, brood, and mourn. Within the hour, an assistant legat named Paul Canton arrived, but by then Parker had become aware of a change of mood in the station. He could sense urgency, and something like fury. He just hoped it wasn't directed at him or his friends.

Canton was in his mid-thirties, and basketball-player tall. He asked for a few minutes alone with Parker before any questioning could commence, put his briefcase on the table, and said:

'What the hell is this?'

'What do you know?'

'I spoke with SAC Ross. He asked if you'd killed anyone, and seemed relieved to learn that you hadn't. He told me you're engaged in an independent investigation, but one that might impact favorably on bureau interests. You had therefore agreed to keep the bureau informed of your progress in return for a certain degree of facilitation, which sounds like ass-covering of the highest order on Ross's part. So how about you give me the short, accurate version?'

Parker decided that he liked Canton. He was probably using the FBI as a stepping stone to a more interesting and lucrative career in the private sector, but at least he'd be good at whatever he ended up doing. Parker offered him a brief but detailed history of the events that had brought the three men to Europe, including the meeting with Hendricksen in Belgium, at which Sellars's name had first come up, and Parker's dealings with Lockwood, Dodson & Fogg, which he believed were directly related to what had occurred at St Bart's. He concluded with a pair of eyes lodged in the sockets of a gilded statue, and what Sellars had said about the death of Bob Johnston.

'And the two men with you? Ross said it would be better if the City of London Police didn't delve too deeply into their histories.'

'They won't find much if they do.'

'Ross indicated that might be the problem. Blank slates tend to arouse suspicion.'

'They haven't committed any crime. Neither have I.'

'That's not the point. Sellars is.'

'He admitted killing some of those women found with beads

in their mouths. We have Dora Coyne as a witness. She heard it all, and I also have it on my phone. I set it to record as soon as I entered the church.'

'There's more to the situation than that.'

'Like what?'

'Murdered British police. That's all I know for now.'

The door of the interview room opened, and two detectives entered: Considine and Woodful. Parker had already been introduced to them.

'What about our friend Bob?' he said to Canton.

'We'll start trying to confirm what we can. We can get blood and DNA from the . . . tissue left in the church.'

Throats were cleared, and folders opened.

It was time.

Priestman wiped her face and mouth with a paper towel, and watched the water swirl down the drain. She checked her eyes. They were puffy, but not markedly so. No one would have blamed her for showing signs of grief, but she would have blamed herself. This was not the moment for them. She would mourn for Hynes and Gackowska later. Already the reports were coming in: Lauren Sellars's car found abandoned off Orange Hill Road in Prestwich, about a quarter of a mile from the scene of the killings; an incident at a church in London; a confession to murder, but not the one Priestman wanted. Someone had slaughtered two of her officers, two of her friends, possibly even the same person who had taken a knife to Douglas Hood in his cottage on the moors.

She left the bathroom. Nabih Uddin was waiting for her, car keys in hand.

'Let's go,' she said.

West, to look upon her dead.

Parker told Considine and Woodful all that he could, but not all he knew. He spoke of Quayle, Mors, and the myth of the Atlas; of a dead mother and a missing child; of bodies left in Indiana, Maine, and by the Mexican border; of the Familists and their god; and, finally, of Sellars. He also informed them of the existence of a cell phone recording from St Bart's, details of which could be corroborated by Dora Coyne. In turn, he learned of the murders of three people at the Sellars home in Prestwich: Lauren Sellars and two Northumbria Police detectives, DS Derek Hynes and DC Lisa Gackowska. The Sellarses' daughters, Kelly and Louise, were missing.

He also discovered that Christopher Sellars was not dead. The needle had entered his brain with force, depositing a massive shot of what was believed to be a strong sedative: the best guess was midazolam or a similar drug, because it would have to be fast-working to take down Parker in seconds. Were Sellars to survive, he wouldn't be answering questions for some time, if at all, depending on the extent of the damage caused by the metal syringe, which was already in the process of being removed from his head by surgeons.

Woodful flicked back through her notes.

'Tell me again when you became certain that Sellars was following you,' said Woodful.

'Charterhouse Street,' said Parker.

'And this man, Glenmore, was the one that told you about the link to St Bart's.'

'Yes.'

'How could he be sure you'd go there?'

'He couldn't, and neither could Sellars. If I hadn't gone to the church, Sellars would probably have tried to kill me somewhere else. But Quayle wanted me to die in there. He wanted me to see that statue, and be reminded of my dead wife and child. He has a taste for the sufferings of others.'

'And you went along with this, even at risk to yourself?'

'I wasn't alone.'

'But all three of you were unarmed?'

'Yes.'

A lie, but a minor one. Parker just hoped that no one tried to play the grand piano at St Bart's before the guns concealed amid its workings could be retrieved. He didn't like the skeptical look on Considine's face, but compared to Woodful, she resembled a picture of credence.

'Your colleagues are somewhat unusual,' said Woodful.

Beside Parker, Canton grunted in what might have been agreement.

'They hear that a lot,' said Parker.

'And you?'

'I often get called something stronger,' said Parker.

There was a knock on the door. A uniformed officer stuck his head in, and addressed Woodful.

'I think we need you outside, ma'am.'

A black man in his sixties was sitting in the reception area of the station. Beside him was a woman perhaps ten years younger than he, and probably his wife. She was holding his right hand in her left. A uniformed policewoman stood between them and the door, just in case one or both experienced any sudden change of heart and tried to escape into the night.

The man looked up as Woodful approached.

'Mr Campbell?' she said.

He stood, and the woman stood with him.

'Nobody calls me Mr Campbell,' he said. 'Mostly, they just call me Glenmore.'

CXXV

It was after ten by the time Parker, Angel, and Louis were permitted to walk free from the station, although they were instructed not to leave the city, or the jurisdiction, without first informing the City of London Police. Parker had even been permitted to keep his cell phone, once the recording from St Bart's had been retrieved from it. Canton remained with them throughout. Woodful offered to have them driven back to their hotel, but they declined her offer. Instead, the four men shared a taxi to Soho, where Canton dropped them off.

'Bob Johnston hasn't returned to Hazlitt's,' Canton told them, as the taxi waited for him by the curb. 'A Rosanna Bellingham left messages at the hotel. It seems he was supposed to meet her for dinner, but never showed. We've traced his physician in Portland, and should have copies of his medical records by now. From there, we can work on finding out if the samples taken from the church give us a match on his blood type. In the meantime, try to get some sleep. I'll see you at your hotel at seven-thirty tomorrow morning.'

They watched him drive away.

'What happens at seven-thirty?' said Angel.

'Nothing,' said Parker, 'but at eight the police are going to raid the offices of Lockwood, Dodson and Fogg. They've already started watching them, not to mention arresting the principals.'

'And you want to be there?'

'That's what I told Canton.'

But Parker's mind was already elsewhere. Three bodies left at the Sellars house: the mother first, killed by a single bullet to the chest, followed by the two detectives, also shot dead. But the Sellarses' neighbors had heard no gunfire, and the police had found no shell casings at the scene.

Who uses a suppressor? Who picks up the brass after a shooting?

A professional.

Who finishes off an injured woman, having first dragged her from the hallway back to the kitchen after she apparently tried to escape?

A sadist. Mors.

But why take the children?

For the same reason that Quayle had instructed Sellars, and at least one other man, Gary Holmby, to abduct and kill young women: because their deaths might be enough to bring the Atlas's reality into being. Sellars believed that Quayle was just one step away from completing his task, and now Mors had two children to offer. Sellars had been set up. If he managed to kill Parker, so much the better, and if Parker killed him, it would be one more loose end tied off; but what really mattered was that Sellars should be drawn away from his children so that Mors could abduct them.

But to take them where? There could be only one place. Johnston had said it himself: '*Everything comes down to that old church.*' The Sellars girls would be brought to Fairford, and if what their father had suggested was true, it would probably be that night. Mors couldn't risk holding on to the children for long, especially if there was a possibility that Sellars might manage to kill Parker before attempting to return to his family. Sellars might have been a fanatic, but was he fanatical enough to sacrifice his own children? Somehow, Parker doubted it.

He could inform the police, of course, and let them swarm Fairford – assuming they bought into his reasoning, and managed to organize themselves quickly enough. But Mors and Quayle would pick up on a large police presence, no matter how cleverly it was disguised. Once they did, they'd dispose of the children before waiting to try again. More people would die; more women, more children.

Or so Parker told himself, but the truth was that he wanted Quayle and Mors for himself.

The church, he knew from Johnston's maps, was at one end of the town of Fairford, but still close enough to the ebb and flow of the community that any attempt to gain access to it while carrying two children would almost certainly be noticed. Quayle and Mors would have to wait until the bars and late-night food joints were closed, and all was quiet.

Fairford was two hours from the center of London. There was still time.

He hailed a cab, and told the driver where he wanted to go.

'And whatever the fare is, you can add another hundred to it,' he said.

'It's your money,' said the driver.

Parker turned to Angel and Louis.

'I guess we're leaving.'

'Without guns?'

'Without much of anything, except hope.'

Louis shook his head, but climbed in the cab nonetheless, Angel behind him.

'We,' said Louis mournfully, 'are running on fumes.'

CXXVI

De Jaager sat in an apartment on Amsterdam's Lijnbaansgracht. The woman before him was old, but then so was everything else in her home. A slice of *boterkoek* had crumbled to dust in his mouth, and the coffee tasted of cheap beans long past their prime. She had money, this one, or so it was said, but elected not to spend it on making her life more comfortable. But who was he to judge? Perhaps she was frightened. In his experience, miserliness and fear went together. The old all had the same dreads: injury, illness, and death. Throw in loneliness and one had a perfect quartet of misery, the only assurance being that mortality would finally bring a close to all. Money wouldn't help the old woman to dodge the grave, but might be of some use in easing the pain that would probably precede it.

She wore spectacles, she informed him, but only to read. She could still see almost perfectly at a distance. To prove this, she called out the license numbers of cars parked on the other side of the canal, and read from the signs in the windows of the stores.

'There,' she said. 'I am no liar.'

Her accent was one De Jaager associated with North Holland, towns like Blaricum and Laren. It was the voice of wealth and privilege. He did not hold it against her. He had wealth of his own, and privilege of a kind. Hers had brought her at last to this place, a realm of scuffed wood and faded rugs, of ticking clocks and stale *boterkoek*. Were he curious enough, he might have delved into her history, but he wanted to hear only what she could tell him about the night of Eva Meertens's death.

The woman was lost in the big armchair at the window, dwarfed by its red leather immensity, and perched on a cushion because she had no flesh of her own to act as a bolster. A tiny, ossified creature: pick her up, and she would rattle in one's arms; a wrin-kled bird, fallen from the nest, clothed as part of some strange child's game.

'You have the money?'

De Jaager showed it to her, the bills counted and banded in a bag. She took one of the bundles in her left hand, eked some spittle from her wasted glands, and wet her right thumb before using it to flick the edges.

'One has to be sure,' she said. 'I don't trust men.'

'No?'

'Nor women either.'

She moved to lodge the cash in the space between her cushion and the arm of the chair, but De Jaager extended a hand to intercept her.

'I have often thought the same myself,' he said, and reclaimed the money, if only temporarily.

The old woman scowled, but voiced no objection.

'Tell me what you saw,' said De Jaager.

'I was dozing in my chair,' she said. 'I sometimes sleep here through the night, if it's too much trouble to get to my bed. I have a blanket, and a stool for my feet.'

She gestured to both nearby.

'And a *pispot* for my needs,' she added, although mercifully for De Jaager, this remained hidden.

Her words brought to mind an old Dutch *tongbreker: Al een potvis in een pispot pist, heb je een pispot vol met potvispis.* If a sperm-whale pisses in a pisspot, you'll have a pisspot full of sperm-whale piss. He had many such *tongbrekers.* He would recite them for his own amusement, and to test the state of his memory. Eva Meertens used to laugh at him for it. He took the recollection as a good omen.

'And?' he said.

'I heard a splash, like something heavy being thrown into the canal.'

'What time was this?'

'It was nine twenty-five. I remember looking at the clock on the mantelpiece.'

'What did you do then?'

'My drapes were open, but I had no lights burning. I could see it all through the gaps in the blinds.'

'You could see what?'

'Ripples on the water, and a woman getting into a car. For a moment, I glimpsed her from head to toe.'

'Why didn't you inform the police?'

'I thought I should wait.'

'For what?'

'For someone to offer a reward for information – or for a man like you to start asking questions, with the promise of greater profit to come.'

'Some might view that as callous.'

'The girl was dead. That was not about to change.'

This much, at least, was inarguable.

'Describe the woman you saw.'

She did, with precision, including her hair and mode of dress. De Jaager did not interrupt. When she was done, she also gave him the color of the car.

'What about the license number?' he said.

'What about it?'

'Did you see that as well?'

'As plain as the money in your possession.'

He reached into the bag, and removed two bundles of euros. She took them, and caused them to vanish before reciting the number from memory.

'Well?' she said.

'Perhaps,' he replied.

'What more do you require?'

'Certainty.'

From the inside pocket of his jacket, De Jaager produced a photograph. Paulus had taken it with a zoom lens, and from some distance, but the image was clear.

'I want to know if this is the woman.'

She stretched out a claw, but De Jaager held on to the picture for a moment longer.

'Understand me,' he said. 'You can have the money anyway,

for the help you have offered, only don't lie. If this is not the same woman, you must say so.'

'I may be a *kut*,' she said, 'but I am not a liar.'

De Jaager blinked at the obscenity, and handed over the photograph. The old woman examined it carefully before returning it.

'Yes,' she said. 'She's the one.'

Armitage, the legat.

Now, at last, he was sure.

De Jaager stood, leaving the bag on the chair.

'Do you know who I am?' he said.

'Yes, of course I—'

'Do you *know* who I *am*?' he repeated.

The bird head wobbled a denial.

'How,' she replied, 'can I know someone that I have never met?'

XIII

There are other places
Which also are the world's end, some at the sea jaws,
Or over a dark lake, in a desert or a city –
But this is the nearest, in place and time,
Now and in England.

T.S. Eliot, 'Little Gidding' from Four Quartets

CXXVII

It was after midnight when Parker and the others reached Fairford. Most of the buildings in the center of the town were dark, but lights still burned in the bar of the Bull Hotel on the market square. Parker experienced a moment of panic, even despair, when he caught signs of activity at the old schoolhouse by the churchyard, but it was only the winding down of a local event that had clearly run late. He and Louis watched from the square as a small group of older men and women dispersed and drove away, while Angel secured a pair of rooms at the Bull. It would give them an excuse to be in the town should the local police find them on the streets at a late hour; and should Quayle and Mors fail to show, they would have somewhere to stay while they waited a second night. They would not remain in Fairford for a third; if there were no sign of their quarry by that time, it would mean Parker had been wrong about the church, and the Sellars children were already dead.

Angel returned with the keys to the rooms, which also gave them access to the hotel after hours. By now the lights were going off in the bar, and they were the only people on the square. A couple of cars passed, but no one showed any interest in their presence. Louis produced a battered pack of cigarettes. None of them smoked, but it was enough that they were holding lit cigarettes in their hands; another reason to be outdoors, although they couldn't remain there indefinitely. Somewhere secure was needed from which to watch the church. They left this to Angel, who headed toward the schoolhouse. Within minutes, Parker's cell phone vibrated once with a missed call, and he and Louis joined Angel inside the old limestone building, entering through a far doorway, out of sight of the main street. The windows on the

663

second floor looked out over the churchyard, and the main entrance porch to St Mary's on the southern wall.

'I checked out the church,' said Angel. 'Three doors, all locked: the main one, another on the west wall under the big window, and a third on the north wall. The main door has a security camera in the porch, but the other two are unwatched.'

'Can you open one of them?'

'Probably.'

'Do it.'

Angel left them for a second time. Moments later, they saw him darting between the gravestones before he faded from view.

'What are you thinking?' said Louis.

'You and Angel stay outside, one watching from the school, the other from those trees to the west. I'll wait inside.'

'You figure they'll kill them in the church? Why not in the churchyard?'

'Because there's less risk of being seen, but mostly because the windows are the key, and the windows and the church are one. If they try to harm the children in the cemetery, you and Angel can stop them, but I think Quayle will want to get inside. Whatever happens, it makes sense to have one of us in there.'

'Maybe Quayle won't come himself. Maybe he'll just send Mors.'

'He'll come,' said Parker. 'This is the final act.'

From the pocket of his jacket, Louis produced a tiny DoubleTap tactical pistol, twin-barreled; a little over five inches in length, and less than an inch wide.

'Two spare rounds in the grip,' said Louis.

'You had this all along?' said Parker. 'Even at the police station?'

'That's right.'

'Where did you keep it hidden?'

'You don't want to know.'

Parker eyed it doubtfully.

'I don't suppose you have a wet wipe?'

CXXVIII

De Jaager met the couple in a room above a shuttered restaurant off Prinsengracht, the building still smelling of grease and Chinese food a year after the departure of the last tenants. He was close to securing a buyer for the premises, which would reduce his portfolio to three properties, one of them his own home. De Jaager no longer had any desire to be involved in real estate, or in business of any kind, legal or illegal. He had already commenced activating the machinery of his retirement when Louis appeared, seeking his assistance. Had it been anyone else, De Jaager would have refused. That decision had cost Eva Meertens her life, and confirmed De Jaager in his wish to be done with it all. Now his final criminal act would be to contract out the killing of an American legat.

The two women before him were of early middle age, with dark hair, dark eyes, and souls to match. They were known only as Lotte and Chris, after a pair of actresses in a Dutch soap opera, and were utterly morally bereft. They did not come cheap, but then the best people rarely did.

'She must vanish without a trace,' said De Jaager.

A body would bring down a different type of investigation by the Americans, one that De Jaager would rather not chance. Disappearances were another matter. He had hoped to punish Eva's killer himself, but under the circumstances it seemed wiser to leave the job to specialists.

'We understand,' said Lotte, the elder of the two. She was attractive in a matronly way, as long as one didn't look too hard. Upon closer inspection, her bone structure became too apparent, like a death's head concealed by a layer of silk.

'There will be a premium,' said Chris. Her face was entirely without blemish, wrinkle, or any defining feature that might have made it memorable. It resembled the head of a doll, or a character sketched on the shell of an egg.

'Of course.' These women would be required to evanesce in the aftermath of the killing.

'Do you want her to suffer?' said Chris. De Jaager could barely detect the movement of her mouth as she spoke.

'Is there a premium for that as well?'

He meant it as a jest.

'No, that's part of the service.'

Retirement, thought De Jaager, could not come soon enough.

Armitage woke on a sweat-soaked sheet. Her skin itched unbearably, and even the interior of her mouth felt swollen – her tongue too large, her cheeks and gums tingling unpleasantly, as in the hours following a difficult dental procedure. Snatches of a song played on repeat in her mind, like a malfunctioning jukebox.

It took a great effort to lift her head from the pillow, and a greater one still to keep it from falling back down. Her eyesight was blurred, but her hand wouldn't rise when she tried to use it to clear her vision. Briefly, she feared that she'd been tied to her bed while sleeping, until she managed to get her right hand moving, then her left. It followed reluctantly, but only after a sharp sting to her forearm, as though she had disturbed an insect in the process of feeding.

She wanted to shower again. She'd been reading up on chronic itching, and found that many sufferers claimed showering eased their discomfort, sometimes for hours. Armitage had showered before going to bed, and applied moisturizer. It must have helped, because she'd managed to get some rest. According to the clock on her locker, it was just after 2 a.m., and she'd been in bed by 11 p.m. Three hours sleep: better than nothing, and she hadn't even taken any pills. She was due at the embassy by 8 a.m., and had hoped to arrive with something resembling a clear head, but what use was it to eschew medication if the result was a night of misery? There was some Benadryl in the medicine cabinet. It might make her drowsy enough to get back to sleep without turning her into a zombie for the rest of the day.

The song resumed, some piece of popular trash she didn't even like, as if her misery wasn't already great enough.

'Stop!' Armitage said, aloud. 'Please, for the love of God!'

She sat on the edge of her bed and rubbed her eyes, but it didn't help; she still couldn't see any better. Tentatively, she got to her feet and made her way to the tiny ensuite bathroom to the left of her bed. She hit the light, shielding her eyes so she didn't blind herself entirely. When she felt it was safe to do so, she lowered her hand. Naked, she stood before the full-length mirror on the wall.

'No,' she said. 'No, no, no . . .'

Her entire body was covered in letters, the same alphabet that had been used to disfigure the books in her library. The ink was purple and faded, in the manner of tattoos that had been in place for many years. They formed words she could not read, snaking along her arms and over her breasts, across her belly and her upper back, over her thighs and calves, her feet and ankles, on her neck and her face—

Jesus, her face.

She opened her mouth. There were letters on her tongue.

And letters on the whites of her eyes.

But one pattern recurred more often than any other, one that was familiar to her:

الجن

Armitage stumbled away from the mirror. Her phone was by her bed. She had to call someone. She needed help. She needed—

Armitage paused. Her body had been marked – no, inscribed – while she slept. An implement had been used to write upon her skin, transforming her into a living page of vellum.

Which meant that someone had done this to her.

Someone had been in her apartment.

Someone might yet be.

She'd disposed of the gun used to kill Gruner, but still had her own service weapon. Officially, as far as the Dutch were concerned, the legats were unarmed. But unofficially, well, that was a different matter.

Armitage stepped back into the bedroom. She had never been so aware of her own nakedness, but she noticed that the music was no longer troubling her. Fear had seen to that. If she could get to the locker, she would have her phone and a weapon. One step, two, three . . .

She was almost at the bed when she heard movement behind her, and smelled something both meaty and rank, like the odor in a butcher's store at the close of a warm day's business. She saw a pair of dark, lidless eyes regarding her from the shadows, and a jagged, circular mouth like a mutilation to the tissue of the face, the whole surrounded by a cloak of flesh that draped itself on the floor. The figure shifted its weight with a wet sound, and a single thin digit reached toward her, topped by a sharp chitinous nib. An inky bubble of purple liquid hung from the tip.

Maggs's demon.

Maggs's *djinni*.

And from the place of his burning, Cornelie Gruner laughed.

CXXIX

Parker sat against the screen between the chancel and tower of St Mary's, hidden by the darkness. Angel had opened the small door on the northern wall, and Parker had told him to lock it again behind him. If Quayle decided to enter the same way – and it seemed likely that he might do so, since it was largely hidden from view – Parker did not want him to be alerted by finding it unlocked.

The interior of the church was cold, and he was grateful for his jacket. He'd found a cushion under one of the benches, which eased his discomfort a little, but he had nothing to do except wait. He thought of Bob Johnston, and the great plans he had been concocting for the final years of his life. He thought of Sam, of Jennifer, and of Rachel. In the solitude of St Mary's, he lived other lives. He had a wife, and another child, although he could put a face to neither. They existed only as nebulous presences, entities unreal, and exuded no more warmth than the stones of the church.

Above and before him only the faintest of moonlight gave life to the stained glass windows, leaving most of their details lost and enshadowed, yet the intentions of their creators remained clear to him. On the windows to the north, the persecutors of the church – among them Judas Iscariot; the High Priests Annas and Caiaphas; and Herod the Great, with a child impaled upon his sword – faced the saints and martyrs, while angels hovered over the heads of the good, and demons capered above those of the foul.

And between them stood the Last Judgment of the great West Window, the final page of the Fractured Atlas.

*   *   *

Sam stood by the window of her bedroom in Vermont, gazing over lawn and forest, but seeing none of it. She looked far to the east, to her father. Her hands lay in her lap, clenched into fists. She was alone, but a second presence was reflected beside her own in the glass: a dead moon in the form of a child.

Such concentration on their faces, such effort, such love; the words of the one spoken aloud, the words of the other a whispered echo, willed over land and sea.

'Daddy.'

daddy

'Don't sleep . . .'

don't sleep

Parker closed his eyes. From the walls above, a voice called to him. He had tried to pray, but this church was too old, too strange. This was not his faith. He no longer even knew what faith he followed. He knew only that he must bleed, and keep bleeding, until he made recompense for his sins. He would assume the burden of pain – his own, and the pain of others – because of all that he had failed to do: he had failed to protect his wife, failed to protect his child. He had failed as a husband, failed as a father.

daddy

And he would fail here too, in the end. He would fail, and light would fade from the earth. When he was dead, and his loss complete, he would wait by a lakeshore in the next world, wait to join the great tide of souls flowing into the eternal sea, but all faces would be turned from him, among them the face of God. Not even Jennifer would be able to save him, and so she would leave him at the last rather than share his exile.

This wasted existence, passed in loneliness and suffering; this self-inflicted punishment, all because it was easier to endure new torments than reach an accommodation with the old; this rage, concealed by a mask of empathy; this sadness, with self-pity as a substitute for remorse.

For someone to take your life would be an act of charity.

For you to take your own would be an act of courage.

daddy

Do it in this place, before your Old God.

Do it in this place, before us.

wake up

Parker opened his eyes. The pistol was between his lips, its barrels pressed against the roof of his mouth.

they're coming

CXXX

N ew light illuminated the windows – light to the north, and
light to the west – although it seemed not to be shining from
outside but from within the glass itself. Where formerly the figures
and motifs had been occluded, now they were entirely distinct,
so that Parker could see clearly the blue-skinned demon looking
down on Judas Iscariot; the creature like a mutated lamb that
might almost have been reaching out from the pane to grasp the
severed head of a martyr raised on the halberd of a soldier; and
the darker, horned entity above Annas, little more than a pair of
bright malevolent eyes in a face otherwise without feature. The
impression they created was less of images fixed in glass and
more of creatures circling the panes from without, pressing their
bodies against them in an effort to gain access.

Across the West Window, in defiance of logic, a darkness was
spreading, so that slowly all those on the right hand of Christ
were lost to sight, the cloud obliterating the top half of the
window and most of the lower, leaving untouched only the three
panes depicting Hell and the affliction of the damned, the flames
from the mouth of the all-consuming Leviathan appearing to
flicker in the altered illumination.

Parker heard footsteps. Rising slightly from his place of
concealment, he was able to see into the Lady Chapel containing
the tomb of John Tame, the great patron of St Mary's. Beside
the tomb stood a small altar draped in blue cloth, but one of
its panels now lay upon the stones, and from the gap emerged
Mors, leading a girl by the right hand. Quayle was already in
the nave of the church, heading toward the West Window, a
second, younger child in his arms. They had not needed to enter
by any of the doors because Quayle, so long lived, knew this

church and its environs better than anyone: what lay within, what lay beneath.

And what lay beyond, because now the vision of Hell flared and vanished, as though finally consumed by its own fires, leaving behind only ash, and charred wastes. The West Window became entirely transparent, its images lost. The ceiling faded away, the church transformed to the status of a ruin with unfamiliar skies above, adorned with constellations no human eye had ever glimpsed. The chill grew deeper, and the stones became so cold that Parker, too slow in lifting his left hand as the temperature dropped, bequeathed to them the skin from his fingertips.

Yet he was also conscious that, somehow, the ceiling remained in place, the decorated windows were still visible, and the stones were no colder than they had been before, even as blood beaded and froze on the ends of his fingers. Were the church doors to have opened, admitting some stranger, he would have seen St Mary's as it had always been. Whether he would also have seen Parker, or Quayle and Mors, or two female children, one now prostrated before the West Window, the other stumbling along beside her captor, was another question. What he might have glimpsed, were he a believer in such matters, were specters and pale relicts, as past, present, and future became one; all pasts, all presents, all futures, now with a single conclusion.

Quayle removed a book from a large leather bag hanging by his side, and placed it on the floor before the West Window. The Fractured Atlas was a more primitive construct than Parker had anticipated. Its spine and cover, both a deep red, were unadorned, its page edges rough and unfinished. Even from a distance, he could pick out the scars and veins in the material that had been used to bind it, the flaws that betrayed its origins in the skin of a once-living creature.

A movement at the West Window distracted him as a monstrosity crawled across the exterior of the glass. It was the corpulent body of a man, with the legs of a spider protruding from either side of his torso. The man's own legs had withered almost to nothing and now dragged along uselessly behind him, but his arms remained mobile, and with them he tested the integrity of the panes, digging at their lead with his fingernails. The top of his head was missing, and small black spiders swarmed from their nest in the cavity. The chimera pressed his face against the glass, and Parker recognized him: Elias Pudd, or some version of him. Pudd, the arachnophile, who had helped to mutilate Angel, and taken a bullet for his troubles; Pudd, whose father had himself created bound tomes celebrating the Apocalypse, the last of them, like the Atlas, formed from skin and bone; Pudd, the son of a man who, Parker now realized, might knowingly or unknowingly have been replicating this same Atlas with his own works; Pudd, consigned to his own particular desolation, because the worst of men received the damnation they deserved.

Now more faces appeared at the windows to the north, and more presences splayed themselves upon the glass. Some were familiar to Parker from the paintings and illustrations sourced by Johnston: the dark spirits that populated the Last Judgments of Hieronymus Bosch, Luca Signorelli, and Fra Angelico; the haunters of the anonymous *Vision of Tundale* and Lorenzo Maitani's bas-relief in Orvieto Cathedral; and the mutant hybrids sent to scourge St Anthony in the paintings of Matthias Grünewald and Jan van der Venne. Humanity had given form to them. They had crept unbidden into the nightmares of artists, invading their fever dreams, becoming concretized in their work. Others were misshapen, unfinished, as though waiting for similar imaginations to imbue them with physicality, while the rest were nebulous, like clouds of polluted smoke. How they might be named, or what shapes they might ultimately assume, was of no consequence. They were all manifestations of the same fear, of what might be waiting for us in the lightless honeycombs of this world and the next. Even Parker himself was not immune; something in his own subconscious, buried all these years, had called out to the dark, and a vision of Pudd had answered.

As quickly as it had appeared, the Pudd mutation was gone, vanished like the images on the glass. Only stars now shone, alien clusters, until one by one they began to flicker out, like the dying of fireflies, and the West Window was transformed once more by a multitude of great presences approaching. They kept to no single configuration, no set disposition, so that they remained eternally in a process of embodiment and disincarnation: wings, eyes, tails, hair, scales, flame, ice; beauty beyond imagining, at once so empyrean yet so blighted that one could not long look upon them without wishing to scour the sight from one's vision, and the taint from one's soul.

But these were only the harbingers. They threw themselves against the glass of the West Window, and Parker felt the church shudder at the impact, before they were gone, lost to the margins, and all that remained was what their coming had presaged.

All that was left was the Not-Gods.

In the void hung two children, their hair perfectly white, their skin translucent, their bodies sexless. Darkness poured from the hollow sockets of their eyes like ink rising through water, flowing from lips moving in silent litany. On the floor of the church, the older of the Sellars girls began to scream. She tried to pull away from Mors, who knocked her to the ground with an open hand, and continued to strike at her until she lay still. Quayle opened the Atlas, revealing a page depicting the interior of the church, an illustration so detailed as to be near photographic in quality, even from Parker's vantage point, an impression confirmed by the presence in it of the figures before the altar: Quayle, Mors, the girls.

'It's time,' said Quayle.

Mors, squatting over the subdued child, produced a blade as though from thin air, the steel seeming to form itself from the atoms of the church. By Quayle's feet, the second Sellars girl had recovered some of her strength, and was trying to crawl away. Quayle knelt on her back, pinning her in place, and drew his own knife from a scabbard on his belt. He raised his face to the window as, unnoticed by him, the page before him changed once more, its contents shifting.

Not four figures near the altar now, but five.

Mors lifted her head in shock, just in time to register the man approaching from the nave, a small, twin-barreled pistol in his raised right hand.

Parker fired, and the first shot took Mors above the right

breast. She was thrown backward, tripping over the prone child, and landed heavily on the floor. Parker fired again, this time not at Mors but at Quayle. A hole burst in the back of Quayle's coat, and he fell on the girl before him. She kicked her way out from under him and ran toward Parker while he fumbled for the speed loader in the butt of the gun. The girl's head hit him heavily in the midriff, and the loader bounced from his hand to be forfeited to the gloom of the church.

But now Mors was back on her feet. She was bleeding from her chest, but she wasn't bleeding enough.

With the last of her strength, she came for Parker.

CXXXI

In a series of existences, all unfolding parallel to one another, versions of the man who called himself Atol Quayle ceased their labors.

Candlelight licked at Josias Quayle as the old Huguenot, Gardiol, breathed his last. Creighton Quayle paused in the act of deciphering the notes of the Jesuit, Martin del Río, in the *Disquisitionum magicarum libri sex*. Jonas Quayle dripped an excess of candlewax on the envelope containing his donation to the Reverend Shipman at Fairfax. Bennett Quayle watched Dea Tacita stand naked before him, her body bathed in Black Mary's blood.

Each feeling Atol's pain, each urging him on.

Each desiring oblivion.

CXXXII

Faced with the advancing Mors, Parker took the only option available to him under the circumstances: he pushed the child away, and threw the empty gun. It hit Mors on the forehead, causing her to reel briefly in shock, and giving Parker enough time to pounce. He struck hard at her right hand, hoping to knock the knife from her grip, but she held tightly to it, and used the blade to slash at him. The tip nicked his jacket but missed his body, and the momentum took the blade far enough to one side for him to be able to grasp Mors's forearm and prevent her from using the weapon again. He feinted at her face, and she lifted her left arm to block him, even as he dipped his fist and used it to strike hard at the wound above her right breast.

Mors screamed, and her face went gray, but she somehow found the strength to butt Parker with the top of her skull. She connected with his nose, and he felt something break wetly inside. The pain briefly blinded him, and he tried to put some space between him and Mors until the redness cleared. He could hear noises from the back of the church, but could not identify them. When his vision returned, he saw that Quayle had disappeared during the struggle with Mors. At the West Window, two childlike figures scratched desperately at the glass, the sound of it like an animal cry, and now their mouths were clearly forming a single word, a name spoken over and over as their faces were transfigured, as they were made beautiful to him.

As they became his daughters.

In Vermont, Jennifer held tightly to her half-sister's hand.
don't answer them
'I won't.'

even if it means he dies
'Even if.'

Quayle was in agony. The bullet was lodged inside him, and each step he took seemed to drive it deeper into the core of his being, but it was only one part of a greater trauma, as though he had been hit not once but multiple times. Yet he was close, so close. He held the Atlas against his chest with one hand, and felt the warmth of it, its life force. In his right hand was the knife, and before him were the Sellars girls. The older one was still dazed, either by the blows from Mors or the lingering effects of the sedative, and moved only with the aid of her sister, but the younger child's strength was failing. As Quayle watched, the older girl's legs collapsed, and she dropped heavily to the floor, her head impacting dully on the stone. Her sister took her by the right arm, and tried to drag her further, but she was dead weight.

'It won't hurt,' said Quayle, as his shadow fell across them. 'I promise. And then we'll all sleep.'

Mors cast aside the knife, and reached for her gun beneath the folds of her jacket. The right side of her body was covered in blood, and the grayness had taken up permanent residence in her face. Only those milky eyes retained hints of brightness, but even these were now fading, like gemstones sinking in lactescent waters. She was swearing, over and over, a string of obscenities directed at a world she would soon leave behind; at every man who had ever hurt or slighted her in a lifetime of baseness; at Quayle, for using her without ever loving her; and at Parker, for having the temerity to believe he could stand against her and prevail.

Mors found the gun, and Parker let his hands fall to his sides. A great lassitude descended upon him. He raised his head and stared at the two children behind the West Window, in all their beauty and strangeness. He felt the fracturing of worlds, heard it as a great exhalation that echoed around the church, and thought that he, like Quayle, would be glad to sleep at last, glad to feel nothing.

Mors, now just a few feet from him, grew rigid. Her eyes

widened, and she opened her mouth to speak words that would never be heard. Behind her stood Louis, his right hand obscured by her body, his left grasping her chin to turn her face toward him, so she might look upon him and know it was he who was responsible for ending her life.

'Remember me?' he said, and his right hand twisted the knife, *her* knife, in her back, and a great gout of blood shot from her lips as the light in her eyes was extinguished at last, as all her pain became one before ceasing forever.

Louis withdrew the blade, and let Mors fall. Parker stepped forward and took the gun from her hand. To his right, he saw Angel running from the direction of the open door in the north wall.

'Quayle!' shouted Angel.

Then Parker, too, was running. He saw the lawyer kneeling on the stones by the chancel, blood spreading across the floor –

And, in a corner, the Sellars children, the younger still protecting the older.

Still breathing.

Still alive.

Parker circled Quayle, keeping his distance, until finally he faced him. The lawyer was sitting back against his calves, his hands splayed, palms up, on his thighs. Parker could see no sign of an exit wound from the .22, which meant the bullet had probably hit bone before ricocheting, tearing through organ, nerve, and tissue before it ran out of energy. Had it passed straight through, Quayle might have survived, but now he was fading. Beside him lay the Atlas, the image of the church already dissolving from its open pages.

Quayle managed to raise his head. He looked at Parker.

'Who are you?' he whispered.

'Nobody,' said Parker.

'Liar. What are you?'

'Nothing.'

'Liar.' Quayle managed an expulsion of air that might have passed for a laugh. 'They told me I couldn't die.'

'It seems they lied too.'

'No, you did this. Just you.' He took a deep, shuddering breath. 'But still you've failed.'

'Really?'

'The Atlas wasn't created by man. It can't be destroyed. It will keep seeking its own completion. Someday, it will find its way back to this church, and unmake the world.'

Quayle stared at the cross on the chancel wall.

'I'm sorry,' he said, but his words were not directed at God. A whiteness flickered in his eyes, like pale light reflected from an unseen source, and then was gone. His chin sank upon his chest as the life left him at last. Upon the West Window, only stained-glass images remained.

Angel looked down at Quayle's body.

'I guess no one ever tried hard enough to kill him before now,' he said, 'or he was just deluded.'

'Fuck him either way,' said Louis.

'Hey,' said Angel disapprovingly, 'we're in a church.'

And they had company.

Canton, the legat, joined them at the chancel. He watched as Angel went to comfort the Sellars girls, gathering them into his arms, before taking in the bodies of Quayle and Mors.

'He arrived just before the shooting started,' said Louis, indicating Canton. Louis sounded apologetic, as though this represented some failure on his part.

'How did you find us?' said Parker.

'I tagged your phone at the police station,' said Canton, 'and your jacket too, just in case. There's a transmitter under the collar. When you didn't return to your hotel, I tracked you.'

He handed Parker a clean white handkerchief to stem some of the bleeding from his broken nose. It hurt like hell. He was tired of hurting.

'The police will be here soon,' said Canton. 'We need to get our story straight.'

'Which is?'

'How badly do you want to be a hero?'

'Not at all.'

'Good, because you'll only be a hero until the police discover you were carrying an illegal firearm, and used it to shoot two people. They won't like that. You'll be arrested, and charged. In the end, you probably won't serve any jail time, but it'll be messy, and public.'

'Do you have a better suggestion?'

'The British are our allies in the War on Terror. Allowances have been made by the authorities when it comes to the possession of firearms by certain representatives of the United States, myself included. I followed you here. In desperation, I was forced to intervene to protect the children. There were fatalities.'

'You think a story like that will stand up?' said Parker.

'Two young girls saved, and two individuals suspected of involvement in any number of murders, including the killing of police officers, dispatched? I think we can make it work. In the end, people prefer easy lies to difficult truths.'

'Then I guess you can be the hero,' said Parker.

'I'll make a better one than you,' said Canton. 'I have a stronger jaw.'

He poked at the Atlas with his foot.

'Is that the book?'

'Yes.'

'Ross wants it.'

'Of course.'

'Do you think he should have it?'

Parker regarded Canton with new interest.

'Probably not.'

'Do you want it?'

'Definitely not.'

'Then what's the alternative?'

Parker removed his jacket, and used it to wrap the Atlas, being careful not to touch it with his bare hands.

'I don't know.'

'Well, while you're thinking about it, I have one other piece of news for you.'

'Which is?'

'Those eyes found at St Bart's? They weren't human.'

CXXXIII

Lotte and Chris climbed the stairs to Armitage's apartment in The Hague. Each wore a black silk ski mask and black gloves, along with cheap black jeans, a long-sleeved black shirt, and black sneakers. Only the fact that Lotte was marginally heavier than Chris distinguished them at all. Both carried Maxim 9 pistols: semiautomatics with an integrated suppressor, capable of delivering a bigger punch than a .22.

Cornelie Gruner had been shot to death, which meant that Armitage, in flagrant breach of Dutch law, was in possession of a firearm for purposes other than hunting or target shooting. Lotte and Chris found this both irritating and presumptuous. It was one thing for them to own any number of illegal firearms, but quite another for a foreigner like Armitage to do so. They were at least Dutch citizens, and if anyone had a right to break Dutch law, they did.

De Jaager had made it clear that no one else was to be hurt, only Armitage. Lotte and Chris had decided to interpret 'hurt' as 'hurt badly', meaning 'shot'. They would only get one run at Armitage. If anyone else in the building should appear before the legat was dealt with, the short stun baton attached to Lotte's belt loop contained enough of a charge – more than two microcoulombs – to put even the biggest man on the ground instantly.

Once De Jaager had confirmed the identity of the woman suspected of killing Eva Meertens – and, in all likelihood, Cornelie Gruner, although De Jaager had yet to lose any sleep over that old man's demise – it had been a simple matter to obtain access to Armitage's place of residence, and the work of minutes to insert a carbon-coated key blank into the two locks on her door which, through pulling, striking, and rocking, produced the marks

683

required to manufacture a duplicate set. Lotte and Chris's only concern was that the new keys to the apartment had not been tested, so if one or the other failed to work they'd either have to pick the lock – which would be time-consuming, and almost certainly alert Armitage to their presence – or kick down the door, which would wake the entire building, and quickly draw the police. De Jaager had assured them that the best locksmith in the city had created the duplicates, a man with decades of experience, both legal and illegal. This had not particularly reassured Lotte and Chris, who were of the opinion that the best man for most jobs was usually a woman.

They reached Armitage's top floor apartment without incident. Lotte inserted the first key into the mortice lock, and it turned easily, but the second lock proved trickier. The key stuck, and Lotte feared that Armitage might have activated the night latch, but after a long minute of jiggling, and the application of some WD-40 from a tiny spray bottle, the lock clicked. Lotte eased the door open with her left hand while keeping her back against the wall. Chris risked the first glance, but no cries or shots came, and seconds later the two women were inside.

The door opened directly into the living area, with a small kitchen to the left. Lotte cleared the kitchen while Chris moved through the other room, ending up at the short hallway leading to the apartment's only bedroom. The main bathroom stood to the right, its door fully open. It was empty, a curtain looped over the shower rail exposing the clean white surface of the bath itself.

Now only the bedroom lay ahead, its door slightly ajar. Chris kept to the left wall, Lotte close behind. From the floor plan, they knew that a private bathroom lay on the far side of the bedroom, which gave Armitage two possible positions from which to fire, assuming she had heard them enter and had not elected to escape through a window instead of risking a confrontation.

Chris kicked the door wide as Lotte came in low, her gun fixed on the bed while Chris aimed her weapon at the door opposite. The bed was unoccupied, the sheets thrown back from the mattress. Chris checked under the bed, but the space was empty even of dust. A large unit stood against the opposite wall, consisting of closet spaces and exposed shelves.

Which left the private bathroom. The door was not quite closed, and the faintest of nightlights shone through the crack at the bottom and along the side. Lotte sniffed the air. It smelled strongly of meat and blood, as well as something more exotic, like cinnamon or nutmeg. Chris caught it, too; Lotte saw her nose wrinkle.

This time, Lotte took care of the door, flipping it open with her right hand. Chris moved back in order to give herself a clear shot. Her gun remained steady, but she lowered it slowly as the interior was revealed. She nodded her head to Lotte, indicating that it was safe to look.

Armitage sat naked in the shower stall, her forearms opened in jagged cuts from wrist to elbow, leaving the legat to bleed out rapidly and copiously. Most of the blood was on the floor of the stall, but some of it had splashed the walls. Lotte checked for a pulse on the woman's neck, but it was a redundant gesture. Armitage was obviously dead, her skin faintly mottled.

'Do you think we'll still get paid?' she said.

But Chris was looking at the tiles, and the blood upon them.

'What is that?' she said, spotting a symbol amid the spray.

'I think it's writing,' said Lotte.

Chris leaned in closer. Even in the glow from the nightlight, she could see that the letters had been scratched into the surface, as though someone had dipped a sharp nib in the blood and used it to etch them into the tiles.

'That looks like Arabic,' said Chris.

They exchanged a glance. A dead federal agent, and a message written in Arabic, meant the kind of heat that set nations alight.

'Do you see a blade?' said Lotte.

'No.'

'Then how did she kill herself?'

'Shit,' said Chris.

'Shit,' echoed Lotte.

But they were already retreating from the apartment, even as the last of the lettering faded from the dead woman's skin, leaving only the barest trace of patterning on the whites of her eyes, like fine blue veins.

Until finally, this too was gone.

CXXXIV

Shortly after 9 a.m., having first secured the offices of Lockwood, Dodson & Fogg, armed police entered the cellars of Lincoln's Inn to begin searching for a means of access to the Old Firm on the other side of Chancery Lane. Following the intervention of a legal historian, a psychogeographer, and a pair of underground explorers familiar with the area, they discovered an entry point, and worked their way under Chancery Lane to a steel door. Upon breaking it down, they found themselves in a basement area beneath the Old Firm, and progressed upward through a series of rooms piled high with books and legal papers going back centuries, until they came to a set of living quarters.

Bob Johnston sat secured to a chair in the main room, his mouth taped shut, but with a hole in the center of the gag. From it protruded a long straw that ended in a near-empty two-liter bottle of water. Johnston was stiff, hungry, and almost delirious with pain from a ruptured eardrum and a damaged hand. What might have befallen him had Glenmore not come forward was unclear, but when asked why Quayle had left him alive, Johnston replied:

'He told me it was because I loved books.'

CXXXV

A week went by. Parker, Angel, and Louis answered a lot of questions, and, on the advice of a lawyer provided by Canton, declined to answer a whole lot more. But Canton was correct: the lie about the events in Fairford was accepted, because the truth would have caused more problems for everyone. Christopher Sellars also inadvertently aided their efforts. It is possible to inject drugs directly and safely into the brain, but not with the kind of force that comes from a gas-propelled aluminum dart. Sellars, who had picked up a pair of pig's eyes while passing through the meat market solely to add extra anguish to Parker's final moments, died without ever regaining consciousness. Whatever he might have had to share about Quayle, or the Atlas, died with him.

Parker spoke with Ross on the morning that he, Angel, and Louis were due to leave for the airport. Bob Johnston would not be joining them, having elected to remain in London for a while. Rosanna Bellingham had offered him a room in her home, which Johnston accepted once she confirmed that the presence in the living room appeared to have departed. He'd had enough of visitations, enough of strangeness. According to the doctors, he would never regain the hearing in his damaged ear. He accepted this news with equanimity, because while he might now be deaf in one ear, with splints and bandages on his broken fingers, he was, at least, still alive.

'I heard things in the walls when I was tied to that chair,' Johnston told Parker, while recovering in his hospital bed. 'I know some might say I was imagining things, but I wasn't.'

'What did you hear?'

'Voices, and a man whistling a tune. I think it was "Pack Up Your Troubles". You know, the old World War One song.'

'I know it.'

'I'd say it was odd, but in the context of all that's happened, that wouldn't be true, would it?'

'No, I guess not.'

And when the Old Firm was searched more thoroughly over the weeks that followed, and its walls were broken down, a number of bodies were found immured there. Most would remain anonymous, but one was identified almost immediately, thanks to a wallet found lodged beneath its feet. The wallet contained some money; a photograph of a man in uniform, seated with a woman and two young children; and a folded, barely intact, certificate of discharge from the military in the name of John Soter.

'What did you see in that church?' Johnston asked Parker, before they parted.

'I'm not sure. I don't think I can tell what was real and what was not.'

'Maybe I don't want to know. Maybe it's enough that I heard John Soter whistling.'

None of this Parker chose to share with Ross in the course of their subsequent conversation. It would not have interested him. He was not a sentimental man.

'This time, you really did make a mess,' said Ross.

'I think you knew I'd make a mess when you sent me after Quayle.'

'I was hoping for a smaller mess. You may be interested to learn that Armitage is dead.'

'How?'

'Someone slit her wrists for her, but they may have saved everyone a lot of embarrassment, as well as the cost of a trial. The Dutch police believe she killed two people: Gruner, the book dealer you were tracking, and a woman named Eva Meertens. You wouldn't know anything about Meertens, would you?'

'No.'

'I thought not.'

'Why do you ask?'

'Because no one cared about Gruner, but I hear the girl may have been better liked. Revenge for her death would have been a compelling motive for killing Armitage.'

'I can't help you.'

'No, you won't help me. I think you often get those two words confused. What about the Atlas?'

'What about it?'

'Don't play games, not with this. I want it.'

'It's lost.'

'Lost where?'

'If I knew that, it wouldn't be lost. It disappeared from the church.'

'Disappeared?'

'There was a lot of confusion. I don't know where it is now.'

'You're lying.'

'On this occasion, I'm not. I really don't know where it is.'

And he didn't.

CXXXVI

The British Library's collection numbers over 150 million items, with a further three million being added every year. Less than half its collection is kept on site at St Pancras, the rest being held in an old ordnance factory at Boston Spa, which alone contains over sixty miles of shelving. The filing and location systems for the library's holdings are second to none. But sometimes, as is the law of averages, books get lost, especially if no one is quite aware of their existence to begin with; and librarians are so very poorly paid for doing their job well that it takes a great deal of money to make one of them do it badly.

If you want to hide a body, find a cemetery.

If you want to hide a book, find a library.

CXXXVII

Quayle opened his eyes. He was standing by a lake. Before him, an endless tide of the dead waded through its waters before being swallowed by the sea beyond.

A girl appeared beside him. He did not know her face.

'I wanted oblivion,' he said.

'I know,' said Jennifer Parker.

'I was promised it.'

'And it was a lie. But the Old God is more merciful.'

The lake was gone. In its place stood a version of Quayle's Chancery lair, with all its books and furnishings.

'What is this?' Quayle asked.

'This is the Old God's mercy. This is your oblivion.'

And in that moment, Quayle was rendered eternally blind.

CXXXVIII

The bar of Boston's Colonial Club was busier than usual, and marginally noisier, if only by the typically hushed standards of that institution. One of the older members had passed away, and a reception was being held in his honor following the cremation. Although he had attended the service, the Principal Backer decided to avoid the reminiscing that followed. He was in no mood for even cursory socializing. Quayle and Mors were dead, which was all to the good, but Armitage, too, was gone, and the location of the Atlas was now unknown. Also, Armitage's murder was being investigated with a rigor that might prove hazardous, given their relationship. The security of the Principal Backer's position depended on knowledge and control, and he was currently running a shortfall of both.

He entered the club's padded elevator in order to access the lobby, preferring to avoid the stairs where some of the mourners had gathered to talk. Just as the doors were about to close, their progress was halted by the appearance of a foot, and they rumbled open again. A man joined him in the elevator: a member familiar to the Principal Backer, if only as one to be avoided. They exchanged a cursory nod. The doors rattled shut, but the elevator did not move. The Principal Backer stabbed at the down button again, but instead the elevator went up, which meant he would be forced to share this man's company for longer than either might have desired.

'A sad occasion,' said the Principal Backer, to break the silence.
'I'm sorry?'
'I suggested that it's a sad occasion.'
'If you say so. Did you know him well?'
'Only barely, but he was well liked by many here.'

693

'That's hardly surprising. He was a crook.'

The doors opened on the top floor, but no one entered. Their descent recommenced, but the Principal Backer was still processing the last comment. Such indiscretion was rare in the Colonial, even if the substance of the rumor was certainly true. The deceased had only been cremated to save the devil the trouble, and there were many in the club who would be reunited with him when their own time came.

'That's very interesting,' said the Principal Backer, for form's sake. 'How do you know he was a crook?'

The doors opened again, and his interlocutor stepped out. He fixed the Principal Backer carefully with the pinpoint of his regard.

'Because,' said SAC Edgar Ross of the Federal Bureau of Investigation, 'it's my job.'

Acknowledgments

I t's odd to begin these acknowledgments by choosing not to thank some people by name, but I'm not sure that all those who were kind enough to help me with my research into St Mary's Church in Fairford would wish to be blamed, however incorrectly, for the use to which I've put its beautiful stained-glass windows. Nevertheless, those windows are stunning, and well worth viewing, so I'm very grateful to those citizens of Fairford who assisted me in understanding their historical and artistic significance. Should you decide to visit St Mary's after reading this book, please leave a donation, if only to assuage my guilt.

Joanne Lee was my guide to the history of legal London, but any errors are my own. Similarly, Jeremy Goulding, formerly of the Northumbria Police, very kindly answered my questions on matters of investigative procedure, and bears no responsibility for whatever mistakes, alterations, inventions or obfuscations may have followed. Thanks also to Andrew Tinkler, Chaplain of Durham University's Josephine Butler College, for his generous assistance, and to my friend, the very fine writer Paul Johnston, for his advice. Meanwhile, Alice Wood's copy edit saved some of my blushes, and the efforts of Cliona O'Neill, Jennie Ridyard, and Ellen Clair Lamb saved more. My gratitude also to Myriam Vidriales for correcting my poor Spanish.

Among the books that proved particularly useful in the course of the writing of this novel were *Fairford Parish Church: A Medieval Church and its Stained Glass* by Sarah Brown and Lindsay MacDonald (Sutton Publishing, 2007); *Occult London* by Merlin Coverley (Oldcastle Books, 2017); *The Old Straight Track* by Alfred Watkins (Abacus, 1974); *Dark Side of the Boom: The Excesses of the Art Market in the 21st Century* by Georgina

Adam (Lund Humphries, 2017); *Folklore, Myths and Legends of Britain* (Reader's Digest, 1973); and *Underworld London* by Catharine Arnold (Simon & Schuster, 2012).

As always, huge thanks to Sue Fletcher, my editor at Hodder & Stoughton, and Emily Bestler, my editor at Atria/Emily Bestler Books, for their advice and support. Thanks also to everyone at Hodder and Atria, particularly Swati Gamble, Carolyn Mays, Kerry Hood, Lucy Hale, Alice Morley, Auriol Bishop, Alasdair Oliver, Lara Jones, and Stephanie Mendoza, and to those publishers and editors in other lands who have been kind enough to translate and distribute these books over the past twenty years. I'd be nothing without you, just as I'd be lost without the booksellers and librarians who continue to find a place for my work on their crowded shelves. Darley Anderson, my long-suffering agent, saw the potential in a young writer when few others did – and continues to see some potential in him after twenty years, which is rather reassuring. I will always be touched by the faith that he and his staff have shown in me. Meanwhile, Ellen Clair Lamb takes care of so much stuff that even listing a fraction of it might require me to pay her more money, so I'll simply thank her for her hard work and friendship.

Lastly, love and gratitude to Jennie, Cameron, and Alistair – and now Megan and Alannah. What would be the point of it all without you?

John Connolly, February 2019

EVERY DEAD THING: TWENTY YEARS AFTER

In my office, to the right of my desk, sits a shelf of my own books. I suppose I keep them there to remind me of what I do, what I have done, and possibly what I have yet to do, although they also theoretically serve a practical purpose.[1] After two decades of writing about the same characters – in the form of seventeen novels, and one novella – I occasionally struggle to remember details of their lives, or plot elements from past stories. The idea is that when such moments arise, I can simply reach for the novel in question, find the relevant section, check the detail, and proceed on my merry way.

The truth is, though, that I rarely take any of those books from the shelf, not unless I'm in the most desperate of straits, memory-wise. No author really wants to go back over his or her old work, or even reread passages written decades before. I hope that I've been improving as a writer over the years – although the lady in Chester who once informed me that I'd never been any good since my first book might beg to differ[2] – but I certainly don't want to be reminded of what I was like when I started. Oh, it's reassuring when readers discover *Every Dead Thing* for the first time, and find that it stands up to scrutiny even after two decades. I'm very happy to take their word for it – relieved, in fact – but I'd prefer not to have to confirm this fact personally. Taking down

---

1 Mind you, one has to be wary of vanity. Twice in recent years I've watched Irish writers admit television crews to their homes, only for the cameras to reveal whole downstairs shelves, and in one case even an entire room, filled with multiple copies of the author's books. In the latter instance, the titles were also colour-coordinated. I felt like staging an intervention.
2 She was unhappy that they had grown markedly less bloody. I was mildly alarmed. She seemed so nice.

one of my books to jog my memory is, quite frankly, agony.

Yet recently I've been forced to do just that, and with *Every Dead Thing*. The book on which I'm working at the moment takes place in the aftermath of the death of Parker's wife and child, and shortly before the events of that first novel. A copy of *Every Dead Thing* now sits on my desk, marked here and there with scraps of paper so I can easily turn to the most relevant passages. In a strange way, it has propelled me back almost a quarter of a century, to a time when I was sitting at a different desk, in a different room, surrounded by notes on a book I never believed would be published, but that I was still determined to finish – because I was afraid that if I didn't finish it, I might never attempt another.

Despite the years, I remember more about the writing of *Every Dead Thing* than I do about a lot of my more recent books. Perhaps it's because the process went on for so long – the best part of five years – or it may be that the journey to publishing one's first novel tends to leave its marks. Whatever the reason, it doesn't take much effort to propel myself back to my twenties, and the gradual emergence of that book.

By the time I was twenty-five, I was working with *The Irish Times* as a freelance journalist, albeit not a particularly good one. I wasn't terrible, but there were many better reporters at the paper, and I would always have been destined to make up the numbers until someone eventually fired me. My heart wasn't really in journalism, though. I'd entered the profession because it was a way to be paid to write, and I learned a lot from it about research and discipline, but my interest lay in fiction.

Well, I say that, but I hadn't actually written much fiction at all since leaving school: one short story, in fact, for the Trinity College literary magazine, *Icarus*. (It was rejected, which might have been for the best.) The entirety of my writing career, from local newspapers and magazines to *The Irish Times*, had revolved around non-fiction and journalism. I think it was because becoming a writer of fiction didn't seem like a realistic prospect, just as becoming an actor hadn't.[3] But the desire to explore fiction was in there somewhere, and slowly it began to emerge in the form of *Every Dead Thing*.

So what would become my first published novel was also the first piece of fiction I'd written since graduation. I know that sounds horribly precocious, but it's not meant to. I don't have half-finished manuscripts or false starts in a drawer somewhere because all my mistakes, all my doubts and missteps, occurred during the writing of *Every Dead Thing*.

I always knew how the book would begin: with a man travelling to visit the grave of his wife and child, the drive to his destination being interspersed with memories of the night they died, and the autopsy report detailing the nature of their injuries.

I spent six months trying to get that prologue right.

Okay, so that was my first mistake, and it didn't help that it happened so early in the creation of the book. I became convinced that I couldn't move on to the first chapter until the prologue was perfect. It would, I thought, be like erecting a building on dodgy foundations. So I kept going over the prologue again and again, near obsessively, until finally I either decided it was perfect – which seems unlikely – or some ounce of common sense prevailed. Whichever it was, a lesson was learned that continues to influence how I write to this day: I never look back over what I've done until the first draft of the novel is finished. At that point, I return to the start and begin rewriting, and move through the book, chapter by chapter, until I reach the end. Then I go back to Chapter One and repeat the process, and keep doing so until it's time to deliver.[4]

---

3 I spent most of my teens attending weekly drama classes. My father indulged it, but he was of the opinion that people like us didn't become actors, or even writers. He might have been right, because we didn't know any actors or writers. Actually, I tell a lie: we knew one poet. Mind you, everyone in Ireland probably knew a poet, so it didn't really count.

4 In the early part of my career, my first draft would often be forty or fifty thousand words shorter than the finished book – closer to an outline, in fact. That was because I would skip over details about which I was uncertain, characters that were not yet fully formed, or scenes that were proving difficult. Unfortunately, that just meant putting off until tomorrow problems

But Parker, at least, was there from the start, even if he didn't always have that name. I think he might have been called Walker for a short time – probably just a day or two – but that didn't have the right ring to it. I'd begun listening to jazz in my twenties, and had accumulated a very small collection of mostly used jazz CDs, although I probably had more affection for the American guitarist Pat Metheny than Charlie Parker. Still, the latter's name interested me – or, more correctly, his nickname, Bird. I liked the associations of flight and spirituality evoked by it, particularly for a man so earthbound, so mired in mortality. Very quickly, though, I ceased to use the nickname in the books. I didn't want readers to think it was a gimmick, and it was enough that those who knew of the musician might make those connections for themselves.

Angel and Louis also wandered on to the page virtually fully formed. (This sometimes happens with characters, although in my experience it's usually the most deranged or vile of them that need little or no work. Often they even arrive with their names attached, as was the case with Elias Pudd in *The Killing Kind*, and the Collector in 'The Reflecting Eye', the Parker novella in the *Nocturnes* collection. They're creatures of the id.) Angel and Louis – although not quite good people at that stage, and still not conventionally good people after a further seventeen stories – were never called anything else. I hope they've grown more complex as the novels have progressed, and I've discovered more about them. I'm always touched by how fond readers are of them, and how much they care about their travails, especially as the characters grow older. 'Whatever you do, don't kill Angel' may be the most frequent comment I receive at signings.[5]

I had also been thinking of *Every Dead Thing* in terms of a two-part novel when I began writing, with the incidents in the

that should really be dealt with today. I no longer write that way, and I tackle difficulties as they arise. The result is that the first draft is now probably just ten per cent shorter than the completed novel.

5 Well, that and 'I thought you'd be taller.' I've also never quite forgiven the reader on the Isle of Man who regarded me in a bookstore, and then stared for some time at the photo of me on my latest novel, before announcing, 'Jesus, that picture on your dust jacket was taken a long time ago . . .'

first part paving the way for what was to come. It was my agent who pointed out that this was asking a lot of readers, and they might prefer not to have their gratification delayed to quite such an extent. Nevertheless, Parker had to go through the events of the earlier part of the book to equip him for his final confrontation with the Traveling Man, which meant that a certain amount of reorganization and interweaving of themes and events occurred during the five years between conception and publication in order to make that hourglass structure work.

When I was about halfway through an early draft, or roughly where the first half of the published book now ends, I sent it out to what seemed like every British agent and publisher in the *Writers' & Artists' Yearbook*. I did this because I was broke, and thought that even a modest advance might fund a research trip to the United States, which would enable me to get to grips with the second half of the novel.[6] In those pre-Internet days, submitting a manuscript meant printing off the first three chapters, and mailing them with an individually addressed covering letter. I think I made about seventy submissions in total, and waited for the money to roll in.

Instead what rolled in, perhaps unsurprisingly, were rejection slips – lots of them. I've kept them all. While most were boiler-plate letters, polite variations on 'Thanks but no thanks', a few were more intemperate in their dismissal of the book. One editor even took the time to express, in biro, her detestation of the style and subject matter. (Two years later, one of her fellow editors at the same publishing house would bid a lot of money for the finished novel, but that was only small consolation. At the time, that letter stung more than any other.)

---

6 I'd exhausted my knowledge of the US in that first half. I used Maine as a setting because I'd worked there in my early twenties, and had since returned there with my first girlfriend, Cliona, as part of a road trip that additionally took in New York, Virginia, and Delaware, where I'd also briefly been employed. All those locations figure in the early part of *Every Dead Thing*, but I wanted Louisiana as a backdrop for the sections dealing with the hunt for the Traveling Man. It was a place that had always fascinated me – a fascination only heightened by the novelist James Lee Burke's writings – but I knew I'd have to experience it in person if I was to make it work in the book.

But it wasn't all bad news. Two agents expressed an interest in representing me, one of whom, Darley Anderson, remains my agent to this day; and one publisher's reader enthused about the outline and sample chapters, leading to a request from that house to see the rest. On the advice of Darley, I concentrated on finishing the second half, which says a lot for how much faith I had in him, even though we'd only spoken a few times on the phone. I took on extra shifts at *The Irish Times*, increased the limit on my credit card, and aided and accompanied by a new, but equally tolerant, girlfriend – Ruth – travelled to Louisiana in the muggy height of summer to figure out the route of the Traveling Man's final rampage. I also went back to Maine, and revised some of those sections. When I returned to Ireland, I was heavily in debt, but I had the substance of what I needed.

That was early in August of 1997, and the remainder of *Every Dead Thing* was completed between then and December. I would work in *The Irish Times* during the day, and write fiction at home deep into the night. Occasionally I would accept Night Town shifts at the newspaper, which meant working from late evening until early the following morning. Because the paper would already be laid out by then, my main responsibility was monitoring the wire services in case someone important died, in which case adjustments might be required to one of the pages. Thankfully, the world's VIPs had the good grace not to pop their clogs while I was manning the desk, which left me free to work on the novel while being paid by *The Irish Times* to do something else entirely.

Finally, shortly before Christmas, I submitted the final draft of *Every Dead Thing* to my agent. Unbeknownst to me, he had sent one chapter from the third quarter of the book to an editor he liked and admired, but wouldn't let her read the rest.[7] She made a pre-emptive bid for the book based on that single chapter, which Darley rejected. (Had I been aware of this, I might well have taken out a contract on him. He had more confidence in me than

---

7 It was Chapter 40, in which Parker recalls a man named Daddy Helms from Maine, and how Helms forces Parker's friend Clarence Johns into an act of betrayal.

I ever had in myself.) Instead, the manuscript went to auction in January 1998, and I travelled to London to meet the two highest bidders. In the end, I went with Hodder & Stoughton, coincidentally the only publisher that had seen something worth pursuing in that earlier submission, while the editor who acquired it, Sue Fletcher, was the same editor who had made that attempt to take the book off the table based on a reading of Chapter 40. Of the four main bidders, Hodder was also the publisher that was happiest with the hourglass structure of the book: two cases, seemingly distinct but actually deeply, intimately connected.[8]

And my first instinct upon being informed of all this was to wonder if I could have the book back so I could write it properly, because surely some error had been made. They couldn't seriously want this novel. After all, it was one thing to submit a book that I'd written, and another entirely to have it accepted. The abstract had suddenly become concrete, and the concrete had wobbly foundations, because that prologue still wasn't right. There's a wonderful scene in the 1987 film *Withnail and I*, Bruce Robinson's

---

8 My colleagues at the paper first became aware of the sale of the book when an article about it appeared in the London *Independent*. The next day, I became the front-page story in *The Irish Times*. That very day, I had to go into the bank to look for an overdraft, because I had less than £100 in my account. About a year or two earlier, I'd sought an overdraft of about £500 from the same bank to buy a used car, and had to fill out enough forms to paper a room, as well as listen to countless warnings about the dire consequences that would befall me should I fail to make up the overdraft in the near future. On this second occasion, I went into the bank, and rather embarrassedly explained that I was a bit short, and would be most grateful if they could see their way clear towards giving me another overdraft. I'd even brought along extra pens to sign the forms, just to spare their ink.

'How much do you want?' asked the woman behind the counter, having called over a manager.

'About two hundred?'

'That's fine,' said the manager, leaping in.

She looked at me. I looked at her.

'Er, don't I have to sign something?' I said.

'Oh, *you* don't have to sign *anything*,' she said, and produced a copy of the newspaper.

This, my friends, is how economies collapse.

blackly funny tale of two unemployed London actors, Withnail and Marwood, who manage to secure the use of a country cottage from Withnail's eccentric Uncle Monty. Unfortunately, nothing goes according to plan, leaving them drenched, starving, and finally reduced to begging for food from the local farmer on the grounds that they've 'gone on holiday by mistake.'

Similarly, it seemed, I was about to become a published novelist by mistake.

Writers are sometimes tempted to reverse-engineer their careers in order to explain how they ended up with lots of published titles to their name. It makes it appear as though they knew what they were doing all along, which is always more impressive than admitting to a series of happy accidents: the right novel, at the right time, finding its way into the hands of the right agent, editor, and publisher.

In a similar fashion, I could claim that *Every Dead Thing*'s unusual combination of two distinct, even opposing, literary forms – mystery, and the supernatural – was the result of some grand plan on my part, a deliberate attempt at subversion in order to create my own little sub-genre, or even sub-sub-genre, but it wouldn't be true. I was just writing what interested me, and what interested me was a product of my own reading.

My reading tastes have always been catholic, although I've gone through phases with writers and genres. The first author whose work I ever consumed voraciously was Ian Fleming, while I was in primary school.[9] Fleming was followed by huge quantities of horror and supernatural fiction, including the work of Stephen King, M.R. James, and anyone else in the genre whose writings I could find in our local library, or the nearest used

9 I admit that Fleming's Bond may not have been the best role model for a pre-pubescent boy, or even a pubescent boy. It resulted in a temporary belief that women needed to be kissed firmly and coldly, regardless of whether they wanted it or not, and preferably after the male party has smoked sixty fags, knocked back the best part of a bottle of vodka, and consumed a meal of Beluga caviar. If I tried that now, I'd die, either from the combination of smokes, booze, and fish eggs, or more likely from Jennie, my better half, beating me to a pulp with one of my own arms.

bookstore.[10] I began reading mystery fiction in my teens, commencing with Ed McBain's 87th Precinct novels, but given a choice between mystery and the supernatural, I'd always plump for horror. Finally, in my twenties, I encountered James Lee Burke, Robert B. Parker, John Sandford, and, crucially, Ross Macdonald.

So this was my grounding, and it wasn't surprising that aspects of some or all of those writers should have influenced the book on which I was working. Looking back, I was conscious of fusing sometimes disparate elements together in *Every Dead Thing*. I recognized that most of the mystery fiction I read eschewed the supernatural entirely – Burke was a notable exception – but I assumed this was because creating hybrids simply didn't interest the majority of practitioners. Only later, after the book was published, did I become aware of the abhorrence that existed in the mystery world for this particular type of hybridization, a product of the genre's roots in rationalism.[11] By then, of course, it was rather too late: *Every Dead Thing* was on the shelves, and *Dark Hollow*, its successor, was already written.[12] The books that followed would become increasingly fascinated by this tension

10 But I never got a handle on H.P. Lovecraft, which may strike some readers as odd given the climax of *A Book of Bones*. Even as a teenager, I found his literary style off-putting. Many of Lovecraft's concepts are remarkable, but the quality of his prose is rarely worthy of them.

11 Incredibly, it persists to this day, although not as strongly as in the past. I recently had dinner with a renowned American bookseller and publisher, of whom I'm very fond, and he continues to consider the blending of the rational and anti-rational as distinctly *infra dig*, and possibly a betrayal of the spirit of the mystery genre itself. To his credit, he did allow that I managed to pull it off. He just wasn't convinced that I should have done it in the first place.

12 *Dark Hollow* would result in my first real disagreement with my British publishers, who didn't like that title one little bit. I recall that they thought it wasn't memorable enough, or didn't sound like a mystery novel, or some combination of the two. Because I was still finding my feet as a writer, I buckled under the pressure, and *Dark Hollow* briefly changed to *Requiem for the Damned*, which I thought was a terrible title – and I'd come up with it – but which they inexplicably loved, to the extent that early proofs of the book went out under that name. In the end, I was too ashamed of *Requiem for the Damned* as a title even to be able to say it aloud, and I prevailed upon them to revert to *Dark Hollow*.

between the rational and anti-rational, and the literary possibilities offered by it. Thankfully, large numbers of readers have proved less conservative, and more adventurous, than commonly held wisdom might have suggested. Mind you, there are still mystery fans who can't abide what I write, which is fine. The mystery genre is a broad church, and some of us don't mind dwelling in its shadows.

Finally, a word on the novel's critical reception. I can remember returning from Maine in early December 1998, shortly before *Every Dead Thing* was due to be published in Ireland. I had with me a draft of *Dark Hollow*, which I'd been revising up in northern Maine, because I had promised to deliver that second novel to my publishers early in 1999. At the airport, I picked up a copy of the *Sunday Times* – no relation to *The Irish Times*, but instead the Irish version of the British News International title – to find a story on its inner pages describing *Every Dead Thing* as a 'Christmas turkey', based on an early review in the trade journal *Books Ireland*. It left me profoundly depressed, because it was the first critical judgement of any kind to appear in print about the novel. I thought it would set the tone for all the reviews that followed, because I really didn't know any better.

Ultimately it didn't, but *Every Dead Thing* still divided critics. The positive reviews were as good as any I could have wished for – better, even – but the bad ones were scathing. In retrospect, this isn't surprising, for a lot of the reasons already mentioned above: the novel's structure, its subject matter, my age (I was 30 when it was published), and even my nationality, given that I was an Irishman attempting to write in an American genre, and an American idiom.

Interestingly, the response in the United States was overwhelmingly positive, with many reviewers not even registering that I wasn't American until they'd finished the book and read the author biography. The British reviews were more mixed, including a couple of scathing takes from writers both inside and outside the mystery genre.[13] It helped that *Dark Hollow* was done and dusted by the time *Every Dead Thing* came under the critical spotlight. It would, I think, have been hard to complete a second novel while the first was being subject to the occasional mauling. Now, twenty years later, I make a point of being well into the writing of a new book before the previous novel appears in print, and I no longer feel the compulsion to read every review. I'm happy enough not to see any at all, in fact: I know that my instinct – and this is not unusual – is probably to believe the bad ones and doubt the good, so it's better to avoid them entirely. As James Lee Burke once told me, 'You have to learn to ignore the catcalls and the applause.' It's sound advice.

I do have one more thing to say: If you've got this far, it's probably because you have some interest in, even affection for, my work. Thank you for that. Thank you for giving me a career, and the encouragement to continue writing. Thank you for showing up at book signings, or dropping the occasional kind word via print or email. Thank you for supporting bookstores, and libraries.

Thank you for the last twenty years.

Thank you for being a reader.

John Connolly, February 2019

---

13 Something similar happened with *The Book of Lost Things* in 1996. The worst reviews for that novel – which was generally well-received, and has gone on, I think, to become the most fondly regarded of my books – came from British fantasy writers, one of whom later apologized for what he'd written, but only, he admitted, after his wife gave him a telling off. 'She said I was just annoyed,' he confessed, 'because it was the kind of book I'd wanted to write.' He had to get very drunk to tell me this, and it didn't help his hangover when I informed him that I had no idea he'd written a review of the book, and could therefore have gotten away without saying anything at all.